George Rhett Cathcart

The literary reader

Typical selections from the best British and American authors

George Rhett Cathcart

The literary reader
Typical selections from the best British and American authors

ISBN/EAN: 9783337278151

Printed in Europe, USA, Canada, Australia, Japan

Cover: Foto ©Andreas Hilbeck / pixelio.de

More available books at **www.hansebooks.com**

CATHCART'S LITERARY READER.

"*Some books are to be tasted, others to be swallowed, and some few to be chewed and digested. That is, some books are to be read only in parts; others, to be read, but not curiously; and some few to be read wholly, and with diligence and attention. Some books also may be read by deputy, and extracts made of them by others. . . . . Reading maketh a full man; conference, a ready man; and writing, an exact man. And therefore, if a man write little, he had need have a great memory; if he confer little, he had need have a present wit; and if he reads little, he had need have much cunning, to seem to know that he doth not. Histories make men wise; poets, witty; the mathematics, subtle; natural philosophy, deep; moral, grave; logic and rhetoric, able to contend.*"

BACON'S ESSAYS.

The American Educational Series.

THE

LITERARY READER:

TYPICAL SELECTIONS FROM SOME OF THE BEST

BRITISH AND AMERICAN AUTHORS,

FROM SHAKESPEARE TO THE PRESENT TIME,

Chronologically Arranged ;

WITH BIOGRAPHICAL AND CRITICAL SKETCHES,
AND NUMEROUS NOTES,
ETC., ETC.

By GEORGE R. CATHCART.

NEW YORK AND CHICAGO:
IVISON, BLAKEMAN, TAYLOR, AND COMPANY.
1876.

PREFACE.

THE compiler of this work has not designed to make a compendium of English Literature, but to provide the means of acquiring a fair knowledge of that literature, for those who may not be able to procure a regular course of study on the subject. So far as gradation is concerned, the book is intended to fill the place usually occupied by the "Sixth" or "Advanced" Reader. The extracts will be found of suitable length, and in other respects well adapted, it is hoped, for this purpose. In the ordinary catalogue of common-school studies literature, practically, holds but a humble place: its value to the mass of scholars has been underestimated, and it has been esteemed a branch of knowledge really useful only to the few who aspire to a "liberal education." Public sentiment has fortunately undergone a change touching this matter, within a few years; and in the hope of furthering that change and confirming literature in its true place among school studies, this book has been prepared. The people of the United States are, above all others, a nation of readers, and no thoughtful person need be told how potent in the formation of character and in the shaping of the national life is the influence of books. The rapid increase of our schools in numbers and efficiency, the multiplication of public libraries, and the ever-growing volume of new publications, indicate beyond the possibility of doubt that, practical people though we are, we find in books the chief source of our intelligence and national strength. Books embody the accumulated wisdom of ages; in them we have the garnered experience of centuries long past; in them we find, so to speak, formulas for our guidance, precedents in the conduct of our fathers, which time has stamped with the validity of rules. Human nature is, in effect, unchanged since the earliest days of the world; and the record of its thought and manifestations, which consti-

tutes the history of civilization, is the most precious inheritance that could
have come down to us. ⎛The literature of a nation is its history in the
subtlest form; and he who intelligently reads it apprehends the spirit of
the time, while history itself gives him only results. Literature is, indeed,
the most faithful expression of the national spirit, which seems to inspire
and inform it ⎞ and the reader of this volume can readily trace in the chronologically arranged extracts from her writers the many stages that mark
the vicissitudes of England's thought: religion, politics, general culture,
all disclose their changing features in the theology, the poetry, and the drama
of succeeding centuries.

English Literature, it is hardly necessary to say, antedates the time at
which our extracts begin. Its birth is generally assigned to the last half
of the fourteenth century. Three chief forces produced it, — classical learning, the influence of Italian culture, and Norman poetry, known as Romance
literature, which was gradually introduced into England after the Conquest.
But of this period — and of the earlier centuries to which belong the Saxon
poem of Beowulf, Caedmon's paraphrase of Scripture, the Ecclesiastical
History of the Venerable Bede (who lived 673 – 735), Layamon's "Brut,"
the metrical Chronicle of Robert of Gloucester, etc., etc. — it has been
thought best to reproduce in this volume no representative fragments, for
the reason that these archaic writings are valuable only to the professed
scholar. The same reason operates, less powerfully indeed, to exclude
specimens of Chaucer's poems. He was, it is true, the founder of English literature, and the first who demonstrated that the English language
was susceptible of forcible and harmonious arrangement in rhythmical
form. But his writings present serious obstacles to the ordinary reader
in their multitude of obsolete words and phrases, and an acquaintance with
them may properly follow the study of more modern writers. Moreover,
the reform which he inaugurated in letters was not steadily progressive.
The century immediately following his life was notably barren of literary
growth; a barrenness mainly due to the stern repression of free inquiry
by the ecclesiastical authorities, and secondarily to the prevalence of civil
wars, which diverted attention from the peaceful pursuit of letters. Near
the close of this century, however, printing was introduced into England,
as if in preparation for the season of intellectual activity which was near
at hand. This season is known as the Elizabethan age, the reign of Queen
Elizabeth, and has been called the creative period in English literature.

It may be regarded as the legitimate result of the Reformation, which loosened the bonds that had trammeled men's minds, and encouraged free investigation and free expression. It has three representatives, *par excellence*, — Hooker of the theological spirit, Bacon of the philosophical, and Shakespeare of the poetic and dramatic. With the last of these, "the most illustrious of the sons of man," our series of glimpses at English literary history begins.

As even the merest mention of all distinguished writers was obviously impracticable, it has been attempted, in the preparation of this volume, to introduce those of the number who most faithfully and forcibly represent the several stages and departments of English literature. In Shakespeare we see a delegate at large from every literary interest known in his time ; Milton gives voice to the thoughtful and devout poetry of Puritanism ; Swift illustrates the power of satire with a brilliancy that has never been surpassed ; Addison inaugurates the revival of classicalism in literature, and gives the world a pattern of rigid, though beautiful, accuracy in style ; Johnson exemplifies ponderousness in matter and manner, and leaves a lasting impress on English letters ; Goldsmith, more thoroughly than any writer had done before his time, transfuses himself into his writings, revealing his own gentle, genial, and poetical nature in his books with almost unequaled fidelity of portraiture ; Gibbon, first of all Englishmen, demonstrated the power of the historian, not only to rescue the past, but to mold the future. But the catalogue is too long to be thus continued. What is here left undone, the student may profitably do for himself, recording briefly his judgment of each writer and specifying his distinguishing services or office in literature.

As helps to history, these brief interviews with typical representatives of different periods cannot fail to be valuable. To the epics of Homer we are largely indebted for our knowledge of the politics, theology, and social customs of the Greeks and Trojans ; and our debt for similar acquisitions to English writers of early times, though rarely acknowledged, is even greater. Chaucer gives us pictures of a life that, but for him, we could only imagine, — a life in which rude ecclesiasticism held unquestioned dominion. Dryden describes or suggests the vicissitudes of religious faith that were the most conspicuous feature of English life in his time, and the pervading corruption that demoralized all classes. Coleridge enlightens us as to the first movements of that spirit of free inquiry whose results have pre-eminently distinguished the nineteenth century. It would be easy to enlarge upon this point if space permitted; but a little reflection will convince the intelligent reader that the literature of a nation is its true history : it is spontaneous and unprejudiced, while formal historical narratives are invariably colored by prejudice, personal, political, or theological. If Hume's and Macaulay's and Froude's Histories were suddenly destroyed, the surviving general literature of England would afford ample materials for their reconstruction.

American Literature has a liberal representation in THE LITERARY READER, which presents one feature that may be said to be unique; that is, its recognition of distinctively scientific writers as contributors to letters. In its early days science was dry and almost repellent to all save its favored students; but its modern exponents have not failed to see the importance of introducing it in an attractive guise, and the writings of Agassiz, Tyndall, Gray, Dana, Maury, Huxley, and others abound in passages of marked beauty even when judged according to the standards of pure literature. This feature of the work seems to mark not only a due acknowledgment of the growing love for scientific study in this country, but also a welcome addition to the treasures of literature.

While this work is primarily intended for the use of schools, as a text-book by the use of which the learner may acquire, simultaneously, proficiency in reading, and no inconsiderable familiarity with what may be called the headlands of English literature, it will, it is believed, also be found serviceable by the general reader. One who desires to acquaint himself with the best literary products of the Anglo-Saxon intellect will find in these pages a convenient and agreeable introduction to them. Indeed, the book may fitly be described as a collection of samples which set forth the peculiar qualities of the chief literary fabrics of England and America, made during nearly three hundred years.

The compiler acknowledges, with pleasure, his obligations to Mr. S. R. Crocker, the accomplished editor of the *Literary World*, for much valuable literary assistance, and also to Messrs. James R. Osgood & Co., Messrs. G. P. Putnam's Sons, Messrs. D. Appleton & Co., and others, for their courtesy in permitting the use of selections from their copyright editions of American writers.

G. R. C.

CONTENTS.

xii

CONTENTS.

INDEX OF AUTHORS.

SHAKESPEARE.

1564–1616.

WILLIAM SHAKESPEARE, dramatist and poet, was born at Stratford-on-Avon, England, in April, 1564. Of his early life almost nothing is known. It is believed that he was a student in the free school at Stratford, and that in his youth he assisted his father in the latter's business, which was that of a wool-dealer and glover. That he formally entered upon any definite calling we have no proof; but critics have found evidence in his writings of his familiarity with various professions: Malone, one of his acutest commentators, firmly insisted that Shakespeare was a lawyer's clerk. At the age of eighteen he married Anne Hathaway, then eight years his senior. Of this union only a vague report that it proved uncongenial has come down to us. In 1586 or 1587 Shakespeare seems to have gone to London, and two years later appears as one of the proprietors of the Blackfriars Theater. In the few years next following he became known as a playwright, and in 1593 he published his first poem, *Venus and Adonis.* The dates of publication of his plays are not settled beyond doubt; but the best authorities place *Henry VI.* first and *The Tempest* last, all included between 1589 and 1611. Shakespeare was an actor as well as a writer of plays, and remained on the stage certainly as late as 1603. Two years later he bought a handsome house at Stratford, and lived therein, enjoying the friendship and respect of his neighbors till his death in 1616.

Meager as is the foregoing sketch, it yet embodies, with a few trifling exceptions, all the known facts as to Shakespeare's life. A mist seems to have settled over "the most illustrious of the sons of man," almost wholly hiding his personality from curious and admiring posterity. Of many of his contemporary writers, and of some who preceded him, comparatively full particulars have come down to us: Edmund Spenser stands out conspicuous among the bright lights of the Elizabethan age; the genial face and the personal habits of "rare Ben Jonson" are almost familiar to us; and even of Chaucer, the father of English literature, we possess a reasonably distinct portraiture; but Shakespeare, *the man,* is lost to us in the darkness of the past. In his works, however, he lives, and will live while written records survive.

The name of Shakespeare is so pre-eminently famous, standing out in the firmament of literature "like the moon among the lesser stars," that no attempt to convey an idea of his greatness seems to be necessary here. We content ourselves, therefore, with quoting the opinions of a few of those who have been worthy to judge him.

Dr. Samuel Johnson says: "The stream of time, which is continually washing the dissolvable fabrics of other poets, passes without injury by the adamant of Shakespeare."

Thomas De Quincey says: "In the gravest sense it may be affirmed of Shakespeare that he is among the modern luxuries of life; it was his prerogative to have thought more finely and more extensively than all other poets combined."

Lord Jeffrey says: "More full of wisdom and ridicule and sagacity than all the moralists that ever existed, he is more wild, airy, and inventive, and more pathetic and fantastic, than all the poets of all regions and ages of the world."

Lord Macaulay pronounced Shakespeare "the greatest poet that ever lived," and esteemed

Othello, the play from which our first selection is taken, as " perhaps the greatest work in the world."

Thomas Carlyle bears this characteristic testimony : " Of this Shakespeare of ours, perhaps the opinion one sometimes hears a little idolatrously expressed is, in fact, the right one ; I think the best judgment is slowly pointing to the conclusion that Shakespeare is the chief of all poets hitherto, the greatest intellect who, in our recorded world, has left record of himself in the way of literature. On the whole, I know not such a power of vision, such a faculty of thought, if we take all the characters of it, in any other man. Such a calmness of depth, placid, joyous strength, all things imaged in that great soul of his so true and clear, as in a tranquil, unfathomable sea ! "

OTHELLO'S SPEECH TO THE SENATE.

MOST potent, grave, and reverend signiors,
My very noble and approved good masters, —
That I have ta'en away this old man's daughter,
It is most true ; true, I have married her ;
The very head and front of my offending
Hath this extent, no more. Rude am I in speech,
And little blessed with the set phrase of peace ;
For since these arms of mine had seven years' pith,
Till now some nine moons wasted, they have used
Their dearest action in the tented field ;
And little of this great world can I speak,
More than pertains to feats of broil and battle ;
And therefore little shall I grace my cause
In speaking for myself. Yet, by your gracious patience,
I will a round unvarnished tale deliver
Of my whole course of love ; what drugs, what charms,
What conjuration, and what mighty magic
(For such proceeding I am charged withal),
I won his daughter with.

Her father loved me ; oft invited me ;
Still questioned me the story of my life,
From year to year ; the battles, sieges, fortunes,
That I have passed.
I ran it through, even from my boyish days,
To the very moment that he bade me tell it.
Wherein I spake of most disastrous chances,
Of moving accidents by flood and field,
Of hair-breadth 'scapes i' the imminent deadly breach ;
Of being taken by the insolent foe,
And sold to slavery ; of my redemption thence,

And portance in my travel's history;
Wherein of antres vast, and deserts idle,
Rough quarries, rocks, and hills whose heads touch heaven,
It was my hint to speak; — such was the process; —
And of the cannibals that each other eat,
The Anthropophagi, and men whose heads
Do grow beneath their shoulders.   This to hear,
Would Desdemona seriously incline:
But still the house affairs would draw her thence;
Which ever as she could with haste despatch,
She 'd come again, and with a greedy ear
Devour up my discourse: which I observing,
Took once a pliant hour, and found good means
To draw from her a prayer of earnest heart,
That I would all my pilgrimage dilate,
Whereof by parcels she had something heard,
But not intentively.   I did consent;
And often did beguile her of her tears,
When I did speak of some distressful stroke
That my youth suffered.   My story being done,
She gave me for my pains a world of sighs:
She swore — In faith, 't was strange, 't was passing strange;
'T was pitiful, 't was wondrous pitiful:
She wished she had not heard it; yet she wished
That Heaven had made her such a man: she thanked me;
And bade me, if I had a friend that loved her,
I should but teach him how to tell my story,
And that would woo her.   Upon this hint, I spake:
She loved me for the dangers I had passed;
And I loved her, that she did pity them.
This only is the witchcraft I have used.

THE WINNING OF JULIET.*

JULIET.   Thou know'st the mask of night is on my face:
Else would a maiden blush bepaint my cheek,
For that which thou hast heard me speak to-night.

* An extract from the love scene in the garden, in the play of *Romeo and Juliet*. Romeo, in ambuscade at night, is discovered by Juliet listening to her declaration of love for him.

Fain would I dwell on form, fain, fain deny
What I have spoke: but farewell compliment!
Dost thou love me? I know thou wilt say, Ay:
And I will take thy word; yet, if thou swear'st,
Thou mayst prove false; at lovers' perjuries,
They say, Jove laughs. O gentle Romeo,
If thou dost love, pronounce it faithfully:
Or if thou think'st I am too quickly won,
I 'll frown and be perverse, and say thee nay,
So thou wilt woo; but else, not for the world.
In truth, fair Montague, I am too fond;
And therefore thou mayst think my 'havior light.
But trust me, gentleman, I 'll prove more true
Than those that have more cunning to be strange.
I should have been more strange, I must confess,
But that thou overheard'st, ere I was 'ware,
My true love's passion: therefore pardon me;
And not impute this yielding to light love,
Which the dark night hath so discovered.

ROMEO. Lady, by yonder blessed moon I swear,
That tips with silver all these fruit-tree tops —

JULIET. O, swear not by the moon, the inconstant moon,
That monthly changes in her circled orb,
Lest that thy love prove likewise variable.

ROMEO. What shall I swear by?

JULIET.   Do not swear at all,
Or, if thou wilt, swear by thy gracious self,
Which is the god of my idolatry,
And I 'll believe thee.

ROMEO.   If my heart's dear love —

JULIET. Well, do not swear: although I joy in thee,
I have no joy of this contract to-night;
It is too rash, too unadvised, too sudden:
Too like the lightning, which doth cease to be
Ere one can say, It lightens. Sweet, good night!
This bud of love, by summer's ripening breath,
May prove a beauteous flower when next we meet.
Good night, good night! as sweet repose and rest
Come to thy heart, as that within my breast!

ROMEO. O, wilt thou leave me so unsatisfied?

JULIET. What satisfaction canst thou have to-night?

ROMEO. The exchange of thy love's faithful vow for mine.

JULIET. I gave thee mine before thou didst request it:
And yet I would it were to give again.

ROMEO. Wouldst thou withdraw it? for what purpose, love?

JULIET. But to be frank, and give it thee again.
And yet I wish but for the thing I have:
My bounty is as boundless as the sea,
My love as deep; the more I give to thee,
The more I have, for both are infinite.

WOLSEY ON THE VICISSITUDES OF LIFE.*

FAREWELL, a long farewell, to all my greatness.
This is the state of man; to-day he puts forth
The tender leaves of hope, to-morrow blossoms,
And bears his blushing honors thick upon him;
The third day comes a frost, a killing frost;
And, when he thinks, good easy man, full surely
His greatness is a-ripening, — nips his root,
And then he falls, as I do. I have ventured,
Like little wanton boys that swim on bladders,
This many summers in a sea of glory;
But far beyond my depth; my high-blown pride
At length broke under me; and now has left me,
Weary, and old with service, to the mercy
Of a rude stream, that must forever hide me.
Vain pomp and glory of this world, I hate ye;
I feel my heart new opened: O, how wretched
Is that poor man that hangs on princes' favors!
There is, betwixt that smile we would aspire to,
That sweet aspect of princes, and their ruin,
More pangs and fears, than wars or women have;
And when he falls, he falls like Lucifer,
Never to hope again.

* Cardinal Wolsey was one of the highest officers of King Henry VIII. of England. Being suddenly deprived of all his honors by the king, and consequently disgraced, Shakespeare represents him as uttering this speech on retiring from office.

HAMLET'S SOLILOQUY.

To be, or not to be, — that is the question : —
Whether 't is nobler in the mind to suffer
The slings and arrows of outrageous fortune ;
Or to take arms against a sea of troubles,
And, by opposing, end them ? — To die, — to sleep, —
No more ; — and, by a sleep, to say we end
The heart-ache, and the thousand natural shocks
That flesh is heir to, — 't is a consummation
Devoutly to be wished.   To die ; — to sleep ; —
To sleep ! perchance to dream ; — ay, there 's the rub :
For in that sleep of death what dreams may come,
When we have shuffled off this mortal coil,
Must give us pause ; there 's the respect
That makes calamity of so long life :
For who would bear the whips and scorns of time,
The oppressor's wrong, the proud man's contumely,
The pangs of despised love, the law's delay,
The insolence of office, and the spurns
That patient merit of the unworthy takes,
When he himself might his quietus make
With a bare bodkin ? who would fardels bear,
To grunt and sweat under a weary life ;
But that the dread of something after death, —
The undiscovered country, from whose bourn
No traveler returns, — puzzles the will ;
And makes us rather bear those ills we have,
Than fly to others that we know not of ?
Thus conscience does make cowards of us all ;
And thus the native hue of resolution
Is sicklied o'er with the pale cast of thought ;
And enterprises of great pith and moment,
With this regard, their currents turn awry,
And lose the name of action.

POLONIUS'S ADVICE TO HIS SON.

GIVE thy thoughts no tongue,
Nor any unproportioned thought his act.
Be thou familiar, but by no means vulgar.
The friends thou hast, and their adoption tried,
Grapple them to thy soul with hooks of steel ;
But do not dull thy palm with entertainment
Of each new-hatched, unfledged comrade.   Beware
Of entrance to a quarrel ; but, being in,
Bear it, that the opposer may beware of thee.
Give every man thine ear, but few thy voice :
Take each man's censure, but reserve thy judgment.
Costly thy habit as thy purse can buy,
But not expressed in fancy ; rich, not gaudy ;
For the apparel oft proclaims the man ;
And they in France, of the best rank and station,
Are most select and generous, chief in that.
Neither a borrower nor a lender be :
For loan oft loses both itself and friend ;
And borrowing dulls the edge of husbandry.
This above all, — to thine own self be true ;
And it must follow, as the night the day,
Thou canst not then be false to any man.
Farewell ; my blessing season this in thee.

THE SEVEN AGES OF MAN.

ALL the world 's a stage;
And all the men and women merely players :
They have their exits and their entrances ;
And one man in his time plays many parts,
His acts being seven ages.   At first, the Infant,
Mewling and puking in the nurse's arms.
And then, the whining School-boy, with his satchel,
And shining morning face, creeping like snail
Unwillingly to school.   And then, the Lover,
Sighing like furnace, with a woful ballad
Made to his mistress' eyebrow.   Then a Soldier ;

Full of strange oaths, and bearded like the pard,
Jealous in honor, sudden and quick in quarrel,
Seeking the bubble reputation
Even in the cannon's mouth. And then, the Justice,
In fair round belly, with good capon lined,
With eyes severe, and beard of formal cut,
Full of wise saws and modern instances ;
And so he plays his part. The sixth age shifts
Into the lean and slippered Pantaloon,
With spectacles on nose, and pouch on side ;
His youthful hose, well saved, a world too wide
For his shrunk shank; and his big manly voice,
Turning again toward childish treble, pipes
And whistles in his sound. Last scene of all,
That ends this strange eventful history,
Is second childishness and mere oblivion,
Sans teeth, sans eyes, sans taste, sans every thing.

MERCY.

THE quality of Mercy is not strained ;
It droppeth, as the gentle rain from heaven,
Upon the place beneath. It is twice blessed ;
It blesseth him that gives and him that takes.
'T is mightiest in the mightiest ; it becomes
The thronéd monarch better than his crown.
His scepter shows the force of temporal power,
The attribute to awe and majesty,
Wherein doth sit the dread and fear of kings ;
But mercy is above this sceptered sway, —
It is enthronéd in the hearts of kings,
It is an attribute to God himself ;
And earthly power doth then show likest God's,
When mercy seasons justice. Therefore, Jew,
Though justice be thy plea, consider this, —
That, in the course of justice, none of us
Should see salvation. We do pray for mercy ;
And that same prayer doth teach us all to render
The deeds of mercy.

ENGLAND.

THIS royal throne of kings, this sceptered isle,
This earth of majesty, this seat of Mars,
This other Eden, demi-paradise;
This fortress, built by Nature for herself,
Against infection and the hand of war;
This happy breed of men, this little world;
This precious stone set in the silver sea,
Which serves it in the office of a wall,
Or as a moat defensive to a house,
Against the envy of less happier lands,
This blessed plot, this earth, this realm, this England.

THE MIND.

FOR 't is the mind that makes the body rich:
And as the sun breaks through the darkest clouds,
So honor peereth in the meanest habit.
What! is the jay more precious than the lark,
Because his feathers are more beautiful?
Or is the adder better than the eel,
Because his painted skin contents the eyes?
O no; good Kate: neither art thou the worse
For this poor furniture and mean array.

PERFECTION.

To gild refinéd gold, to paint the lily,
To throw a perfume on the violet,
To smooth the ice, or add another hue
Unto the rainbow, or with taper-light
To seek the beauteous eye of heaven to garnish,
Is wasteful and ridiculous excess.

1 *

MILTON.

1608 – 1674.

JOHN MILTON — *clarum et venerabile nomen* — was born in London in December, 1608, and died November, 1674. He was the son of John Milton, a respectable scrivener. The younger John entered Christ's College, Cambridge, at the age of sixteen, and became distinguished during his University career for his brilliant poetical abilities. He was destined for the service of the Church; but, on arriving at manhood, he found — to quote his own words — "what tyranny had invaded the Church, and that he who would take orders must subscribe Slave." He therefore turned his thoughts to the law, but soon abandoned it, and gave his undivided attention to literature. The death of his mother, in 1637, affected his health, and he sought to restore it by travel. He visited several continental countries, and, while in Italy, made the acquaintance of Galileo. Returning to England in 1639, he found the nation in a fever of political excitement, and lost no time in declaring himself with reference to the momentous questions then under discussion. In 1641 and 1642 he published his first polemical treatises, which made a profound impression. In 1643 he was married to Mary Powell; but the union, like Shakespeare's, proved a rather unhappy one. The lady was volatile, and fond of gayety, and her family were enthusiastic Royalists, while Milton was a stern Puritan. Soon after the marriage a separation took place; but at last a reconciliation was effected, and the partnership was renewed. Several of his political pamphlets brought Milton into prominence, and led to his being appointed, in 1649, Latin Secretary to the Council of State, which office he held eight years. During that period he wrote his famous *Eikonoklastes*, and several other books. In 1653 his wife died, and three years later he married again, finding, it is believed, real happiness in his new relation. In 1660 the monarchy was re-established, and thenceforward he took no conspicuous part in politics. Having lost his second wife, he took a third in 1664, who survived him nearly fifty years, dying in 1727.

His most famous composition, *Paradise Lost*, was written after he had become totally blind, which happened in 1652, it being dictated to his daughter. It is worthy of note that the whole remuneration received by the poet and his family for this poem, which ranks among the grandest in the world, was only twenty-eight pounds, about one hundred and forty dollars.

Paradise Lost represents the only successful attempt ever made to construct a drama whose principal personages are supernatural; in this character it stands above others unapproached. To the student it offers a field whose exploration never ceases to be delightful and remunerative. It is the finest flower of one of the greatest minds that ever commanded the reverence of the world; and in design, if not in execution, is the noblest poetical product of human genius.

THE INVOCATION AND INTRODUCTION TO PARADISE LOST.

Of man's first disobedience, and the fruit
Of that forbidden tree, whose mortal taste
Brought death into the world, and all our woe,
With loss of Eden, till one greater Man
Restore us, and regain the blissful seat,
Sing, heavenly Muse, that on the secret top
Of Oreb, or of Sinai, didst inspire
That shepherd, who first taught the chosen seed,
In the beginning how the Heavens and Earth
Rose out of Chaos : or, if Sion hill

Delight thee more, and Siloa's brook that flowed
Fast by the oracle of God, I thence
Invoke thy aid to my adventurous song,
That with no middle flight intends to soar
Above the Aonian mount, while it pursues
Things unattempted yet in prose or rhyme.
And chiefly thou, O Spirit, that dost prefer
Before all temples the upright heart and pure,
Instruct me, for thou know'st; thou from the first
Wast present, and, with mighty wings outspread,
Dove-like sat'st brooding on the vast abyss,
And mad'st it pregnant : what in me is dark
Illumine ; what is low raise and support ;
That to the height of this great argument
I may assert eternal Providence,
And justify the ways of God to man.
　　Say first, for Heaven hides nothing from thy view,
Nor the deep tract of Hell ; say first, what cause
Moved our grand parents, in that happy state,
Favored of Heaven so highly, to fall off
From their Creator, and transgress his will,
For one restraint, lords of the world besides ?
Who first seduced them to that foul revolt ?
The infernal serpent ; he it was, whose guile,
Stirred up with envy and revenge, deceived
The mother of mankind, what time his pride
Had cast him out from Heaven, with all his host
Of rebel angels ; by whose aid, aspiring
To set himself in glory above his peers,
He trusted to have equaled the Most High,
If he opposed ; and, with ambitious aim
Against the throne and monarchy of God,
Raised impious war in Heaven, and battle proud,
With vain attempt.　Him the Almighty power
Hurled headlong flaming from the ethereal sky,
With hideous ruin and combustion, down
To bottomless perdition ; there to dwell
In adamantine chains and penal fire,
Who durst defy the Omnipotent to arms.

ADAM AND EVE'S MORNING HYMN.

THESE are thy glorious works, Parent of good,
Almighty! Thine this universal frame,
Thus wondrous fair; Thyself how wondrous then!
Unspeakable, who sit'st above these heavens
To us invisible, or dimly seen
In these thy lowest works; yet these declare
Thy goodness beyond thought, and power divine.
Speak, ye who best can tell, ye sons of light,
Angels; for ye behold him, and with songs
And choral symphonies, day without night,
Circle his throne rejoicing; ye, in Heaven:
On Earth join, all ye creatures, to extol
Him first, him last, him midst, and without end.
Fairest of stars, last in the train of night,
If better thou belong not to the dawn,
Sure pledge of day, that crown'st the smiling Morn
With thy bright circlet, praise him in thy sphere,
While day arises, that sweet hour of prime.
Thou Sun, of this great world both eye and soul,
Acknowledge him thy greater; sound his praise
In thy eternal course, both when thou climb'st,
And when high noon hast gained, and when thou fall'st.
Moon, that now meet'st the orient Sun, now fly'st,
With the fixed stars, fixed in their orb that flies;
And ye five other wandering fires, that move
In mystic dance not without song, resound
His praise, who out of darkness called up light.
Air, and ye elements, the eldest birth
Of Nature's womb, that in quaternion run,
Perpetual circle, multiform; and mix
And nourish all things; let your ceaseless change
Vary to our great Maker still new praise.
Ye mists and exhalations, that now rise
From hill or steaming lake, dusky or gray,
Till the Sun paint your fleecy skirts with gold,
In honor to the world's great Author rise;
Whether to deck with clouds the uncolored sky,

Or wet the thirsty Earth with falling showers,
Rising or falling still advance his praise.
His praise, ye winds, that from four quarters blow,
Breathe soft or loud; and wave your tops, ye pines,
With every plant, in sign of worship, wave.
Fountains, and ye that warble as ye flow,
Melodious murmurs, warbling tune his praise.
Join voices, all ye living souls : ye birds,
That singing up to Heaven-gate ascend,
Bear on your wings and in your notes his praise.
Ye that in waters glide, and ye that walk
The earth, and stately tread, or lowly creep ;
Witness if I be silent, morn or even,
To hill or valley, fountain or fresh shade,
Made vocal by my song, and taught his praise.
Hail, universal Lord, be bounteous still
To give us only good ; and if the night
Have gathered aught of evil or concealed,
Disperse it, as now light dispels the dark !

MAY MORNING.

Now the bright morning star, day's harbinger,
Comes dancing from the East, and leads with her
The flowery May, who from her green lap throws
The yellow cowslip, and the pale primrose.
   Hail bounteous May ! that dost inspire
   Mirth, and youth, and warm desire ;
   Woods and groves are of thy dressing,
   Hill and dale doth boast thy blessing.
Thus we salute thee with our early song,
And welcome thee and wish thee long.

   How charming is divine philosophy !
   Not harsh and crabbed, as dull fools suppose,
   But musical as is Apollo's lute,
   And a perpetual feast of nectared sweets,
   Where no crude surfeit reigns.

DEAN SWIFT.

1667–1745.

JONATHAN SWIFT, commonly known as Dean Swift, was born in Dublin, in November, 1667, and died in October, 1745. He was not proud of his native land, but emphatically declared that his birth in Ireland was a "perfect accident," and lost no opportunity of reviling that country. At Dublin University, where he was matriculated, Swift distinguished himself by his contempt for college laws, and neglect of his studies; and only by special grace did he receive his degree of B. A., in 1685. He entered the family of Sir William Temple in the capacity of secretary; in the same household "Stella," immortalized in Swift's books, was a waiting-maid. King William took a fancy to Swift on account of the latter's services in making the sovereign acquainted with asparagus, and offered him the command of a troop of horse. But the favor was declined. In 1694 Swift was admitted to deacon's orders, and a few years later went to Ireland as chaplain to Lord Berkeley. Here he occupied various ecclesiastical offices, and in 1713 was made Dean of St. Patrick's. He began his career in literature as a writer of political tracts, and was secretly employed by the government to write in its behalf. In 1704 he published *The Tale of a Tub*. From that time till 1725 he was a resident of England, and mainly engaged in political controversy. In 1726 appeared *Gulliver's Travels*, and at frequent intervals thereafter, his other writings, prose and poetry. In 1740 he evinced the first symptoms of the madness which clouded his closing years. The story of his life is a sad one, and goes far to encourage the belief that sometimes, if not always, retribution comes in this life upon the wrong-doer. Swift's career was supremely selfish; nothing was suffered to stand in the way of his interest and gratification; everybody feared him, and nobody, save the three women whose names he has linked with his own, and whose unfaltering affection he requited so brutally,—with these exceptions, nobody loved him. His life furnishes an impressive lesson, the gist of which is, that a man cannot make himself happy by exclusive devotion to himself.

As to Swift's rank as a writer it is not easy to define it; but of his extraordinary abilities there is no chance for doubt. He was, perhaps, the greatest master of satire that has ever written the English language. His originality is remarkable; no writer of his time, probably, borrowed so little from his predecessors; and his versatility—for he succeeded in every department of literature that he attempted—is not less wonderful. All things considered, his *Gulliver's Travels* must be regarded as his greatest work, though several eminent critics, including Hallam, have found it inferior to *The Tale of a Tub*. Perhaps these words of Lord Jeffrey best embody the general estimate of Dean Swift as a literary man: "In humor and in irony, and in the talent of debasing and defiling what he hated, we join with the world in thinking the Dean of St. Patrick's without a rival." We give an extract from *Gulliver's Travels*, which illustrates his best manner as a satirist.

PHILOSOPHERS AND PROJECTORS.

I WAS received very kindly by the warden, and went for many days to the academy. Every room hath in it one or more projectors, and I believe I could not be in fewer than five hundred rooms.

The first man I saw was of a meager aspect, with sooty hands and face, his hair and beard long, ragged, and singed in several places. His clothes, shirt, and skin were all of the same color. He had been eight years upon a project for extracting sunbeams out of cucumbers, which were to be put into vials hermetically sealed, and let out to warm the air in raw, inclement summers. He told me he did not doubt in eight years more that he should be able to supply the governor's gardens with sunshine at a reasonable rate; but he complained that the stock was low, and entreated me to give him something as an encouragement to ingenuity, especially since this had been a very dear season for cucumbers. I made him a small present, for my lord had furnished me with money, on purpose, because he knew their practice of begging from all who go to see them.

I saw another at work to calcine ice into gunpowder, who likewise showed me a treatise he had written concerning the malleability of fire, which he intended to publish.

There was a most ingenious architect, who had contrived a new method for building houses, by beginning at the roof, and working downwards to the foundation; which he justified to me by the like practice of those two prudent insects, the bee and the spider.

In another apartment I was highly pleased with a projector who had found a device of ploughing the ground with hogs, to save the charges of ploughs, cattle, and labor. The method is this: in an acre of ground, you bury, at six inches distance, and eight deep, a quantity of acorns, dates, chestnuts, and other masts or vegetables, whereof these animals are fondest; then you drive six hundred or more of them into the field, where in a few days they will root up the whole ground in search of their food, and make it fit for sowing. It is true, upon experiment they found the charge and trouble very great, and they had little or no crop. However, it is not doubted that this invention may be capable of great improvement.

I went into another room, where the walls and ceilings were all hung round with cobwebs, except a narrow passage for the artist to go in and out. At my entrance he called aloud to me not to disturb his webs. He lamented the fatal mistake the world had been so long in, of using silk-worms, while we had such plenty of domestic insects, who infinitely excelled the former, because they understood how to weave as well as spin. And he proposed, further, that by employing spiders, the charge of dyeing silks would be wholly saved; whereof I was fully convinced when he showed me a vast number of flies most beautifully colored, wherewith he fed his spiders; assuring us that the webs would take a tincture from them; and as he had them of all hues, he hoped to fit everybody's fancy, as soon as he could find proper food for the flies, of certain gums, oils, and other glutinous matter, to give a consistence to the threads.

There was an astronomer who had undertaken to place a sun-dial upon the great weathercock on the town-house, by adjusting the annual and diurnal motions of the earth and sun, so as to answer and coincide with all accidental turning of the winds.

I visited many other apartments, but shall not trouble my reader with all the curiosities I observed, being studious of brevity.

I had hitherto only seen one side of the academy, the other being appropriated to the advancers of speculative learning, of whom I shall say something when I have mentioned one illustrious person more who is called among them the universal artist. He told us he had been thirty years employing his thoughts for the improvement of human life. He had two large rooms full of wonderful curiosities, and fifty men at work; some were condensing air into a dry tangible substance, by extracting the niter, and letting the aqueous or fluid particles percolate; others, softening marble for pillows and pin-cushions; others, petrifying the hoofs of a living horse to preserve them from foundering. The artist himself was at that time busy upon two great designs; first, to sow land with chaff, wherein he affirmed the true seminal virtue to be contained, as he demonstrated by several experiments, which I was not skillful enough to comprehend. The other was, by a certain composition of gums, minerals, and vegetables, outwardly applied, to prevent the growth of wool upon two young lambs, and he hoped in a reasonable time to propagate the breed of naked sheep all over the kingdom.

We crossed a walk to the other part of the academy, where, as I have already said, the projectors in speculative learning resided.

The first professor I saw was in a very large room, with forty pupils about him. After salutation, observing me to look earnestly upon a frame which took up the greatest part of both the length and breadth of the room, he said, perhaps I might wonder to see him employed in a project for improving speculative knowledge by practical and mechanical operations. But the world would soon be sensible of its usefulness, and he flattered himself that a more noble, exalted thought never sprang in any other man's head. Every one knew how laborious the usual method is of attaining to arts and sciences, whereas, by his contrivance, the most ignorant person, at a reasonable charge, and with a little bodily labor, may write books in philosophy, poetry, politics, law, mathematics, and theology, without the least assistance from genius or study. He then led me to the frame, about the sides whereof all his pupils stood in ranks. It was twenty feet square, placed in the middle of the room. The superficies * was composed of several bits of wood, about the bigness of a die, but some larger than others. They were all linked together by slender wires. These bits of wood were covered on every square with paper pasted on them; and on these papers were written all the words of their language in their several moods, tenses, and declensions, but without any order. The professor then desired me to observe, for he was going to set his engine at work. The pupils, at his command, took each of them hold of an iron handle, whereof there were forty fixed round the edges of the frame, and giving them a sudden turn, the whole disposition of the words was entirely changed. He then commanded six-and-thirty of the lads to read the several lines softly as they appeared upon the frame, and where they found three or four words together that might make part of a sentence, they dictated to the four remaining boys, who were scribes. This work was repeated three or four times, and at every turn the engine was so contrived, that the words shifted into new places as the square bits of wood moved upside down.

Six hours a day the young students were employed in this labor; and the professor showed me several volumes in large folio, already collected, of broken sentences, which he intended to piece together, and out of those rich materials to give the world a complete body of all arts and sciences, which, however, might be still improved, and much expedited, if the public would raise a fund for making and employing five hundred such frames in Lagado, and oblige the managers to contribute in common their several collections.

He assured me that this invention had employed all his thoughts from his youth; that he had emptied the whole vocabulary into his frame, and made the strictest computation of the general proportion there is in books, between the numbers of particles, nouns, and verbs, and other parts of speech.

I made my humblest acknowledgments to this illustrious person for his great communicativeness, and promised, if ever I had the good fortune to return to my native country, that I would do him justice, as the sole inventor of this wonderful machine, the form and contrivance of which I desired leave to delineate upon paper. I told him, although it were the custom of our learned in Europe to steal inventions from each other, who had thereby at least this advantage,

* The surface; the exterior part or face of a thing.

that it became a controversy which was the right owner, yet I would take such caution that he should have the honor entire without a rival.

We next went to the school of languages, where three professors sat in consultation upon improving that of their own country.

The first project was to shorten discourse by cutting polysyllables into one, and leaving out verbs and participles; because, in reality, all things imaginable are but nouns.

The other was a scheme for entirely abolishing all words whatsoever; and this was urged as a great advantage in point of health as well as brevity : for it is plain that every word we speak is in some degree a diminution of our lungs by corrosion, and consequently contributes to the shortening of our lives. An expedient was therefore offered, that since words are only names for things, it would be more convenient for all men to carry about them such things as were necessary to express the particular business they are to discourse on. And this invention would certainly have taken place, to the great ease as well as health of the subject, if the women, in conjunction with the vulgar and illiterate, had not threatened to raise a rebellion, unless they might be allowed the liberty to speak with their tongues, after the manner of their forefathers ; such constant irreconcilable enemies to science are the common people.

THE common fluency of speech in many men, and most women, is owing to a scarcity of matter, and a scarcity of words; for whoever is a master of language, and hath a mind full of ideas, will be apt in speaking to hesitate upon the choice of both ; whereas common speakers have only one set of ideas, and one set of words to clothe them in ; and these are always ready at the mouth ; so people come faster out of church when it is almost empty, than when a crowd is at the door.

AN old miser kept a tame jackdaw, that used to steal pieces of money and hide them in a hole, which the cat observing, asked " Why he would hoard up those round shining things that he could make no use of? "   " Why," said the jackdaw, " my master has a whole chest full, and makes no more use of them than I."

ADDISON.

1672 – 1719.

JOSEPH ADDISON was born in 1672, and died in 1719. His name is a synonym of rhetorical elegance; and to say that the style of a composition is " Addisonian " is to give it the highest praise for finish and classic regularity. Addison's style, however admirable it may have seemed to his contemporaries, cannot safely be taken as a model by a writer of the present day : it is too cold and elaborate, and conveys an idea of formality which is not in harmony with the spirit of our time. Addison's fame as a writer rests mainly on his contributions to the *Spectator*, *Tatler*, and *Guardian*, periodicals which clearly illustrate the manners and morals of the time, and which contain many of the finest specimens of English literary workmanship. To these periodicals Addison was the principal contributor, and with these his name will have its most enduring association. He was a poet and a dramatist ; but, except perhaps his tragedy of *Cato*, his efforts in these departments of literature are not held in very high esteem by the authorities of to-day. Addison led an easy and somewhat luxurious life. He held a high office in the government, had an ample income, and in the literary society of that brilliant period occupied, by general acquiescence, the foremost rank. No student of English literature can afford to neglect the essays of Addison, which illustrate the very best literary achievements of English writers, in delicacy of sentiment and felicity of expression.

AMERICAN INDIAN TRADITIONS OF THE SPIRIT-WORLD.

THE American Indians believe that all creatures have souls, not only men and women, but brutes, vegetables, nay, even the most inanimate things, as stocks and stones. They believe the same of all the works of art, as of knives, boats, looking-glasses ; and that, as any of these things perish, their souls go into another world, which is inhabited by the ghosts of men and women. For this reason they always place by the corpse of their dead friend a bow and arrow, that he may make use of the souls of them in the other world, as he did of their wooden bodies in this. How absurd soever such an opinion as this may appear, our European philosophers have maintained several notions altogether as improbable. I shall only instance Albertus Magnus,* who in his dissertation upon the loadstone, observing that fire will destroy its magnetic virtues, tells us that he took particular notice of one as it lay glowing amidst an heap of burning coals, and that he perceived a certain blue vapor to arise from it, which he believed might be the substantial form ; that is, in our West-Indian phrase, the soul of the magnet.

There is a tradition among the Indians, that one of their country-

---

* A Dominican friar and bishop of the eleventh century. He was an eminent mechanician and mathematician, and is said to have been a searcher after the philosopher's stone.

men descended in a vision to the great repository of souls, or, as we call it here, to the other world; and that upon his return he gave his friends a distinct account of everything he saw among those regions of the dead. A friend of mine, whom I have formerly mentioned, prevailed upon one of the interpreters of the Indian kings, to inquire of them, if possible, what tradition they have among them of this matter; which, as well as he could learn by those many questions which he asked them at several times, was in substance as follows.

The visionary, whose name was Marraton, after having traveled for a long space under an hollow mountain, arrived at length on the confines of this world of spirits, but could not enter it by reason of a thick forest made up of bushes, brambles, and pointed thorns, so interwoven with one another, that it was impossible to find a passage through it. Whilst he was looking about for some track or pathway that might be worn in any part of it, he saw a huge lion couched under the side of it, who kept his eye upon him in the same posture as when he watches for his prey. The Indian immediately started back, whilst the lion rose with a spring, and leaped towards him. Being wholly destitute of all other weapons, he stooped down to take up a huge stone in his hand; but to his infinite surprise grasped nothing, and found the supposed stone to be only the apparition of one. If he was disappointed on this side, he was as much pleased on the other, when he found the lion, which had seized on his left shoulder, had no power to hurt him, and was only the ghost of that ravenous creature which it appeared to be. He no sooner got rid of his impotent enemy, but he marched up to the wood, and after having surveyed it for some time, endeavored to press into one part of it that was a little thinner than the rest; when again, to his great surprise, he found the bushes made no resistance, but that he walked through briers and brambles with the same ease as through the open air; and, in short, that the whole wood was nothing else but a wood of shades. He immediately concluded that this huge thicket of thorns and brakes was designed as a kind of fence or quickset hedge to the ghosts it enclosed; and that probably their soft substances might be torn by these subtle points and prickles, which were too weak to make any impressions in flesh and blood. With this thought he resolved to travel through this intricate wood; when by degrees he felt a gale of perfumes breathing upon him, that grew stronger and sweeter in proportion as he advanced. He had not proceeded much farther, when he observed the thorns and briers to end, and give place to a thousand beautiful green trees covered with blossoms of the finest scents and colors, that formed a wilderness of sweets, and were a kind of lining to those rugged scenes which he had before passed through. As he was coming out of this delightful part of the wood, and entering upon the plains it enclosed, he saw several horsemen rushing by him, and a little while after heard the cry of a pack of dogs. He had not listened long before he saw the apparition of a milk-white steed, with a young man on the back of it, advancing upon full stretch after the souls of about an hundred beagles, that were hunting down the ghost of an hare, which ran away before them with an unspeakable swiftness. As the man on the milk-white steed came by him, he looked upon him very attentively, and found him to be the young prince Nicharagua, who died about half a year before, and by reason of his great virtues was at that time lamented over all the western parts of America.

He had no sooner got out of the wood, but he was entertained with such a landscape of flowery plains, green meadows, running streams, sunny hills, and shady vales, as were not to be represented by his own expressions, nor, as he said, by the conceptions of others. This happy region was peopled with innumerable swarms of spirits, who applied themselves to exercises and diversions, according as their fancies led them. Some of them were tossing the figure of a coit; others were pitching the shadow of a bar; others were breaking the apparition of a horse; and multitudes employing themselves upon ingenious handicrafts with the souls of departed utensils, for that is the name which in the Indian language they give their tools when they are burned or broken. As he traveled through this delightful scene, he was very often tempted to pluck the flowers that rose everywhere about him in the greatest variety and profusion, having never seen several of them in his own country; but he quickly found, that though they were objects of his sight, they were not liable to his touch. He at length came to the side of a great river, and being a good fisherman himself, stood upon the banks of it some time to look upon an angler that had taken a great many shapes of fishes, which lay flouncing up and down by him.

I should have told my reader that this Indian had been formerly married to one of the greatest beauties of his country, by whom he had several children. This couple were so famous for their love and constancy to one another, that the Indians to this day, when they give a married man joy of his wife, wish they may live together like Marraton and Yaratilda. Marraton had not stood long by the fisherman, when he saw the shadow of his beloved Yaratilda, who had for some time fixed her eyes upon him before he discovered her. Her arms were stretched out towards him, floods of tears ran down her eyes : her looks, her hands, her voice called him over to her; and at the same time seemed to tell him that the river was impassable. Who can describe the passion, made up of joy, sorrow, love, desire, astonishment, that rose in the Indian upon the sight of his dear Yaratilda? He could express it by nothing but his tears, which ran like a river down his cheeks as he looked upon her. He had not stood in this posture long, before he plunged into the stream that lay before him; and finding it to be nothing but the phantom of a river, walked on the bottom of it till he rose on the other side. At his approach Yaratilda flew into his arms, whilst Marraton wished himself disencumbered of that body which kept her from his embraces. After many questions and endearments on both sides, she conducted him to a bower which she had dressed with all the ornaments that could be met with in those blooming regions. She had made it gay beyond imagination, and was every day adding something new to it. As Marraton stood astonished at the unspeakable beauty of her habitation, and ravished with the fragrancy that came from every part of it, Yaratilda told him that she was preparing this bower for his reception, as well knowing that his piety to his God, and his faithful dealing towards men, would certainly bring him to that happy place, whenever his life should be at an end. She then brought two of her children to him, who died some years before, and resided with her in the same delightful bower; advising him to breed up those others which were still with him in such a manner, that they might hereafter all of them meet together in this happy place.

The tradition tells us further, that he had afterwards a sight of those dismal habitations which are the portion of ill men after death ; and mentions several molten seas of gold into which were plunged the souls of barbarous Europeans, who put to the sword so many thousands of poor Indians for the sake of that precious metal. But having already touched upon the chief points of this tradition, and exceeded the measure of my paper, I shall not give any further account of it.

POPE.

1688 – 1744.

ALEXANDER POPE, the most eminent poet of his time, was born in 1688, and died in 1744. He was blessed with a fair share of wealth, and lived in luxurious retirement in his villa at Twickenham. Afflicted with a bodily deformity, touching which he was keenly sensitive, he mingled but little in the great world, but contented himself with the society which sought him in his home. He was emphatically a literary man, giving his whole time and thought to literary pursuits. Notoriously petulant, a peculiarity which his feeble health goes far toward excusing, he was continually involved in quarrels with contemporary writers; and some of his most brilliant poems were written under the inspiration of personal animosity. His greatest work was the translation of Homer, which in most respects remains unsurpassed by any previous or subsequent version. Of his original compositions *The Essay on Man* is that by which he is best known. From this work we take our extracts.

THE PRESENT CONDITION OF MAN VINDICATED.

HEAVEN from all creatures hides the book of Fate,
All but the page prescribed, their present state;
From brutes what men, from men what spirits know,
Or who could suffer being here below?
The lamb thy riot dooms to bleed to-day,
Had he thy reason, would he skip and play?
Pleased to the last, he crops the flowery food,
And licks the hand just raised to shed his blood.
O blindness to the future! kindly given,
That each may fill the circle marked by Heaven;
Who sees with equal eye, as God of all,
A hero perish or a sparrow fall;
Atoms or systems into ruin hurled,
And now a bubble burst, and now a world.

Hope humbly, then, with trembling pinions soar;
Wait the great teacher, Death; and God adore.
What future bliss, he gives not thee to know,
But gives that hope to be thy blessing now.
Hope springs eternal in the human breast;
Man never IS, but always TO BE blest;
The soul, uneasy and confined from home,
Rests and expatiates in a life to come.

Lo the poor Indian, whose untutored mind
Sees God in clouds, and hears him in the wind;

His soul proud Science never taught to stray
Far as the solar walk, or milky way;
Yet simple Nature to his hope has given,
Behind the cloud-topped hill, a humbler heaven;
Some safer world in depth of woods embraced,
Some happier island in the watery waste,
Where slaves once more their native land behold,
No fiends torment, no Christians thirst for gold.
To BE, contents his natural desire,
He asks no angel's wing, no seraph's fire:
But thinks, admitted to that equal sky,
His faithful dog shall bear him company.
Go, wiser thou! and in thy scale of sense
Weigh thy opinion against Providence;
Call imperfection what thou fanciest such,
Say, here he gives too little, there too much:
Destroy all creatures for thy sport or gust,
Yet cry, if Man's unhappy, God's unjust;
If man alone engross not Heaven's high care,
Alone made perfect here, immortal there:
Snatch from his hand the balance and the rod,
Re-judge his justice, be the God of God.
In Pride, in reasoning Pride, our error lies;
All quit their sphere, and rush into the skies.
Pride still is aiming at the blest abodes,
Men would be Angels, Angels would be Gods.
Aspiring to be Gods, if Angels fell,
Aspiring to be Angels, Men rebel:
And who but wishes to revert the laws
Of Order sins against the Eternal Cause.

GREATNESS.

Honor and shame from no condition rise;
Act well your part, there all the honor lies.
Fortune in men has some small difference made:
One flaunts in rags, one flutters in brocade;
The cobbler aproned, and the parson gowned,
The friar hooded, and the monarch crowned.

" What differ more (you cry) than crown and cowl ? "
I 'll tell you, friend ! a wise man and a fool.
You 'll find, if once the monarch acts the monk,
Or, cobbler-like, the parson will be drunk,
Worth makes the man, and want of it the fellow ;
The rest is all but leather or prunella.
Go ! if your ancient but ignoble blood
Has crept through scoundrels ever since the flood.
Go ! and pretend your family is young,
Nor own your fathers have been fools so long.
What can ennoble sots or slaves or cowards ?
Alas ! not all the blood of all the Howards.

    Look next on greatness ! say where greatness lies ?
" Where, but among the heroes and the wise ? "
Heroes are much the same, the point 's agreed,
From Macedonia's madman to the Swede ; *
The whole strange purpose of their lives, to find
Or make an enemy of all mankind !
Not one looks backward, onward still he goes,
Yet ne'er looks forward farther than his nose.
No less alike the politic and wise ;
All sly slow things, with circumspective eyes :
Men in their loose unguarded hours they take,
Not that themselves are wise, but others weak.
But grant that those can conquer, these can cheat ;
'T is phrase absurd to call a villain great :
Who wickedly is wise, or madly brave,
Is but the more a fool, the more a knave.
Who noble ends by noble means obtains,
Or, failing, smiles in exile or in chains,
Like good Aurelius let him reign, or bleed
Like Socrates, that man is great indeed.

* The allusion is to Alexander the Great and Charles XII. of Sweden. Pope borrowed the idea from Mandeville's *Fable of the Bees.*

DR. JOHNSON.

1709 – 1784.

SAMUEL JOHNSON, one of the great literary men of his time, was born in 1709 and died in 1784. He compiled a celebrated *Dictionary of the English Language* and wrote poems, moral and controversial, essays and biographies, including the well-known *Lives of the Poets*. He was the contemporary of Goldsmith, Burke, Sheridan, and many famous literary men and women, among whom he enjoyed a sort of pre-eminence, yielded rather to his arrogance than to his merits. His manners were incredibly rude, and his general demeanor positively bearish, but his intellectual greatness is beyond question. His prose writings are noted for their formality of style and vigor of thought. Like Addison, he has furnished an adjective descriptive of literary style; and to be "Johnsonian" is to be ponderous and grandiose. *Rasselas, Prince of Abyssinia*, an allegorical story from which we take our extracts, is perhaps the most familiar of his compositions to the general reader. Dr. Johnson was a man of vigorous intellect, acute and argumentative, but narrow in his views, dogmatic and positive in his assertions. He was respected, but not loved. His biography, written by his humble friend Boswell, gives a full and vivid portrait of him as a man and a writer.

A PALACE IN A VALLEY.

YE who listen with credulity to the whispers of fancy, and pursue with eagerness the phantoms of hope; who expect that age will perform the promises of youth, and that the deficiencies of the present day will be supplied by the morrow; attend to the history of Rasselas, Prince of Abyssinia.

Rasselas was the fourth son of the mighty emperor in whose dominions the Father of Waters begins his course; whose bounty pours down the streams of plenty, and scatters over half the world the harvests of Egypt.

According to the custom which has descended from age to age among the monarchs of the torrid zone, Rasselas was confined in a private palace, with the other sons and daughters of Abyssinian royalty, till the order of succession should call him to the throne.

The place which the wisdom or policy of antiquity had destined for the residence of the Abyssinian princes was a spacious valley in the kingdom of Amhara, surrounded on every side by mountains, of which the summits overhang the middle part. The only passage by which it could be entered was a cavern that passed under a rock, of which it has long been disputed whether it was the work of nature or of human industry. The outlet of the cavern was concealed by a thick wood, and the mouth which opened into the valley was closed with gates of iron, forged by the artificers of ancient days, so massy that no man could without the help of engines open or shut them.

From the mountains on every side rivulets descended that filled all the valley with verdure and fertility, and formed a lake in the middle inhabited by fish of every species, and frequented by every fowl whom Nature has taught to dip the wing in water. This lake discharged its superfluities by a stream which entered a dark cleft of the mountain on the northern side, and fell with dreadful noise from precipice to precipice till it was heard no more.

The sides of the mountains were covered with trees, the banks of the brooks were diversified with flowers; every blast shook spices from the rocks, and every month dropped fruits upon the ground. All animals that bite the grass, or browse the shrub, whether wild or tame, wandered in this extensive circuit, secured from beasts of prey by the mountains which confined them. On one part were flocks and herds feeding in the pastures, on another, all beasts of chase frisking in the lawns; the sprightly kid was bounding on the rocks, the subtle monkey frolicking among the trees, and the solemn elephant reposing in the shade. All the diversities of the world were brought together, the blessings of nature were collected, and its evils extracted and excluded.

The valley, wide and fruitful, supplied its inhabitants with the necessaries of life; and all delights and superfluities were added at the annual visit which the emperor paid his children, when the iron gate was opened to the sound of music; and during eight days every one that resided in the valley was required to propose whatever might contribute to make seclusion pleasant, to fill up the vacancies of attention, and lessen the tediousness of time. Every desire was immediately granted. All the artificers of pleasure were called to gladden the festivity; the musicians exerted the power of harmony, and the dancers showed their activity before the princes, in hope that they should pass their lives in this blissful captivity, to which those only were admitted whose performance was thought able to add novelty to luxury. Such was the appearance of security and delight which this retirement afforded, that they to whom it was new always desired that it might be perpetual; and as those on whom the iron gate had once closed were never suffered to return, the effect of long experience could not be known. Thus every year produced new schemes of delight, and new competitors for imprisonment.

The palace stood on an eminence raised about thirty paces above the surface of the lake. It was divided into many squares or courts, built with greater or less magnificence, according to the rank of those for whom they were designed. The roofs were turned into arches of massy stone, joined by a cement that grew harder by time, and the building stood from century to century deriding the solstitial rains and equinoctial hurricanes, without need of reparation.

This house, which was so large as to be fully known to none but some ancient officers who successively inherited the secrets of the place, was built as if Suspicion herself had dictated the plan. To every room there was an open and secret passage; every square had a communication with the rest, either from the upper stories by private galleries, or by subterranean passages from the lower apart-. ments. Many of the columns had unsuspected cavities, in which a long race of monarchs had deposited their treasures. They then closed up the opening with marble, which was never to be removed but in the utmost exigencies of the kingdom; and recorded their accumulations in a book which was itself concealed in a tower not entered but by the emperor, attended by the prince who stood next in succession.

THE DISCONTENT OF RASSELAS.

HERE the sons and daughters of Abyssinia lived only to know the soft vicissitudes of pleasure and repose, attended by all that were skillful to delight, and gratified with whatever the senses can enjoy. They wandered in gardens of fragrance, and slept in the fortresses of security. Every art was practiced to make them pleased with their own condition. The sages who instructed them told them of nothing but the miseries of public life, and described all beyond the mountains as regions of calamity, where discord was always raging, and where man preyed upon man.

To heighten their opinion of their own felicity, they were daily entertained with songs, the subject of which was the *happy valley*. Their appetites were excited by frequent enumerations of different enjoyments, and revelry and merriment was the business of every hour from the dawn of morning to the close of even.

These methods were generally successful; few of the princes had ever wished to enlarge their bounds, but passed their lives in full conviction that they had all within their reach that art or nature could bestow, and pitied those whom fate had excluded from this seat of tranquillity, as the sport of chance and the slave of misery.

Thus they rose in the morning and lay down at night, pleased with each other and with themselves, — all but Rasselas, who in the twenty-sixth year of his age began to withdraw himself from their pastimes and assemblies, and to delight in solitary walks and silent meditation. He often sat before tables covered with luxury, and forgot to taste the dainties that were placed before him; he rose abruptly in the midst of the song, and hastily retired beyond the sound of music. His attendants observed the change, and endeavored to renew his love of pleasure. He neglected their officiousness, repulsed their invitations, and spent day after day on the banks of rivulets sheltered with trees, where he sometimes listened to the birds in the branches, sometimes observed the fish playing in the stream, and anon cast his eyes upon the pastures and mountains filled with animals, of which some were biting the herbage, and some sleeping among the bushes.

This singularity of his humor made him much observed. One of the sages, in whose conversation he had formerly delighted, followed him secretly, in hope of discovering the cause of his disquiet. Rasselas, who knew not that any one was near him, having for some time fixed his eyes upon the goats that were browsing among the rocks, began to compare their condition with his own.

"What," said he, "makes the difference between man and all the rest of the animal creation? Every beast that strays beside me has the same corporal necessities with myself: he is hungry and crops the grass, he is thirsty and drinks the stream; his thirst and hunger are appeased, he is satisfied and sleeps: he rises again and is hungry; he is again fed and is at rest. I am hungry and thirsty, like him; but when thirst and hunger cease I am not at rest: I am, like him, pained with want; but am not, like him, satisfied with fullness. The intermediate hours are tedious and gloomy; I long again to be hungry, that I may again quicken my attention. The birds peck the berries or the corn, and fly away to the groves, where they sit in seeming happiness on the branches, and waste their lives in tuning one unvaried series of sounds. I likewise can call the lutanist and singer, but the sounds that pleased me yesterday weary me to-day, and will grow more wearisome to-morrow. I can discover within me no power of perception which is not glutted with its proper pleasure, yet I do not feel myself delighted. Man surely has some latent sense for which this place affords no gratification, or he has some desires distinct from sense, which must be satisfied before he can be happy."

After this he lifted up his head, and seeing the moon rising, walked toward the palace. As he passed through the fields, and saw the animals around him, "Ye," said he, "are happy, and need not envy me that walk thus among you, burdened with myself; nor do I, ye gentle beings, envy your felicity, for it is not the felicity of man. I have many distresses from which ye are free; I fear pain when I do not feel it; I sometimes shrink at evils recollected, and sometimes start at evils anticipated: surely the equity of Providence has balanced peculiar sufferings with peculiar enjoyments."

With observations like these the prince amused himself as he returned, uttering them with a plaintive voice, yet with a look that discovered him to feel some complacence in his own perspicacity, and to receive some solace of the miseries of life from consciousness of the delicacy with which he bewailed them. He mingled cheerfully in the diversions of the evening, and all rejoiced to find that his heart was lightened.

WE were now treading that illustrious island which was once the luminary of the Caledonian regions, whence savage clans and roving barbarians derived the benefits of knowledge and the blessings of religion. To abstract the mind from all local emotion would be impossible if it were endeavored, and would be foolish if it were possible. Whatever withdraws us from the power of our senses, whatever makes the past the distant, or the future predominate over the present, advances us in the dignity of thinking beings. Far from me and my friends be such frigid philosophy as may conduct us indifferent and unmoved over any ground which has been dignified by wisdom, bravery, or virtue. The man is little to be envied whose patriotism would not gain force on the plains of Marathon,* or whose piety would not grow warmer among the ruins of Iona.† — *Journey to the Hebrides.*

* MARATHON. Among the noted battles of ancient times; fought between the Greeks and Persians 490 B. C.
† IONA. One of the western islands of Scotland. Interesting for the ruins of its ancient religious edifices, established by St. Columba 565 A. D.

GOLDSMITH.

1729-1774

In the long and brilliant list of writers who have made enduring contributions to English literature there is no dearer name than that of Oliver Goldsmith. He seems the personal friend of all who read his writings, and those who are familiar with the strange, sad story of his life cherish his memory with a tender affection. He was born in Ireland in 1729 and died in 1774, spending most of his life in London, where he enjoyed the friendship of Johnson and other eminent authors. His early career was full of vicissitudes; he sauntered through the first years of manhood with empty pockets and smiling lips, studying medicine by fits and starts, wandering through Europe, winning his bread by the exercise of his musical talents, and at last settling down in London to the miserable lot of a literary hack. But he made friends wherever he went; that he won and retained the warm friendship of Samuel Johnson, a notoriously selfish man, is proof positive of the strength of his fascinations. He wrote his most famous works almost literally under the pressure of hunger; the manuscript of one of them was sold to discharge an execution, while the officers of the law waited in the author's lodgings. Goldsmith's nature was eminently lovable; there was no bitterness or guile in it; he loved his fellows and was in turn beloved. The qualities of his heart, as well as those of his intellect, are manifest in his writings, and give them the sweetness that the highest intellectual power or culture could not impart. In *The Vicar of Wakefield* his name will live forever, and, so long as poetry survives, *The Traveler* and *The Deserted Village* will be read and admired. His versatility was astonishing; he was a poet, a novelist, an essayist, and an historian, and won fame in each department of effort. Well has it been said of him, that "he touched nothing which he did not adorn."

THE SAGACITY OF THE SPIDER.

OF all the solitary insects I have ever remarked, the spider is the most sagacious, and its actions, to me, who have attentively considered them, seem almost to exceed belief. This insect is formed by nature for a state of war, not only upon other insects, but upon each other. For this state nature seems perfectly well to have formed it. Its head and breast are covered with a strong natural coat of mail, which is impenetrable to the attempts of every other insect, and its belly is enveloped in a soft pliant skin, which eludes the sting even of a wasp. Its legs are terminated by strong claws, not unlike those of the lobster; and their vast length, like spears, serves to keep every assailant at a distance.

Not worse furnished for observation than for an attack or defense, it has several eyes, large, transparent, and covered with a horny substance, which, however, does not impede its vision. Besides this, it is furnished with a forceps above the mouth, which serves to kill or secure the prey already caught in its claws or its net.

Such are the implements of war with which the body is immediately furnished; but its net to entangle the enemy seems to be what it chiefly trusts to, and what it takes most pains to render as complete as possible. Nature has furnished the body of this little creature with a glutinous liquid, which, proceeding from the lower extremity of the body, it spins into a thread, coarser or finer as it chooses to contract its sphincter.* In order to fix its threads when it begins to weave, it emits a small drop of its liquid against the wall, which, hardening by degrees, serves to hold the thread very firmly. Then receding from the first point, as it recedes the thread lengthens ; and when the spider has come to the place where the other end of the thread should be fixed, gathering up with its claws the thread, which would otherwise be too slack, it is stretched tightly, and fixed in the same manner to the wall as before.

In this manner it spins and fixes several threads parallel to each other, which, so to speak, serve as the warp to the intended web. To form the woof, it spins in the same manner its thread, transversely fixing one end to the first thread that was spun, and which is always the strongest of the whole web, and the other to the wall. All these threads, being newly spun, are glutinous, and therefore stick to each other wherever they happen to touch ; and in those parts of the web most exposed to be torn our natural artist strengthens them, by doubling the thread sometimes six-fold.

Thus far naturalists have gone in the description of this animal : what follows is the result of my own observation upon that species of insect called the house-spider. I perceived, about four years ago, a large spider in one corner of my room, making its web, and though the maid frequently leveled her fatal broom against the labors of the little animal, I had the good fortune then to prevent its destruction, and, I may say, it more than paid me by the entertainment it afforded.

In three days the web was with incredible diligence completed ; nor could I avoid thinking that the insect seemed to exult in its new abode. It frequently traversed it round, and examined the strength of every part of it, retired into its hole, and came out very freq. The first enemy, however, it had to encounter, was another and much larger spider, which having no web of its own, and having probably exhausted all its stock in former labors of this kind, came to invade the property of its neighbor. Soon, then, a terrible encounter ensued, in which the invader seemed to have the victory, and the

---

* SPHINCTER. A muscle that contracts or shuts the mouth of an orifice.

laborious spider was obliged to take refuge in its hole. Upon this I perceived the victor using every art to draw the enemy from its stronghold. He seemed to go off, but quickly returned, and when he found all arts vain, began to demolish the new web without-mercy. This brought on another battle, and, contrary to my expectations, the laborious spider became conqueror, and fairly killed his antagonist.

Now, then, in peaceful possession of what was justly its own, it waited three days with the utmost impatience, repairing the breaches of its web, and taking no sustenance that I could perceive. At last, however, a large blue fly fell into the snare, and struggled hard to get loose. The spider gave it leave to entangle itself as much as possible, but it seemed to be too strong for the cobweb. I must own I was greatly surprised when I saw the spider immediately sally out, and in less than a minute weave a net round its captive, by which the motion of its wings was stopped, and when it was fairly hampered in this manner, it was seized and dragged into the hole.

In this manner it lived, in a precarious state, and nature seemed to have fitted it for such a life; for upon a single fly it subsisted for more than a week. I once put a wasp into the net, but when the spider came out in order to seize it as usual, upon perceiving what kind of an enemy it had to deal with, it instantly broke all the bands that held it fast, and contributed all that lay in its power to disen- . gage so formidable an antagonist. When the wasp was at liberty, I expected the spider would have set about repairing the breaches that were made in its net; but those, it seems, were irreparable, wherefore the cobweb was now entirely forsaken, and a new one begun, which was completed in the usual time.

I had now a mind to try how many cobwebs a single spider could furnish; wherefore I destroyed this, and the insect set about another. When I destroyed the other also, its whole stock seemed entirely exhausted, and it could spin no more. The arts it made use of to support itself, now deprived of its great means of subsistence, were indeed surprising. I have seen it roll up its legs like a ball, and lie motionless for hours together, but cautiously watching all the time; when a fly happened to approach sufficiently near, it would dart out all at once, and often seize its prey.

Of this life, however, it soon began to grow weary, and resolved to invade the possession of some other spider, since it could not make a web of its own. It formed an attack upon a neighboring fortification, with great vigor, and at first was vigorously repulsed. Not daunted, however, with one defeat, in this manner it continued to lay siege to another's web for three days, and at length, having killed the defendant, actually took possession. When smaller flies happen to fall into the snare, the spider does not sally out at once, but very patiently waits till it is sure of them; for upon his immediately approaching, the terror of his appearance might give the captive strength sufficient to get loose; the manner, then, is to wait patiently till, by ineffectual and impotent struggles, the captive has wasted all his strength, and then he becomes a certain and easy conquest.

The insect I am now describing lived three years; every year it changed its skin, and got a new set of legs. At first it dreaded my approach to its web; but at last it became so familiar as to take a fly out of my hand, and upon my touching any part of the web, would immediately leave its hole, prepared either for a defense or an attack.

THE DESERTED VILLAGE.

SWEET Auburn! loveliest village of the plain,
Where health and plenty cheered the laboring swain,
Where smiling spring its earliest visit paid
And parting summer's lingering blooms delayed;
Dear lovely bowers of innocence and ease,
Seats of my youth, when every sport could please;
How often have I loitered o'er thy green,
Where humble happiness endeared each scene;
How often have I paused on every charm, —
The sheltered cot, the cultivated farm,
The never-failing brook, the busy mill,
The decent church that topped the neighboring hill,
The hawthorn bush, with seats beneath the shade,
For talking age and whispering lovers made!
How often have I blest the coming day,
When toil remitting lent its turn to play,
And all the village train, from labor free,
Led up their sports beneath the spreading tree,
While many a pastime circled in the shade,
The young contending as the old surveyed;
And many a gambol frolicked o'er the ground,

And sleights of art and feats of strength went round;
And still as each repeated pleasure tired,
Succeeding sports the mirthful band inspired.
The dancing pair that simply sought renown,
By holding out, to tire each other down;
The swain mistrustless of his smutted face,
While secret laughter tittered round the place;
The bashful virgin's sidelong looks of love,
The matron's glance that would those looks reprove, —
These were thy charms, sweet village! sports like these,
With sweet succession, taught even toil to please;
These round thy bowers their cheerful influence shed,
These were thy charms —   But all these charms are fled.

Sweet smiling village, loveliest of the lawn,
Thy sports are fled, and all thy charms withdrawn;
Amidst thy bowers the tyrant's hand is seen,
And desolation saddens all thy green:
One only master grasps the whole domain,
And half a tillage stints thy smiling plain;
No more thy glassy brook reflects the day,
But, choked with sedges, works its weedy way;
Along thy glades, a solitary guest,
The hollow-sounding bittern guards its nest;
Amidst thy desert walks the lapwing flies,
And tires their echoes with unvaried cries.
Sunk are thy bowers in shapeless ruin all,
And the long grass o'ertops the moldering wall;
And, trembling, shrinking from the spoiler's hand,
Far, far away thy children leave the land.

Ill fares the land, to hastening ills a prey,
Where wealth accumulates, and men decay;
Princes and lords may flourish or may fade;
A breath can make them, as a breath has made;
But a bold peasantry, their country's pride,
When once destroyed, can never be supplied.

A time there was, ere England's griefs began,

When every rood of ground maintained its man ;
For him light labor spread her wholesome store,
Just gave what life required, but gave no more ;
His best companions, innocence and health,
And his best riches, ignorance of wealth.

But times are altered ; trade's unfeeling train
Usurp the land, and dispossess the swain ;
Along the lawn, where scattered hamlets rose,
Unwieldy wealth and cumberous pomp repose :
And every want to luxury allied,
And every pang that folly pays to pride.
Those gentle hours that plenty bade to bloom,
Those calm desires that asked but little room,
Those healthful sports that graced the peaceful scene,
Lived in each look, and brightened all the green ;
These, far departing, seek a kinder shore,
And rural mirth and manners are no more.

HOME.

But where to find that happiest spot below,
Who can direct, when all pretend to know ?
The shuddering tenant of the frigid zone
Boldly proclaims that happiest spot his own ;
Extols the treasures of his stormy seas,
And his long nights of revelry and ease :
The naked negro, panting at the line,
Boasts of his golden sands and palmy wine,
Basks in the glare, or stems the tepid wave,
And thanks his gods for all the good they gave.
Such is the patriot's boast, where'er we roam,
His first, best country ever is at home.
And yet, perhaps, if countries we compare,
And estimate the blessings which they share,
Though patriots flatter, still shall wisdom find
An equal portion dealt to all mankind ;
As different good, by art or nature given,
To different nations makes their blessing even.

BURKE.

1730–1797.

EDMUND BURKE was born in Dublin in 1730 and died in 1797. Unlike his great contemporary, Pitt, he was not a youthful prodigy, but was a warm-hearted boy of apparently average intellectual capacity. Having graduated at Trinity College, Dublin, he went to London and entered upon the study of law. But the profession did not suit him, and he soon abandoned it, and devoted himself to literary labors. His first considerable work was an essay entitled *A Vindication of Natural Society*. It was a parody on the works of Lord Bolingbroke, who had maintained that natural religion is sufficient for man, and that he does not need a revelation. His second book was one which gave him permanent and honorable fame, — *An Inquiry into the Origin of our Ideas on the Sublime and Beautiful*. In 1759 Burke returned to Ireland as private secretary to William Gerard Hamilton (known in history as "Single-Speech Hamilton"), Chief Secretary to the Lord Lieutenant. He held his place but a short time, and left it to become Secretary to the Marquis of Rockingham. Soon obtaining a seat in Parliament he began the brilliant political career the particulars of which are familiar to all. He was especially prominent in the debates upon the American War, and displayed a more thorough knowledge of the subject than any of his colleagues. In 1783 a political scheme, of which he was the organizer, having failed, he retired to private life. Burke was not a popular man; he alienated his closest friends by the singularity and obstinacy of his opinions; but remembering that Goldsmith loved him, and that he had befriended George Crabbe in the hour of the latter's extremity, we cannot doubt that he had a kind heart. As a writer Burke stands in the very front rank. We give extracts from one of his speeches on the American War, and from his very celebrated essay, *Reflections on the French Revolution*.

ON CONCILIATION WITH AMERICA.*

My hold of the Colonies is in the close affection which grows from common names, from kindred blood, from similar privileges, and equal protection. These are ties which, though light as air, are as strong as links of iron. Let the Colonies always keep the idea of their civil rights associated with your government; — they will cling and grapple to you; and no force under heaven will be of power to tear them from their allegiance. But let it be once understood, that your government may be one thing and their privileges another; that these two things may exist without any mutual relation : the cement is gone ; the cohesion is loosened ; and everything hastens to decay and dissolution.• As long as you have the wisdom to keep the sovereign authority of this country as the sanctuary of liberty, the sacred temple consecrated to our common faith, wherever the chosen race and sons of England worship freedom, they will turn their faces towards you. The more they multiply, the more friends you will have ; the

---

* During the Revolutionary War, Burke was a member of the British Parliament. He opposed the coercive policy of George III., being in favor of conciliation.

more ardently they love liberty, the more perfect will be their obedience. Slavery they can have anywhere. It is a weed that grows in every soil. They may have it from Spain, they may have it from Prussia. But, until you become lost to all feeling of your true interest and your natural dignity, freedom they can have from none but you. This is the commodity of price, of which you have the monopoly. This is the true act of navigation, which binds to you the commerce of the Colonies, and through them secures to you the wealth of the world. Deny them this participation of freedom, and you break that sole bond which originally made, and must still preserve, the unity of the empire. Do not entertain so weak an imagination, as that your registers and your bonds, your affidavits and your sufferances, your cockets and your clearances, are what form the great securities of your commerce. Do not dream that your letters of office, and your instructions, and your suspending clauses, are the things that hold together the great contexture of this mysterious whole. These things do not make your government. Dead instruments, passive tools as they are, it is the spirit of the English communion that gives all their life and efficacy to them. It is the spirit of the English constitution, which, infused through the mighty mass, pervades, feeds, unites, invigorates, vivifies every part of the empire, even down to the minutest member.

Is it not the same virtue which does everything for us here in England? Do you imagine, then, that it is the land tax act which raises your revenue? that it is the annual vote in the committee of supply, which gives you your army? or that it is the mutiny bill, which inspires it with bravery and discipline? No! surely no! It is the love of the people; it is their attachment to their government, from the sense of the deep stake they have in such a glorious institution, which gives you your army and your navy, and infuses into both that liberal obedience, without which your army would be a base rabble, and your navy nothing but rotten timber.

All this, I know well enough, will sound wild and chimerical to the profane herd of those vulgar and mechanical politicians, who have no place among us; a sort of people who think that nothing exists but what is gross and material; and who therefore, far from being qualified to be directors of the great movement of empire, are not fit to turn a wheel in the machine. But to men truly initiated and rightly taught, these ruling and master principles, which, in the

opinion of such men as I have mentioned, have no substantial existence, are in truth everything, and all in all. Magnanimity in politics
is not seldom the truest wisdom; and a great empire and little minds
go ill together. If we are conscious of our situation, and glow with
zeal to fill our places as becomes our station and ourselves, we ought
to auspicate our public proceedings on America with the old warning
of the Church, *Sursum Corda!*,* We ought to elevate our minds to
the greatness of that trust to which the order of Providence has
called us. By adverting to the dignity of this high calling, our
ancestors have turned a savage wilderness into a glorious empire;
and have made the most extensive, and the only honorable conquests,
not by destroying, but by promoting the wealth, the number, the
happiness of the human race. Let us get an American revenue as
we have got an American empire. English privileges have made it
all that it is; English privileges alone will make it all it can be.

THE DECAY OF CHIVALROUS SENTIMENT. †

It is now sixteen or seventeen years since I saw the Queen
of France, then the Dauphiness, at Versailles; and surely never
lighted on this orb, which she hardly seemed to touch, a more delightful vision. I saw her just above the horizon, decorating and
cheering the elevated sphere she just began to move in, — glittering
like the morning star, full of life and splendor and joy. O, what a
revolution! and what a heart must I have, to contemplate without
emotion that elevation and that fall! Little did I dream when she
added titles of veneration to those of enthusiastic, distant, respectful
love, that she should ever be obliged to carry the sharp antidote
against disgrace concealed in that bosom; little did I dream that I
should have lived to see such disasters fallen upon her in a nation of
gallant men, in a nation of men of honor, and of cavaliers. I thought
ten thousand swords must have leaped from their scabbards to avenge
even a look that threatened her with insult. But the age of chivalry
is gone. That of sophisters, economists, and calculators has succeeded; and the glory of Europe is extinguished forever. Never,

---

* SURSUM CORDA, *Lift up your hearts.*

† This is justly estimated as one of the finest rhetorical passages in our language. It
refers to the execution of Marie Antoinette, wife of Louis XVI., and Queen of France. She was
guillotined by the Jacobins in 1793, during the celebrated French Revolution. The remarks
about the "age of chivalry" and the "cheap defense of nations" have become famous.

never more shall we behold that generous loyalty to rank and sex,
that proud submission, that dignified obedience, that subordination
of the heart, which kept alive, even in servitude itself, the spirit of an
exalted freedom.   The unbought grace of life, the cheap defense of
nations, the nurse of manly sentiment and heroic enterprise, is gone !
It is gone, that sensibility of principle, that chastity of honor, which
felt a stain like a wound, which inspired courage whilst it mitigated
ferocity, which ennobled whatever it touched, and under which vice
itself lost half its evil, by losing all its grossness.

This mixed system of opinion and sentiment had its origin in the
ancient chivalry ; and the principle, though varied in its appearance
by the varying state of human affairs, subsisted and · influenced
through a long succession of generations, even to the time we live in.
If it should ever be totally extinguished, the loss I fear would be
great.   It is this which has given its character to modern Europe.
It is this which has distinguished it under all its forms of government, and distinguished it to its advantage, from the states of Asia,
and possibly from those states which flourished in the most brilliant
periods of the antique world.   It was this which, without confounding ranks, had produced a noble equality, and handed it down
through all the gradations of social life.   It was this opinion which
mitigated kings into companions, and raised private men to be fellows
with kings.   Without force, or opposition, it subdued the fierceness
of pride and power ; it obliged sovereigns to submit to the soft collar
of social esteem, compelled stern authority to submit to elegance, and
gave a dominating vanquisher of laws, to be subdued by manners.

But now all is to be changed.   All the pleasing illusions, which
made power gentle and obedience liberal, which harmonized the different shades of life, and which, by a bland assimilation, incorporated
into politics the sentiments which beautify and soften private society,
are to be dissolved by this new conquering empire of light and reason.
All the decent drapery of life is to be rudely torn off.   All the
superadded ideas, furnished from the wardrobe of a moral imagination,
which the heart owns and the understanding ratifies as necessary to
cover the defects of our naked, shivering nature, and to raise it to
dignity in our own estimation, are to be exploded as a ridiculous,
absurd, and antiquated fashion.

COWPER.

1731 – 1800.

WILLIAM COWPER was born in 1731 and died in 1800. His life was a sad one, and his last years were shadowed by a mental gloom which almost amounted to insanity. His thoughts dwelt on somber themes, and his poems, with a few exceptions, are didactic to an unpleasant degree. It is not easy to understand how the same mind could have given birth to the melancholy imaginings which constitute the staple of his verse, and the warm, free humor of *John Gilpin's Ride*. Morbid and unsocial though he was, Cowper was able to win and retain the hearty attachment of a few friends, in whose tender care he passed the closing years of his life. Though not one of the greatest English poets, Cowper holds and will hold an honorable place. His sentiments were always elevated, and his expression graceful, if not exceptionally brilliant or vigorous. He is emphatically the poet for thoughtful minds. One of his best-known poems is Alexander Selkirk, of which we give some specimen stanzas.

ALEXANDER SELKIRK.*

I AM monarch of all I survey,
   My right there is none to dispute;
From the center all round to the sea
   I am lord of the fowl and the brute.
O Solitude, where are the charms
   That sages have seen in thy face?
Better dwell in the midst of alarms
   Than reign in this horrible place.

I am out of humanity's reach;
   I must finish my journey alone;
Never hear the sweet music of speech —
   I start at the sound of my own.
The beasts that roam over the plain
   My form with indifference see;
They are so unacquainted with men,
   Their tameness is shocking to me.

Society, friendship, and love,
   Divinely bestowed upon man,
O had I the wings of a dove,
   How soon would I taste you again!

* ALEXANDER SELKIRK was a Scottish sailor, who, having quarreled on one of his voyages with his captain, was left, in 1704, on the uninhabited island of Juan Fernandez, where he remained for more than four years before his rescue. Selkirk's adventures, it is said, suggested to Defoe the celebrated romance of *Robinson Crusoe*, with which all young people are familiar.

My sorrows I then might assuage
  In the ways of religion and truth ;
Might learn from the wisdom of age,
  And be cheered by the sallies of youth.

Religion ! what treasure untold
  Resides in that heavenly word !
More precious than silver and gold,
  Or all that this earth can afford.
But the sound of the church-going bell
  These valleys and rocks never heard, —
Never sighed at the sound of a knell,
  Or smiled when a Sabbath appeared.

Ye winds that have made me your sport,
  Convey to this desolate shore
Some cordial endearing report
  Of a land I shall visit no more.
My friends, do they now and then send
  A wish or a thought after me ?
O tell me I yet have a friend,
  Though a friend I am never to see.

How fleet is a glance of the mind !
  Compared with the speed of its flight,
The tempest itself lags behind,
  And the swift-wingéd arrows of light.
When I think of my own native land,
  In a moment I seem to be there ;
But, alas ! recollection at hand
  Soon hurries me back to despair.

But the sea-fowl is gone to her nest ;
  The beast is laid down in his lair ;
Even here is a season of rest,
  And I to my cabin repair.
There 's mercy in every place ;
  And mercy, encouraging thought !
Gives even affliction a grace,
  And reconciles man to his lot.

GIBBON.

1737 – 1794.

EDWARD GIBBON, the historian, was born in Surrey, England, in 1737, and died in 1794. He entered Magdalen College, Oxford, but remained only a short time. At an early age he became deeply interested in religion, and devoted himself to study, relieving the tedium of his labors by assiduous courtship of Mademoiselle Curchod, whose acquaintance he made in Switzerland. The lady inclined to him; but her father did not, and she finally married M. Necker, and became the mother of Madame de Staël. In 1759 he returned to England and was admitted into the most cultivated society. Two years later he published in French an Essay on the *Study of Literature*, which attracted but little attention in England. In 1763 he went to France, and became the intimate friend of Helvetius, D'Alembert, Diderot, and other eminent men. The next year he went to Rome, and there conceived the project of writing the history of *The Decline and Fall of the Roman Empire*. In 1776 the first volume of this great work was published, and at once made him famous. His attacks on Christianity called out many severe rebukes, which enhanced the popular interest in his book. The concluding volumes of the History appeared in 1787. The author's last literary work was his own Autobiography, which has been pronounced the finest specimen of that kind of composition in the English language. The graces of Gibbon's style have always been the subject of wonder and admiration. In his History he is stately and magnificent; in his Autobiography he is easy, spirited, and charming. The style of his History has been censured by some critics for its excessive elaboration, and its opulence of French phrases; but the general verdict of literary authorities of his own and later ages awards him the highest rank among English historians as a master of the language.

ARABIA.

IN the dreary waste of Arabia, a boundless level of sand is intersected by sharp and naked mountains; and the face of the desert, without shade or shelter, is scorched by the direct and intense rays of a tropical sun. Instead of refreshing breezes, the winds, particularly from the southwest, diffuse a noxious and even deadly vapor; the hillocks of sand which they alternately raise and scatter are compared to the billows of the ocean, and whole caravans, whole armies, have been lost and buried in the whirlwind. The common benefits of water are an object of desire and contest; and such is the scarcity of wood, that some art is requisite to preserve and propagate the element of fire. Arabia is destitute of navigable rivers, which fertilize the soil, and convey its produce to the adjacent regions; the torrents that fall from the hills are imbibed by the thirsty earth; the rare and hardy plants, the tamarind or the acacia, that strike their roots into the clefts of the rocks, are nourished by the dews of the night: a scanty supply of rain is collected in cisterns and aqueducts: the wells and springs are the secret treasure of the desert; and the pilgrim of Mecca,*

* MECCA. A city in Arabia and the birthplace of Mahomet, a celebrated religious teacher and pretended prophet, born about 750 A. D. He was the founder of one of the most widely diffused

after many a dry and sultry march, is disgusted by the taste of the
waters, which have rolled over a bed of sulphur or salt. Such is
the general and genuine picture of the climate of Arabia. The
experience of evil enhances the value of any local or partial enjoyments. A shady grove, a green pasture, a stream of fresh water,
are sufficient to attract a colony of sedentary Arabs to the fortunate
spots which can afford food and refreshment to themselves and
their cattle, and which encourage their industry in the cultivation
of the palm-tree and the vine. The high lands that border on the
Indian Ocean are distinguished by their superior plenty of wood and
water: the air is more temperate, the fruits are more delicious, the
animals and the human race more numerous: the fertility of the soil
invites and rewards the toil of the husbandman; and peculiar gifts of
frankincense and coffee have attracted in different ages the merchants
of the world.

Arabia, in the opinion of the naturalist, is the genuine and original
country of the *horse;* the climate most propitious, not indeed to the
size, but to the spirit and swiftness, of that generous animal. The
merit of the Barb, the Spanish, and the English breed, is derived
from a mixture of Arabian blood; the Bedoweens † preserve, with
superstitious care, the honors and the memory of the purest race:
the males are sold at a high price, but the females are seldom alienated: and the birth of a noble foal was esteemed, among the tribes,
as a subject of joy and mutual congratulation. These horses are
educated in tents, among the children of the Arabs, with a tender
familiarity, which trains them in the habits of gentleness and attachment. They are accustomed only to walk and to gallop: their
sensations are not blunted by the incessant abuse of the spur and the
whip: their powers are reserved for the moments of flight and
pursuit: but no sooner do they feel the touch of the hand or the
stirrup, than they dart away with the swiftness of the wind: and if
their friend be dismounted in the rapid career, they instantly stop till
he has recovered his seat. In the sands of Africa and Arabia the
camel is a sacred and precious gift. That strong and patient beast
of burden can perform, without eating or drinking, a journey of
several days; and a reservoir of fresh water is preserved in a large

religions of the globe. (See Gibbon's *Decline and Fall of the Roman Empire,* Chap. I., and
Irving's *Mahomet and his Successors.*)

† BEDOWEENS, BEDOUINS. A tribe of nomadic Arabs who live in tents, and are scattered
over the deserts of Arabia, Egypt, and parts of Africa.

bag, a fifth stomach of the animal, whose body is imprinted with the marks of servitude: the larger breed is capable of transporting a weight of a thousand pounds; and the dromedary, of a lighter and more active frame, outstrips the fleetest courser in the race. Alive or dead, almost every part of the camel is serviceable to man: her milk is plentiful and nutritious: the young and tender flesh has the taste of veal; and the long hair, which falls each year and is renewed, is coarsely manufactured into the garments, the furniture, and the tents of the Bedoweens.

The perpetual independence of the Arabs has been the theme of praise among strangers and natives; and the arts of controversy transform this singular event into a prophecy and a miracle, in favor of the posterity of Ishmael.* Some exceptions, that can neither be dissembled nor eluded, render this mode of reasoning as indiscreet as it is superfluous. Yet these exceptions are temporary or local; the body of the nation has escaped the yoke of the most powerful monarchies; the armies of Sesostris † and Cyrus,‡ of Pompey § and Trajan,|| could never achieve the conquest of Arabia; the present sovereign of the Turks may exercise a shadow of jurisdiction, but his pride is reduced to solicit the friendship of a people whom it is dangerous to provoke, and fruitless to attack. The obvious causes of their freedom are inscribed on the character and country of the Arabs. Many ages before Mahomet, their intrepid valor had been severely felt by their neighbors, in offensive and defensive war. The patient and active virtues of a soldier are insensibly nursed in the habits and discipline of a pastoral life. The care of the sheep and camels is abandoned to the women of the tribe; but the martial youth, under the banner of the emir, is ever on horseback, and in the field, to practice the exercise of the bow, the javelin, and the scymetar. The long memory of their independence is the firmest pledge of its perpetuity, and succeeding generations are animated to prove their descent, and to maintain their inheritance. In the more simple state of the Arabs, the nation is free, because each of her sons disdains a base submission to the will of a master. His breast is forti-

---

* ISHMAEL. Son of Abraham and Hagar, and the supposed ancestor of the Arabians.

† SESOSTRIS. An Egyptian king and warrior.

‡ CYRUS. The founder of the Persian Empire; one of the great warriors mentioned in the Bible.

§ POMPEY. A famous Roman general, born 106 B. C. (See *Plutarch's Lives.*)

|| TRAJAN. A Roman emperor, born 52 A. D.

fied with the austere virtues of courage, patience, and sobriety; the love of independence prompts him to exercise the habits of self-command; and the fear of dishonor guards him from the meaner apprehension of pain, of danger, and of death. The gravity and firmness of the mind is conspicuous in his outward demeanor: his speech is slow, weighty, and concise; he is seldom provoked to laughter; his only gesture is that of stroking his beard, the venerable symbol of manhood; and the sense of his own importance teaches him to accost his equals without levity, and his superiors without awe.

ARABIA (continued).

THE separation of the Arabs from the rest of mankind has accustomed them to confound the ideas of stranger and enemy; and the poverty of the land has introduced a maxim of jurisprudence which they believe and practice to the present hour. They pretend that, in the division of the earth, the rich and fertile climates were assigned to other branches of the human family; and that the posterity of the outlaw Ishmael might recover, by fraud or force, the portion of inheritance of which he had been unjustly deprived. According to the remark of Pliny,* the Arabian tribes are equally addicted to theft and merchandise: the caravans that traverse the desert are ransomed or pillaged; and their neighbors, since the remote times of Job and Sesostris, have been the victims of their rapacious spirit. If a Bedoween discovers from afar a solitary traveler, he rides furiously against him, crying, with a loud voice, "Undress thyself, thy aunt (*my wife*) is without a garment." A ready submission entitles him to mercy: resistance will provoke the aggressor, and his own blood must expiate the blood which he presumes to shed in legitimate defense.

The nice sensibility of honor, which weighs the insult rather than the injury, sheds its deadly venom on the quarrels of the Arabs: the honor of their women, and of their *beards*, is most easily wounded; an indecent action, a contemptuous word, can be expiated only by the blood of the offender; and such is their patient inveteracy, that they expect whole months and years the opportunity of revenge.

Whatever may be the pedigree of the Arabs, their language is derived from the same original stock with the Hebrew, the Syriac, and the Chaldean tongues: the independence of the tribes was

---

* PLINY. A Roman historian.

marked by their peculiar dialects; but each, after their own, allowed a just preference to the pure and perspicuous idiom of Mecca. In Arabia, as well as in Greece, the perfection of language outstripped the refinement of manners; and her speech could diversify the fourscore names of honey the two hundred of a serpent, the five hundred of a lion the thousand of a sword, at a time when this copious dictionary was intrusted to the memory of an illiterate people. The monuments of the Homerites were inscribed with an obsolete and mysterious character; but the Cufic letters, the groundwork of the present English alphabet, were invented on the banks of the Euphrates; and the recent invention was taught at Mecca by a stranger who settled in that city after the birth of Mahomet. The arts of grammar, of meter, and of rhetoric were unknown to the freeborn eloquence of the Arabians; but their penetration was sharp, their fancy luxuriant, their wit strong and sententious, and their more elaborate compositions were addressed with energy and effect to the minds of their hearers. The genius and merit of a rising poet was celebrated by the applause of his own and kindred tribes. The Arabian poets were the historians and moralists of the age; and if they sympathized with the prejudices, they inspired and crowned the virtues, of their countrymen. The indissoluble union of generosity and valor was the darling theme of their song; and when they pointed their keenest satire against a despicable race, they affirmed, in the bitterness of reproach, that the men knew not how to give, nor the women to deny. The same hospitality, which was practiced by Abraham, and celebrated by Homer, is still renewed in the camps of the Arabs. The ferocious Bedoweens, the terror of the desert, embrace, without inquiry or hesitation, the stranger who dares to confide in their honor and to enter their tent. His treatment is kind and respectful: he shares the wealth, or the poverty, of his host; and, after a needful repose, he is dismissed on his way, with thanks, with blessings, and, perhaps, with gifts. The heart and hand are more largely expanded by the wants of a brother or a friend; but the heroic acts that could deserve the public applause must have surpassed the narrow measure of discretion and experience. A dispute had arisen, who, among the citizens of Mecca, was entitled to the prize of generosity; and a successive application was made to the three who were deemed most worthy of the trial. Abdallah, the son of Abbas, had undertaken a distant journey, and his foot was in the stirrup when he heard the voice of a suppliant. "O son of the uncle of the apostle of God, I am a traveler, and in distress!" He instantly dismounted to present the pilgrim with his camel, her rich caparison, and a purse of four thousand pieces of gold, excepting only the sword, either for its intrinsic value, or as a gift of an honored kinsman. The servant of Kais informed the second suppliant that his master was asleep; but he immediately added, "Here is a purse of seven thousand pieces of gold (it is all we have in the house); and here is an order, that will entitle you to a camel and a slave": the master, as soon as he awoke, praised and enfranchised his faithful steward, with a gentle reproof, that by respecting his slumbers he had stinted his bounty. The third of these heroes, the blind Arabah, at the hour of prayer was supporting his steps on the shoulders of two slaves. "Alas!" he replied, "my coffers are empty! but these you may sell: if you refuse, I renounce them." At these words, pushing away the youths, he groped along the wall with his staff. The character of Hatem is the perfect model of Arabian virtue; he was brave and liberal, an eloquent poet, and a successful robber: forty camels were roasted at his hospitable feast; and at the prayer of a suppliant enemy he restored both the captives and the spoil. The freedom of his countrymen disdained the laws of justice; they proudly indulged the spontaneous impulse of pity and benevolence.

It was on that day or rather night, of the 27th June, 1787, between the hours of eleven and twelve, that I wrote the last line of the last page of the *Rise and Fall of the Roman Empire* in a summer-house in my garden.* After laying down my pen, I took several turns in a covered walk of acacias, which commands a prospect of the country, the lake, and the mountains. The air was temperate, the sky was serene, the silver orb of the moon was reflected from the waters, and all nature was silent. I will not dissemble the first emotions of joy on recovery of my freedom, and perhaps the establishment of my fame. But my pride was soon humbled, and a sober melancholy was spread over my mind, by the idea that I had taken an everlasting leave of an old and agreeable companion, and that, whatsoever might be the future date of my History, the life of the historian must be short and precarious.

* Gibbon was then living at Lausanne, Switzerland.

JEFFERSON.

1743–1826.

Thomas Jefferson was born in Virginia in 1743 and died in 1826. He will live forever in the memory of Americans as the author of *The Declaration of Independence*. He was President of the United States, 1801–9; was Governor of Virginia, Member of Congress, Minister to France, Secretary of State, etc. He is best known in literature by his *Notes on Virginia*, privately printed in Paris in 1782; but none of his writings afford a clearer idea of his style than does this extract from his view of the character of Washington. Hon. Edward Everett said of Jefferson: "On Jefferson rests the imperishable renown of having penned the Declaration of Independence. To have been the instrument of expressing, in one brief, decisive act, the consecrated will and resolution of a whole family of States; of unfolding, in one all-important manifesto, the causes, the motives, and the justification of this great movement in human affairs; to have been permitted to give the impress and peculiarity of his mind to a charter of public rights, destined to an importance in the estimation of men equal to anything human ever borne on parchment or expressed in the visible signs of thought; — this is the glory of Thomas Jefferson."

CHARACTER OF WASHINGTON.

His mind was great and powerful, without being of the very first order; his penetration strong, though not so acute as that of Newton,* Bacon,† or Locke; ‡ and as far as he saw, no judgment was ever sounder. It was slow in operation, being little aided by invention or imagination, but sure in conclusion. Hence the common remark of his officers, of the advantage he derived from councils of war, where, hearing all suggestions, he selected whatever was best; and certainly no general ever planned his battles more judiciously. But if deranged during the course of the action, if any member of his plan was dislocated by sudden circumstances, he was slow in a readjustment. The consequence was, that he often failed in the field, and rarely against an enemy in station, as at Boston and York. He was incapable of fear, meeting personal dangers with the calmest unconcern. Perhaps the strongest feature in his character was prudence, never acting until every circumstance, every consideration, was maturely weighed; refraining if he saw a doubt, but when once decided, going through with his purpose, whatever obstacles opposed. His integrity was most pure, his justice the most inflexible I have ever

* NEWTON. An illustrious English philosopher and mathematician, born 1642. (See Brewster's *Memoirs of Sir Isaac Newton*.)
† BACON. One of the greatest lawyers and philosophers that ever lived, born 1561. (See Campbell's *Lives of the Lord Chancellors*.)
‡ LOCKE. The author of the celebrated *Essay on the Human Understanding*, born in England, 1632.

known; no motives of interest or consanguinity, of friendship or hatred, being able to bias his decision. He was, indeed, in every sense of the words, a wise, a good, and a great man. His temper was naturally irritable and high toned; but reflection and resolution had obtained a firm and habitual ascendency over it. If ever, however, it broke its bounds, he was most tremendous in his wrath. In his expenses he was honorable, but exact; liberal in contributions to whatever promised utility; but frowning and unyielding on all visionary projects, and all unworthy calls on his charity. His heart was not warm in its affections; but he exactly calculated every man's value, and gave him a solid esteem proportioned to it. His person, you know, was fine, his stature exactly what one would wish; his deportment easy, erect, and noble, the best horseman of his age, and the most graceful figure that could be seen on horseback. Although in the circle of his friends, where he might be unreserved with safety, he took a free share in conversation, his colloquial talents were not above mediocrity, possessing neither copiousness of ideas nor fluency of words. In public, when called on for a sudden opinion, he was unready, short, and embarrassed. Yet he wrote readily, rather diffusely, in an easy and correct style. This he had acquired by conversation with the world, for his education was merely reading, writing, and common arithmetic, to which he added surveying at a later day. His time was employed in action chiefly, reading little, and that only in agriculture and English history. His correspondence became necessarily extensive, and with journalizing his agricultural proceedings occupied most of his leisure hours within doors. On the whole, his character was, in its mass, perfect, in nothing bad, in few points indifferent; and it may truly be said, that never did nature and fortune combine more completely to make a man great, and to place him in the same constellation with whatever worthies have merited from man an everlasting remembrance. For his was the singular destiny and merit of leading the armies of his country successfully through an arduous war, for the establishment of its independence; of conducting its councils through the birth of a government, new in its forms and principles, until it had settled down into a quiet and orderly train; and of scrupulously obeying the laws through the whole of his career, civil and military, of which the history of the world furnishes no other example.

BURNS.

1759–1796.

ROBERT BURNS, the son of a small farmer, was born near Ayr, Scotland, in 1759, and died in 1796. He manifested at an early age an eager appetite for learning; but his opportunities for gratifying it were few: in the country school he gained the rudiments of an education in English branches, and in later life learned something of French, Latin, and the higher mathematics. It is worthy of note that one of his favorite books, in boyhood, was Shakespeare's Plays. At the age of sixteen he began to write verses, striving to express in rhyme the emotions excited by his first affair of the heart. These youthful compositions were circulated in manuscript among his acquaintances, and finally came to the notice of some persons of literary taste, who persuaded Burns to publish a volume. The venture brought him fame at once, and twenty pounds, one hundred dollars, in money. He visited Edinburgh on invitation of Dr. Blacklock, and was well received in the brilliant society of that city. A second edition of his poems, published in 1787, yielded him a profit of seven hundred pounds. But his gain in fame and money from his visit to the Scottish capital was more than offset by his acquisition of the dissolute habits which were destined to impede his literary progress and ultimately to bring him to an early grave. His rank among poets it is not easy to determine, though Lord Byron and Allan Cunningham placed him among the first. It is probable that in their estimates they regarded his promise rather than his performance. But it may safely be said that of all poets who have sprung from the people, receiving almost no aid from education, he was surely the greatest. He was the poet of passion and feeling: but his utterances were simple and natural, and owed none of their force or beauty to art. His poems glow with tenderness and the love of freedom, and are rich in a rare, pure humor that none have known how to imitate.

MAN WAS MADE TO MOURN.

WHEN chill November's surly blast
    Made fields and forests bare,
One evening, as I wandered forth
    Along the banks of Ayr,
I spied a man whose aged step
    Seemed weary, worn with care:
His face was furrowed o'er with years,
    And hoary was his hair.

" Young stranger, whither wanderest thou? "
    Began the reverend sage;
" Does thirst of wealth thy step constrain,
    Or youthful pleasures rage?
Or haply, prest with cares and woes,
    Too soon thou hast began
To wander forth, with me, to mourn
    The miseries of man!

" The sun that overhangs yon moors,
 Outspreading far and wide,
Where hundreds labor to support
 A haughty lordling's pride, —
I 've seen yon weary winter sun
 Twice forty times return ;
And every time has added proofs
 That man was made to mourn.

" O man, while in thy early years,
 How prodigal of time !
Misspending all thy precious hours,
 Thy glorious youthful prime !
Alternate follies take the sway :
 Licentious passions burn ;
Which tenfold force gives Nature's law,
 That man was made to mourn.

" Look not alone on youthful prime,
 Or manhood's active might ;
Man then is useful to his kind,
 Supported in his right ;
But see him on the edge of life,
 With cares and sorrows worn,
Then age and want, O ill-matched pair !
 Show man was made to mourn.

" A few seem favorites of fate,
 In pleasure's lap carest ;
Yet think not all the rich and great
 Are likewise truly blest.
But O, what crowds in every land,
 All wretched and forlorn,
Through weary life this lesson learn,
 That man was made to mourn.

" Many and sharp the numerous ills,
 Inwoven with our frame,
More pointed still we make ourselves,
 Regret, remorse, and shame !

And man, whose heaven-erected face
   The smiles of love adorn,
Man's inhumanity to man
   Makes countless thousands mourn !

" See yonder poor, o'erlabored wight,
   So abject, mean, and vile,
Who begs a brother of the earth
   To give him leave to toil ;
And see his lordly fellow-worm
   The poor petition spurn,
Unmindful though a weeping wife
   And helpless offspring mourn.

" If I 'm designed yon lordling's slave, —
   By Nature's law designed, —
Why was an independent wish
   E'er planted in my mind ?
If not, why am I subject to
   His cruelty or scorn ?
Or why has man the will and power
   To make his fellow mourn ?

" Yet let not this too much, my son,
   Disturb thy youthful breast :
This partial view of human-kind
   Is surely not the best !
The poor, oppresséd, honest man
   Had never, sure, been born,
Had there not been some recompense
   To comfort those that mourn !

" O Death ! the poor man's dearest friend,
   The kindest and the best !
Welcome the hour my aged limbs
   Are laid with thee at rest.
The great, the wealthy, fear thy blow,
   From pomp and pleasure torn ;
But O, a blest relief to those
   That weary-laden mourn ! "

FOR A' THAT, AND A' THAT.

Is there, for honest poverty,
   That hangs his head, and a' that?
The coward-slave, we pass him by,
   And dare be poor, for a'.that!
     For a' that, and a' that,
       Our toils obscure, and a' that;
       The rank is but the guinea's stamp;
       The man 's the gowd for a' that.

What tho' on hamely fare we dine,
   Wear hodden-gray, and a' that;
Gie fools their silks, and knaves their wine,
   A man 's a man, for a' that.
     For a' that, and a' that,
       Their tinsel show, and a' that;
       The honest man, tho' ne'er sac poor,
       Is king o' men for a' that.

Ye see yon birkie, ca'ed a lord,
   Wha struts, and stares, and a' that;
Tho' hundreds worship at his word,
   He 's but a coof for a' that:
     For a' that, and a' that,
       His riband, star, and a' that,
       The man of independent mind,
       He looks and laughs at a' that.

A king can mak a belted knight,
   A marquis, duke, and a' that;
But an honest man 's aboon his might,
   Guid faith, he maunna fa' that!
     For a' that, and a' that,
       Their dignities, and a' that,
       The pith o' sense, and pride o' worth,
       Are higher ranks than a' that.

Then let us pray that come it may,
   As come it will for a' that,

That sense and worth, o'er a' the earth,
   May bear the gree, and a' that;
     For a' that, and a' that,
      It 's coming yet, for a' that;
     That man to man, the warld o'er,
      Shall brothers be for a' that.

BANNOCKBURN.*

At Bannockburn the English lay, —
The Scots they were na far away,
But waited for the break o' day
   That glinted in the east.

But soon the sun broke through the heath
And lighted up that field o' death,
When Bruce, wi' saul-inspiring breath,
   His heralds thus addressed : —

" Scots, wha hae wi' Wallace bled,
Scots, wham Bruce has aften led,
Welcome to your gory bed,
   Or to glorious victory !

" Now 's the day, and now 's the hour;
See the front of battle lour ;
See approach proud Edward's power, —
   Edward ! chains and slavery !

" Wha will be a traitor knave ?
Wha can fill a coward's grave ?
Wha sae base as be a slave ?
   Traitor ! coward ! turn and flee !

" Wha for Scotland's king and law
Freedom's sword will strongly draw,
Freeman stand, or freeman fa',
   Caledonia ! on wi' me !

* BANNOCKBURN. See note, page 63.

" By oppression's woes and pains !
By your sons in servile chains !
We will drain our dearest veins,
    But they shall be — shall be free !

" Lay the proud usurpers low !
Tyrants fall in every foe !
Liberty 's in every blow !
    Forward ! let us do or die ! "

OF A' THE AIRTS THE WIND CAN BLAW.

OF a' the airts the wind can blaw,
   I dearly like the west,
For there the bonnie lassie lives,
   The lassie I lo'e best :
Though wild woods grow, and rivers row,
   And mony a hill between ;
Baith day and night, my fancy's flight
   Is ever wi' my Jean.

I see her in the dewy flowers,
   I see her sweet and fair :
I hear her in the tunefu' birds,
   I hear her charm the air :
There 's not a bonnie flower that springs,
   By fountain, shaw, or green ;
There 's not a bonnie bird that sings,
   But minds me o' my Jean.

BUT pleasures are like poppies spread,
You seize the flower, its bloom is shed ;
Or like the snowflake in the river,
A moment white, — then melts forever ;
Or like the borealis race,
That flit ere you can point their place ;
Or like the rainbow's lovely form
Evanishing amid the storm.

WORDSWORTH. ·

1770 – 1850.

WILLIAM WORDSWORTH, a prominent member of the Lake school of poets, was born in Cumberland, England, in 1770, and died in 1850. He was the son of an attorney, and studied at St. John's College, Cambridge. He spent some time in France and Germany, and in 1799 fixed his home — which was presided over by his sister Dorothy (his faithful "guide, philosopher, and friend," throughout his long life) — at Grasmere. Here he lived till 1808. In 1813 he removed his household gods to Rydal Mount, which was ever after his residence, and is closely associated with the most notable products of his genius. He was a favorite of fortune, having inherited a comfortable estate, and for some years holding a lucrative office under government. In 1843 he was appointed Poet Laureate, succeeding Southey, and received the pension of £ 300 attached to that dignity as long as he lived. He was married in 1803 to Mary Hutchinson, who survived him, dying in 1859, at the great age of eighty-eight. In his early manhood Wordsworth was visionary and radical, professing republicanism, and avowing himself an admirer of the principles which were illustrated in the French Revolution; but, as often happens, age tempered his fervor, and during the latter half of his life he was unfaltering in his political and religious conservatism. His first book, *An Evening Walk,* an epistle in verse, was published in 1793; his second, *Descriptive Sketches,* published in the same year, was cordially praised by Coleridge. Between 1798 and 1814 several editions of his poems were issued, receiving praise and censure in nearly equal proportions. When *The Excursion* appeared, in 1814, Lord Jeffrey said of it : "This will never do ; it is longer, weaker, and tamer than any of Mr. Wordsworth's other productions." On the other hand, William Hazlitt pronounced it almost unsurpassed "in power of intellect, lofty conception, and depth of feeling." On the whole, it must be said that during Wordsworth's life, or at least until within a few years prior to his death, the judgment of the critics on his poetry was in effect unfavorable; but with the great public his writings steadily gained popularity. One of the principal reasons for the hostility of the critics was, no doubt, his energetic protest, by precept and example, against the romantic school of poetry, which, conspicuously represented by Byron, was then in high favor. He endeavored to demonstrate the superiority of simplicity in thought and expression, and in the effort incurred the reproach of silliness. During the last twenty years, however, a more candid and accurate estimate of his work has been made, and the deliberate judgment of the reading world has assigned him an enviable rank among English poets of the nineteenth century. One of the most prominent characteristics of his poetical genius is imaginative power, in which quality so high an authority as Coleridge has affirmed that he was surpassed only by Shakespeare. His mind was strongly philosophical, and his writings exhibit a rare union of philosophical and poetical elements. They are distinctively contemplative, and will always be admired for their faithful interpretation of nature. It is not easy to specify Wordsworth's best composition : *The Excursion* is perhaps the greatest; but to the common mind some of his lyrics and ballads are most admirable. Among them are *Hart Leap Well, Lines to a Cuckoo, The Banks of the Wye, Ruth,* etc. Some critics have designated *The Solitary Reaper* as his finest poem.

THE BOY AND THE OWLS.

THERE was a Boy ; ye knew him well, ye cliffs
And islands of Winander! many a time,
At evening, when the earliest stars began
To move along the edges of the hills,
Rising or setting, would he stand alone,
Beneath the trees, or by the glimmering lake ;
And there, with fingers interwoven, both hands

3 *

Pressed closely palm to palm, and to his mouth
Uplifted, he, as through an instrument,
Blew mimic hootings to the silent owls,
That they might answer him; and they would shout
Across the watery vale, and shout again,
Responsive to his call, with quivering peals,
And long halloos, and screams, and echoes loud
Redoubled and redoubled; concourse wild
Of mirth and jocund din! And, when a lengthened pause
Of silence came and baffled his best skill,
Then, sometimes, in that silence, while he hung
Listening, a gentle shock of mild surprise
Has carried far into his heart the voice
Of mountain torrents; or the visible scene
Would enter unawares into his mind
With all its solemn imagery, its rocks,
Its woods, and that uncertain heaven, received
Into the bosom of the steady lake.

This Boy was taken from his mates, and died
In childhood, ere he was full twelve years old.
Fair is the spot, most beautiful the vale
Where he was born: the grassy churchyard hangs
Upon a slope above the village school;
And through that churchyard when my way has led
On summer evenings, I believe that there
A long half-hour together I have stood
Mute,—looking at the grave in which he lies!

RUTH.

WHEN Ruth was left half desolate,
Her father took another mate;
And Ruth, not seven years old,
A slighted child, at her own will
Went wandering over dale and hill,
In thoughtless freedom bold.

And she had made a pipe of straw,
And from that oaten pipe could draw

All sounds of winds and floods ;
Had built a bower upon the green,
As if she from her birth had been
An infant of the woods.

Beneath her father's roof, alone
She seemed to live ; her thoughts her own ;
Herself her own delight ;
Pleased with herself, nor sad, nor gay,
And passing thus the livelong day,
She grew to woman's height.

There came a youth from Georgia's shore, —
A military casque he wore,
With splendid feathers dressed ;
He brought them from the Cherokees ;
The feathers nodded in the breeze,
And made a gallant crest.

From Indian blood you deem him sprung :
Ah, no ! he spake the English tongue,
And bore a soldier's name ;
And, when America was free
From battle and from jeopardy,
He 'cross the ocean came.

With hues of genius on his cheek,
In finest tones the youth could speak.
— While he was yet a boy,
The moon, the glory of the sun,
And streams that murmur as they run,
Had been his dearest joy.

He was a lovely youth ! I guess
The panther in the wilderness
Was not so fair as he ;
And, when he chose to sport and play,
No dolphin ever was so gay
Upon the tropic sea.

Among the Indians he had fought;
And with him many tales he brought
Of pleasure and of fear;
Such tales as, told to any maid
By such a youth, in the green shade,
Were perilous to hear.

He told of girls, a happy rout!
Who quit their fold with dance and shout,
Their pleasant Indian town,
To gather strawberries all day long;
Returning with a choral song
When daylight is gone down.

He spake of plants divine and strange
That every hour their blossoms change,
Ten thousand lovely hues!
With budding, fading, faded flowers,
They stand the wonder of the bowers,
From morn to evening dews.

He told of the magnolia, spread
High as a cloud, high overhead!
The cypress and her spire;
— Of flowers that with one scarlet gleam
Cover a hundred leagues, and seem
To set the hills on fire.

The youth of green savannas spake,
And many an endless, endless lake,
With all its fairy crowds
Of islands, that together lie
As quietly as spots of sky
Among the evening clouds.

And then he said, " How sweet it were
A fisher or a hunter there,
A gardener in the shade,
Still wandering with an easy mind

To build a household fire, and find
A home in every glade!

"What days and what sweet years! Ah me!
Our life were life indeed, with thee
So passed in quiet bliss,
And all the while," said he, "to know
That we were in a world of woe,
On such an earth as this!

"Sweet Ruth! and could you go with me
My helpmate in the woods to be,
Our shed at night to rear;
Or run, my own adopted bride,
A sylvan huntress at my side,
And drive the flying deer!

"Beloved Ruth — " No more he said,
The wakeful Ruth at midnight shed
A solitary tear:
She thought again, — and did agree
With him to sail across the sea,
And drive the flying deer.

"And now, as fitting is and right,
We in the church our faith will plight,
A husband and a wife."
Even so they did; and I may say
That to sweet Ruth that happy day
Was more than human life.

THE SOLITARY REAPER.

BEHOLD her single in the field,
Yon solitary Highland Lass!
Reaping and singing by herself;
Stop here, or gently pass!
Alone she cuts and binds the grain,
And sings a melancholy strain;

O listen ! for the vale profound
Is overflowing with the sound.

No nightingale did ever chant
More welcome notes to weary bands
Of travelers in some shady haunt
Among Arabian sands ;
No sweeter voice was ever heard
In springtime from the cuckoo-bird,
Breaking the silence of the seas
Among the farthest Hebrides.

Will no one tell me what she sings ?
Perhaps the plaintive numbers flow
For old, unhappy, far-off things,
And battles long ago :
Or is it some more humble lay,
Familiar matter of to-day ?
Some natural sorrow, loss, or pain,
That has been, and may be again.

Whate'er the theme, the maiden sang
As if her song could have no ending ;
I saw her singing at her work,
And o'er the sickle bending ;
I listened till I had my fill ;
And as I mounted up the hill
The music in my heart I bore
Long after it was heard no more.

SCOTT.

1771 – 1832.

SIR WALTER SCOTT, the most famous of historical novelists, was born in Edinburgh in 1771 and died in 1832. He studied at the University of Edinburgh, read law, and in 1792 was called to the bar. In 1799 he was appointed Sheriff, in 1806 was made Clerk of the Court of Session, and in 1820, when he was forty-nine years old, received a baronetcy. His first literary effort was a translation of some of Bürger's ballads, which was published in 1796. Other translations followed, with three or four original poems; but not until 1805 did Scott attain the place of literary eminence which he forever after held and adorned. His first grand success was *The Lay of the Last Minstrel*, which appeared in that year, and was received with almost universal praise. *Marmion, The Lady of the Lake, Rokeby*, and other poems, were issued in quick succession, each confirming his poetical reputation and spreading his fame. But Scott is better known to the world as a novelist than as a poet, and a few words descriptive of his remarkable career in fiction seem to be necessary to the completeness of this sketch. In 1814 *Waverley* was issued at Edinburgh, and instantly attracted attention. No author's name appeared on the title-page, and the public was left in a state of painful doubt as to the source of so brilliant a book. Its perplexity was naturally increased, the next year, by the appearance of *Guy Mannering*, and, at brief intervals, of its successors. Scott was suspected of the authorship of these books, but stoutly denied it; and not till many years later did he confess the truth. Space will not permit us to dwell upon the pecuniary troubles which clouded the last years of the great novelist. In all the history of literature there is no record of such labors as his; one admires his lofty sense of honor, his unyielding fortitude, and his almost superhuman power of application with equal warmth. The secret of Scott's success may be said to lie in his felicitous employment of common topics, images, and expressions, such as all readers can appreciate. Another source of his strength was his intense nationality: no writer before him had so vividly illustrated the characteristics of Scottish life and character. His novels were and are popular because they deal with real life, and avoid the meditative and speculative habits which are wearisome to the common reader. Not conspicuously surpassing all other novelists in single qualities, Scott yet possessed and combined all the qualities necessary for his work in such nice and harmonious adjustment as has never been witnessed in any other man. While his novels fascinate and entertain with an enduring yet indescribable charm, they also convey much valuable information as to the life of the times of which they treat.

THE TOMB OF ROBERT BRUCE.*

SUCH of the Scottish knights as remained alive returned to their own country. They brought back the heart of the Bruce and the bones of the good Lord James. These last were interred in the church of St. Bride, where Thomas Dickson and Douglas held so terrible a Palm Sunday. The Bruce's heart was buried below the high altar in Melrose Abbey. As for his body, it was laid in the sepulcher in the midst of the church of Dunfermline, under a marble

---

* Robert Bruce, King of Scots, was born in 1274. He was a man of great valor, and waged, with varying fortune, incessant war against the English. He finally gained a decisive victory over the army of Edward II. at the famous battle of Bannockburn in 1314, which resulted in the independence of Scotland.

stone. But the church becoming afterwards ruinous, and the roof falling down with age, the monument was broken to pieces, and nobody could tell where it stood. But a little while ago, when they were repairing the church at Dunfermline, and removing the rubbish, lo ! they found fragments of the marble tomb of Robert Bruce. Then they began to dig farther, thinking to discover the body of this celebrated monarch ; and at length they came to the skeleton of a tall man, and they knew it must be that of King Robert, both as he was known to have been buried in a winding-sheet of cloth of gold, of which many fragments were found about this skeleton, and also because the breastbone appeared to have been sawed through, in order to take out the heart. So orders were sent from the King's Court of Exchequer to guard the bones carefully, until a new tomb should be prepared, into which they were laid with profound respect. A great many gentlemen and ladies attended, and almost all the common people in the neighborhood ; and as the church could not hold half the numbers, the people were allowed to pass through it, one after another, that each one, the poorest as well as the richest, might see all that remained of the great King Robert Bruce, who restored the Scottish monarchy. Many people shed tears ; for there was the wasted skull which once was the head that thought so wisely and boldly for his country's deliverance ; and there was the dry bone which had once been the sturdy arm that killed Sir Henry de Bohun, between the two armies, at a single blow, on the evening before the battle of Bannockburn.*

It is more than five hundred years since the body of Bruce was first laid into the tomb ; and how many, many millions of men have died since that time, whose bones could not be recognized, nor their names known, any more than those of inferior animals ! It was a great thing to see that the wisdom, courage, and patriotism of a King could preserve him for such a long time in the memory of the people over whom he once reigned. But then, my dear child, you must remember, that it is only desirable to be remembered for praiseworthy and patriotic actions, such as those of Robert Bruce. It would be better for a prince to be forgotten like the meanest peasant, than to be recollected for actions of tyranny or oppression.

* See Burns's poem, page 55.

LOCHINVAR. — LADY HERON'S SONG.

O, YOUNG Lochinvar is come out of the west,
Through all the wide Border his steed was the best,
And save his good broadsword he weapons had none;
He rode all unarmed, and he rode all alone.
So faithful in love, and so dauntless in war,
There never was knight like the young Lochinvar.

He stayed not for brake, and he stopped not for stone,
He swam the Eske river where ford there was none;
But, ere he alighted at Netherby gate,
The bride had consented, the gallant came late:
For a laggard in love, and a dastard in war,
Was to wed the fair Ellen of brave Lochinvar.

So boldly he entered the Netherby hall,
Among bride's-men and kinsmen, and brothers and all:
Then spoke the bride's father, his hand on his sword
(For the poor craven bridegroom spoke never a word),
" O, come ye in peace here, or come ye in war,
Or to dance at our bridal, young Lord Lochinvar?"

" I long wooed your daughter, my suit you denied; —
Love swells like the Solway, but ebbs like its tide, —
And now I am come, with this lost love of mine,
To lead but one measure, drink one cup of wine.
There are maidens in Scotland more lovely by far,
That would gladly be bride to the young Lochinvar."

The bride kissed the goblet; the knight took it up,
He quaffed off the wine, and he threw down the cup,
She looked down to blush, and she looked up to sigh,
With a smile on her lips and a tear in her eye.
He took her soft hand, ere her mother could bar, —
" Now tread we a measure!" said young Lochinvar.

So stately his form, and so lovely her face,
That never a hall such a galliard did grace;

While her mother did fret, and her father did fume,
And the bridegroom stood dangling his bonnet and plume;
And the bride-maidens whispered, " 'T were better by far
To have matched our fair cousin with young Lochinvar."

One touch to her hand, and one word in her ear,
When they reached the hall-door, and the charger stood near;
So light to the croupe the fair lady he swung,
So light to the saddle before her he sprung!
" She is won! we are gone, over bank, bush, and scaur;
They 'll have fleet steeds that follow," quoth young Lochinvar.

There was mounting 'mong Græmes of the Netherby clan;
Forsters, Fenwicks, and Musgraves, they rode and they ran:
There was racing, and chasing, on Cannobie Lee,
But the lost bride of Netherby ne'er did they see.
·So daring in love, and so dauntless in war,
Have ye e'er heard of gallant like young Lochinvar?

THE LAST MINSTREL.

THE way was long, the wind was cold,
The Minstrel was infirm and old;
His withered cheek, and tresses gray,
Seemed to have known a better day;
The harp, his sole remaining joy,
Was carried by an orphan boy:
The last of all the Bards was he,
Who sung of Border chivalry;
For, well-a-day! their date was fled,
His tuneful brethren all were dead;
And he, neglected and oppressed,
Wished to be with them, and at rest.
No more, on prancing palfrey borne,
He caroled, light as lark at morn;
No longer, courted and caressed,
High placed in hall, a welcome guest,
He poured, to lord and lady gay,
The unpremeditated lay:

Old times were changed, old manners gone ;
A stranger fills the Stuarts' throne;
The bigots of the iron time
Had called his harmless art a crime.
A wandering harper, scorned and poor,
He begged his way from door to door ;
And tuned, to please a peasant's ear,
The harp a King had loved to hear.

THE LOVE OF COUNTRY.

BREATHES there the man with soul so dead,
Who never to himself hath said,
   This is my own, my native land ?
Whose heart hath ne'er within him burned
As home his footsteps he hath turned,
   From wandering on a foreign strand ?
If such there breathe, go, mark him well ;
For him no minstrel raptures swell !
High though his titles, proud his name,
Boundless his wealth as wish can claim :
Despite those titles, power, and pelf,
The wretch, concentered all in self,
Living, shall forfeit fair renown,
And doubly dying, shall go down
To the vile dust, from whence he sprung,
Unwept, unhonored, and unsung.

SOME feelings are to mortals given,
With less of earth in them than heaven :
And if there be a human tear
From passion's dross refined and clear,
A tear so limpid and so meek,
It would not stain an angel's cheek,
'T is that which pious fathers shed
Upon a duteous daughter's head !

SYDNEY SMITH.

1771 – 1845.

SYDNEY SMITH's name is a synonym of wit; but he has left behind him evidences of far higher mental powers than those which are called into exercise in the effort to amuse. He was born at Woodford, Essex, England, in 1771, and died in 1845. He was educated at Oxford, took holy orders and held a curacy in Wiltshire; in 1796 he removed to Edinburgh, where, in conjunction with Brougham and other distinguished men, he founded the *Edinburgh Review*. Removing to London in 1804, he continued to write for the *Review*, and speedily won a brilliant reputation as a critic. Ecclesiastical preferment frequently came to him, and at the time of his death he was Canon Residentiary of St. Paul's Cathedral. His writings were mainly in the form of sermons; but he wrote many notable letters on political and religious questions which go far toward justifying Mr. Everett's opinion that if he (Smith) " had not been known as the wittiest man of his day, he would have been accounted one of the wisest." It is believed that his Letters on Catholic Emancipation were largely instrumental in pushing that measure to success. Macaulay said of him: " He is universally admitted to have been a great reasoner, and the greatest master of ridicule that has appeared among us since Swift."

THE PLEASURES OF KNOWLEDGE.

IT is noble to seek Truth, and it is beautiful to find it. It is the ancient feeling of the human heart, that knowledge is better than riches; and it is deeply and *sacredly true*. To mark the course of human passions as they have flowed on in the ages that are past; to see why nations have risen, and why they have fallen; to speak of heat, and light, and the winds; to know what man has discovered in the heavens above and in the earth beneath; to hear the chemist unfold the marvelous properties that the Creator has locked up in a speck of earth; to be told that there are worlds so distant from our own, that the quickness of light, traveling from the world's creation, has never yet reached us; to wander in the creations of poetry, and grow warm again with that eloquence which swayed the democracies of the Old World; to go up with great reasoners to the First Cause of all, and to perceive, in the midst of all this dissolution and decay and cruel separation, that there *is* one thing unchangeable, indestructible, and everlasting; — it is worth while in the days of our youth to strive hard for this great discipline; to pass sleepless nights for it; to give up for it laborious days; to spurn for it present pleasures; to endure for it afflicting poverty; to wade for it through darkness, and sorrow, and contempt, as the great spirits of the world have done in all ages and all times.

I appeal to the experience of any man who is in the habit of exercising his mind vigorously and well, whether there is not a satisfaction in it which tells him he has been acting up to one of the great objects of his existence? The end of nature has been answered: his faculties have done that which they were created to do, — not languidly occupied upon trifles, not enervated by sensual gratification, but exercised in that toil which is so congenial to their nature, and so worthy of their strength.

A life of knowledge is not often a life of injury and crime. Whom does such a man oppress? with whose happiness does he interfere? whom does his ambition destroy? and whom does his fraud deceive? In the pursuit of science he injures no man, and in the acquisition he does good to all. A man who dedicates his life to knowledge, becomes habituated to pleasure which carries with it no reproach: and there is one security that he will never love that pleasure which is paid for by anguish of heart, — his pleasures are all cheap, all dignified, and all innocent; and, as far as any human being can expect permanence in this changing scene, he has secured a happiness which no malignity of fortune can ever take away, but which must cleave to him while he lives, ameliorating every good, and diminishing every evil of his existence.

I solemnly declare, that, but for the love of knowledge, I should consider the life of the meanest hedger and ditcher preferable to that of the greatest and richest man in existence; for the fire of our minds is like the fire which the Persians burn on the mountains, — it flames night and day, and is immortal, and not to be quenched! Upon something it must act and feed, — upon the pure spirit of knowledge, or upon the foul dregs of polluting passions.

Therefore, when I say, in conducting your understanding, love knowledge with a great love, with a vehement love, with a love coeval with life, what do I say but love innocence; love virtue; love purity of conduct; love that which, if you are rich and great, will sanctify the providence which has made you so, and make men call it justice; love that which, if you are poor, will render your poverty respectable, and make the proudest feel it unjust to laugh at the meanness of your fortunes; love that which will comfort you, adorn you, and never quit you, — which will open to you the kingdom of thought, and all the boundless regions of conception, as an asylum against the cruelty, the injustice, and the pain that may be your lot in the outer world, — that which will make your motives habitually great and honorable, and light up in an instant a thousand noble disdains at the very thought of meanness and of fraud?

Therefore, if any young man have embarked his life in the pursuit of knowledge, let him go on without doubting or fearing the event: let him not be intimidated by the cheerless beginnings of knowledge, by the darkness from which she springs, by the difficulties which hover around her, by the wretched habitations in which she dwells, by the want and sorrow which sometimes journey in her train; but let him ever follow her as the Angel that guards him, and as the Genius of his life. She will bring him out at last into the light of day, and exhibit him to the world comprehensive in acquirements, fertile in resources, rich in imagination, strong in reasoning, prudent and powerful above his fellows in all the relations and in all the offices of life.

WIT AND WISDOM.

THERE is an association in men's minds between dullness and wisdom, amusement and folly, which has a very powerful influence in decision upon character, and is not overcome without considerable difficulty. The reason is, that the *outward* signs of a dull man and a wise man are the same, and so are the outward signs of a frivolous man and a witty man; and we are not to expect that the majority will be disposed to look to much *more* than the outward sign. I believe the fact to be, that wit is very seldom the *only* eminent quality which resides in the mind of any man; it is commonly accompanied by many other talents of every description, and ought to be considered as a strong evidence of a fertile and superior understanding. Almost all the great poets, orators, and statesmen of all times have been witty.

The meaning of an extraordinary man is, that he is *eight* men, not one man; that he has as much wit as if he had no sense, and as much sense as if he had no wit; that his conduct is as judicious as if he were the dullest of human beings, and his imagination as brilliant as if he were irretrievably ruined. But when wit is combined with sense and information; when it is softened by benevolence, and restrained by strong principle; when it is in the hands of a man who can use it and despise it, who can be witty, and something much *better* than witty, who loves honor, justice, decency, good-nature, morality, and religion, ten thousand times better than wit; — wit is *then* a beautiful and delightful part of our nature. There is no more interesting spectacle than to see the effects of wit upon the different characters of men; than to observe it expanding caution, relaxing dignity, unfreezing coldness, — teaching age and care and pain to smile, — extorting reluctant gleams of pleasure from melancholy, and charming even the pangs of grief. It is pleasant to observe how it penetrates through the coldness and awkwardness of society, gradually bringing men nearer together, and, like the combined force of wine and oil, giving every man a glad heart and a shining countenance. Genuine and innocent wit like this is surely the *flavor of the mind!* Man could direct his ways by plain reason, and support his life by tasteless food; but God has given us wit, and flavor, and laughter, and perfumes, to enliven the days of man's pilgrimage, and to " charm his painful steps over the burning marle."

SCIENCE OF GOVERNMENT.

It would seem that the science of government is an unappropriated region in the universe of knowledge. Those sciences with which the passions can never interfere are considered to be attainable only by study and by reflection; while there are not many young men who doubt of their ability to make a constitution, or to govern a kingdom, at the same time there cannot, perhaps, be a more decided proof of a superficial understanding than the depreciation of those difficulties which are inseparable from the science of government. To know well the local and the natural man; to track the silent march of human affairs; to seize, with happy intuition, on those great laws which regulate the prosperity of empires; to reconcile principles to circumstances, and be no wiser than the times will permit; to anticipate the effects of every speculation upon the entangled relations and awkward complexity of real life; and to follow out the theorems of the senate to the daily comforts of the cottage, is a task which they will fear most who know it best, — a task in which the great and the good have often failed, and which it is not only wise, but pious and just, in common men to avoid.

COLERIDGE.

1772 – 1834

SAMUEL TAYLOR COLERIDGE was born at Ottery St. Mary, Devonshire, where his father was vicar, in 1772, and died in 1834. He spent two years at Jesus College, Cambridge, but did not complete his course. A little later, being in London without resources or employment, he enlisted in a dragoon regiment. One day he wrote a Latin verse on the stable-wall, which fact coming to the knowledge of his captain, the latter procured his discharge from the service. Coleridge at once entered on a literary and political career, publishing his first work, *The Fall of Robespierre, An Historical Drama*, in 1794, and soon after several pamphlets in which he advocated democratic and Unitarian doctrines. With Southey and Lovell he projected a Pantisocracy to be established in Pennsylvania, but the scheme came to naught, and Coleridge settled down as a writer on the *Morning Post*, in support of the government. In 1798 he visited Germany and studied there diligently. In 1812 his series of Essays, called *The Friend*, was published, and in 1816 *Christabel*. He had acquired the habit of opium-eating, which obtained the mastery over him and reduced him to a condition of unproductive indolence. He passed the last eighteen years of his life in retirement. So able a judge as De Quincey has said that Coleridge's was "the largest and most spacious intellect, the subtlest and most comprehensive, that has yet existed among men." He excelled in every department of literature, and several of his poems rank among the finest in our language. As a conversationist he has never been equaled.

THE IMPORTANCE OF METHOD.

WHAT is that which first strikes us, and strikes us at once, in a man of education, and which, among educated men, so instantly distinguishes the man of superior mind, that (as was observed with eminent propriety of the late Edmund Burke) " we cannot stand under the same archway during a shower of rain, without finding him out"? Not the weight or novelty of his remarks; not any unusual interest of facts communicated by him: for we may suppose both the one and the other precluded by the shortness of our intercourse, and the triviality of the subjects. The difference will be impressed and felt, though the conversation should be confined to the state of the weather or the pavement. Still less will it arise from any peculiarity in his words and phrases. Unless where new things necessitate new terms, he will avoid an unusual word as a rock. It must have been among the earliest lessons of his youth, that the breach of this precept, at all times hazardous, becomes ridiculous in the topics of ordinary conversation. There remains but one other point of distinction possible; and this must be, and in fact is, the true cause of the impression made on us. It is the unpremeditated and evidently habitual arrangement of his words, grounded on the habit of foreseeing, in each integral part, or (more plainly) in every sentence, the whole that he then intends to communicate. However irregular and desultory his talk, there is method in the fragments.

Listen, on the other hand, to an ignorant man, though perhaps shrewd and able in his particular calling, whether he be describing or relating. We immediately perceive, that his memory alone is called into action; and that the objects and events recur in the narration in the same order, and with the same accompaniments, however accidental or impertinent, in which they had first occurred to the narrator. The necessity of taking breath, the efforts of recollection, and the abrupt rectification of its failures, produce all his pauses; and with exception of the "and then," the "and there," and the still less significant, "and so," they constitute likewise all his connections.

Our discussion, however, is confined to method as employed in the formation of the understanding, and in the constructions of science and literature. It would indeed be superfluous to attempt a proof of its importance in the business and economy of active or domestic life. From the cotter's hearth or the workshop of the artisan to the palace or the arsenal, the first merit, that which admits neither substitute nor equivalent, is, that everything be in its place. Where this charm is wanting, every other merit either loses its name, or becomes an additional ground of accusation and regret. Of one, by whom it is eminently possessed, we say proverbially, he is like clock-work. The resemblance extends beyond the point of regularity, and yet falls short of the truth. Both do, indeed, at once, divide and announce the silent and otherwise indistinguishable lapse of time. But the man of methodical industry and honorable pursuits does more; he realizes its ideal divisions, and gives a character and individuality to its moments. If the idle are described as killing time, he may be justly said to call it into life and moral being, while he makes it the distinct object not only of the consciousness, but of the conscience. He organizes the hours, and gives them a soul; and that, the very essence of which is to fleet away, and evermore to have been, he takes up into his own permanence, and communicates to it the imperishableness of a spiritual nature. Of the *good and faithful servant*, whose energies, thus directed, are thus methodized, it is less truly affirmed, that he lives in time, than that time lives in him. His days, months, and years, as the stops and punctual marks in the records of duties performed, will survive the wreck of worlds, and remain extant when time itself shall be no more.

But as the importance of method in the duties of social life is incomparably greater, so are its practical elements proportionably obvious, and such as relate to the will far more than to the understanding. Henceforward, therefore, we contemplate its bearings on the latter.

The difference between the products of a well-disciplined and those of an uncultivated understanding, in relation to what we will now venture to call the science of method, is often and admirably exhibited by our great dramatist. I scarcely need refer my readers to the Clown's evidence, in the first scene of the second act of *Measure for Measure*, or to the Nurse in *Romeo and Juliet*. . . . .

The absence of method, which characterizes the uneducated, is occasioned by an habitual submission of the understanding to mere events and images as such, and independent of any power in the mind to classify or appropriate them. The general accompaniments of time and place are the only relations which persons of this class appear to regard in their statements. As this constitutes their leading feature, the contrary excellence, as distinguishing the well-educated man, must be referred to the contrary habit. Method, therefore, becomes natural to the mind which has been accustomed to contemplate not things only, or for their own sake alone, but likewise and chiefly the relations of things, either their relations to each other, or to the observer, or to the state and apprehensions of the hearers. To enumerate and analyze these relations, with the conditions under which alone they are discoverable, is to teach the science of method. . . . .

Exuberance of mind, on the one hand, interferes with the forms of method; but sterility of mind, on the other, wanting the spring and impulse to mental action, is wholly destructive of method itself. For in attending too exclusively to the relations which the past or passing events and objects bear to general truth, and the moods of his own thought, the most intelligent man is sometimes in danger of overlooking that other relation, in which they are likewise to be placed to the apprehension and sympathies of his hearers. His discourse appears like soliloquy intermixed with dialogue. But the uneducated and unreflecting talker overlooks all mental relations, both logical and psychological; and consequently precludes all method which is not purely accidental. Hence the nearer the things and incidents in time and place, the more distant, disjointed, and impertinent to each other, and to any common purpose, will they appear in his narration; and this from the want of a staple, or starting-post, in the narrator himself; from the absence of the leading thought, which, borrowing a phrase from the nomenclature of legislation, I may not inaptly call the initiative. On the contrary, where the habit of method is present and effective, things the most remote and diverse in time, place, and outward circumstance are brought into mental contiguity and succession, the more striking as the less expected.

KUBLA KHAN; OR, A VISION IN A DREAM.*

A FRAGMENT.

In Xanadu did Kubla Khan
A stately pleasure-dome decree:
Where Alph, the sacred river, ran
Through caverns measureless to man
    Down to a sunless sea.
So twice five miles of fertile ground
With walls and towers were girdled round:
And there were gardens bright with sinuous rills
Where blossomed many an incense-bearing tree;
And here were forests ancient as the hills,
Enfolding sunny spots of greenery.
But oh! that deep romantic chasm which slanted
Down the green hill athwart a cedarn cover!

* Coleridge makes the following reference to this poem: "In consequence of a slight indisposition an anodyne had been prescribed for the author, from the effect of which he fell asleep in his chair at the moment he was reading the following sentence, or words of the same substance, in *Purchas's Pilgrimage:* 'Here the Khan Kubla commanded a palace to be built, and a stately garden thereunto: and thus ten miles of fertile ground were inclosed with a wall.' The author continued for about three hours in a profound sleep, at least of the external senses, during which time he has the most vivid confidence that he could not have composed less than from two to three hundred lines; if that indeed can be called composition in which all the images rose up before him as things, with a parallel production of the correspondent expressions, without any sensation or consciousness of effort. On awaking he appeared to himself to have a distinct recollection of the whole, and taking his pen, ink, and paper, instantly and eagerly wrote down the lines that are here preserved. At this moment he was unfortunately called out and detained above an hour, and on his return to his room, found, to his no small surprise and mortification, that though he still retained some vague and dim recollection of the general purport of the vision, yet, with the exception of some eight or ten scattered lines and images, all the rest had passed away like the images on the surface of a stream into which a stone had been cast, but, alas! without the after restoration of the latter." The fragment is generally ranked among the finest specimens of purely imaginative poetry in our language.

A savage place! as holy and enchanted
As e'er beneath a waning moon was haunted
By woman wailing for her demon-lover!
And from this chasm, with ceaseless turmoil seething,
As if this earth in fast thick pants were breathing,
A mighty fountain momently was forced;
Amid whose swift half-intermitted burst
Huge fragments vaulted like rebounding hail,
Or chaffy grain beneath the thresher's flail:
And 'mid these dancing rocks at once and ever
It flung up momently the sacred river.
Five miles meandering with a mazy motion
Through wood and dale the sacred river ran,
Then reached the caverns measureless to man,
And sank in tumult to a lifeless ocean;
And 'mid this tumult Kubla heard from far
Ancestral voices prophesying war!

The shadow of the dome of pleasure
Floated midway on the waves;
Where was heard the mingled measure
From the fountain and the caves.
It was a miracle of rare device,
A sunny pleasure-dome with caves of ice!
A damsel with a dulcimer
In a vision once I saw:
It was an Abyssinian maid,
And on her dulcimer she played,
Singing of Mount Abora.
Could I revive within me
Her symphony and song,
To such a deep delight 't would win me,
That with music loud and long,
I would build that dome in air,
That sunny dome! those caves of ice!
And all who heard should see them there,
And all should cry, Beware! Beware!
His flashing eyes, his floating hair!
Weave a circle round him thrice,

And close your eyes with holy dread,
For he on honey-dew hath fed,
And drunk the milk of Paradise.

DEAD CALM IN THE TROPICS.

THE fair breeze blew, the white foam flew,
The furrow followed free ;
We were the first that ever burst
Into that silent sea.

Down dropt the breeze, the sails dropt down,
'T was sad as sad could be ;
And we did speak only to break
The silence of the sea !

All in a hot and copper sky,
The bloody Sun, at noon,
Right up above the mast did stand,
No bigger than the Moon.

Day after day, day after day,
We stuck, nor breath nor motion ;
As idle as a painted ship
Upon a painted ocean.

Water, water, everywhere,
And all the boards did shrink ;
Water, water, everywhere,
Nor any drop to drink.

The very deep did rot : O Christ !
That ever this should be !
Yea, slimy things did crawl with legs
Upon the slimy sea.

SEVERED FRIENDSHIP.

ALAS! they had been friends in youth;
But whispering tongues can poison truth;
And constancy lives in realms above;
And life is thorny; and youth is vain;
And to be wroth with one we love
Doth work like madness in the brain.
And thus it chanced, as I divine,
With Roland and Sir Leoline.
Each spake words of high disdain
And insult to his heart's best brother:
They parted — ne'er to meet again!
But never either found another
To free the hollow heart from paining, —
They stood aloof, the scars remaining,
Like cliffs which had been rent asunder:
A dreary sea now flows between; —
But neither heat nor frost nor thunder
Shall wholly do away, I ween,
The marks of that which once hath been.

FLOWERS are lovely; love is flower-like;
Friendship is a sheltering tree;
O, the joys that came down shower-like
Of Friendship, Love, and Liberty,
        Ere I was old!
Dew-drops are the gems of the morning,
But the tears are of mournful eve!
Where no hope is, life's a warning
That only serves to make us grieve,
        When we are old:
That only serves to make us grieve
With oft and tedious taking leave,
Like some poor nigh-related guest,
That may not rudely be dismissed,
Yet hath outstayed his welcome while,
And tells the jest without the smile.

LAMB.

1775–1835.

Charles Lamb, the most charming essayist and humorist of his time, was born in London, 1775, and died 1835. His literary fame may be said to rest upon *Essays of Elia*. The delicate grace and flavor of these papers cannot be described. His style has a peculiar and subtle charm which comes from perfect ease and self-possession, and his humor is of the ripest and richest kind. In all his writings he is a perfect master in delicacy of feeling and happiness of expression. No other writer, save perhaps Goldsmith, enters so closely into his readers' hearts, and so warms them with his genial personality. To all who know him in his writings he is the dear friend, whose voice we seem to hear and whose smile we seem to see. A terrible tragedy shadowed his life; but through its gloom the tender loyalty of his nature shines out with beautiful radiance.

THE ORIGIN OF ROAST-PIG.

Mankind, says a Chinese manuscript, which my friend was obliging enough to read and explain to me, for the first seventy thousand ages ate their meat raw, clawing or biting it from the living animal, just as they do in Abyssinia to this day. This period is not obscurely hinted at by their great Confucius in the second chapter of his Mundane Mutations, where he designates a kind of golden age by the term Chofang, literally the Cooks' Holiday. The manuscript goes on to say, that the art of roasting, or rather broiling (which I take to be the elder brother), was accidentally discovered in the manner following. The swincherd Ho-ti, having gone out into the woods one morning, as his manner was, to collect mast for his hogs, left his cottage in the care of his eldest son, Bo-bo, a great lubberly boy, who being fond of playing with fire, as youngsters of his age commonly are, let some sparks escape into a bundle of straw, which, kindling quickly, spread the conflagration over every part of their poor mansion, till it was reduced to ashes. Together with the cottage (a sorry antediluvian make-shift of a building, you may think it), what was of much more importance, a fine litter of new-farrowed pigs, no less than nine in number, perished. China pigs have been esteemed a luxury all over the East, from the remotest periods that we read of. Bo-bo was in the utmost consternation, as you may think, not so much for the sake of the tenement, which his father and he could easily build up again with a few dry branches, and the labor of an hour or two, at any time, as for the loss of the pigs. While he was thinking what he should say to his father, and wringing his hands over the smoking

remnants of one of those untimely sufferers, an odor assailed his nos-
trils, unlike any scent which he had before experienced. What could
it proceed from? — not from the burnt cottage, — he had smelt that
smell before, — indeed, this was by no means the first accident of the
kind which had occurred through the negligence of this unlucky young
firebrand. Much less did it resemble that of any known herb, weed,
or flower. A premonitory moistening at the same time overflowed
his nether lip. He knew not what to think. He next stooped down
to feel the pig, if there were any signs of life in it. He burnt his
fingers, and to cool them he applied them in his booby fashion to his
mouth. Some of the crumbs of the scorched skin had come away
with his fingers, and for the first time in his life (in the world's life,
indeed, for before him no man had known it) he tasted — *crackling !*
Again he felt and fumbled at the pig. It did not burn him so much
now, still he licked his fingers from a sort of habit. The truth at
length broke into his slow understanding that it was the pig that
smelt so, and the pig that tasted so delicious; and surrendering himself up to the new-born pleasure, he fell to tearing up whole handfuls
of the scorched skin with the flesh next it, and was cramming it down
his throat in his beastly fashion, when his sire entered amid the smoking rafters, armed with retributory cudgel, and finding how affairs
stood, began to rain blows upon the young rogue's shoulders, as
thick as hail-stones, which Bo-bo heeded not any more than if they
had been flies. The tickling pleasure, which he experienced in his
lower regions, had rendered him quite callous to any inconveniences
he might feel in those remote quarters. His father might lay on, but
he could not beat him from his pig, till he had fairly made an end of
it, when, becoming a little more sensible of his situation, something
like the following dialogue ensued : —

"You graceless whelp, what have you got there devouring? Is
it not enough that you have burnt me down three houses with your
dog's tricks, and be hanged to you! but you must be eating fire, and
I know not what? What have you got there, I say ?"

"O father, the pig, the pig! do come and taste how nice the burnt
pig eats."

The ears of Ho-ti tingled with horror. He cursed his son, and he
cursed himself that ever he should beget a son that should eat burnt
pig.

Bo-bo, whose scent was wonderfully sharpened since morning, soon raked out another pig, and fairly rending it asunder, thrust the lesser half by main force into the fists of Ho-ti, still shouting out, " Eat, eat, eat the burnt pig, father, only taste — O Lord ! " — with such-like barbarous ejaculations, cramming all the while as if he would choke.

Ho-ti trembled in every joint while he grasped the abominable thing, wavering whether he should not put his son to death for an unnatural monster, when the crackling scorching his fingers, as it had done his son's, and applying the same remedy to them, he in his turn tasted some of its flavor, which, make what sour mouths he would for pretence, proved not altogether displeasing to him. In conclusion (for the manuscript here is a little tedious), both father and son fairly sat down to the mess, and never left off till they had despatched all that remained of the litter.

Bo-bo was strictly enjoined not to let the secret escape, for the neighbors would certainly have stoned them for a couple of abominable wretches, who could think of improving upon the good meat which God had sent them. Nevertheless, strange stories got about. It was observed that Ho-ti's cottage was burnt down more frequently than ever. Nothing but fires from this time forward. Some would break out in broad day, others in the night-time. As often as the sow farrowed, so sure was the house of Ho-ti to be in a blaze ; and Ho-ti himself, which was more remarkable, instead of chastising his son, seemed to grow more indulgent to him than ever. At length they were watched, the terrible mystery discovered, and father and son summoned to take their trial at Pekin, then an inconsiderable assize town. Evidence was given, the obnoxious food itself produced in court, and verdict about to be pronounced, when the foreman of the jury begged that some of the burnt pig, of which the culprits stood accused, might be handed into the box. He handled it, and they all handled it; and burning their fingers, as Bo-bo and his father had done before them, and nature prompting to each of them the same remedy, against the face of all the facts, and the clearest charge which judge had ever given, — to the surprise of the whole court, townsfolk, strangers, reporters, and all present, — without leaving the box, or any manner of consultation whatever, they brought in a simultaneous verdict of Not Guilty.

The judge, who was a shrewd fellow, winked at the manifest iniquity of the decision ; and when the court was dismissed, went privately, and bought up all the pigs that could be had for love or money. In a few days his Lordship's town house was observed to be on fire. The thing took wing, and now there was nothing to be seen but fires in every direction. Fuel and pigs grew enormously dear all over the district. The insurance-offices one and all shut up shop. People built slighter and slighter every day, until it was feared that the very science of architecture would in no long time be lost to the world. Thus this custom of firing houses continued, till in process of time, says my manuscript, a sage arose, like our Locke, who made a discovery that the flesh of swine, or indeed of any other animal, might be cooked (*burnt*, as they called it) without the necessity of consuming a whole house to dress it. Then first began the rude form of a gridiron. Roasting by the string or spit came in a century or two later, I forget in whose dynasty. By such slow degrees, concludes the manuscript, do the most useful and seemingly the most obvious arts make their way among mankind.

Without placing too implicit faith in the account above given, it must be agreed, that if a worthy pretext for so dangerous an experiment as setting houses on fire (especially in these days) could be assigned in favor of any culinary object, that pretext and excuse might be found in ROAST PIG.

Of all the delicacies in the whole *mundus edibilis*, I will maintain it to be the most delicate.

IN comparing modern with ancient manners, we are pleased to compliment ourselves upon the point of gallantry, — a certain obsequiousness or deferential respect which we are supposed to pay to females as females.

I shall be disposed to admit this when, in polite circles, I shall see the same attentions paid to age as to youth, to homely features as to handsome, to coarse complexions as to clear; to the woman as she is a woman, not as she is a beauty, a fortune, or a title. I shall believe it to be something more than a name when a well-dressed gentleman in a well-dressed company can advert to the topic of *female old age* without exciting, and intending to excite, a sneer; when the phrases, "antiquated virginity," and such a one has "overstood her market," pronounced in good company, shall raise immediate offense in man or woman that shall hear them spoken.

WEBSTER.

1782 – 1852.

DANIEL WEBSTER, the most illustrious of American statesmen, was born in Salisbury, New Hampshire, in 1782, and died at Marshfield, Massachusetts, in 1852. As an orator and a states- man he is chiefly known; but his writings, fragmentary though they are, deservedly rank among the best specimens of our literature. Our first extract is from an article which he contributed to the *North American Review*, and the second is from his memorable speech at the centennial celebration of the birthday of Washington.

THE BATTLE OF BUNKER HILL.*

No national drama was ever developed in a more interesting and splendid first scene. The incidents and the result of the battle itself were most important, and indeed most wonderful. As a mere battle, few surpass it in whatever engages and interests the attention. It was fought on a conspicuous eminence, in the immediate neighborhood of a populous city, and consequently in the view of thousands of spec- tators. The attacking army moved over a sheet of water to the assault. The operations and movements were of course all visible and all dis- tinct. Those who looked on from the houses and heights of Boston had a fuller view of every important operation and event than can ordinarily be had of any battle, or than can possibly be had of such as are fought on a more extended ground, or by detachments of troops acting in different places, and at different times, and in some measure independently of each other. When the British columns were ad- vancing to the attack, the flames of Charlestown (fired, as is generally supposed, by a shell) began to ascend. The spectators, far outnum- bering both armies, thronged and crowded on every height and every point which afforded a view of the scene, themselves constituted a very important part of it. The troops of the two armies seemed like so many combatants in an amphitheater. The manner in which they should acquit themselves was to be judged of, not, as in other cases of military engagements, by reports and future history, but by a vast and anxious assembly already on the spot, and waiting with unspeak- able concern and emotion the progress of the day. In other battles the *recollection* of wives and children has been used as an excitement

* One of the first, and one of the most celebrated battles of the Revolutionary War, fought June 17, 1775. It is commemorated by a granite obelisk, two hundred and twenty feet high, on the battle-ground in Charlestown, Mass., the corner-stone of which was laid by Lafayette in 1825.

to animate the warrior's breast and nerve his arm. Here was not a
mere recollection, but an actual *presence* of them, and other dear connections, hanging on the skirts of the battle, anxious and agitated,
feeling almost as if wounded themselves by every blow of the enemy,
and putting forth, as it were, their own strength, and all the energy
of their own throbbing bosoms, into every gallant effort of their war-
ring friends. But there was a more comprehensive and vastly more
important view of that day's contest than has been mentioned, — a
view, indeed, which ordinary eyes, bent intently on what was immediately before them, did not embrace, but which was perceived in its
full extent and expansion by minds of a higher order. Those men
who were at the head of the colonial councils, who had been engaged
for years in the previous stages of the quarrel with England, and who
had been accustomed to look forward to the future, were well apprised
of the magnitude of the events likely to hang on the business of that
day. They saw in it not only a battle, but the beginning of a civil
war of unmeasured extent and uncertain issue.) All America and all
England were likely to be deeply concerned in the consequences. The
individuals themselves, who knew full well what agency they had in
bringing affairs to this crisis, had need of all their courage, — not that
disregard of personal safety in which the vulgar suppose true courage
to consist, but that high and fixed moral sentiment, that steady and
decided purpose, which enables men to pursue a distant end, with a
full view of the difficulties and dangers before them, and with a conviction that, before they must arrive at the proposed end, should they
ever reach it, they must pass through evil report as well as good
report, and be liable to obloquy as well as to defeat. Spirits that fear
nothing else fear disgrace; and this danger is necessarily encountered
by those who engage in civil war.) (Unsuccessful resistance is not
only ruin to its authors, but is esteemed, and necessarily so, by the
laws of all countries, treasonable.) This is the case, at least, till resistance becomes so general and formidable as to assume the form of
regular war. But who can tell, when resistance commences, whether
it will attain even to that degree of success? Some of those persons
who signed the Declaration of Independence, in 1776, described themselves as signing it "as with halters about their necks." If there
were grounds for this remark in 1776, when the cause had become so
much more general, how much greater was the hazard when the battle
of Bunker Hill was fought! These considerations constituted, to en-

larged and liberal minds, the moral sublimity of the occasion, while to
the outward senses, the movement of armies, the roar of artillery, the
brilliancy of the reflection of a summer's sun from the burnished
armor of the British columns, and the flames of a burning town,
made up a scene of extraordinary grandeur.

EULOGIUM ON WASHINGTON.

I RISE, gentlemen, to propose to you the name of that great man,
in commemoration of whose birth and in honor of whose character
and services we are here assembled.

I am sure that I express a sentiment common to every one present
when I say, that there is something more than ordinarily solemn and
affecting on this occasion.

We are met to testify our regard for him whose name is intimately blended with whatever belongs most essentially to the prosperity, the liberty, the free institutions, and the renown of our
country. That name was of power to rally a nation, in the hour of
thick-thronging public disasters and calamities ; that name shone,
amid the storm of war, a beacon-light, to cheer and guide the
country's friends; it flamed, too, like a meteor, to repel her foes.
That name, in the days of peace, was a loadstone, attracting to
itself a whole people's confidence, a whole people's love, and the
whole world's respect; that name, descending with all time, spreading
over the whole earth, and uttered in all the languages belonging to
the tribes and races of men, will forever be pronounced with affectionate gratitude by every one in whose breast there shall arise an
aspiration for human rights and human liberty.

We perform this grateful duty, gentlemen, at the expiration of a
hundred years from his birth, near the place so cherished and
beloved by him, where his dust now reposes, and in the capital
which bears his own immortal name.

All experience evinces that human sentiments are strongly affected
by associations. The recurrence of anniversaries, or of longer periods
of time, naturally freshens the recollection, and deepens the impression, of events with which they are historically connected. Renowned places, also, have a power to awaken feeling, which all
acknowledge. No American can pass by the fields of Bunker Hill,
Monmouth, and Camden, as if they were ordinary spots on the earth's

surface. Whoever visits them feels the sentiment of love of country kindling anew, as if the spirit that belonged to the transactions which have rendered these places distinguished still hovered round with power to move and excite all who in future time may approach them.

But neither of these sources of emotion equals the power with which great moral examples affect the mind. When sublime virtues cease to be abstractions, when they become embodied in human character, and exemplified in human conduct, we should be false to our own nature, if we did not indulge in the spontaneous effusions of our gratitude and our admiration. A true lover of the virtue of patriotism delights to contemplate its purest models; and that love of country may be well suspected which affects to soar so high into the regions of sentiment as to be lost and absorbed in the abstract feeling, and becomes too elevated, or too refined, to glow with fervor in the commendation or the love of individual benefactors. All this is unnatural. It is as if one should be so enthusiastic a lover of poetry as to care nothing for Homer * or Milton; so passionately attached to eloquence as to be indifferent to Tully † and Chatham ‡; or such a devotee to the arts, in such an ecstasy with the elements of beauty, proportion, and expression, as to regard the masterpieces of Raphael § and Michael Angelo § with coldness or contempt. We may be assured, gentlemen, that he who really loves the thing itself loves its finest exhibitions. A true friend of his country loves her friends and benefactors, and thinks it no degradation to commend and commemorate them. The voluntary outpouring of public feeling made to-day, from the north to the south, and from the east to the west, proves this sentiment to be both just and natural. In the cities and in the villages, in the public temples and in the family circles, among all ages and sexes, gladdened voices to-day bespeak grateful hearts, and a freshened recollection of the virtues of the father of his country. And it will be so in all time to come, so long as public virtue is itself an object of regard. The ingenuous youth of America will hold up to themselves the bright model of Washington's example, and study to be what they behold; they will contemplate his character till all

---

* HOMER. The greatest of the Greek poets: lived about 915 B. C. The *Iliad* stands at the head of all epic poetry.

† TULLY. More commonly known as Cicero, the famous Roman orator. See *Plutarch's Lives.*

‡ CHATHAM. An illustrious English statesman and orator, born 1708.

§ RAPHAEL; MICHAEL ANGELO. Celebrated Italians; the former as a painter, and the latter as a sculptor and architect. Both born in the latter part of the fifteenth century.

its virtues spread out and display themselves to their delighted vision, as the earliest astronomers, the shepherds on the plains of Babylon, gazed at the stars till they saw them form into clusters and constellations, overpowering at length the eyes of the beholders with the united blaze of a thousand lights.

Gentlemen, we are at the point of a century from the birth of Washington; and what a century it has been! During its course the human mind has seemed to proceed with a sort of geometric velocity, accomplishing, for human intelligence and human freedom, more than had been done in fives or tens of centuries preceding. Washington stands at the commencement of a new era, as well as at the head of the new world. A century from the birth of Washington has changed the world. The country of Washington has been the theater on which a great part of that change has been wrought; and Washington himself a principal agent by which it has been accomplished. His age and his country are equally full of wonders, and of both he is the chief.

If the prediction of the poet, uttered a few years before his birth, be true; if indeed it be designed by Providence that the proudest exhibition of human character and human affairs shall be made on this theater of the Western world; if it be true that,

.

> " The four first acts already past,
> A fifth shall close the drama of the day;
> Time's noblest offspring is the last ";

how could this imposing, swelling, final scene be appropriately opened, how could its intense interest be adequately sustained, but by the introduction of just such a character as our Washington?

Washington had attained his manhood when that spark of liberty was struck out in his own country, which has since kindled into a flame, and shot its beams over the earth. In the flow of a century from his birth, the world has changed in science, in arts, in the extent of commerce, in the improvement of navigation, and in all that relates to the civilization of man. But it is the spirit of human freedom, the new elevation of individual man, in his moral, social, and political character, leading the whole long train of other improvements, which has most remarkably distinguished the era. Society, in this century, has not made its progress, like Chinese skill, by a greater acuteness of ingenuity in trifles; it has not merely lashed itself to an increased speed round the old circles of thought and action; but it has assumed a new character; it has raised itself from *beneath* governments to participation *in* governments; it has mixed moral and political objects with the daily pursuits of individual men, and, with a freedom and strength before altogether unknown, it has applied to these objects the whole power of the human understanding. It has been the era, in short, when the social principle has triumphed over the feudal principle; when society has maintained its rights against military power, and established, on foundations never hereafter to be shaken, its competency to govern itself.

THE AMERICAN UNION.

WHEN my eyes turn to behold for the last time the sun in heaven, may they not see him shining on the broken and dishonored fragments of a once glorious Union; on States dissevered, discordant, belligerent; on a land rent with civil feuds; or drenched, it may be, in fraternal blood. Let their last feeble and lingering glance rather behold the gorgeous ensign of the Republic, now known and honored throughout the earth, still full high advanced; its arms and trophies streaming in all their original luster; not a stripe erased or polluted; not a single star obscured; bearing for its motto no such miserable interrogatory as "What is all this worth?" nor those other words of delusion and folly, of Liberty first, and Union afterwards, but everywhere, spread all over in characters of living light, and blazing on all its ample folds, as they float over the sea and over the land, and in every wind under the whole heavens, that other sentiment dear to every American heart, — "Liberty AND Union, — now and forever, — one and inseparable."

OUR fathers raised their flag against a power to which, for purposes of foreign conquest and subjugation, Rome, in the hight of her glory, is not to be compared, — a power which has dotted the surface of the whole globe with her possessions and military posts, whose morning drum-beat, following the sun in his course, and keeping pace with the hours, circles the earth with one continuous and unbroken strain of the martial airs of England.

IRVING.

1783–1859.

No name in our literary annals is more fondly cherished than that of Washington Irving, one of the earliest and most distinguished of American writers. He was born in New York in 1783, and died at Sunnyside, his home on the Hudson, in 1859. He began his literary career by contributing to the columns of the *Morning Chronicle*, of which his brother, Dr. Peter Irving, was editor. His health failing, he went to Europe, where he remained two years. On his return he was admitted to the bar, but gave little attention to his profession. In 1807 appeared the first number of *Salmagundi, or the Whim-Whams and Opinions of Launcelot Langstaff and Others*, a semi-monthly periodical of light and agreeable character, which was very popular during its existence of less than two years. In 1809 the famous *History of New York, by Diedrich Knickerbocker*, was published, and had a most cordial reception. The next year Washington Irving became a partner in the mercantile business conducted by his brothers; but in 1812 the firm failed, and the young author returned to literary labors. *The Sketch-Book* appeared in 1819, and established his fame in England and America. *Bracebridge Hall, The Conquest of Granada, The Life of Columbus*, and other works, were issued at intervals prior to 1832. In 1842 he was appointed United States Minister to Spain, and held that office four years. After his return he wrote a *Life of Goldsmith, The Life of Washington, Mahomet and his Successors*, etc. It is safe to say that no American author has been so generally and heartily loved as Washington Irving, and he was as popular in England as at home. But his fame is by no means wholly due to the qualities of his heart; his intellectual powers were of the first class, but were largely controlled by his native amiability, which shed a sunny radiance over all his writings. His style remains to this day a model of ease, grace, and refinement. Our extracts are from *The Sketch-Book* and *The Life of Columbus*.

ICHABOD CRANE.

In the bosom of one of those spacious coves which indent the eastern shore of the Hudson, at that broad expansion of the river denominated by the ancient Dutch navigators the Tappan Zee, and where they always prudently shortened sail, and implored the protection of St. Nicholas when they crossed, there lies a small market-town or rural port, which by some is called Greensburgh, but which is more generally and properly known by the name of Tarry Town. This name was given, we are told, in former days, by the good housewives of the adjacent country, from the inveterate propensity of their husbands to linger about the village tavern on market-days. Be that as it may, I do not vouch for the fact, but merely advert to it, for the sake of being precise and authentic. Not far from this village, perhaps about two miles, there is a little valley, or rather lap of land, among high hills, which is one of the quietest places in the whole world. A small brook glides through it, with just murmur enough to lull one to repose; and the occasional whistle of a quail, or tapping of a woodpecker, is almost the only sound that ever breaks in upon the uniform tranquillity.

I recollect that, when a stripling, my first exploit in squirrel-shooting was in a grove of tall walnut-trees that shades one side of the valley. I had wandered into it at noon-time, when all nature is peculiarly quiet, and was startled by the roar of my own gun, as it broke the Sabbath stillness around, and was prolonged and reverberated by the angry echoes. If ever I should wish for a retreat, whither I might steal from the world and its distractions, and dream quietly away the remnant of a troubled life, I know of none more promising than this little valley.

From the listless repose of the place, and the peculiar character of its inhabitants, who are descendants from the original Dutch settlers, this sequestered glen has long been known by the name of SLEEPY HOLLOW, and its rustic lads are called the Sleepy Hollow Boys throughout all the neighboring country. A drowsy, dreamy influence seems to hang over the land, and to pervade the very atmosphere. Some say that the place was bewitched by a high German doctor, during the early days of the settlement; others, that an old Indian chief, the prophet or wizard of his tribe, held his powwows there before the country was discovered by Master Hendrick Hudson.* Certain it is, the place still continues under the sway of some witching power, that holds a spell over the minds of the good people, causing them to walk in a continual reverie. They are given to all kinds of marvelous beliefs; are subject to trances and visions; and frequently see strange sights, and hear music and voices in the air. The whole neighborhood abounds with local tales, haunted spots, and twilight superstitions; stars shoot and meteors glare oftener across the valley than in any other part of the country, and the nightmare, with her whole nine fold, seems to make it the favorite scene of her gambols.

The dominant spirit, however, that haunts this enchanted region, and seems to be commander-in-chief of all the powers of the air, is the apparition of a figure on horseback without a head. It is said by some to be the ghost of a Hessian trooper, whose head had been carried away by a cannon-ball, in some nameless battle during the Revolutionary War; and who is ever and anon seen by the country folk, hurrying along in the gloom of night, as if on the wings of the wind. His haunts are not confined to the valley, but extend at times to the adjacent roads, and especially to the vicinity of a church at no

* HENRY HUDSON. An eminent English navigator. He discovered the Hudson River in 1609.

great distance. Indeed, certain of the most authentic historians of those parts, who have been careful in collecting and collating the floating facts concerning this specter, allege that, the body of the trooper having been buried in the church-yard, the ghost rides forth to the scene of battle in nightly quest of his head; and that the rushing speed with which he sometimes passes along the Hollow, like a midnight blast, is owing to his being belated, and in a hurry to get back to the church-yard before daybreak.

Such is the general purport of this legendary superstition, which has furnished materials for many a wild story in that region of shadows; and the specter is known, at all the country firesides, by the name of the Headless Horseman of Sleepy Hollow.

It is remarkable that the visionary propensity I have mentioned is not confined to the native inhabitants of the valley, but is unconsciously imbibed by every one who resides there for a time. However wide awake they may have been before they entered that sleepy region, they are sure, in a little time, to inhale the witching influence of the air, and begin to grow imaginative, — to dream dreams and see apparitions.

I mention this peaceful spot with all possible laud; for it is in such little retired Dutch valleys, found here and there embosomed in the great State of New York, that population, manners, and customs remain fixed; while the great torrent of migration and improvement which is making such incessant changes in other parts of this restless country sweeps by them unobserved. They are like those little nooks of still water which border a rapid stream) where we may see the straw and bubble riding quietly at anchor, or slowly revolving in their mimic harbor, undisturbed by the rush of the passing current. Though many years have elapsed since I trod the drowsy shades of Sleepy Hollow, yet I question whether I should not still find the same trees and the same families vegetating in its sheltered bosom.

In this by-place of nature there abode, in a remote period of American history, that is to say, some thirty years since, a worthy wight of the name of Ichabod Crane; who sojourned, or, as he expressed it, "tarried," in Sleepy Hollow, for the purpose of instructing the children of the vicinity. He was a native of Connecticut; a State which supplies the Union with pioneers for the mind as well as for the forest, and sends forth yearly its legions of frontier woodsmen and country schoolmasters. The cognomen of Crane was not inapplicable to his person. He was tall, but exceedingly lank, with narrow shoulders, long arms and legs, hands that dangled a mile out of his sleeves, feet that might have served for shovels, and his whole frame most loosely hung together. His head was small, and flat at top, with huge ears, large green glassy eyes, and a long snipe nose, so that it looked like a weathercock, perched upon his spindle neck, to tell which way the wind blew. To see him striding along the profile of a hill on a windy day, with his clothes bagging and fluttering about him, one might have mistaken him for the genius of famine descending upon the earth, or some scarecrow eloped from a cornfield.

His school-house was a low building of one large room, rudely constructed of logs; the windows partly glazed, and partly patched with leaves of old copy-books. It was most ingeniously secured at vacant hours by a withe twisted in the handle of the door, and stakes set against the window-shutters; so that, though a thief might get in with perfect ease, he would find some embarrassment in getting out; an idea most probably borrowed by the architect, Yost Van Houten, from the mystery of an eel-pot. The school-house stood in a rather lonely but pleasant situation, just at the foot of a woody hill, with a brook running close by, and a formidable birch-tree growing at one end of it. From hence the low murmur of his pupils' voices, conning over their lessons, might be heard in a drowsy summer's day, like the hum of a beehive, interrupted now and then by the authoritative voice of the master, in the tone of menace or command; or, peradventure, by the appalling sound of the birch, as he urged some tardy loiterer along the flowery path of knowledge. Truth to say, he was a conscientious man, and ever bore in mind the golden maxim, " Spare the rod and spoil the child." — Ichabod Crane's scholars certainly were not spoiled.

I would not have it imagined, however, that he was one of those cruel potentates of the school, who joy in the smart of their subjects; on the contrary, he administered justice with discrimination rather than severity; taking the burden off the backs of the weak, and laying it on those of the strong. Your mere puny stripling, that winced at the least flourish of the rod, was passed by with indulgence; but the claims of justice were satisfied by inflicting a double portion on some little, tough, wrong-headed, broad-skirted Dutch urchin, who sulked and swelled and grew dogged and sullen beneath the birch. All this he called "doing his duty by their parents"; and he never inflicted a chastisement without following it by the assurance, so consolatory to the smarting urchin, that "he would remember it, and thank him for it, the longest day he had to live."

ICHABOD CRANE (*continued*).

WHEN school-hours were over, he was even the companion and playmate of the larger boys; and on holiday afternoons would convoy some of the smaller ones home, who happened to have pretty sisters, or good housewives for mothers, noted for the comforts of the cupboard. Indeed, it behooved him to keep on good terms with his pupils. The revenue arising from his school was small, and would have been scarcely sufficient to furnish him with daily bread, for he was a huge feeder, and, though lank, had the dilating powers of an anaconda; but to help out his maintenance, he was, according to country custom in those parts, boarded and lodged at the houses of the farmers, whose children he instructed. With these he lived successively a week at a time; thus going the rounds of the neighborhood, with all his worldly effects tied up in a cotton handkerchief.

That all this might not be too onerous on the purses of his rustic patrons, who are apt to consider the costs of schooling a grievous burden, and schoolmasters as mere drones, he had various ways of rendering himself both useful and agreeable. He assisted the farmers occasionally in the lighter labors of their farms; helped to make hay; mended the fences; took the horses to water; drove the cows from pasture; cut wood for the winter fire. He laid aside, too, all the dominant dignity and absolute sway with which he lorded it in his little empire, the school, and became wonderfully gentle and ingratiating. He found favor in the eyes of the mothers, by petting the children, particularly the youngest; and like the lion bold, which whilom so magnanimously the lamb did hold, he would sit with a child on one knee, and rock a cradle with his foot for whole hours together.

In addition to his other vocations, he was the singing-master of the neighborhood, and picked up many bright shillings by instructing the young folks in psalmody. It was a matter of no little vanity to him, on Sundays, to take his station in front of the church gallery, with a band of chosen singers; where, in his own mind, he completely carried away the palm from the parson. Certain it is, his voice resounded far above all the rest of the congregation; and there are peculiar quavers still to be heard in that church, and which may even be heard half a mile off, quite to the opposite side of the mill-pond, on a still Sunday morning, which are said to be legitimately descended from the nose of Ichabod Crane. Thus by divers little make-shifts in that ingenious way which is commonly denominated "by hook and by crook," the worthy pedagogue got on tolerably enough, and was thought, by all who understood nothing of the labor of head-work, to have a wonderfully easy life of it.

The schoolmaster is generally a man of some importance in the female circle of a rural neighborhood; being considered a kind of idle gentleman-like personage, of vastly superior taste and accomplishments to the rough country swains, and, indeed, inferior in learning only to the parson. His appearance, therefore, is apt to occasion some little stir at the tea-table of a farm-house, and the addition of a supernumerary dish of cakes or sweetmeats, or, peradventure, the parade of a silver tea-pot. Our man of letters, therefore, was peculiarly happy in the smiles of all the country damsels. How he would figure among them in the church-yard, between services on Sundays! gathering grapes for them from the wild vines that overrun the surrounding trees; reciting for their amusement all the epitaphs on the tombstones; or sauntering, with a whole bevy of them, along the banks of the adjacent mill-pond; while the more bashful country bumpkins hung sheepishly back, envying his superior elegance and address.

From his half itinerant life, also, he was a kind of traveling gazette, carrying the whole budget of local gossip from house to house; so that his appearance was always greeted with satisfaction. He was, moreover, esteemed by the women as a man of great erudition, for he had read several books quite through, and was a perfect master of Cotton Mather's History of New England Witchcraft, in which, by the way, he most firmly and potently believed.

He was, in fact, a mixture of small shrewdness and simple credulity. His appetite for the marvelous, and his powers of digesting it, were equally extraordinary; and both had been increased by his residence in this spell-bound region. No tale was too gross or monstrous for his capacious swallow. It was often his delight, after his school was dismissed in the afternoon, to stretch himself on the rich bed of clover, bordering the little brook that whimpered by his school-house, and there con over old Mather's direful tales, until the gathering dusk of the evening made the printed page a mere mist before his eyes. Then, as he wended his way, by swamp and stream and awful woodland, to the farm-house where he happened to be quartered, every sound of nature, at that witching hour, fluttered his excited imagination; the moan of the whip-poor-will * from the hill-side; the boding cry of the tree-toad, that harbinger of storm; the dreary hooting of the screech-owl, or the sudden rustling in the thicket of birds frightened from their roost. The fire-flies, too, which sparkled most vividly in the darkest places, now and then startled him, as one of uncommon brightness would stream across his path; and if, by chance, a huge blockhead of a beetle came winging his blundering flight against him, the poor varlet was ready to give up the ghost, with the idea that he was struck with a witch's token. His only resource on such occasions, either to drown thought, or drive away evil spirits, was to sing psalm-tunes; and the good people of Sleepy Hollow, as they sat by their doors of an evening, were often filled with awe, at hearing his nasal melody, "in linked sweetness long drawn out," floating from the distant hill, or along the dusky road.

Another of his sources of fearful pleasure was, to pass long winter evenings with the old Dutch wives, as they sat spinning by the fire, with a row of apples roasting and spluttering along the hearth, and listen to their marvelous tales of ghosts and goblins, and haunted fields, and haunted brooks, and haunted bridges, and haunted houses, and particularly of the headless horseman, or Galloping Hessian of the Hollow, as they sometimes called him. He would delight them equally by his anecdotes of witchcraft, and of the direful omens and portentous sights and sounds in the air, which prevailed in the earlier times of Connecticut; and would frighten them wofully with speculations upon comets and shooting stars; and with the alarming fact that the world did absolutely turn round, and that they were half the time topsy-turvy!

But if there was a pleasure in all this, while snugly cuddling in the chimney-corner of a chamber that was all of a ruddy glow from the crackling wood-fire, and where, of course, no specter dared to show

---

* The whip-poor-will is a bird which is only heard at night. It receives its name from its note, which is thought to resemble those words.

his face, it was dearly purchased by the terrors of his subsequent walk homewards. What fearful shapes and shadows beset his path amidst the dim and ghastly glare of a snowy night! — With what wistful look did he eye every trembling ray of light streaming across the waste fields from some distant window! — How often was he appalled by some shrub covered with snow, which, like a sheeted specter, beset his very path! — How often did he shrink with curdling awe at the sound of his own steps on the frosty crust beneath his feet; and dread to look over his shoulder, lest he should behold some uncouth being tramping close behind him! — and how often was he thrown into complete dismay by some rushing blast, howling among the trees, in the idea that it was the Galloping Hessian on one of his nightly scourings!

All these, however, were mere terrors of the night, phantoms of the mind, that walk in darkness; and though he had seen many specters in his time, and been more than once beset by Satan in divers shapes, in his lonely perambulations, yet daylight put an end to all these evils; and he would have passed a pleasant life of it, in despite of the devil and all his works, if his path had not been crossed by a being that causes more perplexity to mortal man than ghosts, goblins, and the whole race of witches put together, and that was — a woman.

THE DISCOVERY OF AMERICA BY COLUMBUS.*

It was on Friday morning, the 12th of October, 1492, that Columbus first beheld the New World. As the day dawned he saw before him a level island, several leagues in extent, and covered with trees like a continual orchard. Though apparently uncultivated, it was populous, for the inhabitants were seen issuing from all parts of the woods and running to the shore. They were perfectly naked, and, as they stood gazing at the ships, appeared by their attitudes and gestures to be lost in astonishment.

Columbus made signals for the ships to cast anchor, and the boats to be manned and armed. He entered his own boat, richly attired in

---

* CHRISTOPHER COLUMBUS, the discoverer of America, was born at Genoa about 1440. A most interesting and instructive account of his marvelous discoveries and career is given in *Irving's Life of Columbus* and in *Prescott's Ferdinand and Isabella*. He died in poverty and neglect, and in ignorance of the grandeur of his discovery. He supposed that he had merely reached remote parts of Asia, having no knowledge whatever that he had discovered a continent.

scarlet, and holding the royal standard; whilst Martin Alonzo Pinzon✗ and Vincent Jañez his brother put off in company in their boats, each with a banner of the enterprise emblazoned with a green cross, having on either side the letters F. and Y., the initials of the Castilian monarchs Fernando and Ysabel, surmounted by crowns.

As he approached the shore, Columbus, who was disposed for all kinds of agreeable impressions, was delighted with the purity and suavity of the atmosphere, the crystal transparency of the sea, and the extraordinary beauty of the vegetation. He beheld, also, fruits of an unknown kind upon the trees which overhung the shores. On landing, he threw himself on his knees, kissed the earth, and returned thanks to God with tears of joy. His example was followed by the rest, whose hearts indeed overflowed with the same feelings of gratitude.

Columbus, then rising, drew his sword, displayed the royal standard, and assembling round him the two captains, with Rodrigo de Escobedo, notary of the armament, Rodrigo Sanchez, and the rest who had landed, he took solemn possession in the name of the Castilian sovereigns, giving the island the name of San Salvador. Having complied with the requisite forms and ceremonies, he called upon all present to take the oath of obedience to him, as admiral and viceroy representing the persons of the sovereigns.

The feelings of the crew now burst forth in the most extravagant transports. They had recently considered themselves devoted men, hurrying forward to destruction; they now looked upon themselves as favorites of fortune, and gave themselves up to the most unbounded joy. They thronged around the admiral with overflowing zeal, some embracing him, others kissing his hands. Those who had been most mutinous and turbulent during the voyage were now most devoted and enthusiastic. Some begged favors of him, as if he had already wealth and honors in his gift. Many abject spirits, who had outraged him by their insolence, now crouched at his feet, begging pardon for all the trouble they had caused him, and promising the blindest obedience for the future.

The natives of the island, when, at the dawn of day, they had beheld the ships hovering on their coast, had supposed them monsters which had issued from the deep during the night. They had crowded to the beach, and watched their movements with awful anxiety. Their veering about, apparently without effort, and the shifting and furling of their sails, resembling huge wings, filled them with astonishment. When they beheld their boats approach the shore, and a number of strange beings clad in glittering steel, or raiment of various colors, landing upon the beach, they fled in affright to the woods.

Finding, however, that there was no attempt to pursue nor molest them, they gradually recovered from their terror, and approached the Spaniards with great awe, frequently prostrating themselves on the earth, and making signs of adoration. During the ceremonies of taking possession, they remained gazing in timid admiration at the complexion, the beards, the shining armor, and splendid dress of the Spaniards. The admiral particularly attracted their attention, from his commanding height, his air of authority, his dress of scarlet, and the deference which was paid him by his companions; all which pointed him out to be the commander.

When they had still further recovered from their fears, they approached the Spaniards, touched their beards, and examined their hands and faces, admiring their whiteness. Columbus was pleased with their gentleness and confiding simplicity, and suffered their scrutiny with perfect acquiescence, winning them by his benignity. They now supposed that the ships had sailed out of the crystal firmament which bounded their horizon, or had descended from above on their ample wings, and that these marvelous beings were inhabitants of the skies.

The natives of the island were no less objects of curiosity to the Spaniards, differing as they did from any race of men they had ever seen. Their appearance gave no promise of either wealth or civilization, for they were entirely naked, and painted with a variety of colors. With some it was confined merely to a part of the face, the nose or around the eyes; with others it extended to the whole body, and gave them a wild and fantastic appearance.

Their complexion was of a tawny or copper hue, and they were entirely destitute of beards. Their hair was not crisped, like the recently discovered tribes of the African coast, under the same latitude, but straight and coarse, partly cut short above the ears, but some locks were left long behind and falling upon their shoulders. Their features, though obscured and discolored by paint, were agreeable; they had lofty foreheads, and remarkably fine eyes. They were of moderate stature and well-shaped; most of them appeared to be under thirty years of age; there was but one female with them, quite young, naked like her companions, and beautifully formed.

As Columbus supposed himself to have landed on an island at the extremity of India, he called the natives by the general appellation of Indians, which was universally adopted before the true nature of his discovery was known, and has since been extended to all the aboriginals of the New World. The islanders were friendly and gentle. Their only arms were lances, hardened at the end by fire, or pointed with a flint, or the teeth or bone of a fish. There was no iron to be seen, nor did they appear acquainted with its properties; for when a drawn sword was presented to them, they unguardedly took it by the edge.

Columbus distributed among them colored caps, glass beads, hawks' bells, and other trifles, such as the Portuguese were accustomed to trade with among the nations of the gold-coast of Africa. They received them eagerly, hung the beads round their necks, and were wonderfully pleased with their finery, and with the sound of the bells. The Spaniards remained all day on shore, refreshing themselves after their anxious voyage amidst the beautiful groves of the island, and returned on board late in the evening, delighted with all they had seen.

On the following morning, at break of day, the shore was thronged with the natives; some swam off to the ships, others came in light barks, which they called canoes, formed of a single tree, hollowed, and capable of holding from one man up to the number of forty or fifty. These they managed dextrously with paddles, and, if overturned, swam about in the water with perfect unconcern, as if in their natural element, righting their canoes with great facility, and baling them with calabashes.

They were eager to procure more toys and trinkets, not, apparently, from any idea of their intrinsic value, but because everything from the hands of the strangers possessed a supernatural virtue in their eyes, as having been brought from heaven; they even picked up fragments of glass and earthenware as valuable prizes. They had but few objects to offer in return, except parrots, of which great numbers were domesticated among them, and cotton yarn, of which they had abundance, and would exchange large balls of five and twenty pounds' weight for the merest trifle.

They brought also cakes of a kind of bread called cassava, which constituted a principal part of their food, and was afterwards an important article of provisions with the Spaniards. It was formed from a great root called yuca, which they cultivated in fields. This they cut into small morsels, which they grated or scraped, and strained in a press, making a broad, thin cake, which was afterwards dried hard, and would keep for a long time, being steeped in water when eaten. It was insipid, but nourishing, though the water strained from it in the preparation was a deadly poison. There was another kind of yuca destitute of this poisonous quality, which was eaten in the root, either boiled or roasted.

The avarice of the discoverers was quickly excited, by the sight of small ornaments of gold, worn by some of the natives in their noses. These the latter gladly exchanged for glass beads and hawks' bells; and both parties exulted in the bargain, no doubt admiring each other's simplicity. As gold, however, was an object of royal monopoly in all enterprises of discovery, Columbus forbade any traffic in it without his express sanction; and he put the same prohibition on the traffic for cotton, reserving to the crown all trade for it, wherever it should be found in any quantity.

He inquired of the natives where this gold was procured. They answered him by signs, pointing to the south, where, he understood them, dwelt a king of such wealth that he was served in vessels of wrought gold. He understood, also, that there was land to the south, the southwest, and the northwest; and that the people from the last-mentioned quarter frequently proceeded to the southwest in quest of gold and precious stones, making in their way descents upon the islands, and carrying off the inhabitants. Several of the natives showed him scars of wounds received in battles with these invaders. It is evident that a great part of this fancied intelligence was self-delusion on the part of Columbus; for he was under a spell of the imagination, which gave its own shapes and colors to every object.

He was persuaded that he had arrived among the islands described by Marco Polo,* as lying opposite Cathay, in the Chinese Sea, and he construed everything to accord with the account given of those opulent regions. Thus the enemies which the natives spoke of as coming from the northwest he concluded to be the people of the mainland of Asia, the subjects of the great Khan of Tartary, who were represented by the Venetian traveler as accustomed to make war upon the islands, and to enslave their inhabitants. The country to the south, abounding in gold, could be no other than the famous island of Cipango; and the king, who was served out of vessels of

---

* MARCO POLO. A renowned Venetian traveler, born about 1252. He was the first European who entered China, or made any extended journey into Central Asia.

gold, must be the monarch whose magnificent city and gorgeous palace, covered with plates of gold, had been extolled in such splendid terms by Marco Polo.

The island where Columbus had thus, for the first time, set his foot upon the New World, was called by the natives Guanahane.* It still retains the name of San Salvador, which he gave to it, though called, by the English, Cat Island. The light which he had seen the evening previous to his making land may have been on Watling's Island, which lies a few leagues to the east. San Salvador is one of the great cluster of the Lucayos or Bahama Islands, which stretch southeast and northwest, from the coast of Florida to Hispaniola, covering the northern coast of Cuba.

THE RETURN OF COLUMBUS.

AFTER a brief interval, the sovereigns requested of Columbus a recital of his adventures. His manner was sedate and dignified, but warmed by the glow of natural enthusiasm. He enumerated the several islands he had visited, expatiated on the temperate character of the climate, and the capacity of the soil for every variety of production, appealing to the samples imported by him as evidence of their natural productiveness. He dwelt more at large on the precious metals to be found in these islands, which he inferred less from the specimens actually obtained than from the uniform testimony of the natives to their abundance in the unexplored regions of the interior. Lastly, he pointed out the wide scope afforded to Christian zeal in the illumination of a race of men whose minds, far from being wedded to any system of idolatry, were prepared by their extreme simplicity for the reception of pure and uncorrupted doctrine. The last consideration touched Isabella's heart most sensibly; and the whole audience, kindled with various emotions by the speaker's eloquence, filled up the perspective with the gorgeous coloring of their own fancies, as ambition or avarice or devotional feeling predominated in their bosoms. When Columbus ceased, the king and queen, together with all present, prostrated themselves on their knees in grateful thanksgivings, while the solemn strains of the Te Deum were poured forth by the choir of the royal chapel, as in commemoration of some glorious victory.

BYRON.

1788 – 1824.

GEORGE GORDON, Lord Byron, was born in 1788 and died in 1824. In youth he was precocious, manifesting remarkable intellectual power, but giving evidence also of a wild and ungovernable temper. Leaving Trinity College, Cambridge, at the age of nineteen, he prepared a volume of poems for publication, which, under the title of *Hours of Idleness*, was severely ridiculed by the *Edinburgh Review*. A year later appeared Byron's reply, *English Bards and Scotch Reviewers*, one of the most powerful and scorching satires ever written. Having traveled for two years on the Continent, Byron returned to England, and in 1812 published the first two cantos of *Childe Harold*, which is generally esteemed his greatest work. In 1816 he left England, which he declared he would never revisit. He spent some time at Geneva, with literary friends, and then settled himself in Italy, where he wrote *Manfred*, the concluding canto of *Childe Harold*, *Mazeppa*, and the first part of *Don Juan*. In 1820 he was associated with Shelley and Leigh Hunt in the publication of a periodical called *The Liberal*, in which *The Vision of Judgment* was first printed. In 1823 he went to Greece, where he intended to aid the Greeks in their resistance to Turkish oppression. But his military career was brief; he was seized with epilepsy, and, rheumatic fever ensuing, he died April 19, 1824. Byron's character presents one of the most interesting studies to be found in literary history. As a man, we must censure even while we pity him; as a poet, he claims our fervent admiration. His poems are marvels of energy and spirit, glittering with poetical beauties and epigrammatic expressions that have become "household words." But a profound morbidness pervades them, and the thoughtful reader feels himself, as he ponders their passionate, defiant, almost savage philosophy, to be in the presence of an unhealthy mind. His poems possess a peculiar fascination for the young; but their charms seem more hollow and unreal to the eye of age and experience. Byron's life was a series of mistakes; and, great poet though he was, his hours of happiness were, no doubt, fewer than those of the most illiterate peasant.

THE SHIPWRECK.

THERE were two fathers in this ghastly crew,
　　And with them their two sons, of whom the one
Was more robust and hardy to the view ;
　　But he died early : and when he was gone,
His nearest messmate told his sire, who threw
　　One glance on him, and said, " Heaven's will be done !
I can do nothing "; and he saw him thrown
Into the deep, without a tear or groan.

The other father had a weaklier child,
　　Of a soft cheek, and aspect delicate ;
But the boy bore up long, and with a mild
　　And patient spirit held aloof his fate :
Little he said, and now and then he smiled,
　　As if to win a part from off the weight

He saw increasing on his father's heart,
With the deep, deadly thought, that they must part.

And o'er him bent his sire, and never raised
  His eyes from off his face, but wiped the foam
From his pale lips, and ever on him gazed :
  And when the wished-for shower at length was come,
And the boy's eyes, which the dull film half glazed,
  Brightened, and for a moment seemed to roam,
He squeezed from out a rag some drops of rain
Into his dying child's mouth ; but in vain !

The boy expired : the father held the clay,
  And looked upon it long ; and when at last
Death left no doubt, and the dead burden lay
  Stiff on his heart, and pulse and hope were past,
He watched it wistfully until away
  'T was borne by the rude wave wherein 't was cast ;
Then he himself sunk down, all dumb and shivering,
And gave no sign of life, save his limbs quivering.

'T was twilight, for the sunless day went down
  Over the waste of waters ; like a veil
Which, if withdrawn, would but disclose the frown
  Of one whose hate is masked but to assail.
Thus to their hopeless eyes the night was shown,
  And grimly darkled o'er their faces pale,
And the dim, desolate deep ; twelve days had Fear
Been their familiar, and now Death was here.

Then rose from sea to sky the wild farewell, —
  Then shrieked the timid, and stood still the brave, —
Then some leaped overboard with dreadful yell,
  As eager to anticipate their grave ;
And the sea yawned around her, like a hell,
  And down she sucked with her the whirling wave,
Like one who grapples with his enemy,
And strives to strangle him before he die.

And first one universal shriek there rushed,
　　Louder than the loud ocean, — like a crash
Of echoing thunder; and then all was hushed,
　　Save the wild wind and the remorseless dash
Of billows; but at intervals there gushed,
　　Accompanied by a convulsive splash,
A solitary shriek, the bubbling cry
Of some strong swimmer in his agony.

MODERN GREECE.

CLIME of the unforgotten brave!
Whose land from plain to mountain cave
Was freedom's home or glory's grave!
Shrine of the mighty! can it be,
That this is all remains of thee?
Approach, thou craven crouching slave:
　　Say, is not this Thermopylæ? *
These waters blue that round you lave,
　　O servile offspring of the free, —
　　Pronounce what sea, what shore is this?
The gulf, the rock of Salamis! †
These scenes, their story not unknown,
Arise and make again your own;
Snatch from the ashes of your sires
The embers of their former fires;
And he who in the strife expires
Will add to theirs a name of fear,
That tyranny shall quake to hear,
And leave his sons a hope, a fame,
They too will rather die than shame;
For freedom's battle once begun,
Bequeathed by bleeding sire to son,
Though baffled oft, is ever won.

---

* THERMOPYLÆ. A mountain defile in Greece where Leonidas (480 B. C.), at the head of three hundred Spartans withstood the whole force of the Persian army for three days. More than twenty thousand Persians perished in the memorable battle, and only one Greek survived. This battle is supposed to have commemorated the finest instance of heroic bravery on record.

† SALAMIS. Refers to a celebrated naval battle between the Greeks and the Persians, where the latter were disastrously defeated.

Bear witness, Greece, thy living page,
Attest it many a deathless age!
While kings, in dusty darkness hid,
Have left a nameless pyramid;
Thy heroes, though the general doom
Hath swept the column from their tomb,
A mightier monument command, —
The mountains of their native land!
There points thy muse to stranger's eye
The graves of those that cannot die.
'T were long to tell, and sad to trace,
Each step from splendor to disgrace;
Enough, — no foreign foe could quell
Thy soul, till from itself it fell;
Yes! self-abasement paved the way
To villain-bonds and despot sway.

ROME.

O ROME! my country! city of the soul!
The orphans of the heart must turn to thee,
Lone mother of dead empires! and control
In their shut breasts their petty misery.
What are our woes and sufferance? Come and see
The cypress, hear the owl, and plod your way
O'er steps of broken thrones and temples, ye!
Whose agonies are evils of a day —
A world is at our feet as fragile as our clay.

The Niobe of nations! there she stands,
Childless and crownless, in her voiceless woe;
An empty urn within her withered hands,
Whose holy dust was scattered long ago;
The Scipios' tomb contains no ashes now;
The very sepulchers lie tenantless
Of their heroic dwellers; dost thou flow,
Old Tiber! through a marble wilderness?
Rise, with thy yellow waves, and mantle her distress.

5 *

The Goth, the Christian, Time, War, Flood, and Fire,
Have dealt upon the seven-hilled city's pride;
She saw her glories star by star expire,
And up the steep barbarian monarchs ride,
Where the car climbed the Capitol; far and wide
Temple and tower went down, nor left a site;
Chaos of ruins! who shall trace the void,
O'er the dim fragments cast a lunar light,
And say, " here was, or is," where all is doubly night?

The double night of ages, and of her,
Night's daughter, Ignorance, hath wrapt and wrap
All round us; we but feel our way to err:
The ocean hath its chart, the stars their map,
And Knowledge spreads them on her ample lap;
But Rome is as the desert, where we steer
Stumbling o'er recollections; now we clap
Our hands, and cry " Eureka!" it is clear, —
When but some false mirage of ruin rises near.

Alas! the lofty city! and alas!
The trebly hundred triumphs! and the day
When Brutus made the dagger's edge surpass
The conqueror's sword in bearing fame away!
Alas, for Tully's voice, and Virgil's lay,
And Livy's pictured page! — but these shall be
Her resurrection; all beside, — decay.
Alas for Earth, for never shall we see
That brightness in her eye she bore when Rome was free!

THE OCEAN.

ROLL on, thou deep and dark blue Ocean, — roll!
Ten thousand fleets sweep over thee in vain;
Man marks the earth with ruin, — his control
Stops with the shore; — upon the watery plain
The wrecks are all thy deed, nor doth remain
A shadow of man's ravage, save his own,
When, for a moment, like a drop of rain,

He sinks into thy depths with bubbling groan,
Without a grave, unknelled, uncoffined, and unknown.

His steps are not upon thy paths, — thy fields
Are not a spoil for him, — thou dost arise
And shake him from thee; the vile strength he wields
For earth's destruction thou dost all despise,
Spurning him from thy bosom to the skies,
And send'st him, shivering in thy playful spray
And howling, to his gods, where haply lies
His petty hope in some near port or bay,
And dashest him again to earth : — there let him lay.

The armaments which thunderstrike the walls
Of rock-built cities, bidding nations quake,
And monarchs tremble in their capitals,
The oak leviathans, whose huge ribs make
Their clay creator the vain title take
Of lord of thee, and arbiter of war;
These are thy toys, and as the snowy flake,
They melt into thy yeast of waves, which mar
Alike the Armada's pride or spoils of Trafalgar.*

Thy shores are empires, changed in all save thee, —
Assyria, Greece, Rome, Carthage, what are they?
Thy waters washed them power while they were free,
And many a tyrant since; their shores obey
The stranger, slave, or savage; their decay
Has dried up realms to deserts; — not so thou; —
Unchangeable, save to thy wild waves' play, —
Time writes no wrinkle on thine azure brow, —
Such as creation's dawn beheld, thou rollest now.

Thou glorious mirror, where the Almighty's form
Glasses itself in tempests; in all time,
Calm or convulsed, — in breeze, or gale, or storm,
Icing the pole, or in the torrid clime
Dark-heaving; — boundless, endless, and sublime, —

* This line refers to two historical naval battles in which the English were victorious.

5 *

The image of Eternity — the throne
Of the Invisible; even from out thy slime
The monsters of the deep are made; each zone
Obeys thee; thou goest forth, dread, fathomless, alone.

And I have loved thee, Ocean! and my joy
Of youthful sports was on thy breast to be
Borne, like thy bubbles, onward: from a boy
I wantoned with thy breakers, — they to me
Were a delight; and if the freshening sea
Made them a terror, — 't was a pleasing fear,
For I was as it were a child of thee,
And trusted to thy billows far and near,
And laid my hand upon thy mane, — as I do here.

I SAW THEE WEEP.

I saw thee weep, — the big bright tear
    Came o'er that eye of blue;
And then methought it did appear
    A violet dropping dew;
I saw thee smile, — the sapphire's blaze
    Beside thee ceased to shine;
It could not match the living rays
    That filled that glance of thine.

As clouds from yonder sun receive
    A deep and mellow dye,
Which scarce the shade of coming eve
    Can banish from the sky,
Those smiles unto the moodiest mind
    Their own pure joy impart;
Their sunshine leaves a glow behind
    That lightens o'er the heart.

COOPER.

1789 – 1851.

JAMES FENIMORE COOPER, who may be called the first, and perhaps the most popular, of American novelists, was born in New Jersey in 1789 and died at Cooperstown, New York, in 1851. The best of his works are *The Spy, The Prairie, The Pilot,* and *The Last of the Mohicans.* His fame is owing mainly to the excellence of his delineation of Indian life and of maritime adventure. In these respects no writer has yet excelled him. His style is peculiarly interesting, being highly dramatic, and pure and scholarly in construction. No American writer has received more cordial treatment at the hands of foreign critics; Victor Hugo went so far as to pronounce him a greater novelist than Scott; the London Athenæum called him "the most original writer that America has yet produced"; and the Revue de Paris said: "Who is there writing English among our contemporaries, if not of him, of whom it can be said that he has a genius of the first order?" These panegyrics will hardly be accepted at their full value by literary authorities of the present day, when American literature is far stronger and richer than at their date. But Mr. Cooper's title to a high, if not the first, place among our writers, is too strong to be impugned. In the assignment of his rank he should have the benefit of the consideration that he was a pioneer in a specialty of authorship, before his time hardly approached by American writers, and which for many years he occupied and honored without a rival. He was intensely patriotic, and resented with spirited indignation the assaults of British writers upon American character and customs. Somewhat reserved and formal in manner, he made few warm personal friends, but his probity and high moral excellence commanded universal respect. Our first extract is from *The Prairie,* a story of Indian life; the second is from *The Pilot,* the best of Mr. Cooper's sea novels.

THE INDIAN ADOPTION.

A LOW, feeble, and hollow voice was heard rising on the ear, as if it rolled from the inmost cavities of the human chest, and gathered strength and energy as it issued into the air. A solemn stillness followed the sounds, and then the lips of the aged man were first seen to move.

"The day of Le Balafré is near its end," were the first words that were distinctly audible. "He is like a buffalo on whom the hair will grow no longer. He will soon be ready to leave his lodge to go in search of another that is far from the villages of the Siouxes; therefore what he has to say concerns not him, but those he leaves behind him. His words are like the fruit on the tree, ripe and fit to be given to chiefs.

"Many snows have fallen since Le Balafré has been found on the war-path. His blood has been very hot, but it has had time to cool. The Wahcondah gives him dreams of war no longer; he sees that it is better to live in peace.

"My brothers, one foot is turned to the happy hunting-grounds, the other will soon follow, and then an old chief will be seen looking for the prints of his father's moccasins, that he may make no mistake, but be sure to come before the Master of Life by the same path that so many good Indians have already traveled. But who will follow? Le Balafré has no son. His oldest has ridden too many Pawnee horses; the bones of the youngest have been gnawed by Konza dogs. Le Balafré has come to look for a young arm on which he may lean, and to find a son, that when he is gone his lodge may not be empty. Tachechana, the skipping fawn of the Tetons, is too weak to prop a warrior who is old. She looks before her and not backwards. Her mind is in the lodge of her husband."

The enunciation of the veteran warrior had been calm, but distinct and decided. His declaration was received in silence; and though several of the chiefs who were in the counsels of Mahtoree turned their eyes on their leader, none presumed to oppose so aged and venerated a brave in a resolution that was strictly in conformity to the usages of the nation. The Teton himself was content to await the result with seeming composure, though the gleams of ferocity that played about his eye occasionally betrayed the nature of those feelings with which he witnessed a procedure that was likely to rob him of that one of all his intended victims whom he most hated.

In the mean time Le Balafré moved with a slow and painful step towards the captives. He stopped before the person of Hard-Heart, whose faultless form, unchanged eye, and lofty mien he contemplated with high satisfaction. Then making a gesture of authority, he waited until his order had been obeyed, and the youth was released from the post and his bonds by the same blow of the knife. When the young warrior was led nearer to his dimmed and failing sight the examination was renewed with strictness of scrutiny.

"It is good," the wary veteran murmured, when he found that all his skill in the requisites of a brave could detect no blemish; "this is a leaping panther. Does my son speak with the tongue of a Teton?"

The intelligence which lighted the eyes of the captive betrayed how well he understood the question, but still he was far too haughty to communicate his ideas through the medium of a language that belonged to a hostile people. Some of the surrounding warriors explained to the old chief that the captive was a Pawnee-Loup.

"My son opened his eyes on the 'waters of the wolves,'" said Le Balafré, in the language of that nation, "but he will shut them in the bend of the 'river with a troubled stream.' He was born a Pawnee, but he will die a Dahcotah. Look at me. I am a sycamore that once covered many with my shadow. The leaves are fallen and the branches begin to drop. But a single sucker is springing from my roots ; it is a little vine, and it winds itself about a tree that is green. I have long looked for one fit to grow by my side. Now have I found him. Le Balafré is no longer without a son ; his name will not be forgotten when he is gone. Men of the Tetons ! I take this youth into my lodge."

No one was bold enough to dispute a right that had so often been exercised by warriors far inferior to the present speaker, and the adoption was listened to in grave and respectful silence. Le Balafré took his intended son by the arm, and leading him into the very centre of the circle, he stepped aside with an air of triumph in order that the spectators might approve of his choice. Mahtoree betrayed no evidence of his intentions, but rather seemed to await a moment better suited to the crafty policy of his character. The more experienced and sagacious chiefs distinctly foresaw the utter impossibility of two partisans so renowned, so hostile, and who had so long been rivals in fame, as their prisoner and their native leader, existing amicably in the same tribe. Still the character of Le Balafré was so imposing, and the custom to which he had resorted so sacred, that none dared to lift a voice in opposition to the measure. They watched the result with increasing interest, but with a coldness of demeanor that concealed the nature of their inquietude. From this state of embarrassment the tribe was relieved by the decision of the one most interested in the success of the aged chief's designs.

During the whole of the foregoing scene, it would have been difficult to have traced a single distinct emotion in the lineaments of the captive. He had heard his release proclaimed, with the same indifference as the order to bind him to the stake. But now that the moment had arrived when it became necessary to make his election, he spoke in a way to prove that the fortitude which had brought him so distinguished a name had in no degree deserted him.

"My father is very old, but he has not yet looked upon everything," said Hard-Heart, in a voice so clear as to be heard by all present. "He has never seen a buffalo change to a bat; he will never see a Pawnee become a Sioux !"

There was a suddenness and yet a calmness in the manner of delivering this decision which assured most of the auditors that it was unalterable. The heart of Le Balafré, however, was yearning towards the youth, and the fondness of age was not so readily repulsed. Reproving the burst of admiration and triumph to which the boldness of the declaration and the freshened hopes of revenge had given rise, by turning his gleaming eye around the band, the veteran again addressed his adopted child as if his purpose was not to be denied.

"It is well," he said; "such are the words a brave should use, that the warriors may see his heart. The day has been when the voice of Le Balafré was loudest among the lodges of the Konzas. But the root of a white hair is wisdom. My child will show the Tetons that he is brave, by striking their enemies. Men of the Dahcotahs, this is my son!"

The Pawnee hesitated a moment, and then stepping in front of the chief, he took his hard and wrinkled hand and laid it with reverence on his head, as if to acknowledge the extent of his obligation. Then recoiling a step, he raised his person to its greatest elevation, and looked upon the hostile band by whom he was environed with an air of loftiness and disdain, as he spoke aloud in the language of the Siouxes, —

"Hard-Heart has looked at himself within and without. He has thought of all he has done in the hunts and in the wars. Everywhere he is the same. There is no change; he is in all things a Pawnee. He has struck so many Tetons that he could never eat in their lodges. His arrows would fly backwards; the point of his lance would be on the wrong end; their friends would weep at every whoop he gave; their enemies would laugh. Do the Tetons know a Loup? Let them look at him again. His head is painted, his arm is flesh, his heart is rock. When the Tetons see the sun come from the Rocky Mountains and move toward the land of the Pale-faces, the mind of Hard-Heart will soften and his spirit will become Sioux. Until that day he will live and die a Pawnee."

A yell of delight, in which admiration and ferocity were strangely mingled, interrupted the speaker, and but too clearly announced the character of his fate. The captive waited a moment for the commotion to subside, and then turning again to Le Balafré, he continued in tones conciliating and kind, as if he felt the propriety of softening his refusal in a manner not to wound the pride of one willing to be his benefactor.

"Let my father lean heavier on the fawn of the Dahcotahs," he said; "she is weak now, but as her lodge fills with young she will be stronger. See!" he added, directing the eyes of the other to the earnest countenance of the attentive trapper; "Hard-Heart is not without a gray-beard to show him the path to the blessed prairies. If he ever has another father it shall be that just warrior."

Le Balafré turned away in disappointment from the youth, and approached the stranger who had thus anticipated his design.

DEATH OF LONG TOM COFFIN.

LIFTING his broad hands high into the air, his voice was heard in the tempest. "God's will be done with me," he cried; "I saw the first timber of the *Ariel* laid, and shall live just long enough to see it turn out of her bottom; after which I wish to live no longer." But his shipmates were far beyond the sounds of his voice before these were half uttered. All command of the boat was rendered impossible, by the numbers it contained, as well as the raging of the surf; and as it rose on the white crest of a wave, Tom saw his beloved little craft for the last time. It fell into a trough of the sea, and in a few moments more its fragments were ground into splinters on the adjoining rocks. The coxswain (Tom) still remained where he had cast off the rope, and beheld the numerous heads and arms that appeared rising, at short intervals, on the waves, some making powerful and well-directed efforts to gain the sands, that were becoming visible as the tide fell, and others wildly tossed in the frantic movements of helpless despair. The honest old seaman gave a cry of joy as he saw Barnstable (the commander whom Tom had forced into the boat) issue from the surf, where one by one several seamen appeared also, dripping and exhausted. Many others of the crew were carried in a similar manner to places of safety; though, as Tom returned to his seat on the bowsprit, he could not conceal from his reluctant eyes the lifeless forms that were, in other spots, driven against the rocks with a fury that soon left them but few of the outward vestiges of humanity.

Dillon and the coxswain were now the sole occupants of their dreadful station. The former stood, in a kind of stupid despair, a witness of the scene; but as his curdled blood began again to flow more warmly to his heart, he crept close to the side of Tom, with that sort of selfish feeling that makes even hopeless misery more tolerable, when endured in participation with another.

"When the tide falls," he said in a voice that betrayed the agony of fear, though his words expressed the renewal of hope, "we shall be able to walk to land."

"There was One and only One to whose feet the waters were the same as a dry deck," returned the coxswain; "and none but such as have His power will ever be able to walk from these rocks to the sands." The old seaman paused, and turning his eyes, which exhibited a mingled expression of disgust and compassion, on his companion, he added, with reverence: "Had you thought more of Him in fair weather, your case would be less to be pitied in this tempest."

"Do you still think there is much danger?" asked Dillon.

"To them that have reason to fear death. Listen! Do you hear that hollow noise beneath ye?"

"'T is the wind driving by the vessel!"

"'T is the poor thing herself," said the affected coxswain, "giving her last groans. The water is breaking upon her decks, and in a few minutes more the handsomest model that ever cut a wave will be like the chips that fell from her in framing!"

"Why, then, did you remain here?" cried Dillon, wildly.

"To die in my coffin, if it should be the will of God," returned Tom. "These waves are to me what the land is to you; I was born on them, and I have always meant that they shall be my grave."

"But — I — I," shrieked Dillon, "I am not ready to die! — I cannot die! — I will not die!"

"Poor wretch!" muttered his companion, "you must go like the rest of us; when the death-watch is called, none can skulk from the muster."

"I can swim," Dillon continued, rushing with frantic eagerness to the side of the wreck. "Is there no billet of wood, no rope, that I can take with me?"

"None; everything has been cut away, or carried off by the sea. If you are about to strive for your life, take with you a stout heart and a clean conscience, and trust the rest to God."

"God!" echoed Dillon, in the madness of his frenzy. "I know no God; there is no God that knows me!"

"Peace!" said the deep tones of the coxswain, in a voice that seemed to speak in the elements; "blasphemer, peace!"

The heavy groaning, produced by the water in the timbers of the *Ariel*, at that moment added its impulse to the raging feelings of Dillon, and he cast himself headlong into the sea. The water, thrown by the rolling of the surf on the beach, was necessarily returned to the ocean in eddies, in different places favorable to such an action of the element. Into the edge of one of these counter-currents, that was produced by the very rocks on which the schooner lay, and which the watermen call the " under-tow," Dillon had unknowingly thrown his person ; and when the waves had driven him a short distance from the wreck he was met by a stream that his most desperate efforts could not overcome. He was a light and powerful swimmer, and the struggle was hard and protracted. With the shore immediately before his eyes, and at no great distance, he was led, as by a false phantom, to continue his efforts, although they did not advance him a foot. The old seaman, who at first had watched his motions with careless indifference, understood the danger of his situation at a glance, and, forgetful of his own fate, he shouted aloud, in a voice that was driven over the struggling victim to the ears of his shipmates on the sands :—

" Sheer to port, and clear the under-tow ! Sheer to the southward ! "

Dillon heard the sounds, but his faculties were too much obscured by terror to distinguish their object ; he, however, blindly yielded to the call, and gradually changed his direction until his face was once more turned towards the vessel. Tom looked around him for a rope, but all had gone over with the spars, or been swept away by the waves. At this moment of disappointment his eyes met those of the desperate Dillon. Calm and inured to horrors as was the veteran seaman, he involuntarily passed his hand before his brow to exclude the look of despair he encountered ; and when, a moment afterwards, he removed the rigid member, he beheld the sinking form of the victim as it gradually settled in the ocean, still struggling with regular but impotent strokes of the arms and feet to gain the wreck, and to preserve an existence that had been so much abused in its hour of allotted probation. " He will soon meet his God, and learn that his God knows him ! " murmured the coxswain to himself. As he yet spoke, the wreck of the *Ariel* yielded to an overwhelming sea, and after a universal shudder, her timbers and planks gave way, and were swept towards the cliffs, bearing the body of the simple-hearted coxswain among the ruins.

BRYANT.

1794 –

WILLIAM CULLEN BRYANT, who may be said to share with Longfellow the first place in the list of American poets, was born in Cummington, Massachusetts, in 1794. His precocity was remarkable. At the age of ten he made translations from the Latin poets, which were published, and three years later, wrote *The Embargo*, a satirical poem of great merit. He studied law, and practiced that profession for some time in Great Barrington, Massachusetts. His early productions were regarded as the work of a precocious genius which would surely spend itself in these premature efforts; but the appearance of *Thanatopsis*, which was written in his nineteenth year, and was published in the *North American Review*, proved conclusively that he was not a mere youthful prodigy. In 1825 he removed to New York, and, with a partner, established the *New York Review* and *Athenæum Magazine*, to which he contributed some of his best poems. The next year he became editor of the *Evening Post*, and still holds that place. While he is best known by his poems, Mr. Bryant is considered by the best authorities one of the finest prose writers in the country. In England his poetry is held in high esteem; *Thanatopsis*, *To a Water-Fowl*, *Green River*, etc., have received earnest praise from the leading English critics. Mr. Bryant is distinctively a student and interpreter of Nature; all her aspects and voices are familiar to him, and are reproduced in his poetry with a solemn and ennobling beauty which has never been attained by any other American poet. In many respects his verse resembles Wordsworth's; but its spirit is less introspective, and appeals more directly to the common understanding. Another striking characteristic of Mr. Bryant's poetry is its lofty moral tone, which is the eloquence of a great intellect warmed and controlled by high and pure impulses.

THE DEATH OF THE FLOWERS.

THE melancholy days are come, the saddest of the year,
Of wailing winds, and naked woods, and meadows brown and sear.
Heaped in the hollows of the grove the withered leaves lie dead ;
They rustle to the eddying gust and to the rabbit's tread.
The robin and the wren are flown, and from the shrubs the jay,
And from the wood-top calls the crow through all the gloomy day.

Where are the flowers, the fair young flowers, that lately sprung and
    stood
In brighter light and softer airs, a beauteous sisterhood ?
Alas ! they all are in their graves ; the gentle race of flowers
Are lying in their lowly beds, with the fair and good of ours.
The rain is falling where they lie ; but the cold November rain
Calls not from out the gloomy earth the lovely ones again.

The wind-flower and the violet, they perished long ago,
And the brier-rose and the orchis died amid the summer's glow ;
But on the hill the golden-rod, and the aster in the wood,

And the yellow sunflower by the brook in autumn beauty stood,
Till fell the frost from the clear cold heaven, as falls the plague on
    men,
And the brightness of their smile was gone from upland, glade, and
    glen.

And now, when comes the calm mild day, as still such days will
    come,
To call the squirrel and the bee from out their winter home;
When the sound of dropping nuts is heard, though all the trees are
    still,
And twinkle in the smoky light the waters of the rill,
The south-wind searches for the flowers whose fragrance late he bore,
And sighs to find them in the wood and by the stream no more.

And then I think of one who in her youthful beauty died,
The fair meek blossom that grew up and faded by my side.
In the cold moist earth we laid her, when the forests cast the leaf,
And we wept that one so lovely should have a life so brief;
Yet not unmeet it was that one, like that young friend of ours,
So gentle and so beautiful, should perish with the flowers.

THANATOPSIS.

    To him who in the love of Nature holds
Communion with her visible forms, she speaks
A various language; for his gayer hours
She has a voice of gladness, and a smile
And eloquence of beauty; and she glides
Into his darker musings, with a mild
And gentle sympathy, that steals away
Their sharpness ere he is aware. When thoughts
Of the last bitter hour come like a blight
Over thy spirit, and sad images
Of the stern agony, and shroud, and pall,
And breathless darkness, and the narrow house,
Make thee to shudder, and grow sick at heart, —
Go forth unto the open sky, and list
To Nature's teachings, while from all around —

Earth and her waters, and the depths of air —
Comes a still voice :—Yet a few days, and thee
The all-beholding sun shall see no more
In all his course; nor yet in the cold ground,
Where thy pale form was laid with many tears,
Nor in the embrace of ocean, shall exist
Thy image.   Earth, that nourished thee, shall claim
Thy growth, to be resolved to earth again,
And, lost each human trace, surrendering up
Thine individual being, shalt thou go
To mix forever with the elements;
To be a brother to the insensible rock,
And to the sluggish clod which the rude swain
Turns with his share and treads upon.   The oak
Shall send his roots abroad, and pierce thy mould.
    Yet not to thy eternal resting-place
Shalt thou retire alone, — nor couldst thou wish
Couch more magnificent.   Thou shalt lie down
With patriarchs of the infant world, — with kings,
The powerful of the earth, — the wise, the good,
Fair forms and hoary seers of ages past,
All in one mighty sepulcher.   The hills,
Rock-ribbed and ancient as the sun; the vales,
Stretching in pensive quietness between;
The venerable woods; rivers that move
In majesty, and the complaining brooks,
That make the meadows green; and, poured round all,
Old ocean's gray and melancholy waste, —
Are but the solemn decorations all
Of the great tomb of man.   The golden sun,
The planets, all the infinite host of heaven,
Are shining on the sad abodes of death
Through the still lapse of ages.   All that tread
The globe are but a handful to the tribes
That slumber in its bosom.   Take the wings
Of morning, traverse Barca's desert sands,
Or lose thyself in the continuous woods
Where rolls the Oregon, and hears no sound
Save his own dashings, — yet the dead are there.

And millions in those solitudes, since first
The flight of years began, have laid them down
In their last sleep ; — the dead reign there alone.
So shalt thou rest ; and what if thou withdraw
In silence from the living, and no friend
Take note of thy departure ? All that breathe
Will share thy destiny. The gay will laugh
When thou art gone, the solemn brood of care
Plod on, and each one, as before, will chase
His favorite phantom ; yet all these shall leave
Their mirth and their employments, and shall come
And make their bed with thee. As the long train
Of ages glide away, the sons of men —
The youth in life's green spring, and he who goes
In the full strength of years, matron and maid,
The bowed with age, the infant in the smiles
And beauty of its innocent age cut off —
Shall one by one be gathered to thy side
By those who in their turn shall follow them.

So live, that when thy summons comes to join
The innumerable caravan that moves
To the pale realms of shade, where each shall take
His chamber in the silent halls of death,
Thou go not, like the quarry-slave at night,
Scourged to his dungeon, but, sustained and soothed
By an unfaltering trust, approach thy grave
Like one who wraps the drapery of his couch
About him, and lies down to pleasant dreams.

TO A WATERFOWL.

Whither, midst falling dew,
While glow the heavens with the last steps of day,
Far, through their rosy depths, dost thou pursue
Thy solitary way ?

Vainly the fowler's eye
Might mark thy distant flight to do thee wrong,
As, darkly painted on the crimson sky,
Thy figure floats along.

Seek'st thou the plashy brink
Of weedy lake, or marge of river wide,
Or where the rocking billows rise and sink
    On the chafed ocean side?

There is a Power whose care
Teaches thy way along that pathless coast, —
The desert and illimitable air, —
    Lone wandering, but not lost.

All day thy wings have fanned,
At that far height, the cold, thin atmosphere;
Yet stoop not, weary, to the welcome land,
    Though the dark night is near.

And soon that toil shall end;
Soon shalt thou find a summer home, and rest,
And scream among thy fellows; reeds shall bend
    Soon o'er thy sheltered nest.

Thou 'rt gone, the abyss of heaven
Hath swallowed up thy form; yet on my heart
Deeply hath sunk the lesson thou hast given,
    And shall not soon depart:

He who, from zone to zone,
Guides through the boundless sky thy certain flight,
In the long way that I must tread alone,
    Will lead my steps aright.

TRUTH, crushed to earth, shall rise again, —
    The eternal years of God are hers;
But Error, wounded, writhes in pain,
    And dies among his worshipers.

CARLYLE.

1795 –   .

THOMAS CARLYLE was born in Scotland in 1795. He is the son of a Dumfriesshire farmer. He studied at Edinburgh University, and is said to have intended to enter the ministry, but abandoned the purpose. His first essay in literature was in contributing to a Cyclopædia, and to several magazines. Next he translated Goethe's *Wilhelm Meister*, and in his labors acquired a warm and lasting love for German literature. *Sartor Resartus*, in which he laid the first substantial foundation of his fame, was published in book-form in 1834. It is one of his most characteristic compositions, exhibiting the originality, depth, and brilliancy of his thought, and the mingled awkwardness and force of his style, in full relief. Three years later appeared his *History of the French Revolution*, a work which has never been surpassed in point of careful research, vigor, and graphic power of narrative. Of his later books we can mention only the names: *Chartism, Hero-Worship, Past and Present, Critical and Miscellaneous Essays, Cromwell's Letters and Speeches, Lives of Schiller and Sterling, The Life of Frederick the Great*, etc. Mr. Carlyle is the most aggressive, and perhaps we may say the most audacious, writer of his age; he attacks on all sides, without fear or favor. His chief bugbear is "shams"; whatever is hollow or false or pretentious invites his relentless denunciation. He has virtually set himself up as the censor and reformer of the world, and has succeeded in his assumed *rôle* as well as any mortal could. His intuitions are wonderfully keen, his judgment quick and generally sound, and his love of right and hatred of wrong are so fervent as to animate all his writings with marvelous potency. He has exercised, perhaps, a mightier influence on the thought of the nineteenth century than any other living man. Our first and third extracts are from his *History of the French Revolution*; the second, from *Sartor Resartus*.

EXECUTION OF MARIE-ANTOINETTE.[*]

ON Monday, the 14th of October, 1793, a Cause is pending in the Palais de Justice, in the new Revolutionary Court, such as these old stone walls never witnessed, — the Trial of Marie-Antoinette. The once brightest of Queens, now tarnished, defaced, forsaken, stands here at Fouquier-Tinville's Judgment-bar, answering for her life. The Indictment was delivered her last night. To such changes of human fortune what words are adequate? Silence alone is adequate. . . . .

Marie-Antoinette, in this her abandonment and hour of extreme need, is not wanting to herself, the imperial woman: Her look, they say, as that hideous indictment was reading, continued calm; "she was sometimes observed moving her fingers, as when one plays on the piano." You discern not without interest, across that dim Revolutionary Bulletin itself, how she bears herself queen-like. Her answers are prompt, clear, often of Laconic brevity; resolution, which has grown

---

[*] Marie-Antoinette, Archduchess of Austria and Queen of France, was condemned by the Revolutionary Tribunal of the French Republicans, and was executed on the 16th October, 1793. See Burke's speech, page 39. Her husband, Louis XVI., had been guillotined on the 21st of January preceding.

contemptuous without ceasing to be dignified, veils itself in calm words. " You persist then in denial?" — " My plan is not denial; it is the truth I have said, and I persist in that." . . . . .

At four o'clock on Wednesday morning, after two days and two nights of interrogating, jury-charging, and other darkening of counsel, the result comes out, — sentence of Death! " Have you anything to say?" The Accused shook her head, without speech. Night's candles are burning out; and with her, too, Time is finishing, and it will be Eternity and Day. This Hall of Tinville's is dark, ill-lighted except where she stands. Silently she withdraws from it, to die.

Two Processions, or Royal Progresses, three-and-twenty years apart, have often struck us with a strange feeling of contrast. The first is of a beautiful Archduchess and Dauphiness, quitting her mother's city, at the age of fifteen, towards hopes such as no other Daughter of Eve then had. " On the morrow," says Weber, an eye-witness, " the Dauphiness left Vienna. The whole city crowded out; at first with a sorrow which was silent. She appeared; you saw her sunk back into her carriage, her face bathed in tears; hiding her eyes now with her handkerchief, now with her hands; several times putting out her head to see yet again this Palace of her Fathers, whither she was to return no more. She motioned her regret, her gratitude, to the good Nation, which was crowding here to bid her farewell. Then arose not only tears, but piercing cries, on all sides. Men and women alike abandoned themselves to such expression of their sorrow. It was an audible sound of wail, in the streets and avenues of Vienna. The last Courier that followed her disappeared, and the crowd melted away."

The young imperial Maiden of Fifteen has now become a worn, discrowned Widow of Thirty-eight, gray before her time. This is the last Procession: " Few minutes after the Trial ended, the drums were beating to arms in all Sections; at sunrise the armed force was on foot, cannons getting placed at the extremities of the Bridges, in the Squares, Crossways, all along from the Palais de. Justice to the Place de la Révolution. By ten o'clock, numerous patrols were circulating in the Streets; thirty thousand foot and horse drawn up under arms. At eleven, Marie-Antoinette was brought out. She had on an undress of *piqué blanc* (white piqué); she was led to the place of execution in the same manner as an ordinary criminal: bound on a Cart, accompanied by a Constitutional Priest in Lay dress, escorted by numerous detachments of infantry and cavalry. These, and the double row of troops all along her road, she appeared to regard with indifference. On her countenance there was visible neither abashment nor pride. To the cries of *Vive la République* (Live the Republic!) and *Down with Tyranny*, which attended her all the way, she seemed to pay no heed. She spoke little to her Confessor. The tricolor Streamers on the house-tops occupied her attention, in the Streets du Roule and Saint-Honoré; she also noticed the Inscriptions on the house-fronts. On reaching the Place de la Révolution her looks turned towards the *Jardin National,* whilom Tuileries; her face at that moment gave signs of lively emotion. She mounted the Scaffold with courage enough; at a quarter past Twelve, her head fell; the Executioner showed it to the people, amid universal long-continued cries of *Vive la République.*"

NIGHT VIEW OF A CITY.

I LOOK down into all that wasp-nest or bee-hive, and witness their wax-laying and honey-making, and poison-brewing, and choking by sulphur. From the Palace esplanade, where music plays while His Serene Highness is pleased to eat his victuals, down the low lane, where in her door-sill the aged widow, knitting for a thin livelihood, sits to feel the afternoon sun, I see it all. Couriers arrive bestrapped and bebooted, bearing Joy and Sorrow bagged-up in pouches of leather; there, top-laden, and with four swift horses, rolls in the country Baron and his household; here, on timber-leg, the lamed Soldier hops painfully along, begging alms: a thousand carriages, and wains, and cars, come tumbling-in with Food, with young Rusticity, and other Raw Produce, inanimate or animate, and go tumbling out again with Produce manufactured. That living flood, pouring through these streets, of all qualities and ages, knowest thou whence it is coming, whither it is going? From Eternity onwards to Eternity! These are apparitions: what else? Are they not souls rendered visible: in Bodies, that took shape and will lose it, melting into air? Their solid Pavement is a Picture of the Sense; they walk on the bosom of Nothing, blank Time is behind them and before them. Or fanciest thou, the red and yellow Clothes-screen yonder, with spurs on its heels and feather in its crown, is but of To-day, without a Yesterday or a To-morrow; and had not rather its Ancestor alive when Hengst and Horsa overran thy Island? Friend, thou seest here a living link in that Tissue of History, which inweaves all Being : watch well, or it will be past thee, and seen no more.   These fringes of lamplight, struggling up through smoke and thousand-fold exhalation, some fathoms into the ancient region of Night, what thinks Boötes of them, as he leads his Hunting-dogs over the Zenith in their leash of side-real fire ?   That stifled hum of Midnight, when Traffic has lain down to rest ; and the chariot-wheels of Vanity, still rolling here and there through distant streets, are bearing her to Halls roofed-in, and lighted to the due pitch for her ; and only Vice and Misery, to prowl or to moan like night-birds, are abroad : that hum, I say, like the stertorous, unquiet slumber of sick Life, is heard in Heaven !   O ! under that hideous coverlet of vapors, and putrefactions, and unimaginable gases, what a Fermenting-vat lies simmering and hid !   The joyful and the sorrowful are there ; men are dying there, men are being born ; men are praying, — on the other side of a brick partition, men are cursing ; and around them all is the vast, void Night.   The proud Grandee still lingers in his perfumed saloons, or reposes within damask curtains ; Wretchedness cowers into truckle-beds, or shivers hunger-stricken into its lair of straw ; in obscure cellars, *Rouge-et-Noir* [*] languidly emits its voice-of-destiny to haggard hungry villains ; while Councilors of State sit plotting, and playing their high chess-game, whereof the pawns are Men.   The Lover whispers his mistress that the coach is ready ; and she, full of hope and fear, glides down, to fly with him over the borders : the Thief, still more silently, sets-to his pick-locks and crowbars, or lurks in wait till the watchmen first snore in their boxes.   Gay mansions, with supper-rooms and dancing-rooms, are full of light and music and high-swelling hearts ; but, in the condemned cells, the pulse of life beats tremulous and faint, and blood-shot eyes look out through the darkness, which is around and within, for the light of a stern last morning.   Six men are to be hanged on the morrow ; their gallows must even now be o' building.   Upwards of five-hundred-thousand two-legged animals without feathers lie round us, in horizontal position ; their heads all in nightcaps, and full of the foolishest dreams.   Riot cries aloud, and staggers and swaggers in his rank dens of shame ; and the Mother, with streaming hair, kneels over her pallid, dying infant, whose cracked lips only her tears now moisten. — All these heaped and huddled together, with nothing but a little carpentry and masonry between them : — crammed-in, like

* A gambler's game.

salted fish, in their barrel; — or weltering, shall I say, like an Egyptian pitcher of tamed vipers, each struggling to get its *head above* the others : *such* work goes on under that smoke-counterpane! — But I sit above it all; I am alone with the Stars!

THE REIGN OF TERROR.

WE are now, therefore, got to that black precipitous abyss, whither all things have long been tending; where, having now arrived on the giddy verge, they hurl down, in confused ruin; headlong, pellmell, down, down ;— till Sansculottism have consummated itself; and in this wondrous French Revolution, as in a Doomsday, a World have been rapidly, if not born again, yet destroyed and engulfed. Terror has long been terrible ; — but to the actors themselves it has now become manifest that their appointed course is one of Terror; and they say, "Be it so." So many centuries had been adding together, century transmitting it with increase to century, the sum of Wickedness, of Falsehood, Oppression of man by man. Kings were sinners, and Priests were, and People. Open-Scoundrels rode triumphant, be-diademed, be-coronetted, be-mitered; or the still fataller species of Secret-Scoundrels, in their fair-sounding formulas, speciosities, respectabilities, hollow within : the race of quacks was grown many as the sands of the sea. Till at length such a sum of quackery had accumulated itself as, in brief, the Earth and the Heavens were weary of. Slow seemed the Day of Settlement ; coming on, all imperceptible, across the bluster and fanfaronade of Courtierisms, Conquering-Heroisms, Most Christian *Grand Monarqueisms*, Well-beloved Pompadourisms : yet, behold, it was always coming : behold, it has come, suddenly, unlooked for by any man ! The harvest of long centuries was ripening and whitening so rapidly of late ; and now it is grown *white*, and is reaped rapidly, as it were, in one day — reaped in this Reign of Terror ; and carried home to Hades and the Pit ! Unhappy Sons of Adam ! it is ever so ; and never do they know it, nor will they know it. With cheerfully-smoothed countenances, day after day, and generation after generation, they, calling cheerfully to one another "Well-speed-ye," are at work *sowing the wind*. And yet, as God lives, they *shall reap the whirlwind ;* no other thing, we say, is possible, — since God is a Truth and His World is a Truth.

PRESCOTT.

1796 – 1859.

WILLIAM HICKLING PRESCOTT, grandson of Colonel William Prescott, commander of the patriot troops at the battle of Bunker Hill, was born at Salem, Mass., in 1796, and died in 1859. He graduated at Harvard in 1814, having won distinction by his attainments in classical learning. An accident during his college course occasioned an injury to his eye, which resulted finally in almost total blindness. He spent two years in Europe, and returned with the purpose of devoting himself to historical labors. His first work, *The History of Ferdinand and Isabella*, was published in 1837, and was almost immediately reprinted in France, Germany, and Spain. The author was overwhelmed with compliments, one of the most notable of which was his election to membership of the Spanish Royal Academy of History. In 1843 he gave to the world his *History of the Conquest of Mexico*, and in 1847 the *History of the Conquest of Peru*. In 1850 Mr. Prescott visited Europe, traveling in Great Britain and on the Continent. Five years later the first two volumes, and in 1858 the third, of the *History of the Reign of Philip the Second of Spain* were issued; but he did not live to complete the work. In addition to the histories named above, Mr. Prescott contributed to our literature a volume of *Biographical and Critical Miscellanies*, which includes a very valuable essay on Spanish Literature. His style is admirably suited to historical composition, presenting a happy compound of the majesty, brilliancy, and elegance which singly characterize those whom the world esteems its greatest historians. His unfinished work, *The History of Philip the Second*, is generally accounted his best. He was a man of kindly nature, and his generous encouragement of younger writers, conspicuous among whom was John Lothrop Motley, was convincing proof of his true nobility.

THE VALLEY AND CITY OF MEXICO.

THE troops, refreshed by a night's rest, succeeded, early on the following day, in gaining the crest of the sierra of Ahualco, which stretches like a curtain between the two great mountains on the north and south. Their progress was now comparatively easy, and they marched forward with a buoyant step as they felt they were treading the soil of Montezuma.*

They had not advanced far, when, turning an angle of the sierra, they suddenly came on a view which more than compensated the toils of the preceding day. It was that of the Valley of Mexico, or ' Tenochtitlan, as more commonly called by the natives; which, with its picturesque assemblage of water, woodland, and cultivated plains, its shining cities, and shadowy hills, was spread out like some gay and gorgeous panorama before them. In the highly rarefied atmosphere of these upper regions, even remote objects have a brilliancy of

* MONTEZUMA. The Montezumas were the Aztec, or native, Emperors of Mexico (1437–1519), and extended the boundaries of their domains by the conquest of several adjacent nations. They built fine cities and temples, and were able and powerful monarchs. In 1519 Cortes with an army of Spaniards invaded the country and conquered it. The extract is from Mr. Prescott's charming work, *The Conquest of Mexico.*

coloring and a distinctness of outline which seem to annihilate distance. Stretching far away at their feet were seen noble forests of oak, sycamore, and cedar, and beyond, yellow fields of maize and the towering maguey, intermingled with orchards and blooming gardens; for flowers, in such demand for their religious festivals, were even more abundant in this populous valley than in other parts of Anahuac. In the center of the great basin were beheld the lakes, occupying then a much larger portion of its surface than at present; their borders thickly studded with towns and hamlets, and, in the midst, like some Indian empress with her coronal of pearls, — the fair city of Mexico, with her white towers and pyramidal temples, reposing, as it were, on the bosom of the waters, — the far-famed " Venice of the Aztecs." High over all rose the royal hill of Chapultepec, the residence of the Mexican monarchs, crowned with the same grove of gigantic cypresses which at this day fling their broad shadows over the land. In the distance beyond the blue waters of the lake, and nearly screened by intervening foliage, was seen a shining speck, the rival capital of Tezcuco, and still farther on, the dark belt of porphyry, girdling the valley around, like a rich setting which Nature had devised for the fairest of her jewels.

Such was the beautiful vision which broke on the eyes of the Conquerors. And even now, when so sad a change has come over the scene; when the stately forests have been laid low, and the soil, unsheltered from the fierce radiance of a tropical sun, is in many places abandoned to sterility; when the waters have retired, leaving a broad and ghastly margin white with the incrustation of salts, while the cities and hamlets on their borders have moldered into ruins; even now that desolation broods over the landscape, so indestructible are the lines of beauty which Nature has traced on its features, that no traveler, however cold, can gaze on them with any other emotions than those of astonishment and rapture.

What, then, must have been the emotions of the Spaniards, when, after working their toilsome way into the upper air, the cloudy tabernacle parted before their eyes, and they beheld these fair scenes in all their pristine magnificence and beauty? It was like the spectacle which greeted the eyes of Moses from the summit of Pisgah, and, in the warm glow of their feelings, they cried out, " It is the promised land ! "

But these feelings of admiration were soon followed by others of a very different complexion; as they saw in all this the evidences of a civilization and power far superior to anything they had yet encountered.   The more timid, disheartened by the prospect, shrunk from a contest so unequal, and demanded, as they had done on some former occasions, to be led back again to Vera Cruz.   Such was not the effect produced on the sanguine spirit of the general.   His avarice was sharpened by the display of the dazzling spoil at his feet; and, if he felt a natural anxiety at the formidable odds, his confidence was renewed, as he gazed on the lines of his veterans, whose weather-beaten visages and battered armor told of battles won and difficulties surmounted, while his bold barbarians, with appetites whetted by the view of their enemies' country, seemed like eagles on the mountains, ready to pounce upon their prey.   By argument, entreaty, and menace, he endeavored to restore the faltering courage of the soldiers, urging them not to think of retreat, now that they had reached the goal for which they had panted, and the golden gates were opened to receive them.   In these efforts he was well seconded by the brave cavaliers, who held honor as dear to them as fortune; until the dullest spirits caught somewhat of the enthusiasm of their leaders, and the general had the satisfaction to see his hesitating columns, with their usual buoyant step, once more on their march down the slopes of the sierra.

THE COLONIZATION OF AMERICA.

IT is not easy at this time to comprehend the impulse given to Europe by the discovery of America.   It was not the gradual acquisition of some border territory, a province or a kingdom, that had been gained, but a new world that was now thrown open to the European. The races of animals, the mineral treasures, the vegetable forms, and the varied aspects of nature, man in the different phases of civilization, filled the mind with entirely new sets of ideas, that changed the habitual current of thought, and stimulated it to indefinite conjecture. The eagerness to explore the wonderful secrets of the new hemisphere became so active, that the principal cities of Spain were, in a manner, depopulated, as emigrants thronged one after another to take their chance upon the deep.   It was a world of romance that was thrown open; for, whatever might be the luck of the adventurer, his reports on his return were tinged with a coloring of romance that stimulated still higher the sensitive fancies of his countrymen, and nourished the chimerical sentiments of an age of chivalry. They listened with attentive ears to tales of Amazons, which seemed to realize the classic legends of antiquity; to stories of Patagonian giants; to flaming pictures of an *El Dorado* (Golden Land), where the sands sparkled with gems, and golden pebbles as large as birds' eggs were dragged in nets out of the rivers.

Yet that the adventurers were no impostors, but dupes, too easy dupes, of their own credulous fancies, is shown by the extravagant character of their enterprises; by expeditions in search of the magical Fountain of Health, of the golden Temple of Doboyba, of the golden Sepulchres of Yenu, — for gold was ever floating before their distempered vision, and the name of *Castilla del Oro* (Golden Castle), the most unhealthy and unprofitable region of the Isthmus, held out a bright promise to the unfortunate settler, who too frequently instead of gold found there only his grave.

In this realm of enchantment all the accessories served to maintain the illusion. The simple natives, with their defenseless bodies and rude weapons, were no match for the European warrior, armed to the teeth in mail. The odds were as great as those found in any legend of chivalry, where the lance of the good knight overturned hundreds at a touch. The perils that lay in the discoverer's path, and the sufferings he had to sustain, were scarcely inferior to those that beset the knight-errant. Hunger and thirst and fatigue, the deadly effluvia of the morass, with its swarms of venomous insects, the cold of mountain snows, and the scorching sun of the tropics, — these were the lot of every cavalier who came to seek his fortunes in the New World. It was the reality of romance. The life of the Spanish adventurer was one chapter more, and not the least remarkable, in the chronicles of knight-errantry.

The character of the warrior took somewhat of the exaggerated coloring shed over his exploits. Proud and vainglorious, swelled with lofty anticipations of his destiny, and an invincible confidence in his own resources, no danger could appall and no toil could tire him. The greater the danger, indeed, the higher the charm; for his soul reveled in excitement, and the enterprise without peril wanted that spur of romance which was necessary to rouse his energies into action. Yet in the motives of action meaner influences were strangely mingled with the loftier, the temporal with the spiritual. Gold was the incentive and the recompense, and in the pursuit of it his inflexible

nature rarely hesitated as to the means. His courage was sullied
with cruelty, the cruelty that flowed equally, strange as it may seem,
from his avarice and his religion; religion as it was understood in
that age, — the religion of the Crusader. It was the convenient cloak
for a multitude of sins, which covered them even from himself. The
Castilian, too proud for hypocrisy, committed more cruelties in the
name of religion than were ever practised by the pagan idolater or the
fanatical Moslem. The burning of the infidel was a sacrifice acceptable to Heaven, and the conversion of those who survived amply
atoned for the foulest offences. It is a melancholy and mortifying
consideration that the most uncompromising spirit of intolerance —
the spirit of the Inquisitor at home, and of the Crusader abroad —
should have emanated from a religion which preached " peace upon
earth and good-will towards man " !

What a contrast did these children of Southern Europe present to
the Anglo-Saxon races, who scattered themselves along the great
northern division of the Western Hemisphere ! For the principle of
action with these latter was not avarice, nor the more specious pretext
of proselytism; but independence, — independence religious and political. To secure this, they were content to earn a bare subsistence by
a life of frugality and toil. They asked nothing from the soil but
the reasonable returns of their own labor. No golden visions threw a
deceitful halo around their path, and beckoned them onwards through
seas of blood to the subversion of an unoffending dynasty. They
were content with the slow but steady progress of their social polity.
They patiently endured the privations of the wilderness, watering the
tree of liberty with their tears and with the sweat of their brow, till
it took deep root in the land and sent up its branches high towards
the heavens, while the communities of the neighboring continent,
shooting up into the sudden splendors of a tropical vegetation, exhibited, even in their prime, the sure symptoms of decay.

It would seem to have been especially ordered by Providence, that
the discovery of the two great divisions of the American Hemisphere
should fall to the two races best fitted to conquer and colonize them.
Thus the northern section was consigned to the Anglo-Saxon race,
whose orderly, industrious habits found an ample field for development under its colder skies and on its more rugged soil; while the
southern portion, with its rich tropical products and treasures of mineral wealth, held out the most attractive bait to invite the enterprise of

the Spaniard. How different might have been the result, if the bark of Columbus had taken a more northerly direction, as he at one time meditated, and landed its band of adventurers on the shores of what is now Free America.

STORMING THE TEMPLE OF MEXICO.

THE parties closed with the desperate fury of men who had no hope but in victory. Quarter was neither asked nor given; and to fly was impossible. The edge of the area was unprotected by parapet or battlement. The least slip would be fatal; and the combatants, as they struggled in mortal agony, were sometimes seen to roll over the sheer sides of the precipice together. The battle lasted with unintermitting fury for three hours. The number of the enemy was double that of the Christians; and it seemed as if it were a contest which must be determined by numbers and brute force, rather than by superior science. But it was not so. The invulnerable armor of the Spaniard, his sword of matchless temper, and his skill in the use of it gave him advantages which far outweighed the odds of physical strength and numbers. After doing all that the courage of despair could enable men to do, resistance grew fainter and fainter on the side of the Aztecs. One after another they had fallen. Two or three priests only survived to be led away in triumph by the victors. Every other combatant was stretched a corpse on the bloody arena, or had been hurled from the giddy heights. The loss of the Spaniards amounted to forty-five of their best men; and nearly all the remainder were more or less injured in the desperate conflict. The victorious cavaliers now rushed towards the sanctuaries. Penetrating into their recesses, they had the mortification to find the image of the Virgin and Cross removed. But in the other edifice they still beheld the grim figure of the Mexican Idol, with his censer of smoking hearts, and the walls of his oratory reeking with gore, — not improbably of their own countrymen. With shouts of triumph the Christians tore the uncouth monster from his niche, and tumbled him, in the presence of the horror-struck Aztecs, down the steps of the teocalli. They then set fire to the accursed building. The flame speedily ran up the slender towers, sending forth an ominous light over city, lake, and valley, to the remotest hut among the mountains. It was the funeral pyre of paganism, and proclaimed the fall of that sanguinary religion which had so long hung like a dark cloud over the fair regions of Anahuac.

LYELL.

1797 – 1875.

Sir Charles Lyell, an eminent English geologist, was born in 1797, and lived in the enjoyment of full intellectual vigor until the early part of 1875, when he died. He ranks among the foremost of scientific discoverers and writers of the present century. His best-known works, *The Principles of Geology*, *The Geological Evidences of the Antiquity of Man*, *Travels in North America*, and its sequel, *A Second Visit to the United States*, have been widely read in this country, and valued for their candid views of American institutions, and for the vast fund of geological information which they contain. His style is well suited to scientific composition, and invests his books with a charm which is rarely found in works of such solid character.

THE DISMAL SWAMP.

There are many swamps or morasses in this low, flat region, and one of the largest of these occurs between the towns of Norfolk and Weldon. We traversed several miles of its northern extremity on the railway, which is supported on piles. It bears the appropriate and very expressive name of the " Great Dismal," and is no less than forty miles in length from north to south, and twenty-five miles in its greatest width from east to west, the northern half being situated in Virginia, the southern in North Carolina. I observed that the water was obviously in motion in several places, and the morass had somewhat the appearance of a broad inundated river-plain, covered with all kinds of aquatic trees and shrubs, the soil being as black as in a peat-bog. The accumulation of vegetable matter going on here in a hot climate, over so vast an area, is a subject of such high geological interest, that I shall relate what I learnt of this singular morass. It is one enormous quagmire, soft and muddy, except where the surface is rendered partially firm by a covering of vegetables and their matted roots ; yet, strange to say, instead of being lower than the level of the surrounding country, it is actually higher than nearly all the firm and dry land which encompasses it, and, to make the anomaly complete, in spite of its semi-fluid character, it is higher in the interior than towards its margin.

The only exception to both these statements is found on the western side, where, for the distance of about twelve or fifteen miles, the streams flow from slightly elevated but higher land, and supply all its abundant and overflowing water. Towards the north, the east, and the south the waters flow from the swamp to different rivers, which give abundant evidence, by the rate of their descent, that the Great Dismal is higher than the surrounding firm ground. This fact is also confirmed by the measurements made in leveling for the railway from Portsmouth to Suffolk, and for two canals cut through different parts of the morass, for the sake of obtaining timber. The railway itself, when traversing the Great Dismal, is literally higher than when on the land some miles distant on either side, and is six to seven feet higher than where it passes over dry ground near to Suffolk and Portsmouth. Upon the whole, the center of the morass seems to lie more than twelve feet above the flat country round it. If the streams which now flow in from the west had for ages been bringing down black fluid mire instead of water, over the firm subsoil, we might suppose the ground so inundated as to have acquired its present configuration. Some small ridges, however, of land must have existed in the original plain or basin, for these now rise like low islands in various places above the general surface. But the streams to the westward do not bring down liquid mire, and are not charged with any sediment. The soil of the swamp is formed of vegetable matter, usually without any admixture of earthy particles. We have here, in fact, a deposit of peat from ten to fifteen feet in thickness, in a latitude where, owing to the heat of the sun and length of the summer, no peat-mosses like those of Europe would be looked for under ordinary circumstances.

In countries like Scotland and Ireland, where the climate is damp, and the summer short and cool, the natural vegetation of one year does not rot away during the next in moist situations. If water flows into such land it is absorbed, and promotes the vigorous growth of mosses and other aquatic plants, and when they die the same water arrests their putrefaction. But, as a general rule, no such accumulation of peat can take place in a country like that of Virginia, where the summer's heat causes annually as large a quantity of dead plants to decay as is equal in amount to the vegetable matter produced in one year.

There are many trees and shrubs in the region of the Pine Barrens (and the same may be said of the United States generally) which, like our willows, flourish luxuriantly in water. The juniper trees, or white cedar, stand firmly in the softest part of the quagmire, supported by their long tap-roots, and afford, with many other evergreens, a dark shade, under which a multitude of ferns, reeds, and shrubs, from nine to eighteen feet high, and a thick carpet of mosses, four or five inches high, spring up, and are protected from the rays of the sun. When these are most powerful, the large cedar and many other deciduous trees are in full leaf. The black soil formed beneath this shade, to which the mosses and the leaves make annual additions, does not perfectly resemble the peat of Europe, most of the plants being so decayed as to leave little more than soft black mud, without any traces of organization. This loose soil is called sponge by the laborers; and it has been ascertained that when exposed to the sun and thrown out on the bank of a canal where clearings have been made, it rots entirely away. Hence it is evident that it owes its preservation in the swamp to moisture and the shade of the dense foliage. The evaporation continually going on in the wet, spongy soil during summer cools the air and generates a temperature resembling that of a more northern climate, or a region more elevated above the level of the sea.

Numerous trunks of large and tall trees lie buried in the black mire of the morass. In so loose a soil they are easily overthrown by winds, and nearly as many have been found lying beneath the surface of the peaty soil as standing erect upon it. When thrown down, they are soon covered by water, and keeping wet, they never decompose, except the sap-wood, which is less than an inch thick. Much of the timber is obtained by sounding a foot or two below the surface, and it is sawn into planks while half under water.

The Great Dismal has been described as being highest towards its center. Here, however, there is an extensive lake of an oval form, seven miles long and more than five wide, the depth, where greatest, fifteen feet; and its bottom consisting of mud like the swamp, but sometimes with a pure white sand, a foot deep, covering the mud. The water is transparent, though tinged of a pale brown color, like that of our peat-mosses, and contains abundance of fish. This sheet of water is usually even with its banks, on which a thick and tall forest grows. There is no beach, for the bank sinks perpendicularly, so that if the waters are lowered several feet, it makes no alteration in the breadth of the lake.

Much timber has been cut down and carried out from the swamp by means of canals, which are perfectly straight for long distances, with the trees on each side arching over, and almost joining their branches across, so that they throw a dark shade on the water, which of itself looks black, being colored as before mentioned. When the boats emerge from the gloom of these avenues into the lake, the scene is said to be "as beautiful as fairy-land."

The bears inhabiting the swamp climb trees in search of acorns and gum-berries, breaking off large boughs of the oaks in order to draw the acorns near to them. These same bears are said to kill hogs, and even cows. There are also wild-cats, and occasionally a solitary wolf, in the morass.

That the ancient seams of coal were produced for the most part by terrestrial plants of all sizes, not drifted but growing on the spot, is a theory more and more generally adopted in modern times; and the growth of what is called sponge in such a swamp, and in such a climate as the Great Dismal, already covering so many square miles of a low level region, bordering the sea, and capable of spreading itself indefinitely over the adjacent country, helps us greatly to conceive the manner in which the coal of the ancient carboniferous rocks may have been formed. The heat, perhaps, may not have been excessive when the coal-measures originated, but the entire absence of frost, with a warm and damp atmosphere, may have enabled tropical forms to flourish in latitudes far distant from the line. Huge swamps in a rainy climate, standing above the level of the surrounding firm land, and supporting a dense forest, may have spread far and wide, invading the plains, like some European peat-mosses when they burst; and the frequent submergence of these masses of vegetable matter beneath seas or estuaries, as often as the land sank down during subterranean movements, may have given rise to the deposition of strata of mud, sand, or limestone immediately upon the vegetable matter. The conversion of successive surfaces into dry land where other swamps supporting trees may have formed, might give origin to a continued series of coal-measures of great thickness. In some kinds of coal the vegetable texture is apparent throughout under the microscope; in others, it has only partially disappeared; but even in this coal, the flattened trunks of trees, converted into pure coal, are occasionally met with, and erect fossil trees are observed in the overlying strata, terminating downwards in seams of coal.

MACAULAY.

1800-1859.

THOMAS BABINGTON MACAULAY, who may fairly be described as the most accomplished literary man of his time, was born in Leicestershire, England, in 1800, and died in 1859. . His father, Zachary Macaulay, was an eminent philanthropist. The subject of this notice entered Trinity College, Cambridge, graduating B. A. in 1822, with a reputation for varied and readily available learning such as few collegians have ever won. In 1826 he was called to the bar, and in 1830 was elected to represent the borough of Calne in Parliament. In that body he was an active supporter of the Reform Measures. In 1834 he was sent to India as a member of the Supreme Council of Calcutta; in 1839 he was made Secretary of War; in 1841 he went out of office, on the accession of Sir Robert Peel; in 1846, the Whigs returning to power, he was appointed Paymaster-General of the Forces, and had a seat in the Cabinet. In 1847 he was defeated in the Parliamentary elections, his Edinburgh constituents disapproving his course on the Maynooth Grant question. Five years later, however, these same constituents chose him as their representative in Parliament, where he served them till 1856, when he withdrew finally from political life. Meantime, in 1849, he was elected Lord Rector of the University of Glasgow, and delivered an inaugural address of great brilliancy. In 1857 his genius and services in literature and politics received merited recognition in his elevation to the peerage, with the title of Baron or Lord Macaulay.

Macaulay's first essays in literature were in the department of poetry; during his university career he won two high prizes for poetical composition, and he was a frequent contributor of verse to Knight's Quarterly Magazine. Among his best-known youthful productions were *The Battle of Ivry* and *The Spanish Armada*, poems which foreshadowed the maturer excellence of his *Lays of Ancient Rome*, which were first published in 1842. In the periodical above mentioned Macaulay made his *début* as an essayist; but his first great triumph in this character is connected with the pages of the Edinburgh Review, in which, in 1825, appeared his masterly essay on Milton, which instantly gave him acknowledged rank among the ablest English critics. This essay was followed by many others, which are familiar to all readers of English, and which as a collection are unsurpassed, perhaps unequaled, in the literature of any nation. The essay on Bacon, though less popular than some of its associates, illustrates with admirable effect the original intellectual power and vast acquired resources of the author. As an essayist Macaulay very closely approaches perfection. His poetry lacks the sensuous element which the public seems to demand in that form of composition, and, vigorous and dramatic though it is in an almost unequaled degree, it has never become popular with the mass of readers. His history has been assailed for its manifestations of partisanship and its occasional inaccuracies. But in the presence of his essays unfriendly criticism has stayed its hand; and even the eye of envy and personal animosity has failed to find any serious blemishes in their beautiful and symmetrical fabric. There is little risk in pronouncing them the most perfect literary products of the nineteenth century. The first and second volumes of Macaulay's *History of England* " from the time of James II. down to a time which is within the memory of men still living," appeared in 1849, and won immediate success. The work did not, however, escape censure; John Wilson Croker attacked it violently, though his judgment was said to be biased by personal feeling, and Sir Archibald Alison deplored its general lack of candor. But these few protesting voices were drowned in the chorus of applause with which the literary leaders of England and America welcomed the history. All things considered, the writings of Macaulay offer a more remunerative field to the student than do those of any other English writer, except of course Shakespeare. In point of style, construction, and effective utilization of knowledge, they may safely be used as models.

THE PURITANS.

WE would speak of the Puritans, the most remarkable body of men, perhaps, which the world has ever produced. The odious and ridiculous parts of their character lie on the surface. He that runs may read them ; nor have there been wanting attentive and malicious observers to point them out. For many years after the Restoration, they were the theme of unmeasured invective and derision. They were exposed to the utmost licentiousness of the press and of the stage, at the time when the press and the stage were most licentious. They were not men of letters; they were, as a body, unpopular : they could not defend themselves; and the public would not take them under its protection. They were therefore abandoned, without reserve, to the tender mercies of the satirists and dramatists. The ostentatious simplicity of their dress, their sour aspect, their nasal twang, their stiff posture, their long graces, their Hebrew names, the Scriptural phrases which they introduced on every occasion, their contempt of human learning, their detestation of polite amusements, were indeed fair game for the laughers. But it is not from the laughers alone that the philosophy of history is to be learnt. And he who approaches this subject should carefully guard against the influence of that potent ridicule which has already misled so many excellent writers.

Those who roused the people to resistance, who directed their measures through a long series of eventful years, who formed, out of the most unpromising materials the finest army that Europe had ever seen, who trampled down King, Church, and Aristocracy, who, in the short intervals of domestic sedition and rebellion, made the name of England terrible to every nation on the face of the earth, were no vulgar fanatics. Most of their absurdities were mere external badges, like the signs of freemasonry or the dresses of friars. We regret that these badges were not more attractive. We regret that a body to whose courage and talents mankind has owed inestimable obligations had not the lofty elegance which distinguished some of the adherents of Charles the First, or the easy good-breeding for which the Court of Charles the Second was celebrated. But, if we must make our choice, we shall, like Bassanio in the play, turn from the specious caskets which contain only the Death's head and the Fool's head, and fix on the plain leaden chest which conceals the treasure.

The Puritans were men whose minds had derived a peculiar character from the daily contemplation of superior beings and eternal interests. Not content with acknowledging, in general terms, an overruling Providence, they habitually ascribed every event to the will of the Great Being for whose power nothing was too vast, for whose inspection nothing was too minute. To know him, to serve him, to enjoy him was with them the great end of existence. They rejected with contempt the ceremonious homage which other sects substituted for the pure worship of the soul. Instead of catching occasional glimpses of the Deity through an obscuring veil, they aspired to gaze full on his intolerable brightness, and to commune with him face to face. Hence originated their contempt for terrestrial distinctions. The difference between the greatest and the meanest of mankind seemed to vanish, when compared with the boundless interval which separated the whole race from him on whom their own eyes were constantly fixed. They recognized no title to superiority but his favor; and, confident of that favor, they despised all the accomplishments and all the dignities of the world. If they were unacquainted with the works of philosophers and poets, they were deeply read in the oracles of God. If their names were not found in the registers of heralds, they were recorded in the Book of Life. If their steps were not accompanied by a splendid train of menials, legions of ministering angels had charge of them.

Their palaces were houses not made with hands; their diadems crowns of glory which should never fade away. On the rich and the eloquent, on nobles and priests, they looked down with contempt: for they esteemed themselves rich in a more precious treasure, and eloquent in a more sublime language, nobles by the right of an earlier creation, and priests by the imposition of a mightier hand. The very meanest of them was a being to whose fate a mysterious and terrible importance belonged, on whose slightest action the spirits of light and darkness looked with anxious interest, who had been destined, before heaven and earth were created, to enjoy a felicity which should continue when heaven and earth should have passed away. Events which short-sighted politicians ascribed to earthly causes, had been ordained on his account. For his sake empires had risen, and flourished, and decayed. For his sake the Almighty had proclaimed his will by the pen of the evangelist and the harp of the prophet. He had been wrested by no common deliverer from the grasp of no common foe. He had been ransomed by the sweat of no vulgar agony, by the blood of no earthly sacrifice. It was for him that the sun had been darkened, that the rocks had been rent, that the dead had risen, that all nature had shuddered at the sufferings of her expiring God.

Thus the Puritan was made up of two different men, — the one all self-abasement, penitence, gratitude, passion; the other proud, calm, inflexible, sagacious. He prostrated himself in the dust before his Maker; but he set his foot on the neck of his king. In his devotional retirement he prayed with convulsions and groans and tears. He was half-maddened by glorious or terrible illusions. He heard the lyres of angels or the tempting whispers of fiends. He caught a gleam of the Beatific Vision, or woke screaming from dreams of ever-lasting fire. Like Vane, he thought himself entrusted with the scepter of the millennial year. Like Fleetwood, he cried in the bitterness of his soul that God had hid his face from him. But when he took his seat in the council, or girt on his sword for war, these tempestuous workings of the soul had left no perceptible trace behind them. People who saw nothing of the godly but their uncouth visages, and heard nothing from them but their groans and their whining hymns, might laugh at them. But those had little reason to laugh who en-countered them in the hall of debate or in the field of battle.

These fanatics brought to civil and military affairs a coolness of judgment and an immutability of purpose which some writers have thought inconsistent with their religious zeal, but which were in fact the necessary effects of it. The intensity of their feelings on one sub-ject made them tranquil on every other. One overpowering sentiment had subjected to itself pity and hatred, ambition and fear. Death had lost its terrors and pleasure its charms. They had their smiles and their tears, their raptures and their sorrows, but not for the things of this world. Enthusiasm had made them Stoics, had cleared their minds from every vulgar passion and prejudice, and raised them above the influence of danger and of corruption. It sometimes might lead them to pursue unwise ends, but never to choose unwise means. They went through the world, like Sir Artegal's iron man Talus with his flail, crushing and trampling down oppressors, mingling with human beings, but having neither part nor lot in human infirmities, insensible to fatigue, to pleasure, and to pain, not to be pierced by any weapon, not to be withstood by any barrier.

THE PROGRESS OF ENGLAND.

THE history of England is emphatically the history of progress. It is the history of a constant movement in the public mind, of a con-stant change in the institutions of a great society. We see that society, at the beginning of the twelfth century, in a state more miserable than the state in which the most degraded nations of the East now are. We see it subjected to the tyranny of a handful of armed foreigners. We see a strong distinction of caste separating the victorious Norman from the vanquished Saxon. We see the great body of the population in a state of personal slavery. We see the most debasing and cruel superstition exercising boundless dominion over the most elevated and benevolent minds. We see the multitude sunk in brutal ignorance, and the studious few engaged in acquiring what did not deserve the name of knowledge.

In the course of seven centuries the wretched and degraded race have become the greatest and most highly civilized people that ever the world saw, — have spread their dominion over every quarter of the globe, — have scattered the seeds of mighty empires and republics over vast continents of which no dim intimation had ever reached Ptolemy * or Strabo, † — have created a maritime power which would annihilate in a quarter of an hour the navies of Tyre, Athens, Carthage, Venice, and Genoa together, — have carried the science of healing, the means of locomotion and correspondence, every mechanical art, every manufacture, everything that promotes the convenience of life, to a perfection which our ancestors would have thought magical, — have produced a literature which may boast of works not inferior to the noblest which Greece has bequeathed to us, — have discovered the laws which regulate the motions of the heavenly bodies, — have speculated with exquisite subtilty on the operations of the human mind, — have been the acknowledged leaders of the human race in the career of political improvement.

The history of England is the history of this great change in the moral, intellectual, and physical state of the inhabitants of our own island. There is much amusing and instructive episodical matter, but this is the main action. To us, we will own, nothing is so interesting and delightful as to contemplate the steps by which the England of the Domesday Book, the England of the Curfew and the Forest Laws, the England of crusaders, monks, schoolmen, astrologers, serfs, outlaws, became the England which we know and love, the classic ground of liberty and philosophy, the school of all knowledge, the mart of all trade.

* PTOLEMY. The founder of the Greek dynasty of kings of Egypt. He was a friend of Alexander the Great, and like him was a great warrior; he was noted also for political wisdom. Died 283 B. C.

† STRABO. An eminent Greek geographer, born about 60 B. C.

BUNYAN'S PILGRIM'S PROGRESS.

THE characteristic peculiarity of the Pilgrim's Progress is, that it is the only work of its kind which possesses a strong human interest. Other allegories only amuse the fancy. The allegory of Bunyan has been read by many thousands with tears. There are some good allegories in Johnson's works, and some of still higher merit by Addison. In these performances there is, perhaps, as much wit and ingenuity as in the Pilgrim's Progress. But the pleasure which is produced by the Vision of Mirza, the Vision of Theodore, the Genealogy of Wit, or the Contest between Rest and Labor, is exactly similar to the pleasure which we derive from one of Cowley's odes or from a canto of Hudibras. It is a pleasure which belongs wholly to the understanding, and in which the feelings have no part whatever.

It is not so with the Pilgrim's Progress. That wonderful book, while it obtains admiration from the most fastidious critics, is loved by those who are too simple to admire it. Doctor Johnson, all whose studies were desultory, and who hated, as he said, to read books through, made an exception in favor of the Pilgrim's Progress. That work, he said, was one of the two or three works which he wished longer. In the wildest parts of Scotland the Pilgrim's Progress is the delight of the peasantry. In every nursery the Pilgrim's Progress is a greater favorite than Jack the Giant-Killer. Every reader knows the strait and narrow path as well as he knows a road in which he has gone backward and forward a hundred times. This is the highest miracle of genius, — that things which are not should be as though they were; that the imaginations of one mind should become the personal recollections of another. And this miracle the tinker * has wrought.

There is no ascent, no declivity, no resting-place, no turnstile, with which we are not perfectly acquainted. The wicket-gate, and the desolate swamp which separates it from the City of Destruction ; the long line of road, as straight as a rule can make it ; the Interpreter's house and all its fair shows ; all the stages of the journey, all the forms which cross or overtake the pilgrims, giants and hobgoblins, ill-favored ones and shining ones ; the tall, comely, swarthy Madam Bubble, with her great purse by her side, and her fingers playing with the money ; the black man in the bright vesture ; Mr. Worldly Wiseman

---

* Bunyan was a tinker.

and my Lord Hategood, Mr. Talkative and Mrs. Timorous; — all are actually existing beings to us. We follow the travelers through their allegorical progress with interest not inferior to that with which we follow Elizabeth from Siberia to Moscow, or Jeanie Deans from Edinburgh to London.

Bunyan is almost the only writer that ever gave to the abstract the interest of the concrete. In the works of many celebrated authors men are mere personifications. We have not an Othello, but jealousy; not an Iago, but perfidy; not a Brutus, but patriotism. The mind of Bunyan, on the contrary, was so imaginative that personifications, when he dealt with them, became men. A dialogue between two qualities, in his dream, has more dramatic effect than a dialogue between two human beings in most plays.

The style of Bunyan is delightful to every reader, and invaluable as a study to every person who wishes to obtain a wide command over the English language. The vocabulary is the vocabulary of the common people. There is not an expression, if we except a few technical terms of theology, which would puzzle the rudest peasant. We have observed several pages which do not contain a single word of more than two syllables. Yet no writer has said more exactly what he meant to say. For magnificence, for pathos, for vehement exhortation, for subtile disquisition, for every purpose of the poet, the orator, and the divine, this homely dialect, the dialect of plain workingmen, was perfectly sufficient. There is no book in our literature on which we would so readily stake the fame of the old unpolluted English language; no book which shows so well how rich that language is, in its own proper wealth, and how little it has been improved by all that it has borrowed.

Cowper said, fifty or sixty years ago, that he dared not name John Bunyan in his verse, for fear of moving a sneer. We live in better times; and we are not afraid to say, that though there were many clever men in England during the latter half of the seventeenth century, there were only two great creative minds. One of these produced the PARADISE LOST, the other the PILGRIM'S PROGRESS.

BANCROFT.

1800 – 1891

GEORGE BANCROFT was born in Worcester, Massachusetts, in 1800. He recently returned from Berlin, where for several years he discharged, with honor to himself and his country, the duties of United States Minister. In 1817 he graduated at Harvard, bearing off, despite his tender age, the second honors of his class. The next year he went to Germany, where he studied under the direction of Heeren and Schlosser, and other eminent scholars. He prepared himself for a clerical life; but his love of literature was stronger than his "drawing" to the pulpit, and he soon abandoned the idea of adopting the sacred profession. In 1823 he made his first public literary essay in a' volume of poems, and, in the next following year, put forth a translation of Heeren's *Reflections on the Politics of Ancient Greece*. About this time he associated himself with the late Dr. Joseph G. Cogswell in the establishment of the Round Hill School at Northampton. The duties of a pedagogue, however, proved uncongenial to him, and, although the school enjoyed a fair degree of prosperity, he found its management irksome, and turned his attention to politics. In 1838 he was appointed Collector of the Port of Boston; was an unsuccessful candidate for Governor of Massachusetts in 1844, and in 1845 was made Secretary of the Navy. This office he held about one year, displaying marked ability in the discharge of its duties, and effecting many important reforms in the department. In 1846 he was appointed Minister to England, and remained abroad till 1849. From that time till the date of his appointment as Minister to Berlin by President Grant, he devoted himself assiduously to the writing of his *History of the United States*, which is now completed. The first volume of this work was published in 1834, and the succeeding volumes, down to the tenth, which is just ready, have followed at long intervals. It is safe to say that Mr. Bancroft's History is unrivaled as a record of the origin and growth of the United States. In its preparation, or at least in that of those volumes which treat of the years immediately preceding the Revolution, he had the use of a vast number of manuscripts to which no earlier historian had access. His natural qualifications, reinforced by wide reading, for the historian's work are exceptionally great. It has been charged by some English critics that his democratic prejudices are too manifest in his History; but this allegation has had little weight with those who are most competent to form a judgment in the case, — his own countrymen; and his judicial candor is generally reckoned among the most admirable components of his intellectual equipment. His style has received warm and universal praise; it is eminently scholarly, yet not pedantic, brilliant, yet not flashy, in narrative animated and picturesque, and in philosophical passages massive and majestic. This history is one of the proudest monuments of American scholarship.

INDIAN MASSACRES OF THE EARLY SETTLERS.

BETWEEN the Indians and the English there had been quarrels, but no wars. From the first landing of colonists in Virginia, the power of the natives was despised: their strongest weapons were such arrows as they could shape without the use of iron, such hatchets as could be made from stone; and an English mastiff seemed to them a terrible adversary. Nor were their numbers considerable. Within sixty miles of Jamestown,* it is computed, there were no more than five thousand souls, or about fifteen hundred warriors. The whole

* JAMESTOWN. A town in Virginia, on the James River, now in ruins. The first English settlement in the United States was made here in 1608.

territory of the clans which listened to Powhatan * as their leader or their conqueror comprehended about eight thousand square miles, thirty tribes, and twenty-four hundred warriors; so that the Indian population amounted to about one inhabitant to a square mile. The natives, naked and feeble compared with the Europeans, were nowhere concentrated in considerable villages; but dwelt dispersed in hamlets, with from forty to sixty in each company. Few places had more than two hundred, and many had less. It was also unusual for any large portion of these tribes to be assembled together. An idle tale of an ambuscade of three or four thousand is perhaps an error for three or four hundred; otherwise it is an extravagant fiction, wholly unworthy of belief. Smith once met a party, that seemed to amount to seven hundred; and so complete was the superiority conferred by the use of fire-arms, that with fifteen men he was able to withstand them all.

The savages were therefore regarded with contempt or compassion. No uniform care had been taken to conciliate their good-will, although their condition had been improved by some of the arts of civilized life. The degree of their advancement may be judged by the intelligence of their chieftain. A house having been built for Opechancanough after the English fashion, he took such delight in the lock and key, that he would lock and unlock the door a hundred times a day, and thought the device incomparable. When Wyatt arrived, the natives expressed a fear lest his intentions should be hostile; he assured them of his wish to preserve inviolable peace, and the emigrants had no use for fire-arms except against a deer or a fowl. Confidence so far increased that the old law which made death the penalty for teaching the Indians to use the musket was forgotten; and they were now employed as fowlers and huntsmen. The plantations of the English were widely extended, in unsuspecting confidence, along the James River and towards the Potomac, wherever rich grounds invited to the culture of tobacco; nor were solitary places, remote from neighbors, avoided; since there would there be less competition for the ownership of the soil.

Powhatan, the father of Pocahontas, remained, after the marriage of his daughter, the firm friend of the English. He died in 1618; and his younger brother was now the heir to his influence. Should the

---

* POWHATAN. An Indian chief, father of Pocahontas. The familiar story of the heroism of Pocahontas in saving the life of Captain John Smith is now generally considered a myth. She married John Rolfe, an Englishman, and died in 1617.

native occupants of the soil consent to be driven from their ancient patrimony? Should their feebleness submit patiently to contempt, injury, and the loss of their lands? The desire of self-preservation, the necessity of self-defense, seemed to demand an active resistance; to preserve their dwelling-places, the English must be exterminated; in open battle the Indians would be powerless; conscious of their weakness, they could not hope to accomplish their end except by a preconcerted surprise. The crime was one of savage ferocity; but it was suggested by their situation. They were timorous and quick of apprehension, and consequently treacherous; for treachery and false-hood are the vices of cowardice. The attack was prepared with impenetrable secrecy. To the very last hour the Indians preserved the language of friendship; they borrowed the boats of the English to attend their own assemblies; on the very morning of the massacre they were in the houses and at the tables of those whose death they were plotting. "Sooner," said they, "shall the sky fall, than peace be violated on our part." At length, on the 22d of March (1622), at midday, at one and the same instant of time, the Indians fell upon an unsuspecting population, which was scattered through distant villages, extending one hundred and forty miles on both sides of the river. The onset was so sudden that the blow was not discerned till it fell. None were spared; children and women, as well as men; the missionary, who had cherished the natives with untiring gentleness; the liberal benefactors, from whom they had received daily benefits, — all were murdered with indiscriminate barbarity, and every aggravation of cruelty. The savages fell upon the dead bodies, as if it had been possible to commit on them a fresh murder.

In one hour three hundred and forty-seven persons were cut off. Yet the carnage was not universal; and Virginia was saved from so disastrous a grave. The night before the execution of the conspiracy it was revealed by a converted Indian to an Englishman, whom he wished to rescue; Jamestown and the nearest settlements were well prepared against an attack; and the savages, as timid as they were ferocious, fled with precipitation from the appearance of wakeful resistance. Thus the larger part of the colony was saved.

7   J

THE DISCOVERY OF THE MISSISSIPPI RIVER.

ALL the disasters which had been encountered, far from diminishing the boldness of De Soto,* served only to confirm his obstinacy by wounding his pride. Should he, who had promised greater booty than Mexico or Peru had yielded, now return as a defeated fugitive, so naked that his troops were clad only in skins and mats of ivy? The search for some wealthy region was renewed; the caravan marched still farther to the west.

For seven days it struggled through a wilderness of forests and marshes, and at length came to Indian settlements in the vicinity of the Mississippi. The lapse of nearly three centuries has not changed the character of the stream. It was then described as more than a mile broad, flowing with a strong current, and, by the weight of its waters, forcing a channel of great depth. The water was always muddy; trees and timber were continually floating down the stream.

The Spaniards were guided to the Mississippi by the natives; and were directed to one•of the usual crossing-places, probably at the lowest Chickasa Bluff, not far from the thirty-fifth parallel of latitude. The arrival of the strangers awakened curiosity and fear. A multitude of people from the western banks of the river, painted and gayly decorated with great plumes of white feathers, the warriors standing in rows with bow and arrows in their hands, the chieftains sitting under awnings as magnificent as the artless manufactures of the natives could weave, came rowing down the stream in a fleet of two hundred canoes, seeming to the admiring Spaniards "like a fair army of galleys."

They brought gifts of fish and loaves made of the fruit of the persimmon. At first they showed some desire to offer resistance; but, soon becoming conscious of their relative weakness, they ceased to defy an enemy who could not be overcome, and suffered injury without attempting open retaliation. The boats of the natives were too weak to transport horses; almost a month expired before barges large enough to hold three horsemen each were constructed for crossing the river. At length the Spaniards embarked upon the Mississippi, and were borne to its western bank.

---

* HERNANDO DE SOTO. A Spanish explorer, born about 1500, discovered the Mississippi River in 1541, and died in Louisiana in 1542. He was one of the boldest and bravest of the many brave leaders who figured in the discoveries, and distinguished themselves in the wild warfare of the Western World.

The Dacotah tribes, doubtless, then occupied the country south-west of the Missouri. De Soto had heard its praises; he believed in its vicinity to mineral wealth, and he determined to visit its towns. In ascending the Mississippi the party was often obliged to wade through morasses; at length they came, as it would seem, upon the district of Little Prairie, and the dry and elevated lands which extend towards New Madrid.

Here the religions of the invaders and the natives came in contrast. The Spaniards were adored as children of the sun, and the blind were brought into their presence, to be healed by the sons of light. "Pray only to God, who is in heaven, for whatsoever ye need," said De Soto in reply; and the sublime doctrine which, thousands of years before, had been proclaimed in the deserts of Arabia, now first found its way into the prairies of the Far West.

The wild fruits of that region were abundant; the pecan-nut, the mulberry, and the two kinds of wild plums, furnished the natives with articles of food. At Pacaha, the northernmost point which De Soto reached near the Mississippi, he remained forty days. The spot cannot be identified; but the accounts of the amusements of the Spaniards confirm the truth of the narrative of their ramblings. Fish were taken, such as are now found in the fresh waters of that region; one of them, the spade fish, — the strangest and most whim-sical production of the muddy streams of the west, so rare that, even now, it is hardly to be found in any museum, — is accurately de-scribed by the best historian of the expedition.

An exploring party, which was sent to examine the regions to the north, reported that they were almost a desert. The country still nearer the Missouri was said by the Indians to be thinly inhabited; the bison abounded there so much that no maize could be cultivated, and the few inhabitants were hunters. De Soto turned, therefore, to the west and northwest, and plunged still more deeply into the inte-rior of the continent. The highlands of White River, more than two hundred miles from the Mississippi, were probably the limit of his ramble in this direction.

The mountains offered neither gems nor gold; and the disappointed adventurers marched to the south. They passed through a succession of towns, of which the position cannot be fixed, till at length we find them among the Tunicas, near the hot springs and saline tributaries of the Washita. It was at Autiamque, a town on the same river, that they passed the winter; they had arrived at the settlement through the country of the Kappaws.

The native tribes, everywhere on the route, were found in a state of civilization beyond that of nomadic hordes. They were an agricultural people, with fixed places of abode, and subsisted upon the produce of the fields more than upon the chase. Ignorant of the arts of life, they could offer no resistance to their unwelcome visitors; the bow and arrow were the most effective weapons with which they were acquainted. They seem not to have been turbulent or quarrelsome; but as the population was moderate, and the earth fruitful, the tribes were not accustomed to contend with each other for the possession of territories.

Their dress was, in part, mats wrought of ivy and bulrushes, or of the bark and lint of trees; in cold weather they wore mantles woven of feathers. The settlements were by tribes, — each tribe occupied what the Spaniards called a province; their villages were generally near together, but were composed of few habitations. The Spaniards treated them with no other forbearance than their own selfishness demanded, and enslaved such as offended, employing them as porters and guides.

On a slight suspicion, they would cut off the hands of numbers of the natives, for punishment or intimidation; while the young cavaliers, from desire of seeming valiant, ceased to be merciful, and exulted in cruelties and carnage. The guide who was unsuccessful, or who purposely led them away from the settlements of his tribe, would be seized and thrown to the hounds. Sometimes a native was condemned to the flames. Any trifling consideration of safety would induce the governor to set fire to a hamlet. He did not delight in cruelty; but the happiness, the life, and the rights of the Indians were held of no account. The approach of the Spaniards was heard with dismay; and their departure hastened by the suggestion of wealthier lands at a distance.

In the spring of the following year De Soto determined to descend the Washita to its junction, and to get tidings of the sea. As he advanced he was soon lost amidst the bayous and marshes which are found along the Red River and its tributaries. Near the Mississippi he came upon the country of Nilco, which was well peopled. The river was there larger than the Guadalquiver at Seville. At last he arrived at the province where the Washita, already united with the Red River, enters the Mississippi. The province was called Guachoya.

De Soto anxiously inquired the distance to the sea; the chieftain of Guachoya could not tell. Were there settlements extending along the river to its mouth? It was answered that its lower banks were an uninhabited waste. Unwilling to believe so disheartening a tale, De Soto sent one of his men with eight horsemen to descend the banks of the Mississippi, and explore the country. They traveled eight days, and were able to advance not much more than thirty miles, they were so delayed by the frequent bayous, the impassable cane-brakes, and the dense woods.

The governor received the intelligence with concern; he suffered from anxiety and gloom. His horses and men were dying around him, so that the natives were becoming dangerous enemies. He attempted to overawe a tribe of Indians near Natchez by claiming a supernatural birth, and demanding obedience and tribute. "You say you are the child of the sun," replied the undaunted chief; "dry up the river, and I will believe you. Do you desire to see me? Visit the town where I dwell. If you come in peace, I will receive you with special good-will; if in war, I will not shrink one foot back."

But De Soto was no longer able to abate the confidence or punish the temerity of the natives. His stubborn pride was changed by long disappointments into a wasting melancholy; and his health sunk rapidly and entirely under a conflict of emotions. A malignant fever ensued, during which he had little comfort, and was neither visited nor attended as the last hours of life demand. Believing his death near at hand, he held the last solemn interview with his faithful followers; and, yielding to the wishes of his companions, who obeyed him to the end, he named a successor. On the next day he died.

EMERSON.

1803 - 18.8 :.

RALPH WALDO EMERSON was born in Boston in 1803. He graduated at Harvard College in 1821, and, after pursuing a course of theological study, was ordained pastor of the Second Unitarian Church of Boston. His ministry was brief, however: a difference of opinion as to points of doctrine arose between himself and his people, and he resigned his charge. Retiring to the town of Concord, he gave himself up to the study of mental and moral philosophy. His first published writings — *Man Thinking, Literary Ethics*, and *Nature, an Essay* — instantly attracted the attention of thoughtful readers, and he at once took the position of a leader of philosophical opinion, not only in this country but in England. In 1847 he published his first volume of poems. He is best known by his *Essays* and his *Representative Men*. His impress on the thought of his time has been deep and lasting; he has founded a school of philosophy and a literary style which are called Emersonian; and though he has failed to win a numerous following, he has done much towards molding the ethical opinions of New England, and, in a less degree, of the whole country. His influence has not been limited to his own country. His books have been widely read in England and Germany, and during his several visits to Europe he has been received by the foremost representatives of modern culture with the honors due to one of the master-minds of the age. His style can hardly be recommended as a model, though it possesses many striking beauties. In order thoroughly to appreciate it, one must be in such full sympathy with the writer's spirit as it is the privilege of few to attain.

NAPOLEON BONAPARTE.

NAPOLEON understood his business. Here was a man who in each moment and emergency knew what to do next. It is an immense comfort and refreshment to the spirits, not only of kings, but of citizens. Few men have any next; they live from hand to mouth, without plan, and are ever at the end of their line, and, after each action, wait for an impulse from abroad. Napoleon had been the first man of the world, if his ends had been purely public. As he is, he inspires confidence and vigor by the extraordinary unity of his action.

He is firm, sure, self-denying, self-postponing, sacrificing everything to his aim, — money, troops, generals, and his own safety also; not misled, like common adventurers, by the splendor of his own means. "Incidents ought not to govern policy," he said, "but policy incidents." "To be hurried away by every event, is to have no political system at all." His victories were only so many doors, and he never for a moment lost sight of his way onward in the dazzle and uproar of the present circumstance. He knew what to do, and he flew to his mark.

He would shorten a straight line to come at his object. Horrible anecdotes may, no doubt, be collected from his history, of the price at which he bought his successes; but he must not, therefore, be set down as cruel, but only as one who knew no impediment to his will: not bloodthirsty, not cruel; but woe to what thing or person stood in his way! "Sire, General Clarke cannot combine with General Junot for the dreadful fire of the Austrian battery." "Let him carry the battery." "Sire, every regiment that approaches the heavy artillery is sacrificed. Sire, what orders?" "*Forward! forward!*"

In the plenitude of his resources every obstacle seemed to vanish. "There shall be no Alps," he said; and he built his perfect roads, climbing by graded galleries their steepest precipices, until Italy was as open to Paris as any town in France. Having decided what was to be done, he did that with might and main. He put out all his strength. He risked everything, and spared nothing, — neither ammunition, nor money, nor troops, nor generals, nor himself. If fighting be the best mode of adjusting national differences (as large majorities of men seem to agree), certainly Bonaparte was right in making it thorough.

"The grand principle of war," he said, "was, that an army ought always to be ready, by day and by night, and at all hours, to make all the resistance it is capable of making." He never economized his ammunition, but on a hostile position rained a torrent of iron, — shells, balls, grape-shot, — to annihilate all defense. He went to the edge of his possibility, so heartily was he bent on his object. It is plain that in Italy he did what he could, and all that he could; he came several times within an inch of ruin, and his own person was all but lost. He was flung into the marsh at Arcola.* The Austrians were between him and his troops in the confusion of the struggle, and he was brought off with desperate efforts. At Lonato,† and at other places, he was on the point of being taken prisoner.

He fought sixty battles. He had never enough. Each victory was a new weapon. "My power would fall, were I not to support it by new achievements. Conquest has made me what I am, and conquest must maintain me." He felt, with every wise man, that as much life is needed for conservation as for creation. We are always in peril, always in a bad plight, just on the edge of destruction, and only to be saved by invention and courage. This vigor was guarded

---

* ARCOLA. A village of Northern Italy.
† LONATO. A small town near Lake Garda in Italy.

and tempered by the coldest prudence and punctuality. A thunderbolt in the attack, he was found invulnerable in his intrenchments. His very attack was never the inspiration of courage, but the result of calculation. His idea of the best defense consisted in being always the attacking party. "My ambition," he says, "was great, but was of a cold nature."

Everything depended on the nicety of his combinations: the stars were not more punctual than his arithmetic. His personal attention descended to the smallest particulars. "At Montebello I ordered Kellermann to attack with eight hundred horse; and with these he separated the six thousand Hungarian grenadiers before the very eyes of the Austrian cavalry. This cavalry was half a league off, and required a quarter of an hour to arrive on the field of action; and I have observed it is always these quarters of an hour that decide the fate of a battle."

Before he fought a battle Bonaparte thought little about what he should do in case of success, but a great deal about what he should do in case of a reverse of fortune. The same prudence and good sense marked all his behavior. His instructions to his secretary at the palace are worth remembering: "During the night, enter my chamber as seldom as possible. Do not awake me when you have any good news to communicate; with that there is no hurry: but when you bring bad news, rouse me instantly, for then there is not a moment to be lost." His achievement of business was immense, and enlarges the known powers of man. There have been many working kings, from Ulysses to William of Orange, but none who accomplished a tithe of this man's performance.

To these gifts of nature Napoleon added the advantage of having been born to a private and humble fortune. In his later days he had the weakness of wishing to add to his crowns and badges the prescription of aristocracy; but he knew his debt to his austere education, and made no secret of his contempt for the born kings, and for "the hereditary donkeys," as he coarsely styled the Bourbons. He said that, in their exile, "they had learned nothing, and forgot nothing." Bonaparte had passed through all the degrees of military service; but, also, was citizen before he was emperor, and so had the key to citizenship. His remarks and estimates discovered the information and justness of measurement of the middle class.

Those who had to deal with him found that he was not to be imposed upon, but could cipher as well as another man. When the expenses of the empress, of his household, of his palaces, had accumulated great debts, Napoleon examined the bills of the creditors himself, detected overcharges and errors, and reduced the claims by considerable sums. His grand weapon, namely, the millions whom he directed, he owed to the representative character which clothed him. He interests us as he stands for France and for Europe; and he exists as captain and king only as far as the Revolution or the interests of the industrious masses found an organ and a leader in him.

In the social interests he knew the meaning and value of labor, and threw himself naturally on that side. The principal works that have survived him are his magnificent roads. He filled his troops with his spirit, and a sort of freedom and companionship grew up between him and them, which the forms of his court never permitted between the officers and himself. They performed under his eye that which no others could do. The best document of his relation to his troops is the order of the day on the morning of the battle of Austerlitz, in which Napoleon promises the troops that he will keep his person out of reach of fire. This declaration, which is the reverse of that ordinarily made by generals and sovereigns on the eve of a battle, sufficiently explains the devotion of the army to their leader.

GOOD BY, PROUD WORLD!

Good by, proud world! I'm going home;
   Thou art not my friend; I am not thine:
Too long through weary crowds I roam, —
   A river ark on the ocean brine,
Too long I am tossed like the driven foam;
But now, proud world, I'm going home.

Good by to Flattery's fawning face;
To Grandeur with his wise grimace:
To upstart Wealth's averted eye;
To supple Office, low and high;
To crowded halls, to court and street,
To frozen hearts, and hasting feet,
To those who go, and those who come,
Good by, proud world, I'm going home.

7 *

I go to seek my own hearth-stone,
Bosomed in yon green hills alone;
A secret lodge in a pleasant land,
Whose groves the frolic fairies planned,
Where arches green, the livelong day,
Echo the blackbird's roundelay,
And evil men have never trod
A spot that is sacred to thought and God.

O, when I am safe in my sylvan home,
I mock at the pride of Greece and Rome;
And when I am stretched beneath the pines,
Where the evening star so holy shines,
I laugh at the lore and the pride of man,
At the sophist schools, and the learned clan;
For what are they all in their high conceit,
When man in the bush with God may meet?

THE SEA.

BEHOLD the Sea,
The opaline, the plentiful and strong,
Yet beautiful as is the rose in June,
Fresh as the trickling rainbow of July:
Sea full of food, the nourisher of kinds,
Purger of earth, and medicine of men;
Creating a sweet climate by my breath,
Washing out harms and griefs from memory,
And, in my mathematic ebb and flow,
Giving a hint of that which changes not.
Rich are the sea-gods: — who gives gifts but they?
They grope the sea for pearls, but more than pearls:
They pluck Force thence, and give it to the wise.
For every wave is wealth to Dædalus,
Wealth to the cunning artist who can work
This matchless strength.   Where shall he find, O waves!
A load your Atlas shoulders cannot lift?

HAWTHORNE.

●

1804 – 1864.

NATHANIEL HAWTHORNE, the most brilliant and original writer of romance that America has yet produced, was born in Salem in 1804 and died in 1864. He graduated at Bowdoin College in 1825, being a classmate of Henry Wadsworth Longfellow. He began to write at an early age; but his first efforts received little encouragement. Modest, retiring, and singularly sensitive, he was unwilling to thrust himself forward, but patiently awaited the recognition of his claims to literary honors, and the rewards which accrue to the successful author. During the early years of his manhood he filled offices in the Custom Houses of Boston and Salem; but while discharging his duties with fidelity, he gave his thought and heart to literary labor. His first book, *Twice Told Tales*, found few readers; and it may be said that ten years after its publication his name would hardly have found a place in a catalogue of American writers. In *The Scarlet Letter*, however, he vindicated his right to the title of author, and from the publication of that book his reputation steadily and rapidly increased in brilliancy. In 1853 he was appointed Consul to Liverpool by his friend and classmate, President Pierce, and held that office several years, receiving flattering attentions in the most cultivated circles of England. During his residence in that country he gathered material for *Our Old Home*, one of the most delightful records of travel and observation ever written. At the expiration of his term of office he proceeded to Italy, where he lived for some time, and, as the fruit of this sojourn, gave to the world *The Marble Faun*. During the last years of his life the condition of his health obliged him to abstain, measurably, from literary work; but he left behind him several chapters of *The Dolliver Romance* which warrant the opinion that the completed work would have been his masterpiece. Several years after his death there was discovered among his papers the manuscript of *Septimius Felton*, a weird and repulsive, but strikingly characteristic, story. Mr. Hawthorne died at Plymouth, New Hampshire, while on a journey with Ex-President Pierce.

On the whole, Hawthorne must be esteemed the foremost writer of prose among Americans; and it would not be easy to select a name from the crowded annals of English literature that is more closely and honorably associated with the marriage of fine thoughts to fine language, which constitutes the charm of prose. As a romancist, he stands alone and unapproached. His psychological insight was simply marvelous, and gave a distinguishing and inimitable character to all his writings. The dark side of things especially attracted him; he dwelt broodingly and with the devotion of an enthusiast upon abnormal manifestations of human nature, and delighted in delineating the intricacies of human passion. Yet to those who knew him intimately he was eminently lovable; and in his writings one can catch glimpses of moods of genuine sunny humor. His style is remarkable for its purity and gracefulness. *The Scarlet Letter* and *The House of The Seven Gables* are generally esteemed his best works. The extracts are from *Our Old Home* and *Mosses from an Old Manse*.

CIVIC BANQUETS IN ENGLAND.

IT has often perplexed me to imagine how an Englishman will be able to reconcile himself to any future state of existence from which the earthly institution of dinner shall be excluded. Even if he fail to take his appetite along with him (which it seems to me hardly possible to believe, since this endowment is so essential to his composition), the immortal day must still admit an interim of two or three hours during which he will be conscious of a slight distaste, at all events, if not an absolute repugnance, to merely spiritual nutriment. The idea of dinner has so imbedded itself among his highest and deepest characteristics, so illuminated itself with intellect and softened itself with the kindest emotions of his heart, so linked itself with Church and State, and grown so majestic with long hereditary customs and ceremonies, that by taking it utterly away, Death, instead of putting the final touch to his perfection, would leave him infinitely less complete than we have already known him. In this connection I should be glad to invite the reader to the official dinner-table of his Worship the Mayor, at a large English seaport where I spent several years.

The Mayor's dinner-parties occur as often as once a fortnight, and, inviting his guests by fifty or sixty at a time, his Worship probably assembles at his board most of the eminent citizens and distinguished personages of the town and neighborhood more than once during his year's incumbency, and very much, no doubt, to the promotion of good feeling among individuals of opposite parties and diverse pursuits in life. A miscellaneous party of Englishmen can always find more comfortable ground to meet upon than as many Americans, their differences of opinion being incomparably less radical than ours, and it being the sincerest wish of all their hearts, whether they call themselves Liberals or what not, that nothing in this world shall ever be greatly altered from what it has been and is. Thus there is seldom such a virulence of political hostility that it may not be dissolved in a glass or two of wine, without making the good liquor any more dry or bitter than accords with English taste.

The first dinner of this kind at which I had the honor to be present took place during assize-time, and included among the guests the judges and the prominent members of the bar. Reaching the Town Hall at seven o'clock, I communicated my name to one of several splendidly dressed footmen, and he repeated it to another on the first staircase, by whom it was passed to a third, and thence to a fourth at the door of the reception-room, losing all resemblance to the original sound in the course of these transmissions; so that I had the advantage of making my entrance in the character of a stranger, not only to the whole company, but to myself as well. His Worship, however, kindly recognized me, and put me on speaking terms with two or three gentlemen, whom I found very affable, and all the more hospitably attentive on the score of my nationality. It is very singular how kind an Englishman will almost invariably be to an individual

American, without ever bating a jot of his prejudice against the American character in the lump. My new acquaintances took evident pains to put me at my ease; and, in requital of their good-nature, I soon began to look round at the general company in a critical spirit, making my crude observations apart, and drawing silent inferences, of the correctness of which I should not have been half so well satisfied a year afterwards as at that moment.

There were two judges present, a good many lawyers, and a few officers of the army in uniform. The other guests seemed to be principally of the mercantile class, and among them was a ship-owner from Nova Scotia, with whom I coalesced a little, inasmuch as we were born with the same sky over our heads, and an unbroken continuity of soil between his abode and mine. There was one old gentleman, whose character I never made out, with powdered hair, clad in black breeches and silk stockings, and wearing a rapier at his side; otherwise, with the exception of the military uniforms, there was little or no pretence of official costume. It being the first considerable assemblage of Englishmen that I had seen, my honest impression about them was, that they were a heavy and homely set of people, with a remarkable roughness of aspect and behavior, not repulsive, but beneath which it required more familiarity with the national character than I then possessed always to detect the good breeding of a gentleman. Being generally middle-aged, or still farther advanced, they were by no means graceful in figure; for the comeliness of the youthful Englishman rapidly diminishes with years, his body appearing to grow longer, his legs to abbreviate themselves, and his stomach to assume the dignified prominence which justly belongs to that metropolis of his system. His face (what with the acridity of the atmosphere, ale at lunch, wine at dinner, and a well-digested abundance of succulent food) gets red and mottled, and develops at least one additional chin, with a promise of more; so that, finally, a stranger recognizes his animal part at the most superficial glance, but must take time and a little pains to discover the intellectual. Comparing him with an American, I really thought that our national paleness and lean habit of flesh gave us greatly the advantage in an æsthetic point of view. It seemed to me, moreover, that the English tailor had not done so much as he might and ought for these heavy figures, but had gone on wilfully exaggerating their uncouthness by the roominess of their garments; he had evidently no idea of accuracy of fit, and smartness was entirely out of his line. But, to be quite open with the reader, I afterwards learned to think that this aforesaid tailor has a deeper art than his brethren among ourselves, knowing how to dress his customers with such individual propriety that they look as if they were born in their clothes, the fit being to the character rather than the form. If you make an Englishman smart (unless he be a very exceptional one, of whom I have seen a few), you make him a monster; his best aspect is that of ponderous respectability.

In due time we were summoned to the table, and went thither in no solemn procession, but with a good deal of jostling, thrusting behind, and scrambling for places when we reached our destination. The legal gentlemen, I suspect, were responsible for this indecorous zeal, which I never afterwards remarked in a similar party. The dining-hall was of noble size, and, like the other rooms of the suite, was gorgeously painted and gilded and brilliantly illuminated. There was a splendid table-service, and a noble array of footmen, some of them in plain clothes, and others wearing the town-livery, richly decorated with gold lace, and themselves excellent specimens of the blooming young manhood of Britain. When we were fairly seated, it was certainly an agreeable spectacle to look up and down the long vista of earnest faces, and behold them so resolute, so conscious that there was an important business in hand, and so determined to be equal to the occasion.

During the dinner I had a good deal of pleasant conversation with the gentlemen on either side of me. One of them, a lawyer, expatiated with great unction on the social standing of the judges. Representing the dignity and authority of the Crown, they take precedence, during assize-time, of the highest military men in the kingdom, of the Lord-Lieutenant of the county, of the Archbishops, of the royal Dukes, and even of the Prince of Wales. For the nonce, they are the greatest men in England. With a glow of professional complacency that amounted to enthusiasm, my friend assured me, that, in case of a royal dinner, a judge, if actually holding an assize, would be expected to offer his arm and take the Queen herself to the table. Happening to be in company with some of these elevated personages, on subsequent occasions, it appeared to me that the judges are fully conscious of their paramount claims to respect, and take rather more pains to impress them on their ceremonial inferiors than men of high hereditary rank are apt to do. Bishops, if it be not irreverent to say so, are sometimes marked by a similar characteristic. Dignified position is so sweet to an Englishman that he needs to be born in it, and to feel it thoroughly incorporated with his nature from its original germ, in order to keep him from flaunting it obtrusively in the faces of innocent bystanders.

After an hour or two of valiant achievement with knife and fork came the dessert; and at the point of the festival where finger-glasses are usually introduced, a large silver basin was carried round to the guests, containing rose-water, into which we dipped the ends of our napkins and were conscious of a delightful fragrance, instead of that heavy and weary odor, the hateful ghost of a defunct dinner.

When the cloth was removed, a goodly group of decanters were set before the Mayor, who sent them forth on their outward voyage, full freighted with Port, Sherry, Madeira, and Claret, of which excellent liquors, methought, the latter found least acceptance among the guests. When every man had filled his glass, his Worship stood up and proposed a toast. It was, of course, "Our gracious Sovereign," or words to that effect; and immediately a band of musicians, whose preliminary tootings and thrummings I had already heard behind me, struck up "God save the Queen," and the whole company rose with one impulse to assist in singing that famous national anthem.

MOSSES FROM AN OLD MANSE.

WE stand now on the river's brink. It may well be called the Concord, — the river of peace and quietness, — for it is certainly the most unexcitable and sluggish stream that ever loitered imperceptibly towards its eternity, the sea. Positively, I had lived three weeks beside it, before it grew quite clear to my perception which way the current flowed. It never has a vivacious aspect, except when a north-western breeze is vexing its surface, on a sunshiny day.

From the incurable indolence of its nature, the stream is happily incapable of becoming the slave of human ingenuity, as is the fate of so many a wild, free, mountain torrent. While all things else are compelled to subserve some useful purpose, it idles its sluggish life away in lazy liberty, without turning a solitary spindle, or affording even water-power enough to grind the corn that grows upon its banks.

The torpor of its movement allows it nowhere a bright, pebbly shore, nor so much as a narrow strip of glistening sand, in any part of its course. It slumbers between broad prairies, kissing the long meadow-grass, and bathes the overhanging boughs of elder-bushes and willows, or the roots of elm and ash trees, and clumps of maples. Flags and rushes grow along its plashy shore; the yellow water-lily spreads its broad, flat leaves on the margin; and the fragrant white pond-lily abounds, generally selecting a position just so far from the river's bank that it cannot be grasped, save at the hazard of plunging in.

It is a marvel whence this perfect flower derives its loveliness and perfume, springing, as it does, from the black mud over which the river sleeps, and where lurk the slimy eel, and speckled frog, and the mud-turtle, whom continual washing cannot cleanse. It is the same black mud out of which the yellow lily sucks its rank life and noisome odor. Thus we see, too, in the world, that some persons assimilate only what is ugly and evil from the same moral circumstances which supply good and beautiful results — the fragrance of celestial flowers — to the daily life of others.

The Old Manse! — we had almost forgotten it, but will return thither through the orchard. This was set out by the last clergyman, in the decline of his life, when the neighbors laughed at the hoary-headed man for planting trees from which he could have no prospect of gathering fruit. Even had that been the case, there was only so much the better motive for planting them, in the pure and unselfish hope of benefiting his successors, — an end so seldom achieved by more ambitious efforts. But the old minister, before reaching his patriarchal age of ninety, ate the apples from this orchard during many years, and added silver and gold to his annual stipend by disposing of the superfluity.

It is pleasant to think of him, walking among the trees in the quiet afternoons of early autumn, and picking up here and there a windfall; while he observes how heavily the branches are weighed down, and computes the number of empty flour-barrels that will be filled by their burden. He loved each tree, doubtless, as if it had been his own child. An orchard has a relation to mankind, and readily connects itself with matters of the heart. The trees possess a domestic character; they have lost the wild nature of their forest kindred, and have grown humanized by receiving the care of man, as well as by contributing to his wants.

I have met with no other such pleasant trouble in the world, as that of finding myself, with only the two or three mouths which it was my privilege to feed, the sole inheritor of the old clergyman's wealth of fruits. Throughout the summer, there were cherries and currants ; and then came Autumn, with his immense burden of apples, dropping them continually from his overladen shoulders as he trudged along. In the stillest afternoon, if I listened, the thump of a great apple was audible, falling without a breath of wind, from the mere necessity of perfect ripeness. And, besides, there were pear-trees, that flung down bushels upon bushels of heavy pears ; and peach-trees, which, in a good year, tormented me with peaches, neither to be eaten nor kept, nor, without labor and perplexity, to be given away.

The idea of an infinite generosity and inexhaustible bounty, on the part of our mother Nature, was well worth obtaining through such cares as these. That feeling can be enjoyed in perfection not only by the natives of summer islands, where the bread-fruit, the cocoa, the palm, and the orange grow spontaneously, and hold forth the ever-ready meal ; but, likewise, almost as well, by a man long habituated to city life, who plunges into such a solitude as that of the Old Manse, where he plucks the fruit of trees that he did not plant ; and which, therefore, to my heterodox taste, bear the closer resemblance to those that grew in Eden.

Not that it can be disputed that the light toil requisite to cultivate a moderately sized garden imparts such zest to kitchen vegetables as is never found in those of the market-gardener. Childless men, if they would know something of the bliss of paternity, should plant a seed, — be it squash, bean, Indian corn, or perhaps a mere flower, or worthless weed, — should plant it with their own hands, and nurse it from infancy to maturity, altogether by their own care. If there be not too many of them, each individual plant becomes an object of separate interest.

My garden, that skirted the avenue of the Manse, was of precisely the right extent. An hour or two of morning labor was all that it required. But I used to visit and revisit it a dozen times a day, and stand in deep contemplation over my vegetable progeny, with a love that nobody could share or conceive of, who had never taken part in the process of creation. It was one of the most bewitching sights in the world to observe a hill of beans thrusting aside the soil, or a row of early peas just peeping forth sufficiently to trace a line of delicate green.

LYTTON.

1805 – 1873.

Sir Edward Bulwer (raised to the peerage with the title of Lord Lytton) was born in England in 1805 and died in 1873. He graduated at Trinity College, Cambridge, in 1826. In 1832 he entered Parliament, continuing a member till 1841; in 1852 he was re-elected to a seat in that body, where he served until his elevation to the peerage. In 1856 he was chosen Lord Rector of the University of Glasgow. At a very tender age he began to write verses, and long before he reached his majority, had published a volume. His first book, *Ismael, an Oriental Tale*, bears the date of 1820. It was followed by several volumes of verse, and his first novel, *Falkland*, appeared in 1827, the year of his marriage. The next year he gave to the world his famous novel, *Pelham*, which established his reputation on a firm basis. It was surpassed in merit, however, by some of his subsequent works, especially by *Rienzi*. Lord Lytton distinguished himself in almost every department of literature, — as poet, essayist, novelist, and dramatist. Several of his plays, *The Lady of Lyons* and *Richelieu*, rank among the most popular plays on the modern stage. He was a most prolific writer; even a catalogue of his productions would be too long for a place here. During the ten years preceding his death Lord Lytton published almost nothing, but found time, amid his political duties, to do a good deal of literary work. Since his death two of his novels have been given to the world, *Kenelm Chillingly* and *The Parisians*. The former is superior to any of his earlier books, representing the high culture of the author in its fullest development. Judged by his first compositions, he won the reputation of a literary fop, to whose ultra-fastidious taste finish was the chief merit in composition. He seemed to hold himself aloof from the world, as from possible contamination. In his later novels this tendency was less marked; and in *Kenelm Chillingly* it disappears wholly, being replaced by a catholic, warm-hearted philosophy that bespeaks a healthy and genial nature. For the work of the novelist he was most happily equipped. The art of delineating the passion of love was his in full measure, and he was a master of graphic and dramatic narrative. In his earlier books, *Falkland* and *Paul Clifford*, he exhibits the license and levity of youth; but these vices were corrected in later life, and morally, his last novels are unexceptionable. Regarded as a whole, Lord Lytton's literary career was conspicuously successful, and he left behind him not only an honored name, but many enduring fruits of his genius and industry. The first extract is from *My Novel*, the second is from *Leila, or the Siege of Granada*; the poetry from *The Lady of Lyons*.

ON REVOLUTION.

"My dear boy," cried Riccabocca kindly, "the only thing sure and tangible to which these writers would lead you lies at the first step, and that is what is commonly called a Revolution. Now, I know what that is. I have gone, not indeed through a revolution, but an attempt at one."

Leonard raised his eyes towards his master with a look of profound respect and great curiosity.

"Yes," added Riccabocca, and the face on which the boy gazed exchanged its usual grotesque and sardonic expression for one animated, noble, and heroic. "Yes, not a revolution for chimeras, but for that cause which the coldest allow to be good, and which, when successful, all time approves as divine, — the redemption of our native soil from the rule of the foreigner! I have shared in such an attempt. And," continued the Italian, mournfully, "recalling now all the evil passions it arouses, all the ties it dissolves, all the blood that it commands to flow, all the healthful industry it arrests, all the madmen that it arms, all the victims that it dupes, I question whether one man really honest, pure, and humane, who has once gone through such an ordeal, would ever hazard it again, unless he was assured that the victory was certain, — ay, and the object for which he fights not to be wrested from his hands amidst the uproar of the elements that the battle has released."

The Italian paused, shaded his brow with his hand, and remained long silent. Then, gradually resuming his ordinary tone, he continued : —

" Revolutions that have no definite objects made clear by the positive experience of history, — revolutions, in a word, that aim less at substituting one law or one dynasty for another, than at changing the whole scheme of society, have been little attempted by real statesmen. Even Lycurgus * is proved to be a myth who never existed. Such organic changes are but in the day-dreams of philosophers who lived apart from the actual world, and whose opinions (though generally they were very benevolent, good sort of men, and wrote in an elegant poetical style) one would no more take on a plain matter of life than one would look upon Virgil's Eclogues as a faithful picture of the ordinary pains and pleasures of the peasants who tend our sheep. Read them as you would read poets, and they are delightful. But attempt to shape the world according to the poetry, and fit yourself for a madhouse. The farther off the age is from the realization of such projects, the more these poor philosophers have indulged them. Thus, it was amidst the saddest corruption of court manners that it became the fashion in Paris to sit for one's picture, with a crook in one's hand, as Alexis or Daphne. Just as liberty was fast dying out of Greece, and the successors of Alexander were founding their monarchies, and Rome was growing up to crush in its iron grasp all states save its own, Plato withdraws his eyes from the world, to open them in his dreamy Atlantis.† Just in the grimmest period of English history, with the ax hanging over his head, Sir Thomas More gives

---

* LYCURGUS. A famous Spartan lawgiver, supposed to have lived about 850 B. C. See *Plutarch's Lives.*

† Plato's idea of a perfect state is unfolded in the *Laws* and the *Republic.*

you his Utopia.*   Just when the world is to be the theater of a new
Sesostris, the sages of France tell you that the age is too enlightened
for war, that man is henceforth to be governed by pure reason and
live in a paradise.   Very pretty reading all this to a man like me,
Lenny, who can admire and smile at it.   But to you, to the man who
has to work for his living, to the man who thinks it would be so
much more pleasant to live at his ease in a phalanstery † than to work
eight or ten hours a day; to the man of talent and action and industry, whose future is invested in that tranquillity and order of a state
in which talent and action and industry are a certain capital; why,
the great bankers had better encourage a theory to upset the system
of banking !   Whatever disturbs society, yea, even by a causeless
panic, much more by an actual struggle, falls first upon the market of
labor, and thence affects prejudicially every department of intelligence.
In such times the arts are arrested, literature is neglected, people are
too busy to read anything save appeals to their passions.   And capital, shaken in its sense of security, no longer ventures boldly through
the land, calling forth all the energies of toil and enterprise, and extending to every workman his reward.   Now, Lenny, take this piece
of advice.   You are young, clever, and aspiring : men rarely succeed
in changing the world ; but a man seldom fails of success if he lets
the world alone, and resolves to make the best of it.   You are in the
midst of the great crisis of your life ; it is the struggle between the
new desires knowledge excites, and that sense of poverty, which those
desires convert either into hope and emulation or into envy and
·despair.   I grant that it is an up-hill work that lies before you ; but
don't you think it is always easier to climb a mountain than it is to level
it ?   These books call on you to level the mountain ; and that moun-

---

* UTOPIA. (See note, page 317.) This work, named from a king Utopus, written in Latin, was
published at Louvain in 1516. The first English edition, translated by Robynson, was published
in London in 1551. Bishop Burnet's translation appeared in 1684. Hallam says: "The *Republic*
of Plato no doubt furnished More with the germ of his perfect society: but it would be unreasonable to deny him the merit of having struck out the fiction of its real existence from his own fertile
imagination; and it is manifest that some of his most distinguished successors in the same walk
of romance, especially Swift, were largely indebted to his reasoning as well as inventive talents.
Those who read the *Utopia* in Burnet's translation may believe that they are in Brobdingnag; so
similar is the vein of satirical humor and easy language. If false and impracticable theories are
found in the *Utopia* (and, perhaps, he knew them to be such), this is in a much greater degree
true of the Platonic republic." In a note to a later edition of his *Literary History*, Hallam qualifies
the assertion that More borrowed the germ of his *Utopia* from Plato, and says, "Neither the *Republic* nor the *Laws* of Plato bear any resemblance to the *Utopia.*" Lord Bacon's treatise on the
same subject, *The New Atlantis, a Fragment*, was published in 1635, and Swift's *Gulliver's
Travels* in 1726 – 27.

† PHALANSTERY. An organized community of socialists.

tain is the property of other people, subdivided amongst a great many proprietors and protected by law. At the first stroke of the pickax it is ten to one but what you are taken up for a trespass. But the path up the mountain is a right of way uncontested. You may be safe at the summit before (even if the owners are fools enough to let you) you could have leveled a yard. It is more than two thousand years ago," quoth the doctor, "since poor Plato began to level it, and the mountain is as high as ever!"

Thus saying, Riccabocca came to the end of his pipe, and stalking thoughtfully away, left Leonard Fairfield trying to extract light from the smoke.

SURRENDER OF GRENADA.

DAY dawned upon Grenada, and the beams of the winter sun, smiling away the clouds of the past night, played cheerily upon the murmuring waves of the Xenil and the Darro. Alone, upon a balcony commanding a view of the beautiful landscape, stood Boabdil,* the last of the Moorish kings. He had sought to bring to his aid all the lessons of the philosophy he had so ardently cultivated.

"What are we," said the musing prince, "that we should fill the earth with ourselves, — we kings! Earth resounds with the crash of my falling throne; on the ear of races unborn the echo will live prolonged. But what have I lost? Nothing that was necessary to my happiness, my repose; nothing save the source of all my wretchedness, the Marah of my life! Shall I less enjoy heaven and earth, or thought and action, or man's more material luxuries of food and sleep, — the common and cheap desires of all? At the worst, I sink but to a level with chiefs and princes; I am but leveled with those whom the multitude admire and envy. . . . . But it is time to depart." So saying, he descended to the court, flung himself on his barb, and, with a small and saddened train passed through the gate which we yet survey, by a blackened and crumbling tower, overgrown with vines and ivy; thence, amid gardens, now appertaining to the convent of the victor faith, he took his mournful and unnoticed way.

When he came to the middle of the hill that rises above those gar-

---

* BOABDIL. The last Moorish king of Granada. Ferdinand of Aragon dethroned him, 1491. Boabdil returned to Africa, and died about 1536. For nearly eight centuries the Moors had held possession of Granada, it being the last province of the Peninsula recovered by the Christians. The reader will find a delightful history of this romantic country and its perpetual wars in Irving's *Conquest of Granada*.

dens, the steel of the Spanish armor gleamed upon him, as the detachment sent to occupy the palace marched over the summit in steady
order and profound silence.   At the head of the vanguard rode, upon
a snow-white palfrey, the Bishop of Avila, followed by a long train of
barefooted monks.   They halted as Boabdil approached, and the grave
bishop saluted him with the air of one who addresses an infidel and
an inferior.   With the quick sense of dignity common to the great,
and yet more to the fallen, Boabdil felt, but resented not the pride
of the ecclesiastic.   "Go, Christian," said he, mildly ; "the gates of
the Alhambra are open, and Allah has bestowed the palace and the
city upon your king.   May his virtues atone the faults of Boabdil ! "
So saying, and waiting no answer, he rode on, without looking to the
right or the left.   The Spaniards also pursued their way.

The sun had fairly risen above the mountains, when Boabdil and
his train beheld, from the eminence on which they were, the whole
armament of Spain ; and at the same moment, louder than the tramp
of horse or the clash of arms, was heard distinctly the solemn chant of
Te Deum, which preceded the blaze of the unfurled and lofty standards.
Boabdil, himself still silent, heard the groans and acclamations of his
train : he turned to cheer or chide them, and then saw, from his own
watch-tower, with the sun shining full upon its pure and dazzling
surface, the silver cross of Spain.   His Alhambra was already in the
hands of the foe ; while beside that badge of the holy war waved the
gay and flaunting flag of St. Jago, the canonized Mars of the chivalry
of Spain.   At that sight the king's voice died within him ; he gave the
rein to his barb, impatient to close the fatal ceremonial, and slackened
not his speed till almost within bow-shot of the first rank of the army.

Never had Christian war assumed a more splendid and imposing
aspect.   Far as the eye could reach extended the glittering and gorgeous lines of that goodly power, bristling with sun-lighted spears
and blazoned banners ; while beside murmured and glowed and
danced the silver and laughing Xenil, careless what lord should
possess, for his little day, the banks that bloomed by its everlasting
course.   By a small mosque halted the flower of the army.   Surrounded by the arch-priests of that mighty hierarchy, the peers and
princes of a court that rivaled the Roland of Charlemagne, was seen
the kingly form of Ferdinand himself, with Isabel at his right hand,
and the high-born dames of Spain, relieving, with their gay colors
and sparkling gems, the sterner splendor of the crested helmet and

polished mail. Within sight of the royal group, Boabdil halted, composed his aspect so as best to conceal his soul, and a little in advance of his scanty train, but never in mien and majesty more a king, the son of Abdallah met his haughty conqueror.

At the sight of his princely countenance and golden hair, his comely and commanding beauty, made more touching by youth, a thrill of compassionate admiration ran through that assembly of the brave and fair. Ferdinand and Isabel slowly advanced to meet their late rival, — their new subject; and as Boabdil would have dismounted, the Spanish king placed his hand upon his shoulder. "Brother and prince," said he, "forget thy sorrows; and may our friendship hereafter console thee for reverses against which thou hast contended as a hero and a king; resisting man, but resigned at length to God."

Boabdil did not affect to return this bitter but unintentional mockery of compliment. He bowed his head, and remained a moment silent; then motioning to his train, four of his officers approached, • and, kneeling beside Ferdinand, proffered to him, upon a silver buckler, the keys of the city. "O king!" then said Boabdil, "accept the keys of the last hold which has resisted the arms of Spain. The empire of the Moslem is no more. Thine are the city and the people of Grenada; yielding to thy prowess, they yet confide in thy mercy." "They do well," said the king; "our promises shall not be broken. But since we know the gallantry of Moorish cavaliers, not to us, but to gentler hands, shall the keys of Grenada be surrendered."

Thus saying, Ferdinand gave the keys to Isabel, who would have addressed some soothing flatteries to Boabdil, but the emotion and excitement were too much for her compassionate heart, heroine and queen though she was; and when she lifted her eyes upon the calm and pale features of the fallen monarch, the tears gushed from them irresistibly, and her voice died in murmurs. A faint flush overspread the features of Boabdil, and there was a momentary pause of embarrassment, which the Moor was the first to break.

"Fair queen," said he, with mournful and pathetic dignity, "thou canst read the heart that thy generous sympathy touches and subdues: this is my last, but not least glorious conquest. But I detain ye; let not my aspect cloud your triumph. Suffer me to say farewell." "Farewell, my brother," replied Ferdinand, "and may fair fortune go with you! Forget the past!" Boabdil smiled bitterly, saluted the royal pair with profound respect and silent reverence, and rode

slowly on, leaving the army below, as he ascended the path that led
to his new principality beyond the Alpuxarras.   As the trees snatched
the Moorish cavalcade from the view of the king, Ferdinand ordered
the army to recommence its march ; and trumpet and cymbal presently
sent their music to the ear of the Moslem.

Boabdil spurred on at full speed, till his panting charger halted at
the little village where his mother, his slaves, and his faithful wife,
Armine (sent on before), awaited him.   Joining these, he proceeded
without delay upon his melancholy path.   They ascended that eminence which is the pass into the Alpuxarras.   From its height, the
vale, the rivers, the spires, and the towers of Grenada broke gloriously
upon the view of the little band.   They halted mechanically and abruptly ; every eye was turned to the beloved scene.   The proud shame
of baffled warriors, the tender memories of home, of childhood, of
fatherland, swelled every heart, and gushed from every eye.

Suddenly the distant boom of artillery broke from the citadel, and
rolled along the sun-lighted valley and crystal river.   A universal
wail burst from the exiles ; it smote, it overpowered the heart of the
ill-starred king, in vain seeking to wrap himself in Eastern pride or
stoical philosophy.   The tears gushed from his eyes, and he covered
his face with his hands.   The band wound slowly on through the
solitary defiles ; and that place, where the king wept at the last view
of his lost empire, is still called THE LAST SIGH OF THE MOOR.

CLAUDE MELNOTTE'S APOLOGY AND DEFENSE.*

PAULINE, by pride ·
Angels have fallen ere thy time ; by pride, —
That sole alloy of thy most lovely mould, —
The evil spirit of a bitter love
And a revengeful heart, had power upon thee.
From my first years my soul was filled with thee ;
I saw thee midst the flowers the lowly boy
Tended, unmarked by thee, — a spirit of bloom,
And joy and freshness, as spring itself
Were made a living thing, and wore thy shape !
I saw thee, and the passionate heart of man
Entered the breast of the wild-dreaming boy ;

* The extract is from the play, *The Lady of Lyons*.

And from that hour I grew — what to the last
I shall be — thine adorer! Well, this love,
Vain, frantic, — guilty, if thou wilt, — became
A fountain of ambition and bright hope;
I thought of tales that by the winter hearth
Old gossips tell, — how maidens sprung from kings
Have stooped from their high sphere; how Love, like Death,
Levels all ranks, and lays the shepherd's crook
Beside the scepter. Thus I made my home
In the soft palace of a fairy Future!
My father died; and I, the peasant-born,
Was my own lord. Then did I seek to rise
Out of the prison of my mean estate;
And, with such jewels as the exploring mind
Brings from the caves of Knowledge, buy my ransom
From those twin jailers of the daring heart, —
Low birth and iron fortune. Thy bright image,
Glassed in my soul, took all the hues of glory,
And lured me on to those inspiring toils
By which man masters men! For thee, I grew
A midnight student o'er the dreams of sages!
For thee, I sought to borrow from each Grace
And every Muse such attributes as lend
Ideal charms to Love. I thought of thee,
And passion taught me poesy, — of thee,
And on the painter's canvas grew the life
Of beauty! — Art became the shadow
Of the dear starlight of thy haunting eyes!
Men called me vain, — some, mad, — I heeded not;
But still toiled on, hoped on, — for it was sweet,
If not to win, to feel more worthy, thee!

At last, in one mad hour, I dared to pour
The thoughts that burst their channels into song,
And sent them to thee, — such a tribute, lady,
As beauty rarely scorns, even from the meanest.
The name — appended by the burning heart
That longed to show its idol what bright things
It had created — yea, the enthusiast's name,

8

That should have been thy triumph, was thy scorn!
That very hour — when passion, turned to wrath,
Resembled hatred most; when thy disdain
Made my whole soul a chaos — in that hour
The tempters found me a revengeful tool
For their revenge! Thou hadst trampled on the worm, —
It turned, and stung thee!

A LOVER'S DREAM OF HOME.

NAY, dearest, nay, if thou wouldst have me paint
The home to which, could love fulfil its prayer,
This hand would lead thee, listen : a deep vale,
Shut out by Alpine hills from the rude world,
Near a clear lake,* margined by fruits of gold
And whispering myrtles; glassing softest skies
As cloudless, save with rare and roseate shadows,
As I would have thy fate!
A palace lifting to eternal summer
Its marble walls, from out a glossy bower
Of coolest foliage musical with birds,
Whose songs should syllable thy name! At noon
We'd sit beneath the arching vines, and wonder
Why Earth could be unhappy, while the Heaven
Still left us youth and love; we'd have no friends
That were not lovers; no ambition, save
To excel them all in love; we'd read no books
That were not tales of love, — that we might smile
To think how poorly eloquence of words
Translates the poetry of hearts like ours!
And when night came, amidst the breathless heavens
We'd guess what star should be our home when love
Becomes immortal; while the perfumed light
Stole through the mists of alabaster lamps,
And every air was heavy with the sighs
Of orange groves and music from sweet lutes,
And murmurs of low fountains that gush forth
I' the midst of roses! Dost thou like the picture?

* Lake Como.

DISRAELI.

1805 - 1881.

BENJAMIN DISRAELI, eminent in literature and politics, was born in London in 1805. He is the son of Isaac Disraeli, author of several unique and valuable books, *The Curiosities of Literature, The Calamities of Authors*, etc. Benjamin produced his first book, *Vivian Grey*, a novel of extraordinary merit, in his twenty-first year. After several defeats he was elected to Parliament for the Borough of Maidstone, in 1837, and since that time, when not in high office, has been an active member of the House of Commons. He has three times been Chancellor of the Exchequer, was Prime Minister in 1868, and in February, 1874, on the dissolution of Gladstone's Ministry, was called by the Queen to form a new Cabinet. His literary efforts have been mainly in the line of fiction, and several of his novels rank among the best of the century. Of these may be mentioned *The Young Duke, Contarini Fleming, Coningsby, The Wondrous Tale of Alroy*, and his latest production, *Lothair*, which profoundly stirred the literary and political circles of British society. Although Disraeli will be remembered as a statesman rather than as an author, he has shown that he possesses abilities which entitle him to a high place in English literature. In descriptive power, he is hardly surpassed by any living writer, and in the exposition of politics, social theories, and the illustration of real public life by means of fictitious personages and incidents, he is without a rival. He is of Jewish descent. Our first extract, taken from *Coningsby*, is one of the finest tributes ever paid to the Hebrew character, and has special weight and significance as coming from his hand.

THE HEBREW RACE.

You never observe a great intellectual movement in Europe in which the Jews do not greatly participate. The first Jesuits were Jews; that mysterious Russian diplomacy which so alarms Western Europe is organized and principally carried on by Jews; that mighty revolution which is at this moment preparing in Germany, and which will be, in fact, a second and greater Reformation, and of which so little is as yet known in England, is entirely developing under the auspices of Jews, who almost monopolize the professorial chairs of Germany. Neander, the founder of spiritual Christianity, and who is Regius Professor of Divinity in the University of Berlin, is a Jew. Benary, equally famous and in the same University, is a Jew. Wehl, the Arabic professor of Heidelberg, is a Jew. Years ago, when I was in Palestine, I met a German student who was accumulating materials for the history of Christianity, and studying the genius of the place; a modest and learned man. It was Wehl; then unknown, since become the first Arabic scholar of the day, and the author of the life of Mohammed. But for the German professors of this race, their name is Legion. I think there are more than ten at Berlin alone.

I told you just now that I was going up to town to-morrow, because I always made it a rule to interpose when affairs of state were on the carpet. Otherwise, I never interfere. I hear of peace and war in newspapers, but I am never alarmed, except when I am informed that the sovereigns want treasure; then I know that monarchs are serious. A few years back we were applied to by Russia. Now, there has been no friendship between the court of St. Petersburg and my family. It has Dutch connections which have generally supplied it, and our representations in favor of the Polish Hebrews — a numerous race, but the most suffering and degraded of all the tribes — have not been very agreeable to the czar. However, circumstances drew to an approximation between the Romanoffs and the Sidonias. I resolved to go myself to St. Petersburg. I had on my arrival an interview with the Russian Minister of Finance, Count Cancrin; I beheld the son of a Lithuanian Jew. The loan was connected with the affairs of Spain; I resolved on repairing to Spain from Russia. I traveled without intermission. I had an audience immediately on my arrival with the Spanish minister, Señor Mendizabel; I beheld one like myself, a Jew of Aragon.

In consequence of what transpired at Madrid, I went straight to Paris, to consult the President of the French Council; I beheld the son of a French Jew, a hero, an imperial marshal, and very properly so, for who should be military heroes if not those who worship the Lord of Hosts? "And is Soult a Hebrew?" "Yes, and several of the French marshals, and the most famous; Massena, for example, — his real name was Manasseh." But to my anecdote. The consequence of our consultations was, that some Northern power should be applied to in a friendly and mediative capacity. We fixed on Prussia, and the President of the Council made an application to the Prussian Minister, who attended a few days after our conference. Count Arnim entered the cabinet, and I beheld a Prussian Jew. So you see, my dear Coningsby, that the world is governed by very different personages to what is imagined by those who are not behind the scenes. Favored by nature and by nature's God, we produced the lyre of David; we gave you Isaiah and Ezekiel; they are our Olynthiacs, our Philippics. Favored by nature we still remain; but in exact proportion as we have been favored by nature we have been persecuted by man. After a thousand struggles, — after acts of heroic courage that Rome has never equaled, — deeds of divine patriotism

that Athens and Sparta and Carthage have never excelled, — we have
endured fifteen hundred years of supernatural slavery; during which
every device that can degrade or destroy man has been the destiny
that we have sustained and baffled.

The Hebrew child has entered adolescence only to learn that he
was the Pariah of that ungrateful Europe that owes to him the best
part of its laws, a fine portion of its literature, all its religion. Great
poets require a public; we have been content with the immortal
melodies that we sung more than two thousand years ago by the
waters of Babylon and wept. They record our triumphs; they solace
our affliction. Great orators are the creatures of popular assemblies;
we were permitted only by stealth to meet even in our temples. And
as for great writers, the catalogue is not blank. What are all the
schoolmen, Aquinas himself, to Maimonides? * and as for modern
philosophy, all springs from Spinoza! † But the passionate and
creative genius that is the nearest link to divinity, and which no
human tyranny can destroy, though it can divert it; that should have
stirred the hearts of nations by its inspired sympathy, or governed
senates by its burning eloquence, has found a medium for its expression, to which, in spite of your prejudices and your evil passions,
you have been obliged to bow.

The ear, the voice, the fancy teeming with combinations, — the imagination fervent with picture and emotion, that came from Caucasus,
and which we have preserved unpolluted, — have endowed us with
almost the exclusive privilege of music; that science of harmonious
sounds which the ancients recognized as most divine, and deified in
the person of their most beautiful creation. I speak not of the past;
though were I to enter into the history of the lords of melody, you
would find it the annals of Hebrew genius. But at this moment,
even, musical Europe is ours. There is not a company of singers, not
an orchestra in a single capital, that are not crowded with our children, under the feigned names which they adopt to conciliate the dark
aversion which your posterity will some day disclaim with shame and

---

* MAIMONIDES. A Jewish Rabbi and philosopher of great celebrity, born in Spain about
1135. He acquired a great reputation for sagacity and learning.

† SPINOZA. A celebrated pantheistical philosopher born of Jewish parents in Holland, in 1632.
At an early age he announced opinions which were considered heretical and for which he was
excommunicated by the Jews. He passed his life as a solitary recluse, his character being, according to an eminent writer, "one of the most devout on record, for his life was, in a manner,
one unbroken hymn." See Froude's *Short Studies on Great Subjects.*

disgust.   Almost every great composer, skilled musician, almost every
voice that ravishes you with its transporting strains, spring from our
tribes.   The catalogue is too vast to enumerate; too illustrious to
dwell for a moment on secondary names, however eminent.   Enough
for us that the three great creative minds to whose exquisite inventions
all nations at this moment yield — Rossini, Meyerbeer, Mendelssohn,
— are of Hebrew race; and little do your men of fashion, your "Mus-
cadins" of Paris and your dandies of London, as they thrill into raptures at the notes of a Pasta or a Grisi, — little do they suspect that
they are offering homage to the sweet singers of Israel.

ON THE DEATH OF THE DUKE OF WELLINGTON.*

THE House of Commons is called upon to-night to fulfil a sorrowful, but a noble, duty.   It has to recognize, in the face of the
country, and of the civilized world, the loss of the most illustrious of
our citizens, and to offer to the ashes of the great departed the solemn
anguish of a bereaved nation.   The princely personage who has left
us was born in an age more fertile of great events than any period of
recorded time.   Of those vast incidents the most conspicuous were
his own deeds, and these were performed with the smallest means,
and in defiance of the greatest obstacles.   He was, therefore, not only
a great man, but the greatest man of a great age. · Amid the chaos
and conflagration which attended the end of the last century there rose
one of those beings who seem born to master mankind.   It is not
too much to say that Napoleon combined the imperial ardor of Alexander with the strategy of Hannibal.   The kings of the earth fell
before his fiery and subtile genius, and at the head of all the powers of
Europe he denounced destruction to the only land which dared to be
free.   The Providential superintendence of this world seems seldom
more manifest than in the dispensation which ordained that the French
Emperor and Wellesley should be born in the same year; that in the
same year they should have embraced the same profession; and that,
natives of distant islands, they should both have sought their military
education in that illustrious land which each in his turn was destined

---

* The extract is from a speech on the death of the Duke of Wellington delivered by Mr. Disraeli in the House of Commons while Chancellor of the Exchequer. Wellington was the greatest
general England ever produced. His most famous victory was gained over Napoleon at the
historic battle of Waterloo. He was born in Ireland in 1769 and died in 1852.

to subjugate. During the long struggle for our freedom, our glory, I may say our existence, Wellesley fought and won fifteen pitched battles, all of the highest class, — concluding with one of those crowning victories which give a color and aspect to history. During this period that can be said of him which can be said of no other captain, — that he captured three thousand cannon from the enemy, and never lost a single gun. The greatness of his exploits was only equaled by the difficulties he overcame. He had to encounter at the same time a feeble government, a factious opposition, and a distrustful people, scandalous allies, and the most powerful enemy in the world. He gained victories with starving troops, and carried on sieges without tools; and, as if to complete the fatality which in this sense always awaited him, when he had succeeded in creating an army worthy of Roman legions, and of himself, this invincible host was broken up on the eve of the greatest conjuncture of his life, and he entered the field of Waterloo with raw levies, and discomfited allies.

But the star of Wellesley never paled. He has been called fortunate, for fortune is a divinity that ever favors those who are alike s gacious and intrepid, inventive and patient. It was his character that created his career. This alike achieved his exploits and guarded him from vicissitudes. It was his sublime self-control that regulated his lofty fate. It has been the fashion of late years to disparage the military character. Forty years of peace have hardly qualified us to be aware how considerable and how complex are the qualities which are necessary for the formation of a great general. It is not enough to say that he must be an engineer, a geographer, learned in human nature, adroit in managing mankind; that he must be able to perform the highest duties of a minister of state, and sink to the humblest offices of a commissary and a clerk; but he has to display all this knowledge, and he must do all these things at the same time, and under extraordinary circumstances. At the same moment he must think of the eve and the morrow, — of his flanks and of his reserves; he must carry with him ammunition, provisions, hospitals; he must calculate at the same time the state of the weather and the moral qualities of man; and all these elements, which are perpetually changing, he must combine amid overwhelming cold or overpowering heat; sometimes amid famine, often amid the thunder of artillery. Behind all this, too, is the ever-present image of his country, and the dreadful alternative whether that country is to receive him with cypress or laurel. But all these conflicting ideas must be driven from the mind of the military leader, for he must think — and not only think — he must think with the rapidity of lightning, for on a moment, more or less, depends the fate of the finest combination, and on a moment, more or less, depends glory or shame. Doubtless, all this may be done in an ordinary manner, by an ordinary man; as we see every day of our lives ordinary men making successful ministers of state, successful speakers, successful authors. But to do all this with genius is sublime. Doubtless, to think deeply and clearly in the recess of a cabinet is a fine intellectual demonstration, but to think with equal depth and equal clearness amid bullets is the most complete exercise of the human faculties. Although the military career of the Duke of Wellington fills so large a space in history, it was only a comparatively small section of his prolonged and illustrious life. Only eight years elapsed from Vimiera to Waterloo, and from the date of his first commission to the last cannon-shot on the field of battle scarcely twenty years can be counted. After all his triumphs he was destined for another career, and if not in the prime, certainly in the perfection of manhood, he commenced a civil career scarcely less eminent than those military achievements which will live forever in history. Thrice was he the ambassador of his sovereign to those great historic congresses that settled the affairs of Europe; twice was he Secretary of State; twice was he Commander-in-Chief; and once he was Prime Minister of England. His labors for his country lasted to the end; and he died the active chieftain of that famous army to which he has left the tradition of his glory.

The Duke of Wellington left to his countrymen a great legacy, — greater even than his glory. He left them the contemplation of his character. I will not say his conduct revived the sense of duty in England. I would not say that of our country. But that his conduct inspired public life with a purer and more masculine tone I cannot doubt. His career rebukes restless vanity, and reprimands the irregular ebullitions of a morbid egotism. I doubt not that, among all orders of Englishmen, from those with the highest responsibilities of our society to those who perform the humblest duties, I dare say there is not a man who in his toil and his perplexity has not sometimes thought of the duke and found in his example support and solace.

Though he lived so much in the hearts and minds of his countrymen, — though he occupied such eminent posts and fulfilled such august duties, — it was not till he died that we felt what a space he filled in the feelings and thoughts of the people of England. Never was the influence of real greatness more completely asserted than on his decease. In an age whose boast of intellectual equality flatters all our self-complacencies, the world suddenly acknowledged that it had lost the greatest of men; in an age of utility the most industrious and common-sense people in the world could find no vent for their woe and no representative for their sorrow but the solemnity of a pageant; and we — we who have met here for such different purposes — to investigate the sources of the wealth of nations, to enter into statistical research, and to encounter each other in fiscal controversy — we present to the world the most sublime and touching spectacle that human circumstances can well produce, — the spectacle of a Senate mourning a Hero !

THERE have been some, and those, too, among the wisest and the wittiest of the northern and western races, who, touched by a presumptuous jealousy of the long predominance of that Oriental intellect to which they owed their civilization, would have persuaded themselves and the world that the traditions of Sinai and Calvary were fables. Half a century ago Europe made a violent and apparently successful effort to disembarrass itself of its Asian faith. The most powerful and the most civilized of its kingdoms,* about to conquer the rest, shut up its churches, desecrated its altars, massacred and persecuted their sacred servants, and announced that the Hebrew creeds which Simon Peter brought from Palestine, and which his successors revealed to Clovis, were a mockery and a fiction. What has been the result? In every city, town, village, and hamlet of that great kingdom, the divine image of the most illustrious of Hebrews has been again raised amid the homage of kneeling millions; while, in the heart of its bright and witty capital, the nation has erected the most gorgeous of modern temples,† and consecrated its marble and golden walls to the name, and memory, and celestial efficacy of a Hebrew woman.

* FRANCE. When the celebrated French Revolution was at its height, the rulers and their followers, for the time being, repudiated the Christian religion, and set up Paganism in its stead. The Communists, while they held possession of Paris, during the recent Franco-German War, did much the same thing, but it was shorter lived.
† The Church of the Madeleine in Paris.

MAURY.

1806–1873.

MATTHEW FONTAINE MAURY, an eminent astronomer and hydrographer, was born in Spottsylvania County, Virginia, in 1806, and entered the United States Navy in 1825. He devoted himself assiduously to the duties of his profession, and in 1835 published a *Treatise on Navigation*, which was adopted as a text-book in the Navy. An accident having rendered him incapable of performing sea-service, he devoted himself to scientific and literary work, writing extensively on such subjects as the *Gulf Stream, National Defenses, Overland Communication with the Pacific,* etc. To his foresight and influence are due the expeditions for exploring the Amazon and the Rio de la Plata. Under his direction the National Observatory speedily assumed an equal rank with the best similar institutions in the world. Lieutenant Maury's labors in the department of Hydrography give him a title to lasting and honorable fame. His wind and current charts and the accompanying book of *Sailing Directions* must be regarded as the most important work of the century in its bearing on navigation. In 1854 Mr. Maury visited Europe and excited attention by his inquiry into the ocean current, local winds, etc. In illustration of these subjects he published his celebrated *Physical Geography of the Sea*, with charts and diagrams, which has been translated into several languages. Both of our extracts are from this work.

THE GULF STREAM.

THERE is a river in the ocean. In the severest droughts it never fails, and in the mightiest floods it never overflows. Its banks and its bottom are of cold water, while its current is of warm. The Gulf of Mexico is its fountain, and its mouth is in the Arctic Seas. It is the Gulf Stream. There is in the world no other such majestic flow of waters. Its current is more rapid than the Mississippi or the Amazon, and its volume more than a thousand times greater.

The currents of the ocean are among the most important of its movements. They carry on a constant interchange between the waters of the poles and those of the equator, and thus diminish the extremes of heat and cold in every zone.

The sea has its climates as well as the land. They both change with the latitude; but one varies with the elevation above, the other with the depression below, the sea level. The climates in each are regulated by circulation: but the regulators are, on the one hand, winds; on the other, currents.

The inhabitants of the ocean are as much the creatures of climate as are those of the dry land; for the same Almighty hand which decked the lily and cares for the sparrow fashioned also the pearl and feeds the great whale, and adapted each to the physical conditions by which his providence has surrounded it. Whether of the land or the sea, the inhabitants are all his creatures, subjects of his laws, and agents in his economy. The sea, therefore, we may safely infer, has its offices and duties to perform; so, may we infer, have its currents; and so, too, its inhabitants: consequently, he who undertakes to study its phenomena must cease to regard it as a waste of waters. He must look upon it as a part of that exquisite machinery by which the harmonies of nature are preserved, and then he will begin to perceive the developments of order and the evidences of design.

From the Arctic Seas a cold current flows along the coasts of America, to replace the warm water sent through the Gulf Stream to moderate the cold of Western and Northern Europe. Perhaps the best indication as to these cold currents may be derived from the fishes of the sea. The whales first pointed out the existence of the Gulf Stream by avoiding its warm waters. Along the coasts of the United States all those delicate animals and marine productions which delight in warmer waters are wanting; thus indicating, by their absence, the cold current from the north now known to exist there. In the genial warmth of the sea about the Bermudas on one hand, and Africa on the other, we find in great abundance those delicate shell-fish and coral formations which are altogether wanting in the same latitudes along the shores of South Carolina.

No part of the world affords a more difficult or dangerous navigation than the approaches of the northern coasts of the United States in winter. Before the warmth of the Gulf Stream was known, a voyage at this season from Europe to New England, New York, and even to the capes of the Delaware or Chesapeake, was many times more trying, difficult, and dangerous than it now is. In making this part of the coast vessels are frequently met by snow-storms and gales which mock the seaman's strength and set at naught his skill. In a little while his bark becomes a mass of ice; with her crew frosted and helpless, she remains obedient only to her helm, and is kept away for the Gulf Stream. After a few hours' run she reaches its edge, and almost at the next bound passes from the midst of winter into a sea at summer heat. Now the ice disappears from her apparel, and the sailor bathes his stiffened limbs in tepid waters. Feeling himself invigorated and refreshed with the genial warmth about him, he realizes out there at sea the fable of Antæus and his mother Earth. He rises up and attempts to make his port again, and is again, perhaps, as rudely met and beat back from the northwest; but each time that he is driven off from the contest, he comes forth from this stream, like the ancient son of Neptune, stronger and stronger, until, after many days, his freshened strength prevails, and he at last triumphs and enters his haven in safety, though in this contest he sometimes falls to rise no more.

The ocean currents are partly the result of the immense evaporation which takes place in the tropical regions, where the sea greatly exceeds the land in extent. The enormous quantity of water there carried off by evaporation disturbs the equilibrium of the seas; but this is restored by a perpetual flow of water from the poles. When these streams of cold water leave the poles they flow directly toward the equator; but, before proceeding far, their motion is deflected by the diurnal motion of the earth. At the poles they have no rotary motion, and although they gain it more and more in their progress to the equator, which revolves at the rate of a thousand miles an hour, they arrive at the tropics before they have gained the same velocity of rotation with the intertropical ocean. On that account they are left behind, and, consequently, flow in a direction contrary to the diurnal rotation of the earth. Hence the whole surface of the ocean for thirty degrees on each side of the equator flows in a stream or current three thousand miles broad from east to west. The trade winds, which constantly blow in one direction, combine to give this great Equatorial Current a mean velocity of ten or eleven miles in twenty-four hours.

Were it not for the land, such would be the uniform and constant flow of the waters of the ocean. The presence of the land interrupts the regularity of this great western movement of the waters, sending them to the north or south, according to its conformation.

The principal branch of the Equatorial Current of the Atlantic takes a northwesterly direction from off Cape St. Roque, in South America. It rushes along the coast of Brazil, and, after passing through the Caribbean Sea, and sweeping round the Gulf of Mexico, it flows between Florida and Cuba, and enters the North Atlantic under the name of the Gulf Stream, the most beautiful of all the oceanic currents.

In the Strait of Florida the Gulf Stream is thirty-two miles wide, two thousand two hundred feet deep, and flows at the rate of four miles an hour. Its waters are of the purest ultramarine blue as far as the coasts of Carolina; and so completely are they separated from the sea through which they flow, that a ship may be seen at times half in the one and half in the other.

As a rule, the hottest water of the Gulf Stream is at or near the surface; and as the deep-sea thermometer is sent down, it shows that these waters, though still much warmer than the water on either side at corresponding depths, gradually become less and less warm until the bottom of the current is reached. There is reason to believe that the warm waters of the Gulf Stream are nowhere permitted, in the oceanic economy, to touch the bottom of the sea. There is everywhere a cushion of cool water between them and the solid parts of the earth's crust. This arrangement is suggestive, and strikingly beautiful. One of the benign offices of the Gulf Stream is to convey heat from the Gulf of Mexico, — where otherwise it would become excessive, — and to dispense it in regions beyond the Atlantic, for the amelioration of the climates of the British Islands and of all Western Europe. Now, cold water is one of the best non-conductors of heat, but if the warm water of the Gulf Stream were sent across the Atlantic in contact with the solid crust of the earth, comparatively a good conductor of heat, instead of being sent across, as it is, in contact with a non-conducting cushion of cool water to fend it from the bottom, all its heat would be lost in the first part of the way, and the soft climates of both France and England would be as that of Labrador, severe in the extreme, and ice-bound.

It has been estimated that the quantity of heat discharged over the Atlantic from the waters of the Gulf Stream, in a winter's day, would be sufficient to raise the whole column of atmosphere that rests upon France and the British Islands from the freezing point to summer heat. /

Every west wind that blows crosses the stream on its way to Europe, and carries with it a portion of this heat to temper there the northern winds of winter. It is the influence of this stream that makes Erin the "Emerald Isle of the Sea," and that clothes the shores of Albion in evergreen robes; while, in the same latitude, the coasts of Labrador are fast bound in fetters of ice.

As the Gulf Stream proceeds on its course, it gradually increases in width. It flows along the coast of North America to Newfoundland, where it turns to the east, one branch setting towards the British Islands, and away to the coasts of Norway and the Arctic Ocean. Another branch reaches the Azores, from which it bends round to the

south, and, after running along the African coast, it rejoins the great
equatorial flow, leaving a vast space of nearly motionless water between the Azores, the Canaries, and Cape de Verd Islands.) This
great area is the Grassy or Sargasso Sea, covering a space many
times larger than the British Islands. It is so thickly matted over
with gulf weeds that the speed of vessels passing through it is often
much retarded. When the companions of Columbus saw it, they
thought it marked the limits of navigation, and became alarmed. To
the eye, at a little distance, it seems substantial enough to walk upon.
Patches of the weed are always to be seen floating along the outer
edge of the Gulf Stream. Now, if bits of cork or chaff, or any floating substance, be put into a basin, and a circular motion be given to
the water, all the light substances will be found crowding together
near the centre of the pool where there is the least motion. Just
such a basin is the Atlantic Ocean to the Gulf Stream; and the Sargasso Sea is the center of the whirl. Columbus first found this
weedy sea, in his voyage of discovery; there it has remained to this
day, moving up and down, and changing its position like the calms
of Cancer, according to the seasons, the storms, and the winds.
Exact observations as to its limits and their range, extending back for
fifty years, assure us that its mean position has not been altered since
that time.

THE AIR AND SEA.

WE have already said that the atmosphere forms a spherical shell,
surrounding the earth to a depth which is unknown to us, by reason
of its growing tenuity, as it is released from the pressure of its own
superincumbent mass. Its upper surface cannot be nearer to us than
fifty, and can scarcely be more remote than five hundred miles. It
surrounds us on all sides, yet we see it not; it presses on us with a
load of fifteen pounds on every square inch of surface of our bodies,
or from seventy to one hundred tons on us in all, yet we do not so
much as feel its weight. Softer than the finest down, more impalpable than the finest gossamer, it leaves the cobweb undisturbed, and
scarcely stirs the lightest flower that feeds on the dew it supplies; yet it
bears the fleets of nations on its wings around the world, and crushes
the most refractory substances with its weight. When in motion,
its force is sufficient to level with the earth the most stately forests
and stable buildings, to raise the waters of the ocean into ridges like

mountains, and dash the strongest ships to pieces like toys. It warms and cools by turns the earth and the living creatures that inhabit it. It draws up vapors from the sea and land, retains them dissolved in itself or suspended in cisterns of clouds, and throws them down again as rain or dew, when they are required. It bends the rays of the sun from their path to give us the aurora of the morning and twilight of evening ; it disperses and refracts their various tints to beautify the approach and the retreat of the orb of day. But for the atmosphere, sunshine would burst on us in a moment and fail us in the twinkling of an eye, removing us in an instant from midnight darkness to the blaze of noon. We should have no twilight to soften and beautify the landscape, no clouds to shade us from the scorching heat ; but the bald earth, as it revolved on its axis, would turn its tanned and weakened front to the full unmitigated rays of the lord of day.

The atmosphere affords the gas which vivifies and warms our frames ; it receives into itself that which has been polluted by use, and is thrown off as noxious. It feeds the flame of life exactly as it does that of the fire. It is in both cases consumed, in both cases it affords the food of consumption, and in both cases it becomes combined with charcoal, which requires it for combustion, and which removes it when combustion is over. It is the girdling, encircling air that makes the whole world kin. The carbonic acid with which body our breathing fills the air, to-morrow seeks its way round the world. The date-trees that grow round the falls of the Nile will drink it in by their leaves ; the cedars of Lebanon will take of it to add to their stature ; the cocoa-nuts of Tahiti will grow rapidly upon it ; and the palms and bananas of Japan will change it into flowers. The oxygen we are breathing was distilled for us some short time ago by the magnolias of the Susquehanna, and the great trees that skirt the Orinoco and the Amazon ; the giant rhododendrons of the Himalayas contributed to it, and the roses and myrtles of Cashmere, the cinnamon-tree of Ceylon, and the forest, older than the flood, that lies buried deep in the heart of Africa, far behind the Mountains of the Moon, gave it out. The rain we see descending was thawed for us out of the icebergs which have watched the Polar Star for ages, or it came from snows that rested on the summits of the Alps, but which the lotus lilies have soaked up from the Nile, and exhaled as vapor again into the ever-present air.

There are processes no less interesting going on in other parts of this magnificent field of research. Water is Nature's carrier: with its currents it conveys heat away from the torrid zone and ice from the frigid; or, bottling the caloric away in the vesicles of its vapor, it first makes it impalpable, and then conveys it, by unknown paths, to the most distant parts of the earth. The materials of which the coral builds the island and the sea-conch its shell are gathered by this restless leveler from mountains, rocks, and valleys in all latitudes. Some it washes down from the Mountains of the Moon, or out of the gold-fields of Australia, or from the mines of Potosi, others from the battle-fields of Europe, or from the marble-quarries of ancient Greece and Rome. These materials, thus collected and carried over falls or down rapids, are transported from river to sea, and delivered by the obedient waters to each insect and to every plant in the ocean at the right time and temperature, in proper form and in due quantity.

Treating the rocks less gently, it grinds them into dust, or pounds them into sand, or rolls and rubs them until they are fashioned into pebbles, rubble, or bowlders; the sand and shingle on the sea-shore are monuments of the abrading, triturating power of water. By water the soil has been brought down from the hills, and spread out into valleys, plains, and fields for man's use. Saving the rocks on which the everlasting hills are established, every thing on the surface of our planet seems to have been removed from its original foundation and lodged in its present place by water. Protean in shape, benignant in office, water, whether fresh or salt, solid, fluid, or gaseous, is marvelous in its powers.

It is one of the chief agents in the manifold workshops in which and by which the earth has been made a habitation fit for man.

WILLIS.

1806 – 1867.

Nathaniel Parker Willis was born in Portland, Maine, in January, 1806. He was the son of Nathaniel Willis, and the brother of Sarah Payson Willis (Fanny Fern). Graduating at Yale College in 1827, he at once entered upon a literary life. In 1829 he established the American Monthly Magazine, which, three years later, was merged in the New York Mirror, of which Mr. Willis became editor, in association with George P. Morris. He made several voyages to Europe, and was admitted to the best literary society of England. He died at Idlewild, his beautiful home on the Hudson River, January 20, 1867. His first volume of verse, called *Sketches*, was published in 1827. His first prose book, *Pencillings by the Way* (1835), attracted a good deal of notice in England, and a review of it, written by Captain Marryat, led to a duel between himself and Mr. Willis. Among the most notable of the twenty-seven volumes of prose and verse which bear his name, are *Letters from under a Bridge, Loiterings by the Way, People I Have Met*, and *Dashes at Life with a Free Pencil*. One of his latest works was *Paul Fane*, a novel, which did not enhance his reputation. Mr. Willis is best known in literature as a writer of sketches of society. He was at once a "society man" and a *littérateur*, and rejoiced in such opportunities of appearing in his twofold character as were afforded in such sketches, in the writing of which he displayed peculiar grace, ease, and admirable audacity. While the bulk of his writings is of a somewhat ephemeral character, he was sometimes moved by a loftier ambition, and produced matter of more substantial value. Specimens of this may be found in some of his notes of travel, — *A Health Trip to the Tropics*, and *A Summer Cruise in the Mediterranean*, and in several religious poems of marked dignity and beauty. These poems must be regarded as his best productions; and, indeed, few poets have equaled him in this poetical specialty. In *The Death of Absalom*, the dramatic harmony, the sober beauty of the descriptive passages, and the noble grief of David, combine with singular felicity to produce a powerful and enduring effect on the reader's mind. Mr. Willis's versatility was remarkable; but it is to be regretted that he lavished so much of his talent upon such frivolous subjects.

THE DEATH OF ABSALOM.

The waters slept. Night's silvery veil hung low
On Jordan's bosom, and the eddies curled
Their glassy rings beneath it, like the still,
Unbroken beating of the sleeper's pulse.
The reeds bent down the stream; the willow leaves,
With a soft cheek upon the lulling tide,
Forgot the lifting winds; and the long stems,
Whose flowers the water, like a gentle nurse,
Bears on its bosom, quietly gave way,
And leaned, in graceful attitudes, to rest.
How strikingly the course of nature tells,
By its light heed of human suffering,
That it was fashioned for a happier world!

King David's limbs were weary. He had fled
From far Jerusalem; and now he stood,
With his faint people, for a little rest
Upon the shores of Jordan. The light wind
Of morn was stirring, and he bared his brow
To its refreshing breath; for he had worn
The mourner's covering, and he had not felt
That he could see his people until now.
They gathered round him on the fresh green bank,
And spoke their kindly words; and, as the sun
Rose up in heaven, he knelt among them there,
And bowed his head upon his hands to pray.
Oh! when the heart is full, — when bitter thoughts
Come crowding thickly up for utterance,
And the poor common words of courtesy
Are such an empty mockery, — how much
The bursting heart may pour itself in prayer!
He prayed for Israel, — and his voice went up
Strongly and fervently. He prayed for those
Whose love had been his shield, — and his deep tones
Grew tremulous. But, oh! for Absalom, —
For his estranged, misguided Absalom, —
The proud, bright being, who had burst away
In all his princely beauty, to defy
The heart that cherished him, — for him he poured,
In agony that would not be controlled,
Strong supplication, and forgave him there,
Before his God, for his deep sinfulness.

   . . . . .

The pall was settled. He who slept beneath
Was straightened for the grave; and, as the folds
Sank to the still proportions, they betrayed
The matchless symmetry of Absalom.
His hair was yet unshorn, and silken curls
Were floating round the tassels as they swayed
To the admitted air, as glossy now
As when, in hours of gentle dalliance, bathing
The snowy fingers of Judæa's daughters.
His helm was at his feet; his banner, soiled

With trailing through Jerusalem, was laid,
Reversed, beside him ; and the jeweled hilt,
Whose diamonds lit the passage of his blade,
Rested, like mockery, on his covered brow.
The soldiers of the king trod to and fro,
Clad in the garb of battle ; and their chief,
The mighty Joab, stood beside the bier,
And gazed upon the dark pall steadfastly,
As if he feared the slumberer might stir.
A slow step startled him.   He grasped his blade
As if a trumpet rang ; but the bent form
Of David entered, and he gave command,
In a low tone, to his few followers,
And left him with his dead.   The king stood still
Till the last echo died ; then, throwing off
The sackcloth from his brow, and laying back
The pall from the still features of his child,
He bowed his head upon him, and broke forth
In the resistless eloquence of woe : —

" Alas ! my noble boy ! that thou shouldst die !
    Thou, who wert made so beautifully fair !
That death should settle in thy glorious eye,
    And leave his stillness in this clustering hair !
How could he mark thee for the silent tomb !
        My proud boy, Absalom !

" Cold is thy brow, my son ! and I am chill,
    As to my bosom I have tried to press thee !
How was I wont to feel my pulses thrill,
    Like a rich harp-string, yearning to caress thee,
And hear thy sweet ' *My father !* ' from these dumb
        And cold lips, Absalom !

" But death is on thee.   I shall hear the gush
    Of music, and the voices of the young ;
And life will pass me in the mantling blush,
    And the dark tresses to the soft winds flung ;
But thou no more, with thy sweet voice, shalt come
        To meet me, Absalom !

" And oh ! when I am stricken, and my heart,
　　Like a bruised reed, is waiting to be broken,
How will its love for thee, as I depart,
　　Yearn for thine ear to drink its last deep token !
It were so sweet, amid death's gathering gloom,
　　　　To see thee, Absalom !

" And now, farewell !　'T is hard to give thee up,
　　With death so like a gentle slumber on thee ; —
And thy dark sin ! — Oh ! I could drink the cup,
　　If from this woe its bitterness had won thee.
May God have called thee, like a wanderer, home,
　　. My lost boy, Absalom ! "

He covered up his face, and bowed himself
A moment on his child : then, giving him
A look of melting tenderness, he clasped
His hands convulsively, as if in prayer ;
And, as if strength were given him of God,
He rose up calmly, and composed the pall
Firmly and decently — and left him there —
As if his rest had been a breathing sleep.

THE BELFRY PIGEON.

On the cross-beam under the Old South bell
The nest of a pigeon is builded well.
In summer and winter that bird is there,
Out and in with the morning air ;
I love to see him track the street,
With his wary eye and active feet ;
And I often watch him as he springs,
Circling the steeple with easy wings,
Till across the dial his shade has passed,
And the belfry edge is gained at last ;
'T is a bird I love, with its brooding note,
And the trembling throb in its mottled throat ;
There 's a human look in its swelling breast,
And the gentle curve of its lowly crest ;

And I often stop with the fear I feel, —
He runs so close to the rapid wheel.
    Whatever is rung on that noisy bell, —
Chime of the hour, or funeral knell, —
The dove in the belfry must hear it well.
When the tongue swings out to the midnight moon,
When the sexton cheerly rings for noon,
When the clock strikes clear at morning light,
When the child is waked with " nine at night,"
When the chimes play soft in the Sabbath air,
Filling the spirit with tones of prayer, —
Whatever tale in the bell is heard,
He broods on his folded feet unstirred,
Or, rising half in his rounded nest,
He takes the time to smooth his breast,
Then drops again, with filméd eyes,
And sleeps as the last vibration dies.
    Sweet bird ! I would that I could be
A hermit in the crowd like thee !
With wings to fly to wood and glen,
Thy lot, like mine, is cast with men ;
And daily, with unwilling feet,
I tread, like thee, the crowded street ;
But, unlike me, when day is o'er,
Thou canst dismiss the world and soar ;
Or, at a half-felt wish for rest,
Canst smooth the feathers on thy breast,
And drop, forgetful, to thy nest.
    I would that in such wings of gold
I could my weary heart upfold ;
I would I could look down unmoved
(Unloving as I am unloved),
And while the world throngs on beneath,
Smooth down my cares and calmly breathe ;
And never sad with others' sadness,
And never glad with others' gladness,
Listen, unstirred, to knell or chime,
And, lapped in quiet, bide my time.

SIMMS.

1806 - 1870.

WILLIAM GILMORE SIMMS was born in Charleston, South Carolina, in 1806, and died in 1870. He adopted the profession of the law, but, like Irving and many other *littérateurs*, abandoned it for the more congenial pursuits of literature. He published his first volume, *Lyrical and other Poems*, in 1827, and during the next twenty-seven years produced no less than thirteen additional volumes of verse. He labored in almost every department of literature, writing plays, histories, biographies, criticisms, and novels of various kinds. It is as a novelist that he is best known, and as such he will be regarded in the future. His best work in this specialty may be found in some of his historical romances, such as *The Yemassee*, *The Partisan*, and *Eutaw*. What Cooper did for the pioneer life of the Middle States was done by Simms for that of the South, the characteristic features of whose colonial and revolutionary history he has preserved in a series of spirited and faithfully colored narratives. He is a picturesque and vigorous writer, evidently inspired by his subject (i. e. in his historical romances), cherishing a generous pride in the annals of his native section and the chivalrous character of her people. Although his books have, to a great extent, been superseded, as have Cooper's, by novels which deal with later times, they are still widely read and admired. Taking into account the variety and amount of Mr. Simms's literary work, its distinctively American character, and the positive merit possessed by much of it, his name deserves to be cherished among those of the most honored representatives of our literature.

THE CHARM OF THE RATTLESNAKE.

How beautiful was the green and garniture of that little copse of wood! The leaves were thick, and the grass around lay folded over and over in bunches, with here and there a wild-flower gleaming from its green, and making of it a beautiful carpet of the richest and most beautiful texture. A small tree arose from the center of a clump around which a wild grape gadded luxuriantly; and with an incoherent sense of what she saw, the maiden lingered before the little cluster, seeming to survey that which, though it fixed her eye, failed to fill her thought. Her mind wandered, her soul was far away; and the objects in her vision were far other than those which occupied her imagination. Things grew indistinct beneath her eye. The eye rather slept than saw. The musing spirit had given holiday to the ordinary senses, and took no heed of the forms that rose, and floated or glided away before them.

In this way the leaf detached made no impression upon the sight that was yet bent upon it; she saw not the bird, though it whirled, untroubled by a fear, in wanton circles around her head; and the black snake, with the rapidity of the arrow, darted over her path without arousing a single terror in the form that otherwise would have shivered at its mere appearance. And yet, though thus indistinct were all things around her to the musing eye of the maiden, her eye was singularly fixed, — fastened, as it were, to a single spot, — gathered and controlled by a single object, and glazed apparently beneath a curious fascination.

Before the maiden rose a little clump of bushes, bright tangled leaves flaunting widely in glossiest green, with vines trailing over them, thickly decked with blue and crimson flowers. Her eye communed vacantly with these; fastened by a starlike shining glance, — a subtile ray that shot out from the circle of green leaves, — seeming to be their very eye, and sending out a lurid luster that seemed to stream across the space between, and find its way into her own eyes. Very piercing and beautiful was that subtile brightness, of the sweetest, strangest power.

And now the leaves quivered and seemed to float away, only to return, and the vines wavered and swung around in fantastic mazes, unfolding ever-changing varieties of form and color to her gaze; but the starlike eye was ever steadfast, bright, and gorgeous, gleaming in their midst, and still fastened in strange fondness upon her own. How beautiful, with wondrous intensity, did it gleam and dilate, growing larger and more lustrous with every ray which it sent forth. And her own glance became intense, fixed also; but with a dreaming sense, that conjured up the wildest fancies, terribly beautiful, that took her soul away from her, and wrapt it about as with a spell.

She would have fled; but she had not power to move. The will was wanting to her flight. She felt that she could have bent forward to pluck the gemlike thing from the bosom of the leaf in which it seemed to grow, and which it irradiated with its bright gleam; but even as she aimed to stretch forth her hand, and bend forward, she heard a rush of wings and a shrill scream from the tree above her, — such a scream as the mocking-bird makes, when angrily it raises its dusky crest, and flaps its wings furiously against its slender sides. Such a scream seemed like a warning, and, though yet unawakened to full consciousness, it startled her and forbade her effort.

More than once in her survey of this strange object had she heard that shrill note, and still had it carried to her ear the same note of warning, and to her mind the same vague consciousness of an evil presence. But the starlike eye was yet upon her own, — a small, bright eye, quick like that of a bird, now steady in its place, and observant seemingly only of hers, now darting forward with all the clustering leaves about it, and shooting up toward her as if wooing her to seize.   At another moment, riveted to the vine which lay around it, it would whirl round and round, dazzlingly bright and beautiful, even as a torch, waving hurriedly by night in the hands of some playful boy : but in all this time the glance was never taken from her own ; there it grew fixed, — a very principle of light; and such a light ! a subtile, burning, piercing, fascinating gleam, such as gathers in vapor above the old grave, and binds us as we look ; shooting, darting directly into her eye, dazzling her gaze, defeating its sense of discrimination, and confusing strangely that of perception.

She felt dizzy ; for, as she looked, a cloud of colors, bright, gay, various colors, floated and hung like so much drapery around the single object that had so secured her attention and spellbound her feet. Her limbs felt momently more and more insecure, her blood grew cold, and she seemed to feel the gradual freeze of vein by vein throughout her person.   At that moment a rustling was heard in the branches of the tree beside her, and the bird which had repeatedly uttered a single cry above her, as it were of warning, flew away from his station with a scream more piercing than ever.

This movement had the effect, for which it really seemed intended, of bringing back to her a portion of the consciousness she seemed to have been so totally deprived of before.   She strove to move from before the beautiful yet terrible presence, but for a while strove in vain. The rich starlike glance still riveted her own, and the subtile fascination kept her bound.

The mental energies, however, with the moment of their greatest trial, now gathered suddenly to her aid ; and with a desperate effort, but with a feeling still of most annoying uncertainty and dread, she succeeded partially in the attempt, and threw her arms backward, her hands grasping the neighboring tree, feeble, tottering, and depending upon it for that support which her own limbs almost entirely denied her.   With her movement, however, came the full development of the powerful spell and dreadful mystery before her.   As her feet receded, though but a single pace, to the tree against which she now rested, the audibly articulate ring, like that of a watch when wound up with the verge broken, announced the nature of that splendid yet dangerous presence, in the form of the monstrous rattlesnake, now but a few feet before her, lying coiled at the bottom of a beautiful shrub, with which, to her dreaming eye, many of its own glorious hues had become associated.

THE SHADED WATER.

WHEN that my mood is sad, and in the noise
    And bustle of the crowd I feel rebuke,
I turn my footsteps from its hollow joys
    And sit me down beside this little brook;
The waters have a music to mine ear
It glads me much to hear.

It is a quiet glen, as you may see,
    Shut in from all intrusion by the trees,
That spread their giant branches, broad and free,
    The silent growth of many centuries;
And make a hallowed time for hapless moods,
A Sabbath of the woods.

Few know its quiet shelter, — none, like me,
    Do seek it out with such a fond desire,
Poring in idlesse mood on flower and tree,
    And listening as the voiceless leaves respire, —
When the far-traveling breeze, done wandering,
Rests here his weary wing.

And all the day, with fancies ever new,
    And sweet companions from their boundless store,
Of merry elves bespangled all with dew,
    Fantastic creatures of the old-time lore,
Watching their wild but unobtrusive play,
I fling the hours away.

A gracious couch — the root of an old oak
    Whose branches yield it moss and canopy —
Is mine, and, so it be from woodman's stroke
    Secure, shall never be resigned by me;
It hangs above the stream that idly flies,
Heedless of any eyes.

9   M

There, with eye sometimes shut, but upward bent,
   Sweetly I muse through many a quiet hour,
While every sense on earnest mission sent,
   Returns, thought-laden, back with bloom and flower;
Pursuing, though rebuked by those who moil,
A profitable toil.

And still the waters trickling at my feet
   Wind on their way with gentlest melody,
Yielding sweet music, which the leaves repeat,
   Above them, to the gay breeze gliding by, —
Yet not so rudely as to send one sound
Through the thick copse around.

Sometimes a brighter cloud than all the rest
   Hangs o'er the archway opening through the trees,
Breaking the spell that, like a slumber, pressed
   On my worn spirit its sweet luxuries, —
And, with awakened vision upward bent,
I watch the firmament.

How like — its sure and undisturbed retreat,
   Life's sanctuary at last, secure from storm —
To the pure waters trickling at my feet,
   The bending trees that overshade my form!
So far as sweetest things of earth may seem
Like those of which we dream.

Such, to my mind, is the philosophy
   The young bird teaches, who, with sudden flight,
Sails far into the blue that spreads on high,
   Until I lose him from my straining sight, —
With a most lofty discontent to fly,
Upward, from earth to sky.

MRS. BROWNING.

1807 – 1861.

ELIZABETH BARRETT was born in Hertfordshire, England, in 1807, and died at Florence in 1861. Her marked precocity was encouraged by her admiring relatives, who greeted her juvenile feats in literature with unbounded commendation, and lavished upon her every educational advantage that wealth could procure. At the age of ten years she began to compose, and seven years later put forth her first volume, *An Essay on Mind, with other Poems.* Although possessing unquestionable merit, these juvenile productions did not warrant the expectation of such literary triumphs as she afterwards achieved. But they must be regarded as preliminary exercises, perhaps essential to the great and enduring work in which she was about to engage. This work is represented to the public by several volumes of poems, issued between 1838 and the year of her death, *The Seraphim, The Romaunt of the Page, The Drama of Exile,* etc. In 1846 Miss Barrett became the wife of Robert Browning, their marriage marking one of the most remarkable and felicitous unions on record. Although distinctively a poet, Mrs. Browning was not merely a poet. Her scholarship was extensive and accurate, and some of her critical papers on abstruse subjects entitle her to high rank as a writer of prose. For several years the poetical pair had their home in Italy, and Mrs. Browning, sympathizing ardently with the Italian heart in its struggles toward political independence, wrote many of her finest poems on Italian themes and inspired by Italian enthusiasm. Her last work of magnitude was *Aurora Leigh,* a long poem, in which she gave vehement, though somewhat mystical and obscure, expression to her very positive opinions as to the nature and mission of woman. Her literary faults are many and grave, the chief of them being intentional obscurity, affectation in style, and carelessness in details; but with the basic qualities of the poet she was grandly endowed, and her place in the front ranks of English singers is not likely to be questioned.

A DEAD ROSE.

O ROSE! who dares to name thee?
No longer roseate now, nor soft, nor sweet;
But barren, and hard, and dry as stubble-wheat,
    Kept seven years in a drawer, — thy titles shame thee.

The breeze that used to blow thee
Between the hedge-row thorns, and take away
An odor up the lane, to last all day, —
    If breathing now, — unsweetened would forego thee.

The sun that used to smite thee,
And mix his glory in thy gorgeous urn,
Till beam appeared to bloom and flower to burn, —
    If shining now, — with not a hue would light thee.

The dew that used to wet thee,
And, white first, grew incarnadined, because

It lay upon thee where the crimson was, —
  If dropping now, — would darken where it met thee.

The fly that lit upon thee,
To stretch the tendrils of its tiny feet
Along the leaf's pure edges after heat, —
  If lighting now, — would coldly overrun thee.

The bee that once did suck thee,
And build thy perfumed ambers up his hive,
And swoon in thee for joy, till scarce alive, —
  If passing now, — would blindly overlook thee.

The heart doth recognize thee,
Alone, alone! The heart doth smell thee sweet,
Doth view thee fair, doth judge thee most complete, —
  Though seeing now those changes that disguise thee.

Yes, and the heart doth owe thee
More love, dead rose! than to such roses bold
As Julia wears at dances, smiling cold ! —
  Lie still upon this heart, which breaks below thee !

SLEEP.

Of all the thoughts of God that are
Borne inward unto souls afar,
Along the Psalmist's music deep,
Now tell me if that any is
For gift or grace surpassing this, —
" He giveth his beloved sleep " ?

What would we give to our beloved ?
The hero's heart, to be unmoved, —
The poet's star-tuned harp, to sweep, —
The patriot's voice, to teach and rouse, —
The monarch's crown, to light the brows ?
" He giveth his beloved sleep."

What do we give to our beloved?
A little faith, all undisproved, —
A little dust to overweep, —
And bitter memories, to make
The whole earth blasted for our sake;
" He giveth his beloved sleep."

" Sleep soft, beloved!" we sometimes say,
But have no tune to charm away
Sad dreams that through the eyelids creep;
But never doleful dream again
Shall break the happy slumber when
" He giveth his beloved sleep."

O earth, so full of dreary noises!
O men, with wailing in your voices!
O delvéd gold the wailers heap!
O strife, O curse, that o'er it fall!
God strikes a silence through you all,
And " giveth his beloved sleep."

His dews drop mutely on the hill,
His cloud above it saileth still,
Though on its slope men sow and reap;
More softly than the dew is shed,
Or cloud is floated overhead,
" He giveth his beloved sleep."

For me, my heart, that erst did go
Most like a tired child at a show,
That sees through tears the jugglers leap,
Would now its wearied vision close,
Would childlike on His love repose
Who " giveth his beloved sleep."

LOVE: A SONNET.

I THOUGHT once how Theocritus had sung
Of the sweet years, the dear and wished-for years,
Who each one, in a gracious hand, appears

To bear a gift for mortals, old and young;
And as I mused it in his antique tongue,
I saw a gradual vision through my tears,
The sweet sad years, the melancholy years,
Those of my own life, who by turns had flung
A shadow across me.   Straightway I was 'ware,
So weeping, how a mystic shape did move
Behind me, and drew me backwards by the hair,
And a voice said in mastery, while I strove,
"Guess now who holds thee?"   "Death," I said; but there
The silver answer rang, — "Not Death, but Love."

THE CRY OF THE CHILDREN.*

Do ye hear the children weeping, O my brothers,
    Ere the sorrow comes with years?
They are leaning their young heads against their mothers, —
    And *that* cannot stop their tears.
The young lambs are bleating in the meadows,
    The young birds are chirping in the nest,
The young fawns are playing with the shadows,
    The young flowers are blowing towards the west;
But the young, young children, O my brothers,
        They are weeping bitterly! —
They are weeping in the playtime of the others,
        In the country of the free.

And well may the children weep before you!
        They are weary ere they run;
They have never seen the sunshine, nor the glory
        Which is brighter than the sun:
They know the grief of man, without his wisdom;
        They sink in man's despair, without his calm, —
Are slaves, without the liberty in Christdom, —
        Are martyrs, by the pang without the palm, —
Are worn, as if with age, yet unretrievingly
        The blessings of its memory cannot keep, —
Are orphans of the earthly love and heavenly:
        Let them weep! let them weep!

* This extract is from a very pathetic poem on the factory children of England.

AGASSIZ.

1807–1873.

LOUIS JEAN RODOLPHE AGASSIZ, in whose death the nation has lost one of her most honored citizens, and Science one of her ablest representatives, was born in the canton of Vaud, Switzerland, in 1807. While still very young he became a zealous student of scientific subjects, and early gave promise of the eminence which he afterwards attained in that department of intellectual effort. For several years he occupied the chair of Natural History at Neufchâtel, and in the discharge of his duties and the prosecution of independent investigations commended himself to the attention and respect of leading scientists in all parts of Europe. He was the intimate and trusted friend of Cuvier, the great naturalist. He was urgently invited by several universities of the highest grade ; but he felt a powerful attraction towards the vigorous young Republic of the West, and when in 1847 there came a call to him from Harvard University, he instantly accepted it. The history of his work in the twenty-five years of his life in this country is too familiar to require a detailed statement; it is sufficient to say that for many years he was esteemed by universal consent the foremost *savant* in the United States and the peer of the greatest of the brotherhood in Europe. It should be added that the recent rapid growth of popular interest in science and the establishment and gratifying progress of many scientific institutions in this country are fairly attributable to his example and influence. Long before his emigration to America Agassiz had become a famous author, and had won an enviable fame in connection with the Glacial Theory, which he promulgated in 1837. During his residence here he was a frequent contributor to scientific periodicals, and produced several works of marked originality and permanent value. Conspicuous among these are *Methods of Study in Natural History* and *Geological Sketches*. In 1865 Professor Agassiz made a voyage to Brazil in the interests of science. The labors resulting from this enterprise, and his arduous efforts in behalf of the Museum of Comparative Zoölogy at Cambridge, proved too severe for his physical strength, and within the year just preceding his death it was evident to his friends that he was failing. Their forebodings were too soon realized, and near the close of his sixty-sixth year the great naturalist passed away. It is simple justice to his memory to add that he was no less conspicuous and admirable for the qualities of his heart than for the powers and stores of his mind. The first extract is from *A Journey in Brazil*, the joint work of Professor and Mrs. Agassiz ; the second is from *Geological Sketches*.

A COFFEE PLANTATION IN BRAZIL.

THE Fazenda da Fortaleza de Santa Anna lies at the foot of the Serra da Babylonia. The house itself forms a part of a succession of low white buildings, enclosing an oblong square divided into neat lots for the drying of coffee. This drying of the coffee in the immediate vicinity of the house, though a very general custom, must be an uncomfortable one ; for the drying-lots are laid in a dazzling white cement, from the glare of which, in this hot climate, the eye turns wearily away. Just behind the house, on the slope of the hill, is the orangery. I am never tired of these golden orchards, and this was one of especial beauty. The small, deep-colored tangerines, sometimes twenty or thirty in one cluster, the large, choice orange, "Laranja selecta," as it is called, often ten or twelve together in a single bunch, and bearing the branches to the ground with their weight, the paler "Limaô dôce," or sweet lemon, rather insipid, but greatly esteemed here for its cool, refreshing properties, — all these, with many others, make a mass of color in which gold, deep orange, and pale yellow blend wonderfully with the background of green. Beyond the house enclosure, on the opposite side of the road, are the gardens, with aviary and fish-ponds in the center. With these exceptions, all the property not forest is devoted to coffee, covering the hillsides for miles around. The seed is planted in nurseries especially prepared, where it undergoes its first year's growth. It is then transplanted to its permanent home, and begins to bear in about three years, the first crop being of course a very light one. From that time forward, under good care and with favorable soil, it will continue to bear, and even to yield two crops or more annually for thirty years in succession. At that time the shrubs and the soil are alike exhausted, and, according to the custom of the country, the fazendeiro cuts down the forest for a new plantation, completely abandoning his old one, without a thought of redeeming or fertilizing the exhausted land.

One of the long-sighted reforms undertaken by Mr. Lage is the manuring of all the old, deserted plantations on his estate; he has already a number of vigorous young plantations, which promise to be as good as if a virgin forest had been sacrificed to produce them. He wishes not only to preserve the wood on his own estate, and to show that agriculture need not be promoted at the expense of taste and beauty, but to remind his country people also, that, extensive as are the forests, they will not last forever, and that it will be necessary to emigrate before long to find new coffee-grounds, if the old ones are treated as worthless. Another of his reforms is that of the roads. The ordinary roads in the coffee plantations, like the mule-tracks all over the country, go straight up the sides of the hills between the lines of shrubs, and besides being gullied by every rain, they form so steep an ascent that even with eight or ten oxen it is often impossible to drive the clumsy, old-fashioned carts up the slope, and the negroes are obliged to bring a great part of the harvest down on their heads. On Senhor Lage's estate all these old roads are abandoned, except where they are planted here and there with alleys of orange-trees for the use of the negroes; and he has substituted for them winding roads in the side of the hill with a very gradual ascent, so that light carts drawn by a single mule can transport all the harvest from the summit of the plantation to the drying-ground.

It was the harvesting season, and the spectacle was a pretty one. The negroes, men and women, were scattered about the plantations with broad, shallow trays, made of plaited grass or bamboo, strapped over their shoulders and supported at their waists ; into these they were gathering the coffee ; some of the berries being brilliantly red, some already beginning to dry and turn brown, while here and there was a green one not yet quite ripe, but soon to ripen in the scorching sun. Little black children were sitting on the ground and gathering what fell under the bushes, singing at their work a monotonous but rather pretty snatch of song, in which some took the first and others the second, making a not inharmonious music. As their baskets were filled they came to the Administrador to receive a little metal ticket on which the amount of their work was marked.

A task is allotted to each one, — so much to a full-grown man, so much to a woman with young children, so much to a child, — and each one is paid for whatever he may do over and above it. The requisition is a very moderate one, so that the industrious have an opportunity of earning a little money independently. At night they all present their tickets and are paid on the spot, for any extra work. From the harvesting-ground we followed the carts down to the place where their burden is deposited. On their return from the plantation the negroes divide the day's harvest, and dispose it in little mounds on the drying-ground. When pretty equally dried, the coffee is spread out in thin even layers over the whole enclosure, where it is baked for the last time. It is then hulled by a very simple machine in use on almost all the fazendas, and the process is complete.

Yesterday we succeeded in obtaining living specimens of the insect so injurious to the coffee-tree, the larva of a little moth akin to those which destroy the vineyards in Europe, and among them was one just spinning his cocoon on the leaf. We watched him for a long time with the lens as he wove his filmy tent. He had arched the threads upwards in the center, so as to leave a little hollow space into which he could withdraw ; this tiny vault seemed to be completed at the moment we saw him, and he was drawing threads forward and fastening them at a short distance beyond, thus lashing his house to the leaf, as it were. The exquisite accuracy of the work was amazing. He was spinning the thread with his mouth, and with every new stitch he turned his body backward, attached his thread to the same spot, then drew it forward and fastened it exactly on a line with the last, with a precision and rapidity that machinery could hardly imitate.

It is a curious question how far this perfection of workmanship in many of the lower animals is simply identical with their organization, and therefore to be considered a function, as inevitable in its action as digestion or respiration, rather than an instinct. In this case the body of the little animal was his measure : it was amazing to see him lay down his threads with such accuracy, till one remembered that he could not make them longer or shorter ; for, starting from the center of his house, and stretching his body its full length, they must always reach the same point. The same is true of the so-called mathematics of the bee. The bees stand as close as they can together in their hive for economy of space, and each one deposits his wax around him, his own form and size being the mould for the cells, the regularity of which when completed excites so much wonder and admiration. The mathematical secret of the bee is to be found in his structure, not in his instinct. But in the industrial work of some of the lower animals, the ant for instance, there is a power of adaptation which is not susceptible of the same explanation. Their social organization, too intelligent, it seems, to be the work of any reasoning powers of their own, yet does not appear to be directly connected with their structure. While we were watching our little insect, a breath stirred the leaf and he instantly contracted himself and drew back under his roof, but presently came out again and returned to his work.

AMERICA THE OLD WORLD.

First-born among the Continents, though so much later in culture and civilization than some of more recent birth, America, so far as her physical history is concerned, has been falsely denominated the *New World*. Hers was the first dry land lifted out of the waters, hers the first shore washed by the ocean that enveloped all the earth beside ; and while Europe was represented only by islands rising here and there above the sea, America already stretched an unbroken line of land from Nova Scotia to the Far West.*

In the present state of our knowledge, our conclusions respecting the beginning of the earth's history, the way in which it took form and shape as a distinct, separate planet, must, of course, be very

---

* " It would be inexpedient to encumber this essay," Mr. Agassiz remarks, " with references to all the authorities on which such geological results rest. They are drawn from the various *State Surveys*, including that of the mineral lands of Lake Superior, in which the early rise of the American Continent is for the first time affirmed, and other more general works on American geology."

vague and hypothetical. Yet the progress of science is so rapidly reconstructing the past that we may hope to solve even this problem; and to one who looks upon man's appearance upon the earth as the crowning work in a succession of creative acts, all of which have had relation to his coming in the end, it will not seem strange that he should at last be allowed to understand a history which was but the introduction to his own existence. It is my belief that not only the future, but the past also, is the inheritance of man, and that we shall yet conquer our lost birthright.

Even now our knowledge carries us far enough to warrant the assertion that there was a time when our earth was in a state of igneous fusion, when no ocean bathed it and no atmosphere surrounded it, when no wind blew over it, and no rain fell upon it, but an intense heat held all its materials in solution. In those days the rocks which are now the very bones and sinews of our mother Earth — her granites, her porphyries, her basalts, her sienites — were melted into a liquid mass. As I am writing for the unscientific reader, who may not be familiar with the facts through which these inferences have been reached, I will answer here a question which, were we talking together, he might naturally ask in a somewhat skeptical tone. How do you know that this state of things ever existed, and, supposing that the solid materials of which our earth consists were ever in a liquid condition, what right have you to infer that this condition was caused by the action of heat upon them? I answer, Because it is acting upon them still; because the earth we tread is but a thin crust floating on a liquid sea of molten materials; because the agencies that were at work then are at work now, and the present is the logical sequence of the past. From Artesian wells, from mines, from geysers, from hot springs, a mass of facts has been collected, proving incontestably the heated condition of all substances at a certain depth below the earth's surface; and if we need more positive evidence, we have it in the fiery eruptions that even now bear fearful testimony to the molten ocean seething within the globe and forcing its way out from time to time. The modern progress of Geology has led us by successive and perfectly connected steps back to a time when what is now only an occasional and rare phenomenon was the normal condition of our earth; when those internal fires were inclosed in an envelop so thin that it opposed but little resistance to their frequent outbreak, and they constantly forced themselves through this crust, pouring out melted materials that subsequently cooled and consolidated on its surface. So constant were these eruptions, and so slight was the resistance they encountered, that some portions of the earlier rock-deposits are perforated with numerous chimneys, narrow tunnels as it were, bored by the liquid masses that poured out through them and greatly modified their first condition.

There is, perhaps, no part of the world, certainly none familiar to science, where the early geological periods can be studied with so much ease and precision as in the United States. Along their northern borders, between Canada and the United States, there runs the low line of hills known as the Laurentian Hills. Insignificant in height, nowhere rising more than fifteen hundred or two thousand feet above the level of the sea, these are nevertheless the first mountains that broke the uniform level of the earth's surface, and lifted themselves above the waters. Their low stature, as compared with that of other more lofty mountain-ranges, is in accordance with an invariable rule, by which the relative age of mountains may be estimated. The oldest mountains are the lowest, while the younger and more recent ones tower above their elders, and are usually more torn and dislocated also. This is easily understood when we remember that all mountains and mountain-chains are the result of upheavals, and that the violence of the outbreak must have been in proportion to the strength of the resistance. When the crust of the earth was so thin that the heated masses within easily broke through it, they were not thrown to so great a height, and formed comparatively low elevations, such as the Canadian hills or the mountains of Bretagne and Wales. But in later times, when young, vigorous giants, such as the Alps, the Himalayas, or, later still, the Rocky Mountains, forced their way out from their fiery prison-house, the crust of the earth was much thicker, and fearful indeed must have been the convulsions which attended their exit.

The Laurentian Hills form, then, a granite range, stretching from Eastern Canada to the Upper Mississippi, and immediately along its base are gathered the Azoic deposits, the first stratified beds, in which the absence of life need not surprise us, since they were formed beneath a heated ocean. As well might we expect to find the remains of fish or shells or crabs at the bottom of geysers or of boiling springs, as on those early shores bathed by an ocean of which the heat must have been so intense. Although from the condition in which we find it, this first granite range has evidently never been disturbed by any violent convulsion since its first upheaval, yet there has been a gradual rising of that part of the continent, for the Azoic beds do not lie horizontally along the base of the Laurentian Hills in the position in which they must originally have been deposited, but are lifted and rest against their slopes. They have been more or less dislocated in this process, and are greatly metamorphosed by the intense heat to which they must have been exposed. Indeed, all the oldest stratified rocks have been baked by the prolonged action of heat.

It may be asked how the materials for those first stratified deposits were provided. In later times, when an abundant and various soil covered the earth, when every river brought down to the ocean, not only its yearly tribute of mud or clay or lime, but the *débris* of animals and plants that lived and died in its waters or along its banks, when every lake and pond deposited at its bottom in successive layers the lighter or heavier materials floating in its waters and settling gradually beneath them, the process by which stratified materials are collected and gradually harden into rock is more easily understood. But when the solid surface of the earth was only just beginning to form, it would seem that the floating matter in the sea can hardly have been in sufficient quantity to form any extensive deposits. No doubt there was some abrasion even of that first crust; but the more abundant source of the earliest stratification is to be found in the submarine volcanoes that poured their liquid streams into the first ocean. At what rate these materials would be distributed and precipitated in regular strata it is impossible to determine; but that volcanic materials were so deposited in layers is evident from the relative position of the earliest rocks. I have already spoken of the innumerable chimneys perforating the Azoic beds, narrow outlets of Plutonic rock, protruding through the earliest strata. Not only are such funnels filled with the crystalline mass of granite that flowed through them in a liquid state, but it has often poured over their sides, mingling with the stratified beds around. In the present state of our knowledge, we can explain such appearances only by supposing that the heated materials within the earth's crust poured out frequently, meeting little resistance, — that they then scattered and were precipitated in the ocean around, settling in successive strata at its bottom, — that through such strata the heated masses within continued to pour again and again, forming for themselves the chimney-like outlets above mentioned.

Such, then, was the earliest American land, — a long, narrow island, almost continental in its proportions, since it stretched from the eastern borders of Canada nearly to the point where now the base of the Rocky Mountains meets the plain of the Mississippi Valley. We may still walk along its ridge and know that we tread upon the ancient granite that first divided the waters into a northern and southern ocean; and if our imaginations will carry us so far, we may look down toward its base and fancy how the sea washed against this earliest shore of a lifeless world. This is no romance, but the bald, simple truth; for the fact that this granite band was lifted out of the waters so early in the history of the world, and has not since been submerged, has, of course, prevented any subsequent deposits from forming above it. And this is true of all the northern part of the United States. It has been lifted gradually, the beds deposited in one period being subsequently raised, and forming a shore along which those of the succeeding one collected, so that we have their whole sequence before us. In regions where all the geological deposits, Silurian, Devonian, Carboniferous, Permian, Triassic, etc., are piled one upon another, and we can get a glimpse of their internal relations only where some rent has laid them open, or where their ragged edges, worn away by the abrading action of external influences, expose to view their successive layers, it must, of course, be more difficult to follow their connection. For this reason the American continent offers facilities to the geologist denied to him in the so-called Old World, where the earlier deposits are comparatively hidden, and the broken character of the land, intersected by mountains in every direction, renders his investigation still more difficult. Of course, when I speak of the geological deposits as so completely unveiled to us here, I do not forget the sheet of drift which covers the continent from north to south; but the drift is only a superficial and recent addition to the soil, resting loosely above the other geological deposits, and arising from very different causes.

In this article I have intended to limit myself to a general sketch of the formation of the Laurentian Hills with the Azoic stratified beds resting against them. In the Silurian epoch following the Azoic we have the first beach on which any life stirred; it extended along the base of the Azoic beds, widening by its extensive deposits the narrow strip of land already upheaved.

LONGFELLOW.

1807—

HENRY WADSWORTH LONGFELLOW, the most distinguished of American poets, was born in Portland, Maine, in 1807. He graduated at Bowdoin College in the class of 1825, of which Nathaniel Hawthorne and President Pierce were members. The next year he was appointed Professor of Modern Languages in this institution, and in 1835 was elected to the chair of Belles-Lettres in Harvard University, which position he held for many years, finally resigning it in order that he might give his attention wholly to literary labor. Between these two dates he spent much time in Europe, assiduously studying modern languages and literature. Mr. Longfellow's poetry is distinguished for refinement and grace rather than for vigor of thought or expression. His sympathies are quick and strong, and this fact, together with the directness and simplicity of his verse, accounts mainly for the extraordinary popularity of his writings, not only in this country, but in England, where they are almost universally read and admired. Perhaps his best — as it is his most famous — poem is *Evangeline*, which contains some of the most perfect idyllic passages in the language, and is eloquent with a sweet pathos that touches every heart. He is an accomplished student of foreign literature, and has translated many poems from the Spanish, German, and Scandinavian languages into his own graceful measures. He may fairly be regarded as one of the most influential founders of American literature, as he is one of its brightest ornaments. As a representative of our national culture in European eyes, he is undoubtedly the most conspicuous of American poets.

THE WRECK OF THE HESPERUS.

IT was the schooner Hesperus
  That sailed the wintry sea ;
And the skipper had taken his little daughter,
  To bear him company.

Blue were her eyes as the fairy-flax,
  Her cheeks like the dawn of day,
And her bosom white as the hawthorn buds
  That ope in the month of May.

The skipper he stood beside the helm,
  His pipe was in his mouth,
And he watched how the veering flaw did blow
  The smoke now west, now south.

Then up and spake an old sailor,
  Had sailed the Spanish Main,
" I pray thee put into yonder port,
  For I fear a hurricane.

" Last night the moon had a golden ring,
    And to-night no moon we see ! "
The skipper, he blew a whiff from his pipe,
    And a scornful laughed he.

Colder and louder blew the wind,
    A gale from the northeast ;
The snow fell hissing in the brine,
    And the billows frothed like yeast.

Down came the storm, and smote amain
    The vessel in its strength ;
She shuddered and paused, like a frighted steed,
    Then leaped her cable's length.

" Come hither ! come hither ! my little daughter,
    And do not tremble so ;
For I can weather the roughest gale
    That ever wind did blow."

He wrapped her warm in his seaman's coat
    Against the stinging blast ;
He cut a rope from a broken spar,
    And bound her to the mast.

" O father ! I hear the church-bells ring,
    O say what may it be ? "
" 'T is a fog-bell on a rock-bound coast ! "
    And he steered for the open sea.

" O father ! I hear the sound of guns,
    O say what may it be ? "
" Some ship in distress, that cannot live
    In such an angry sea ! "

" O father ! I see a gleaming light,
    O say what may it be ? "
But the father answered never a word, —
    A frozen corpse was he.

Lashed to the helm, all stiff and stark,
  With his face turned to the skies,
The lantern gleamed through the gleaming snow
  On his fixed and glassy eyes.

Then the maiden clasped her hands and prayed
  That savéd she might be;
And she thought of Christ, who stilled the wave
  On the Lake of Galilee.

And fast through the midnight dark and drear,
  Through the whistling sleet and snow,
Like a sheeted ghost, the vessel swept
  Towards the reef of Norman's Woe.

And ever the fitful gusts between
  A sound came from the land;
It was the sound of the trampling surf,
  On the rocks and the hard sea-sand.

The breakers were right beneath her bows,
  She drifted a dreary wreck,
And a whooping billow swept the crew
  Like icicles from her deck.

She struck where the white and fleecy waves
  Looked soft as carded wool,
But the cruel rocks, they gored her side
  Like the horns of an angry bull.

Her rattling shrouds, all sheathed in ice,
  With the masts went by the board;
Like a vessel of glass, she stove and sank,
  Ho! ho! the breakers roared!

At daybreak, on the bleak sea-beach,
  A fisherman stood aghast,
To see the form of a maiden fair
  Lashed close to a drifting mast.

The salt sea was frozen on her breast,
   The salt tears in her eyes;
And he saw her hair, like the brown sea-weed,
   On the billows fall and rise.

Such was the wreck of the Hesperus,
   In the midnight and the snow!
Christ save us all from a death like this,
   On the reef of Norman's Woe!

THE SHIP OF STATE.

THOU too sail on, O Ship of State!
Sail on, O Union, strong and great!
Humanity, with all its fears,
With all the hopes of future years,
Is hanging breathless on thy fate!
We know what Master laid thy keel,
What Workmen wrought thy ribs of steel,
Who made each mast, and sail, and rope,
What anvils rang, what hammers beat,
In what a forge and what a heat
Were shaped the anchors of thy hope!
Fear not each sudden sound and shock,
 T is of the wave and not the rock;
'T is but the flapping of the sail,
And not a rent made by the gale!
In spite of rock and tempest's roar,
In spite of false lights on the shore,
Sail on, nor fear to breast the sea!
Our hearts, our hopes, are all with thee;
Our hearts, our hopes, our prayers, our tears,
Our faith triumphant o'er our fears,
Are all with thee, — are all with thee!

A PSALM OF LIFE.

TELL me not, in mournful numbers,
   "Life is but an empty dream!"
For the soul is dead that slumbers,
   And things are not what they seem.

Life is real! life is earnest!
　And the grave is not its goal;
"Dust thou art, to dust returnest,"
　Was not spoken of the soul.

Not enjoyment, and not sorrow,
　Is our destined end or way;
But to act that each to-morrow,
　Find us farther than to-day *is our des. ender*

Art is long, and Time is fleeting,
　And our hearts, though stout and brave,
Still, like muffled drums, are beating
　Funeral marches to the grave.

In the world's broad field of battle,
　In the bivouac of Life,
Be not like dumb, driven cattle!
　Be a hero in the strife!

Trust no Future, howe'er pleasant!
　Let the dead Past bury its dead!
Act, — act in the living Present!
　Heart within, and God o'erhead!

Lives of great men all remind us
　We can make our lives sublime,
And, departing, leave behind us
　Footprints on the sands of time;

Footprints, that perhaps another,
　Sailing o'er life's solemn main,
A forlorn and shipwrecked brother,
　Seeing, shall take heart again.

Let us, then, be up and doing,
　With a heart for any fate;
Still achieving, still pursuing,
　Learn to labor and to wait.

THE LAUNCHING OF THE SHIP.

ALL is finished ! and at length
Has come the bridal day
Of beauty and of strength.
To-day the vessel shall be launched !
With fleecy clouds the sky is blanched,
And o'er the bay,
Slowly, in all his splendors dight,
The great Sun rises to behold the sight.

The Ocean old,
Centuries old,
Strong as youth, and as uncontrolled,
Paces restless to and fro,
Up and down the sands of gold.
His beating heart is not at rest ;
And far and wide,
With ceaseless flow,
His beard of snow
Heaves with the heaving of his breast.

He waits impatient for his bride.
There she stands,
With her foot upon the sands,
Decked with flags and streamers gay,
In honor of her marriage day,
Her snow-white signals, fluttering, blending,
Round her like a veil descending,
Ready to be
The bride of the gray old Sea.

.   .   .   .   .

Then the master,
With a gesture of command,
Waved his hand ;
And at the word,
Loud and sudden there was heard,
All around them and below,

The sound of hammers, blow on blow,
Knocking away the shores and spurs.
And see! she stirs!
She starts, — she moves, — she seems to feel
The thrill of life along her keel,
And, spurning with her foot the ground,
With one exulting, joyous bound,
She leaps into the Ocean's arms!

DISASTER.

NEVER stoops the soaring vulture
On his quarry in the desert,
On the sick or wounded bison,
But another vulture, watching
From his high aerial lookout,
Sees the downward plunge, and follows;
And a third pursues the second,
Coming from the invisible ether,
First a speck, and then a vulture,
Till the air is dark with pinions.

So disasters come not singly;
But as if they watched and waited,
Scanning one another's motions,
When the first descends, the others
Follow, follow, gathering flock-wise
Round their victim, sick and wounded,
First a shadow, then a sorrow,
Till the air is dark with anguish.

THOUGH the mills of God grind slowly,
Yet they grind exceeding small;
Though with patience he stands waiting,
With exactness grinds he all.

WHITTIER.

1808– .

John Greenleaf Whittier, the Quaker poet, was born in Haverhill, Massachusetts, in 1808. His youth was spent on the paternal farm, and his educational opportunities were not first-rate. He possessed a keen appetite for knowledge, however, and at the age of twenty-one had so enriched and disciplined his mind that he was thought competent to fill the editorial chair of a Boston paper. One year later he went to Hartford, where he edited the *New England Weekly*. In 1831 he returned to Haverhill, where he remained five years, engaged in agriculture, and serving the State as Representative in the Legislature through two terms. From boyhood he had been deeply interested in the subject of slavery, and his convictions of the sinfulness of that institution were strengthened with his growth. He was one of the original members of the American Antislavery Society, and having been appointed one of its secretaries, he took up his residence at Philadelphia in 1836, and for four years wrote constantly for antislavery periodicals. In 1840 he established himself at Amesbury, Massachusetts, which has ever since been his home. His first volume, *Legends of New England in Prose and Verse*, was published in 1831. This has been followed at frequent intervals by nearly thirty volumes, mostly of verse. During the late war he poured forth a multitude of strong and stirring lyrics which helped not a little to sustain and energize public sentiment; and the literature of the antislavery struggle, from its beginning to its end, had in him an active and efficient contributor. Mr. Whittier's earlier poems deal largely with the colonial annals of New England, and some of the most interesting traditions of that region have been preserved for remote posterity in his graphic and vigorous lines. Two of Mr. Whittier's poems have enjoyed an exceptional popularity, *Maud Muller* and *Snow-Bound*; the first, telling the story of a universal experience, appeals to every heart, while the second affords the most faithful and finished pictures of winter life in rural New England that have ever been drawn by a poet. No American poet, it may be said, is so free as Mr. Whittier from obligations to English writers; his poems show no evidence of appropriation, or even of a study of masterpieces so assiduous and appreciative as almost inevitably to entail a general resemblance. He is eminently original, and eminently American. One principal charm of his poetry consists in its catholicity; he sings not of himself, but for humanity, and his voice is heeded as if it bore a special call to all who heard it. The moral tone of his writings is uncompromisingly high; his highest inspiration is found in the thought of elevating or helping his fellow-man, or widening the bounds of his freedom. The sentiment of Mr. Whittier's verse is generally elevated, and is expressed with mingled tenderness and dignity. His style lacks elegance, and is sometimes marred by positive faults; but these are more than balanced by the vigor of his lyrics and the intensity of his didactic passages.

MAUD MULLER.

Maud Muller, on a summer's day,
Raked the meadow sweet with hay.

Beneath her torn hat glowed the wealth
Of simple beauty and rustic health.

Singing, she wrought, and her merry glee
The mock-bird echoed from his tree.

But, when she glanced to the far-off town,
White from its hill-slope looking down,

The sweet song died, and a vague unrest
And a nameless longing filled her breast, —

A wish, that she hardly dared to own,
For something better than she had known.

The Judge rode slowly down the lane,
Smoothing his horse's chestnut mane.

He drew his bridle in the shade
Of the apple-trees, to greet the maid,

And ask a draught from the spring that flowed
Through the meadows across the road.

She stooped where the cool stream bubbled up,
And filled for him her small tin cup,

And blushed as she gave it, looking down
On her feet so bare, and her tattered gown.

"Thanks!" said the Judge, "a sweeter draught
From a fairer hand was never quaffed."

He spoke of the grass, and flowers, and trees,
Of the singing birds and the humming bees;

Then talked of the haying, and wondered whether
The cloud in the west would bring foul weather.

And Maud forgot her brier-torn gown,
And her graceful ankles bare and brown;

And listened, while a pleased surprise
Looked from her long-lashed hazel eyes.

At last, like one who for delay
Seeks a vain excuse, he rode away.

Maud Muller looked and sighed: "Ah, me!
That I the Judge's bride might be!

"He would dress me up in silks so fine,
And praise and toast me at his wine.

" My father should wear a broadcloth coat;
My brother should sail a painted boat.

" I 'd dress my mother so grand and gay,
And the baby should have a new toy each day.

" And I 'd feed the hungry and clothe the poor,
And all should bless me who left our door."

The Judge looked back as he climbed the hill,
And saw Maud Muller standing still.

" A form more fair, a face more sweet,
Ne'er hath it been my lot to meet.

" And her modest answer and graceful air,
Show her wise and good as she is fair.

" Would she were mine, and I to-day,
Like her, a harvester of hay :

" No doubtful balance of rights and wrongs,
Nor weary lawyers with endless tongues,

" But low of cattle and song of birds,
And health and quiet and loving words."

But he thought of his sisters, proud and cold,
And his mother, vain of her rank and gold.

So, closing his heart, the Judge rode on,
And Maud was left in the field alone.

But the lawyers smiled that afternoon,
When he hummed in court an old love-tune;

And the young girl mused beside the well,
Till the rain on the unraked clover fell.

He wedded a wife of richest dower,
Who lived for fashion, as he for power.

Yet oft, in his marble hearth's bright glow,
He watched a picture come and go :

And sweet Maud Muller's hazel eyes
Looked out in their innocent surprise.

Oft when the wine in his glass was red
He longed for the wayside well instead;

And closed his eyes on his garnished rooms,
To dream of meadows and clover blooms.

And the proud man sighed, with a secret pain,
" Ah, that I were free again !

" Free as when I rode that day,
Where the barefoot maiden raked her hay."

She wedded a man unlearned and poor,
And many children played round her door.

But care and sorrow, and childbirth pain,
Left their traces on heart and brain.

And oft, when the summer sun shone hot
On the new-mown hay in the meadow lot,

And she heard the little spring brook fall
Over the roadside, through the wall,

In the shade of the apple-tree again
She saw a rider draw his rein :

And, gazing down with timid grace,
She felt his pleased eyes read her face.

Sometimes her narrow kitchen walls
Stretched away into stately halls ;

The weary wheel to a spinnet turned,
The tallow candle an astral burned,

And for him who sat by the chimney lug,
Dozing and grumbling o'er pipe and mug,

A manly form at her side she saw,
And joy was duty, and love was law.

10

Then she took up her burden of life again,
Saying only, " It might have been ! "

Alas for maiden, alas for Judge,
For rich repiner and household drudge !

God pity them both ! and pity us all,
Who vainly the dreams of youth recall.

For of all sad words of tongue or pen,
The saddest are these : " It might have been ! "

Ah, well ☞ for us all some sweet hope lies,
Deeply buried from human eyes ;

And, in the hereafter, angels may
Roll the stone from its grave away !

THE BAREFOOT BOY.

BLESSINGS on thee, little man,
Barefoot boy, with cheek of tan !
With thy turned-up pantaloons,
And thy merry whistled tunes ;
With thy red lip, redder still
Kissed by strawberries on the hill ;
With the sunshine on thy face,
Through thy torn brim's jaunty grace ;
From my heart I give thee joy, —
I was once a barefoot boy !
Prince thou art, — the grown-up man
Only is republican.
Let the million-dollared ride !
Barefoot, trudging at his side,
Thou hast more than he can buy
In the reach of ear and eye, —
Outward sunshine, inward joy ;
Blessings on thee, barefoot boy !

O for boyhood's painless play,
Sleep that wakes in laughing day,

Health that mocks the doctor's rules,
Knowledge never learned of schools,
Of the wild bee's morning chase,
Of the wild-flower's time and place,
Flight of fowl and habitude
Of the tenants of the wood ;
How the tortoise bears his shell,
How the woodchuck digs his cell,
And the ground-mole sinks his well ;
How the robin feeds her young,
How the oriole's nest is hung ;
Where the whitest lilies blow,
Where the freshest berries grow,
Where the ground-nut trails its vine,
Where the wood-grape's clusters shine ;
Of the black wasp's cunning way,
Mason of his walls of clay,
And the architectural plans
Of gray hornet artisans ! —
For, eschewing books and tasks,
Nature answers all he asks ;
Hand in hand with her he walks,
Face to face with her he talks,
Part and parcel of her joy, —
Blessings on the barefoot boy !

O for boyhood's time of June,
Crowding years in one brief moon,
When all things I heard or saw,
Me, their master, waited for.
I was rich in flowers and trees,
Humming-birds and honey-bees ;
For my sport the squirrel played,
Plied the snouted mole his spade ;
For my taste the blackberry cone
Purpled over hedge and stone ;
Laughed the brook for my delight
Through the day and through the night,
Whispering at the garden wall,

Talked with me from fall to fall;
Mine the sand-rimmed pickerel pond,
Mine the walnut slopes beyond,
Mine, on bending orchard trees,
Apples of Hesperides !
Still as my horizon grew,
Larger grew my riches too ;
All the world I saw or knew
Seemed a complex Chinese toy,
Fashioned for a barefoot boy !

O for festal dainties spread,
Like my bowl of milk and bread, —
Pewter spoon and bowl of wood,
On the door-stone, gray and rude !
O'er me, like a regal tent,
Cloudy-ribbed, the sunset bent,
Purple-curtained, fringed with gold,
Looped in many a wind-swung fold ;
While for music came the play
Of the pied frogs' orchestra ;
And, to light the noisy choir,
Lit the fly his lamp of fire.
I was monarch : pomp and joy
Waited on the barefoot boy !

Cheerily, then, my little man,
Live and laugh, as boyhood can !
Though the flinty slopes be hard,
Stubble-speared the new-mown sward,
Every morn shall lead thee through
Fresh baptisms of the dew ;
Every evening from thy feet
Shall the cool wind kiss the heat :
All too soon these feet must hide
In the prison cells of pride,
Lose the freedom of the sod,
Like a colt's for work be shod,
Made to tread the mills of toil,

Up and down in ceaseless moil :
Happy if their track be found
Never on forbidden ground ;
Happy if they sink not in
Quick and treacherous sands of sin.
Ah ! that thou couldst know thy joy,
Ere it passes, barefoot boy !

WINTER.

SHUT in from all the world without,
We sat the clean-winged hearth about,
Content to let the north-wind roar
In baffled rage at pane and door,
While the red logs before us beat
The frost-line back with tropic heat ;
And ever, when a louder blast
Shook beam and rafter as it passed,
The merrier up its roaring draught
The great throat of the chimney laughed.
The house-dog on his paws outspread,
Laid to the fire his drowsy head,
The cat's dark silhouette on the wall
A couchant tiger's seemed to fall ;
And, for the winter fireside meet,
Between the andirons' straddling feet,
The mug of cider simmered slow,
The apples sputtered in a row,
And, close at hand, the basket stood
With nuts from brown October's wood.

MERIVALE.

1808 – 1875.

Rev. Charles Merivale, Dean of Ely, and a distinguished historian, was born in England in 1808, and died in 1875. His *History of Rome under the Emperors* is a scholarly, calm, and unprejudiced representation of the period of Roman history which lies between the establishment of the first Triumvirate and the last of the Cæsars. This work is written with great care, and exhibits marked opulence of scholarship and thorough comprehension of the subject. The author was a profound rather than brilliant historian, and is especially to be praised for his accuracy and fullness. The extracts are from his History above named.

AUGUSTUS CÆSAR.*

In stature Augustus hardly exceeded the middle height, but his person was lightly and delicately formed, and its proportions were such as to convey a favorable and even a striking impression. His countenance was pale, and testified to the weakness of his health, and almost constant bodily suffering; but the hardships of military service had imparted a swarthy tinge to a complexion naturally fair, and his eyebrows meeting over a sharp and aquiline nose gave a serious and stern expression to his countenance. His hair was light, and his eyes blue and piercing; he was well pleased if any one on approaching him looked on the ground and affected to be unable to meet their dazzling brightness. It was said that his dress concealed many imperfections and blemishes on his person; but he could not disguise all the infirmities under which he labored; the weakness of the forefinger of his right hand and a lameness in the left hip were the results of wounds he incurred in a battle with the Iapydæ in early life; he suffered repeated attacks of fever of the most serious kind, especially in the course of the campaign of Philippi and that against the Cantabrians, and again two years afterward at Rome, when his recovery was despaired of. From that time, although constantly liable to be affected by cold and heat, and obliged to nurse himself throughout with the care of a valetudinarian, he does not appear to have had any return of illness so serious as the preceding; and dying at the age of seventy-

---

* Augustus Cæsar, one of the Emperors of Rome and the heir of Julius Cæsar, the greatest of warriors and rulers, was born 63 B. C. He was a liberal patron of literature and art, and his reign was so illustrious that it is called the Augustan Age. He was the friend of Virgil and Horace, the most eminent of the Roman poets, and so increased the architectural splendor of Rome as to be able to boast that he had transformed it from a city of brick to a city of marble. (See *Plutarch's Life of Marcus Antonius.*)

four, the rumor obtained popular currency that he was prematurely cut off by poison administered by the empress. As the natural consequence of this bodily weakness and sickly constitution, Augustus did not attempt to distinguish himself by active exertions or feats of personal prowess.

The splendid examples of his uncle the dictator, and of Antonius his rival, might have early discouraged him from attempting to shine as a warrior and hero : he had not the vivacity and animal spirits necessary to carry him through such exploits as theirs ; and, although he did not shrink from exposing himself to personal danger, he prudently declined to allow a comparison to be instituted between himself and rivals whom he could not hope to equal. Thus necessarily thrown back upon other resources, he trusted to caution and circumspection, first to preserve his own life, and afterwards to obtain the splendid prizes which had hitherto been carried off by daring adventure, and the good fortune which is so often its attendant. From his youth upwards accustomed to overreach, not the bold and reckless only, but the most considerate and wily of his contemporaries, he succeeded in the end in deluding the senate and people of Rome in the establishment of his tyranny ; and finally deceived the expectations of the world, and falsified the lessons of the Republican history, reigning himself forty years in disguise, and leaving a throne to be claimed without a challenge by his successors for fourteen centuries.

But although emperor in name, and in fact absolute master of his people, the manners of the Cæsar, both in public and private life, were still those of a simple citizen. On the most solemn occasions he was distinguished by no other dress than the robes and insignia of the offices which he exercised ; he was attended by no other guards than those which his consular dignity rendered customary and decent. In his court there was none of the etiquette of modern monarchies to be recognized, and it was only by slow and gradual encroachment that it came to prevail in that of his successors. Many anecdotes are recorded of the moderation with which the emperor received the opposition, and often the rebukes, of individuals in public as well as in private. These stories are not without their importance as showing how little formality there was in the tone of addressing the master of the Roman world, and how entirely different the ideas of the nation were, with regard to the position occupied by the Cæsar and his family, from those with which modern associations have imbued us.

We have already noticed the rude freedom with which Tiberius was attacked, although step-son of the emperor, and participating in the eminent functions of the tribunitian power, by a declaimer in the schools at Rhodes; but Augustus himself seems to have suffered almost as much as any private citizen from the general coarseness of behavior which characterized the Romans in their public assemblies, and the rebukes to which he patiently submitted were frequently such as would lay the courtier of a constitutional sovereign in modern Europe under perpetual disgrace.

On one occasion, for instance, in the public discharge of his functions as corrector of manners, he had brought a specific charge against a certain knight for having squandered his patrimony. The accused proved that he had, on the contrary, augmented it. "Well," answered the emperor, somewhat annoyed by his error, "but you are at all events living in celibacy contrary to recent enactments." The other was able to reply that he was married, and was the father of three legitimate children; and when the emperor signified that he had no further charge to bring, added aloud, "Another time, Cæsar, when you give ear to informations against honest men, take care that your informants are honest themselves." Augustus felt the justice of the rebuke thus publicly administered, and submitted to it in silence.

THE BURNING OF ROME.*

PROVIDENCE was preparing an awful chastisement; and was about to overwhelm Rome, like the Cities of the Plain, in a sheet of retributive fire. Crowded, as the mass of the citizens were, in their close wooden dwelling-chambers, accidents were constantly occurring which involved whole streets and quarters of the city in wide-spreading conflagrations, and the efforts of the night-watch to stem these outbursts of fire, with few of the appliances, and little, perhaps, even of the discipline of our modern police, were but imperfectly effectual. But the greatest of all the fires which desolated Rome was that which broke out on the 19th of July, in the year 817, the tenth of Nero, which began at the eastern end of the Circus, abutting on the valley between

---

* In A. D. 64 Rome was nearly destroyed by a fire which the Emperor Nero was himself accused of instigating. In order to remove this suspicion he charged the crime upon the Christians, many of whom were in consequence subjected to the most cruel tortures. But for this fire we should have, perhaps, still left many of the beautiful structures for which ancient Rome was so famous, only the ruins of which now remain.

the Palatine and the Cælian hills. Against the outer walls of this edifice leaned a mass of wooden booths and stores filled chiefly with combustible articles. The wind from the east drove the flames towards the corner of the Palatine, whence they forked in two directions, following the draught of the valleys. At neither point were they encountered by the massive masonry of halls or temples, till they had gained such head that the mere intensity of the heat crumbled brick and stone like paper. The Circus itself was filled from end to end with wooden galleries, along which the fire coursed with a speed which defied all check and pursuit.

The flames shot up to the heights adjacent, and swept the basements of many noble structures on the Palatine and Aventine. Again they plunged into the lowest levels of the city, the dense habitations and narrow winding streets of the Velabrum and Forum Boarium, till stopped by the river and the walls. At the same time another torrent rushed towards the Velia and the Esquiline, and sucked up all the dwellings within its reach; till it was finally arrested by the cliffs beneath the gardens of Mæcenas.

Amidst the horror and confusion of the scene, the smoke, the blaze, the din, and the scorching heat, with half the population, bond and free, cast loose and houseless into the streets, ruffians were seen to thrust blazing brands into the buildings, who affirmed, when seized by the indignant sufferers, that they were acting with orders; and the crime, which was probably the desperate resource of slaves and robbers, was imputed by fierce suspicions to the government itself.

At such a moment of sorrow and consternation every trifle is seized to confirm the suspicion of foul play. The flames, it seems, had subsided after raging for six days, and the wretched outcasts were beginning to take breath and visit the ruins of their habitations, when a second conflagration burst out in a different quarter. This fire commenced at the point where the Æmilian gardens of Tigellinus abutted on the outskirts of the city beneath the Pincian hill; and it was on Tigellinus himself, the object already of popular scorn if not of anger, that the suspicion now fell. The wind, it seems, had now changed, for the fire spread from the northwest towards the Quirinal and the Viminal, destroying the buildings, more sparsely planted, of the quarter denominated the Via Lata. Three days exhausted the fury of this second visitation, in which the loss of life and property was less, but the edifices it overthrew were generally of greater interest, shrines and temples of the gods, and halls and porticos devoted to the amusement or convenience of the people. Altogether, the disaster, whether it sprang from accident or design, involved nearly the whole of Rome.

Of the fourteen regions of the city, three we are assured were entirely destroyed, while seven others were injured more or less severely; four only of the whole number escaped unhurt. The fire made a complete clearance of the central quarters, leaving perhaps but few public buildings erect, even on the Palatine and Aventine; but it was, for the most part, hemmed in by the crests of the surrounding eminences, and confined to the seething crater which had been the cradle of the Roman people. The day of its outburst, it was remarked, was that of the first burning of Rome by the Gauls, and some curious calculators computed that the addition of an equal number of years, months, and days together would give the complete period which had elapsed in the long interval of her greatness. Of the number of houses and insulæ destroyed Tacitus does not venture to hazard a statement; he only tantalizes us by his slender notice of the famous fanes and monuments which sank in the common ruin. Among them were the temple of Diana, which Servius Tullius had erected; the shrine and altar of Hercules, consecrated by Evander, as affirmed in the tradition impressed upon us by Virgil; the Romulean temple of Jupiter Stator, the remembrance of which thrilled the soul of the banished Ovid; the little Regia of Numa, which armed so many a sarcasm against the pride of consuls and imperators; the sanctuary of Vesta herself, with the Palladium, the Penates, and the ever-glowing hearth of the Roman people.

But the loss of these decayed though venerable objects was not the worst disaster. Many an unblemished masterpiece of the Grecian pencil or chisel or graver — the prize of victory — was devoured by the flames; and amidst all the splendor with which Rome rose afterwards from her ashes, old men could lament to the historian the irreparable sacrifice of these ancient glories. Writings and documents of no common interest may have perished at the same time irrecoverably; and with them, trophies, images, and family devices. At a moment when the heads of patrician houses were falling rapidly by the sword, the loss of such memorials was the more deplorable.

HOLMES.

1809 – 1894

OLIVER WENDELL HOLMES, one of the wittiest and wisest of American writers, was born in Cambridge, Massachusetts, in 1809, and graduated at Harvard University in 1829. He began the study of law, but feeling a stronger bent toward the profession of medicine, applied himself zealously to preparation for its practice. In 1836, having spent several years in study abroad, he received his medical degree at Cambridge; two years later was appointed to a professorship in the Dartmouth Medical School, and in 1847 succeeded Dr. Warren as Professor of Anatomy in Harvard University. His first considerable literary effort was a poem delivered before the Phi Beta Kappa Society of Harvard in 1836. It received warm praise from competent critics, and its success undoubtedly confirmed his not yet openly confessed *penchant* for literary labors. The first edition of his collected poems was published in 1836, and at least a dozen editions have followed it in this country and England. His range in poetry is limited, though perhaps not necessarily; he confined his efforts in former years almost exclusively to long poems, like *Urania* and *Astræa*, metrical essays, melodious, polished, and glittering with wit, and in later days he has been content to throw off short lyrics and "occasional pieces," which are so exquisite that the public reasonably asks for more. The most conspicuous characteristic of Dr. Holmes's verse is humor, of indescribable and rarely equaled delicacy and brilliancy. Several of his humorous poems, like the *One-Hoss Shay*, have by common consent been elevated to the rank of classics in our literature. Not less felicitous has he been in a few pieces in which a fine pathos relieves the glow of his wit. But admirable as are his poems, his greatest triumphs have been won in prose. He was one of the founders of the *Atlantic Monthly*, and in its first years was a regular and favorite contributor to its pages. For it he wrote *The Autocrat of the Breakfast-Table*, and later, *The Professor* and *The Poet at the Breakfast-Table*, a series of papers which are unique in our literature, combining in a marvelous degree the rarest qualities of the light essay, — freshness of thought, deftness of touch, keen, but good-humored satire, and a pervading atmosphere of wit that keeps the reader in a state of continual exhilaration. As a novelist, Dr. Holmes has succeeded in spite of, rather than in accordance with, the rules which govern the composition of fiction; the abounding riches of his fancy and the play of his unfailing wit overleap the ordinary bounds prescribed to the novelist, to the delight of his readers, if not to the honor of literary canons. In no writer of the present day, in Europe or America, is there found so potent a combination of those intellectual qualities which mainly contribute to a writer's power, as is seen in Dr. Holmes. While he is surpassed by some of his contemporaries in single gifts, — though by none in wit and grace of style, — of the harmonious and fruitful union of them all he seems to stand out the superior representative. His success in prose and poetry may be mainly attributed to his dexterous avoidance of the didactic; he is never tedious, and always presents even his driest matter in a guise that commends it to readers of all tastes.

ON AMATEUR WRITERS.

IF I were a literary Pope sending out an Encyclical, I would tell inexperienced persons that nothing is so frequent as to mistake an ordinary human gift for a special and extraordinary endowment. The mechanism of breathing and that of swallowing are very wonderful, and if one had seen and studied them in his own person only, he might well think himself a prodigy. Everybody knows these and other bodily faculties are common gifts; but nobody except editors and school-teachers and here and there a literary man knows how common is the capacity of rhyming and prattling in readable prose, especially among young women of a certain degree of education. In my character of Pontiff, I should tell these young persons that most of them labored under a delusion. It is very hard to believe it; one feels so full of intelligence and so decidedly superior to one's dull relations and schoolmates; one writes so easily and the lines sound so prettily to one's self; there are such felicities of expression, just like those we hear quoted from the great poets; and besides one has been told by so many friends that all one had to do was to print and be famous! Delusion, my poor dear, delusion at least nineteen times out of twenty, yes, ninety-nine times in a hundred.

But as private father confessor, I always allow as much as I can for the one chance in the hundred. I try not to take away all hope, unless the case is clearly desperate, and then to direct the activities into some other channel.

Using kind language, I can talk pretty freely. I have counselled more than one aspirant after literary fame to go back to his tailor's board or his lapstone. I have advised the *dilettanti*, whose foolish friends praised their verses or their stories, to give up all their deceptive dreams of making a name by their genius, and go to work in the study of a profession which asked only for the diligent use of average, ordinary talents. It is a very grave responsibility which these unknown correspondents throw upon their chosen counselors. One whom you have never seen, who lives in a community of which you know nothing, sends you specimens more or less painfully voluminous of his writings, which he asks you to read over, think over, and pray over, and send back an answer informing him whether fame and fortune are awaiting him as the possessor of the wonderful gifts his writings manifest, and whether you advise him to leave all, — the shop he sweeps out every morning, the ledger he posts, the mortar in which he pounds, the bench at which he urges the reluctant plane, — and follow his genius whithersoever it may lead him. The next correspondent wants you to mark out a whole course of life for him, and the means of judgment he gives you are about as adequate as the brick which the simpleton of old carried round as an advertisement of the house he had to sell. My advice to all young men that write to me depends somewhat on the handwriting and spelling. If these are of a certain character, and they have reached a mature age, I recommend some honest manual calling, such as they have very probably been bred to, and which will, at least, give them a chance of becoming President of the United States by and by, if that is any object to them. What would *you* have done with the young person who called on me a good many years ago, — so many that he has probably forgotten his literary effort, — and read as specimens of his literary workmanship lines like those which I will favor you with presently? He was an able-bodied, grown-up young person, whose ingenuousness interested me; and I am sure if I thought he would ever be pained to see his maiden effort in print, I would deny myself the pleasure of submitting it to the reader. The following is an exact transcript of the lines he showed me, and which I took down on the spot: —

> " Are you in the vein for cider?
> Are you in the tune for pork?
> Hist! for Betty 's cleared the larder
> And turned the pork to soap."

Do not judge too hastily this sincere effort of a maiden muse. Here was a sense of rhythm, and an effort in the direction of rhyme; here was an honest transcript of an occurrence of daily life, told with a certain idealizing expression, recognizing the existence of impulses, mysterious instincts, impelling us even in the selection of our bodily sustenance. But I had to tell him that it wanted dignity of incident and grace of narrative, that there was no atmosphere to it, nothing of the light that never was and so forth. I did not say this in these very words, but I gave him to understand, without being too hard upon him, that he had better not desert his honest toil in pursuit of the poet's bays. This, it must be confessed, was a rather discouraging case. A young person like this may *pierce*, as the Frenchmen say, by and by, but the chances are all the other way.

I advise aimless young men to choose some profession without needless delay, and so get into a good strong current of human affairs, and find themselves bound up in interests with a compact body of their fellow-men.

I advise young women who write to me for counsel, — perhaps I do not advise them at all, only sympathize a little with them, and listen to what they have to say (eight closely written pages on the average, which I always read from beginning to end, thinking of the widow's cruse and myself in the character of Elijah) and — and — come now, I don't believe Methuselah would tell you what he said in his letters to young ladies, written when he was in his nine hundred and sixty-ninth year.

But, dear me! how much work all this private criticism involves! An editor has only to say "respectfully declined," and there is the end of it. But the confidential adviser is expected to give the reasons of his likes and dislikes in detail, and sometimes to enter into an argument for their support. *That* is more than any martyr can stand, but what trials he must go through, as it is! Great bundles of manuscripts, verse or prose, which the recipient is expected to read, perhaps to recommend to a publisher, at any rate to express a well-digested and agreeably flavored opinion about; which opinion, nine times out of ten, disguise it as we may, has to be a bitter draught; every form of egotism, conceit, false sentiment, hunger for notoriety, and eagerness for display of anserine plumage before the admiring public; — all these come in by mail or express, covered with postage-stamps of so much more cost than the value of the waste words they overlie, that one comes at last to groan and change color at the very sight of a package, and to dread the postman's knock as if it were that of the other visitor whose naked knuckles rap at every door.

Still there are experiences which go far towards repaying all these inflictions. My last young man's case looked desperate enough; some of his sails had blown from the rigging, some were backing in the wind, and some were flapping and shivering, but I told him which way to head, and to my surprise he promised to do just as I directed, and I do not doubt is under full sail at this moment.

What if I should tell my last, my very recent experience with the other sex? I received a paper containing the inner history of a young woman's life, the evolution of her consciousness from its earliest record of itself, written so thoughtfully, so sincerely, with so much firmness and yet so much delicacy, with such truth of detail and such grace in the manner of telling, that I finished the long manuscript almost at a sitting, with a pleasure rarely, almost never experienced in voluminous communications which one has to spell out of handwriting. This was from a correspondent who made my acquaintance by letter when she was little more than a child, some years ago. How easy at that early period to have silenced her by indifference, to have wounded her by a careless epithet, perhaps even to have crushed her as one puts his heel on a weed! A very little encouragement kept her from despondency, and brought back one of those overflows of gratitude which make one more ashamed of himself for being so over-paid, than he would be for having committed any of the lesser sins.

But what pleased me most in the paper lately received was to see how far the writer had outgrown the need of any encouragement of mine; that she had strengthened out of her tremulous questionings into a self-reliance and self-poise which I had hardly dared to anticipate for her.

Some of my readers who are also writers have very probably had more numerous experiences of this kind than I can lay claim to; self-revelations from unknown and sometimes nameless friends, who write from strange corners where the winds have wafted some stray words of theirs which have lighted in the minds and reached the hearts of those to whom they were as the angel that stirred the pool of Bethesda. Perhaps this is the best reward authorship brings; it may not imply much talent or literary excellence, but it means that your way of thinking and feeling is just what some one of your fellow-creatures needed.

I know nothing in the world tenderer than the pity that a kind-hearted young girl has for a young man who feels lonely. It is true that these dear creatures are all compassion for every form of human woe, and anxious to alleviate all human misfortunes. They will go to Sunday schools through storms their brothers are afraid of, to teach the most unpleasant and intractable classes of little children the age of Methuselah and the dimensions of Og the King of Bashan's bedstead. They will stand behind a table at a fair all day until they are ready to drop, dressed in their prettiest clothes and their sweetest smiles, and lay hands upon you, — to make you buy what you do not want, at prices which you cannot afford; all this as cheerfully as if it were not martyrdom to them as well as to you. Such is their love for all good objects, such their eagerness to sympathize with all their suffering fellow-creatures! But there is nothing they pity as they pity a lonely young man. — *From " The Poet at the Breakfast-Table."*

When we are as yet small children there comes up to us a youthful angel, holding in his right hand cubes like dice, and in his left spheres like marbles. The cubes are of stainless ivory, and on each is written in letters of gold, — Truth. The spheres are veined and streaked and spotted beneath, with a dark crimson flush above, where the light falls on them, and in a certain aspect you can make out upon every one of them the three letters L, I, E. The child to whom they are offered very probably clutches at both. The spheres are the most convenient things in the world; they roll with the least possible impulse just where the child would have them. The cubes will not roll at all; they have a great talent for standing still, and always keep right side up. But very soon the young philosopher finds that things which roll so easily are very apt to roll into the wrong corner, and to get out of his way when he most wants them, while he always knows where to find the others, which stay where they are left. Thus he learns — thus we learn — to drop the streaked and speckled globes of falsehood and to hold fast the white angular blocks of truth. But then comes Timidity, and after her Good-nature, and last of all Polite-behavior, all insisting that truth must *roll*, or nobody can do anything with it; and so the first with her coarse rasp, and the second with her broad file, and the third with her silken sleeve, do so round off and smooth and polish the snow-white cubes of truth, that, when they have got a little dingy by use, it becomes hard to tell them from the rolling spheres of falsehood.

The schoolmistress was polite enough to say that she was pleased with this, and that she would read it to her little flock the next day. But she should tell the children, she said, that there were better reasons for truth than could be found in mere experience of its convenience and the inconvenience of lying. — *From " The Autocrat at the Breakfast-Table."*

UNDER THE VIOLETS.

HER hands are cold; her face is white;
  No more her pulses come and go;
Her eyes are shut to life and light; —
  Fold the white vesture, snow on snow,
  And lay her where the violets blow.

But not beneath a graven stone,
  To plead for tears with alien eyes;
A slender cross of wood alone
  Shall say, that here a maiden lies
  In peace beneath the peaceful skies.

And gray old trees of hugest limb
  Shall wheel their circling shadows round,
To make the scorching sunlight dim
    That drinks the greenness from the ground,
    And drop their dead leaves on her mound.

When o'er their boughs the squirrels run,
  And through their leaves the robins call,
And, ripening in the autumn sun,
    The acorns and the chestnuts fall,
    Doubt not that she will heed them all.

For her the morning choir shall sing
  Its matins from the branches high,
And every minstrel-voice of spring,
    That trills beneath the April sky,
    Shall greet her with its earliest cry.

When, turning round their dial-track,
  Eastward the lengthening shadows pass,
Her little mourners, clad in black,
    The crickets, sliding through the grass,
    Shall pipe for her an evening mass.

At last the rootlets of the trees
  Shall find the prison where she lies,
And bear the buried dust they seize
    In leaves and blossoms to the skies.
    So may the soul that warmed it rise!

If any, born of kindlier blood,
  Should ask, What maiden lies below?
Say only this: A tender bud,
    That tried to blossom in the snow,
    Lies withered where the violets blow.

TENNYSON.

1810-1894

ALFRED TENNYSON, unquestionably the first of living poets, was born in Lincolnshire, England, in 1810. He is the youngest of three brothers, all of whom were educated at Trinity College, Cambridge, and gave promise of marked intellectual greatness. Indeed, Wordsworth, estimating a volume of poems, published in 1829, and the joint work of Charles and Alfred Tennyson, found the contributions of Charles to be entitled to the highest praise. Alfred Tennyson's first volume, *Poems, chiefly Lyrical*, was published in 1830, and had a favorable reception, though its merits hardly warranted the expectation of his later masterpieces. Two editions of his *Poems* followed, in 1832 and 1842, the latter showing a marked increase of strength in the poet. *The Princess*, appearing in 1847, elicited various comment, though there was but one opinion among critics as to the delicacy and grace of its execution. In 1850 Tennyson gave to the world a poem which instantly quieted all doubts as to his title to the highest rank among contemporary poets, and which was universally received as an ample warrant for his appointment to the post of Poet Laureate, which was made in the same year. This was *In Memoriam*, a lament for the poet's friend, Arthur Hallam. In it noble thoughts are conveyed in a guise of ideal beauty, — a combination which has hardly, if ever, been surpassed in our literature. *Maud*, published in 1855, added nothing to the poet's fame; and the same may be said of the many short poems from his pen which preceded the publication of *The Idyls of the King*, in 1859. These poems must be regarded as his masterpieces, and can fairly be compared with no compositions less lofty than Milton's. It should be remarked, however, that they are unequal in merit, the earlier Idyls being superior to their successors. Yet to the mass of readers the Laureate is best known by his shorter pieces, some of which are familiar as household words. Among them are *The Queen of the May, Locksley Hall, Lady Clara Vere de Vere*, and the exquisite songs which are scattered through *The Princess*, and some of the longer poems. The charm of Tennyson's poetry lies mainly in his unequaled felicity of diction : his choice and arrangement of words and adjustment of epithets almost seem to be the result of inspiration, so happy are they. The most striking characteristic of his verse is refinement, — a delicacy of sentiment and expression that has rarely, if ever, been attained by any poet. His influence upon the poetical spirit of his age has been very potent, and to the purity of his muse is due, in a great degree, the comparative health of our poetical literature.

CHARGE OF THE LIGHT BRIGADE.*

HALF a league, half a league,
Half a league onward,
All in the valley of death
Rode the six hundred.
"Forward the Light Brigade !
Charge for the guns," he said ;
Into the valley of death
Rode the six hundred.

---

* The poem refers to a celebrated cavalry charge of the British at the battle of Balaclava, 25th October, 1854, in the war in the Crimea between Russia on the one side and England and France on the other.

" Forward the Light Brigade ! "
Was there a man dismayed ?
Not though the soldier knew
Some one had blundered :
Theirs not to make reply,
Theirs not to reason why,
Theirs but to do and die ;
Into the valley of death
Rode the six hundred.

Cannon to right of them,
Cannon to left of them,
Cannon in front of them,
Volleyed and thundered ;
Stormed at with shot and shell,
Boldly they rode and well,
Into the jaws of death,
Into the mouth of hell
Rode the six hundred.

Flashed all their sabers bare,
Flashed as they turned in air,
Sabring the gunners there,
Charging an army, while
All the world wondered :
Plunged in the battery smoke,
Right through the line they broke ;
Cossack and Russian
Reeled from the saber stroke
Shattered and sundered :
Then they rode back, but not —
Not the six hundred.

Cannon to right of them,
Cannon to left of them,
Cannon behind them,
Volleyed and thundered ;
Stormed at with shot and shell,
While horse and hero fell,
They that had fought so well

Came through the jaws of death
Back from the mouth of hell,
All that was left of them,
Left of six hundred.

When can their glory fade?
Oh! the wild charge they made!
All the world wondered.
Honor the charge they made;
Honor the Light Brigade,
Noble Six Hundred!

LADY CLARA VERE DE VERE.

LADY Clara Vere de Vere,
  Of me you shall not win renown:
You thought to break a country heart
  For pastime, ere you went to town.
At me you smiled, but unbeguiled
  I saw the snare, and I retired:
The daughter of a hundred earls,
  You are not one to be desired.

Lady Clara Vere de Vere,
  I know you proud to bear your name,
Your pride is yet no mate for mine,
  Too proud to care from whence I came.
Nor would I break for your sweet sake
  A heart that doats on truer charms.
A simple maiden in her flower
  Is worth a hundred coats-of-arms.

Lady Clara Vere de Vere,
  Some meeker pupil you must find,
For were you queen of all that is,
  I could not stoop to such a mind.
You sought to prove how I could love,
  And my disdain is my reply.
The lion on your old stone gates
  Is not more cold to you than I.

Lady Clara Vere de Vere,
   You put strange memories in my head.
Not thrice your branching limes have blown
   Since I beheld young Laurence dead.
Oh! your sweet eyes, your low replies;
   A great enchantress you may be;
But there was that across his throat
   Which you had hardly cared to see.

Lady Clara Vere de Vere,
   . When thus he met his mother's view,
She had the passions of her kind,
   She spake some certain truths of you.
Indeed, I heard one bitter word
   That scarce is fit for you to hear;
Her manners had not that repose
   Which stamps the caste of Vere de Vere.

Lady Clara Vere de Vere,
   There stands a specter in your hall:
The guilt of blood is at your door:
   You changed a wholesome heart to gall.
You held your course without remorse,
   To make him trust his modest worth,
And, last, you fixed a vacant stare,
   And slew him with your noble birth.

Trust me, Clara Vere de Vere,
   From yon blue heavens above us bent
The grand old gardener and his wife
   Smile at the claims of long descent.
Howe'er it be, it seems to me,
   'T is only noble to be good.
Kind hearts are more than coronets,
   And simple faith than Norman blood.

I know you, Clara Vere de Vere:
   You pine among your halls and towers:
The languid light of your proud eyes
   Is wearied of the rolling hours.
In glowing health, with boundless wealth,
   But sickening of a vague disease,

You know so ill to deal with time,
    You needs must play such pranks as these.

Clara, Clara Vere de Vere,
    If time be heavy on your hands,
Are there no beggars at your gate,
    Nor any poor about your lands?
Oh! teach the orphan-boy to read,
    Or teach the orphan girl to sew,
Pray Heaven for a human heart,
    And let the foolish yeoman go.

THE BROOK.

I SLIP, I slide, I gloom, I glance,
    Among my skimming swallows;
I make the netted sunbeam dance
    Against my sandy shallows.

I murmur under moon and stars
    In brambly wildernesses;
I linger by my shingly bars;
    I loiter round my cresses;

And out again I curve and flow
    To join the brimming river,
For men may come, and men may go,
    But I go on forever.

ENOCH ARDEN SHIPWRECKED.

THE mountain wooded to the peak, the lawns
And winding glades high up like ways to Heaven,
The slender coco's drooping crown of plumes,
The lightning flash of insect and of bird,
The luster of the long convolvuluses
That coiled around the stately stems, and ran
Even to the limit of the land, the glows
And glories of the broad belt of the world,
All these he saw; but what he fain had seen
He could not see, the kindly human face,
Nor ever hear a kindly voice, but heard

The myriad shriek of wheeling ocean-fowl,
The league-long roller thundering on the reef,
The moving whisper of huge trees that branched
And blossomed in the zenith, or the sweep
Of some precipitous rivulet to the wave,
As down the shore he ranged, or all day long
Sat often in the seaward-gazing gorge,
A shipwrecked sailor, waiting for a sail;
No sail from day to day, but every day
The sunrise broken into scarlet shafts
Among the palms and ferns and precipices;
The blaze upon the waters to the east;
The blaze upon his island overhead;
The blaze upon the waters to the west;
Then the great stars that globed themselves in Heaven,
The hollower-bellowing ocean, and again
The scarlet shafts of sunrise, — but no sail.

THE BUGLE SONG.

THE splendor falls on castle walls
    And snowy summits, old in story;
The long light shakes across the lakes,
    And the wild cataract leaps in glory.
Blow, bugle, blow, set the wild echoes flying,
Blow, bugle; answer, echoes, dying, dying, dying.

O hark, O hear! how thin and clear,
    And thinner, clearer, farther going!
O sweet and far from cliff and scar
    The horns of Elfland faintly blowing!
Blow, let us hear the purple glens replying:
Blow, bugle; answer, echoes, dying, dying, dying.

O love, they die in yon rich sky,
    They faint on hill or field or river:
Our echoes roll from soul to soul,
    And grow forever and forever.
Blow, bugle, blow, set the wild echoes flying,
And answer, echoes, answer, dying, dying, dying.

GRAY.

1810-1888

PROFESSOR ASA GRAY, the eminent botanist, was born in Paris, Oneida County, New York, November 18, 1810. He studied medicine, but his enthusiastic love of botanical investigation withheld him from the practice of his profession. In 1834 he received the appointment of Botanist to the United States Exploring Expedition, but, impatient of the delays which hindered that enterprise, he resigned his office in 1837. About that time he was chosen Professor of Botany in the University of Michigan; before that institution was opened he accepted the Fisher Professorship of Natural History in Harvard University, and has ever since filled it with honor to himself and great advantage to science. His first contribution to the literature of botany was *North American Gramineæ and Cyperaceæ*, of which two volumes were published in 1834–35. This brought him prominently before the scientific world. His botanical career, however, may be said to date from his reading in December, 1834, before the New York Lyceum of Natural History, of *A Notice of some New, Rare, or otherwise Interesting Plants from the Northern and Western Portions of the State of New York.* In 1838, in conjunction with John Torrey, M. D., he prepared the first part of *The Flora of North America.* This work has never been completed; but in its fragmentary state it is esteemed one of the most valuable contributions ever made in America to the science of Botany. The collections made by the Exploring Expedition of Commodore Wilkes, during the years 1838–42, except those obtained from the Pacific Coast, were placed in the hands of Professor Gray for elaboration, and the fruits of his labors are preserved in two volumes on the *Botany of the United States Exploring Expedition.* His numerous papers in the memoirs of the learned societies, although not of a popular character, comprise a large part of his most important contributions to science. The most generally interesting one is his *Memoir on the Botany of Japan in its Relations to that of the United States*, which subject was followed up in his Address as President of the American Association for the Advancement of Science, delivered at Dubuque, August, 1872. But while, by the works above-mentioned and many others unnamed, Professor Gray has won fame at home and abroad, he has established a still stronger claim upon the grateful respect of humanity by his untiring and successful efforts to popularize the study of Botany by means of elementary books. His *Structural Botany* has gone through a multitude of editions, and is universally accepted as one of the best expositions of vegetable physiology and morphology ever written, while his *Manual of Botany* has long been known as a standard work. Within a few years he has produced several books of an elementary character, which combine literary grace and substantial instruction in singularly happy union. Among these are *How Plants Grow, How Plants Behave, Lessons in Botany, The School and Field Book of Botany*, etc. Professor Gray possesses remarkable qualifications for this work, his expositions being singularly clear, and his style in all respects attractive. As a representative of science in America, he enjoys an enviable reputation abroad, and his works are quoted with admiring respect by the most distinguished European *savans*.

HOW CERTAIN PLANTS CAPTURE INSECTS.

THIS is not a common habit of plants. Insects are fed and allowed to depart unharmed. When captures are made they must sometimes be purely accidental and meaningless; as in those species of *Silene* called Catch-fly, because small flies and other weak insects, sticking fast to a clammy exudation of the calyxes in some species, of a part of the stem in others, are unable to extricate themselves and so perish. But in certain cases insects are caught in ways so remarkable that we cannot avoid regarding them as contrivances, as genuine *fly-traps*.

Flower fly-traps are certainly to be found in some plants of the Orchis family. One instance is that of Cypripedium or Lady's-Slipper, which is a contrivance for cross-fertilization. Here the insect is entrapped for the purpose of securing its services; and the detention is only temporary. If it did not escape from one flower to enter into another, the whole purpose of the contrivance would be defeated. Not so, however, in leaf fly-traps. These all take the insect's life, — whether with intent or not it may be difficult to make out. The commonest and the most ambiguous leaf fly-traps are such as Pitchers, of which those of our *Sarracenia* or Sidesaddle-flower are most familiar. A common yellow-flowered species of the Southern States has them so very long and narrow, that they are popularly named *Trumpets*. In these pitchers or tubes water is generally found, sometimes caught from rain, but in other cases evidently furnished by the plant, the pitcher being so constructed that water cannot rain in: this water abounds with drowned insects, commonly in all stages of decay. One would suppose that insects which have crawled into the pitcher might as readily crawl out; but they do not, and closer examination shows that escaping is not as easy as entering. In most pitchers of this sort there are sharp and stiff hairs within, all pointing downward, which offer considerable obstruction to returning, but none to entering.

Why plants which are rooted in wet bogs or in moist ground need to catch water in pitchers, or to secrete it there, is a mystery, unless it is wanted to drown flies in. And what they gain from a solution of dead flies is equally hard to guess, unless this acts as a liquid manure.

Into such pitchers as those of the common species rain may fall; but not readily into others, not at all into those of the Parrot-headed species of the Southern States, for the inflated lid or cover arches over the mouth of the pitcher completely. This is even more strikingly so in *Darlingtonia*, the curious Californian Pitcher-plant lately made known and cultivated: in this the contracted entrance to the pitcher is concealed under the hood and looks downward instead of upward; and even the small chance of any rain entering by aid of the wind is, as it were, guarded against by a curious appendage, resembling the forked tail of some fish, which hangs over the front. Any water found in this pitcher must come from the plant itself. So it also must in the combined Pitcher and Tendril of Nepenthes. These Pitcher-plants are woody climbers, natives of the Indian Archipelago, and not rarely cultivated in hothouses, as a curiosity. Some of their leaves lengthen the tip into the tendril only ; some of the lower bear a pitcher only ; but the best developed leaves have both, — the tendril for climbing, the pitcher one can hardly say for what purpose. The pitcher is tightly closed by a neatly fitting lid when young; and in strong and healthy plants there is commonly a little water in it, which could not possibly have been introduced from without. After they are fully grown the lid opens by a hinge ; then a little water might be supposed to rain in. In the humid, sultry climates they inhabit it probably does so freely ; and the leaves are found partly filled with dead flies, as in our wild Pitcher-plants.

The drowning of insects in plant-pitchers is of course an accidental occurrence, and any supposed advantage of this to the plant may be altogether fanciful. But we cannot deny that the supply of liquid manure may be useful. Before concluding that they are of no account, it may be well to contemplate other sorts of leaf fly-traps.

All species of Sundew (*Drosera*) have their leaves, and some their stalks also, beset with bristles tipped with a gland from which oozes a drop of clear but very glutinous liquid, making the plant appear as if studded with dew-drops. These remain, glistening in the sun, long after dew-drops would have been dissipated. Small flies, gnats, and such-like insects, seemingly enticed by the glittering drops, stick fast upon them, and perish by starvation, one would suppose without any benefit whatever to the plant. But in the broad-leaved wild species of our bogs, such as the common Round-leaved Sundew, the upper face and edges of the blade of the leaf bear stronger bristles, tipped with a larger glutinous drop, and the whole forms what we must allow to be a veritable fly-trap.

For, when a small fly alights on the upper face, and is held by some of the glutinous drops long enough for the leaf to act, the surrounding bristles slowly bend inwards so as to bring their glutinous tips also against the body of the insect, adding, one by one, to the bonds, and rendering captivity and death certain. This movement of the bristles must be of the same nature as that by which tendrils and some leafstalks bend or coil. It is much too slow to be visible except in the result, which takes a few hours or even a day or two to be completed. Here, then, is a contrivance for catching flies, a most elaborate one, in action slow but sure. And the different species of Sundew offer all gradations between those with merely scattered and motionless dewy-tipped bristles, to which flies may chance to stick, and this more complex arrangement, which we cannot avoid regarding as intended for fly-catching. Moreover, in both of our commoner species, the blade of the leaf itself incurves, so as to fold round its victim!

And a most practiced observer, whose observations are not yet published, declares that the leaves of the common Round-leaved Sundew act differently when different objects are placed upon them. For instance, if a particle of raw meat be substituted for the living fly, the bristles will close upon it in the same manner; but to a particle of chalk or wood they remain nearly indifferent. If any doubt should still remain whether the fly-catching in Sundews is accidental or intentional, — in other words, whether the leaf is so constructed and arranged in order that it may capture flies, — the doubt may perhaps disappear upon the contemplation of another and even more extraordinary plant of the same family of the Sundew, namely, Venus's Flytrap, or *Dionæa muscipula*. This plant abounds in the low savannas around Wilmington, North Carolina, and is native nowhere else. It is not very difficult to cultivate, at least for a time, and it is kept in many choice conservatories as a vegetable wonder.

The trap is the end of the leaf. It is somewhat like the leaf of Sundew, only larger, about an inch in diameter, with bristles still stouter, but only round the margin, like a fringe, and no clammy liquid or gland at their tips. The leaf folds on itself as if hinged at the midrib. Three more delicate bristles are seen on the face upon close inspection. When these are touched by the finger or the point of a pencil, the open trap shuts with a quick motion, and after a considerable interval it reopens. When a fly or other insect alights on the surface and brushes against these sensitive bristles, the trap closes promptly, generally imprisoning the intruder. It closes at first with the sides convex and the bristles crossing each other like the fingers of interlocked hands or the teeth of a steel trap. But soon the sides of the trap flatten down and press firmly upon the victim; and it now requires a very considerable force to open the trap. If nothing is caught, the trap presently reopens of itself and is ready for another attempt. When a fly or any similar insect is captured it is retained until it perishes, — is killed, indeed, and consumed; after which it opens for another capture. But after the first or second it acts sluggishly and feebly, it ages and hardens, at length loses its sensibility, and slowly decays.

It cannot be supposed that plants, like boys, catch flies for pastime or in objectless wantonness. Living beings though they are, yet they are not of a sufficiently high order for that. · It is equally incredible that such an exquisite apparatus as this should be purposeless. And in the present case the evidence of the purpose and of the meaning of the strange action is wellnigh complete. The face of this living trap is thickly sprinkled with glands immersed in its texture, of elaborate structure under the microscope, but large enough to be clearly discerned with a hand-lens; these glands, soon after an insect is closed upon, give out a saliva-like liquid, which moistens the insect, and in a short time (within a week) dissolves all its soft parts, — digests them, we must believe; and the liquid, with the animal matter it has dissolved, is re-absorbed into the leaf! We are forced to conclude that, in addition to the ordinary faculties and function of a vegetable, this plant is really carnivorous.

That, while all plants are food for animals, some few should, in turn and to some extent, feed upon them, will appear more credible when it is considered that whole tribes of plants of the lowest grade (Mould-Fungi and the like) habitually feed upon living plants and living animals, or upon their juices when dead. An account of them would make a volume of itself, and an interesting one. But all goes to show that the instances of extraordinary behavior which have been recounted in these chapters * are not mere prodigies, wholly out of the general order of Nature, but belong to the order of Nature, and indeed are hardly different in kind from, or really more wonderful than, the doings of many of the commonest plants, which, until our special attention is called to them, ordinarily pass unregarded.

---

* *How Plants Behave: How they move, climb, employ insects to work for them, etc.* A charming elementary work, from which this extract is taken.

POE.

1811 – 1849.

EDGAR ALLAN POE, perhaps the most brilliant, and surely the most unfortunate, of young American poets, was born in Baltimore, Maryland, in 1811, and died in 1849. Left a penniless orphan on the death of his parents, who were members of the theatrical profession, he was adopted by a rich merchant of Baltimore, and sent to school. In 1822 he entered the University of Virginia, but his habits soon became so dissolute as to compel his expulsion. His benefactor refusing young Poe's demands for money to be squandered at the gaming-table, the latter resolved to go, like Byron, to the aid of the struggling Greeks. He went to Europe, but never reached the theater of war, and in about a year was sent home by the United States Consul at St. Petersburg. His long-suffering benefactor next procured him an appointment to West Point; but the high-spirited youth could not endure the strict discipline of cadet-life, and in less than a year he was again expelled. Again he was received at the house of his benefactor, but his stay, this time, was short; for some offense whose nature has never been clearly explained, he was shut out forever from the house that had been his only home. He at once entered upon that career of literary Bohemianism which was to end only with his life. In 1829 a small collection of his poems was published in Baltimore, and was received with encouraging favor; but his literary work done prior to his twenty-fourth year had little permanent value. While editing the Southern Literary Messenger, at Richmond, Virginia, 1835 – 37, he married his cousin, Virginia Clemm. In 1839 he went to New York, where he wrote for newspapers and magazines, and in 1840 to Philadelphia, where he edited Graham's Magazine. Returning to the first-named city, he engaged in miscellaneous literary labor, contributing his most famous poem, *The Raven*, to Colton's Whig Review, in February, 1845. His life, during the next four years, was a sad one; poverty continually oppressed him; his loving and suffering wife was taken from him; and, at last, having become almost a vagabond, he was carried to the Baltimore Hospital, where he died, October 7, 1849, aged thirty-eight years. Although Poe is best known as a poet, many of the ablest critics agree that he was even greater as a writer of tales. In this department of literature he occupied a niche in which he has had no successor. His imagination was exceptionally powerful, his love of the weird and marvelous very strong, and his skill in producing somber and uncanny effects was extraordinary. Though he wrote a good deal of verse, but a small proportion of it is worthy of his genius. As a critic he was remarkable mainly for his violent abusiveness, and his *Literati of New York City*, though spicy reading, gives no evidence of high critical power. Two or three of his poems, *The Raven, The Bells, Annabel Lee,* and perhaps some others, will always be read and admired. The story of his short life conveys a solemn warning, and suggests the thought that the most brilliant intellectual gifts are a curse rather than a blessing, if unaccompanied by a vigorous directing and controlling moral sense. It confirms, too, the notion that marked precocity is unfavorable to, if not absolutely incompatible with, healthy and fruitful intellectual development. In the most prosperous natures, the moral growth precedes the mental, — is its guide and support. Yet Poe is to be pitied rather than condemned: his faults grew out of his misfortunes.

ANNABEL LEE.

IT was many and many a year ago,
  In a kingdom by the sea,
That a maiden lived, whom you may know
  By the name of Annabel Lee;
And this maiden she lived with no other thought
  Than to love, and be loved by me.

I was a child and she was a child,
　In this kingdom by the sea;
But we loved with a love that was more than love,
　I and my Annabel Lee, —
With a love that the wingéd seraphs of heaven
　Coveted her and me.

And this was the reason that long ago,
　In this kingdom by the sea,
A wind blew out of a cloud, chilling
　My beautiful Annabel Lee;
So that her high-born kinsmen came,
　And bore her away from me,
To shut her up in a sepulcher,
　In this kingdom by the sea.

The angels, not so happy in heaven,
　Went envying her and me.
Yes! that was the reason (as all men know)
　In this kingdom by the sea, .
That the wind came out of the cloud by night,
　Chilling and killing my Annabel Lee.

But our love it was stronger by far than the love
　Of those who were older than we,
　Of many far wiser than we;
And neither the angels in heaven above,
　Nor the demons down under the sea,
Can ever dissever my soul from the soul
　Of the beautiful Annabel Lee.

For the moon never beams without bringing me dreams
　Of the beautiful Annabel Lee,
And the stars never rise but I feel the bright eyes
　Of the beautiful Annabel Lee.
And so, all the night-tide I lie down by the side
Of my darling, my darling, my life, and my bride,
　In her sepulcher there by the sea,
　In her tomb by the sounding sea.

FROM THE RAVEN.

ONCE upon a midnight dreary, while I pondered, weak and weary,
Over many a quaint and curious volume of forgotten lore, —
While I nodded, nearly napping, suddenly there came a tapping,
As of some one gently rapping, rapping at my chamber door.
" 'T is some visitor," I muttered, " tapping at my chamber door;
     Only this, and nothing more."

.   .   .   .   .

Open then I flung the shutter, when, with many a flirt and flutter,
In there stepped a stately raven of the saintly days of yore.
Not the least obeisance made he; not an instant stopped or stayed
     he ;
But, with mien of lord or lady, perched above my chamber door, —
Perched upon a bust of Pallas, just above my chamber door, —
     Perched, and sat, and nothing more.

Then this ebony bird beguiling my sad fancy into smiling,
By the grave and stern decorum of the countenance it wore,
" Though thy crest be shorn and shaven, thou," I said, " art sure no
     craven ;
Ghastly, grim, and ancient raven, wandering from the nightly shore,
Tell me what thy lordly name is on the night's Plutonian shore ? "
     Quoth the raven, " Nevermore ! "

THE BELLS.

I.

     HEAR the sledges with the bells, —
       Silver bells, —
What a world of merriment their melody foretells !
     How they tinkle, tinkle, tinkle,
      In the icy air of night !
     While the stars that oversprinkle
     All the heavens seem to twinkle
      With a crystalline delight, —
     Keeping time, time, time,
     In a sort of Runic rhyme,

To the tintinnabulation that so musically wells
From the bells, bells, bells, bells,
Bells, bells, bells, —
From the jingling and the tinkling of the bells.

II.

Hear the mellow wedding bells, —
Golden bells !
What a world of happiness their harmony foretells !
Through the balmy air of night
How they ring out their delight !
From the molten-golden notes,
And all in tune,
What a liquid ditty floats
To the turtle-dove that listens, while she gloats
On the moon !
O, from out the sounding cells,
What a gush of euphony voluminously wells !
How it swells !
How it dwells
On the Future ! how it tells
Of the rapture that impels
To the swinging and the ringing
Of the bells, bells, bells,
Of the bells, bells, bells, bells,
Bells, bells, bells, —
To the rhyming and the chiming of the bells.

III.

Hear the loud alarum bells, —
Brazen bells !
What a tale of terror, now, their turbulency tells !
In the startled ear of night
How they scream out their affright !
Too much horrified to speak,
They can only shriek, shriek,
Out of tune,
In the clamorous appealing to the mercy of the fire,
In a mad expostulation with the deaf and frantic fire

Leaping higher, higher, higher,
With a desperate desire,
And a resolute endeavor,
Now — now to sit or never,
By the side of the pale-faced moon.
O the bells, bells, bells,
What a tale their terror tells
Of despair !
How they clang and clash and roar !
What a horror they outpour
On the bosom of the palpitating air !
Yet the ear it fully knows,
By the twanging,
And the clanging,
How the danger ebbs and flows ;
Yet the ear distinctly tells,
In the jangling,
And the wrangling,
How the danger sinks and swells,
By the sinking or the swelling in the anger of the bells, —
Of the bells, —
Of the bells, bells, bells, bells,
Bells, bells, bells, —
In the clamor and the clangor of the bells !

IV.

Hear the tolling of the bells, —
Iron bells !
What a world of solemn thought their monody compels !
In the silence of the night,
How we shiver with affright
At the melancholy menace of their tone ;
For every sound that floats
From the rust within their throats
Is a groan.
And the people, — ah, the people,
They that dwell up in the steeple,
All alone,
And who tolling, tolling, tolling,

11 *

In that muffled monotone,
Feel a glory in so rolling
  On the human heart a stone, —
They are neither man nor woman, —
They are neither brute nor human, —
    They are ghouls:
And their king it is who tolls;
And he rolls, rolls, rolls,
    Rolls,
  A pæan from the bells!
And his merry bosom swells
  With the pæan of the bells!
And he dances and he yells;
Keeping time, time, time,
In a sort of Runic rhyme,
  To the pæan of the bells, —
    Of the bells;
Keeping time, time, time,
In a sort of Runic rhyme,
  To the throbbing of the bells, —
Of the bells, bells, bells, —
  To the sobbing of the bells;
Keeping time, time, time,
  As he knells, knells, knells,
In a happy Runic rhyme,
  To the rolling of the bells, —
Of the bells, bells, bells, —
  To the tolling of the bells,
Of the bells, bells, bells, bells, —
  Bells, bells, bells, —
To the moaning and the groaning of the bells.

GREELEY.

1811 – 1873.

HORACE GREELEY, the greatest of American journalists, and eminent as a writer of pure and vigorous English, was born in Amherst, New Hampshire, in 1811 and died in 1872. He was the son of a poor farmer, and was in every sense "a self-made man." Pure in mind, honest and upright to such an extent that he was called by many an eccentric man, he made his way, by his own unaided efforts, from poverty to well-deserved fame as a writer and philosopher. His style is better in certain respects than that of any of his contemporary writers. It is terse and masculine, so evenly balanced and nicely constructed, so simple and yet so graceful that it is equally admired by the uneducated farmer and the fastidious literary critic. Mr. Greeley will always be best known as the founder and first editor of the *New York Tribune*, but his collected writings will hold a place in standard American literature. The best known of these are: *Recollections of a Busy Life*, *What I know of Farming*, and *The American Conflict*, a history of the late civil war.

THE EDITOR.

IT only remains to me to speak more especially of my own vocation, — the Editor's, — which bears much the same relation to the Author's that the Bellows-blower's bears to the Organist's, the Player's to the Dramatist's. The Editor, from the absolute necessity of the case, cannot speak deliberately; he must write to-day of to-day's incidents and aspects, though these may be completely overlaid and transformed by the incidents and aspects of to-morrow. He must write and strive in the full consciousness that whatever honor or distinction he may acquire must perish with the generation that bestowed them. No other public teacher lives so wholly in the present as the Editor; and the noblest affirmations of unpopular truth — the most self-sacrificing defiance of a base and selfish Public Sentiment that regards only the most sordid ends, and values every utterance solely as it tends to preserve quiet and contentment, while the dollars fall jingling into the merchant's drawer, the land-jobber's vault, and the miser's bag — can but be noted in their day, and with their day forgotten. It is his cue to utter silken and smooth sayings, — to condemn Vice so as not to interfere with the pleasures or alarm the consciences of the vicious, — to commend and glorify Labor without attempting to expose or repress any of the gainful ·contrivances by which Labor is plundered and degraded. Thus sidling dexterously between somewhere and nowhere, the Able Editor of the Nineteenth Century may glide through life respectable and in good case, and lie down to his long rest with the non-achievements of his life emblazoned on the very whitest marble, surmounting and glorifying his dust.

There is a different and sterner path, — I know not whether there be any now qualified to tread it, — I am not sure that even one has ever followed it implicitly, in view of the certain meagerness of its temporal rewards and the haste wherewith any fame acquired in a sphere so thoroughly ephemeral as the Editor's must be shrouded by the dark waters of oblivion.   This path demands an ear ever open to the plaints of the wronged and the suffering, though they can never repay advocacy, and those who mainly support newspapers will be annoyed and often exposed by it; a heart as sensitive to oppression and degradation in the next street as if they were practiced in Brazil or Japan; a pen as ready to expose and reprove the crimes whereby wealth is amassed and luxury enjoyed in our own country at this hour, as if they had only been committed by Turks or Pagans in Asia some centuries ago.   Such an Editor, could one be found or trained, need not expect to lead an easy, indolent, or wholly joyous life, — to be blessed by Archbishops or followed by the approving shouts of ascendant majorities : but he might find some recompense for their loss in the calm verdict of an approving conscience ; and the tears of the despised and the friendless, preserved from utter despair by his efforts and remonstrances, might freshen for a season the daisies that bloomed above his grave.

THE REFORMER.

AND, indeed, though the life of the Reformer may seem rugged and arduous, it were hard to say considerately that any other were worth living at all.   Who can thoughtfully affirm that the career of the conquering, desolating, subjugating warrior, — of the devotee of Gold, or Pomp, or Sensual Joys ; the monarch in his purple, the Miser by his chest, the wassailer over his bowl, — is not a libel on Humanity and an offense against God ?   But the earnest, unselfish Reformer, — — born into a state of darkness, evil, and suffering, and honestly striving to replace these by light and purity and happiness, — he may fall and die, as so many have done before him, but he cannot fail. His vindication shall gleam from the walls of his hovel, his dungeon, his tomb ; it shall shine in the radiant eyes of uncorrupted Childhood, and fall in blessings from the lips of high-hearted, generous Youth.

As the untimely death of the good is our strongest moral assurance of the Resurrection, so the life wearily worn out in doubtful and perilous conflict with Wrong and Woe is our most conclusive evidence that Wrong and Woe shall yet vanish forever. Luther, dying amid the agonizing tears and wild consternation of all Protestant Germany, — Columbus, borne in regal pomp to his grave by the satellites of the royal miscreant whose ingratitude and perfidy had broken his mighty heart,* — these teach us, at least, that all true greatness is ripened and tempered and proved in life-long struggle against vicious beliefs, traditions, practices, institutions; and that not to have been a Reformer is not to have truly lived.

Life is a bubble which any breath may dissolve; Wealth or Power a snow-flake, melting momently into the treacherous deep across whose waves we are floated on to our unseen destiny: but to have lived so that one less orphan is called to choose between starvation and infamy, to have lived so that some eyes of those whom Fame shall never know are brightened and others suffused at the name of the beloved one, — so that the few who knew him truly shall recognize him as a bright, warm, cheering presence, which was here for a season and left the world no worse for his stay in it, — this surely is to have really *lived*, — and not wholly in vain.

AGRICULTURE.

Is agriculture a repulsive pursuit? That what has been called farming has repelled many of the youth of our day, I perceive; and I glory in the fact. An American boy, who has received a fair common-school education and has an active, inquiring mind, does not willingly consent merely to drive oxen and hold the plow forever. He will do these with alacrity, if they come in his way; he will not accept them as the be-all and the end-all of his career. He will not sit down in a rude, slovenly, naked home, devoid of flowers, and trees, and books, and periodicals, and intelligent, inspiring, refining conversation, and there plod through a life of drudgery as hopeless and cheerless as any mule's. He has needs, and hopes, and aspirations, which this life does not and ought not to satisfy. This might have served his progenitor in the ninth century; but this is the nineteenth, and the young American knows it.

He needs to feel the intellectual life of the period flowing freely

* See note, page 98.

into and through him, — needs to feel that, though the city and the railroad are out of sight, the latter is daily bringing within his reach all that is noblest and best in the achievements and attractions of the former. He may not listen to our ablest orators in the senate or in the pulpit; but the press multiplies their best thoughts and most forcible expressions at the rate of ten to twenty thousand copies per hour; and its issues are within the reach of every industrious family.

To arrest the rush of our youth to the cities, we have only to diffuse what is best of the cities through the country; and this the latest triumphs of civilization enable us easily to do. A home irradiated by the best thoughts of the sages and heroes of all time, even though these be compressed within a few rusty volumes, cheered by the frequent arrival of two or three choice periodicals, and surrounded by such floral evidences of taste and refinement as are within the reach of the poorest owner of the soil he tills, will not be spurned as a prison by any youth not thoroughly corrupted and depraved.

Any American farmer, who has two hands and knows how to use them, may, at fifty years of age, have a better library than King Solomon ever dreamed of, though he declared that "of making of many books there is no end"; any intelligent farmer's son may have a better knowledge of Nature and her laws when twenty years old than Aristotle or Pliny ever attained. The steam-engine, the electric telegraph, and the power-press have brought knowledge nearer to the humblest cabin than it was, ten centuries since, to the stateliest mansion; let the cabin be careful not to disparage or repel it.

But thousands of farmers are more intent on leaving money and lands to their children than on informing and enriching their minds. They starve their souls in order to pamper their bodies. They grudge their sons that which would make them truly wise, in order to provide them with what can at best but make them rich in corn and cattle, while poor in manly purpose and generous ideas.

Modern agriculture is an art — or rather a circle of arts — based upon natural science, which is a methodical exposition of divine law. The savage is Nature's thrall, whom she scorches, freezes, starves, drowns, as her caprice may dictate. He lives in constant dread of her frosts, her tornadoes, her lightnings. Science teaches his civilized successor to turn her wildest eccentricities to his own use and profit. Her floods and gales saw his timber and grind his grain; in time, they will chop his trees, speed his plow, and till his crops as well.

Science transforms and exalts him from the slave into the master of the elements. If he does not yet harness the electric fluid to his plow, his boat, his wagon, and make the most docile and useful of his servants, it is because he is still but little advanced from barbarism. Essentially, the lightning garnered in a summer cloud should be as much at his command, and as subservient to his needs, as the water that refreshes his thirsty fields and starts his hitherto lifeless wheels.

Only good farming pays. He who sows or plants without reasonable assurance of good crops annually, might better earn wages of some capable neighbor than work for so poor a paymaster as he is certain to prove himself. The good farmer is proved such by the steady appreciation of his crops. Any one may reap an ample harvest from a fertile, virgin soil; the good farmer alone grows good crops at first, and better and better ever afterward.

It is far easier to maintain the productive capacity of a farm than to restore it. To exhaust its fecundity, and then attempt its restoration by buying costly commercial fertilizers, is wasteful and irrational. The good farmer sells mainly such products as are least exhaustive. Necessity may constrain him, for the first year or two, to sell grain, or even hay; but he will soon send off his surplus mainly in the form of cotton, or wool, or meat, or butter and cheese, or something else that returns to the soil nearly all that is taken from it. A bank account daily drawn upon, while nothing is deposited to its credit, must soon respond, " No funds " : so with a farm similarly treated.

Wisdom is never dear, provided the article be genuine. I have known farmers who toiled constantly from daybreak to dark, yet died poor, because, through ignorance, they wrought to disadvantage. If every farmer would devote two hours of each day to reading and reflection, there would be fewer failures in farming than there are. The best investment a farmer can make for his children is that which surrounds their youth with the rational delights of a beauteous, attractive home. The dwelling may be small and rude, yet a few flowers will embellish, as choice fruit-trees will enrich and gladden it; while grass and shade are within the reach of the humblest. Hardly any labor done on a farm is so profitable as that which makes the wife and children fond and proud of their home.

A good, practical education, including a good trade, is a better outfit for a youth than a grand estate with the drawback of an empty mind. Many parents have slaved and pinched to leave their children rich, when half the sum thus lavished would have profited them far more had it been devoted to the cultivation of their minds, the enlargement of their capacity to think, observe, and work. The one structure that no neighborhood can afford to do without is the school-house.

A small library of well-selected books in his home has saved many a youth from wandering into the baleful ways of the prodigal son. Where paternal strictness and severity would have bred nothing but dislike and a fixed resolve to abscond at the first opportunity, good books and pleasant surroundings have weaned many a youth from his first wild impulse to go to sea or cross the continent, and made him a docile, contented, obedient, happy lingerer by the parental fireside. In a family, however rich or poor, no other good is so cheap or so precious as thoughtful, watchful love.

Most men are born poor, but no man, who has average capacities and tolerable luck, need remain so. And the farmer's calling, though proffering no sudden leaps, no ready short-cuts to opulence, is the surest of all ways from poverty and want to comfort and independence. Other men must climb; the temperate, frugal, diligent, provident farmer may *grow* into competence and every external accessory to happiness. Each year of his devotion to his homestead may find it more valuable, more attractive than the last, and leave it better still.

There are discoveries in natural science and improvements in mechanics which conduce to the efficiency of agriculture; but the principles which underlie this first of arts are old as agriculture itself. Greek and Roman sages made observations so acute and practical that the farmers of to-day may ponder them with profit, while modern literature is padded with essays on farming not worth the paper they have spoiled. And yet the generation whereof I am part has witnessed great strides in your vocation, while the generation preparing to take our places will doubtless witness still greater. I bid you hold fast to the good, with minds receptive of and eager for the better, and rejoice in your knowledge that there is no nobler pursuit and no more inviting soil than those which you proudly call your own.

THACKERAY.

1811 – 1863.

WILLIAM MAKEPEACE THACKERAY, one of the great writers of fiction of the nineteenth century, was born in Calcutta in 1811, but was sent to England while a child, and educated in the Charterhouse School, which he has immortalized in *The Newcomes*, and at Cambridge University. On the death of his parents he found himself in possession of a handsome fortune; but it soon vanished, and he was compelled to earn a subsistence. He dallied with Law, courted Art with greater earnestness, and finally — a resolution for which the lovers of high fiction will never cease to be grateful — resolved to devote himself to Literature. His first essay in letters was in the department of journalism; he wrote for the Times, The New Monthly Magazine, and Punch, to which latter periodical he contributed the inimitable *Snob Papers*, *Jeames's Diary*, etc. His first volume, *The Paris Sketch-Book*, was published in 1840, and was followed during the next seven years by several collections of essays, sketches, etc. In 1848 appeared his first novel, *Vanity Fair*, a work that deserves rank among the masterpieces of English fiction. Two years later *The History of Pendennis* was given to the world, which, if it did not enhance the author's reputation, confirmed his title to a high place among English novelists. *The History of Henry Esmond*, *The Virginians*, *The Newcomes*, appeared at short intervals, the latter, which was issued in 1855, being pronounced by high literary authority his masterpiece. *Lovel the Widower* (1861) and *The Adventures of Philip* (1862) mark the decay of the author's powers. At his death in 1863 he left unfinished a novel called *Denis Ducal*. *The Four Georges*, lectures first delivered in the principal American cities, were published in book form in 1860. It is a remarkable fact that while Thackeray's writings were comparatively neglected in England, they enjoyed an extensive popularity in the United States, where they are still read with eagerness and delight by all who look beneath the surface of novels into the soul that animates them. It is impossible to do justice to the characteristics of Thackeray as a writer in the limits of this notice; but two or three of them may be briefly mentioned. He was a cynic, though a kindly one: he was a keen student of human nature, quick to recognize and to denounce its weaknesses; yet he apparently found his deepest pleasure in depicting its lovely features and recording its noblest manifestations. The character of Colonel Newcome is, we think, unsurpassed, if equaled, as a type of true manhood; its pathos is indescribable, and the memory of it lingers in the reader's mind, softening and refining. Thackeray's humor was nimble rather than rich; but it is not, though commonly held to be, a very important component of his intellectual strength. He was a reformer, who exposed and denounced social wrongs, not with rude force, but with polished satire. His mastery of English was wonderful; in the purity and vigor of his language he was unequaled by any writer of his time. The first extract is from *The Four Georges*; the others are from *Pendennis*.

GEORGE THE THIRD.*

WE have to glance over sixty years in as many minutes. To read the mere catalogue of characters who figured during that long period, would occupy our allotted time, and we should have all text and no sermon. England has to undergo the revolt of the American colonies; to submit to defeat and separation; to shake under the volcano

---

* George the Third was king of England during our Revolutionary War. He was born in 1738, ascended the throne in 1760, and reigned for sixty years. He became insane in 1810, and died in 1820. His weaknesses are most mercilessly criticised by Thackeray in his *Lectures on the Four Georges*, as will be seen from the extract.

of the French Revolution; to grapple and fight for the life with her gigantic enemy Napoleon; to gasp and rally after that tremendous struggle. The old society, with its courtly splendors, has to pass away; generations of statesmen to rise and disappear; Pitt to follow Chatham to the tomb; the memory of Rodney and Wolfe to be superseded by Nelson's and Wellington's glory; the old poets who unite us to Queen Anne's time to sink into their graves; Johnson to die, and Scott and Byron to arise, Garrick to delight the world with his dazzling dramatic genius, and Kean to leap on the stage and take possession of the astonished theater. Steam has to be invented; kings to be beheaded, banished, deposed, restored; Napoleon to be but an episode, and George III. is to be alive through all these varied changes, to accompany his people through all these revolutions of thought, government, society, — to survive out of the old world into ours.

His mother's bigotry and hatred George inherited with the courageous obstinacy of his own race; but he was a firm believer where his fathers had been free-thinkers, and a true and fond supporter of the Church, of which he was the titular defender. Like other dull men, the king was all his life suspicious of superior people. He did not like Fox; he did not like Reynolds; he did not like Nelson, Chatham, Burke: he was testy at the idea of all innovations, and suspicious of all innovators. He loved mediocrities; Benjamin West was his favorite painter; Beattie was his poet. The king lamented, not without pathos, in his after life, that his education had been neglected. He was a dull lad, brought up by narrow-minded people. The cleverest tutors in the world could have done little probably to expand that small intellect, though they might have improved his tastes and taught his perceptions some generosity.

George married the Princess Charlotte of Mecklenburg Strelitz, and for years they led the happiest, simplest lives, sure, ever led by married couple. It is said the king winced · when he first saw his homely little bride; but, however that may be, he was a true and faithful husband to her, as she was a faithful and loving wife. They had the simplest pleasures, — the very mildest and simplest, — little country dances, to which a dozen couple were invited, and where the honest king would stand up and dance for three hours at a time to one tune; after which delicious excitement they would go to bed without any supper (the Court people grumbling sadly at that absence of supper), and get up quite early the next morning, and perhaps the next night have another dance; or the queen would play on the spinnet, — she played pretty well, Haydn said; or the king would read to her a paper out of the *Spectator*, or perhaps one of Ogden's sermons. O Arcadia! what a life it must have been!

The theater was always his delight. His bishops and clergy used to attend it, thinking it no shame to appear where that good man was seen. He is said not to have cared for Shakespeare or tragedy much; farces and pantomimes were his joy; and especially when clown swallowed a carrot or a string of sausages, he would laugh so outrageously that the lovely princess by his side would have to say, " My gracious monarch, do compose yourself." But he continued to laugh, and at the very smallest farces, as long as his poor wits were left him.

" George, be a king! " were the words which his mother was forever croaking in the ears of her son; and a king the simple, stubborn, affectionate, bigoted man tried to be.

He did his best, — he worked according to his lights: what virtue he knew, he tried to practice; what knowledge he could master, he strove to acquire. But, as one thinks of an office almost divine, performed by any mortal man, — of any single being pretending to control the thoughts, to direct the faith, to order implicit obedience of brother millions; to compel them into war at his offense or quarrel; to command, " In this way you shall trade, in this way you shall think; these neighbors shall be your allies, whom you shall help, — these others your enemies, whom you shall slay at my orders; in this way you shall worship God "; — who can wonder that, when such a man as George took such an office on himself, punishment and humiliation should fall upon people and chief?

Yet there is something grand about his courage. The battle of the king with his aristocracy remains yet to be told by the historian who shall view the reign of George more justly than the trumpery panegyrists who wrote immediately after his decease. It was he, with the people to back him, that made the war with America; it was he and the people who refused justice to the Roman Catholics; and on both questions he beat the patricians. He bribed, he bullied, he darkly dissembled on occasion; he exercised a slippery perseverance, and a vindictive resolution, which one almost admires as one thinks his character over. His courage was never to be beat. It trampled North underfoot; it bent the stiff neck of the younger Pitt; even his illness never conquered that indomitable spirit. As soon as his brain was clear, it resumed the scheme, only laid aside when his reason left him: as soon as his hands were out of the strait-waistcoat, they took up the pen and the plan which had engaged him up to the moment of his malady. I believe, it is by persons believing themselves in the right, that nine tenths of the tyranny of this world has been perpetrated. Arguing on that convenient premise, the Dey of Algiers would cut off twenty heads of a morning; Father Dominic would burn a score of Jews in the presence of the Most Catholic King, and the Archbishops of Toledo and Salamanca sing Amen. Protestants were roasted, Jesuits hung and quartered at Smithfield, and witches burned at Salem; and all by worthy people, who believed they had the best authority for their actions. And so with respect to old George, even Americans, whom he hated and who conquered him, may give him credit for having quite honest reasons for oppressing them.

Of little comfort were the king's sons to the king. But the pretty Amelia was his darling; and the little maiden, prattling and smiling in the fond arms of that old father, is a sweet image to look on.

From November, 1810, George III. ceased to reign. All the world knows the story of his malady; all history presents no sadder figure than that of the old man, blind and deprived of reason, wandering through the rooms of his palace, addressing imaginary parliaments, reviewing fancied troops, holding ghostly courts. I have seen his picture as it was taken at this time, hanging in the apartment of his daughter, the Landgravine of Hesse Homburg, — amidst books and Windsor furniture, and a hundred fond reminiscences of her English home. The poor old father is represented in a purple gown, his snowy beard falling over his breast, — the star of his famous Order still idly shining on it. He was not only sightless, — he became utterly deaf. All light, all reason, all sound of human voices, all the pleasures of this world of God, were taken from him. Some slight lucid moments he had; in one of which, the queen, desiring to see him, entered the room, and found him singing a hymn, and accompanying himself at the harpsichord. When he had finished, he knelt down and prayed aloud for her, and then for his family, and then for the nation, concluding with a prayer for himself, that it might please God to avert his heavy calamity from him, but if not, to give him resignation to submit. He then burst into tears, and his reason again fled.

What preacher need moralize on this story; what words save the simplest are requisite to tell it? It is too terrible for tears. The thought of such a misery smites me down in submission before the Ruler of kings and men, the Monarch Supreme over empires and republics, the inscrutable Dispenser of life, death, happiness, victory. " O brothers," I said to those who heard me first in America, — " O brothers! speaking the same dear mother tongue, — O comrades! enemies no more, let us take a mournful hand together as we stand by this royal corpse, and call a truce to battle! Low he lies to whom the proudest used to kneel once, and who was cast lower than the poorest; dead, whom millions prayed for in vain. Driven off his throne; buffeted by rude hands; with his children in revolt; the darling of his old age killed before him untimely; our Lear hangs over her breathless lips and cries, ' Cordelia, Cordelia, stay a little! '

> ' Vex not his ghost — oh ! let him pass — he hates him
> That would upon the rack of this tough world
> Stretch him out longer ! '

Hush! Strife and Quarrel, over the solemn grave! Sound, Trumpets, a mournful march. Fall, Dark Curtain, upon his pageant, his pride, his grief, his awful tragedy! "

THE MAJOR'S ADVICE TO HIS NEPHEW.

Like a wary and patient man of the world, Major Pendennis did not press poor Pen any farther for the moment, but hoped the best from time, and that the young fellow's eyes would be opened before long to see the absurdity of which he was guilty. And having found out how keen the boy's point of honor was, he worked kindly upon that kindly feeling with great skill, discoursing him over their wine after dinner, and pointing out to Pen the necessity of a perfect uprightness and openness in all his dealings, and entreating that his communications with his interesting young friend (as the Major politely called Miss Fotheringay) should be carried on with the knowledge, if not approbation, of Mrs. Pendennis. "After all, Pen," the Major said, with a convenient frankness that did not displease the boy, whilst it advanced the interests of the negotiator, "you must bear in mind that you are throwing yourself away. Your mother may submit to your marriage as she would to anything else you desired, if you did but cry long enough for it : but be sure of this, that it can never please her. You take a young woman off the boards of a country theater and prefer her, for such is the case, to one of the finest ladies in England. And your mother will submit to your choice, but you can't suppose that she will be happy under it.

"I have often fancies that my sister had it in her eye to make a marriage between you and that little ward of hers — Flora, Laura, — what's her name? And I always determined to do my small endeavor to prevent any such match. The child has but two thousand pounds, I am given to understand. It is only with the utmost economy and care that my sister can provide for the decent maintenance of her house, and for your appearance and education as a gentleman; and I don't care to own to you that I had other and much higher views for you. With your name and birth, sir, — with your talents, which I suppose are respectable, with the friends whom I have the honor to possess, I could have placed you in an excellent position, — a remarkable position for a young man of such exceeding small means, and had hoped to see you, at least, try to restore the honors of our name. Your mother's softness stopped one prospect, or you might have been a general like our gallant ancestor who fought at Ramillies and Malplaquet. I had another plan in view: my excellent and kind friend, Lord Bagwig, who is very well disposed towards me, would, I have little doubt, have attached you to his mission at Pumpernickel, and you might have advanced in the diplomatic service. But, pardon me for recurring to the subject; how is a man to serve a young gentleman of eighteen, who proposes to marry a lady of thirty, whom he has selected from a booth in a fair? — well, not a fair, — barn. That profession at once is closed to you. The public service is closed to you. Society is closed to you. You see, my good friend, to what you bring yourself. You may get on at the bar, to be sure, where I am given to understand that gentlemen of merit occasionally marry out of their kitchens; but in no other profession. Or you may come and live down here — down here, dear Pen, forever!" (said the Major, with a dreary shrug, as he thought with inexpressible fondness of Pall Mall) "where your mother will receive the Mrs. Arthur that is to be, with perfect kindness; where the good people of the county won't visit you; and where, my dear sir, I shall be shy of visiting you myself, for I 'm a plain-spoken man, and I own to you that I like to live with gentlemen for my companions; where you will have to live, with rum-and-water drinking gentlemen-farmers, and drag through your life the young husband of an old woman, who, if she does n't quarrel with your mother, will at least cost that lady her position in society, and drag her down into that dubious caste into which you must inevitably fall. It is no affair of mine, my good sir. I am not angry. Your downfall will not hurt me farther than that it will extinguish the hopes I had of seeing my family once more taking its place in the world. It is only your mother and yourself that will be ruined. And I pity you both from my soul. Pass the claret: it is some I sent to your poor father; I remember I bought it at poor Lord Levant's sale. But of course," added the Major, smacking the wine, "having engaged yourself, you will do what becomes you as a man of honor, however fatal your promise may be. However, promise us on our side, my boy, what I set out by entreating you to grant, — that there shall be nothing clandestine, that you will pursue your studies, that you will only visit your interesting friend at proper intervals. Do you write to her much?"

Pen blushed and said, "Why, yes, he had written."

"I suppose verses, eh! as well as prose? I was a dab at verses myself. I recollect when I first joined, I used to write verses for the fellows in the regiment; and did some pretty things in that way. I was talking to my old friend General Hobbler about some lines I dashed off for him in the year 1806, when we were at the Cape, and, Gad, he remembered every line of them still; for he 'd used 'em so often, the old rogue, and had actually tried 'em on Mrs. Hobbler, sir, who brought him sixty thousand pounds. I suppose you 've tried verses, eh, Pen?"

Pen blushed again, and said, "Why, yes, he had written verses."

"And does the fair one respond in poetry or prose?" asked the Major, eying his nephew with the queerest expression, as much as to say, "O Moses and Green Spectacles! what a fool the boy is."

Pen blushed again. She had written, but not in verse, the young lover owned, and he gave his breast-pocket the benefit of a squeeze with his left arm, which the Major remarked, according to his wont.

"You have got the letters there, I see," said the old campaigner, nodding at Pen, and pointing to his own chest (which was manfully wadded with cotton by Mr. Stultz). "You know you have. I would give twopence to see 'em."

"Why," said Pen, twiddling the stalks of the strawberries, "I —

I," but this sentence never finished; for Pen's face was so comical and embarrassed, as the Major watched it, that the elder could contain his gravity no longer, and burst into a fit of laughter, in which chorus Pen himself was obliged to join after a minute : when he broke out fairly into a guffaw.

It sent them with great good-humor into Mrs. Pendennis's drawing-room. She was pleased to hear them laughing in the hall as they crossed it.

"You sly rascal!" said the Major, putting his arm gayly on Pen's shoulder, and giving a playful push at the boy's breast-pocket. He felt the papers crackling there sure enough. The young fellow was delighted — conceited — triumphant — and in one word, a spooney.

The pair came to the tea-table in the highest spirits. The Major's politeness was beyond expression. He had never tasted such good tea, and such bread was only to be had in the country. He asked Mrs. Pendennis for one of her charming songs. He then made Pen sing, and was delighted and astonished at the beauty of the boy's voice; he made his nephew fetch his maps and drawings, and praised them as really remarkable works of talent in a young fellow : he complimented him on his French pronunciation : he flattered the simple boy as adroitly as ever lover flattered a mistress : and when bedtime came, mother and son went to their several rooms perfectly enchanted with the kind Major.

When they had reached those apartments, I suppose Helen took to her knees as usual; and Pen read over his letters before going to bed : just as if he did n't know every word of them by heart already. In truth there were but three of those documents; and to learn their contents required no great effort of memory.

In No. 1 Miss Fotheringay presents grateful compliments to Mr. Pendennis, and in her papa's name and her own begs to thank him for his *most beautiful presents*. They will always be *kept carefully ;* and Miss F. and Captain C. will never forget the *delightful evening* which they passed on *Tuesday last*.

No. 2 said — Dear Sir, we shall have a small quiet party of *social friends* at our *humble board*, next Tuesday evening, at an *early tea*, when I shall wear the *beautiful scarf* which, with its *accompanying delightful verses*, I shall *ever, ever cherish :* and papa bids me say how happy he will be if you will join "*the feast of reason and the flow of soul*" in our *festive little party*, as I am sure will be your *truly grateful*

EMILY FOTHERINGAY.

No. 3 was somewhat more confidential, and showed that matters had proceeded rather far. You were *odious* yesterday night, the letter said. Why did you not come to the stage-door? Papa could not escort me on account of his eye; he had an accident, and fell down over a loose carpet on the stair on Sunday night. I saw you looking at Miss Diggle all night; and you were *so enchanted* with Lydia Languish you scarcely once looked at Julia. I could have *crushed* Bingley, I was so *angry*. I play *Ella Rosenberg* on Friday: will you come then? *Miss Diggle performs* — ever your

E. F.

These three letters Mr. Pen used to read at intervals, during the day and night, and embrace with that delight and fervor which such beautiful compositions surely warranted. A thousand times at least he had kissed fondly the musky satin paper, made sacred to him by the hand of Emily Fotheringay. This was all he had in return for his passion and flames, his vows and protests, his rhymes and similes, his wakeful nights and endless thoughts, his fondness, fears, and folly. The young wiseacre had pledged away his all for this: signed his name to endless promissory-notes, conferring his heart upon the bearer: bound himself for life, and got back twopence as an equivalent. For Miss Costigan was a young lady of such perfect good conduct and self-command, that she never would have thought of giving more, and reserved the treasures of her affection until she could transfer them lawfully at church.

Howbeit, Mr. Pen was content with what tokens of regard he had got, and mumbled over his three letters in a rapture of high spirits, and went to sleep delighted with his kind old uncle from London, who must evidently yield to his wishes in time; and, in a word, a preposterous state of contentment with himself and all the world.*

---

* It may be remarked that Mr. Pen did not marry Miss Fotheringay, and that Captain Costigan, her father, and Major Pendennis came near having a duel on the subject. For a full and interesting account of young Pendennis's trials and tribulations in this matter, and his happy issue therefrom, together with the charmingly described record of his life after this episode, you must read *Pendennis*, one of the best of Mr. Thackeray's stories.

SUMNER.

1811 – 1874.

CHARLES SUMNER, one of the most prominent actors in the public affairs of the United States for a quarter of a century, was born in Boston, Massachusetts, in January, 1811. Graduating at Harvard College in 1830, he studied law under the direction of Judge Story, and began practice in 1834. In 1837 he went abroad and mingled in the most cultivated society in England and on the Continent. Returning to Boston, after an absence of three years, he resumed his profession and his studies. In 1845, being invited by the city government to deliver a Fourth of July Oration, he spoke on *The True Grandeur of Nations* with such eloquence and force as at once gave him high rank as an orator. Made conspicuous by this success, he naturally entered into political associations, and became an active member of the Free Soil party. By its aid, five years later, in 1850, he was elected to the seat in the United States Senate made vacant by Mr. Webster's appointment to be Secretary of State. On his entrance into that body Mr. Sumner declared himself the uncompromising enemy of slavery, and never ceased his assaults upon that institution until it ceased to exist. He was repeatedly re-elected to the Senate, and had completed his twenty-third year of honorable service, when he was suddenly stricken by *angina pectoris*, and died March 11, 1874. Mr. Sumner's efforts in literature were almost exclusively in the department of oratory, and the many volumes of his published works are mainly filled with speeches. Many of these have a place among the masterpieces of American eloquence. Unlike most American public men, he was not a politician; he held himself aloof from the petty obligations and entanglements of party, and maintained a lofty and unswerving independence. His integrity and purity of purpose were never questioned even by those to whom his political doctrines were most abhorrent. By his profound intellectual ability, his thorough and elegant scholarship, and above all by his high-mindedness and unimpeachable probity, he commanded the respect of the whole country. His speeches were rather scholarly than statesman-like. Though his mastery of whatever subjects he grappled with was thorough, and his presentation of them vigorous and effective, there is an excess of elaboration, an ultra-classicism in all his writings that never, or very rarely, accompanies the highest spontaneous oratory. As specimens of careful, finished composition, his speeches are hardly surpassed in the annals of American eloquence.

THE LAW OF HUMAN PROGRESS.

THE way is now prepared to consider the character, conditions, and limitations of this law, the duties it enjoins, and the encouragements it affords.

Let me state the law as I understand it. Man as an individual is capable of indefinite improvement. Societies and nations, which are but aggregations of men, and, finally, the Human Family, or collectively Humanity, are capable of indefinite improvement. And this is the destiny of man, of societies, of nations, and of the Human Family.

Restricting the proposition to the capacity for indefinite improvement, I believe I commend it to the candor and intelligence of all who have meditated upon this subject. And this brings me to the remarkable words of Leibnitz. He boldly says, as we have already seen, that man seems able to arrive at perfection. Turgot and Condorcet also speak of his " perfectibility," — a term adopted by recent French writers. If by this is meant simply that man is capable of indefinite improvement, then it will not be questioned. But whatever the heights of virtue and intelligence to which he may attain in future ages, who can doubt that to his grander vision new summits will ever present themselves, provoking him to still grander aspirations? God only is perfect. Knowledge and goodness, his attributes, are infinite; nor can man hope, in any lapse of time, to comprehend this immensity. In the infinitude of the universe, he will seem, like Newton, with all his acquisitions, only to have gathered a few pebbles by the seaside. In a similar strain Leibnitz elsewhere says that the place which God assigns to man in space and time necessarily limits the perfections he is able to acquire. As in Geometry the asymptote constantly approaches its curve, so that the distance between them is constantly diminishing, and yet, though prolonged indefinitely, they never meet, so, according to him, are infinite souls the asymptotes of God.

There are revolutions in history seeming on a superficial view inconsistent with this law. From early childhood attention is directed to Greece and Rome ; and we are sometimes taught that these two powers reached heights which subsequent nations cannot hope to equal, much less to surpass. I would not disparage the triumphs of the ancient mind. The eloquence, the poetry, the art of Athens still survive, and bear no mean sway upon earth. Rome, too, yet lives in her jurisprudence, which, next after Christianity, has exerted a paramount influence over the laws of modern communities.

But exalted as these productions may be, it is impossible not to perceive that something of their present importance is derived from the early period when they appeared, something from the unquestioning and high-flown admiration of them transmitted through successive generations until it became a habit, and something also from the disposition, still prevalent, to elevate Antiquity at the expense of subsequent ages. Without undertaking to decide if the genius of Antiquity, as displayed by individuals, can justly claim supremacy, it would be easy to show that the ancient plane of civilization never reached our common level. The people were ignorant, vicious, and poor, or degraded to abject slavery, — itself the sum of all injustice and all vice. Even the most illustrious characters, whose names still shine from that distant night, were little more than splendid barbarians. Archi-

tecture, sculpture, painting, and vases of exquisite perfection attest
an appreciation of beauty in form; but our masters in these things
were strangers to the useful arts, as to the comforts and virtues of
home. Abounding in what to us are luxuries, they had not what to
us are necessaries.

Without knowledge there can be no sure Progress. Vice and barbarism are the inseparable companions of ignorance. Nor is it too
much to say, that, except in rare instances, the highest virtue is attained only through intelligence. This is natural; for to do right we
must first understand what is right. But the people of Greece and
Rome, even in the brilliant days of Pericles and Augustus, could not
arrive at this knowledge. The sublime teachings of Plato and Socrates
—calculated in many respects to promote the best interests of the race
— were limited in influence to a small company of listeners, or to the
few who could obtain a copy of the costly manuscripts in which they
were preserved. Thus the knowledge and virtue acquired by individuals were not diffused in their own age or secured to posterity.

Now, at last, through an agency all unknown to Antiquity, knowledge of every kind has become general and permanent. It can no
longer be confined to a select circle. It cannot be crushed by tyranny,
or lost by neglect. It is immortal as the soul from which it proceeds.
This alone renders all relapse into barbarism impossible, while it
affords an unquestionable distinction between ancient and modern
times. The Press, watchful with more than the hundred eyes of
Argus, strong with more than the hundred arms of Briareus, not only
guards all the conquests of civilization, but leads the way to future
triumphs. Through its untiring energies, the meditation of the
closet, or the utterance of the human voice, which else would die away
within the precincts of a narrow room, is prolonged to the most distant nations and times, with winged words circling the globe. We
admire the genius of Demosthenes, Sophocles, Plato, and Phidias;
but the printing-press is a higher gift to man than the eloquence, the
drama, the philosophy, and the art of Greece.

THE LOVE OF GLORY.

THE Love of Glory is a motive of human conduct. But the same
Heavenly Father who endowed us with the love of approbation has
placed in us other sentiments of a higher order, more kindred to his

own divine nature. These are Justice and Benevolence, both of which, however imperfectly developed or ill-directed, are elements of every human soul. The desire of Justice, filling us with the love of Duty, is the sentiment which fits us to receive and comprehend the sublime injunction of doing unto others as we would have them do to us. In the predominance of this sentiment, enlightened by intelligence, injustice becomes impossible. The desire of Benevolence goes farther. It leads all who are under its influence to those acts of kindness, dis-interestedness, humanity, love to neighbor, which constitute the crown of Christian character. Such sentiments are celestial, godlike in their office.

In determining proper motives of conduct, it is easy to perceive that the higher are more commendable than the lower, and that even an act of Justice and Benevolence loses something of its charm when known to be inspired by the selfish desire of human applause. It was the gay poet of antiquity who said that concealed virtue differed little from sepulchered sluggishness : —

> " Paulum sepultæ distat inertiæ
> Celata virtus."

But this is a heathen sentiment, alien to reason and to truth.

It is hoped that men will be honest, but from a higher motive than because honesty is the best policy. It is hoped that they will be hu-mane, but for a nobler cause than the fame of humanity.

The love of approbation may properly animate the young, whose minds have not yet ascended to the appreciation of that virtue which is its own exceeding great reward. It may justly strengthen those of maturer age who are not moved by the simple appeals of duty, unless the smiles of mankind attend them. It were churlish not to offer homage to those acts by which happiness is promoted, even though inspired by a sentiment of personal ambition, or by considerations of policy. But such motives must always detract from the perfect beauty even of good works. The Man of Ross, who was said to

> " Do good by stealth, and blush to find it Fame,"

was a character of real life, and the example of his virtue may still be prized, like the diamond, for its surpassing rarity. It cannot be dis-guised, however, that much is gained where the desire of praise acts in conjunction with the higher sentiments. If ambition be our lure, it will be well for mankind if it unite with Justice and Benevolence.

It may be demanded if we should be indifferent to the approbation of men. Certainly not. It is a proper source of gratification, and is one of the just rewards on earth. It may be enjoyed when virtuously won, though it were better if not proposed as the object of desire. The great English magistrate, Lord Mansfield, while confessing a wish for popularity, added, in words which cannot be too often quoted, " But it is that popularity which follows, not that which is run after ; it is that popularity which, sooner or later, never fails to do justice to the pursuit of noble ends by noble means." And the historian of the Decline and Fall of the Roman Empire, who was no stranger to the Love of Glory, has given expression to the satisfaction which he derived from the approbation of those whose opinions were valuable. " If I listened to the music of praise," says Gibbon in his Autobiography, " I was more seriously satisfied with the approbation of my judges. The candor of Dr. Robertson embraced his disciple. A letter from Mr. Hume overpaid the labor of ten years." It would be difficult to declare the self-gratulation of the successful author in language more sententious or expressive.

While recognizing praise as an incidental reward, though not a commendable motive, we cannot disregard the evil which ensues when the desire for it predominates over the character, and fills the soul, as is too often the case, with a blind emulation chiefly solicitous for personal success. The world, which should be a happy scene of constant exertion and harmonious co-operation, becomes a field of rivalry, competition, and hostile struggle. It is true that God has not given to all the same excellences of mind and heart ; but he naturally requires more of the strong than of the many less blessed. The little we can do will not be cast vainly into his treasury ; nor need the weak and humble be filled with any idle emulation of others. Let each act earnestly, according to the measure of his powers, — rejoicing always in the prosperity of his neighbor ; and though we may seem to accomplish little, yet we shall do much, if we be true to the convictions of the soul, and give the example of unselfish devotion to duty. This of itself is success ; and this is within the ambition of all. Life is no Ulyssean bow, to be bent only by a single strong arm. There is none so weak as not to use it.

In the growth of the individual the intellect advances before the moral powers ; for it is necessary to know what is right before we can practice it ; and this same order of progress is observed in the

Human Family. Moral excellence is the bright, consummate flower of all progress. It is often the peculiar product of age. And it is then, among other triumphs of virtue, that Duty assumes her commanding place, while personal ambition is abased. Burke, in that marvelous passage of elegiac beauty where he mourns his only son, says, " Indeed, my Lord, I greatly deceive myself, if, in this hard season, I would give a peck of refuse wheat for all that is called Fame and Honor in the world." And Channing, with a sentiment most unlike the ancient Roman orator, declares that he sees " nothing worth living for but the divine virtue which endures and surrenders all things for truth, duty, and mankind." Such an insensibility to worldly objects, and such an elevation of spirit, may not be expected at once from all men, — certainly not without something of the trials of Burke or the soul of Channing. But it is within the power of all to strive after that virtue which it may be difficult to reach ; and just in proportion as duty becomes the guide and the aim of life shall we learn to close the soul against the allurements of praise and the asperities of censure, while we find satisfactions and compensations such as man cannot give or take away. The world, with ignorant or intolerant judgment, may condemn ; the countenance of companion may be averted ; the heart of friend may grow cold ; but the consciousness of duty done will be sweeter than the applause of the world, than the countenance of companion, or the heart of friend.

The age of chivalry has gone. An age of humanity has come. The horse, whose importance, more than human, gave the name to that early period of gallantry and war, now yields his foremost place to man. In serving him, in promoting his elevation, in contributing to his welfare, in doing him good, there are fields of bloodless triumph, nobler far than any in which the bravest knights ever conquered. Here are spaces of labor wide as the world, lofty as heaven.

Let me say, then, in the language once bestowed upon the youthful knights, scholars, jurists, artists, philanthropists, heroes of a Christian age, companions of a celestial knighthood, " Go forth. Be brave, loyal, and successful ! " And may it be our office to light a fresh beacon-fire sacred to truth ! Let the flame spread from hill to hill, from island to island, from continent to continent, till the long lineage of fires shall illumine all the nations of the earth, animating them to the holy contests of knowledge, justice, beauty, love.

DICKENS.

1812 – 1870.

CHARLES DICKENS, the most popular novelist of his time, was born at Portsmouth, England, in 1812, and died June 9, 1870. His childhood was spent in poverty and menial toil, and how, amid such unfavorable surroundings, he acquired an education sufficient for his work in life will always remain a subject of wonder. His father was at one time a reporter of Parliamentary debates, and Charles adopted the same calling. He became attached to the Morning Chronicle, and in its columns first appeared *Sketches by Boz*, afterwards published in book form, 1836 – 37. These *Sketches* had a very cordial reception, and their success induced a publisher to engage Dickens and Seymour the artist to prepare an illustrated narrative of the adventures of a party of Cockney sportsmen. The result of this contract was *The Pickwick Papers*, which at once became the most popular book of the day, and still ranks among the first favorites of all classes of readers. It was followed at short intervals by *Nicholas Nickleby, Oliver Twist, The Old Curiosity Shop*, and *Barnaby Rudge*. In 1842 Dickens visited America, where he had a very cordial reception. With ingratitude for which he has never been fully forgiven, he repaid the sincere kindness of his American entertainers by writing a record of his tour, called *American Notes*, in which he ridiculed the people and institutions of the United States with unsparing hand. In *Martin Chuzzlewit*, published in 1844, he returned to the attack with great keenness and vigor of satire. In 1845 he established the Daily News in London, but conducted it only for a short time, returning to the more congenial work of novel-writing. In 1853 he began to give public readings from his own books, and was no less successful as a reader than he had been as a writer. In 1868 he visited America for the second time, and gave readings in the principal cities to immense and delighted audiences. The profits of his tour are said to have been over $200,000. During the last year of his life he was engaged on a novel, *The Mystery of Edwin Drood*, which he left unfinished. His death was very sudden, and the announcement of it caused universal grief throughout the English-speaking world. His books are too familiar to the reading public to demand enumeration here. Of them all, *The Pickwick Papers, Nicholas Nickleby*, and *David Copperfield* are generally esteemed the best; the latter is specially interesting as being largely autobiographical. His later novels, *Great Expectations* and *Our Mutual Friend*, were less popular than their predecessors. Among English novelists Dickens stands alone; he occupies a field that none other has cultivated, and may justly be esteemed the creator of a new school of fiction. He was a man of strong sympathies, quick to feel and plead for the poor and oppressed, and in his books he has done yeoman service in the work of social and legal reform. His most conspicuous characteristic is humor, natural, rich, and seemingly inexhaustible, and in this quality lies the chief charm of his writings. Yet many pages in *Dombey and Son* exhibit a not less thorough mastery of pathos. The secret of his success seems to have consisted in his intuitive apprehension of the popular needs and tastes; no other novelist has ever lived who was so thoroughly *en rapport* with the heart of the people: he wrote for them and to them, and they acknowledged his efforts with unbounded good-will and admiration. Brilliant, genial, and uniformly entertaining though they are, Dickens's books have little moral depth or weight: they please, warm, soften, but they are, in effect, material. The extracts, each of which represents fairly his humor, pathos, and descriptive power, are from *The Pickwick Papers, Dombey and Son*, and *American Notes*.

MR. PICKWICK'S EXTRAORDINARY DILEMMA.

MR. PICKWICK's apartments in Goswell Street, although on a limited scale, were not only of a very neat and comfortable description, but peculiarly adapted for the residence of a man of his genius and observation.

His landlady, Mrs. Bardell — the relict and sole executrix of a deceased custom-house officer — was a comely woman of bustling manners and agreeable appearance, with a natural genius for cooking, improved by study and long practice into an exquisite talent. There were no children, no servants, no fowls. The only other inmates of the house were a large man and a small boy; the first a lodger, the second a production of Mrs. Bardell's. The large man was always home precisely at ten o'clock at night, at which hour he regularly condensed himself into the limits of a dwarfish French bedstead in the back parlor; and the infantine sports and gymnastic exercises of Master Bardell were exclusively confined to the neighboring pavements and gutters. Cleanliness and quiet reigned throughout the house; and in it Mr. Pickwick's will was law.

To any one acquainted with these points of the domestic economy of the establishment, and conversant with the admirable regulation of Mr. Pickwick's mind, his appearance and behavior, on the morning previous to that which had been fixed upon for the journey to Eatanswill, would have been most mysterious and unaccountable. He paced the room to and fro with hurried steps, popped his head out of the window at intervals of about three minutes each, constantly referred to his watch, and exhibited many other manifestations of impatience, very unusual with him. It was evident that something of great importance was in contemplation; but what that something was, not even Mrs. Bardell herself had been enabled to discover.

"Mrs. Bardell," said Mr. Pickwick, at last, as that amiable female approached the termination of a prolonged dusting of the apartment.

"Sir," said Mrs. Bardell.

"Your little boy is a very long time gone."

"Why, it 's a good long way to the Borough, sir," remonstrated Mrs. Bardell.

"Ah," said Mr. Pickwick, "very true; so it is."

Mr. Pickwick relapsed into silence, and Mrs. Bardell resumed her dusting.

"Mrs. Bardell," said Mr. Pickwick, at the expiration of a few minutes.

"Sir," said Mrs. Bardell again.

"Do you think it 's a much greater expense to keep two people than to keep one?"

"La, Mr. Pickwick," said Mrs. Bardell, coloring up to the very
border of her cap, as she fancied she observed a species of matrimo-
nial twinkle in the eyes of her lodger, — "la, Mr. Pickwick, what a
question !"

"Well, but *do* you?" inquired Mr. Pickwick.

"That depends," said Mrs. Bardell, approaching the duster very
near to Mr. Pickwick's elbow, which was planted on the table, —
"that depends a good deal upon the person, you know, Mr. Pickwick; and whether it's a saving and careful person, sir."

"That's very true," said Mr. Pickwick; "but the person I have
in my eye" (here he looked very hard at Mrs. Bardell) "I think possesses these qualities; and has, moreover, a considerable knowledge
of the world, and a great deal of sharpness, Mrs. Bardell; which may
be of material use to me."

"La, Mr. Pickwick," said Mrs. Bardell; the crimson rising to her
cap-border again.

"I do," said Mr. Pickwick, growing energetic, as was his wont in
speaking of a subject which interested him, — "I do, indeed; and,
to tell you the truth, Mrs. Bardell, I have made up my mind."

"Dear me, sir," exclaimed Mrs. Bardell.

"You'll think it not very strange now," said the amiable Mr.
Pickwick, with a good-humored glance at his companion, "that I
never consulted you about this matter, and never mentioned it, till
I sent your little boy out this morning, — eh?"

Mrs. Bardell could only reply by a look.   She had long worshiped
Mr. Pickwick at a distance, but here she was, all at once, raised to a
pinnacle to which her wildest and most extravagant hopes had never
dared to aspire.   Mr. Pickwick was going to propose, — a deliberate
plan, too, — sent her little boy to the Borough to get him out of the
way, — how thoughtful, — how considerate!

"Well," said Mr. Pickwick, "what do you think?" ·

"O Mr. Pickwick!" said Mrs. Bardell, trembling with agitation,
"you're very kind, sir."

"It will save you a great deal of trouble, won't it?" said Mr.
Pickwick.

"O, I never thought anything of the trouble, sir," replied Mrs.
Bardell; "and of course, I should take more trouble to please you
then than ever; but it is so kind of you, Mr. Pickwick, to have so
much consideration for my loneliness."

"Ah, to be sure," said Mr. Pickwick; "I never thought of that. When I am in town, you'll always have somebody to sit with you. To be sure, so you will."

"I'm sure I ought to be a very happy woman," said Mrs. Bardell.

"And your little boy — " said Mr. Pickwick.

"Bless his heart," interposed Mrs. Bardell, with a maternal sob.

"He, too, will have a companion," resumed Mr. Pickwick, — "a lively one, who'll teach him, I'll be bound, more tricks in a week than he would ever learn in a year." And Mr. Pickwick smiled placidly.

"O you dear — " said Mrs. Bardell.

Mr. Pickwick started.

"O you kind, good, playful dear," said Mrs. Bardell; and without more ado she rose from her chair, and flung her arms round Mr. Pickwick's neck, with a cataract of tears, and a chorus of sobs.

"Bless my soul!" cried the astonished Mr. Pickwick; — "Mrs. Bardell, my good woman, — dear me, what a situation, — pray consider. Mrs. Bardell, don't, — if anybody should come — "

"O, let them come," exclaimed Mrs. Bardell, frantically. "I'll never leave you, — dear, kind, good soul"; and, with these words, Mrs. Bardell clung the tighter.

"Mercy upon me," said Mr. Pickwick, struggling violently. "I hear somebody coming up the stairs. Don't, don't, there's a good creature, don't." But entreaty and remonstrance were alike unavailing, for Mrs. Bardell had fainted in Mr. Pickwick's arms; and before he could gain time to deposit her on a chair, Master Bardell entered the room, ushering in Mr. Tupman, Mr. Winkle, and Mr. Snodgrass.

Mr. Pickwick was struck motionless and speechless. He stood with his lovely burden in his arms, gazing vacantly on the countenances of his friends, without the slightest attempt at recognition or explanation. They, in their turn, stared at him; and Master Bardell, in his turn, stared at everybody.

The astonishment of the Pickwickians was so absorbing, and the perplexity of Mr. Pickwick was so extreme, that they might have remained in exactly the same relative situations until the suspended animation of the lady was restored, had it not been for a most beautiful and touching expression of filial affection on the part of her youthful son. Clad in a tight suit of corduroy, spangled with brass buttons of a very considerable size, he at first stood at the door astounded and un-certain; but by degrees, the impression that his mother must have suffered some personal damage pervaded his partially developed mind, and, considering Mr. Pickwick the aggressor, he set up an ap-palling and semi-earthly kind of howling, and, butting forward with his head, commenced assailing that immortal gentleman about the back and legs with such blows and pinches as the strength of his arm and the violence of his excitement allowed.

"Take this little villain away," said the agonized Mr. Pickwick, "he 's mad."

"What *is* the matter?" said the three tongue-tied Pickwickians.

"I don't know," replied Mr. Pickwick, pettishly. "Take away the boy" (here Mr. Winkle carried the interesting boy, screaming and struggling, to the farther end of the apartment). "Now help me to lead this woman down stairs."

"O, I 'm better now," said Mrs. Bardell, faintly.

"Let me lead you down stairs," said the ever-gallant Mr. Tup-man.

"Thank you, sir, — thank you," exclaimed Mrs. Bardell, hysteri-cally. And down stairs she was led accordingly, accompanied by her affectionate son.

"I cannot conceive," said Mr. Pickwick, when his friend returned, — "I cannot conceive what has been the matter with that woman. I had merely announced to her my intention of keeping a man-servant, when she fell into the extraordinary paroxysm in which you found her. Very extraordinary thing!"

"Very," said his three friends.

"Placed me in such an extremely awkward situation," continued Mr. Pickwick.

"Very," was the reply of his followers, as they coughed slightly, and looked dubiously at each other.

This behavior was not lost upon Mr. Pickwick. He remarked their incredulity. They evidently suspected him.

"There is a man in the passage now," said Mr. Tupman.

"It 's the man that I spoke to you about," said Mr. Pickwick. "I sent for him to the Borough this morning. Have the goodness to call him up, Snodgrass."

THE LAST HOURS OF LITTLE PAUL DOMBEY.

PAUL had never risen from his little bed. He lay there, listening to the noises in the street, quite tranquilly; not caring much how the time went, but watching everything about him with observing eyes.

When the sunbeams struck into his room through the rustling blinds, and quivered on the opposite wall like golden water, he knew that evening was coming on, and that the sky was red and beautiful. As the reflection died away, and the gloom went creeping up the wall, he watched it deepen, deepen, deepen into night. Then he thought how the long streets were dotted with lamps, and how the peaceful stars were shining overhead. His fancy had a strange tendency to wander to the river, which he knew was flowing through the great city; and now he thought how black it was, and how deep it would look, reflecting the hosts of stars, and more than all, how steadily it rolled away to meet the sea.

As it grew later in the night, and footsteps in the street became so rare that he could hear them coming, count them as they passed, and lose them in the hollow distance, he would lie and watch the many-colored ring about the candle, and wait patiently for day. His only trouble was, the swift and rapid river. He felt forced, sometimes, to try to stop it, — to stem it with his childish hands, or choke its way with sand, — and when he saw it coming on, resistless, he cried out! But a word from Florence, who was always at his side, restored him to himself; and leaning his poor head upon her breast, he told Floy of his dream, and smiled.

When day began to dawn again, he watched for the sun; and when its cheerful light began to sparkle in the room, he pictured to himself — pictured! he saw — the high church-towers rising up into the morning sky, the town reviving, waking, starting into life once more, the river glistening as it rolled (but rolling fast as ever), and the country bright with dew. Familiar sounds and cries came by degrees into the street below; the servants in the house were roused and busy; faces looked in at the door, and voices asked his attendants softly how he was. Paul always answered for himself, "I am better. I am a great deal better, thank you! Tell papa so!"

By little and little he got tired of the bustle of the day, the noise of carriages and carts, people passing and repassing; and would fall asleep, or be troubled with a restless and uneasy sense again — the child could hardly tell whether this were in his sleeping or his waking moments — of that rushing river. "Why, will it never stop, Floy?" he would sometimes ask her. "It is bearing me away, I think!"

But Floy could always soothe and reassure him; and it was his daily delight to make her lay her head down on his pillow, and take some rest.

"You are always watching me, Floy. Let me watch *you*, now!" They would prop him up with cushions in a corner of his bed, and there he would recline the while she lay beside him; bending forward oftentimes to kiss her, and whispering to those who were near that she was tired, and how she had sat up so many nights beside him.

Thus, the flush of the day, in its heat and light, would gradually decline; and again the golden water would be dancing on the wall.

He was visited by as many as three grave doctors, — they used to assemble down stairs, and come up together, — and the room was so quiet, and Paul was so observant of them (though he never asked of anybody what they said), that he even knew the difference in the sound of their watches. But his interest centered in Sir Parker Peps, who always took his seat on the side of the bed. For Paul had heard them say long ago, that that gentleman had been with his mamma when she clasped Florence in her arms and died. And he could not forget it now. He liked him for it. He was not afraid. . . . .

Paul closed his eyes with those words, and fell asleep. When he awoke, the sun was high, and the broad day was clear and warm. He lay a little, looking at the windows, which were open, and the curtains rustling in the air, and waving to and fro: then he said, "Floy, is it to-morrow? Is she come?"

Some one seemed to go in quest of her. Perhaps it was Susan. Paul thought he heard her telling him, when he had closed his eyes again, that she would soon be back; but he did not open them to see. She kept her word — perhaps she had never been away — but the next thing that happened was a noise of footsteps on the stairs, and then Paul woke — woke mind and body — and sat upright in his bed. He saw them now about him. There was no gray mist before them, as there had been sometimes in the night. He knew them every one, and called them by their names.

"And who is this? Is this my old nurse?" said the child, regarding, with a radiant smile, a figure coming in.

Yes, yes. No other stranger would have shed those tears at the sight of him, and called him her dear boy, her pretty boy, her own poor blighted child. No other woman would have stooped down by his bed, and taken up his wasted hand, and put it to her lips and breast, as one who had some right to fondle it. No other woman would have so forgotten everybody there but him and Floy, and been so full of tenderness and pity.

"Floy! this is a kind good face!" said Paul. "I am glad to see it again. Don't go away, old nurse! Stay here!"

His senses were all quickened, and he heard a name he knew.

"Who was that? who said Walter?" he asked, looking round. "Some one said Walter. Is he here? I should like to see him very much."

Nobody replied directly, but his father soon said to Susan, "Call him back, then: let him come up!" After a short pause of expectation, during which he looked with smiling interest and wonder on his nurse, and saw that she had not forgotten Floy, Walter was brought into the room. His open face and manner, and his cheerful eyes, had always made him a favorite with Paul; and when Paul saw him, he stretched out his hand, and said, "Good by!"

"Good by, my child!" cried Mrs. Pipchin, hurrying to his bed's head. "Not good by?"

For an instant, Paul looked at her with the wistful face with which he had so often gazed upon her in his corner by the fire. "Ah, yes," he said, placidly, "good by! Walter dear, good by!" turning his head to where he stood, and putting out his hand again. "Where is papa?"

He felt his father's breath upon his cheek, before the words had parted from his lips.

"Remember Walter, dear papa," he whispered, looking in his face, — "remember Walter. I was fond of Walter!" The feeble hand waved in the air, as if it cried "good by!" to Walter once again.

"Now lay me down again," he said; "and, Floy, come close to me, and let me see you!"

Sister and brother wound their arms around each other, and the golden light came streaming in, and fell upon them, locked together.

"How fast the river runs between its green banks and the rushes, Floy! But it's very near the sea. I hear the waves. They always said so!"

Presently he told her that the motion of the boat upon the stream was lulling him to rest. How green the banks were now, how bright the flowers growing on them, and how tall the rushes! Now the boat was out at sea, but gliding smoothly on. And now there was a shore before him. Who stood on the bank!

He put his hands together, as he had been used to do at his prayers. He did not remove his arms to do it, but they saw him fold them so behind her neck.

"Mamma is like you, Floy. I know her by the face! But tell them that the print upon the stairs at school is not divine enough. The light about the head is shining on me as I go!"

The golden ripple on the wall came back again, and nothing else stirred in the room. The old, old fashion! The fashion that came in with our first garments, and will last unchanged until our race has run its course, and the wide firmament is rolled up like a scroll. The old, old fashion — Death!

O, thank God, all who see it, for that older fashion yet, of immortality! And look upon us, angels of young children, with regards not quite estranged, when the swift river bears us to the ocean!

A HEAD-WIND IN THE ATLANTIC.

IT is the third morning. I am awakened out of my sleep by a dismal shriek from my wife, who demands to know whether there's any danger. I rouse myself and look out of bed. The water-jug is plunging and leaping like a lively dolphin; all the smaller articles are afloat, except my shoes, which are stranded on a carpet-bag, high and dry, like a couple of coal-barges. Suddenly I see them spring into the air, and behold the looking-glass, which is nailed to the wall, sticking fast upon the ceiling. At the same time the door entirely disappears, and a new one is opened in the floor. Then I begin to comprehend that the state-room is standing on its head.

Before it is possible to make any arrangement at all compatible with this novel state of things, the ship rights. Before one can say, "Thank Heaven!" she wrongs again. Before one can cry she is wrong, she seems to have started forward, and to be a creature actively running of its own accord, with broken knees and failing legs, through every variety of hole and pitfall, and stumbling constantly. Before one can so much as wonder, she takes a high leap into the air. Before she has well done that, she takes a deep dive into the water.

Before she has gained the surface, she throws a somerset. The instant she is on her legs, she rushes backward. And so she goes on staggering, heaving, wrestling, leaping, diving, jumping, pitching, throbbing, rolling, and rocking; and going through all these movements, sometimes by turns, and sometimes all together; until one feels disposed to roar for mercy.

A steward passes. " Steward ! " " Sir ? " " What is the matter ? what do you call this? " " Rather a heavy sea on, sir, and a head-wind."

A head-wind! Imagine a human face upon the vessel's prow, with fifteen thousand Samsons in one, bent upon driving her back, and hitting her exactly between the eyes whenever she attempts to advance an inch. Imagine the ship herself, with every pulse and artery of her huge body swollen and bursting under this maltreatment, sworn to go on or die. Imagine the wind howling, the sea roaring, the rain beating; all in furious array against her. Picture the sky both dark and wild, and the clouds, in fearful sympathy with the waves, making another ocean in the air. Add to all this, the clattering on deck and down below; the tread of hurried feet; the loud hoarse shouts of seamen; the gurgling in and out of water through the scuppers; with, every now and then, the striking of a heavy sea upon the planks above, with the deep, dead, heavy sound of thunder heard within a vault; — and there is the head-wind of that January morning.

I say nothing of what may be called the domestic noises of the ship : such as the breaking of glass and crockery, the tumbling down of stewards, the gambols, overhead, of loose casks and truant dozens of bottled porter, and the very remarkable and far from exhilarating sounds raised in their various state-rooms by the seventy passengers who were too ill to get up to breakfast. I say nothing of them; for, although I lay listening to this concert for three or four days, I don't think I heard it for more than a quarter of a minute, at the expiration of which term I lay down again, excessively sea-sick.

The laboring of the ship in the troubled sea on this night I shall never forget. " Will it ever be worse than this ? " was a question I had often heard asked, when everything was sliding and bumping about, and when it certainly did seem difficult to comprehend the possibility of anything afloat being more disturbed, without toppling over and going down. But what the agitation of a steam-vessel is, on a bad winter's night in the wild Atlantic, it is impossible for the most vivid imagination to conceive. To say that she is flung down on her side in the waves, with her masts dipping into them, and that, spring-.. ing up again, she rolls over on the other side, until a heavy sea strikes her with the noise of a hundred great guns, and hurls her back, — that she stops, and staggers, and shivers, as though stunned, and then, with a violent throbbing at her heart, darts onward like a monster goaded into madness, to be beaten down, and battered, and crushed, and leaped on by the angry sea, — that thunder, lightning, hail, and rain, and wind are all in fierce contention for the mastery, — that every plank has its groan, every nail its shriek, and every drop of water in the great ocean its howling voice, — is nothing. To say that all is grand, and all appalling and horrible in the last degree, is noth- ing. Words cannot express it. Thoughts cannot convey it. Only a dream can call it up again, in all its fury, rage, and passion.

And yet, in the very midst of these terrors, I was placed in a situa- tion so exquisitely ridiculous that even then I had as strong a sense of its absurdity as I have now : and could no more help laughing than I can at any other comical incident, happening under circumstances the most favorable to its enjoyment. About midnight we shipped a sea, which forced its way through the skylights, burst open the doors above, and came raging and roaring down into the ladies' cabin, to the unspeakable consternation of my wife and a little Scotch lady, — who, by the way, had previously sent a message to the captain by the stew- ardess, requesting him, with her compliments, to have a steel conduc- tor immediately attached to the top of every mast, and to the chimney, in order that the ship might not be struck by lightning. They, and the handmaid before mentioned, being in such ecstasies of fear that I scarce- ly knew what to do with them, I naturally bethought myself of some restorative or comforting cordial; and nothing better occurring to me, at the moment, than hot brandy and water, I procured a tumbler- ful without delay. It being impossible to sit or stand without hold- ing on, they were all heaped together in one corner of a long sofa, — a fixture extending entirely across the cabin, — where they clung to each other in momentary expectation of being drowned. When I ap- proached this place with my specific, and was about to administer it, with many consolatory expressions, to the nearest sufferer, what was my dismay to see them all roll slowly down to the other end ! And when I staggered to that end, and held out the glass once more, how immensely baffled were my good intentions by the ship giving another lurch, and their all rolling back again! I suppose I dodged them up and down this sofa for at least a quarter of an hour, without reaching them once ; and by the time I did catch them, the brandy and water was diminished, by constant spilling, to a teaspoonful. To complete the group, it is necessary to recognize, in this disconcerted dodger, an individual very pale from sea-sickness ; who had shaved his beard and brushed his hair last at Liverpool ; and whose only articles of dress (linen not included) were a pair of dreadnought trousers, a blue jacket, formerly admired upon the Thames at Richmond, no stockings, and one slipper.

THE NOBLE SAVAGE.

To come to the point at once, I beg to say that I have not the least belief in the Noble Savage. I consider him a prodigious nuisance, and an enormous superstition. His calling rum fire-water, and me a pale-face, wholly fail to reconcile me to him. I don't care what he calls me. I call him a savage, and I call a savage a something highly desirable to be civilized off the face of the earth. I think a mere gent (which I take to be the lowest form of civilization) better than a howling, whistling, clucking, stamping, jumping, tearing savage. It is all one to me whether he sticks a fish-bone through his visage, or bits of trees through the lobes of his ears, or birds' feathers in his head ; whether he flattens his hair between two boards, or spreads his nose over the breadth of his face, or drags his lower lip down by great weights, or blackens his teeth, or knocks them out, or paints one cheek red and the other blue, or tattoos himself, or oils himself, or rubs his body with fat, or crimps it with knives. Yielding to whichsoever of these agreeable eccentricities, he is a savage, — cruel, false, thievish, murderous ; addicted more or less to grease, entrails, and beastly customs ; a wild animal with the questionable gift of boasting ; a conceited, tiresome, bloodthirsty, monotonous humbug.

Yet it is extraordinary to observe how some people will talk about him, as they talk about the good old times ; how they will regret his disappearance, in the course of this world's development, from such and such lands, — where his absence is a blessed relief and an indispensable preparation for the sowing of the very first seeds of an influence that can exalt humanity, — how, even with the evidence of himself before them, they will either be determined to believe, or will suffer themselves to be persuaded into believing, that he is something which their five senses tell them he is not.

acb, Byron's life ## MRS. STOWE.

1812–   .

HARRIET BEECHER STOWE, born in Litchfield, Connecticut, June 14, 1812, has a world-wide fame as the author of *Uncle Tom's Cabin.* She is the daughter of Rev. Dr. Lyman Beecher, an eminent clergyman, and the sister of Rev. Henry Ward Beecher. In 1833 she became the wife of Professor Calvin E. Stowe, a distinguished Hebrew scholar and theologian. Her first book, *Mayflower; or, Sketches of the Descendants of the Pilgrims,* was published in 1849, and was favorably noticed at home and abroad. Three years later she gave to the world what must be regarded as the most remarkable book of the century, its subject and its popularity being considered, — *Uncle Tom's Cabin.* This story was first published as a serial in the National Era, in 1851 – 52, and appeared in book form in 1852. Its sales must be reckoned by millions, and through translations and dramatizations it has reached every civilized nation under the sun. This extraordinary popularity was due not so much to the author's genius as to the novelty and intrinsic interest of her subject and the excited state of public sentiment with reference to it. Read to-day, removed from the heat of a great conflict of opinions, the book discloses many and grave faults, errors of fact and literary infelicities. It is a significant and gratifying fact that the author is now a resident of the South, whose enemy she has been accounted; and in her recent book, *Palmetto Leaves,* she exhibits a more accurate knowledge of that section, and a sincere interest in its welfare. Mrs. Stowe has written many other books; but none of them have added to the fame which she derived from *Uncle Tom's Cabin.* Perhaps *Oldtown Folks* may be ranked next to this in real ability. *The True Story of Lady Byron's Life,* in which Mrs. Stowe defamed the memory of Lord Byron, drew upon her a torrent of indignation such as few authors have ever endured. Her recent novels, *Pink and White Tyranny* and *My Wife and I,* deal with social subjects in vigorous style; but, like all her compositions, they are disfigured by many literary blemishes. She is a very industrious writer, contributing to the periodical press papers on religious and social topics, and manifests a hearty interest in the improvement of society through its moral elevation. The extract is from *Oldtown Folks.*

TYRANNY OF MISS ASPHYXIA.

MATTERS between Miss Asphyxia and her little subject began to show evident signs of approaching some crisis, for which that valiant virgin was preparing herself with mind resolved. It was one of her educational tactics that children, at greater or less intervals, would require what she was wont to speak of as *good* whippings, as a sort of constitutional stimulus to start them in the ways of well-doing. As a school-teacher, she was often fond of rehearsing her experiences, — how she had her eye on Jim or Bob through weeks of growing carelessness or obstinacy or rebellion, suffering the measure of iniquity gradually to become full, until, in an awful hour, she pounced down on the culprit in the very blossom of his sin, and gave him such a lesson as he would remember, as she would assure him, the longest day he had to live.

The burning of rebellious thoughts in the little breast, of internal hatred and opposition, could not long go on without slight whiffs of external smoke, such as mark the course of subterranean fire. As the child grew more accustomed to Miss Asphyxia, while her hatred of her increased, somewhat of that native hardihood which had characterized her happier days returned; and she began to use all the subtlety and secretiveness which belonged to her feminine nature in contriving how *not* to do the will of her tyrant, and yet not to seem designedly to oppose. It really gave the child a new impulse in living to devise little plans for annoying Miss Asphyxia without being herself detected. In all her daily toils she made nice calculations how slow she could possibly be, how blundering and awkward, without really bringing on herself a punishment; and when an acute and capable child turns all its faculties in such a direction, the results may be very considerable.

Miss Asphyxia found many things going wrong in her establishment in most unaccountable ways. One morning her sensibilities were almost paralyzed, on opening her milk-room door, to find there, with creamy whiskers, the venerable Tom, her own model cat, — a beast who had grown up in the very sanctities of household decorum, and whom she was sure she had herself shut out of the house, with her usual punctuality, at nine o'clock the evening before. She could not dream that he had been enticed through Tina's window, caressed on her bed, and finally sped stealthily on his mission of revenge, while the child returned to her pillow to gloat over her success.

Miss Asphyxia also, in more than one instance, in her rapid gyrations, knocked down and destroyed a valuable bit of pottery or earthenware, that somehow had contrived to be stationed exactly in the wind of her elbow or her hand. It was the more vexatious because she broke them herself. And the child assumed stupid innocence: "How could she know Miss Sphyxy was coming that way?" or, "She didn't see her." True, she caught many a hasty cuff and sharp rebuke; but, with true Indian spirit, she did not mind singeing her own fingers if she only tortured her enemy.

It would be an endless task to describe the many vexations that can be made to arise in the course of household experience when there is a shrewd little elf watching with sharpened faculties for every opportunity to inflict an annoyance or do a mischief. In childhood the passions move with a simplicity of action unknown to any other period of life, and a child's hatred and a child's revenge have an intensity of bitterness entirely unalloyed by moral considerations;

and when a child is without an object of affection, and feels itself unloved, its whole vigor of being goes into the channels of hate.

Religious instruction, as imparted by Miss Asphyxia, had small influence in restraining the immediate force of passion. That "the law worketh wrath" is a maxim as old as the times of the Apostles. The image of a dreadful Judge — a great God, with ever-watchful eyes, that Miss Asphyxia told her about — roused that combative element in the child's heart which says in the heart of the fool, "There is no God." "After all," thought the little skeptic, "how does she know? She never saw him." Perhaps, after all, then, it might be only a fabrication of her tyrant to frighten her into submission. There was a dear Father that mamma used to tell her about; and perhaps he was the one, after all. As for the bear story, she had a private conversation with Sol, and was relieved by his confident assurance that there "had n't been no bears seen round in them parts these ten year"; so that she was safe in that regard, even if she should call Miss Asphyxia a bald-head, which she perfectly longed to do, just to see what would come of it.

In like manner, though the story of Ananias and Sapphira, struck down dead for lying, had been told her in forcible and threatening tones, yet still the little sinner thought within herself that such things must have ceased in our times, as she had told more than one clever lie which neither Miss Asphyxia nor any one else had found out.

In fact, the child considered herself and Miss Asphyxia as in a state of warfare which suspends all moral rules. In the stories of little girls who were taken captives by goblins or giants or witches, she remembered many accounts of sagacious deceptions which they had practised on their captors. Her very blood tingled when she thought of the success of some of them, — how Hensel and Grettel had heated an oven red-hot, and persuaded the old witch to get into it by some cock-and-bull story of what she would find there; and how, the minute she got in, they shut up the oven door and burnt her all up! Miss Asphyxia thought the child a vexatious, careless, troublesome little baggage, it is true; but if she could have looked into her heart and seen her imaginings, she would probably have thought her a little fiend.

At last, one day, the smothered fire broke out. The child had had a half-hour of holiday, and had made herself happy in it by furbishing up her little bedroom. She had picked a peony, a yellow lily, and one or two blue irises, from the spot of flowers in the garden, and put them in a tin dipper on the table in her room, and ranged around them her broken bits of china, her red berries and fragments of glass, in various zigzags. The spirit of adornment thus roused within her, she remembered having seen her brother make pretty garlands of oak-leaves; and, running out to an oak hard by, she stripped off an apronful of the leaves, and, sitting down in the kitchen door, began her attempts to plait them into garlands. She grew good-natured and happy as she wrought, and was beginning to find herself in charity even with Miss Asphyxia, when down came that individual, broom in hand, looking vengeful as those old Greek Furies who used to haunt houses, testifying their wrath by violent sweeping.

"What under the canopy you up to now, making such a litter on my kitchen floor?" she said. "Can't I leave you a minute 'thout your gettin' into some mischief, I want to know? Pick 'em up, every leaf of 'em, and carry 'em and throw 'em over the fence; and don't you never let me find you bringing no such rubbish into my kitchen agin!"

In this unlucky moment she turned, and, looking into the little bedroom, whose door stood open, saw the arrangements there. "What!" she said; "you been getting down the tin cup to put your messes into? Take 'em all out!" she said, seizing the flowers with a grasp that crumpled them, and throwing them into the child's apron. "Take 'em away, every one of 'em! You'd get everything out of place, from one end of the house to the other, if I did n't watch you!" And forthwith she swept off the child's treasures into her dust-pan.

In a moment all the smothered wrath of weeks blazed up in the little soul. She looked as if a fire had been kindled in her which reddened her cheeks and burned in her eyes; and, rushing blindly at Miss Asphyxia, she cried, "You are a wicked woman, a hateful old witch, and I hate you!"

"Hity-tity! I thought I should have to give you a lesson before long, and so I shall," said Miss Asphyxia, seizing her with stern determination. "You've needed a good sound whipping for a long time, miss, and you are going to get it now. I'll whip you so that you'll remember it, I'll promise you."

And Miss Asphyxia kept her word, though the child, in the fury of despair, fought her with tooth and nail, and proved herself quite a dangerous little animal; but at length strength got the better in the fray, and, sobbing, though unsubdued, the little culprit was put to bed without her supper.

In those days the literal use of the rod·in the education of children was considered as a direct Bible teaching. The wisest, the most loving parent felt bound to it in many cases, even though every stroke cut into his own heart. The laws of New England allowed masters to correct their apprentices, and teachers their pupils, — and even the public whipping-post was an institution of New England towns. It is not to be supposed, therefore, that Miss Asphyxia regarded herself otherwise than as thoroughly performing a most necessary duty. She was as ignorant of the blind agony of mingled shame, wrath, sense of degradation, and burning for revenge, which had been excited by her measures, as the icy east-wind of Boston flats is of the stinging and shivering it causes in its course. There is a class of coldly-conscientious, severe persons, who still, as a matter of duty and conscience, justify measures like these in education. Such persons are commonly both obtuse in sensibility and unimaginative in temperament; but if their imaginations could once be thoroughly enlightened to see the fiend-like passions, the terrific convulsions, which are roused in a child's soul by the irritation and degradation of such correction, they would shrink back appalled. With sensitive children left in the hands of stolid and unsympathizing force, such convulsions and mental agonies often are the beginning of a sort of slow moral insanity which gradually destroys all that is good in the soul.

As the child lay sobbing in a little convulsed heap in her bed, a hard, horny hand put back the curtain of the window, and the child felt something thrown on the bed. It was Sol, who, on coming in to his supper, had heard from Miss Asphyxia the whole story, and who, as a matter of course, sympathized entirely with the child. He had contrived to slip a doughnut into his pocket, when his hostess was looking the other way. When the child rose up in the bed and showed her swelled and tear-stained face, Sol whispered : "There's a doughnut I saved for ye. Don't dare say a word, ye know. She'll hear me."

The child was comforted, and actually went to sleep hugging the doughnut. She felt as if she loved Sol, and said so to the doughnut many times, — although he had great horny fists, and eyes like oxen. With these he had a heart in his bosom, and the child loved him.

STEPHENS.

1812–

ALEXANDER HAMILTON STEPHENS, a distinguished statesman and political writer, was born in Taliaferro County, Georgia, in February, 1812. Graduating at Franklin College, Georgia, in 1832, he studied law, and in 1834 began the practice of his profession at Crawfordsville, in the same State. He soon took an active interest in politics, and served for six successive years in the State Legislature. In 1843 he was elected to the National House of Representatives, of which body he continued a prominent and respected member till the end of the Thirty-fifth Congress, when he declined a re-election. A zealous Whig, so long as that party existed, on its dissolution he acted with the Democrats, and supported the measures of the Buchanan administration. At the outbreak of the late civil war he stoutly opposed secession, as a question of expediency, though he defended the right of it. In February, 1861, he was elected Vice-President of the Confederacy, under the Provisional Constitution, and in November of that year was chosen to the same office under the regular Constitution. In 1873 he was elected to Congress as a Representative of Georgia. His writings have been almost exclusively on political subjects, and the chief of them are: *A Constitutional View of the War between the States*, and *The Reviewers Reviewed*, a reply to strictures on the first-named work. He is also the author of *A Compendium of the History of the United States*. Mr. Stephens possesses a very acute and vigorous intellect, admirably equipped for analytical service, and for careful ratiocination. He has been an earnest student of the science of government, and his writings in illustration of it possess great philosophical value. His utterances have always commanded the respectful attention of his political antagonists, and his long and brilliant public career has, by universal consent, given him a title to rank among the foremost of American statesmen.

DECISION AND ENERGY.

For success in life, it is essential that there should be a fixedness of purpose as to the object and designs to be attained. There should be a clear conception of the outlines of that character which is to be established. The business of life, in whatever pursuit it may be directed, is a great work. And in this, as in all other undertakings, it is important in the outset to have a clear conception of what is to be done. This is the first thing to be settled. What profession, what vocation, is to be followed? The only rule for determining this is natural ability and natural aptitude, or suitableness for the particular business selected. The decision in such case should always be governed by that ideal of character which a man, with high aspirations, should always form for himself.

The artist who has laid before him the huge misshapen block of marble, from which the almost living and breathing statue is to spring, under the operation of his chisel, first has the ideal in his mind. The magnificent Temple at Jerusalem, with all its halls and porticos, entrances, stairways, and arches, was designed by Solomon, in all its grand proportions and arrangements, before the foundation-stone was laid. The first thing with the sculptor, the architect, or the painter is the grand design. This being fixed, everything afterward is directed toward its perfect consummation. So it should be with the great work of life. When the course is determined upon, to secure the object in view it should be steadily pursued. You will pardon an illustration of the importance of this consideration by a reference to an incident in the life of one of the most distinguished men of our own country. I allude to Mr. Webster.

He, it may be known to you, was the son of a New Hampshire farmer of very limited means. All the hopes of the father were centered in his son. To put him through college was an object of great desire to him. This he succeeded in doing, but not without some pecuniary embarrassment, as may be the case with some of those fathers whom I now address, in their efforts to give an education to some of these young gentlemen now about to leave this seat of learning.* Before young Daniel had left the walls of his *Alma Mater* he had made up his mind to devote himself to the law. For the first year after his graduation he taught school for the stipulated salary of three hundred and fifty dollars. At the expiration of that time, with this small capital in hand, he set out for Boston to enter upon the course that he had marked out for himself. He was admitted as a student of law in the office of a distinguished counselor in that city. Soon after, and while he was still pursuing his studies, the clerkship of the Court of Common Pleas of his native county of Hillsborough, in New Hampshire, became vacant. The emoluments of that office were about fifteen hundred dollars per annum. Some of his friends, from the best of motives, no doubt, procured the appointment for young Webster, supposing that it would be very acceptable to him. The information was first given to his father, and he was requested to forward it to his son. The father was delighted, and he conveyed the intelligence to the son in language that left no doubt of his earnest desire for its prompt acceptance. Such was his respect for the feelings of his father, that Mr. Webster would not send a reply in writing, but went immediately, in person, to make known to him that he could not accept the place. This he did by gradually unfolding his views and inclinations on the subject.

* The extract is from an address delivered by Mr. Stephens before the Literary Societies of Emory College, Oxford, Georgia, July 21, 1852.

" What," said the father, after he found from the son's conversation that he was speaking against accepting the place, — " what, do you intend to decline this office ? "

" Most assuredly," replied the son, when the question came direct, " I cannot think of doing otherwise."

The father at first seemed angry ; then assuming the air of one who feels the pangs of disappointment in realizing long-cherished hopes, he said, " Well, my son, your mother always said that you would come to something or nothing ; become a somebody or a nobody." The emphasis showed that he thought his son was about to become a " nobody."

The reply of the son was : " I intend, sir, to use my tongue in court, and not my pen ; to be an actor, and not a register of other men's actions."

Nobly has that pledge been redeemed.

The decision with Webster, though young, as to his future course, had been made. The ideal of that character which he desired to establish had been formed. And to the fixedness of purpose with which he adhered to it on that trying occasion, when the strongest inducements of parental entreaty and pecuniary gain were presented to divert him from it, the world is indebted for that name and fame which are the pride and admiration of his countrymen, and that towering reputation which sends its light and effulgence to the remotest regions of civilization.

Another example of the same principle of fixedness of purpose may be given in the character of Mr. Calhoun, who was so long one of Mr. Webster's most distinguished rivals in the Senate of the United States. They both entered life about the same time, though under very different circumstances. And the lives of both afford striking illustrations of that element of character of which I am now speaking. Mr. Calhoun from his earliest youth fixed his mind upon politics. Not the arts and tricks and chicanery of the mere politician or diplomatist, but what may be more properly termed the *science* of government ; the knowledge and thorough understanding of those principles and laws of human action which lie at the foundation of all civil society, in whatever form it may be found ; and the regulations and modifications of which are necessary for the surest enjoyment of rational constitutional liberty.

In no branch of learning, perhaps, has mankind been slower in

their progress than in understanding the true principles of government, the origin of its necessity, the sanction of its obligations, together with the correlative powers and duties of those who govern
and those who are governed.

To this most abstruse subject, which had engaged so much of the
time and attention of the profoundest thinkers that the world ever
produced, the great Carolinian brought all the energies of his subtile
and powerful intellect. It seems to have been the absorbing theme
of his life. Nothing diverted him from it. To master it was his
object. Nor was he unequal to the work undertaken. All questions
of public policy, whether in the cabinet or in the legislative councils,
seem to have been considered, examined, and analyzed by him according to the strictest principles of abstract philosophy. But his labors
were not confined to the consideration and investigation of temporary
questions connected with the administration of his own government.
His objects were higher. His purposes were more comprehensive.
He looked to achievements more permanent, as well as more substantial, than the acquisition of those transitory honors which accompany
a forensic display or a triumphant reply in debate. To such an end
his efforts for years were directed. The result was the production of
a Treatise, or Disquisition as he calls it, on Government, which has
been published since his death, and which, though it has as yet produced but little sensation in the public mind, at no distant day will
doubtless be regarded as the crowning glory of his illustrious life.
This treatise has no particular reference to the government of the
United States; but it discusses the elements and principles of all
forms of government, — reduces them to system and the rules of
science.

I have one other point only to present; that is, energy in execution.
By this I mean application, attention, activity, perseverance, and
untiring industry in that business or pursuit, whatever it may be, that
is undertaken. Nothing great or good can ever be accomplished without labor and toil. Motion is the law of living nature. Inaction is the
symbol of death, if it is not death itself. The hugest engines, with
strength and capacity sufficient to drive the mightiest ships "across the
stormy deep," are utterly useless without a moving power. Energy
is the steam power, the motive principle, of intellectual capacity. It is
the propelling force; and as in physics, *momentum* is resolvable into
quantity of matter and velocity, so in metaphysics, the extent of hu-

man accomplishment may be resolvable into the degree of intellectual endowment and the energy with which it is directed. A small body driven by a great force will produce a result equal to, or even greater than, that of a much larger body moved by a considerably less force. So it is with minds. Hence we often see men of comparatively small capacity, by greater energy alone, leave, and justly leave, their superiors in natural gifts far behind them in the race for honors, distinction, and preferment.

This is, perhaps, the most striking characteristic of those great minds and intellects which never fail to impress their names, their views, ideas, and opinions, indelibly upon the history of the times in which they live. To this class belong Columbus, Luther, Cromwell, Watt, Fulton, Franklin, and Washington. It was to the same class that General Jackson belonged. He had not only a clear conception of his purpose, but a will and energy to execute it. And it is in the same class, or amongst the first order of men, that Henry Clay will be assigned a place; that great man whose recent loss the nation still mourns. Mr. Clay's success, and those civic achievements which will render his name as lasting as the history of his country, were the result of nothing so much as that element of character which I have denominated energy. Thrown upon life at an early age, without any means or resources save his natural powers and abilities, and without the advantages of anything above a common-school education, he had nothing to rely upon but himself, and nothing upon which to place a hope but his own exertions. But, fired with a high and noble ambition, he resolved, as young as he was, and cheerless as were his prospects, to meet and surmount every embarrassment and obstacle by which he was surrounded. His aims and objects were high, and worthy the greatest efforts; they were not to secure the laurels won upon the battle-field, but those wreaths which adorn the brow of the wise, the firm, the sagacious and far-seeing statesman. The honor and glory of his life was, —

> " Th' applause of list'ning senates to command,
> The threats of pain and ruin to despise,
> To scatter plenty o'er a smiling land,
> And read his history in a nation's eyes."

This great end he most successfully accomplished. In his life and character you have a most striking example of what energy and indomitable perseverance can do, even when opposed by the most adverse circumstances.

BEECHER.

1813–   .

HENRY WARD BEECHER, the most distinguished preacher of his day, not only in America, but in the world, was born at Litchfield, Connecticut, in 1813.   He is the son of Rev. Dr. Lyman Beecher, himself a clergyman of positive character and commanding abilities, and is one of a large family of brothers and sisters, each of whom has won distinction in literature or the pulpit.   Henry Ward graduated at Amherst College in 1834, and in 1837 was settled as pastor of a Presbyterian church at Lawrenceburgh, Indiana.   Two years later he removed to Indianapolis, whence the first glimmer of his great genius surprised and fascinated the public. After eight years' service at this post, he accepted a call to the pastorate of Plymouth Church, Brooklyn, which is still the theater of his labors.   His rank as a pulpit orator has already been indicated in the first lines of this paragraph.   In that character he has won his fame, and in it he will go down in history with Massillon and Bossuet, and the great preachers of the English Church.   His connection with literature is almost exclusively *ria* the pulpit ; what he speaks to attentive thousands in his church reappears in his many books, lacking, it is true, the magnetic and intensifying charm of his personal presence, yet instinct and eloquent with the lofty thoughts and the noble catholicity which are fundamental constituents of his nature.   The limitations which restrict this notice forbid any adequate analysis of the sources of his power; but it may be suggested that Mr. Beecher's success as a moral teacher is largely due to the practical and sympathetic qualities of his mind.   He knows how to put himself in direct *rapport* with his hearers or readers, knows their needs, their modes of thinking; puts himself in their place, in fact, and manipulates an audience of thousands as easily and effectively as he would conduct his part of a colloquy.   A briefer definition of his exceptional intellectual equipment would be, — a marvelous knowledge of human nature, touching which he would almost seem to have received a special illumination.   In his sermons and addresses every one recognizes a personal application, so many-sided and many-eyed is Mr. Beecher's mind ; he speaks not merely to those in his presence, but to all humanity.   His first book, *Lectures to Young Men*, was published in 1850, and has passed through nearly a score of editions.   *The Star Papers, First and Second Series*, two volumes made up of his contributions to a New York weekly paper, and *Life Thoughts*, a collection of extracts from his extemporaneous sermons, have had great popularity.   Within a year has been issued his *Yale Lectures on Preaching*, a series of vigorous and suggestive discourses delivered before the students of the Yale Divinity School.   Mr. Beecher's most ambitious literary work is *The Life of Jesus, the Christ*, which is still unfinished, only one volume having been published.   One of the most noteworthy advantages possessed by Mr. Beecher is his power of adapting his style to his subject.   Our extracts illustrate this, and an examination of other specimens of his composition would disclose a still wider range of his versatility.   His homiletic style is simple, yet singularly vigorous, compact in form, yet euphonious and flowing ; his rhetoric is marked by frequent illustrations drawn from universal knowledge or experience, and by occasional passages of dramatic fervor and picturesque beauty.   But in all his writings all considerations are held strictly subordinate to strength and substance.

THE MONTHS.

1. JANUARY !   Darkness and light reign alike.   Snow is on the ground.   Cold is in the air.   The winter is blossoming in frost-flowers.   Why is the ground hidden ?   Why is the earth white ?   So hath God wiped out the past, so hath he spread the earth like an unwritten page for a new year !   Old sounds are silent in the forest and in the air.   Insects are dead, birds are gone, leaves have perished, and

all the foundations of soil remain. Upon this lies, white and tranquil, the emblem of newness and purity, the virgin robes of the yet unstained year.

2. FEBRUARY! The day gains upon the night. The strife of heat and cold is scarce begun. The winds that come from the desolate north wander through forests of frost-cracking boughs, and shout in the air the weird cries of the northern bergs and ice-resounding oceans. Yet, as the month wears on, the silent work begins, though storms rage. The earth is hidden yet, but not dead. The sun is drawing near. The storms cry out. But the Sun is not heard in all the heavens. Yet he whispers words of deliverance into the ears of every sleeping seed and root that lies beneath the snow. The day opens; but the night shuts the earth with its frost-lock. They strive together; but the darkness and the cold are growing weaker. On some nights they forget to work.

3. MARCH! The conflict is more turbulent; but the victory is gained. The world awakes. There come voices from long-hidden birds. The smell of the soil is in the air. The sullen ice, retreating from open field and all sunny places, has slunk to the north of every fence and rock. The knolls and banks that face the east or south sigh for release, and begin to lift up a thousand tiny palms.

4. APRIL! The singing month. Many voices of many birds call for resurrection over the graves of flowers, and they come forth. Go see what they have lost. What have ice and snow and storm done unto them? How did they fall into the earth stripped and bare? — how do they come forth opening and glorified? Is it, then, so fearful a thing to lie in the grave? In its wild career, shaking and scourged of storms through its orbit, the earth has scattered away no treasures. The Hand that governs in April governed in January. You have not lost what God has only hidden. · You lose nothing in struggle, in trial, in bitter distress. If called to shed thy joys as trees their leaves, if the affections be driven back into the heart as the life of flowers to their roots, yet be patient. Thou shalt lift up thy leaf-covered boughs again. Thou shalt shoot forth from thy roots new flowers. Be patient. Wait. When it is February, April is not far off. Secretly the plants love each other.

5. MAY! O flower-month! perfect the harvests of flowers; be not niggardly. Search out the cold and resentful nooks that refused the sun, casting back its rays from disdainful ice, and plant flowers

even there. There is goodness in the worst. There is warmth in the coldness. The silent, hopeful, unbreathing sun, that will not fret or despond, but carries a placid brow through the unwrinkled heavens, at length conquers the very rocks ; and lichens grow, and inconspicuously blossom. What shall not Time do that carries in its bosom Love?

6. June! Rest! This is the year's bower. Sit down within it. Wipe from thy brow the toil. The elements are thy servants. The dews bring thee jewels. The winds bring perfume. The Earth shows thee all her treasure. The forests sing to thee. The air is all sweetness, as if all the angels of God had gone through it, bearing spices homeward. The storms are but as flocks of mighty birds that spread their wings, and sing in the high heaven. Speak to God now, and say, " O Father! where art thou?" and out of every flower and tree, and silver pool, and twined thicket, a voice will come, " God is in me." The earth cries to the heavens, " God is here!" and the heavens cry to the earth, " God is here!" The sea claims him. The land hath him. His footsteps are upon the deep. He sitteth upon the circle of the earth. O sunny joys of the sunny month, yet soft and temperate, how soon will the eager months that come burning from the equator scorch you!

7. July! Rouse up! The temperate heats that filled the air are raging forward to glow and overfill the earth with hotness. Must it be thus in everything, that June shall rush toward August? Or is it not that there are deep and unreached places for whose sake the probing sun pierces down its glowing hands? There is a deeper work than June can perform. The Earth shall drink of the heat before she knows her nature or her strength. Then shall she bring forth to the uttermost the treasures of her bosom ; for there are things hidden far down, and the deep things of life 'are not known till the fire reveals them.

8. August! Reign, thou fire-month! What canst thou do? Neither shalt *thou* destroy the earth, whom frosts and ice could not destroy. The vines droop, the trees stagger, the broad-palmed leaves give thee their moisture, and hang down ; but every night the dew pities them. Yet there are flowers that look thee in the eye, fierce Sun, all day long, and wink not. This is the rejoicing month for joyful insects. If our unselfish eye would behold it, it is the most populous and the happiest month. The herds plash in the sedge ; fish

seek the deeper pools; forest fowl lead out their young; the air is resonant of insect orchestras, each one carrying his part in Nature's grand harmony. August, thou art the ripeness of the year! Thou art the glowing center of the circle!

9. SEPTEMBER! There are thoughts in thy heart of death. Thou art doing a secret work, and heaping up treasures for another year. The unborn infant-buds which thou art tending are more than all the living leaves. Thy robes are luxuriant, but worn with softened pride. More dear, less beautiful, than June, thou art the heart's month. Not till the heats of summer are gone, while all its growths remain, do we know the fullness of life. Thy hands are stretched out, and clasp the glowing palm of August and the fruit-smelling hand of October. Thou dividest them asunder, and art thyself molded of them both.

10. OCTOBER! Orchard of the year, bend thy boughs to the earth, redolent of glowing fruit! Ripened seeds shake in their pods. Apples drop in the stillest hours. Leaves begin to let go when no wind is out, and swing in long waverings to the earth, which they touch without sound, and lie looking up, till winds rake them, and heap them in fence-corners. When the gales come through the trees, the yellow leaves trail like sparks at night behind the flying engine. The woods are thinner, so that we can see the heavens plainer as we lie dreaming on the yet warm moss by the singing spring. The days are calm. The nights are tranquil. The Year's work is done. She walks in gorgeous apparel, looking upon her long labor; and her serene eye saith, " It is good."

11. NOVEMBER! Patient watcher, thou art asking to lay down thy tasks. Life to thee now is only a task accomplished. In the night-time thou liest down, and the messengers of winter deck thee with hoar-frosts for thy burial. The morning looks upon thy jewels, and they perish while it gazes. Wilt thou not come, O December?

12. DECEMBER! Silently the month advances. There is nothing to destroy, but much to bury. Bury then, thou snow, that slumberously fallest through the still air, the hedge-rows of leaves! Muffle thy cold wool about the feet of shivering trees! Bury all that the year hath known! and let thy brilliant stars, that never shine as they do in thy frostiest nights, behold the work! But know, O month of destruction! that in thy constellation is set that Star, whose rising is

13 *

the sign, forevermore, that there is life in death. Thou art the month of resurrection. In thee the Christ came. Every star that looks down upon thy labor and toil of burial knows that all things shall come forth again. Storms shall sob themselves to sleep. Silence shall find a voice. Death shall live; Life shall rejoice; Winter shall break forth, and blossom into Spring; Spring shall put on her glorious apparel, and be called Summer. It is life, it is life, through the whole year!

COMING AND GOING.

Once came to our fields a pair of birds that had never built a nest nor seen a winter. O, how beautiful was everything! The fields were full of flowers, and the grass was growing tall, and the bees were humming everywhere. Then one of the birds fell to singing; and the other bird said, "Who told you to sing?" And he answered, "The flowers told me, and the bees told me, and the winds and leaves told me, and the blue sky told me, and you told me to sing." Then his mate answered, "When did I tell you to sing?" And he said, "Every time you brought in tender grass for the nest, and every time your soft wings fluttered off again for hair and feathers to line the nest." Then his mate said, "What are you singing about?" And he answered, "I am singing about everything and nothing. It is because I am so happy that I sing."

By and by, five little speckled eggs were in the nest; and his mate said, "Is there anything in all the world as pretty as my eggs?" Then they both looked down on some people that were passing by, and pitied them because they were not birds, and had no nests with eggs in them. Then the father-bird sang a melancholy song because he pitied folks that had no nests, but had to live in houses.

In a week or two, one day, when the father-bird came home, the mother-bird said, "O, what do you think has happened?" "What?" "One of my eggs has been peeping and moving!" Pretty soon another egg moved under her feathers, and then another and another, till five little birds were born.

Now the father-bird sung louder and louder than ever. The mother-bird, too, wanted to sing; but she had no time, and so she turned her song into work. So hungry were these little birds, that it kept both parents busy feeding them. Away each one flew. The moment the little birds heard their wings fluttering again among the leaves, five yellow mouths flew open so wide that nothing could be seen but five yellow mouths.

"Can anybody be happier?" said the father-bird to the mother-bird. "We will live in this tree always; for there is no sorrow here. It is a tree that always bears joy."

The very next day one of the birds dropped out of the nest, and a cat ate it up in a minute, and only four remained; and the parent-birds were very sad, and there was no song all that day nor the next. Soon the little birds were big enough to fly; and great was their parents' joy to see them leave the nest, and sit crumpled up upon the branches. There was then a great time. One would have thought the two old birds were two French dancing-masters, talking and chattering, and scolding the little birds to make them go alone. The first bird that tried flew from one branch to another, and the parents praised him; and the other little birds wondered how he did it. And he was so vain of it that he tried again, and flew and flew, and could n't stop flying, till he fell plump down by the house-door; and then a little boy caught him and carried him into the house, and only three birds were left. Then the old birds thought that the sun was not as bright as it used to be, and they did not sing as often.

In a little time the other birds had learned to use their wings; and they flew away and away, and found their own food, and made their own beds; and their parents never saw them any more.

Then the old birds sat silent, and looked at each other a long while.

At last the wife-bird said, —

"Why don't you sing?"

And he answered, —

"I can't sing: I can only think and think."

"What are you thinking of?"

"I am thinking how everything changes. The leaves are falling down from off this tree, and soon there will be no roof over our heads; the flowers are all gone, or going; last night there was a frost; almost all the birds are flown away, and I am very uneasy. Something calls me, and I feel restless as if I would fly far away."

"Let us fly away together!"

Then they rose silently; and, lifting themselves far up in the air, they looked to the north: far away they saw the snow coming. They looked to the south: there they saw green leaves. All day they flew, and all night they flew and flew, till they found a land where there was no winter; where there was summer all the time; where flowers always blossom, and birds always sing.

But the birds that staid behind found the days shorter, the nights longer, and the weather colder. Many of them died of cold; others crept into crevices and holes, and lay torpid. Then it was plain that it was better to go than to stay.

PURITY OF CHARACTER.

OVER the plum and apricot there may be seen a bloom and beauty more exquisite than the fruit itself, — a soft, delicate flush that overspreads its blushing cheek. Now, if you strike your hand over that, and it is once gone, it is gone forever; for it never grows but once. The flower that hangs in the morning, impearled with dew, arrayed with jewels, — once shake it so that the beads roll off, and you may sprinkle water over it as you please, yet it can never be made again what it was when the dew fell lightly upon it from heaven.

On a frosty morning you may see the panes of glass covered with landscapes, mountains, lakes, and trees, blended in a beautiful fantastic picture. Now, lay your hand upon the glass, and by the scratch of your fingers, or by the warmth of the palm, all the delicate tracery will be immediately obliterated. So in youth there is a purity of character which, when once touched and defiled, can never be restored, — a fringe more delicate than frostwork, and which, when torn and broken, will never be re-embroidered.

A man who has spotted and soiled his garments in youth, though he may seek to make them white again, can never wholly do it, even were he to wash them with his tears. When a young man leaves his father's house, with the blessing of his mother's tears still wet upon his forehead, if he once loses that early purity of character, it is a loss he can never make whole again. Such is the consequence of crime. Its effects cannot be eradicated, they can only be forgiven.

DANA.

1813- .

PROFESSOR JAMES DWIGHT DANA, one of the most eminent of American geologists and naturalists, was born at Utica, New York, in 1813. At the age of twenty he graduated at Yale College, where he was distinguished for his scientific tastes and attainments. Devoting himself assiduously to this specialty in knowledge, he soon acquired a reputation which justified his appointment to be the geologist and mineralogist of Commodore Wilkes's Exploring Expedition, sent out by the United States government in 1838. During his four years' absence in this capacity he gathered materials for some of the most notable contributions that have ever been made to the literature of science. Among these are his *Report on Zoöphytes*, *Report on the Geology of the Pacific*, and *Report on Crustacea*. The amount of labor demanded by the preparation of these Reports may be inferred from the fact that they comprised 3,100 pages of text, in quarto form, and 178 plates in folio. Prior to his departure with this expedition he published his *System of Mineralogy*, the fourth edition of which was issued in 1854, and the descriptive part of the fifth, in 1868. In 1850 he was called to the chair of Natural History and Geology at Yale College, but did not begin its occupancy until five years later. Since 1846 he has been a principal editor of the American Journal of Science. Professor Dana's *Manual of Geology*, a new and thoroughly revised edition of which has recently been issued, is a standard text-book, not only in this country, but in Europe. His latest work is a volume entitled *Corals and Coral Islands*. Professor Dana has long been recognized in the scientific circles of Europe as one of the foremost living naturalists; he is a member of many English and Continental scientific societies, and last year received the high compliment of an election to membership in the French Academy. Professor Dana's fame rests upon the sound basis of practical achievement. He has been a hard student and a close observer of nature, and his special qualifications for scientific investigation are happily supplemented by general intellectual powers of exceptional breadth and strength, which admirably fit him for the office of leader and instructor in his chosen department of science.

KNOWLEDGE OF NATURE.

WHEN man, at the word of his Maker, stood up to receive his birthright, God pronounced a benediction, and gave him this commission: "*Replenish the earth: subdue it: and have dominion over every living thing.*"

"*Subdue and have dominion.*" These were the first recorded words that fell on the human ear; and Heaven's blessing was in them.

But what is this subduing of the earth? How is nature brought under subjection? Man's highest glory consists in obedience to the Eternal Will; and in this case, is he actually taking the reins into his own hands? Far from it. He is but yielding submission. He is learning that will, and placing himself, as Lord Bacon has said, in direct subserviency to divine laws. When he sets his sails, and drives over the waves before the blast, feeling the pride of power in that the gale has been broken into a willing steed, he still looks up reverently, and acknowledges that God in nature has been his teacher, and is his strength. When he strikes the rock, and out flows the brilliant metal, he admits that it is in obedience to a higher will than his own, and a reward of careful searching for truth, in complete subjection to that will. When he yokes together a plate of copper and zinc, and urges them to action by a cup of acid, — and then despatches burdens of thought on errands of thousands of miles, — man may indeed claim that he has nature at his bid, subdued, a willing messenger; and yet it is so, because man himself acts in perfect obedience to law. He may well feel exalted : but his exaltation proceeds from the fact that he has drawn from a higher source of strength than himself; and a mind not morally perverted will give the glory where it is due.

These are the rewards of an humble and teachable spirit, kneeling at the shrine of nature ; and if there is indeed that forgetfulness of self, and that unalloyed love of truth, which alone can insure the highest success in research, this shrine will be viewed as only the portal to a holier temple, where God reigns in his purity and love.

The command, " subdue, and have dominion," is, then, a mark both of man's power, and of God's power. It requires man to study his Maker's works, that he may adapt himself to his laws, and use them to his advantage ; — to become wise, that he may be strong ; — to elevate and ennoble mind, that matter may take its true place of subjection. It involves not merely a study of nature in the ordinary sense of those words, but also a study of man himself, and the utmost exaltation of the moral and mental qualities ; for man is a part of nature ; and moreover, to understand the teachings of Infinite Wisdom, the largest expansion of intellect and loftiest elevation of soul are requisite.

Solomon says, that, in his day, " there was nothing new under the sun." What is, is what has been, and what shall be. The sentiment was not prompted by any modern scientific spirit, — impatience of so little progress ; for it is immediately connected with sighings for the good *old* times. Much the same spirit is often shown in these days, and elaborate addresses are sometimes written to prove that, after all our boasted progress, Egypt and Greece were the actual sources of existing knowledge. They point to the massy stones of the pyramids ; the sublime temples and palaces of the old empires ; the occasional utensils of half-transparent glass, and implements of bronze or iron, found among their buried ruins; the fine fabrics and costly Tyrian dyes; — they descant upon the wonderful perfection attained in the fine arts, in poetry and rhetoric, and the profound thought of the ancient philosophers : and then are almost ready to echo, "There is nothing new under the sun." What is, is what has been. *Those good old times !*

But what had those old philosophers, or the whole ancient world, done toward bringing nature under subjection, in obedience to the command, "subdue it"?

They had, it is true, built magnificent temples. But the taste of the architect, or that of the statuary or poet, is simply an emanation from the divine breath within man, and is cultivated by contemplation, and only surface contact with nature.

They piled up Cyclopean rocks into walls and pyramids. But the use of the lever and pulley comes also from the workings of mind, and but shallow views of the world. And adding man to man till thousands have worked together, as in one harness, has been a common feat of despots from the time of the Pharaohs onward.

They educed profound systems of philosophy, showing a depth of thought since unsurpassed. But these again were the results of cogitating mind, acting in its own might, — glancing, it may be, at the landscape and the stars in admiration, but centering on man and mind; and often proving to be as erroneous as profound.

They cultivated the intellect, and made progress in political knowledge. But in their attempts to control nature, they brought to bear little beyond *mere physical force.*

Although ancient wisdom treats of air, earth, fire, and water, not one of these so-called elements was, in any proper sense, brought under subjection.

The *Air :* — Was it subdued, when the old Roman still preferred his banks of oars, and on the land, the wind was trained only to turn a wind-mill, carry off chaff, or work in a bellows?

Was the *Earth* subdued, when, instead of being forced to pour out in streams its wealth of various ores, but half a dozen metals were known? and, instead of being explored and found to be marshaled, for man's command, under sixty or more elements, each with its laws of combination, and all bound to serve the arts, the wisest minds saw only a mass of earth, something to tread upon, and grow grain and grass?

Was *Fire* subdued, when almost its only uses were to warm, and cook, and to bake clay, and few of its other powers were known, besides those of destruction? or *Light*, when not even its component colors were recognized, and it served simply as a means of sight, in which man shared its use with brutes?

Was *Water* subdued, when it was left to run wild along the water-courses, and its ocean-waves were a terror to all the sailors of the age? when steam was only the ephemeral vapor of a boiling kettle, yet unknown in its might, and unharnessed? when the clouds sent their shafts where they willed? when the constituents of water — the life-element *oxygen* and the inflammable *hydrogen* — had not yet yielded themselves to man as his vassals?

KNOWLEDGE OF NATURE (*continued*).

HARDLY the initial step had been taken, through the thousands of years of the earth's existence, to acquire that control of nature which mind should have, and God had ordered. The sciences of observation and experiment had not emerged from the mists of empiricism and superstition. There were few ascertained principles beyond those that flow from mathematical law, or from cogitations of mind after surface surveys of the world.

No wonder that nature unsubdued should have proved herself a tyrant. She *is* powerful. Vast might is embodied in her forces, that may well strike terror into the uninstructed: and man has shown his greatness in that he has at last dared to claim obedience. The air, earth, water, fire, had become filled with fancied fiends, which any priest or priestess could evoke; and even the harmless moon, or two approaching or receding planets, or the accidental flight of a thoughtless bird, caused fearful forebodings; and a long-tailed comet made the whole world to shake with terror.

Christianity, although radiant with hope, could not wholly break the spell. The Christian's trust, Heaven's best gift to man, makes the soul calm and strong mid dangers, real or unreal; yet it leaves the sources of terror in nature untouched, to be assailed by that power which comes from knowledge.

Man thus suffered for his disobedience. He was the slave, — nature, the feared master; to many, even the evil demon himself.

Is this now true of nature? We know that, to a large extent, nature is yet unsearched and unsubdued. Still, vast progress has been made toward gaining control of her ten thousand agencies.

In gathering this knowledge, we have not sought for it among the faded monuments and rolls of the *ancients*, as we call the inhabitants of the earth's childhood: but have looked to records of vaster antiquity, — the writings of the infinite God in creation, which are now as fresh with beauty and wisdom as when His finger first mapped out the heavens, or traced the flowers and crystals of the earth. This is the fountain whence we have drawn; and what is the result?

How is it with *water* in these last times? Instead of wasting its powers in gambols down valleys, or in sluggish quiet about " sleepy hollows," it is trained to toil. With as much glee as it ever displayed running and leaping in its free channel, a single stream now turns over a million of spindles in this New England.

Changed to steam, there is terror in its strength even now. Yet the laws of steam, of its production, condensation, and elasticity, have been so carefully studied, and also the strength and other qualities of the metal used to confine it, as well as the nature and effects of fuel, that if we are careful not to defy established principles, steam is our most willing worker, — turning saw-mills, printing-presses, cotton-gins, — speeding over our roads with indefinite trains of carriages and freight, — bearing away floating mansions, against wind and tide, across the oceans, — cooking, heating, searching out dyes from coarse logwood, and the like, — and applying itself to useful purposes, one way or another, in almost all the arts. Again, if we will it, and follow nature's laws, water gives up its oxygen and hydrogen, and thus the chemist secures the means of burning even the diamond; the aëronaut makes wings for his adventurous flight, and the lighthouse derives the famous Drummond light for its work of mercy.

Light is no longer a mere colorless medium of sight. We may evoke from it any color we please, either for use or pleasure. We may also take its chemical rays from the rest, or its light rays, or its heat rays, and employ them separately or together; for we have found out where its strength lies in these particulars, so that at will, light may pass from our manipulations, shorn of its heating power, or of its power of promoting growth, or chemical change. Ay, the subtile agent will now use its pencil in taking sketches from nature, or portraits, if we desire it: and the work is well done.

The ancient wise men, discoursing on the power which holds matter together, sometimes attributed to the particles convenient hooks for clinging to one another. Little was it dreamed that the force of combination in matter — now called attraction — included the lightning among its effects, and would be made to run errands and do hard work for man. Electricity, galvanism, magnetism, are modern names for some of the different moods under which this agent appears; and none of nature's powers now do better service. It is kept on constant run with messages over the continents, scaling mountains or traversing seas with equal facility. It does our gilding and silverplating. Give it an engraved plate as a copy, and it will make a hundred such in a short time. If taken into employ, it will, in case of fire, set all the bells of a city ringing at once; or it will strike a common beat for all the clocks of a country; or be the astronomer's best and surest aid in observing phases in the heavens, or measuring longitude on the earth. All this and more it accomplishes for us, or can if we wish, besides opening to our inquiring eyes the profound philosophy which God has inscribed in his works.

Nature is not now full of gloom and terror. Her fancied fiends have turned out friends. Although God still holds supreme control, and often makes man remember whence his strength, yet every agent, however mighty in itself, is becoming a gentle and ready assistant, both in our work and play, — in the material progress of nations, as well as their moral and intellectual advancement.

MOTLEY.

1814-1877

John Lothrop Motley, one of the most eminent of American historians, was born in Dorchester, Massachusetts, in 1814. Graduating at Harvard College at the age of seventeen, he went to Europe, where he spent several years in preparation for a task to which he had early devoted himself, — the writing of a *History of the Rise of the Dutch Republic*. Young as he was, he had already produced two novels, *Morton's Hope, or The Memoirs of a Provincial*, and *Merry Mount, A Romance of the Massachusetts Colony*, which were long ago forgotten. After fifteen years of arduous labor he finished his *History*, and its reception on both sides of the Atlantic was exceptionally cordial. Mr. Everett said of it that it was, in his judgment, "a work of the highest merit," and placed "the name of Motley by the side of those of our great American historical trio, — Bancroft, Irving, and Prescott." The instantaneous success of this History — the work of a young and unknown writer — is unprecedented in the annals of historical literature. Not content with this triumph, which assured him of an immortality of fame, Mr. Motley at once set about a new enterprise, the results of which appear in *The History of the United Netherlands*, in which the career of the young nation, the story of whose birth had been told in the previous work, is described with equal spirit and accuracy. During the current year (1874) Mr. Motley's third historical work, *Life and Death of John of Barneveld*, has been published. In common with the eminent historians with whom Edward Everett classed him, Mr. Motley possesses in rare combination the highest intellectual qualifications for his work. He is especially remarkable for a certain breadth of mind which impels him to take comprehensive and exhaustive views of his subject. His style is a model of vigor and grace, and in dramatic quality it is equaled by that of no other historian of this century. It would be, perhaps, impossible to indicate any other historical works than his, of comparatively modern issue, touching which the judgment of critics has been so unanimously favorable. Some foreign reviewers, unable to appreciate, or, perhaps, eager to rebuke, the sturdy Republican spirit that animates this American writer, have charged him with excessive severity in his denunciation of Spanish despotism ; but with this exception his candor and conscientious accuracy have never been impugned. Mr. Motley was appointed United States Minister to Austria by President Lincoln, and, after honorable service at Vienna, was transferred to England, where he represented this government with conspicuous ability. The exigencies of partisan politics required his removal, and he is now, a private citizen, fully occupied with congenial literary labors.

HISTORIC PROGRESS.

We talk of History. No man can more highly appreciate than I do the noble labors of your Society,* and of others in this country, for the preservation of memorials belonging to our brief but most important past. We can never collect too much of them, nor ponder them too carefully, for they mark the era of a new civilization. But that interesting past presses so closely upon our sight that it seems still a portion of the present ; the glimmering dawn preceding the noontide of to-day.

* The New York Historical Society. The extract is from an address delivered by Mr. Motley before this society, December 16, 1868, the subject being *Historic Progress and American Democracy*.

I shall not be misunderstood, then, if I say that there is no such thing as human history. Nothing can be more profoundly, sadly true. The annals of mankind have never been written, never can be written ; nor would it be within human capacity to read them if they were written. We have a leaf or two torn from the great book of human fate as it flutters in the storm-winds ever sweeping across the earth. We decipher them as we best can with purblind eyes, and endeavor to learn their mystery as we float along to the abyss ; but it is all confused babble, hieroglyphics of which the key is lost. Consider but a moment. The island on which this city stands is as perfect a site as man could desire for a great, commercial, imperial city. Byzantium,* which the lords of the ancient world built for the capital of the earth ; which the temperate and vigorous Turk in the days of his stern military discipline plucked from the decrepit hands which held the scepter. of Cæsar and Constantine, and for the succession to which the present lords of Europe are wrangling, — not Byzantium, nor hundred-gated Thebes,† nor London nor Liverpool, Paris nor Moscow, can surpass the future certainties of this thirteen-mile-long Manhattan.

And yet it was but yesterday — for what are two centuries and a half in the boundless vista of the past ? — that the Mohawk and the Mohican were tomahawking and scalping each other throughout these regions, and had been doing so for centuries ; while the whole surface of this island, now groaning under millions of wealth which oppress the imagination, hardly furnished a respectable hunting-ground for a single sachem, in his war-paint and moccasins, who imagined himself proprietor of the soil.

But yesterday Cimmerian darkness, primeval night. To-day, grandeur, luxury, wealth, power. I come not here to-night to draw pictures or pour forth dithyrambics that I may gratify your vanity or my own, whether municipal or national. To appreciate the unexampled advantages bestowed by the Omnipotent upon this favored Republic, this youngest child of civilization, is rather to oppress the thoughtful mind with an overwhelming sense of responsibility ; to

---

* BYZANTIUM. The original name of Constantinople, the present capital of the Turkish Empire. The beauty and convenience of its situation were observed by Constantine the Great, who made it the capital of the Eastern Roman Empire A. D. 328, and called it Constantinopolis, i. e. the City of Constantine.

† THEBES. A great city of Egypt which was formerly the capital of that country. It is now in ruins, its remains extending for seven miles along both banks of the Nile.

sadden with quick-coming fears ; to torture with reasonable doubts. The world's great hope is here. The future of humanity — at least for that cycle in which we are now revolving — depends mainly upon the manner in which we deal with our great trust.

The good old times ! Where and when were those good old times ?

> " All times when old are good,"

says Byron.

> " And all our yesterdays have lighted fools
> The way to dusty death,"

says the great master of morals and humanity.

But neither fools nor sages, neither individuals nor nations, have any other light to guide them along the track which all must tread, save that long glimmering vista of yesterdays which grows so swiftly fainter and fainter as the present fades into the past.

And I believe it possible to discover a law out of all this apparently chaotic whirl and bustle, this tangled skein of human affairs, as it spins itself through the centuries. That law is Progress, — slow, confused, contradictory, but ceaseless development, intellectual and moral, of the human race.

It is of Human Progress that I speak to-night. It is of Progress that I find a startling result when I survey the spectacle which the American Present displays.

This nation stands on the point towards which other people are moving, — the starting-point, not the goal. It has put itself — or rather Destiny has placed it — more immediately than other nations in subordination to the law governing all bodies political as inexorably as Kepler's law controls the motions of the planets.

The law is Progress ; the result, Democracy.

Sydney Smith once alluded, if I remember rightly, to a person who allowed himself to speak disrespectfully of the equator. I have a strong objection to be suspected of flattering the equator. Yet were it not for that little angle of 23° 27' 26", which it is good enough to make with the plane of the ecliptic, the history of this earth and of " all which it inherit " would have been essentially modified, even if it had not been altogether a blank.

Out of the obliquity of the equator has come forth our civilization. It was long ago observed by one of the most thoughtful writers that ever dealt with human history, John von Herder, that it was to the gradual shading away of zones and alternation of seasons that the vigor and variety of mankind were attributable.

I have asked where and when were the good old times? This earth of ours has been spinning about in space, great philosophers tell us, some few hundred millions of years. We are not very familiar with our predecessors on this continent. For the present, the oldest inhabitant must be represented here by the man of Natchez, whose bones were unearthed not long ago under the Mississippi bluffs in strata which were said to argue him to be at least one hundred thousand years old. Yet he is a mere modern, a *parvenu* on this planet, if we are to trust illustrious teachers of science, compared with the men whose bones and whose implements have been found in high mountain-valleys and gravel-pits of Europe; while these again are thought by the same authorities to be descendants of races which flourished many thousands of years before, and whose relics science is confidently expecting to discover, although the icy sea had once ingulfed them and their dwelling-places.

We of to-day have no filial interest in the man of Natchez. He was no ancestor of ours, nor have he and his descendants left traces along the dreary track of their existence to induce a desire to claim relationship with them.

We are Americans; but yesterday we were Europeans, — Netherlanders, Saxons, Normans, Swabians, Celts; and the day before yesterday, Asiatics, Mongolians, what you will.

The orbit of civilization, so far as our perishing records enable us to trace it, seems preordained from East to West. China, India, Palestine, Egypt, Greece, Rome, are successively lighted up as the majestic orb of day moves over them; and as he advances still farther through his storied and mysterious zodiac, we behold the shadows of evening as surely falling on the lands which he leaves behind him.

Man still reeled on, — falling, rising again, staggering forward with hue and cry at his heels, — a wounded felon daring to escape from the prison to which the grace of God had inexorably doomed him. And still there was progress. Besides the sword, two other instruments grew every day more potent, — the pen and the purse.

The power of the pen soon created a stupendous monopoly. Clerks obtained privilege of murder because of their learning; a Norman king gloried in the appellation of "fine clerk," because he could spell; the sons of serfs and washerwomen became high pontiffs, put their feet on the necks of emperors, through the might of education, and appalled the souls of tyrants with their weird anathemas. Naturally, the priests kept the talisman of learning to themselves. How should education help them to power and pelf, if the people could participate in the mystic spell? The icy Deadhand of the Church, ever extended, was filled to overflowing by trembling baron and superstitious hind.

But there was another power steadily augmenting, — the magic purse of Fortunatus with its clink of perennial gold. Commerce changed clusters of hovels, cowering for protection under feudal castles, into powerful cities. Burghers wrested or purchased liberties from their lords and masters.

And still man struggled on. An experimenting friar, fond of chemistry, in one corner of Europe, put niter, sulphur, and charcoal together; * a sexton or doctor, in another obscure nook, carved letters on blocks of wood; † and lo! there were explosions shaking the solid earth, and causing the iron-clad man on horseback to reel in his saddle.

It was no wonder that Dr. Faustus was supposed to have sold his soul to the fiend. Whence but from devilish alliance could he have derived such power to strike down the grace of God?

Speech, the alphabet, Mount Sinai, Egypt, Greece, Rome, Nazareth, the wandering of the nations, the feudal system, Magna Charta, gunpowder, printing, the Reformation, the mariner's compass, America, — here are some of the great landmarks of human motion.

As we pause for a moment's rest, after our rapid sweep through the eons and the centuries, have we not the right to record proof of man's progress since the days of the rhinoceros-eaters of Bedfordshire, of the man of Natchez?

---

* The discovery of gunpowder by Bertholdus, a German monk, in 1320.

† GUTENBERG, born in Germany about 1400, is generally called the inventor of printing. He was the first to print from letters cut on blocks of wood and metal. He was associated with Dr. Faustus, mentioned below. Having printed off numbers of copies of the Bible, to imitate those which were commonly sold in manuscript, Hayden says Dr. Faustus undertook the sale of them at Paris where printing was then unknown. As he sold his copies for sixty crowns, while the scribes demanded five hundred, he created universal astonishment; but when he produced copies as fast as they were wanted, and lowered the price to thirty crowns, all Paris was agitated. The uniformity of the copies increased the wonder: informations were given to the police against him as a magician, and his lodgings being searched and a great number of copies being found, they were seized. The red ink with which they were embellished was supposed to be his blood, and it was seriously adjudged that he was in league with the Devil; and if he had not fled, he would have shared the fate of those whom superstitious judges condemned in those days for witchcraft, A. D. 1460. The career of Dr. Faustus has formed the subject of numerous dramas, romances, and poems, the most notable of which are Goethe's *Faust*, and the celebrated opera of that name.

And for details and detached scenes in the general phantasmagoria, which has been ever shifting before us, we may seek for illustration, instruction, or comfort in any age or land where authentic record can be found. We may take a calm survey of passionate, democratic Greece in her great civil war through the terse, judicial narrative of Thucydides;[*] we may learn to loathe despotism in that marvelous portrait-gallery of crime which the somber and terrible Tacitus[†] has bequeathed; we may cross the yawning abysses and dreary deserts which lie between two civilizations over that stately viaduct of a thousand arches which the great hand of Gibbon has constructed; we may penetrate to the inmost political and social heart of England, during a period of nine years, by help of the magic wand of Macaulay; we may linger in the stately portico to the unbuilt dome which the daring genius of Buckle consumed his life in devising; we may yield to the sweet fascinations which ever dwell in the picturesque pages of Prescott; we may investigate rules, apply and ponder examples: but the detail of history is essentially a blank, and nothing could be more dismal than its pursuit, unless the mind be filled by a broad view of its general scheme.

THE RELIEF OF LEYDEN.[‡]

THE besieged city [§] was at its last gasp. The burghers had been in a state of uncertainty for many days; being aware that the fleet had set forth for their relief, but knowing full well the thousand obstacles which it had to surmount. They had guessed its progress by the illumination from the blazing villages, they had heard its salvos of artillery on its arrival at North Aa; but since then all had been dark and mournful again, — hope and fear, in sickening alternation,

---

[*] THUCYDIDES. One of the most illustrious of the Greek historians, born 471 B. C. His celebrity rests upon his unfinished *History of the Peloponnesian War.* (See Grote's *History of Greece.*)

[†] TACITUS. A celebrated Roman historian, born about 55 A. D. His reputation is chiefly founded on his *Annals,* in sixteen books, which record the history of the Roman Empire from the death of Augustus A. D. 14 to the death of Nero A. D. 68. Excepting the seventh, eighth, ninth, and tenth books, the work still exists.

[‡] The extract is from Mr. Motley's brilliant history, *The Rise of the Dutch Republic.*

[§] LEYDEN, now a flourishing manufacturing town of South Holland. It was besieged by the Spaniards in 1574, when they tried to subdue the Netherlands under their yoke. The siege began on 31st October, 1573, and ended on 3d October, 1574. It was relieved by the dikes being cut, and the sea let in on the Spanish works. Fifteen hundred Spaniards were slain or drowned. The University of Leyden was erected as a memorial of this gallant defense and happy deliverance. The relief of Leyden was a fatal blow to Spanish power in the Netherlands.

distracting every breast. They knew that the wind was unfavorable, and at the dawn of each day every eye was turned wistfully to the vanes of the steeples. So long as the easterly breeze prevailed, they felt, as they anxiously stood on towers and house-tops, that they must look in vain for the welcome ocean.

Yet, while thus patiently waiting, they were literally starving; for even the misery endured at Haarlem* had not reached that depth and intensity of agony to which Leyden was now reduced. Bread, malt-cake, horse-flesh, had entirely disappeared; dogs, cats, rats, and other vermin were esteemed luxuries. A small number of cows, kept as long as possible for their milk, still remained; but a few were killed from day to day, and distributed in minute portions, hardly sufficient to support life, among the famishing population. Starving wretches swarmed daily around the shambles where these cattle were slaughtered, contending for any morsel which might fall, and lapping eagerly the blood as it ran along the pavement; while the hides, chopped and boiled, were greedily devoured.

Women and children, all day long, were seen searching gutters and elsewhere for morsels of food, which they disputed fiercely with the famishing dogs. The green leaves were stripped from the trees, every living herb was converted into human food; but these expedients could not avert starvation. The daily mortality was frightful. Infants starved to death on the maternal breasts which famine had parched and withered; mothers dropped dead in the streets, with their dead children in their arms.

In many a house the watchmen, in their rounds, found a whole family of corpses — father, mother, children — side by side; for a disorder, called "the Plague," naturally engendered of hardship and famine, now came, as if in kindness, to abridge the agony of the people. Pestilence stalked at noonday through the city, and the doomed inhabitants fell like grass beneath his scythe. From six to eight thousand human beings sank before this scourge alone; yet the people resolutely held out, women and men mutually encouraging each other to resist the entrance of their foreign foe,† — an evil more horrible than pest or famine.

---

* HAARLEM. Frederick, the son of Alva, starved the little garrison of Haarlem (20 miles north of Leyden) into a surrender (1573); and then, enraged at the gallant defense they had made, butchered them without mercy. When the executioners were worn out with their bloody work, he tied the three hundred citizens that remained back to back, and flung them into the sea.

† The Spaniards.

13 *

Leyden was sublime in its despair. A few murmurs were, however, occasionally heard at the steadfastness of the magistrates; and a dead body was placed at the door of the burgomaster, as a silent witness against his inflexibility. A party of the more faint-hearted even assailed the heroic Adrian Van der Werf * with threats and reproaches as he passed along the streets. A crowd had gathered around him as he reached a triangular place in the center of the town, into which many of the principal streets emptied themselves, and upon one side of which stood the Church of St. Pancras.

There stood the burgomaster, a tall, haggard, imposing figure, with dark visage and a tranquil but commanding eye. He waved his broad-leaved felt hat for silence, and then exclaimed, in language which has been almost literally preserved, "What would ye, my friends? Why do ye murmur that we do not break our vows and surrender the city to the Spaniards, — a fate more horrible than the agony which she now endures? I tell you I have made an oath to hold the city; and may God give me strength to keep my oath! I can die but once, whether by your hands, the enemy's, or by the hand of God. My own fate is indifferent to me; not so that of the city intrusted to my care. I know that we shall starve if not soon relieved; but starvation is preferable to the dishonored death which is the only alternative. Your menaces move me not. My life is at your disposal. Here is my sword; plunge it into my breast, and divide my flesh among you. Take my body to appease your hunger, but expect no surrender so long as I remain alive."

On the 28th of September a dove flew into the city, bringing a letter from Admiral Boisot.† In this despatch the position of the fleet at North Aa was described in encouraging terms, and the inhabitants were assured that, in a very few days at furthest, the long-expected relief would enter their gates.

The tempest came to their relief. A violent equinoctial gale, on the night of the 1st and 2d of October, came storming from the northwest, shifting after a few hours fully eight points, and then blowing still more violently from the southwest. The waters of the North Sea were piled in vast masses upon the southern coast of Holland, and then dashed furiously landward, the ocean rising over the earth and sweeping with unrestrained power across the ruined dikes.

---

* ADRIAN VAN DER WERF, the burgomaster, or chief magistrate of Leyden.

† ADMIRAL BOISOT, the commander of the Dutch fleet.

In the course of twenty-four hours the fleet at North Aa, instead of nine inches, had more than two feet of water.

On it went, sweeping over the broad waters. As they approached some shallows which led into the great Mere, the Zeelanders dashed into the sea, and with sheer strength shouldered every vessel through!

It was resolved that a sortie, in conjunction with the operations of Boisot, should be made against Lammen * with the earliest dawn. Night descended upon the scene, — a pitch-dark night, full of anxiety to the Spaniards, to the Armada, to Leyden. Strange sights and sounds occurred at different moments to bewilder the anxious sentinels. A long procession of lights issuing from the fort was seen to flit across the black face of the waters, in the dead of night; and the whole of the city wall between the Cowgate and the town of Burgundy fell with a loud crash. The horror-struck citizens thought that the Spaniards were upon them at last; the Spaniards imagined the noise to indicate a desperate sortie of the citizens. Everything was vague and mysterious.

Day dawned at length after the feverish night, and the admiral prepared for the assault. Within the fortress reigned a death-like stillness, which inspired a sickening suspicion. Had the city indeed been carried in the night? Had the massacre already commenced? Had all this labor and audacity been expended in vain?

Suddenly a man was descried wading breast-high through the water from Lammen towards the fleet, while at the same time one solitary boy was seen to wave his cap from the summit of the fort. After a moment of doubt, the happy mystery was solved. The Spaniards had fled panic-struck during the darkness. Their position would still have enabled them, with firmness, to frustrate the enterprise of the patriots; but the hand of God, which had sent the ocean and the tempest to the deliverance of Leyden, had struck her enemies with terror likewise.

The lights which had been seen moving during the night were the lanterns of the retreating Spaniards; and the boy who was now waving his triumphant signal from the battlements had alone witnessed the

---

* LAMMEN, a fort occupied by the Spaniards, which formed the sole remaining obstacle between the fleet and the city. It swarmed with soldiers and bristled with cannon; and so serious an impediment did Boisot consider it, that he wrote that very night in desponding terms regarding it to the Prince of Orange.

spectacle. So confident was he in the conclusion to which it led him, that he had volunteered at daybreak to go thither alone.

The magistrates, fearing a trap, hesitated for a moment to believe the truth, which soon, however, became quite evident. Valdez,* flying himself from Leyderdorp, had ordered Colonel Borgia to retire with all his troops from Lammen.

Thus the Spaniards had retreated at the very moment that an extraordinary accident had laid bare a whole side of the city for their entrance! The noise of the wall as it fell only inspired them with fresh alarm; for they believed that the citizens had sallied forth in the darkness to aid the advancing flood in the work of destruction.

All obstacles being now removed, the fleet of Boisot swept by Lammen, and entered the city on the morning of the 3d of October. Leyden was relieved!

THE HERO OF THE DUTCH REPUBLIC.

No man — not even Washington — has ever been inspired by a purer patriotism than that of William of Orange. Whether originally of a timid temperament or not, he was certainly possessed of perfect courage at last. In siege and battle, in the deadly air of pestilential cities, in the long exhaustion of mind and body which comes from unduly protracted labor and anxiety, amid the countless conspiracies of assassins, he was daily exposed to death in every shape. Within two years five different attempts against his life had been discovered. Rank and fortune were offered to any malefactor who would compass the murder. He had already been shot through the head, and almost mortally wounded. He went through life bearing the load of a people's sorrows upon his shoulders with a smiling face. Their name was the last word upon his lips, save the simple affirmative with which the soldier who had been battling for the right all his lifetime commended his soul, in dying, "to the great Captain, Christ." The people were grateful and affectionate, for they trusted the character of their "Father William," and not all the clouds which calumny could collect ever dimmed to their eyes the radiance of that lofty mind to which they were accustomed, in their darkest calamities, to look for light. As long as he lived he was the guiding-star of a whole brave nation, and when he died the little children cried in the streets.

---

* VALDEZ, the Spanish commander. His head-quarters were at Leyderdorp, a mile and a half to the right of Lammen.

FROUDE.

1818–

JAMES ANTHONY FROUDE, the historian, was born in Devonshire, England, in 1818. He graduated at Oxford University, and became a Fellow of Exeter College. His first book was a novel, *The Shadows of the Clouds*, which had much merit, but is now forgotten. His second was *The Nemesis of Faith*, a theological work which attracted much attention. But his third essay, in the field of history, was conspicuously successful. His *History of England* embraces the period between the Fall of Wolsey and the Death of Elizabeth, and furnishes the completest view of that time that has ever been written. In its preparation the author availed himself of a large collection of manuscripts never before discovered, and which threw a strong light upon his subject. Mr. Froude is not absolutely impartial as an historian; he often gives way to his prejudices, and seems to pervert testimony in aid of his own opinions. His treatment of the case of Mary Queen of Scots has been shown to be thoroughly unjust. But he has admirable qualifications for historical writing; his philosophical reflections are judicious, and his style is spirited and forcible. Some of his dramatic passages are equal to any in our historical literature. Although best known, in this country, at least, by his *History*, Mr. Froude has written many able essays on moral, social, and educational topics, some of which have been collected in a volume entitled *Short Studies on Great Subjects*, from which the second extract is taken. He is now engaged on a book entitled *The English in Ireland*, the first volume of which has been published. In 1872 Mr. Froude visited this country on a lecturing tour, and was received with marked cordiality.

EXECUTION OF SIR THOMAS MORE.*

At daybreak More was awoke by the entrance of Sir Thomas Pope, who had come to confirm his anticipations, and to tell him it was the king's pleasure that he should suffer at nine o'clock that morning. He received the news with utter composure. "I am much bounden to the king," he said, "for the benefits and honors he has bestowed on me; and, so help me God, most of all I am bounden to him that it pleaseth his Majesty to rid me so shortly out of the miseries of this present world."

Pope told him the king desired that he would not "use many words on the scaffold." "Mr. Pope," he answered, "you do well to give me warning, for otherwise I had purposed somewhat to have spoken; but no matter wherewith his Grace should have cause to be offended.

---

* SIR THOMAS MORE, a celebrated English philosopher and statesman, born in London in 1480. He was the author of the famous *Utopia*, a fanciful production written in Latin, describing an imaginary commonwealth in the imaginary island of Utopia, the citizens of which had all things in common. He was a strong Roman Catholic, and wrote tracts against Luther. In October, 1529, he was appointed Lord Chancellor by Henry VIII. in place of the famous Cardinal Wolsey (see extract from Shakespeare's King Henry the Eighth, page 5). Sir Thomas refused to sanction the divorce of Queen Catherine and the marriage of King Henry to Anne Boleyn, for which he was beheaded in the Tower on the 6th of July, 1535. (See *Campbell's Lives of the Lord Chancellors*, and *Froude's History of England.*)

Howbeit, whatever I intended, I shall obey his Highness's command."

He afterwards discussed the arrangements for the funeral, at which he begged that his family might be present; and when all was settled, Pope rose to leave him. He was an old friend. He took More's hand and wrung it, and, quite overcome, burst into tears.

"Quiet yourself, Mr. Pope," More said, "and be not discomfited, for I trust we shall once see each other full merrily, when we shall live and love together in eternal bliss."

As soon as he was alone he dressed in his most elaborate costume. It was for the benefit, he said, of the executioner who was to do him so great a service.* Sir William Kingston remonstrated, and with some difficulty induced him to put on a plainer suit; but that his intended liberality should not fail, he sent the man a gold angel in compensation, "as a token that he maliced him nothing, but rather loved him extremely."

So about nine of the clock he was brought by the Lieutenant out of the Tower; his beard being long, which fashion he had never before used, his face pale and lean, carrying in his hands a red cross, casting his eyes often towards heaven. He had been unpopular as a judge, and one or two persons in the crowd were insolent to him; but the distance was short and soon over, as all else was nearly over now.

The scaffold had been awkwardly erected, and shook as he placed his foot upon the ladder. "See me safe up," he said to Kingston. "For my coming down I can shift for myself." He began to speak to the people, but the sheriff begged him not to proceed, and he contented himself with asking for their prayers, and desiring them to bear witness for him that he died in the faith of the holy Catholic Church, and a faithful servant of God and the king. He then repeated the Miserere psalm† on his knees; and when he had ended and had risen, the executioner, with an emotion which promised ill for the manner in which his part in the tragedy would be accomplished, begged his forgiveness. More kissed him. "Thou art to do me the greatest benefit that I can receive," he said. "Pluck up thy spirit, man, and be not afraid to do thine office. My neck is very short. Take heed, therefore, that thou strike not awry for saving of thine honesty." The executioner offered to tie his eyes. "I will cover them myself,"

---

* The executioner received the clothes worn by the sufferer.
† Psalm li.

he said; and binding them in a cloth which he had brought with him, he knelt, and laid his head upon the block. The fatal stroke was about to fall, when he signed for a moment's delay while he moved aside his beard. "Pity that should be cut," he murmured, "that has not committed treason." With which strange words, the strangest, perhaps, ever uttered at such a time, the lips most famous through Europe for eloquence and wisdom closed forever.

"So," concludes his biographer, "with alacrity and spiritual joy he received the fatal ax, which no sooner had severed the head from the body, but his soul was carried by angels into everlasting glory, where a crown of martyrdom was placed upon him which can never fade nor decay; and then he found those words true which he had often spoken, that a man may lose his head and have no harm."

This was the execution of Sir Thomas More, an act which sounded out into the far corners of the earth, and was the world's wonder as well for the circumstances under which it was perpetrated, as for the preternatural composure with which it was borne. Something of his calmness may have been due to his natural temperament, something to an unaffected weariness of a world which in his eyes was plunging into the ruin of the latter days. But those fair hues of sunny cheerfulness caught their color from the simplicity of his faith; and never was there a Christian's victory over death more grandly evidenced than in that last scene lighted with its lambent humor.

THE BOOK OF JOB.

WITH the Book of Job analytical criticism has only served to clear up the uncertainties which have hitherto always hung about it. It is now considered to be beyond all doubt a genuine Hebrew original, completed by its writer almost in the form in which it now remains to us. It is the most difficult of all the Hebrew compositions, — many words occurring in it, and many thoughts, not to be found elsewhere in the Bible. How difficult our translators found it may be seen by the number of words which they were obliged to insert in italics, and the doubtful renderings which they have suggested in the margin. There are many mythical and physical allusions scattered over the poem, which, in the sixteenth century, there were positively no means of understanding; and perhaps, too, there were mental tendencies in the translators themselves which prevented them from adequately apprehending even the drift and spirit of the composition.

The form of the story was too stringent to allow such tendencies any latitude ; but they appear, from time to time, sufficiently to produce serious confusion. With these recent assistances, therefore, we propose to say something of the nature of this extraordinary book, — a book of which it is to say little to call it unequaled of its kind, and which will one day, perhaps, when it is allowed to stand on its own merits, be seen towering up alone, far away above all the poetry of the world. How it found its way into the canon, smiting as it does through and through the most deeply seated Jewish prejudices, is the chief difficulty about it now ; to be explained only by a traditional acceptance among the sacred books, dating back from the old times of the national greatness, when the minds of the people were hewn in a larger type than was to be found among the Pharisees of the great synagogue. But its authorship, its date, and its history are alike a mystery to us ; it existed at the time when the canon was composed ; and this is all that we know beyond what we can gather out of the language and contents of the poem itself.

The conjectures which have been formed upon the date of this book are so various that they show of themselves on how slight a foundation the best of them must rest. The language is no guide, for although unquestionably of Hebrew origin, the poem bears no analogy to any of the other books in the Bible ; while of its external history nothing is known at all, except that it was received into the canon at the time of the great synagogue. Ewald decides, with some confidence, that it belongs to the great prophetic period, and that the writer was a contemporary of Jeremiah. Ewald is a high authority in these matters, and this opinion is the one which we believe is now commonly received among biblical scholars. In the absence of proof, however (and the reasons which he brings forward are really no more than conjectures), these opposite considerations may be of moment. It is only natural that at first thought we should ascribe the grandest poem in a literature to the time at which the poetry of the nation to which it belongs was generally at its best ; but, on reflection, the time when the poetry of prophecy is the richest, is not likely to be favorable to compositions of another kind. The prophets wrote in an era of decrepitude, dissolution, sin, and shame, when the glory of Israel was falling round them into ruin, and their mission, glowing as they were with the ancient spirit, was to rebuke, to warn, to threaten, and to promise. Finding themselves too late to save, and only, like

Cassandra, despised and disregarded, their voices rise up singing the swan song of a dying people, now falling away in the wild wailing of despondency over the shameful and desperate present, now swelling in triumphant hope that God will not leave them forever, and in his own time will take his chosen to himself again. But such a period is an ill occasion for searching into the broad problems of human destiny; the present is all-important and all-absorbing; and such a book as that of Job could have arisen only out of an isolation of mind, and life, and interest, which we cannot conceive of as possible under such conditions.

The more it is studied, the more the conclusion forces itself upon us that, let the writer have lived when he would, in his struggle with the central falsehood of his own people's creed, he must have divorced himself from them outwardly as well as inwardly; that he traveled away into the world, and lived long, perhaps all his matured life, in exile. Everything about the book speaks of a person who had broken free from the narrow littleness of "the peculiar people." The language, as we said, is full of strange words. The hero of the poem is of a strange land and parentage, — a Gentile certainly, not a Jew. The life, the manners, the customs, are of all varieties and places: Egypt, with its river and its pyramids, is there; the description of mining points to Phœnicia; the settled life in cities, the nomad Arabs, the wandering caravans, the heat of the tropics, and the ice of the north, all are foreign to Canaan, speaking of foreign things and foreign people. No mention, or hint of mention, is there throughout the poem of Jewish traditions or Jewish certainties. We look to find the three friends vindicate themselves, as they so well might have done, by appeals to the fertile annals of Israel, to the Flood, to the cities of the plain, to the plagues of Egypt, or the thunders of Sinai. But of all this there is not a word; they are passed by as if they had no existence; and instead of them, when witnesses are required for the power of God, we have strange un-Hebrew stories of the Eastern astronomic mythology, the old wars of the giants, the imprisoned Orion, the wounded dragon, "the sweet influences of the seven stars," and the glittering fragments of the sea-snake Rahab * trailing across the northern sky. Again, God is not the God of Israel, but the father of mankind; we hear nothing of a chosen people, nothing of a special revelation, nothing of peculiar privileges; and in the court of heaven

---

* See Ewald on Job ix. 13, and xxvi. 14.

there is a Satan, not the prince of this world and the enemy of God, but the angel of judgment, the accusing spirit whose mission was to walk to and fro over the earth, and carry up to heaven an account of the sins of mankind. We cannot believe that thoughts of this kind arose out of Jerusalem in the days of Josiah. The scenes, the names, and the incidents are all contrived as if to baffle curiosity, — as if, in the very form of the poem, to teach us that it is no story of a single thing which happened once, but that it belongs to humanity itself, and is the drama of the trial of man, with Almighty God and the angels as the spectators of it.

No reader can have failed to have been struck with the simplicity of the opening. Still, calm, and most majestic, it tells us everything which is necessary to be known in the fewest possible words. The history of Job was probably a tradition in the East; his name, like that of Priam in Greece, the symbol of fallen greatness, and his misfortunes the problem of philosophers. In keeping with the current belief, he is described as a model of excellence, the most perfect and upright man upon the earth, "and the same was the greatest man in all the east." So far, greatness and goodness had gone hand in hand together, as the popular theory required. The details of his character are brought out in the progress of the poem. He was "the father of the oppressed, and of those who had none to help them." When he sat as a judge in the market-places, "righteousness clothed him" there, and "his justice was a robe and a diadem." He "broke the jaws of the wicked, and plucked the spoil out of his teeth"; and, humble in the midst of his power, he "did not despise the cause of his man-servant, or his maid-servant, when they contended with him," knowing that "He who had made him had made them," and *one* "had fashioned them both in the womb." Above all, he was the friend of the poor; "the blessing of him that was ready to perish came upon him," and he "made the widow's heart to sing for joy."

Setting these characteristics of his daily life by the side of his unaffected piety, as it is described in the first chapter, we have a picture of the best man who could then be conceived; not a hard ascetic, living in haughty or cowardly isolation, but a warm figure of flesh and blood, a man full of all human loveliness, and to whom God himself bears the emphatic testimony, that "there was none like him upon the earth, a perfect and upright man, who feared God and eschewed evil."

HELPS.

1818–1875.

Sir Arthur Helps was born in England in 1818, and died in 1875. He has written two dramatic poems of more than average merit, but is best known by his essays, in which department of literature he occupies a unique and very honorable place. His most popular books are *Friends in Council* and *Companions of my Solitude*. In these volumes are reported the conversations of a company of friends, who discuss questions of various kinds, — ethical, social, and literary. English literature contains nothing in the shape of colloquial essays that approaches these in merit. The individuality of the interlocutors is carefully preserved, and the reader acquires a personal interest in each hardly subordinate to the general effect of the wisdom which they interchange. The thought of these essays is effective not only by its intrinsic vigor and its wonderful affinity for the mind of average intelligence, but by the inimitable grace and almost insidious gentleness of its expression. No writer is more remote from dogmatism than Mr. Helps; but his opinions bear unmistakable marks of maturity and fixedness. His felicity of illustration is hardly surpassed, and the tender human sympathy which warms all his writings brings him very near to his readers. Mr. Helps was not a powerful original thinker; but he had the art of presenting the best thought in the most impressive and persuasive shape, in an almost unequaled degree, and of calling out or reanimating ideas which have been latent in the minds of his readers. There are no essays in the language, save perhaps those of Macaulay, that are at once so delightful and so instructive as Mr. Helps's. The subtile and sweet influence of Mr. Helps's writings is cordially acknowledged by Mr. Ruskin, and other authoritative critics have united in praise of the serene beauty of his style and the stimulating and suggestive potency of his philosophy. He was the author of two novels, or rather essays, in the form of novels, *Realmah* and *Casimir Maremma*, and had lately produced an historical novel of Russian life called *Ivan de Biron*. For many years Mr. Helps held an office in the personal service of Queen Victoria, and a short time before his death he received the honor of knighthood.

DISCOVERY OF THE PACIFIC OCEAN.

Vasco Nuñez * resolved, therefore, to be the discoverer of that sea and of those rich lands to which Comagre's son had pointed, when, after rebuking the Spaniards for their " brabbling " about the division of the gold, he turned his face towards the south. In the peril which so closely impended over Vasco Nuñez there was no use in waiting for reinforcements from Spain : when those reinforcements should come, his dismissal would come too. Accordingly, early in September, 1513, he set out on his renowned expedition for finding " the other sea," accompanied by a hundred and ninety men well armed,

---

* Vasco Nuñez de Balboa. A celebrated Spanish navigator and discoverer, born about 1475. Dissensions having arisen between the partisans of an expedition which had landed on the Isthmus of Panama in 1510, of which Balboa was a member, he was chosen leader of the expedition, and, having obtained reinforcements from Columbus at Hispaniola, he proceeded to explore the Isthmus of Darien, and on the 29th of September, 1513, discovered from the summit of a mountain the vast expanse of the Pacific Ocean. Like Columbus he was traduced by jealous rivals, and was finally executed on a charge of treasonable designs in 1517. (See Irving's *Voyages and Discoveries of the Companions of Columbus*.)

and by dogs, which were of more avail than men, and by Indian slaves to carry the burdens.

Following Poncha's guide, Vasco Nuñez and his men commenced the ascent of the mountains, until he entered the country of an Indian chief called Quarequa, whom they found fully prepared to resist them. The brave Indian advanced at the head of his troops, intending to make a vigorous attack; but they could not withstand the discharge of the fire-arms. Indeed, they believed the Spaniards to have thunder and lightning in their hands, — not an unreasonable fancy, — and, flying in the utmost terror from the place of battle, a total rout ensued. The rout was a bloody one, and is described by an author, who gained his information from those who were present at it, as a scene to remind one of the shambles. The king and his principal men were slain, to the number of six hundred.

Speaking of these people, Peter Martyr makes mention of "the sweetness of their language, saying that all the words in it might be written in Latin letters, as was also to be remarked in that of the inhabitants of Hispaniola. This writer also mentions, and there is reason for thinking that he was correctly informed, that there was a region, not two days' journey from Quarequa's territory, in which Vasco Nuñez found a race of black men, who were conjectured to have come from Africa, and to have been shipwrecked on this coast. Leaving several of his men, who were ill, or over-weary, in Quarequa's chief town, and taking with him guides from this country, the Spanish commander pursued his way up the most lofty sierras there, until, on the 25th of September, 1513, he came near the top of a mountain from whence the South Sea was visible. The distance from Poncha's chief town to this point was forty leagues, reckoned then six days' journey; but Vasco Nuñez and his men took twenty-five days to accomplish it, as they suffered much from the roughness of the ways and from the want of provisions.

A little before Vasco Nuñez reached the height, Quarequa's Indians informed him of his near approach to the sea. It was a sight in beholding which for the first time any man would wish to be alone. Vasco Nuñez bade his men sit down while he ascended, and then, in solitude, looked down upon the vast Pacific, — the first man of the Old World, so far as we know, who had done so. Falling on his knees, he gave thanks to God for the favor shown to him, in his being permitted to discover the sea of the South. Then with his hand he beckoned to his men to come up. When they had come, both he and they knelt down, and poured forth their thanks to God.

He then addressed them in these words : " You see here, gentlemen and children mine, how our desires are being accomplished, and the end of our labors. Of that we ought to be certain ; for, as it has turned out true, what King Comagre's son told of this sea to us, who never thought to see it, so I hold for certain that what he told us of there being incomparable treasures in it will be fulfilled. God and His Blessed Mother, who have assisted us, so that we should arrive here and behold this sea, will favor us, that we may enjoy all that there is in it." Afterward, they all devoutly sang the " Te Deum Laudamus " ; and a list was drawn up, by a notary, of those who were present at this discovery, which was made upon St. Martin's day.

Every great and original action has a prospective greatness, — not alone from the thought of the man who achieves it, but from the various aspects and high thoughts which the same action will continue to present and call up in the minds of others to the end, it may be, of all time. And so a remarkable event may go on acquiring more and more significance. In this case, our knowledge that the Pacific, which Vasco Nuñez then beheld, occupies more than one half of the earth's surface, is an element of thought which in our minds lightens up and gives an awe to this first gaze of his upon those mighty waters.

Having thus addressed his men, Vasco Nuñez proceeded to take formal possession, on behalf of the kings of Castile, of the sea, and of all that was in it ; and in order to make memorials of the event, he cut down trees, formed crosses, and heaped up stones. He also inscribed the names of the monarchs of Castile upon great trees in the vicinity.

READING.

As the world grows older and as civilization advances, there is likely to be more and more time given to reading. In several parts of the earth where mankind are most active, and where the proportion of those who need to labor by their hands is less than in other countries, and likely to go on becoming less, the climate is such as to confine, if it does not repress, out-of-door amusements ; and, in all climates, for the lovers of ease, the delicate in health, the reserved, the fastidious, and the musing, books are amongst the chief sources of delight, and such as will more probably intrench upon other joys and occupations than give way to them.

If we consider what are the objects men pursue, when conscious of any object at all, in reading, they are these : amusement, instruction, a wish to appear well in society, and a desire to pass away time. Now even the lowest of these objects is facilitated by reading with method. The keenness of pursuit thus engendered enriches the most trifling gain, takes away the sense of dullness in details, and gives an interest to what would, otherwise, be most repugnant. No one who has never known the eager joy of some intellectual pursuit, can understand the full pleasure of reading. In considering the present subject, the advantage to the world in general of many persons being really versed in various subjects cannot be passed by. And were reading wisely undertaken, much more method and order would be applied to the consideration of the immediate business of the world.

It must not be supposed that this choice and maintenance of one or more subjects of study must necessarily lead to pedantry or narrowness of mind. The Arts are sisters ; Languages are close kindred ; Sciences are fellow-workmen ; almost every branch of human knowledge is immediately connected with biography ; biography falls into history, which, after drawing into itself various minor streams, such as geography, jurisprudence, political and social economy, issues forth upon the still deeper waters of general philosophy. There are very few, if any, vacant spaces between various kinds of knowledge : any track in the forest, steadfastly pursued, leads into one of the great highways ; just as you often find, in considering the story of any little island, that you are perpetually brought back into the general history of the world, and that this small rocky place has partaken the fate of mighty thrones and distant empires. In short, all things are so connected together, that a man who knows one subject well cannot, if he would, fail to have acquired much besides : and that man will not be likely to keep fewer pearls who has a string to put them on, than he who picks them up and throws them together without method. This, however, is a very poor metaphor to represent the matter ; for what I would aim at producing, not merely holds together what is gained, but has vitality in itself, is always growing. And anybody will confirm this who, in his own case, has had any branch of study or human affairs to work upon ; for he must have observed how all he meets seems to work in with, and assimilate itself to, his own peculiar subject. During his lonely walks, or in society, or in action, it seems as if this one pursuit were something almost independent of himself, always on the watch, and claiming its share in whatever is going on.

Again, by recommending some choice of subject, and method in the pursuit of it, I do not wish to be held to a narrow interpretation of that word "subject." For example, I can imagine a man saying, I do not care particularly to investigate this or that question in history ; I am not going to pursue any branch of science ; but I have a desire to know what the most renowned men have written : I will see what the twenty or thirty great poets have said ; what in various ages has appeared the best expression of the things nearest to the heart and fancy of man. A person of more adventure and more time might seek to include the greatest writers in morals or history. There are not so many of them. If a man were to read a hundred great authors, he would, I suspect, have heard what mankind has yet had to say upon most things. I am aware of the culture that would be required for such an enterprise ; but I merely give it as an instance of what may justly come under the head of the pursuit of one subject, as I mean it, and which certainly would not be called a narrow purpose.

There is another view of reading, which, though it is obvious enough, is seldom taken, I imagine, or at least acted upon ; and that is, that, in the course of our reading, we should lay up in our minds a store of goodly thoughts in well-wrought words, which should be a living treasure of knowledge always with us, and from which at various times, and amidst all the shifting of circumstances, we might be sure of drawing some comfort, guidance, and sympathy. We see this with regard to the sacred writings. " A word spoken in due season, how good is it ! " But there is a similar comfort on a lower level to be obtained from other sources than sacred ones. In any work that is worth carefully reading there is generally something that is worth remembering accurately. A man whose mind is enriched with the best sayings of the poets of his own country is a more independent man, walks the streets in a town, or the lanes in the country, with far more delight than he otherwise would have ; and is taught, by wise observers of man and nature, to examine for himself. Sancho Panza with his proverbs is a great deal better than he would have been without them : and I contend that a man has something in himself to meet troubles and difficulties, small or great, who has stored in his mind some of the best things which have been said about troubles and difficulties. Moreover, the loneliness of sorrow is thereby diminished.

It need not be feared that a man whose memory is rich in such resources will become a quoting pedant. Often, the sayings which are dearest to our hearts are least frequent on our lips; and those great ideas which cheer men in their direst struggles, are not things which they are likely to inflict by frequent repetition upon those they live with. There is a certain reticence with us as regards anything we deeply love.

I have not hitherto spoken of the indirect advantage of methodical reading in the culture of the mind. One of the dangers supposed to be incident upon a life of study is, that purpose and decisiveness are worn away. Not, as I contend, upon a life of study, such as it ought to be. For, pursued methodically, there must be some, and not a little, of the decision, resistance, and tenacity of pursuit which create, or further, greatness of character in action. Though, as I have said, there are times of keen delight to a man who is engaged in any distinct pursuit, there are also moments of weariness, vexation, and vacillation, which will try the metal in him and see whether he is worthy to understand and master anything. For this you may observe that, in all times and all nations, sacrifice is needed. The savage Indian who was to obtain any insight into the future had to starve for it for a certain time. Even the fancy of this power was not to be gained without paying for it. And was anything real ever gained without sacrifice of some kind?

It cannot have escaped the notice of any one who has had much experience, that human life is a system of cunningly devised checks and counter-checks. This is easily seen in considering physical things, — such, for instance, as the human body. One of these bodies has a particular disorder. You could cure it by a certain remedy, if that remedy could be continued far enough; but it cannot, as it would produce another disorder. The same law holds good throughout life; and sometimes, where there is an appearance of the power of free movement in many directions, there is in reality a check to movement in every one.

RUSKIN.

1819 – .

John Ruskin, who has risen to be an authority of last resort in all questions pertaining to Art, is a native of London, where he was born in 1819. He was educated at Oxford, where he won the Newdigate Prize for English Poetry, and has devoted his whole life to the study and exposition of Art. He has written many books, most of which treat of architecture and painting. His first work was *Modern Painters*, which at once established his reputation. It elicited profuse criticism, which in effect was favorable; but high authorities severely censured it as illogical and as extravagant in style. Among his best-known works are *The Seven Lamps of Architecture*, *The Stones of Venice*, and *Lectures on Architecture and Painting*. Within a few years he has given much attention to questions of Political Economy. On no modern writer have praise and blame been bestowed in so great volumes and in so nearly equal measures. In the early years of his career it is undoubtedly true that the weight of critical authority was against him; but to-day his hold upon the popular respect seems to be firmer than ever. His arrogance and dogmatism have cost him many friends, and the eccentricities of his style — which, however, is marvelously forcible, and vigorous with a certain wild beauty — have repelled many readers from his books. But it is impossible not to admire his earnestness, his unquestionable love of truth, and his honest detestation of shams. He has done more than any other living writer to stimulate the public interest in Art, and to formulate sound theories about it.

WATER.

Of all inorganic substances, acting in their own proper nature, and without assistance or combination, water is the most wonderful. If we think of it as the source of all the changefulness and beauty which we have seen in clouds; then as the instrument by which the earth we have contemplated was modeled into symmetry, and its crags chiseled into grace; then as, in the form of snow, it robes the mountains it has made with that transcendent light which we could not have conceived if we had not seen; then as it exists in the foam of the torrent, — in the iris which spans it, in the morning mist which rises from it, in the deep crystalline pools which mirror its hanging shore, in the broad lake and glancing river; finally, in that which is to all human minds the best emblem of unwearied, unconquerable power, the wild, various, fantastic, tameless unity of the sea; what shall we compare to this mighty, this universal element, for glory and for beauty? or how shall we follow its eternal changefulness of feeling? It is like trying to paint a soul.

Few people, comparatively, have ever seen the effect on the sea of a powerful gale continued without intermission for three or four days and nights, and to those who have not I believe it must be unimaginable, not from the mere force or size of surge, but from the complete annihilation of the limit between sea and air. The water from its prolonged agitation is beaten, not into mere creaming foam, but into masses of accumulated yeast, which hang in ropes and wreaths from wave to wave, and where one curls over to break, form a festoon like a drapery, from its edge ; these are taken up by the wind, not in dissipating dust, but bodily, in writhing, hanging, coiling masses, which make the air white and thick as with snow, only the flakes are a foot or two long each ; the surges themselves are full of foam in their very bodies, underneath, making them white all through, as the water is under a great cataract ; and their masses, being thus half water and half air, are torn to pieces by the wind, whenever they rise, and carried away in roaring smoke, which chokes and strangles like actual water. Add to this, that when the air has been exhausted of its moisture by long rain, the spray of the sea is caught by it, and covers its surface not merely with the smoke of finely divided water, but with boiling mist ; imagine also the low rain-clouds brought down to the very level of the sea, as I have often seen them, whirling and flying in rags and fragments from wave to wave ; and, finally, conceive the surges themselves in their utmost pitch of power, velocity, vastness, and madness, lifting themselves in precipices and peaks, furrowed with their whirl of ascent, through all this chaos, and you will understand that there is, indeed, no distinction left between the sea and air ; that no object, nor horizon, nor any landmark or natural evidence of position is left ; that the heaven is all spray, and the ocean all cloud, and that you can see no farther in any direction than you could see through a cataract. Few people have had the opportunity of seeing the sea at such a time, and when they have, cannot face it. To hold by a mast or a rock, and watch it, is a prolonged endurance of drowning which few people have courage to go through. To those who have, it is one of the noblest lessons of nature.

All rivers, small or large, agree in one character ; they like to lean a little on one side ; they cannot bear to have their channels deepest in the middle, but will always, if they can, have one bank to sun themselves upon, and another to get cool under ; one shingly shore to play over, where they may be shallow, and foolish, and childlike ; and another steep shore, under which they can pause and purify themselves, and get their strength of waves fully together for due occasions. Rivers in this way are just like wise men, who keep one side of their life for play and another for work ; and can be brilliant, and chattering, and transparent when they are at ease, and yet take deep counsel on the other side when they set themselves to the main purpose. And rivers are just in this divided, also, like wicked and good men; the good rivers have serviceable deep places all along their banks that ships can sail in, but the wicked rivers go scoopingly, irregularly, under their banks until they get full of strangling eddies, which no boat can row over without being twisted against the rocks, and pools like wells which no one can get out of but the water-kelpie that lives at the bottom; but, wicked or good, the rivers all agree in having two sides.

When water, not in very great body, runs in a rocky bed much interrupted by hollows, so that it can rest every now and then in a pool as it goes along, it does not acquire a continuous velocity of motion. It pauses after every leap, and curdles about, and rests a little, and then goes on again; and if in this comparatively tranquil and rational state of mind it meets with an obstacle, as a rock or stone, it parts on each side of it with a little bubbling foam, and goes round; if it comes to a step in its bed, it leaps it lightly, and then after a little plashing at the bottom, stops again to take breath. But if its bed be on a continuous slope, not much interrupted by hollows, so that it cannot rest, or if its own mass be so increased by flood that its usual resting-places are not sufficient for it, but that it is perpetually pushed out of them by the following current, before it has had time to tranquilize itself, it of course gains velocity with every yard that it runs; the impetus got at one leap is carried to the credit of the next, until the whole stream becomes one mass of unchecked, accelerating motion. Now when water in this state comes to an obstacle, it does not part at it, but clears it like a race-horse; and when it comes to a hollow, it does not fill it up and run out leisurely at the other side, but it rushes down into it and comes up again on the other side, as a ship into the hollow of the sea. Hence the whole appearance of the bed of the stream is changed, and all the lines of the water altered in their nature.

The quiet stream is a succession of leaps and pools; the leaps are light and springy, and parabolic, and make a great deal of splashing when they tumble into the pool; then we have a space of quiet curdling water, and another similar leap below. But the stream when it has gained an impetus takes the shape of its bed, never stops, is equally deep and equally swift everywhere, goes down into every hollow, not with a leap, but with a swing, not foaming, nor splashing, but in the bending line of a strong sea-wave, and comes up again on the other side, over rock and ridge, with the ease of a bounding leopard; if it meet a rock three or four feet above the level of its bed, it will neither part nor foam, nor express any concern about the matter, but clear it in a smooth dome of water, without apparent exertion, coming down again as smoothly on the other side; the whole surface of the surge being drawn into parallel lines by its extreme velocity, but foamless, except in places where the form of the bed opposes itself at some direct angle to such a line of fall, and causes a breaker; so that the whole river has the appearance of a deep and raging sea, with this only difference, that the torrent-waves always break backwards, and sea-waves forwards. Thus, then, in the water which has gained an impetus, we have the most exquisite arrangements of curved lines, perpetually changing from convex to concave, and *vice versa*, following every swell and hollow of the bed with their modulating grace, and all in unison of motion, presenting perhaps the most beautiful series of inorganic forms which nature can possibly produce; for the sea runs too much into similar and concave curves with sharp edges, but every motion of the torrent is united, and all its curves are modifications of beautiful lines.

THE CLOUDS.

STAND upon the peak of some isolated mountain at daybreak, when the night-mists first rise from off the plains, and watch their white and lake-like fields as they float in level bays and winding gulfs about the islanded summits of the lower hills, untouched yet by more than dawn, colder and more quiet than a windless sea under the moon of midnight. Watch when the first sunbeam is sent upon the silver channels, how the foam of their undulating surface parts and passes away; and down under their depths the glittering city and green pasture lie, like Atlantis, between the white paths of winding rivers; the flakes of light falling every moment faster and broader among the spires, starry as the wreathed surges break and vanish above them, and the confused crests and ridges of the dark hills shorten their gray shadows upon the plain.

Wait a little longer, and you shall see those scattered mists rallying in the ravines and floating up towards you, along the winding valleys, till they couch in quiet masses, iridescent with the morning light,

upon the broad breasts of the higher hills, whose leagues of massy
undulation will melt back and back into that robe of material light,
until they fade away, lost in its luster, to appear again above, in the
serene heaven, like a wild, bright, impossible dream, foundationless
and inaccessible, their very bases vanishing in the unsubstantial and
mocking blue of the deep lake below. Wait yet a little longer,
and you shall see those mists gather themselves into white towers,
and stand like fortresses along the promontories, massy and motionless, only piling with every instant higher and higher into the sky,
and casting longer shadows athwart the rocks; and out of the pale
blue of the horizon you will see forming and advancing a troop of
narrow, dark, pointed vapors, which will cover the sky, inch by inch,
with their gray network, and take the light off the landscape with an
eclipse which will stop the singing of the birds and the motion of the
leaves together; and then you will see horizontal bars of black
shadow forming under them, and lurid wreaths create themselves, you
know not how, along the shoulders of the hills; you never see them
form, but when you look back to a place which was clear an instant
ago, there is a cloud on it, hanging by the precipices, as a hawk
pauses over his prey.

And then you will hear the sudden rush of the awakened wind, and
you will see those watch-towers of vapor swept away from their foundations, and waving curtains of opaque rain let down to the valleys,
swinging from the burdened clouds in black, bending fringes, or pacing
in pale columns along the lake level, grazing its surface into foam as
they go. And then, as the sun sinks, you shall see the storm drift
for an instant from off the hills, leaving their broad sides smoking,
and loaded yet with snow-white, torn, steam-like rags of capricious
vapor, now gone, now gathered again; while the smoldering sun,
seeming not far away, but burning like a red-hot ball beside you, and
as if you could reach it, plunges through the rushing wind and rolling
cloud with headlong fall, as if it meant to rise no more, dyeing all the
air about it with blood. And then you shall hear the fainting tempest
die in the hollow of the night, and you shall see a green halo kindling
on the summit of the eastern hills, brighter — brighter yet, till the
large white circle of the slow moon is lifted up among the barred
clouds, step by step, line by line; star after star she quenches with
her kindling light, setting in their stead an army of pale, penetrable,
fleecy wreaths in the heaven, to give light upon the earth, which move

together hand in hand, company by company, troop by troop, so measured in their unity of motion, that the whole heaven seems to roll with them, and the earth to reel under them.

And then wait yet for one hour, until the east again becomes purple, and the heaving mountains, rolling against it in darkness, like waves of a wild sea, are drowned one by one in the glory of its burning; watch the white glaciers blaze in their winding paths about the mountains, like mighty serpents with scales of fire; watch the columnar peaks of solitary snow, kindling downwards, chasm by chasm, each in itself a new morning; their long avalanches cast down in keen streams brighter than the lightning, sending each his tribute of driven snow, like altar-smoke, up to the heaven; the rose-light of their silent domes flushing that heaven about them and above them, piercing with purer light through its purple lines of lifted cloud, casting a new glory on every wreath as it passes by, until the whole heaven — one scarlet canopy — is interwoven with a roof of waving flame, and tossing, vault beyond vault, as with the drifted wings of many companies of angels; and then, when you can look no more for gladness, and when you are bowed down with fear and love of the Maker and Doer of this, tell me who has best delivered this his message unto men!

NATURE has a thousand ways and means of rising above herself, but incomparably the noblest manifestations of her capability of color are in the sunsets among the high clouds. I speak especially of the moment before the sun sinks, when his light turns pure rose-color, and when this light falls upon a zenith covered with countless cloud-forms of inconceivable delicacy, threads and flakes of vapor, which would in common daylight be pure snow-white, and which give therefore fair field to the tone of light. There is then no limit to the multitude, and no check to the intensity of the hues assumed. The whole sky from the zenith to the horizon becomes one molten, mantling sea of color and fire; every black bar turns into massy gold, every ripple and wave into unsullied, shadowless crimson, and purple, and scarlet, and colors for which there are no words in language and no ideas in the mind, — things which can only be conceived while they are visible, — the intense hollow blue of the upper sky melting through it all, — showing here deep and pure and lightless, there modulated by the filmy, formless body of the transparent vapor, till it is lost imperceptibly in its crimson and gold.

LOWELL.

1819- .

JAMES RUSSELL LOWELL, poet, critic, and essayist, was born at Cambridge, Massachusetts, in 1819. Having graduated at Harvard College, he studied law, but, after a brief experience of the profession, he abandoned the courts for the more congenial walks of literature. His first volume of poetry, *A Year's Life*, was published in 1841. In 1844 appeared a second collection of his poems, and in 1848 a third. This latter year is a memorable one in his literary career, having witnessed the publication of some of his most famous compositions. Among these are *The Vision of Sir Launfal, A Fable for Critics*, and *The Biglow Papers*, besides a fresh collection of his shorter poems. In 1855 Mr. Lowell succeeded to the chair of Belles-Lettres in Harvard College, for many years occupied by Mr. Longfellow. Since his accession to this post he has undertaken no important literary enterprises. He has, however, contributed to the magazines, and written occasional poems (e. g. the *Commemoration Ode*) which exhibit his powers at their best. The only volumes bearing his name issued within the last ten years are two collections of essays, — *My Study Windows* and *Among my Books*. Professor Lowell is, perhaps, the most scholarly of American writers; yet he is far from sacrificing vigor to finish, and his compositions illustrate the highest American attainment in culture and style. His *Fable for Critics* marked a new departure in American letters, and exhibited him as a successful pioneer in a department of poetical effort which had been almost untried in this country. Its execution would do credit to the poet in his maturity; but its spirit smacked of acerbity and arrogance, and strikingly exemplified one of his characteristics, — an almost finical fastidiousness, which has always prevented him from becoming a popular writer. *The Biglow Papers* are a unique product of American humor, and, though written with reference to a temporary condition of public sentiment, will always be admired for their graphic and faithful representations of Yankee character, and for the mingled wit and wisdom with which they abound. As an essayist, Mr. Lowell is at his best in dealing with literary topics: his essays on certain old English writers are hardly surpassed in English literature. He has been a loving student of nature as well as of books, and his essay on *My Garden Acquaintance* is as admirable as anything he has written. In 1872 Mr. Lowell went to Europe, where he remained two years.

MY GARDEN ACQUAINTANCE.

DR. WATTS's statement that " birds in their little nests agree," like too many others intended to form the infant mind, is very far from being true. On the contrary, the most peaceful relation of the different species to each other is that of armed neutrality. They are very jealous of neighbors. A few years ago, I was much interested in the housebuilding of a pair of summer yellow-birds. They had chosen a very pretty site near the top of a tall white lilac, within easy eyeshot of a chamber window. A very pleasant thing it was to see their little home growing with mutual help, to watch their industrious skill interrupted only by little flirts and snatches of endearment, frugally cut short by the common-sense of the tiny housewife. They had brought their work nearly to an end, and had already begun to line it with fern-down, the gathering of which demanded more distant

journeys and longer absences.   But, alas! the syringa, immemorial
manor of the catbirds, was not more than twenty feet away, and these
"giddy neighbors" had, as it appeared, been all along jealously watchful, though silent, witnesses of what they deemed an intrusion of
squatters.   No sooner were the pretty mates fairly gone for a new
load of lining, than

> " To their unguarded nest these weasel Scots
> Came stealing."

Silently they flew back and forth, each giving a vengeful dab at the
nest in passing.   They did not fall-to and deliberately destroy it, for
they might have been caught at their mischief.   As it was, whenever
the yellow-birds came back, their enemies were hidden in their own
sight-proof bush.   Several times their unconscious victims repaired
damages, but at length, after counsel taken together, they gave it up.
Perhaps, like other unlettered folk, they came to the conclusion that
the Devil was in it, and yielded to the invisible persecutions of witchcraft.

The robins, by constant attacks and annoyances, have succeeded in
driving off the blue-jays who used to build in our pines, their gay
colors and quaint noisy ways making them welcome and amusing
neighbors.   I once had the chance of doing a kindness to a household of them, which they received with very friendly condescension.
I had had my eye for some time upon a nest, and was puzzled by a
constant fluttering of what seemed full-grown wings in it whenever I
drew nigh.   At last I climbed the tree, in spite of angry protests from
the old birds against my intrusion.   The mystery had a very simple
solution.   In building the nest, a long piece of packthread had been
somewhat loosely woven in.   Three of the young had contrived to
entangle themselves in it, and had become full-grown without being
able to launch themselves upon the air.   One was unharmed; another
had so tightly twisted the cord about its shank that one foot was
curled up and seemed paralyzed; the third, in its struggles to escape,
had sawn through the flesh of the thigh and so much harmed itself
that I thought it humane to put an end to its misery.   When I took
out my knife to cut their hempen bonds, the heads of the family
seemed to divine my friendly intent.   Suddenly ceasing their cries
and threats, they perched quietly within reach of my hand, and
watched me in my work of manumission.   This, owing to the fluttering terror of the prisoners, was an affair of some delicacy; but erelong

I was rewarded by seeing one of them fly away to a neighboring tree, while the cripple, making a parachute of his wings, came lightly to the ground, and hopped off as well as he could with one leg, obsequiously waited on by his elders. A week later I had the satisfaction of meeting him in the pine-walk, in good spirits, and already so far recovered as to be able to balance himself with the lame foot. I have no doubt that in his old age he accounted for his lameness by some handsome story of a wound received at the famous Battle of the Pines, when our tribe, overcome by numbers, was driven from its ancient camping-ground. Of late years the jays have visited us only at intervals; and in winter their bright plumage, set off by the snow, and their cheerful cry, are especially welcome. They would have furnished Æsop with a fable, for the feathered crest in which they seem to take so much satisfaction is often their fatal snare. Country boys make a hole with their finger in the snow-crust just large enough to admit the jay's head, and, hollowing it out somewhat beneath, bait it with a few kernels of corn. The crest slips easily into the trap, but refuses to be pulled out again, and he who came to feast remains a prey.

Twice have the crow-blackbirds attempted a settlement in my pines, and twice have the robins, who claim a right of pre-emption, so successfully played the part of border-ruffians as to drive them away, — to my great regret, for they are the best substitute we have for rooks. At Shady Hill (now, alas! empty of its so long loved household) they build by hundreds, and nothing can be more cheery than their creaking clatter (like a convention of old-fashioned tavern-signs) as they gather at evening to debate in mass meeting their windy politics, or to gossip at their tent-doors over the events of the day. Their port is grave, and their stalk across the turf as martial as that of a second-rate ghost in Hamlet. They never meddled with my corn, so far as I could discover.

For a few years I had crows, but their nests are an irresistible bait for boys, and their settlement was broken up. They grew so wonted as to throw off a great part of their shyness, and to tolerate my near approach. One very hot day I stood for some time within twenty feet of a mother and three children, who sat on an elm bough over my head, gasping in the sultry air, and holding their wings half spread for coolness. All birds during the pairing season become more or less sentimental, and murmur soft nothings in a tone very unlike the grinding-organ repetition and loudness of their habitual song. The

crow is very comical as a lover, and to hear him trying to soften his
croak to the proper Saint Preux standard has something the effect of
a Mississippi boatman quoting Tennyson. Yet there are few things
to my ear more melodious than his caw of a clear winter morning as
it drops to you filtered through five hundred fathoms of crisp blue air.
The hostility of all smaller birds makes the moral character of the
crow, for all his deaconlike demeanor and garb, somewhat questionable.   He could never sally forth without insult.   The golden robins,
especially, would chase him as far as I could follow with my eye,
making him duck clumsily to avoid their importunate bills.   I do not
believe, however, that he robbed any nests hereabouts, for the refuse
of the gas-works, which, in our free-and-easy community, is allowed to
poison the river, supplied him with dead alewives in abundance.   I
used to watch him making his periodical visits to the salt-marshes
and coming back with a fish in his beak to his young savages, who,
no doubt, like it in that condition which makes it savory to the
Kanakas and other corvine races of men.

YUSSOUF.

A STRANGER came one night to Yussouf's tent,
Saying, "Behold one outcast and in dread,
Against whose life the bow of power is bent,
Who flies, and hath not where to lay his head;
I come to thee for shelter and for food,
To Yussouf, called through all our tribes 'The Good.'"

"This tent is mine," said Yussouf, "but no more
Than it is God's; come in, and be at peace;
Freely shalt thou partake of all my store
As I of His who buildeth over these
Our tents his glorious roof of night and day,
And at whose door none ever yet heard Nay."

So Yussouf entertained his guest that night,
And, waking him ere day, said: "Here is gold,
My swiftest horse is saddled for thy flight,
Depart before the prying day grow bold."
As one lamp lights another, nor grows less,
So nobleness enkindleth nobleness.

That inward light the stranger's face made grand,
Which shines from all self-conquest; kneeling low,
He bowed his forehead upon Yussouf's hand,
Sobbing: "O Sheik, I cannot leave thee so;
I will repay thee; all this thou hast done
Unto that Ibrahim who slew thy son!"

"Take thrice the gold," said Yussouf, "for with thee
Into the desert, never to return,
My one black thought shall ride away from me;
First-born, for whom by day and night I yearn,
Balanced and just are all of God's decrees;
Thou art avenged, my first-born, sleep in peace!"

THE CHANGELING.

I HAD a little daughter,
    And she was given to me
To lead me gently backward
    To the Heavenly Father's knee,
That I, by the force of nature,
    Might in some dim wise divine
The depth of his infinite patience
    To this wayward soul of mine.

I know not how others saw her,
    But to me she was wholly fair,
And the light of the heaven she came from
    Still lingered and gleamed in her hair;
For it was as wavy and golden,
    And as many changes took,
As the shadows of sun-gilt ripples
    On the yellow bed of a brook.

To what can I liken her smiling
    Upon me, her kneeling lover,
How it leaped from her lips to her eyelids,
    And dimpled her wholly over,

Till her outstretched hands smiled also,
   And I almost seemed to see
The very heart of her mother
   Sending sun through her veins to me !

She had been with us scarce a twelvemonth,
   And it hardly seemed a day,
When a troop of wandering angels
   Stole my little daughter away ;
Or perhaps those heavenly Zingari
   But loosed the hampering strings,
And when they had opened her cage-door,
   My little bird used her wings.

But they left in her stead a changeling,
   A little angel child,
That seems like her bud in full blossom,
   And smiles as she never smiled :
When I wake in the morning, I see it
   Where she always used to lie,
And I feel as weak as a violet
   Alone 'neath the awful sky ;

As weak, yet as trustful also ;
   For the whole year long I see
All the wonders of faithful Nature
   Still worked for the love of me ;
Winds wander, and dews drip earthward,
   Rain falls, suns rise and set,
Earth whirls, and all but to prosper
   A poor little violet.

This child is not mine as the first was,
   I cannot sing it to rest,
I cannot lift it up fatherly
   And bliss it upon my breast ;
Yet it lies in my little one's cradle
   And sits in my little one's chair,
And the light of the heaven she 's gone to
   Transfigures its golden hair.

ON A CERTAIN CONDESCENSION IN FOREIGNERS.

PERHAPS one reason why the average Briton spreads himself here with such an easy air of superiority may be owing to the fact that he meets with so many bad imitations as to conclude himself the only real thing in a wilderness of shams. He fancies himself moving through an endless Bloomsbury, where his mere apparition confers honor as an avatar of the court-end of the universe. Not a Bull of them all but is persuaded he bears Europa upon his back. This is the sort of fellow whose patronage is so divertingly insufferable. Thank Heaven he is not the only specimen of cater-cousinship from the dear old Mother Island that is shown to us! Among genuine things, I know nothing more genuine than the better men whose limbs were made in England. So manly-tender, so brave, so true, so warranted to wear, they make us proud to feel that blood is thicker than water.

But it is not merely the Englishman; every European candidly admits in himself some right of primogeniture in respect to us, and pats this shaggy continent on the back with a lively sense of generous unbending. The German who plays the bass-viol has a well-founded contempt, which he is not always nice in concealing, for a country so few of whose children ever take that noble instrument between their knees.

So long as we continue to be the most common-schooled and the least cultivated people in the world, I suppose we must consent to endure this condescending manner of foreigners toward us. The more friendly they mean to be, the more ludicrously prominent it becomes. They can never appreciate the immense amount of silent work that has been done here making this continent slowly fit for the abode of man, and which will demonstrate itself, let us hope, in the character of the people. Outsiders can only be expected to judge a nation by the amount it has contributed to the civilization of the world; the amount, that is, that can be seen and handled. A great place in history can only be achieved by competitive examinations, nay, by a long course of them. How much new thought have we contributed to the common stock? Till that question can be triumphantly answered, or needs no answer, we must continue to be simply interesting as an experiment, to be studied as a problem, and not respected as an attained result or an accomplished solution. Perhaps, as I have hinted, their patronizing manner toward us is the fair result of their failing to see here any thing more than a poor imitation, a plaster-cast of Europe. And are they not partly right? If the tone of the uncultivated American has too often the arrogance of the barbarian, is not that of the cultivated as often vulgarly apologetic? In the American they meet with is there the simplicity, the manliness, the absence of sham, the sincere human nature, the sensitiveness to duty and implied obligation, that in any way distinguishes us from what our orators call "the effete civilization of the Old World"? Is there a politician among us daring enough to risk his future on the chance of our keeping our word with the exactness of superstitious communities like England? Is it certain that we shall be ashamed of a bankruptcy of honor, if we can only keep the letter of our bond? I hope we shall be able to answer all these questions with a frank *yes*. At any rate, we would advise our visitors that we are not merely curious creatures, but belong to the family of man, and that, as individuals, we are not to be always subjected to the competitive examination above mentioned, even if we acknowledged their competence as an examining board. Above all, we beg them to remember that America is not to us, as to them, a mere object of external interest to be discussed and analyzed, but *in* us, part of our very marrow. Let them not suppose that we conceive of ourselves as exiles from the graces and amenities of an older date than we, though very much at home in a state of things not yet all it might be or should be, but which we mean to make so, and which we find both wholesome and pleasant for men to live in. "The full tide of human existence" may be felt here as keenly as Johnson felt it at Charing Cross, and in a larger sense. I know one person who is singular enough to think Cambridge the very best spot on the habitable globe.* "Doubtless God *could* have made a better, but doubtless he never did."

It will take England a great while to get over her airs of patronage toward us, or even passably to conceal them. She cannot help confounding the people with the country, and regarding us as lusty juveniles. She has a conviction that whatever good there is in us is wholly English, when the truth is that we are worth nothing except so far as we have disinfected ourselves of Anglicism. She is especially condescending just now, and lavishes sugar-plums on us as if we

---

* Mr. Lowell resides at Cambridge.

had not outgrown them. I am no believer in sudden conversions, especially in sudden conversions to a favorable opinion of people who have just proved you to be mistaken in judgment and therefore unwise in policy. I never blamed her for not wishing well to democracy, — how should she? The only sure way of bringing about a healthy relation between the two countries is for Englishmen to clear their minds of the notion that we are always to be treated as a kind of inferior and deported Englishman whose nature they perfectly understand, and whose back they accordingly stroke the wrong way of the fur with amazing perseverance. Let them learn to treat us naturally on our merits as human beings, as they would a German or a Frenchman, and not as if we were a kind of counterfeit Briton whose crime appeared in every shade of difference, and before long there would come that right feeling which we naturally call a good understanding. The common blood, and still more the common language, are fatal instruments of misapprehension. Let them give up *trying* to understand us, still more thinking that they do, and acting in various absurd ways as the necessary consequence; for they will never arrive at that devoutly-to-be-wished consummation, till they learn to look at us as we are and not as they suppose us to be. Dear old long-estranged mother-in-law, it is a great many years since we parted. Since 1660, when you married again, you have been a stepmother to us. Put on your spectacles, dear madam. Yes, we *have* grown, and changed likewise. You would not let us darken your doors, if you could help it. We know that perfectly well. But pray, when we look to be treated as men, don't shake that rattle in our faces, nor talk baby to us any longer.

> "Do, child, go to it grandam, child ;
> Give grandam kingdom, and it grandam will
> Give it a plum, a cherry, and a fig."

MRS. LE VERT.

1820-   .

MRS. OCTAVIA WALTON LE VERT, a distinguished Southern writer, was born near Augusta, Georgia, in 1820. She was the daughter of Colonel George Walton. While a mere girl she selected a name for the capital of Florida, — of which State her father was at that time governor, — Tallahassee, an Indian word meaning "beautiful land." In 1836 she became the wife of Dr. Henry S. Le Vert of Mobile, Alabama. She has traveled much, both in America and Europe. The observations made during two tours in Europe are given in her *Souvenirs of Travel*, a duodecimo of two volumes, published in 1858. She has contributed occasionally to current literature; and since the war has given readings from her writings. Of Mrs. Le Vert's tours in Europe N. P. Willis says: "There probably was never a more signal success in the way of access to foreign society, friendly attentions from the nobility, and notice from royalty, than fell to the share of Madame Le Vert." Her style is spontaneous, often conversational, but always graceful, natural, and easy, and never dull. The best portions are *The Eruption of Vesuvius, The Coliseum, The Way over the Simplon, The Brownings in Florence, Moonlight in Venice, A Visit to the Pope,* and *The Farewell to Italy.* In 1869 a similar work, *Souvenirs of Distinguished People,* by Mrs. Le Vert, was announced as in press; but it has never appeared, owing, the public were advised, to circumstances of a personal nature.

THE STUDY OF LANGUAGE.

> " Greek 's a harp we love to hear:
> Latin is a trumpet clear;
> Spanish like an organ swells;
> Italian rings its silver bells;
> France, with many a frolic mien,
> Tunes her sprightly violin;
> Loud the German rolls his drum
> When Russia's clashing cymbals come;
> But Briton's sons may well rejoice,
> For English is the human voice."

THERE is not a more useful or delightful occupation for the leisure hours of young ladies than the study of foreign languages. It is the bridge spanning the deep waters which divide our own from the rich and varied literature of other lands. When once we have passed over it, a new world of enjoyment is open to us, and we are quickly brought *en rapport* with the brilliant intellects that have illustrated the grand and glorious in prose and poetry.

The best translation is but a shadow of the original. We may transplant a tropical flower to our climate, and cherish it with infinite care; still its blossoms will never possess the beauty and fragrance of its own sunny clime. Thus it is with foreign literature. To enjoy perfectly the noble utterances of great minds, we must read them in the language with which Genius first draped them. The subtile charm of originality, — the delicate shades of thought, radiant and evanescent as the hues of the rainbow, — vanish away before the realities of a translation.

A few hours, or even one hour, each day, snatched from the exigencies of society, and devoted to the study of any one of the languages of Europe, would prove a profitable investment of time, and yield a sure reward. Madame Campan did not consider the education of a young girl completed because she had left school. In one of her admirable letters of advice to a friend, she writes : " Continue still to devote daily some hours to study, that you may speak fluently in German, sing sweetly in Italian, and write charmingly in French."

Although the fashionable world may be very exacting and absorb much of the attention of our young ladies, still, even in its whirl of gayety there are many weary and listless hours, which might be pleasantly occupied in learning a foreign language. The Persian poet exclaims, " Count every hour enjoyed as a treasure gained." May we not paraphrase this by saying, " Count every hour well employed as a treasure gained ? " One of those weary hours given each day to German would soon afford you the satisfaction of reading the grandly eloquent works of Goethe, of Schiller, of Jean Paul Richter, of Heine, and of other authors, to which no translation can ever render justice.

Many young ladies study Latin at school ; hence the acquisition of any of the languages of Southern Europe would be vastly facilitated. It is a fascinating occupation to follow all these different streams which flow from the great fountain of the Latin.

First, the Spanish, — resembling it closely, with many of its noble characteristics, while it is enriched with the sonorous grandeur of the Moorish, — vehement, expressive, and forcible, — peculiarly powerful and majestic in oratory and declamation.

Next, the Italian, — soft and graceful, the type of its own rose-tinted skies and delicious clime. Music, which gives laws to harmony, has chosen that idiom as the most exquisite for the sweet breathings of its melody ; while Poetry, the sister spirit of Music, revels in the full and swelling beauty of its tones.

Then, the French, — bright as the flight of a shining arrow, — emphatic and concise, — the language of society and of diplomacy. Through all changes of " clime and time," we will trace their allegiance to the Latin. It lingers around them as the remembrance of a mother's love clings to the human heart.

Among the happy visions which float in the mind of nearly every American girl is that of a visit to Europe; therefore, to her, a knowledge of foreign languages would be especially agreeable. Many persons travel through classic lands with no more enjoyment than the deaf and dumb, whose only pleasure is derived from sight. How charmingly might a young lady utilize her accomplishments as a linguist by contributing to the information, the happiness, and the comfort of those of her family who accompany her, and who, perhaps, have been too much occupied with the hard actualities of life to acquire these languages!

It is always a joy to woman's heart to know she increases the happiness of the loved ones. Thus many amusing incidents and sparkling conversations are constantly occurring as we travel through "lands beyond the seas," which might be translated for their enjoyment also. Pleasure and usefulness are combined in the knowledge of foreign languages. It is an admirable training for the memory, and genial exercise for the mind; and the acquisition of every new language is another delight added to existence.

THE ESCURIAL.

At dawn we left Madrid, passing through the deserted Puerto del Sol, by the great palace of the queen, and on to the avenue called *La Florida*. The trees are planted near the Manzanares, and their vigorous life is in strong contrast with the sterility around them. The plains are parched, and the hills gray, and entirely without verdure. At intervals we saw the peasants working amid the rocks, for there did not seem to be a vestige of soil upon them. The snow-capped peaks of the Guadarama Mountains soon met our eyes, gleaming brightly in the morning sunlight, as we journeyed pleasantly along the *camino real* — the royal road — which leads from the capital to the Escurial, a distance of twenty-five miles. The road is really magnificent, with a parapet rising up on each side, and grand bridges spanning deep chasms, where far below trickle slowly on diminutive streamlets dignified with the name of river.

Many leagues away we caught sight of the Escurial, rising in gloomy yet majestic grandeur near the highest point of the mountain region of the Guadarama. It is built of granite, and absolutely seems a part and portion of the "everlasting hills." It is a glorious old palace, monastery, and mausoleum, erected in 1563 by Philip the Second, son of the famous Charles the Fifth, in compliance with a vow made to St. Lorenzo — so says tradition — during the battle of St. Quentin. The saint granting the monarch's prayer for victory, this colossal and sacred edifice was dedicated to his honor, and constructed in the form of a *parilla*, — gridiron, — as St. Lorenzo suffered martyrdom by being broiled upon one. Hence it presents a most singular appearance. Four enormous towers indicate the feet of the gridiron, while the interior is divided into cloisters like its bars. The handle contains the palace. In the center of the building is the immense dome, and beneath it the church. We drove through a poor little village near the palace, and stopping at the *posada*, obtained a guide, and went immediately to the Escurial. Its proportions are gigantic, and it seems intended for eternity, — with its arched corridors, its spacious · porticos and wide courts, its lofty galleries and noble saloons. There are eleven thousand windows, in holy remembrance of the "Virgins of Cologne, slain by the Huns," and fourteen thousand doors. Twenty-two years were occupied in its construction, and it cost six millions of crowns.

We spent all the day following our guide Cornelio through the windings of the building, almost as intricate as those of the Cretan labyrinth. Cornelio was entirely blind, and had been so for forty-eight years. Still, in his " mind's eye," he sees all the glories of the Escurial. It was so strange to hear the sightless old man exclaim, " Now, Señora, remark the effect of the sunlight upon that picture ! " And then he would stop as though looking upon it, and point out all its beauty. " See the deep shadows cast by those columns ; they have the form of a king upon his throne," again would he say, as we passed along with him up the great granite stairways, and through vaulted cloisters to the royal apartments, where Isabel the Second spends her summers. These are fitted up with luxurious elegance, but not by far so exquisite as that portion of the palace embellished and adorned by Charles the Third. It is quite unique in style. The floors and walls are composed of a mosaic of different colored wood, and the furniture inlaid with ivory and pearl-shell, and glittering with stones and gems.

The view from the balcony of these rooms is admirably picturesque, looking down upon the *lonja* — terrace — planted with box, cut into fanciful shapes. Beyond this terrace are the hanging gardens, and the little lakes and fountains; then great groves of elm and oak trees, all brought from England. Inclosing the lovely picture, as though in a dark frame, were the gray summits of the Guadarama chain. Gazing over the wide expanse, it appeared to me the realization of the wild dream of an enthusiast. The creation of such a paradise, beneath the shadow of the snow-topped mountains, upon whose highest peak is the grand Escurial, is justly styled by the Castilians *la octava maravilla del mundo*, — the eighth wonder of the world. Philip the Second was a man of most indomitable will and religious zeal. Thus, inspired by a holy purpose, and aided by the great magician of the earth, mighty gold, he accomplished almost a miracle. Possessing infinite taste in the fine arts, and a love of the beautiful, he adorned the vast halls, galleries, and libraries with the works of distinguished artists and authors.

When we came to the door of the great library, blind Cornelio gave me to the charge of an aged monk, who became the cicerone of our wanderings through it. There are thirty-five thousand volumes resting upon the shelves, and multitudes of manuscripts in Arabic; then noble portraits of Philip the Second, in his early youth and in his manhood. There is a superb picture of Charles the Fifth, taken in the glorious days of his life, when he ruled nearly one half of Europe. We also saw the portraits of Herrera, architect of the Escurial, and of Montano, the first librarian. The ceiling, which is extremely lofty, was painted by Carducho, and is now as fresh and bright as when painted, some three hundred years ago.

The old monk was learned, kind, and courteous. He gave us most interesting and valuable information concerning the former occupants of this wonderful place. He showed us the small room in which Philip died, in 1598, at the age of seventy-two. His last illness was of frightful duration, and he commanded his people to remove him to a spot whence his eyes could look constantly upon the great altar of the church. We also saw the seat where he was wont to place himself among the monks in the *coro*, and listen to the music swelling out from the giant organ. In his old age he was rigid in the observance of his religious duties, casting aside all the regal splendor of the monarch. Just in the rear of the *coro* is the statue of Christ upon the cross, carved by Benvenuto Cellini, and given to Philip by the King of Sardinia. It is of exquisite workmanship, but painful to look upon. So precious was it deemed, that it was brought all the distance from Barcelona on the shoulders of men, for fear the shaking of a carriage might injure it.

Although many of the paintings have been removed to the *Museo* of Madrid, multitudes still remain, of rare excellence. There are many of Raphael, of Tintoretto, of Murillo, of Titian and Velasquez. The monk often paused before pictures by *Navarrette el Mudo* — Navarrette the Dumb — and commended them to my special attention. They all portray the sufferings of our Saviour, and were indescribably affecting. This Navarrette was a poor deaf-and-dumb boy, who was permitted to wander unheeded through the long cloisters and amid the picture-galleries of the Escurial. At last his genius and his talent found utterance through the pencil and brush. The eloquence of the soul seems infused into them. "The Temptation of Christ upon the Mount" is a perfect history of the fierce struggle and trial of the passions. "Christ bound to the Column" touched me even to tears. The divine face of our Lord, although bitterness and humiliation are expressed in it, has also a holy calm in the beautiful eyes irresistibly impressive. There were other paintings of Navarrette the Dumb besides these, which were remarkable for the coloring and admirable life-like attitudes. From the saints and martyrs his subjects were all taken.

In the private chapel is the grand painting of Titian, representing San Lorenzo bound to the gridiron, and the fire just kindled beneath it. A most gloomy and sad picture it is, with the stern and fierce faces clustering around to gaze upon the agonies and martyrdom of the saint.

We passed through a long subterranean passage, under a portion of the edifice, and came out just near our inn.

TYNDALL.

1820– .

JOHN TYNDALL, LL. D., one of the most distinguished scientists of the day, is a native of Ireland, where he was born about 1820. At an early age he devoted himself to the study of physics, and soon achieved a reputation which warranted his appointment, at the age of thirty-three years, to the chair of Natural Philosophy in the Royal Institution of London. He has won fame as a writer and lecturer on subjects of natural science, and has of all men most exhaustively discussed the important theory of the mutual convertibility of heat and motion. He is a vigorous and fascinating writer, and his books may fairly be said to represent the poetry of science. His best-known work is a treatise on *Heat, Considered as a Mode of Motion*; others are *Hours of Exercise in the Alps, Fragments of Science for Unscientific People*, and *Six Lectures on Light.* These lectures were delivered by the author, recently, in the principal cities of the United States, and were cordially admired for their rhetorical beauty and their instructiveness. It is worthy of note that Professor Tyndall first gave evidence of his great powers of mind in the capacity of teacher. His experience in this capacity, at Queenswood College, though brief, seems to have had an important part in the molding of his intellectual character, and in confirming his predilection for the special field of labor in which he has toiled with a success so signal. Though best known as an explorer in experimental physics, he is highly esteemed as a philosophic thinker, and his opinions on some of the momentous questions in science as opposed to theology, that are now disturbing the thinking world, command the highest respect.

AN ADDRESS TO STUDENTS.

THE doctrine has been held that the mind of the child is like a sheet of white paper, on which by education we can write what characters we please. This doctrine assuredly needs qualification and correction. In physics, when an external force is applied to a body with a view of affecting its inner texture, if we wish to predict the result, we must know whether the external force conspires with or opposes the internal forces of the body itself; and in bringing the influence of education to bear upon the new-born man his inner powers must be also taken into account. He comes to us as a bundle of inherited capacities and tendencies, labeled " from the indefinite past to the indefinite future "; and he makes his transit from the one to the other through the education of the present time. The object of that education is, or ought to be, to provide wise exercise for his capacities, wise direction for his tendencies, and through this exercise and this direction to furnish his mind with such knowledge as may contribute to the usefulness, the beauty, and the nobleness of his life.

How is this discipline to be secured, this knowledge imparted? Two rival methods now solicit attention, — the one organized and equipped, the labors of centuries having been expended in bringing it to its present state of perfection; the other, more or less chaotic, but becoming daily less so, and giving signs of enormous power, both as a source of knowledge and as a means of discipline. These two methods are the classical and the scientific method. I wish they were not rivals; it is only bigotry and short-sightedness that make them so; for assuredly it is possible to give both of them fair play. Though hardly authorized to express any opinion whatever upon the subject, I nevertheless hold the opinion that the proper study of a language is an intellectual discipline of the highest kind. If I except discussions on the comparative merits of Popery and Protestantism, English grammar was the most important discipline of my boyhood. The piercing through the involved and inverted sentences of Paradise Lost; the linking of the verb to its often distant nominative, of the relative to its distant antecedent, of the agent to the object of the transitive verb, of the preposition to the noun or pronoun which it governed; the study of variations in mood and tense, the transformations often necessary to bring out the true grammatical structure of a sentence, — all this was to my young mind a discipline of the highest value, and, indeed, a source of unflagging delight. How I rejoiced when I found a great author tripping, and was fairly able to pin him to a corner from which there was no escape! As I speak, some of the sentences which exercised me when a boy rise to my recollection. "He that hath ears to hear let him hear." That was one of them, where the "He" is left, as it were, floating in mid-air without any verb to support it. I speak thus of English, because it was of real value to me. I do not speak of other languages; because their educational value for me was almost insensible. But, knowing the value of English so well, I should be the last to deny, or even to doubt, the high discipline involved in the proper study of Latin and Greek.

That study, moreover, has other merits and recommendations which have been already slightly touched upon. It is organized and systematized by long-continued use. It is an instrument wielded by some of the best intellects of the country in the education of youth; and it can point to results in the achievements of our foremost men. What, then, has science to offer which is in the least degree likely to compete with such a system? Speaking of the world and all that therein is, of the sky and the stars around it, the ancient writer says, "And God saw all that he had made, and behold it was very good."

It is the body of things thus described which science offers to the study of man.

The ultimate problem of physics is to reduce matter by analysis to its lowest condition of divisibility, and force to its simplest manifestations, and then by synthesis to construct from these elements the world as it stands. We are still a long way from the final solution of this problem; and when the solution comes, it will be one more of spiritual insight than of actual observation. But though we are still a long way from this complete intellectual mastery of Nature, we have conquered vast regions of it, have learned their politics and the play of their powers. We live upon a ball of matter eight thousand miles in diameter, swathed by an atmosphere of unknown height. This ball has been molten by heat, chilled to a solid, and sculptured by water; it is made up of substances possessing distinctive properties and modes of action, properties which have an immediate bearing upon the continuance of man in health, and on his recovery from disease, on which moreover depend all the arts of industrial life. These properties and modes of action offer problems to the intellect, some profitable to the child, and others sufficient to tax the highest powers of the philosopher. Our native sphere turns on its axis and revolves in space. It is one of a band which do the same. It is illuminated by a sun which, though nearly a hundred millions of miles distant, can be brought virtually into our closets and there subjected to examination. It has its winds and clouds, its rain and frost, its light, heat, sound, electricity, and magnetism. And it has its vast kingdoms of animals and vegetables. To a most amazing extent the human mind has conquered these things, and reveals the logic which runs through them. Were they facts only, without logical relationship, science might, as a means of discipline, suffer in comparison with language. But the whole body of phenomena is instinct with law; the facts are hung on principles, and the value of physical science as a means of discipline consists in the motion of the intellect, both inductively and deductively, along the lines of law marked out by phenomena. As regards that discipline to which I have already referred as derivable from the study of languages, — that, and more, are involved in the study of physical science. Indeed, I believe it would be possible so to limit and arrange the study of a portion of physics as to render the mental exercise involved in it almost qualitatively the same as that involved in the unraveling of a language.

I have thus far limited myself to the purely intellectual side of this question. But man is not all intellect. If he were so, science would, I believe, be his proper nutriment. But he feels as well as thinks; he is receptive of the sublime and the beautiful as well as of the true. Indeed, I believe that even the intellectual action of a complete man is, consciously or unconsciously, sustained by an undercurrent of the emotions. It is vain, I think, to attempt to separate moral and emotional nature from intellectual nature. Let a man but observe himself, and he will, if I mistake not, find that, in nine cases out of ten, moral or immoral considerations, as the case may be, are the motive force which pushes his intellect into action. The reading of the works of two men, neither of them imbued with the spirit of modern science, neither of them, indeed, friendly to that spirit, has placed me here to-day. These men are the English Carlyle and the American Emerson. I never should have gone through Analytical Geometry and the Calculus had it not been for those men. I never should have become a physical investigator, and hence without them I should not have been here to-day. They told me what I ought to do in a way that caused me to do it, and all my consequent intellectual action is to be traced to this purely moral source. To Carlyle and Emerson I ought to add Fichte, the greatest representative of pure idealism. These three unscientific men made me a practical scientific worker. They called out, " Act ! " I hearkened to the summons, taking the liberty, however, of determining for myself the direction which effort was to take.

And I may now cry, " Act ! " but the potency of action must be yours. I may pull the trigger, but if the gun be not charged there is no result. We are creators in the intellectual world as little as in the physical. We may remove obstacles, and render latent capacities active, but we cannot suddenly change the nature of man. The " new birth " itself implies the pre-existence of the new character which requires not to be created but brought forth. You cannot by any amount of missionary labor suddenly transform the savage into the civilized Christian. The improvement of man is *secular*, — not the work of an hour or of a day. But, though indubitably bound by our organizations, no man knows what the potentialities of any human mind may be, which require only release to be brought into action.

The circle of human nature is not complete without the arc of feeling and emotion. The lilies of the field have a value for us beyond their botanical ones, — a certain lightening of the heart accompanies the declaration that "Solomon in all his glory was not arrayed like one of these." The sound of the village bell which comes mellowed from the valley to the traveler upon the hill, has a value beyond its acoustical one. The setting sun when it mantles with the bloom of roses the alpine snows, has a value beyond its optical one. The starry heavens, as you know, had for Immanuel Kant a value beyond their astronomical one. Round about the intellect sweeps the horizon of emotions from which all our noblest impulses are derived. I think it very desirable to keep this horizon open; not to permit either priest or philosopher to draw down his shutters between you and it. And here the dead languages, which are sure to be beaten by science in the purely intellectual fight, have an irresistible claim. They supplement the work of science by exalting and refining the æsthetic faculty, and must on this account be cherished by all who desire to see human culture complete. There must be a reason for the fascination which these languages have so long exercised upon the most powerful and elevated minds, — a fascination which will probably continue for men of Greek and Roman mold to the end of time.

Let me utter one practical word in conclusion, — take care of your health. There have been men who by wise attention to this point might have risen to any eminence, — might have made great discoveries, written great poems, commanded armies, or ruled states, but who by unwise neglect of this point have come to nothing. Imagine Hercules as oarsman in a rotten boat; what can he do there but by the very force of his stroke expedite the ruin of his craft? Take care, then, of the timbers of your boat, and avoid all practices likely to introduce either wet or dry rot among them. And this is not to be accomplished by desultory or intermittent efforts of the will, but by the formation of *habits*. The will, no doubt, has sometimes to put forth its strength in order to strangle or crush the special temptation. But the formation of right habits is essential to your permanent security. They diminish your chance of falling when assailed, and they augment your chance of recovery when overthrown.

GEORGE ELIOT.

1820 - 1880

GEORGE ELIOT is the *nom de plume* of Marian C. Evans, who was born in the North of England about 1820. Of her origin and early history little is publicly known. During her girlhood she went to London, and was fortunate enough to attract the kindly notice of several eminent men of letters, who detected in her the signs of extraordinary intellectual power. Under their direction she entered upon a course of study more severe than is usually attempted by members of her sex. She did not hasten to test her abilities by public appearance in literature, but, for several years before the publication of her first book, pursued her studies assiduously, unknown to the world, yet recognized by the few judicious friends who surrounded and counseled her, as the possessor of exceptional genius. In 1858 her first novel, *Adam Bede*, appeared, and its reception fully justified the anticipations of her literary sponsors. A few years later it was followed by *The Mill on the Floss*, and, at intervals, by *Romola*, etc. With each production her fame increased, and for many years she has held unquestioned rank as first among the novelists of this century. Her last novel, *Middlemarch*, has had a deserved, and an almost unprecedented, popularity. Two volumes of poetry have come from her pen, both full of strength and beauty, but serving to show that prose fiction is her *forte*. Her intellect is rather masculine than feminine, and her knowledge of human nature is surprising in one whose sphere of observation must necessarily have been restricted. The careful reader will notice what may be called a lack of cosmopolitanism in her books; she dwells on ground that is familiar to her, — the details of country life, with which she made acquaintance in her youth, and the operations of the human heart and the delineation of character of which her studies and the associations of her later life have made her an intelligent student. Her novels are distinctively intellectual, lacking spirituality and warmth; but as literary compositions, combining profound thought and vigorous, if not brilliant, imagination, they are unsurpassed in English literature. A few years ago Miss Evans became the wife of George Henry Lewes, the celebrated philosophical writer. The extracts are from *Middlemarch*.

DR. LYDGATE.

A GREAT historian,* as he insisted on calling himself, who had the happiness to be dead a hundred and twenty years ago, and so to take his place among the colossi whose huge legs our living pettiness is observed to walk under, glories in his copious remarks and digressions as the least imitable part of his work, and especially in those initial chapters to the successive books of his history, where he seems to bring his arm-chair to the proscenium, and chat with us in all the lusty ease of his fine English. But Fielding lived when the days were longer (for time, like money, is measured by our needs), when summer afternoons were spacious, and the clock ticked slowly in the winter evenings. We belated historians must not linger after his example; and if we did so it is probable that our chat would be thin and eager, as if delivered from a camp-stool in a parrot-house. I, at least, have so much to do in unraveling certain human lots, and seeing

* HENRY FIELDING, an eminent author of the eighteenth century.

how they were woven and interwoven, that all the light I can command must be concentrated on this particular web, and not dispersed over that tempting range of relevancies called the universe.

At present I have to make the new settler Lydgate better known to any one interested in him than he could possibly be even to those who had seen the most of him since his arrival in Middlemarch. For surely all must admit that a man may be puffed and belauded, envied, ridiculed, counted upon as a tool, and fallen in love with, or at least selected as a future husband, and yet remain virtually unknown, — known merely as a cluster of signs for his neighbors' false suppositions. There was a general impression, however, that Lydgate was not altogether a common country doctor, and in Middlemarch at that time such an impression was significant of great things being expected from him. For everybody's family doctor was remarkably clever, and was understood to have immeasurable skill in the management and training of the most skittish or vicious diseases. The evidence of his cleverness was of the higher intuitive order, lying in his lady patients' immovable conviction, and was unassailable by any objection except that their intuitions were opposed by others equally strong. Nobody's imagination had gone so far as to conjecture that Mr. Lydgate could know as much as Dr. Sprague and Dr. Minchin, the two physicians who alone could offer any hope when danger was extreme, and when the smallest hope was worth a guinea. Still, I repeat, there was a general impression that Lydgate was something rather more uncommon than any general practitioner in Middlemarch. And this was true. He was but seven-and-twenty, an age at which many men are not quite common, — at which they are hopeful of achievement, resolute in avoidance, thinking that Mammon shall never put a bit in their mouths and get astride their backs, but rather that Mammon, if they have anything to do with him, shall draw their chariot.

He had been left an orphan when he was fresh from a public school. His father, a military man, had made but little provision for three children; and when the boy Tertius asked to have a medical education, it seemed easier to his guardians to grant his request by apprenticing him to a country practitioner than to make any objections on the score of family dignity. He was one of the rarer lads who early get a decided bent, and make up their minds that there is something particular in life which they would like to do for its own sake, and not because their fathers did it. Most of us who turn to any subject with love remember some morning or evening hour when we got on a high stool to reach down an untried volume, or sat with parted lips listening to a new talker, or for very lack of books began to listen to the voices within, as the first traceable beginning of our love. Something of that sort happened to Lydgate. He was a quick fellow, and, when hot from play, would toss himself in a corner, and in five minutes be deep in any sort of book that he could lay his hands on : if it were Rasselas or Gulliver, so much the better; but Bailey's Dictionary would do, or the Bible with the Apocrypha in it. Something he must read when he was not riding the pony, or running and hunting, or listening to the talk of men. All this was true of him at ten years of age ; he had then read through Chrysal, or the Adventures of a Guinea, which was neither milk for babes nor any chalky mixture meant to pass for milk ; and it had already occurred to him that books were stuff, and that life was stupid. His school-studies had not much modified that opinion ; for though he " did " his classics and mathematics, he was not pre-eminent in them.

It was said of him that Lydgate could do anything he liked, but he had certainly not yet liked to do anything remarkable. He was a vigorous animal, with a ready understanding, but no spark had yet kindled in him an intellectual passion ; knowledge seemed to him a very superficial affair, easily mastered. Judging from the conversation of his elders, he had apparently got already more than was necessary for mature life. Probably this was not an exceptional result of expensive teaching at that period of short-waisted coats, and other fashions which have not yet recurred. But, one vacation, a wet day sent him to the small home library to hunt once more for a book which might have some freshness for him : in vain! unless, indeed, he took down a dusty row of volumes with gray paper backs and dingy labels, — the volumes of an old Cyclopedia which he had never disturbed. It would at least be a novelty to disturb them. They were on the highest shelf, and he stood on a chair to get them down. But he opened the volume he first took from the shelf : somehow, one is apt to read in a make-shift attitude, just where it might seem inconvenient to do so. The page he opened on was under the head of Anatomy, and the first passage that drew his eyes was on the valves of the heart. He was not much acquainted with valves of any sort, but he knew that *valvæ* were folding-doors, and through this crevice came a sudden light, startling him with his first vivid notion of finely adjusted mechanism in the human frame. A liberal education had, of course, left him free to read the indecent passages in the school classics, but, beyond a general sense of secrecy and obscenity in connection with his internal structure, had left his imagination quite unbiased, so that for anything he knew his brains lay in small bags at his temples, and he had no more thought of representing to himself how his blood circulated than how paper served instead of gold. But the moment of vocation had come, and before he got down from his chair, the world was made new to him by a presentiment of endless processes filling the vast spaces planked out of his sight by that wordy ignorance which he had supposed to be knowledge. From that hour Lydgate felt the growth of an intellectual passion.

We are not afraid of telling over and over again how a man comes to fall in love with a woman and be wedded to her, or else be fatally parted from her. Is it due to excess of poetry or of stupidity that we are never weary of describing what King James called a woman's "makdom and her fairnesse," never weary of listening to the twanging of the old Troubadour strings, and are comparatively uninterested in that other kind of "makdom and fairnesse" which must be wooed with industrious thought and patient renunciation of small desires? In the story of this passion, too, the development varies: sometimes it is the glorious marriage, sometimes frustration and final parting. And not seldom the catastrophe is wound up with the other passion, sung by the Troubadours. For in the multitude of middle-aged men who go about their vocations in a daily course determined for them much in the same way as the tie of their cravats, there is always a good number who once meant to shape their own deeds and alter the world a little. The story of their coming to be shapen after the average, and fit to be packed by the gross, is hardly ever told even in their consciousness; for perhaps their ardor for generous, unpaid toil cooled as imperceptibly as the ardor of other youthful loves, till one day their earlier self walked like a ghost in its old home and made the new furniture ghastly. Nothing in the world more subtle than the process of their gradual change! In the beginning they inhaled it unknowingly: you and I may have sent some of our breath toward infecting them, when we uttered our conforming falsities or drew our silly conclusions; or perhaps it came with the vibrations from a woman's glance.

Lydgate did not mean to be one of those failures, and there was the better hope of him because his scientific interest soon took the form of a professional enthusiasm; he had a youthful belief in his bread-winning work, not to be stifled by that initiation in make-shift called his 'prentice days; and he carried to his studies in London, Edinburgh, and Paris the conviction that the medical profession as it might be was the finest in the world; presenting the most perfect interchange between science and art; offering the most direct alliance between intellectual conquest and the social good. Lydgate's nature demanded this combination: he was an emotional creature, with a flesh-and-blood sense of fellowship which withstood all the abstractions of special study. He cared not only for "cases," but for John and Elizabeth, especially Elizabeth.

DR. LYDGATE (continued).

DOES it seem incongruous to you that a Middlemarch surgeon should dream of himself as a discoverer? Most of us, indeed, know little of the great originators until they have been lifted up among the constellations, and already rule our fates. But that Herschel, for example, who "broke the barriers of the heavens" — did he not once play a provincial church organ, and give music-lessons to stumbling pianists? Each of those Shining Ones had to walk on the earth among neighbors who perhaps thought much more of his gait and his garments than of anything which was to give him a title to everlasting fame; each of them had his little local personal history sprinkled with small temptations and sordid cares, which made the retarding friction of his course toward final companionship with the immortals. Lydgate was not blind to the dangers of such friction, but he had plenty of confidence in his resolution to avoid it as far as possible; being seven-and-twenty, he felt himself experienced.

Perhaps that was a more cheerful time for observers and theorizers than the present; we are apt to think it the finest era of the world when America was beginning to be discovered, when a bold sailor, even if he were wrecked, might alight on a new kingdom; and about 1829 the dark territories of Pathology were a fine America for a spirited young adventurer. Lydgate was ambitious above all to contribute toward enlarging the scientific, rational basis of his profession. The more he became interested in special questions of disease, such as the nature of fever or fevers, the more keenly he felt the need for that fundamental knowledge of structure which just at

the beginning of the century had been illuminated by the brief and
glorious career of Bichat, who died when he was only one-and-thirty,
but, like another Alexander, left a realm large enough for many heirs.
That great Frenchman first carried out the conception that living
bodies, fundamentally considered, are not associations of organs
which can be understood by studying them first apart, and then, as it
were, federally; but must be regarded as consisting of certain primary
webs or tissues, out of which the various organs — brain, heart, lungs,
and so on — are compacted, as the various accommodations of a house
are built up in various proportions of wood, iron, stone, brick, zinc,
and the rest, each material having its peculiar composition and proportions.   No man, one sees, can understand and estimate the entire
structure or its parts, what are its frailties and what its repairs,
without knowing the nature of the materials.   And the conception
wrought out by Bichat, with his detailed study of the different
tissues, acted necessarily on medical questions as the turning of gas-
light would act on a dim, oil-lit street, showing new connections and
hitherto hidden facts of structure which must be taken into account in
considering the symptoms of maladies and the action of medicaments.

   But results which depend on human conscience and intelligence
work slowly, and now most medical practice was still strutting or
shambling along the old paths, and there was still scientific work to
be done which might have seemed to be a direct sequence of Bichat's.
This great seer did not go beyond the consideration of the tissues as
ultimate facts in the living organism, marking the limit of anatomical
analysis; but it was open to another mind to say, Have not these
structures some common basis from which they have all started, as
your sarcenet, gauze, net, satin, and velvet from the raw cocoon?
Here would be another light, as of oxyhydrogen, showing the very
grain of things, and revising all former explanations.   Of this sequence to Bichat's work, already vibrating along many currents of
the European mind, Lydgate was enamored; he longed to demonstrate the more intimate relations of living structure, and help to
define men's thought more accurately after the true order.   The work
had not yet been done, but only prepared for those who knew how to
use the preparation.   What was the primitive tissue?   In that way
Lydgate put the question, — not quite in the way required by the
awaiting answer; but such missing of the right word befalls many
seekers.   And he counted on quiet intervals to be watchfully seized

for taking up the threads of investigation;— on many hints to be won from diligent application, not only of the scalpel, but of the micro-scope, which research had begun to use again with new enthusiasm of reliance. Such was Lydgate's plan of his future : to do good small work for Middlemarch, and great work for the world.

He was certainly a happy fellow at this time; to be seven-and-twenty, without any fixed vices, with a generous resolution that his action should be beneficent, and with ideas in his brain that made life interesting, he was at a starting-point which makes many a man's career a fine subject for betting, if there were any gentlemen given to that amusement who could appreciate the complicated probabilities of an arduous purpose, with all the possible thwartings and furtherings of circumstance, all the niceties of inward balance, by which a man swims and makes his point, or else is carried headlong. The risk would remain, even with close knowledge of Lydgate's character; for character, too, is a process and an unfolding. The man was still in the making, as much as the Middlemarch doctor and immortal dis-coverer, and there were both virtues and faults capable of shrinking or expanding. The faults will not, I hope, be a reason for the with-drawal of your interest in him. Among our valued friends is there not some one or other who is a little too self-confident and disdainful, whose distinguished mind is a little spotted with commonness, who is a little pinched here and protuberant there with native prejudices, or whose better energies are liable to lapse down the wrong channel under the influence of transient solicitations? All these things might be alleged against Lydgate, but then they are the periphrases of a polite preacher, who talks of Adam, and would not like to mention anything painful to the pew-renters. The particular faults from which these delicate generalities are distilled have distinguishable physiognomies, diction, accent, and grimaces; filling up parts in very various dramas. Our vanities differ as our noses do; all conceit is not the same conceit, but varies in correspondence with the minutiæ of mental make in which one of us differs from another.

Lydgate's conceit was of the arrogant sort, never simpering, never impertinent, but massive in its claims, and benevolently contemptuous. He would do a great deal for noodles, being sorry for them, and feeling quite sure that they could have no power over him; he had thought of joining the Saint Simonians when he was in Paris, in order to turn them against some of their own doctrines. All his faults were marked by kindred traits, and were those of a man who had a fine baritone, whose clothes hung well upon him, and who even in his ordinary gestures had an air of inbred distinction. Where, then, lay the spots of commonness? says a young lady, enamored of that careless grace. How could there be any commonness in a man so well bred, so ambitious of social distinction, so generous and unusual in his views of social duty? As easily as there may be stupidity in a man of genius if you take him unawares on the wrong subject, or as many a man who has the best will to advance the social millennium might be ill inspired in imagining its lighter pleasures; unable to go beyond Offenbach's music, or the brilliant punning in the last burlesque. Lydgate's spots of commonness lay in the complexion of his prejudices, which, in spite of noble intention and sympathy, were half of them such as are found in ordinary men of the world: that distinction of mind which belonged to his intellectual ardor did not penetrate his feeling and judgment about furniture, or women, or the desirability of its being known (without his telling) that he was better born than other country surgeons. He did not mean to think of furniture at present; but whenever he did so, it was to be feared that neither biology nor schemes of reform would lift him above the vulgarity of feeling that there would be an incompatibility in his furniture not being of the best.

A WORLDLY PICTURE.

EVERY limit is a beginning as well as an ending. Who can quit young lives after being long in company with them, and not desire to know what befell them in their after-years? For the fragment of a life, however typical, is not the sample of an even web; promises may not be kept, and an ardent outset may be followed by declension; latent powers may find their long-waited opportunity; a past error may urge a grand retrieval.

Marriage, which has been the bourne of so many narratives, is still a great beginning, as it was to Adam and Eve, who kept their honeymoon in Eden, but had their first little one among the thorns and thistles of the wilderness. It is still the beginning of the home epic, —the gradual conquest or irremediable loss of that complete union which makes the advancing years a climax, and age the harvest of sweet memories in common.

Some set out, like Crusaders of old, with a glorious equipment of hope and enthusiasm, and get broken by the way, wanting patience with each other and the world.

All who have cared for Fred Vincy and Mary Garth will like to know that these two made no such failure, but achieved a solid mutual happiness. Fred surprised his neighbors in various ways. He became rather distinguished in his side of the county as a theoretic and practical farmer, and produced a work on the Cultivation of Green Crops and the Economy of Cattle-Feeding which won him high congratulations at agricultural meetings; but in Middlemarch admiration was more reserved: most persons there were inclined to believe that the merit of Fred's authorship was due to his wife, since they had never expected Fred Vincy to write on turnips and mangel-wurzel.

But when Mary wrote a little book for her boys, called Stories of Great Men, taken from Plutarch, and had it printed and published by Gripp & Co., Middlemarch, every one in the town was willing to give the credit of this work to Fred, observing that he had been to the University, "where the ancients were studied," and might have been a clergyman if he had chosen.

In this way it was made clear that Middlemarch had never been deceived, and that there was no need to praise anybody for writing a book, since it was always done by somebody else.

Moreover, Fred remained unswervingly steady. Some years after his marriage he told Mary that his happiness was half owing to Farebrother, who gave him a strong pull-up at the right moment. I cannot say that he was never again misled by his hopefulness: the yield of crops. or the profits of a cattle sale usually fell below his estimate; and he was always prone to believe that he could make money by the purchase of a horse which turned out badly, — though this, Mary observed, was of course the fault of the horse, not of Fred's judgment. He kept his love of horsemanship, but he rarely allowed himself a day's hunting; and when he did so, it was remarkable that he submitted to be laughed at for cowardliness at the fences, seeming to see Mary and the boys sitting on the five-barred gate, or showing their curly heads between hedge and ditch.

There were three boys: Mary was not discontented that she brought forth men-children only; and when Fred wished to have a girl like her, she said laughingly, "That would be too great a trial to your mother." Mrs. Vincy in her declining years, and in the diminished luster of her housekeeping, was much comforted by her perception that two at least of Fred's boys were real Vincys, and did not "feature the Garths." But Mary secretly rejoiced that the youngest of the three was very much what her father must have been when he wore a round jacket, and showed a marvelous nicety of aim in playing at marbles, or in throwing stones to bring down the mellow pears.

Ben and Letty Garth, who were uncle and aunt before they were well in their teens, disputed much as to whether nephews or nieces were more desirable; Ben contending that it was clear girls were good for less than boys, else they would not be always in petticoats, which showed how little they were meant for; whereupon Letty, who argued much from books, got angry in replying that God made coats of skins for both Adam and Eve alike, — also it occurred to her that in the East the men too wore petticoats. But this latter argument, obscuring the majesty of the former, was one too many, for Ben answered, contemptuously, "The more spooneys they!" and immediately appealed to his mother whether boys were not better than girls. Mrs. Garth pronounced that both were alike naughty; but that boys were undoubtedly stronger, could run faster, and throw with more precision to a greater distance. With this oracular sentence Ben was well satisfied, not minding the naughtiness; but Letty took it ill, her feeling of superiority being stronger than her muscles.

Fred never became rich, — his hopefulness had not led him to expect that; but he gradually saved enough to become owner of the stock and furniture at Stone Court, and the work which Mr. Garth put into his hands carried him in plenty through those "bad times" which are always present with farmers. Mary, in her matronly days, became as solid in figure as her mother; but, unlike her, gave the boys little formal teaching, so that Mrs. Garth was alarmed lest they should never be well grounded in grammar and geography. Nevertheless, they were found quite forward enough when they went to school; perhaps because they had liked nothing so well as being with their mother. When Fred was riding home on winter evenings, he had a pleasant vision beforehand of the bright hearth in the wainscoted parlor, and was sorry for other men who could not have Mary for their wife; especially for Mr. Farebrother. "He was ten times worthier of you than I was," Fred could now say to her, magnanimously. "To be sure he was," Mary answered; "and for that reason he could do better without me. But you — I shudder to think what you would have been, — a curate in debt for horse-hire and cambric pocket-handkerchiefs ! "

Lydgate's hair never became white. He died when he was only fifty, leaving his wife and children provided for by a heavy insurance on his life. He had gained an excellent practice, alternating, according to the season, between London and a Continental bathing-place ; having written a treatise on Gout, a disease which has a good deal of wealth on its side. His skill was relied on by many paying patients, but he always regarded himself as a failure ; he had not done what he once meant to do. His acquaintances thought him enviable to have so charming a wife, and nothing happened to shake their opinion. Rosamond never committed a second compromising indiscretion. She simply continued to be mild in her temper, inflexible in her judgment, disposed to admonish her husband, and able to frustrate him by stratagem. As the years went on, he opposed her less and less, whence Rosamond concluded that he had learned the value of her opinion ; on the other hand, she had a more thorough conviction of his talents now that he gained a good income, and instead of the threatened cage in Bride Street provided one all flowers and gilding, fit for the bird-of-paradise that she resembled. In brief, Lydgate was what is called a successful man. But he died prematurely of diphtheria, and Rosamond afterward married an elderly and wealthy physician, who took kindly to her four children.

Dorothea never repented that she had given up position and fortune to marry Will Ladislaw, and he would have held it the greatest shame as well as sorrow to him if she had repented. They were bound to each other by a love stronger than any impulses which could have marred it. No life would have been possible to Dorothea which was not filled with emotion, and she had now a life filled also with a beneficent activity which she had not the doubtful pains of discovering and marking out for herself. Will became an ardent public man, working well in those times when reforms were begun with a young hopefulness of immediate good which has been much checked in our days, and getting at last returned to Parliament by a constituency who paid his expenses. Dorothea could have liked nothing better, since wrongs existed, than that her husband should be in the thick of a struggle against them, and that she should give him wifely help. Many who knew her thought it a pity that so substantive and rare a creature should have been absorbed into the life of another, and be only known in a certain circle as a wife and mother.

Sir James never ceased to regard Dorothea's second marriage as a mistake; and indeed this remained the tradition concerning it in Middlemarch, where she was spoken of to a younger generation as a fine girl who married a sickly clergyman, old enough to be her father, and in little more than a year after his death gave up her estate to marry his cousin, — young enough to have been his son, with no property, and not well-born. Those who had not seen anything of Dorothea usually observed that she could not have been " a nice woman," else she would not have married either the one or the other.

Certainly those determining acts of her life were not ideally beautiful. They were the mixed result of young and noble impulse struggling under prosaic conditions. Among the many remarks passed on her mistakes, it was never said in the neighborhood of Middlemarch that such mistakes could not have happened if the society into which she was born had not smiled on propositions of marriage from a sickly man to a girl less than half his own age, — on modes of education which make a woman's knowledge another name for motley ignorance, — on rules of conduct which are in flat contradiction with its own loudly asserted beliefs. While this is the social air in which mortals begin to breathe, there will be collisions such as those in Dorothea's life, where great feelings will take the aspect of error, and great faith the aspect of illusion. For there is no creature whose inward being is so strong that it is not greatly determined by what lies outside it. A new Theresa will hardly have the opportunity of reforming a conventual life, any more than a new Antigone will spend her heroic piety in daring all for the sake of a brother's burial; the medium in which their ardent deeds took shape is forever gone. But we insignificant people, with our daily words and acts, are preparing the lives of many Dorotheas, some of which may present a far sadder sacrifice than that of the Dorothea whose story we know.

Her finely touched spirit had still its fine issues, though they were not widely visible. Her full nature, like that river of which Alexander broke the strength, spent itself in channels which had no great name on the earth. But the effect of her being on those around her was incalculably diffusive; for the growing good of the world is partly dependent on unhistoric acts; and that things are not so ill with you and me as they might have been is half owing to the number who lived faithfully a hidden life, and rest in unvisited tombs.

PARTON.

1822–   .

JAMES PARTON, though a native of England, where he was born in 1822, has lived in the United States since his early childhood. He has been an industrious writer, chiefly in the field of biography, in which he has done some admirable work. His first book was *The Life of Horace Greeley*, which was published in 1855, and it has been followed by biographies of *Aaron Burr*, *Andrew Jackson, Benjamin F. Butler, John Jacob Astor*, and *Thomas Jefferson*. He has labored in other departments of literature, editing *The Humorous Poetry of the English Language*, and writing several pamphlets on New York politics, etc.; but his fame as a writer will rest on his biographical work. In this specialty he has been signally successful in presenting vivid and attractive portraits of his subjects, supported by dramatic pictures of their times. In reaching this result he has been forced to disregard in many instances the strict records of history, and his biographies are, therefore, not absolutely unimpeachable in point of facts. He displays great industry in the collection of material and great skill in its arrangement; and, by availing himself of many personal particulars which most biographers would deem too insignificant for use, has made his books exceptionally readable. His *Life of Thomas Jefferson*, recently published, furnishes good specimens of his faults and his merits: it is full of matter, and very fascinating; but it is marred somewhat by historical inaccuracies.

PATRICK HENRY'S SPEECH ON CONCILIATION WITH ENGLAND.

PATRICK HENRY had been coming and going during Jefferson's student years,* dropping in when the General Court met in the autumn, and riding homeward, with a book or two of Jefferson's in his saddlebags, when the court adjourned over till the spring; then returning with the books unread. The wondrous eloquence which he had displayed in the Parsons Case in December, 1763, does not seem to have been generally known in Williamsburg in 1764; for he moved about the streets and public places unrecognized, though not unmarked. It would not have been extraordinary if our young student had been a little ashamed of his oddity of a guest as they walked together towards the Capitol, at the time when the young ladies were abroad, — Sukey Potter, Betsy Moore, Judy Burwell, and the rest; for Henry's dress was coarse, worn, and countrified, and he walked with such an air of thoughtless unconcern that he was taken by some for an idiot. But he had a cause to plead that winter; and when he sat down he had become "Mr. Henry" to all Williamsburg. You will observe in

* The extract is from Parton's *Life of Jefferson*. Jefferson at this time was a law-student and a warm personal friend of Patrick Henry, who was himself a young man and just becoming known as a skillful lawyer and popular speaker. The speech referred to was delivered in the Virginia House of Burgesses — a body somewhat resembling the State Legislature of to-day — in 1765, and is generally familiar to school-children, extracts from it being given in nearly all school "Speakers."

the memorials of Old Virginia, from 1765 to 1800, that, whoever else may be named without a prefix of honor, this "forest-born Demosthenes," as Byron styled him, is generally styled *Mr.* Henry. To Washington, to Jefferson, to Madison, to all that circle of eminent men, he ever remained "Mr. Henry." On that day in 1764 he gave such an exhibition of his power, that, during the next session of the House of Burgesses, a vacancy was made for him, and he was elected to a seat. The up-country yeomen, whose idol he had become, gladly gave their votes to such a man, when the Stamp Act was expected to be a topic of debate.

And so, in May, 1765, the new member was in Williamsburg to take his seat, a guest again of his young friend Jefferson. He sat, day after day, waiting for some of the older members to open the subject. But no one seemed to know just what to do. A year before the House had gently denied the right of Parliament to tax the colonies, and softly remonstrated against the threatened measure; but as the act had been passed, in spite of their objections, what more could a loyal colony do? No one thought of formal resistance, and remonstrance had failed. What else? What next? However frequently the two friends may have conversed upon this perplexity, it was Patrick Henry who, to use his own words, "alone, unadvised, and unassisted," hit upon the proper expedient.

Only three days of the session remained. On the blank leaf of an old Coke upon Lyttleton * — perhaps Jefferson's own copy — the new member wrote his celebrated five resolutions, of this purport : We, Englishmen, living in America, have all the rights of Englishmen living in England ; the chief of which is, that we can only be taxed by our own representatives ; and any attempt to tax us otherwise menaces British liberty on both continents. In all probability, Jefferson knew that something of the kind was intended on that memorable day, for he was present in the House. There was no gallery then, nor any other provision for spectators ; but there could be no objection to the friend and relative of so many members standing in the doorway between the lobby and the chamber ; and there he took his stand. He saw his tall, gaunt, coarsely attired guest rise in his awkward way, and break with stammering tongue the silence which had brooded over the loudest debates, as week after week of the session had passed. He observed, and felt, too, the thrill which ran through

* A celebrated law text-book.

the House at the mere introduction of a subject with which every
mind was surcharged, and marked the rising tide of feeling as the
reading of the resolutions went on, until the climax of audacity was
reached in the last clause of the last resolution. How moderate, how
tame, the words seem to us ! " Every attempt to invest such power
[of taxation] in any person or persons whatever, other than the General Assembly aforesaid, has a manifest tendency to destroy British
and American freedom."

When the reading was finished, Jefferson heard his friend utter the
opening sentences of his speech, with faltering tongue as usual, and
giving little promise of the strains that were to follow. But it was the
nature of this great genius, as of all genius, to rise to the occasion.
Soon Jefferson saw him stand erect, and, swinging free of all impedi-
ments, launch into the tide of his oration ; every eye captivated by
the large and sweeping grace of his gesticulation, every ear charmed
with the swelling music of his voice, every mind thrilled or stung by
the vivid epigrams into which he condensed his opinions. He never
had a listener so formed to be held captive by him as the student at
the lobby door, who, as a boy, had found the oratory of the Indian
chief so impressive, and could not now resist a slurring translation of
Ossian's majestic phrases. After the lapse of fifty-nine years, Jefferson still spoke of this great day with enthusiasm, and described anew
the closing moment of Henry's speech, when the orator, interrupted
by cries of treason, uttered the well-known words of defiance, " If this
be treason, make the most of it ! "

The debate which followed Mr. Henry's opening speech was, as
Jefferson has recorded, " most bloody." It is impossible for a reader
of this generation to conceive the mixture of fondness, pride, and
veneration with which these colonists regarded the mother country, its
parliament and king, its church and its literature, and all the glorious
names and events of its history. Whig as Jefferson was by nature and
conviction, he could not give up England as long as there was any
hope of a just union with her. What, then, must have been the feelings of the Tories of the House, — Tories by nature and by party, —
upon hearing this yeoman from the West speak of the natural rights
of man in the spirit of a Sidney, and use language in reference to the
king which sounded to them like the prelude to an assassin's stab ?
They had to make a stand, too, for their position as leaders of the
House, unquestioned for a century. To the matter of the resolutions

no one objected. All that Wythe, Pendleton, Bland, and Peyton Randolph could urge against them was, that they were unbecoming and unnecessary. The House had already remonstrated without effect, and it became a loyal people to submit. "Torrents of sublime eloquence" from Patrick Henry, as Jefferson observes, swept away their arguments, and the resolutions were carried; the last one, however, by only a single vote.

Doubtless the young gentlemen went home exulting. Patrick Henry, unused to the artifices of legislation, and always impatient of detail, supposing now that the work for which he had come to Williamsburg was done, mounted that very evening and rode away. Jefferson, perhaps, was not too sure of this; for the next morning, some time before the hour of meeting, he was again at the Capitol, and in the Burgesses' Chamber. His uncle, Colonel Peter Randolph, one of the Tory members, came in, and, sitting down at the clerk's table, began to turn over the journals of the House. He had a dim recollection, he said, of a resolution of the House, many years ago, having been *expunged!* He was trying to find the record of the transaction. He wanted a precedent. The student of law looked over his shoulder, as he turned the leaves; a group of members standing near, in trepidation at the thought of yesterday's doings. The House-bell rang; the House convened; the student resumed his stand in the doorway. A motion was made to expunge the last resolution of yesterday's series; and, in the absence of the mighty orator whose eloquence had yesterday made the dull intelligent and the timid brave, the motion was carried, and the resolution was expunged.

THE DECLARATION OF INDEPENDENCE.*

IT was on the 7th of June, 1776, that Mr. R. H. Lee obeyed the instructions of the Virginia legislature by moving that Congress should declare independence. Two days' debate revealed that the measure,

* The Declaration of Independence was signed by the Continental Congress July 4th, 1776. Edward Everett said of this great charter and of Mr. Jefferson, its author: "To have been the instrument of expressing, in one brief, decisive act, the concentrated will and resolution of a whole family of States; of unfolding, in one all-important manifesto, the causes, the motives, and the justification of this great movement in human affairs; to have been permitted to give the impress and peculiarity of his own mind to a charter of public right, destined — or rather, let me say, already elevated — to an importance, in the estimation of men, equal to anything human, ever borne on parchment, or expressed in the visible signs of thought, — this is the glory of Thomas Jefferson."

though still a little premature, was destined to pass; and therefore the further discussion of the subject was postponed for twenty days, and a committee of five was appointed to draught a declaration, — Thomas Jefferson, Dr. Franklin, John Adams, Roger Sherman, and R. R. Livingston. Mr. Jefferson was naturally urged to prepare the draught. He was chairman of the committee, having received the highest number of votes; he was also its youngest member, and therefore bound to do an ample share of the work; he was noted for his skill with the pen; he was particularly conversant with the points of the controversy; he was a Virginian. The task, indeed, was not very arduous or difficult. Nothing was wanted but a careful and brief recapitulation of wrongs familiar to every patriotic mind, and a clear statement of principles hackneyed from eleven years' iteration. Jefferson made no difficulty about undertaking it, and probably had no anticipation of the vast celebrity that was to follow so slight an exercise of his faculties.

He was ready with his draught in time. His colleagues upon the committee suggested a few verbal changes, none of which were important; but during the three days' discussion of it in the House, it was subjected to a review so critical and severe, that the author sat in his place silently writhing under it, and Dr. Franklin felt called upon to console him with the comic relation of the process by which the sign-board of *John Thompson, hatter, makes and sells hats for ready money*, was reduced to the name of the hatter and the figure of a hat. Congress made eighteen suppressions, six additions, and ten alterations; and nearly every one of these changes was an improvement. The noblest utterance of the whole composition is the reason given for making the Declaration, — "A DECENT RESPECT FOR THE OPINIONS OF MANKIND." This touches the heart. Among the best emotions that human nature knows is the veneration of man for man. This recognition of the public opinion of the world, — the sum of human sense, — as the final arbiter in all such controversies, is the single phrase of the document which Jefferson alone, perhaps, of all the Congress, would have originated; and, in point of merit, it was worth all the rest.

During the 2d, 3d, and 4th of July Congress were engaged in reviewing the Declaration. Thursday, the fourth, was a hot day; the session lasted many hours; members were tired and impatient. Every one who has watched the sessions of a deliberative body knows

how the most important measures are retarded, accelerated, even
defeated, by physical causes of the most trifling nature. Mr. Kinglake intimates that Lord Raglan's invasion of the Crimea was due
rather to the after-dinner slumbers of the British Cabinet, than to
any well-considered purpose. Mr. Jefferson used to relate, with much
merriment, that the final signing of the Declaration of Independence
was hastened by an absurdly trivial cause. Near the hall in which
the debates were then held was a livery-stable, from which swarms of
flies came into the open windows, and assailed the silk-stockinged
legs of honorable members. Handkerchief in hand, they lashed the
flies with such vigor as they could command on a July afternoon;
but the annoyance became at length so extreme as to render them
impatient of delay, and they made haste to bring the momentous
business to a conclusion.

After such a long and severe strain upon their minds, members
seem to have indulged in many a jocular observation as they stood
around the table. Tradition has it, that when John Hancock had
affixed his magnificent signature to the paper, he said, " *There*, John
Bull may read *my* name without spectacles! "

No composition of man was ever received with more rapture than
this. It came at a happy time. Boston was delivered, and New
York, as yet, but menaced; and in all New England there was not a
British soldier who was not a prisoner, nor a king's ship that was
not a prize. Between the expulsion of the British troops from Boston, and their capture of New York, was the period of the Revolutionary War when the people were most confident and most united.
From the newspapers and letters of the times, we should infer that the
contest was ending rather than beginning, so exultant is their tone;
and the Declaration of Independence, therefore, was received more
like a song of triumph than a call to battle.

The paper was signed late on Thursday afternoon, July 4. On
the Monday following, at noon, it was publicly read for the first time,
in Independence Square, from a platform erected by Rittenhouse for
the purpose of observing the transit of Venus. Captain John Hopkins, a young man commanding an armed brig of the navy of the
new nation, was the reader; and it required his stentorian voice to
carry the words to the distant verge of the multitude who had come
to hear it. In the evening, as a journal of the day has it, " our *late*
king's coat-of-arms were brought from the hall of the State House,

where the said king's courts were formerly held, and burned amid the acclamations of a crowd of spectators." Similar scenes transpired in every center of population, and at every camp and post. Usually the militia companies, the committee of safety, and other revolutionary bodies, marched in procession to some public place, where they listened decorously to the reading of the Declaration, at the conclusion of which cheers were given and salutes fired; and, in the evening, there were illuminations and bonfires. In New York, after the reading, the leaden statue of the *late* king in Bowling Green was "laid prostrate in the dirt," and ordered to be run into bullets. The debtors in prison were also set at liberty. Virginia, before the news of the Declaration had reached her (July 5, 1776), had stricken the king's name out of the prayer-book; and now (July 30), Rhode Island made it a misdemeanor to pray for the king *as* king, under penalty of a fine of one hundred thousand pounds!

The news of the Declaration was received with sorrow by all that was best in England. Samuel Rogers used to give American guests at his breakfasts an interesting reminiscence of this period. On the morning after the intelligence reached London, his father, at family prayers, added a prayer for the *success* of the colonies, which he repeated every day until the peace.

The deed was done. A people not formed for empire ceased to be imperial; and a people destined to empire began the political education that will one day give them far more and better than imperial sway.

JEAN INGELOW.

1825-

JEAN INGELOW was born in England about 1825. Little is known of her private life, which has been very retired; but her name has become familiar and beloved throughout the English-speaking world. Her first important literary essay was a volume of poems published in England in 1863, and immediately reprinted in this country, where it was received with such favor as is rarely accorded to a book of verse. It has been followed by two or three volumes of poems, which have been less popular than the author's first venture, for the reason, perhaps, that they have dealt with more ambitious themes. In prose, Miss Ingelow has written little, but very well. Her *Studies for Stories* is one of the best collections of stories for children in print, and *Poor Mat* is a tale of singular beauty, though, perhaps, too sad. In 1872 she produced her first novel, *Off the Skelligs*, which, however faulty in artistic respects, in purity of sentiment, and freshness and wholesomeness of atmosphere, has hardly been surpassed in modern literature. But poetry is evidently this author's *forte:* there is a simple sweetness, an earnest goodness, in her verse which is irresistibly winning, and which appeals powerfully to the hearts of the people. While her general mood is calmly contemplative, *The High Tide* and a few other poems prove her possession of a high degree of dramatic vigor.

SEVEN TIMES ONE.

THERE 's no dew left on the daisies and clover,
    There 's no rain left in heaven.
I 've said my " seven times " over and over, —
    Seven times one are seven.

I am old, — so old I can write a letter;
    My birthday lessons are done.
The lambs play always, — they know no better;
    They are only one times one.

O Moon! in the night I have seen you sailing
    And shining so round and low.
You were bright — ah, bright — but your light is failing;
    You are nothing now but a bow.

You Moon! have you done something wrong in heaven,
    That God has hidden your face?
I hope, if you have, you will soon be forgiven,
    And shine again in your place.

O velvet Bee! you 're a dusty fellow, —
    You 've powdered your legs with gold.
O brave marsh Mary-buds, rich and yellow,
    Give me your money to hold!

O Columbine! open your folded wrapper,
  Where two twin turtle-doves dwell!
O Cuckoo-pint! toll me the purple clapper
  That hangs in your clear green bell!

And show me your nest, with the young ones in it, —
  I will not steal them away:
I am old! you may trust me, linnet, linnet!
  I am seven times one to-day.

A MAIDEN WITH A MILKING-PAIL.

I.

WHAT change has made the pastures sweet,
And reached the daisies at my feet,
  And cloud that wears a golden hem?
This lovely world, the hills, the sward, —
They all look fresh, as if our Lord
  But yesterday had finished them.

And here's the field with light aglow:
How fresh its boundary lime-trees show!
  And how its wet leaves trembling shine!
Between their trunks come through to me
The morning sparkles of the sea,
  Below the level browsing line.

I see the pool, more clear by half
Than pools where other waters laugh
  Up at the breasts of coot and rail.
There, as she passed it on her way,
I saw reflected yesterday
  A maiden with a milking-pail.

There, neither slowly nor in haste, —
One hand upon her slender waist,
  The other lifted to her pail, —
She, rosy in the morning light,
Among the water-daisies white,
  Like some fair sloop appeared to sail.

Against her ankles as she trod
The lucky buttercups did nod:
   I leaned upon the gate to see.
The sweet thing looked, but did not speak;
A dimple came in either cheek,
   And all my heart was gone from me.

Then, as I lingered on the gate,
And she came up like coming fate,
   I saw my picture in her eyes, —
Clear dancing eyes, more black than sloes!
Cheeks like the mountain pink, that grows
   Among white-headed majesties!

I said, "A tale was made of old
That I would fain to thee unfold.
   Ah! let me, — let me tell the tale."
But high she held her comely head:
"I cannot heed it now," she said,
   "For carrying of the milking-pail."

She laughed. What good to make ado?
I held the gate, and she came through,
   And took her homeward path anon.
From the clear pool her face had fled;
It rested on my heart instead,
   Reflected when the maid was gone.

With happy youth, and work content,
So sweet and stately, on she went,
   Right careless of the untold tale.
Each step she took I loved her more,
And followed to her dairy door
   The maiden with the milking-pail.

II.

For hearts where wakened love doth lurk,
How fine, how blest a thing is work!
   For work does good when reasons fail, —

Good; yet the ax at every stroke
The echo of a name awoke, —
   Her name is Mary Martindale.

I 'm glad that echo was not heard
Aright by other men.   A bird
   Knows doubtless what his own notes tell;
And I know not, — but I can say
I felt as shamefaced all that day
   As if folks heard her name right well.

And when the west began to glow
I went — I could not choose but go —
   To that same dairy on the hill;
And while sweet Mary moved about
Within, I came to her without, ⁀
   And leaned upon the window-sill.

The garden border where I stood
Was sweet with pinks and southernwood.
   I spoke, — her answer seemed to fail.
I smelt the pinks, — I could not see.
The dusk came down and sheltered me,
   And in the dusk she heard my tale.

And what is left that I should tell?
I begged a kiss, — I pleaded well:
   The rosebud lips did long decline;
But yet, I think — I think 't is true —
That, leaned at last into the dew,
   One little instant they were mine!

O life! how dear thou hast become!
She laughed at dawn, and I was dumb!
   But evening counsels best prevail.
Fair shine the blue that o'er her spreads,
Green be the pastures where she treads,
   The maiden with the milking-pail!

BAYARD TAYLOR.

1825 –   .

BAYARD TAYLOR, famous as a traveler, was born in Kennett Square, Chester County, Pennsylvania, in January, 1825. At the age of seventeen he became an apprentice in a printing-office; but soon growing weary of the drudgery of his calling, he set out on a tour of Europe, where he traveled two years at a cost of only five hundred dollars. The story of this journey, published in a volume entitled *Views Afoot*, at once gave the author an enviable place in literature. After a brief residence in Pennsylvania and New York, where he was engaged in journalism, Mr. Taylor resumed his wanderings, and traveled extensively in California, Mexico, Europe, Asia, and Africa. In 1862 he was appointed Secretary of the United States Legation at St. Petersburg. The list of this author's books is too long to be printed entire; it includes records of travel, poems, novels, etc. Of the latter, *The Story of Kennett*, a picture of life in his native region, is perhaps the best. His latest work is a translation of Goethe's *Faust* complete. Mr. Taylor married, in 1864, Marie, daughter of Professor Hansen, the distinguished German astronomer recently deceased, and since that date has lived mainly abroad. His highest success in authorship has been in books of travel; his qualifications for the work which they represent are exceptionally good; he has a spirited and flowing style, and a happy faculty of conveying instruction. The extracts are from *Views Afoot*.

A DAY IN LONDON.

AFTER breakfast, on the first day, we set out for a walk through London. Entering the main artery of this mighty city, we passed on, through Aldgate and Cornhill, to St. Paul's, with still increasing wonder. Farther on, through Fleet Street and the Strand, — what a world! Here come the ever-thronging, ever-rolling waves of life, pressing and whirling on in their tumultuous career. Here, day and night, pours the stream of human beings, seeming, amid the roar and din and clatter of the passing vehicles, like the tide of some great combat. How lonely it makes one to stand still and feel that of all the mighty throng which divides itself around him, not a being knows or cares for him! What knows, he too, of the thousands who pass him by! How many who bear the impress of godlike virtue, or hide beneath a goodly countenance a heart black with crime! How many fiery spirits, all glowing with hope for the yet unclouded future, or brooding over a darkened and desolate past in the agony of despair! There is a sublimity in this human Niagara that makes one look on his own race with something of awe.

St. Paul's is on a scale of grandeur excelling everything I have yet seen. The dome seems to stand in the sky, as you look up to it; the distance from which you view it, combined with the atmosphere of London, gives it a dim, shadowy appearance, that startles one with its immensity. The roof from which the dome springs is itself as high as the spires of most other churches ; blackened for two hundred years with the coal-smoke of London, it stands like a relic of the giant architecture of the early world. The interior is what one would expect to behold, after viewing the outside. A maze of grand arches on every side encompasses the dome, at which you gaze up as at the sky ; and from every pillar and wall look down the marble forms of the dead. There is scarcely a vacant niche left in all this mighty hall, so many are the statues that meet one on every side. With the exception of John Howard, Sir Astley Cooper, and Wren, whose monument is the church itself, they are all to military men. I thought if they had all been removed except Howard's, it would better have suited such a temple, and the great soul it commemorated.

I never was more impressed with the grandeur of human invention, than when ascending the dome. I could with difficulty conceive the means by which such a mighty edifice had been lifted into the air. The small frame of Sir Christopher Wren must have contained a mind capable of vast conceptions. The dome is like the summit of a mountain ; so wide is the prospect, and so great the pile upon which you stand. London lay beneath us, like an ant-hill, with the black insects swarming to and fro in their long avenues, the sound of their employments coming up like the roar of the sea. A cloud of coal-smoke hung over it, through which many a pointed spire was thrust up ; sometimes the wind would blow it aside for a moment, and the thousands of red roofs would shine out clearer. The bridged Thames, covered with craft of all sizes, wound beneath us like a ringed and spotted serpent.

It was a relief to get into St. James's Park, among the trees and flowers again. Here beautiful winding walks led around little lakes, in which were hundreds of waterfowl, swimming. Groups of merry children were sporting on the green lawn, enjoying their privilege of roaming everywhere at will, while the older bipeds were confined to the regular walks. At the western end stood Buckingham Palace, looking over the trees towards St. Paul's ; and through the grove, on the eminence above, the towers of St. James's could be seen. But there was a dim building with two lofty square towers, decorated with a profusion of pointed Gothic pinnacles, that I looked at with more interest than these appendages of royalty. I could not linger long in its vicinity, but, going back again by the Horse Guards, took the road to *Westminster Abbey.*

We approached by the general entrance, Poet's Corner. I hardly stopped to look at the elaborate exterior of Henry the Seventh's Chapel, but passed on to the door. On entering, the first thing that met my eyes were the words " OH RARE BEN JONSON," under his bust. Near by stood the monuments of Spenser and Gay, and a few paces farther looked down the sublime countenance of Milton. Never was a spot so full of intense interest. The light was just dim enough to give it a solemn, religious air, making the marble forms of poets and philosophers so shadowy and impressive that I felt as if standing in their living presence. Every step called up some mind linked with the associations of my childhood. There was the gentle feminine countenance of Thomson, and the majestic head of Dryden; Addison with his classic features, and Gray, full of the fire of lofty thought. In another chamber, I paused long before the tablet to Shakespeare; and while looking at the monument of Garrick, started to find that I stood upon his grave. What a glorious galaxy of genius is here collected, — what a constellation of stars whose light is immortal! The mind is fettered by their spirit, everything is forgotten but the mighty dead, who still " rule us from their urns."

The side-chapels are filled with tombs of knightly families, the husband and wife lying on their backs on the tombs, with their hands clasped, while their children, about the size of dolls, are kneeling around. Numberless are the Barons and Earls and Dukes, whose grim effigies stare from their tombs. In opposite chapels are the tombs of Mary and Elizabeth, and near the former that of Darnley. After having visited many of the scenes of her life, it was with no ordinary emotion that I stood by the sepulcher of Mary. How differently one looks upon it and upon that of the proud Elizabeth!

We descended to the Chapel of Edward the Confessor, within the splendid shrine of which his ashes repose. Here the chair on which the English monarchs have been crowned for several hundred years was exhibited. Under the seat is the stone, brought from the Abbey of Scone, whereon the Kings of Scotland were crowned. The chair is of oak, carved and hacked over with names, and on the bottom some one has recorded his name with the fact that he once slept in it. We sat down and rested in it without ceremony. Near this is the hall where the Knights of the Order of the Bath met. Over each seat their dusty banners are still hanging, each with its crest, and their armor is rusting upon the wall. It resembled a banqueting-hall of the olden time, where the knights had left their seats for a moment vacant. Entering the nave, we were lost in the wilderness of sculpture. Here stood the forms of Pitt, Fox, Burke, Sheridan, and Watts, from the chisels of Chantrey, Bacon, and Westmacott. Farther down were Sir Isaac Newton, and Sir Godfrey Kneller, — opposite André, and Paoli, the Italian, who died here in exile. How can I convey an idea of the scene! Notwithstanding all the descriptions I had read, I was totally unprepared for the reality, nor could I have anticipated the hushed and breathless interest with which I paced the dim aisles, gazing, at every step, on the last resting-place of some great and familiar name. A place so sacred to all who inherit the English tongue is worthy of a special pilgrimage across the deep. To those who are unable to visit it a description may be interesting ; but so far does it fall short of the scene itself, that if I thought it would induce a few of our wealthy idlers, or even those who, like myself, must travel with toil and privation, to come hither, I would write till the pen dropped from my hand.

We walked down the Thames through the narrow streets of Wapping. Over the mouth of the Tunnel is a large circular building, with a dome to light the entrance below. Paying a fee of a penny, we descended by a winding staircase to the bottom, which is seventy-three feet below the surface. The carriage-way, still unfinished, will extend farther into the city. From the bottom the view of the two arches of the Tunnel, brilliantly lighted with gas, is very fine ; it has a much less heavy and gloomy appearance than I expected. As we walked along under the bed of the river, two or three girls at one end began playing on the French horn and bugle, and the echoes, when not sufficient to confuse the melody, were remarkably beautiful. Between the arches of the division separating the two passages are shops, occupied by venders of fancy articles, views of the Tunnel, engravings, etc. In the middle is a small printing-press, where a sheet containing a description of the whole work is printed for those who desire it. As I was no stranger to this art, I requested the boy to let me print one myself, but he had such a bad roller I did not succeed in getting a good impression. The air within is somewhat damp, but fresh and agreeably cool, and one can scarcely realize, in walking along the light passage, that a river is rolling above his head.

The immense solidity and compactness of the structure precludes the danger of accident, each of the sides being arched outwards, so that the heaviest pressure only strengthens the work.   It will long remain a noble monument of human daring and ingenuity.

ROME AND ST. PETER'S.

ONE day's walk through Rome, — how shall I describe it?   The Capitol, the Forum, St. Peter's, the Coliseum, — what few hours' ramble ever took in places so hallowed by poetry, history, and art? It was a golden leaf in my calendar of life.   In thinking over it now, and drawing out the threads of recollection from the varied web of thought I have woven to-day, I almost wonder how I dared so much at once; but within reach of them all, how was it possible to wait? Let me give a sketch of our day's ramble.

Hearing that it was better to visit the ruins by evening or moonlight (alas! there is no moon now), we set out to hunt St. Peter's. Going in the direction of the Corso, we passed the ruined front of the magnificent Temple of Antoninus, now used as the Papal Custom House.   We turned to the right on entering the Corso, expecting to have a view of the city from the hill at its southern end.   It is a magnificent street, lined with palaces and splendid edifices of every kind, and always filled with crowds of carriages and people.   On leaving it, however, we became bewildered among the narrow streets, — passed through a market of vegetables, crowded with beggars and *contadini*, — threaded many by-ways between dark old buildings, — saw one or two antique fountains and many modern churches, and finally arrived at a hill.

We ascended many steps, and then, descending a little towards the other side, saw suddenly below us the *Roman Forum!*   I knew it at once, — and those three Corinthian columns that stood near us, — what could they be but the remains of the temple of Jupiter Stator? We stood on the Capitoline Hill; at the foot was the Arch of Septimius Severus, brown with age and shattered; near it stood the majestic front of the Temple of Fortune, its pillars of polished granite glistening in the sun, as if they had been erected yesterday, while on the left the rank grass was waving from the arches and mighty walls of the Palace of the Cæsars!   In front ruin upon ruin lined the way for half a mile, where the Coliseum towered grandly through the blue morning mist, at the base of the Esquiline Hill! Good heavens, what a scene! Grandeur, such as the world has never since beheld, once rose through that blue atmosphere; splendor inconceivable, the spoils of a world, the triumphs of a thousand armies, had passed over that earth; minds which for ages moved the ancient world had thought there; and words of power and glory from the lips of immortal men had been syllabled on that hallowed air. To call back all this on the very spot, while the wreck of what once was rose moldering and desolate around, kindled a glow of thought and feeling too powerful for words.

Returning at hazard through the streets, we came suddenly upon the column of Trajan, standing in an excavated square below the level of the city, amid a number of broken granite columns, which formed part of the Forum dedicated to him by Rome, after the conquest of Dacia. The column is one hundred and thirty-two feet high, and entirely covered with bas-reliefs representing his victories, winding about it in a spiral line to the top. The number of figures is computed at two thousand five hundred, and they were of such excellence that Raphael used many of them for his models. They are now much defaced, and the column is surmounted by a statue of some saint. The inscription on the pedestal has been erased, and the name of Sixtus V. substituted. Nothing can exceed the ridiculous vanity of the old popes in thus mutilating the finest monuments of ancient art. You cannot look upon any relic of antiquity in Rome, but your eyes are assailed by the words " PONTIFEX MAXIMUS," in staring modern letters. Even the magnificent bronzes of the Pantheon were stripped to make the baldachin under the dome of St. Peter's.

Finding our way back again, we took a fresh start, happily in the right direction, and after walking some time came out on the Tiber, at the Bridge of St. Angelo. The river rolled below in his muddy glory, and in front, on the opposite bank, stood "the pile which Hadrian reared on high," — now, the Castle of St. Angelo. Knowing that St. Peter's was to be seen from this bridge, I looked about in search of it. There was only one dome in sight, large and of beautiful proportions. I said at once, "Surely that cannot be St. Peter's!" On looking again, however, I saw the top of a massive range of building near it, which corresponded so nearly with the pictures of the Vatican that I was unwillingly forced to believe the mighty dome was really before me. I recognized it as one of those we had seen from the Capitol, but it appeared so much smaller when viewed from a greater distance that I was quite deceived. On considering we were still three fourths of a mile from it, and that we could see its minutest parts distinctly, the illusion was explained.

Going directly down the *Borgo Vecchio*, it seemed a long time before we arrived at the square of St. Peter's; and when at length we stood in front, with the majestic colonnade sweeping around, the fountains on each side sending up their showers of silvery spray, the mighty obelisk of Egyptian granite piercing the sky, and beyond, the great façade and dome of the Cathedral, I confessed my unmingled admiration. It recalled to my mind the grandeur of ancient Rome, and mighty as her edifices must have been, I doubt if she could boast many views more overpowering than this. The façade of St. Peter's seemed close to us, but it was a third of a mile distant, and the people ascending the steps dwindled to pygmies.

I passed the obelisk, went up the long ascent, crossed the portico, pushed aside the heavy leathern curtain at the entrance, and stood in the great nave. I need not describe my feelings at the sight, but I will give the dimensions, and the reader may then fancy what they were. Before me was a marble plain six hundred feet long, and under the cross four hundred and seventeen feet wide! One hundred and fifty feet above sprang a glorious arch, dazzling with inlaid gold, and in the center of the cross there were four hundred feet of air between me and the top of the dome! The sunbeam, stealing through the lofty window at one end of the transept, made a bar of light on the blue air, hazy with incense, one tenth of a mile long, before it fell on the mosaics and gilded shrines of the other extremity. The grand cupola alone, including lantern and cross, is two hundred and eighty-five feet high, or sixty feet higher than the Bunker Hill Monument, and the four immense pillars on which it rests are each one hundred and thirty-seven feet in circumference! It seems as if human art had outdone itself in producing this temple, — the grandest which the world ever erected for the worship of the Living God! The awe I felt in looking up at the colossal arch of marble and gold did not humble me; on the contrary, I felt exalted, ennobled; beings in the form I wore planned the glorious edifice, and it seemed that, in godlike power and perseverance, they were indeed but a little lower than the angels. I felt that, if fallen, my race was still mighty and immortal.

The Vatican is only open twice a week, on days which are not *festas ;* most fortunately, to-day happened to be one of these, and we took a run through its endless halls. The extent and magnificence of the gallery of sculpture is amazing. The halls, which are filled to overflowing with the finest works of ancient art, would, if placed side by side, make a row more than two miles in length! You enter at once into a hall of marble, with a magnificent arched ceiling, a third of a mile long ; the sides are covered for a great distance with Roman inscriptions of every kind, divided into compartments according to the era of the empire to which they refer. One which I examined appeared to be a kind of index of the roads in Italy, with the towns on them; and we could decipher, on that time-worn block, the very route we had followed from Florence hither.

Then came the statues, and here I am bewildered how to describe them. Hundreds upon hundreds of figures, — statues of citizens, generals, emperors, and gods, — fauns, satyrs, and nymphs, — children, Cupids, and Tritons; in fact, they seemed inexhaustible. Many of them, too, were forms of matchless beauty ; there were Venuses and nymphs, born of the loftiest dreams of grace ; fauns on whose faces shone the very soul of humor, and heroes and divinities with an air of majesty worthy the "land of lost gods and godlike men"!

I am lost in astonishment at the perfection of art attained by the Greeks and Romans. There is scarcely a form of beauty, that has ever met my eye, which is not to be found in this gallery. I should almost despair of such another blaze of glory on the world, were it not my devout belief that what has been done may be done again, and had I not faith that the dawn in which we live will bring on another day equally glorious. And why should not America, with the experience and added wisdom which three thousand years have slowly yielded to the old world, joined to the giant energy of her youth and freedom, re-bestow on the world the divine creations of Art ?

But let us step on to the hemicycle of the Belvedere, and view some works greater than any we have yet seen, or even imagined. The adjoining gallery is filled with masterpieces of sculpture, but we will keep our eyes unwearied and merely glance along the rows. At length we reach a circular court with a fountain flinging up its waters in the center. Before us is an open cabinet; there is a beautiful, manly form within, but you would not for an instant take it for the Apollo. By the Gorgon head it holds aloft, we recognize Canova's Perseus, — he has copied the form and attitude of the Apollo, but he could not breathe into it the same warming fire. It seemed to me particularly lifeless, and I greatly preferred his Boxers, who stand on either side of it.

Now we look on a scene of the deepest physical agony. Mark how every muscle of old Laocoön's body is distended to the utmost in the mighty struggle! What intensity of pain in the quivering, distorted features! Every nerve which despair can call into action is excited in one giant effort, and a scream of anguish seems just to have quivered on those marble lips. The serpents have rolled their strangling coils around father and sons, but terror has taken away the strength of the latter, and they make but feeble resistance. After looking with indifference on the many casts of this group, I was the more moved by the magnificent original. It deserves all the admiration that has been heaped upon it.

I absolutely trembled on approaching the cabinet of the Apollo. I had built up in fancy a glorious ideal, drawn from all that bards have sung or artists have rhapsodized about its divine beauty. I feared disappointment, — I dreaded to have my ideal displaced and my faith in the power of human genius overthrown by a form less than perfect. However, with a feeling of desperate excitement, I entered and looked upon it. Now what shall I say of it? How describe its immortal beauty? To what shall I liken its glorious perfection of form, or the fire that imbues the cold marble with the soul of a god? Not with sculpture, for it stands alone and above all other works of art, nor with men, for it has a majesty more than human. I gazed on it, lost in wonder and joy, — joy that I could at last take into my mind a faultless ideal of godlike, exalted manhood. The figure seems actually to possess a soul, and I looked on it, not as on a piece of marble, but as on a being of loftier mold, and waited to see him step forward when the arrow had reached its mark. I would give worlds to feel one moment the sculptor's triumph when his work was completed; that one exulting thrill must have repaid him for every ill he might have suffered on earth.

HUXLEY.

1825 –　.

Thomas Henry Huxley, one of the most distinguished of living physiologists and naturalists, was born in Middlesex, England, in 1825. At an early age he entered the royal navy in the capacity of surgeon. In 1848 he produced his first book, *On the Anatomy and Affinities of the Family of the Medusæ.* In 1854 he became Professor of Palæontology in the School of Mines, and a few years later was appointed Professor of Physiology in the Royal Institution. To the recent controversy as to the origin of man Professor Huxley has been an important contributor. His *Man's Place in Nature* was largely instrumental in directing public attention to this subject, and the ability of the book made a profound impression on thoughtful minds. His later work, *Protoplasm, or The Physical Basis of Life,* was not less stimulating and impressive. Professor Huxley is one of the ablest supporters of the Darwinian theory. From the lecture platform he has won the admiring attention of the best minds of England, and through his published words has gained the ear of the whole scientific world. To no man now living does science owe a larger debt, whether as an investigator or as an expounder. His style is peculiarly attractive, and in his hands the driest themes of science take on a charm which compels attention and quickens interest.

ON SCIENTIFIC EDUCATION.

I HOPE you will consider that the arguments I have now stated, even if there were no better ones, constitute a sufficient apology for urging the introduction of science into schools. The next question to which I have to address myself is, What sciences ought to be thus taught? And this is one of the most important of questions. (There are other forms of culture beside physical science) (and I should be profoundly sorry to see the fact forgotten, or even to observe a tendency to starve or cripple literary or æsthetic culture for the sake of science.) Such a narrow view of the nature of education has nothing to do with my firm conviction that a complete and thorough scientific culture ought to be introduced into all schools.) (By this, however, I do not mean that every school-boy should be taught everything in science.) That would be a very absurd thing to conceive, and a very mischievous thing to attempt. What I mean is, that no boy or girl should leave school without possessing a grasp of the general character of science, and without having been disciplined, more or less, in the methods of all sciences; so that, when turned into the world to make their own way, they shall be prepared to face scientific problems, not by knowing at once the conditions of every problem, or by being able at once to solve it, but by being familiar with the general current of scientific thought, and by being able to apply the methods of science in the proper way, when they have acquainted themselves with the conditions of the special problem.

That is what I understand by scientific education. To furnish a
boy with such an education, it is by no means necessary that he
should devote his whole school existence to physical science ; in fact,
no one would lament so one-sided a proceeding more than I. Nay,
more, it is not necessary for him to give up more than a moderate
share of his time to such studies, if they be properly selected and
arranged, and if he be trained in them in a fitting manner.

I conceive the proper course to be somewhat as follows : To begin
with, let every child be instructed in those general views of the phenomena of nature for which we have no exact English name. The
nearest approximation to a name for what I mean, which we possess,
is " physical geography "; that is to say, a general knowledge of the
earth, and what is on it, in it, and about it. If any one who has
had experience of the ways of young children will call to mind their
questions, he will find that, so far as they can be put into any scientific category, they come under this head. The child asks," What is
the moon, and why does it shine ? " " What is this water, and where
does it run ? " " What is the wind ? " " What makes the waves in
the sea ? " " Where does this animal live, and what is the use of that
plant ? " And if not snubbed and stunted by being told not to ask
foolish questions, there is no limit to the intellectual craving of a
young child, nor any bounds to the slow but solid accretion of
knowledge and development of the thinking faculty in this way. To
all such questions answers which are necessarily incomplete, though
true as far as they go, may be given by any teacher whose ideas represent real knowledge, and not mere book learning ; and a panoramic
view of nature, accompanied by a strong infusion of the scientific
habit of mind, may thus be placed within the reach of every child
of nine or ten.

After this preliminary opening of the eyes to the great spectacle of
the daily progress of nature, as the reasoning faculties of the child grow,
and he becomes familiar with the use of the tools of knowledge, —
reading, writing, and elementary mathematics, — he should pass on
to what is, in the more strict sense, physical science. Now, there are
two kinds of physical science. The one regards form and the relation of forms to one another ; the other deals with causes and effects.
In many of what we term our sciences, these two kinds are mixed up
together ; but systematic botany is a pure example of the former
kind, and physics of the latter kind, of science. Every educational

advantage which training in physical science can give is obtainable from the proper study of these two ; and I should be contented for the present if they, added to physical geography, furnished the whole of the scientific curriculum of schools. Indeed, I conceive it would be one of the greatest boons which could be conferred upon England, if henceforward every child in the country were instructed in the general knowledge of the things about it, in the elements of physics and of botany ; but I should be still better pleased if there could be added somewhat of chemistry, and an elementary acquaintance with human physiology.

So far as school education is concerned, I want to go no further just now ; and I believe that such instruction would make an excellent introduction to that preparatory scientific training which, as I have indicated, is so essential for the successful pursuit of our most important professions. But this modicum of instruction must be so given as to insure real knowledge and practical discipline. If scientific education is to be dealt with as mere book-work, it will be better not to attempt it, but to stick to the Latin Grammar, which makes no pretence to be anything but book-work.

If the great benefits of scientific training are sought, it is essential that such training should be real ; that is to say, that the mind of the scholar should be brought into direct relation with fact, that he should not merely be told a thing, but made to see by the use of his own intellect and ability that the thing is *so* and no otherwise. The great peculiarity of scientific training, that in virtue of which it cannot be replaced by any other discipline whatsoever, is this bringing of the mind directly into contact with fact, and practicing the intellect in the completest form of induction ; that is to say, in drawing conclusions from particular facts made known by immediate observation of nature.

The other studies which enter into ordinary education do not discipline the mind in this way. Mathematical training is almost purely deductive. The mathematician starts with a few simple propositions, the proof of which is so obvious that they are called self-evident, and the rest of his work consists of subtile deductions from them. The teaching of languages, at any rate as ordinarily practiced, is of the same general nature, — authority and tradition furnish the data, and the mental operations of the scholar are deductive.

Again, if history be the subject of study, the facts are still taken upon the evidence of tradition and authority. You cannot make a boy see the Battle of Thermopylæ for himself, or know, of his own knowledge, that Cromwell once ruled England. There is no getting into direct contact with natural fact by this road; there is no dispensing with authority, but rather a resting upon it.

In all these respects science differs from other educational discipline, and prepares the scholar for common life. What have we to do in every-day life? Most of the business which demands our attention is matter of fact, which needs, in the first place, to be accurately observed or apprehended; in the second, to be interpreted by inductive and deductive reasonings, which are altogether similar in their nature to those employed in science. In the one case, as in the other, whatever is taken for granted is so taken at one's own peril. Fact and reason are the ultimate arbiters, and patience and honesty are the great helpers out of difficulty.

But if scientific training is to yield its most eminent results, it must, I repeat, be made practical. That is to say, in explaining to a child the general phenomena of nature, you must, as far as possible, give reality to your teaching by object-lessons. In teaching him botany, he must handle the plants and dissect the flowers for himself; in teaching him physics and chemistry, you must not be solicitous to fill him with information, but you must be careful that what he learns he knows of his own knowledge. Don't be satisfied with telling him that a magnet attracts iron. Let him see that it does; let him feel the pull of the one upon the other for himself. And, especially, tell him that it is his duty to doubt, until he is compelled by the absolute authority of nature to believe, that which is written in books. Pursue this discipline carefully and conscientiously, and you may make sure that, however scanty may be the measure of information which you have poured into the boy's mind, you have created an intellectual habit of priceless value in practical life.

One is constantly asked, When should this scientific education be commenced? I should say with the dawn of intelligence. As I have already said, a child seeks for information about matters of physical science as soon as it begins to talk. The first teaching it wants is an object-lesson of one sort or another; and as soon as it is fit for systematic instruction of any kind, it is fit for a modicum of science.

People talk of the difficulty of teaching young children such

matters, and in the same breath insist upon their learning their Cate-
chism, which contains propositions far harder to comprehend than
anything in the educational course I have proposed. Again, I am
incessantly told that we who advocate the introduction of science
into schools make no allowance for the stupidity of the average boy
or girl; but, in my belief, that stupidity, in nine cases out of ten,
is unnatural, and is developed by a long process of parental and
pedagogic repression of the natural intellectual appetites, accompanied
by a persistent attempt to create artificial ones for food which is not
only tasteless, but essentially indigestible.

Those who urge the difficulty of instructing young people in
science are apt to forget another very important condition of success;
important in all kinds of teaching, but most essential, I am disposed
to think, when the scholars are very young. This condition is, that
the teacher should himself really and practically know his subject.
If he does, he will be able to speak of it in the easy language, and
with the completeness of conviction, with which he talks of any ordinary every-day matter. If he does not, he will be afraid to wander
beyond the limits of the technical phraseology which he has got up;
and a dead dogmatism, which oppresses or raises opposition, will take
the place of the lively confidence, born of personal conviction, which
cheers and encourages the eminently sympathetic mind of childhood.

TIMROD.

1829–1867.

HENRY TIMROD was born in Charleston, South Carolina, on the 8th of December, 1829. His father, William Henry Timrod, was also a poet. The son received his collegiate education at the University of Georgia, although he left a short time before the graduating commencement. He taught as private tutor several years in his native city; and during the civil war for a year or two was upon the editorial staff of the South Carolinian newspaper in Columbia. In 1860 Ticknor and Fields of Boston issued a small volume of *Poems* by Timrod; and since his death — in 1872 — a complete edition has appeared, with a sketch of the poet's brief and painful life. He died on the 7th of October, 1867.

Mr. Timrod's best poems are the patriotic and the idyllic; and his reputation, especially in the South, rests just now mainly upon the former. In this vein his *Carolina* is his strongest and best, and is as terse and vehement in movement as a Greek war-cry. *A Cry to Arms* has also many admirers; and if we transfer the scene of it to Greece or Germany, substituting Tyrtaios or Körner for Timrod, its musical vehemence would be striking. This stanza especially is notable for its fanciful realism: —

> " Come, with the weapons at your call, —
> With musket, pike, or knife;
> He wields the deadliest blade of all
> Who lightest holds his life.
> The arm that drives its unbought blows
> With all a patriot's scorn,
> Might brain a tyrant with a rose
> Or stab him with a thorn."

But clearly the poet was more at home among the beauties of nature, to which he was exquisitely alive. In this vein *Katie* is one of his happiest efforts. It is earnest, natural, musical, chaste, and at the same time sensuous. His longest poem is *A Vision of Poesy*, — the story of aspiration, struggle, and heart-failure, — a foreshadowing of his own brief, eager, and unattaining struggle for success.

SPRING.

SPRING, with that nameless pathos in the air
Which dwells with all things fair, —
Spring, with her golden suns and silver rain,
Is with us once again.

Out in the lonely woods the jasmine burns
Its fragrant lamps, and turns
Into a royal court with green festoons
The banks of dark lagoons.

In the deep heart of every forest tree
The blood is all aglee,
And there's a look about the leafless bowers
As if they dreamed of flowers.

Yet still on every side we trace the hand
Of Winter in the land,
Save where the maple reddens on the lawn,
Flushed by the season's dawn;

Or where, like those strange semblances we find
That age to childhood bind,
The elm puts on, as if in Nature's scorn,
The brown of Autumn corn.

As yet the turf is dark, although you know
That, not a span below,
A thousand germs are groping through the gloom,
And soon will burst their tomb.

Already, here and there, on frailest stems
Appear some azure gems,
Small as might deck, upon a gala day,
The forehead of a fay.

In gardens you may note amid the dearth
The crocus breaking earth;
And near the snowdrop's tender white and green,
The violet in its screen.

But many gleams and shadows needs must pass
Along the budding grass,
And weeks go by, before the enamored South
Shall kiss the rose's mouth.

Still there's a sense of blossoms yet unborn
In the sweet airs of morn;
One almost looks to see the very street
Grow purple at his feet.

At times a fragrant breeze comes floating by,
And brings, you know not why,
A feeling as when eager crowds await,
Before a palace gate,

17 *

Some wondrous pageant ; and you scarce would start,
If from a beech's heart
A blue-eyed Dryad, stepping forth, should say,
" Behold me !   I am May ! "

Ah ! who would couple thoughts of war and crime
With such a blessed time !
Who, in the west wind's aromatic breath,
Could hear the call of Death !

Yet not more surely shall the Spring awake
The voice of wood and brake,
Than she shall rouse, for all her tranquil charms,
A million men to arms.

There shall be deeper hues upon her plains
Than all her sunlit rains,
And every gladdening influence around,
Can summon from the ground.

Oh ! standing on this desecrated mold,
Methinks that I behold,
Lifting her bloody daisies up to God,
Spring, kneeling on the sod,

And calling, with the voice of all her rills,
Upon the ancient hills
To fall and crush the tyrants and the slaves
Who turn her meads to graves.

A MOTHER'S WAIL.

My babe ! my tiny babe ! my only babe !
My single rose-bud in a crown of thorns !
My lamp that in that narrow hut of life,
Whence I looked forth upon a night of storm,
Burned with the luster of the moon and stars !

My babe ! my tiny babe ! my only babe !
Behold, the bud is gone ! the thorns remain !

My lamp hath fallen from its niche — ah, me!
Earth drinks the fragrant flame, and I am left
Forever and forever in the dark!

My babe! my babe! my own and only babe!
Where art thou now?   If somewhere in the sky
An angel hold thee in his radiant arms,
I challenge him to clasp thy tender form
With half the fervor of a mother's love!

Forgive me, Lord! forgive my reckless grief!
Forgive me that this rebel, selfish heart
Would almost make me jealous for my child,
Though thy own lap enthroned him.   Lord, thou hast
So many such!   I have — ah! had — but one!

O yet once more, my babe, to hear thy cry!
O yet once more, my babe, to see thy smile!
O yet once more to feel against my breast
Those cool, soft hands, that warm, wet, eager mouth,
With the sweet sharpness of its budding pearls!

But it must never, never more be mine
To mark the growing meaning in thine eyes,
To watch thy soul unfolding leaf by leaf,
Or catch, with ever fresh surprise and joy,
Thy dawning recognitions of the world!

Three different shadows of thyself, my babe,
Change with each other while I weep.   The first,
The sweetest, yet the not least fraught with pain,
Clings like my living boy around my neck,
Or purs and murmurs softly at my feet!

Another is a little mound of earth;
That comes the oftenest, darling!   In my dreams,
I see it beaten by the midnight rain,
Or chilled beneath the moon.   Ah! what a couch
For that which I have shielded from a breath
That would not stir the violets on thy grave!

The third, my precious babe ! the third, O Lord !
Is a fair cherub face beyond the stars,
Wearing the roses of a mystic bliss,
Yet sometimes not unsaddened by a glance
Turned earthward on a mother in her woe !

This is the vision, Lord, that I would keep
Before me always.   But, alas ! as yet,
It is the dimmest and the rarest too !
O touch my sight, or break the cloudy bars
That hide it, lest I madden where I kneel !

A COMMON THOUGHT.*

SOMEWHERE on this earthly planet
    In the dust of flowers to be,
In the dew-drop in the sunshine,
    Sleeps a solemn day for me.

At this wakeful hour of midnight
    I behold it dawn in mist,
And I hear a sound of sobbing
    Through the darkness, — hist ! O, hist !

In a dim and musky chamber,
    I am breathing life away ;
Some one draws a curtain softly
    And I watch the broadening day.

As it purples in the zenith,
    As it brightens on the lawn,
There 's a hush of death about me,
    And a whisper, " He is gone ! "

* This little poem, written several years before the poet's death, was prophetic.   He died at the very hour here predicted.   The whisper, " He is gone," went forth as the day was purpling in the zenith, on that October morning of 1867.

BRET HARTE.

1838 –

FRANCIS BRET HARTE was born in the State of New York in 1838. When quite young he went to California, where he remained until within a few years. His early occupations were various, including teaching and journalism. His success in the latter field of effort led him suddenly into literature and fame. His earliest essays in prose and verse were contributed to California periodicals, but speedily found their way to the Atlantic coast and even to Europe, being admired for their positive originality and as representative of a new phase of social life. In 1868 the Overland Monthly was started in San Francisco, and Mr. Harte was called to the editorial chair, which he filled very creditably for a year or two. But he had outgrown the sphere of a Pacific coast constituency, and there was a general demand for his removal to the larger field of the East. He yielded to this, and during the last few years has been a resident of New York. Mr. Harte is, perhaps, equally distinguished as a writer of prose and poetry: *The Luck of Roaring Camp* and *The Heathen Chinee*, representing these two forms of composition, are unique in literature, and their merit has never been approximated by the author's many imitators. Their marvelous popularity is due, primarily, to the strangeness of the life whose products they are, — the wild society of newly-settled regions, in which violence is the ruling, and humanity the exceptional, social force; and, secondarily, to a peculiar quality of the author's genius, exclusively peculiar to him, it may be said, by which he is enabled to besiege the reader's mind with almost simultaneous humor and pathos. The power of employing these two agencies in apparently antagonistic, yet practically harmonious combination, is, perhaps, the secret of Mr. Harte's literary success. Surely it is possessed in equal development by no other living writer. His range in composition seems to be limited, and he seems to draw inspiration only from the scenes which first engaged his pen; when he ventures across the Rocky Mountains into regions of conventional life, his wings fail him and he falls to the level of commonplace. In proof of this it is only necessary to cite the fact that since his removal to the Atlantic coast he has written but little, and that little far inferior in quality to his Pacific productions. The volume entitled *The Luck of Roaring Camp* contains his best work in prose; his verses have been published in a volume called *Poems*.

JOHN CHINAMAN.

THE expression of the Chinese face in the aggregate is neither cheerful nor happy. In an acquaintance of half a dozen years, I can only recall one or two exceptions to this rule. There is an abiding consciousness of degradation, — a secret pain or self-humiliation visible in the lines of the mouth and eye. Whether it is only a modification of Turkish gravity, or whether it is the dread Valley of the Shadow of the Drug through which they are continually straying, I cannot say. They seldom smile, and their laughter is of such an extraordinary and sardonic nature — so purely a mechanical spasm, quite independent of any mirthful attribute — that to this day I am doubtful whether I ever saw a Chinaman laugh.

I have often been struck with the delicate pliability of the Chinese expression and taste, that might suggest a broader and deeper criti-

cism than is becoming these pages. A Chinaman will adopt the
American costume, and wear it with a taste of color and detail that
will surpass those(" native, and to the manner born.") To look at a
Chinese slipper, one might imagine it impossible to shape the original
foot to anything less cumbrous and roomy, yet a neater-fitting boot
than that belonging to the Americanized Chinaman is rarely seen on this
side of the Continent.   When the loose sack or paletot takes the place
of his brocade blouse, it is worn with a refinement and grace that
might bring a jealous pang to the exquisite of our more refined civilization.   Pantaloons fall easily and naturally over legs that have known
unlimited freedom and bagginess, and even garrote collars meet correctly around sun-tanned throats.   The new expression seldom overflows in gaudy cravats.   I will back my Americanized Chinaman
against any neophyte of European birth in the choice of that article.
While in our own State, the Greaser resists one by one the garments
of the Northern invader, and even wears the livery of his conqueror
with a wild and buttonless freedom, the Chinaman, abused and degraded as he is, changes by correctly graded transition to the garments of Christian civilization.   There is but one article of European
wear that he avoids.   These Bohemian eyes have never yet been
pained by the spectacle of a tall hat on the head of an intelligent
Chinaman.

My acquaintance with John has been made up of weekly interviews, involving the adjustment of the washing accounts, so that I
have not been able to study his character from a social view-point or
observe him in the privacy of the domestic circle.   I have gathered
enough to justify me in believing him to be generally honest, faithful,
simple, and painstaking.   Of his simplicity let me record an instance
where a sad and civil young Chinaman brought me certain shirts with
most of the buttons missing and others hanging on delusively by a
single thread.   In a moment of unguarded irony I informed him that
unity would at least have been preserved if the buttons were removed
altogether.   He smiled sadly and went away.   I thought I had hurt
his feelings, until the next week when he brought me my shirts with
a look of intelligence, and the buttons carefully and totally erased.
At another time, to guard against his general disposition to carry off
anything as soiled clothes that he thought could hold water, I requested him to always wait until he saw me.   Coming home late one
evening, I found the household in great consternation, over an im-

movable Celestial who had remained seated on the front door-step during the day, sad and submissive, firm but also patient, and only betraying any animation or token of his mission when he saw me coming. This same Chinaman evinced some evidences of regard for a little girl in the family, who in her turn reposed such faith in his intellectual qualities as to present him with a preternaturally uninteresting Sunday-school book, her own property. This book John made a point of carrying ostentatiously with him in his weekly visits. It appeared usually on the top of the clean clothes, and was sometimes painfully clasped outside of the big bundle of soiled linen. Whether John believed he unconsciously imbibed some spiritual life through its pasteboard cover, as the Prince in the Arabian Nights imbibed the medicine through the handle of the mallet, or whether he wished to exhibit a due sense of gratitude, or whether he had n't any pockets, I have never been able to ascertain. In his turn he would sometimes cut marvelous imitation roses from carrots for his little friend. I am inclined to think that the few roses strewn in John's path were such scentless imitations. The thorns only were real. From the persecutions of the young and old of a certain class, his life was a torment. I don't know what was the exact philosophy that Confucius taught, but it is to be hoped that poor John in his persecution is still able to detect the conscious hate and fear with which inferiority always regards the possibility of even-handed justice, and which is the keynote to the vulgar clamor about servile and degraded races.

BOONDER.

I NEVER knew how the subject of this memoir came to attach himself so closely to the affections of my family. He was not a prepossessing dog. He was not a dog of even average birth and breeding. His pedigree was involved in the deepest obscurity. He may have had brothers and sisters, but in the whole range of my canine acquaintance (a pretty extensive one), I never detected any of Boonder's peculiarities in any other of his species. His body was long, and his forelegs and hind legs were very wide apart, as though Nature originally intended to put an extra pair between them, but had unwisely allowed herself to be persuaded out of it. This peculiarity was annoying on cold nights, as it always prolonged the interval of keeping the door open for Boonder's ingress long enough to allow two or three dogs of a reasonable length to enter. Boonder's feet were decided; his toes turned out considerably, and in repose his favorite attitude was the first position of dancing. Add to a pair of bright eyes ears that seemed to belong to some other dog, and a symmetrically pointed nose that fitted all apertures like a pass-key, and you have Boonder as we knew him.

I am inclined to think that his popularity was mainly owing to his quiet impudence. His advent in the family was that of an old member, who had been absent for a short time, but had returned to familiar haunts and associations. In a Pythagorean point of view this might have been the case, but I cannot recall any deceased member of the family who was in life partial to bone-burying (though it might be *post mortem* a consistent amusement), and this was Boonder's great weakness. He was at first discovered coiled up on a rug in an upper chamber, and was the least disconcerted of the entire household. From that moment Boonder became one of its recognized members, and privileges, often denied the most intelligent and valuable of his species, were quietly taken by him and submitted to by us. Thus, if he were found coiled up in a clothes-basket, or any article of clothing assumed locomotion on its own account, we only said, "O, it's Boonder," with a feeling of relief that it was nothing worse.

I have spoken of his fondness for bone-burying. It could not be called an economical faculty, for he invariably forgot the locality of his treasure, and covered the garden with purposeless holes; but although the violets and daisies were not improved by Boonder's gardening, no one ever thought of punishing him. He became a synonym for fate; a Boonder to be grumbled at, to be accepted philosophically, — but never to be averted. But although he was not an intelligent dog, nor an ornamental dog, he possessed some gentlemanly instincts. When he performed his only feat, — begging upon his hind legs (and looking remarkably like a penguin), — ignorant strangers would offer him crackers or cake, which he did n't like, as a reward of merit. Boonder always made a great show of accepting the proffered dainties, and even made hypocritical contortions as if swallowing, but always deposited the morsel when he was unobserved in the first convenient receptacle, — usually the visitor's overshoes.

In matters that did not involve courtesy, Boonder was sincere in his likes and dislikes. He was instinctively opposed to the railroad.

When the track was laid through our street, Boonder maintained a defiant attitude toward every rail as it went down, and resisted the cars shortly after to the fullest extent of his lungs. I have a vivid recollection of seeing him, on the day of the trial trip, come down the street in front of the car, barking himself out of all shape, and thrown back several feet by the recoil of each bark. But Boonder was not the only one who has resisted innovations, or has lived to see the innovation prosper and even crush — But I am anticipating. Boonder had previously resisted the gas, but although he spent one whole day in angry altercation with the workmen, — leaving his bones unburied and bleaching in the sun, — somehow the gas went in. The Spring Valley water was likewise unsuccessfully opposed, and the grading of an adjoining lot was for a long time a personal matter between Boonder and the contractor.

These peculiarities seemed to evince some decided character and embody some idea. A prolonged debate in the family upon this topic resulted in an addition to his name, — we called him "Boonder the Conservative," with a faint acknowledgment of his fateful power. But, although Boonder had his own way, his path was not entirely of roses. Thorns sometimes pricked his sensibilities. When certain minor chords were struck on the piano, Boonder was always painfully affected and howled a remonstrance. If he were removed for company's sake to the back yard, at the recurrence of the provocation, he would go his whole length (which was something) to improvise a howl that should reach the performer. But we got accustomed to Boonder, and as we were fond of music the playing went on.

One morning Boonder left the house in good spirits with his regular bone in his mouth, and apparently the usual intention of burying it. The next day he was picked up lifeless on the track, — run over, apparently, by the first car that went out of the depot.

THE AGED STRANGER.

"I was with Grant — " the stranger said;
    Said the farmer, "Say no more,
But rest thee here at my cottage porch,
    For thy feet are weary and sore."

"I was with Grant — " the stranger said;
    Said the farmer, "Nay, no more, —

I prithee sit at my frugal board,
    And eat of my humble store.

"How fares my boy, — my soldier boy,
    Of the old Ninth Army Corps?
I warrant he bore him gallantly
    In the smoke and the battle's roar!"

"I know him not," said the aged man,
    "And, as I remarked before,
I was with Grant — " "Nay, nay, I know,"
    Said the farmer, "say no more;

"He fell in battle, — I see, alas!
    Thou 'dst smooth these tidings o'er, —
Nay: speak the truth, whatever it be,
    Though it rend my bosom's core.

"How fell he, — with his face to the foe,
    Upholding the flag he bore?
O, say not that my boy disgraced
    The uniform that he wore!"

"I cannot tell," said the aged man,
    "And should have remarked, before,
That I was with Grant, — in Illinois, —
    Some three years before the war."

Then the farmer spake him never a word,
    But beat with his fist full sore
That aged man, who had worked for Grant
    Some three years before the war.

VOCABULARY.

A-boon' (*Scotch*), above.

Ab-o-rig'i-nals, the first inhabitants of a country. (Usually written *Aborigines*.)

A-brad'ing, rubbing or wearing off.

A-ca'ci-a, a tree growing chiefly in tropical countries.

Ac-ces'so-ry, aiding; additional; an accompaniment.

A-crid'i-ty, sharpness and bitterness to the taste.

Ad-a-man'tine (*-in*), hard like adamant; incapable of being broken.

Ad'e-quate-ly, in an equal degree; sufficiently.

Ad-hĕr'ents, followers; partisans.

Ad-o-les'cence, the period of growth; youth.

A-dop'tion, receiving as one's own; acceptance.

A'er-o-naut, a navigator of the air; a balloonist.

Æs-thet'ic, pertaining to, or cultivating, the taste.

Af'fa-ble, easy in conversation; courteous.

Ag-gre-ga'tion, a collection into one sum or mass.

A-glee' (page 392), aglow; active.

Airts (*Scotch*), winds.

A-lac'ri-ty, cheerful readiness; sprightliness.

Al-le-gor'i-cal, having the nature of an allegory; figurative.

Al'le-go-ry, a fable or parable; a description of anything under the image of something else which resembles it.

Al'ma Ma'ter (*Latin*), fostering mother; the college or seminary where one is educated.

Al-ter-ca'tion, dispute in words; angry debate.

Al-ter-na'tion, following one after the other by turns.

Am-big'u-ous, having a doubtful or double meaning.

Am-bus-cade', a lying concealed in wait to attack an enemy.

A-me-li-o-ra'tion, the act of making better; improvement.

A-men'i-ty, pleasantness; civility.

Am-phi-the'a-ter, an oval or circular theater.

A-nath'e-ma, a curse pronounced with solemnity and authority.

And'i-rons, utensils for supporting wood in a fireplace.

An'gli-cism, a form of expression peculiar to the English language.

An'nals, a history of events year by year.

A-nom'a-ly, an irregularity; a deviation from law or rule.

An'ser-ine, relating to or resembling a goose.

An-tag'o-nist, an opponent; an adversary.

An-te-di-lu'vi-an, existing before the flood.

An'them, a sacred song.

An-thro-poph'a-gi, cannibals.

An'ti-dote, that which counteracts the effects of any drug.

An'tres (*Latin*), caves.

A-o'ni-an, relating to Aonia, a country of Greece, sacred to the Muses.

Ap-pa-rā'tus, instruments or utensils provided for the performance of any work.

Ap-pa-ri'tion, a supernatural appearance; a ghost.

Ap-prox-i-ma'tion, near approach.

A-quat'ic, relating to the water.

Aq'ui-line (*-lin* or *-lin*), resembling an eagle; like an eagle's beak.

Ar-ca'di-a, a country in Greece, noted for the simple, peaceful life of its inhabitants.

Ar'gus, a fabled being of antiquity, said to have had a hundred eyes.

Ar-is-toc'ra-cy, government by the nobles; the nobility.

Ar-te'si-an, relating to Artois, in France; a term applied to wells formed by boring into the earth.

As-cen'den-cy, controlling influence; power.

As-cet'ic, one who too rigorously applies himself to religious practices.

As-sim-i-la'tion, the act of bringing to a likeness.

As-size', an inquest; a measure or adjustment.

As-trol'o-ger, one who professes to foretell future events by observing the stars.

As'ymp-tote, a line which constantly approaches a curve, but which can never meet it.

At-trib'ute, to assign or impute to.

Au-ro'ra, the dawn, or a light in the heavens resembling it.

Au'spi-cate, to foreshow.

Au-to-bi-og'ra-phy, an account of one's own life.

Av'a-lanche, a mass of snow and ice, sliding down a mountain.

Av-a-tar', the descent of a Hindoo deity.

A-zo'ic, before the existence of animal life.

Bar'y-tone, a deep male voice, but higher than the bass.

Ba-salt', a greenish-black stone.

Bass-re-lief', carved work in which the figures stand partly from the surface.

Bat'tle-ment, the upper part of the wall of a fortification, notched or indented.

Bay'ou, an inlet of the sea, connected with rivers or lakes.

Be-a-tif'ic, producing bliss.

Bel-lig'er-ent, waging war.

Ben-e-dic'tion, act of pronouncing a blessing.

Be-nef'i-cent, doing good.

Be-nig'ni-ty, kindness of disposition; goodwill.

Bib'li-cal, relating to the Bible.

Bi-og'ra-phy, a history of any person's life.

Bi-ol'o-gy, the science of life.

Bi'peds, animals having two legs.

Bir'kie (*Scotch*), a clever fellow.

Biv'ou-ac (*biv'wak*), night rest of soldiers in the open air.

Boon, anything granted as a benefit or favor.

Bo-re-a'lis, relating to the north; northern.

Bowl'der, a large mass of stone worn smooth by the action of water.

Brake, a place overgrown with shrubs; a thicket.

Bri-a're-us, a fabled giant having a hundred hands.

Bro-cade', silk stuff, wrought or woven with ornaments.

Burgh'er, one who belongs to a burgh, or corporate town; a citizen.

Bur'go-mas-ter, a Dutch magistrate.

Cal'a-bash, a vessel made from a gourd.

Cal-cine', to reduce to powder by heat.

Cal'en-dar, a register of the year; an almanac.

Ca-lor'ic, heat.

Ca'lyx, a flower-cup.

Cam-paign'er, a soldier in active service.

Can'on-ize, to declare a saint.

Can'on, a law; catalogue of the saints.

Can'o-py, a covering over the head; an awning or tent.

Can'to, a division of a poem.

Can'yon, a gorge; a ravine; a gulch.

Ca-par'i-son, trappings for a horse.

Car-a-van', a company of travelers in the East.

Car-bon-if'er-ous, containing carbon, or coal.

Car'nage, slaughter; bloodshed.

Car'ni-val, a festival celebrated just before Lent.

Car-niv'o-rous, subsisting on flesh; flesh-eating.

Casque, a helmet.

Cas-sa'va, the plant from which tapioca is obtained; manioc.

Ca-tas'tro-phe, the termination of an event; a disaster.

Cat'e-go-ry, a class of things.

Ca-the'dral, the principal church in a diocese.

Ce-leb'ri-ty, fame; distinction.

Ce-les'tial, heavenly.

Cel'i-ba-cy, unmarried state; single life.

Cen'ser, a vessel for burning perfumes.

Cen'sure, blame; reproof; judgment.

Cha'os, a confused mass; disorder.

Cha-ot'ic, in a state of chaos; disorganized.

Chi-ca'ner-y, trickery; deception.

Chi-mer'i-cal, fanciful; unreal.

Chiv'al-rous, gallant; valiant; brave.

Chiv'al-ry, knighthood; gallantry.

Ci-ce-ro'ne (*chē-che-ro'ne*), one who shows strangers the curiosities of a place.

Cim-me'ri-an, very black or dark.

Cir-cum-spec'tion, caution; prudent watchfulness.

Civ'ic, civil; not military; municipal.

Clam'or-ous, noisy.

Clan-des'tine (*-in*), secret; underhand.

Clang'or, a loud and shrill sound.

Cli'max, gradual rise; highest point.

Clois'ter, a convent; a nunnery.

Co-a-lesce', to unite; to blend into one.

Cock'et, a custom-house certificate.

Co-e'val, of the same age.

Cog'i-tate, to think; to meditate.

Coil, a series of rings of rope, etc; noise; tumult.

Col-lo'qui-al, conversational.

Col'lo-quy, a conversation.

Co-los'sal, like the Colossus; gigantic.

Co-los'si, plural of *Colossus*; giants.

Com-mem-o-ra'tion, keeping in memory by formal celebration.

Com-pat'i-ble, suitable to; consistent with.

Con-cen'ter, to concentrate; to bring into one point.

Con'crete, firm; solid; not abstract.

Con-ge'ni-al, of the same nature, or disposition.

Con-ju-ra'tion, sorcery; incantation.

Con-san-guin'i-ty, relationship by blood or birth.

Con-serv'a-tive, opposed to change.

Con-serv'a-to-ry, a place for preserving things; a greenhouse.

Con-stit'u-ent, composing; component.

Con'sum-mate, to complete; to perfect.

Con-tem'po-ra-ry, living at the same time.

Con-text'ure, framework; structure.

Con-ti-gu'i-ty, contact; state of being adjacent.

Con'tu-me-ly, scornful treatment; disdain.

Con-vent'u-al, relating to a convent; monastic.

Con-vol'vu-lus, a vine; bindweed.

Coot Scotch, a blockhead; a simpleton.

Cor-du-roy', a thick cotton stuff, having a ribbed surface.

Cor-rel'a-tive, having mutual relations; reciprocal.

Couch'ant, lying down.

Cra'ven, a coward.

Cre-du'li-ty, readiness to believe without proof.

Croupe or Croup, the part of a horse's back behind the saddle.

Cu'li-na-ry, pertaining to cooking.

Cu'po-la, a dome; an arched roof.

Cur-ric'u-lum, course of studies.

Cy'cle, a circle of time; a round of years; a period.

Cy-clo-pe'an, pertaining to the Cyclops, a fabled giant; huge.

Cy-clo-pæ'di-a, a book in which the various sciences are treated.

Cym'bals, a musical instrument.

De-bris (da-bre') rubbish; remains; ruins.

De-cid'u-ous, falling off; not evergreen (of trees).

De-ci'pher, to unravel; to explain.

De-co'rum, propriety of behavior; decency.

De-crep'it, weak from old age.

De-duct'ive-ly, by deduction, or inference.

Def-er-en'tial, respectful.

De-flect', to turn or bend aside.

De-funct', dead; deceased.

De'i-fied, made or declared a god.

De-mure'ly, soberly; modestly.

De-nom'i-nate, to name; to entitle.

Des'cant, a song; the variation of an air or melody.

Des'e-crate, to abuse what is sacred; to profane.

Des'pot, one who rules with absolute power; a tyrant.

Des'ul-to-ry, unconnected; fitful; wandering.

De-vo'ni-an, pertaining to certain geological strata abounding in Devonshire, England.

Di'a-dem, a crown.

Di'a-lect, a form of language peculiar to a place or district.

Dic'tion, style of language, or expression.

Dight (lite), dressed; adorned.

Di-gres'sion, departure from the main subject.

Dike, a ditch; a mound to prevent the overflow of water.

Dil-et-tan'ti, lovers of the fine arts.

Di-min'u-tive, of small size; little.

Di-plo'ma-cy, the art of negotiating treaties.

Dip-lo-mat'ic, pertaining to diplomacy.

Dis-com'fit-ed, defeated.

Dis-con-cert'ed, frustrated; confused.

Dis-en-cum'ber, to disburden; to set free.

Dis'lo-cate, to displace; to disjoint.

Dis-par'age, to undervalue; to depreciate.

Dis-qui-si'tion, a discourse; a treatise.

Dis-sem'ble, to conceal; to feign.

Dis-ser-ta'tion, a discourse; a treatise.

Dis-sev'er, to disjoin; to separate.

Dis-so-lu'tion, decomposition; death.

Dis-tend'ed, expanded; enlarged.

Dith-y-ram'bics, poems of a wild, enthusiastic character; (anciently) songs to Bacchus.

Dit'ty, a song.

Dog'ma-tism, positiveness of assertion.

Du'bi-ous-ly, doubtfully; with uncertainty.

Dul'ci-mer, a kind of musical instrument.

Dy'nas-ty, a succession of sovereigns of the same race.

Ec-cen-tric'i-ties, peculiarities; oddities.

Ec'logue, a pastoral poem, i. e. relating to shepherds, or the country.

E-con'o-mist, one who studies or practices economy.

Ef-flu'vi-a (plural of effluvium), noxious or noisome exhalations.

Ef-ful'gence, splendor; brightness.

E'go-tism, conceit; vanity.

E-jac-u-la'tion, exclamation.

E-lab'o-rate, to improve or perfect by labor.

E-le'gi-ac or El-e-gi'ac, pertaining to an elegy, or funereal song; plaintive.

Elves (plural of elf), fairies.

Em-a-na'tion, a flowing out; an efflux.

Em-bla'zoned, decked with showy ornaments.

E'mir (Arabic), a governor, prince, or military commander.

E-mol'u-ment, gain; pecuniary profit.

Em-pir'i-cism, dependence on experiment; quackery.

En-am'ored, charmed; inflamed with love.

En-cyc'li-cal, circular.

En-dow'ment, a natural gift.

E-ner'vat-ed, deprived of strength; weakened.

En-fran'chised, set free; admitted as a freeman.

E-nor'mous, huge; prodigious; very wicked.

En rap-port' (*French*), in relation; related.

E-nu-mer-a'tion, numbering; summing up.

E-nun-ci-a'tion, utterance; declaration.

E'on, the time a person or thing exists; a period of time; an age.

E-phem'e-ral, lasting for a day; of short duration.

Ep'i-gram, a short, witty poem.

Ep'i-sode, a digression.

Ep-i-sod'i-cal, pertaining to an episode.

Ep'i-thet, a name; a title; a qualifying term.

E-qui-lib'ri-um, even balance; equality of weight.

E-qui-noc'tial, a great circle in the heavens in the plane of the equator.

E-quipped', furnished; arrayed.

E'ra, a fixed point or period of time; an epoch.

E-rad'i-cate, to root out; to destroy.

E-ru-di'tion, knowledge obtained from books; learning.

Es-chew'ing, avoiding; shunning.

Es'pla-nade, a clear space used for rides or walks.

Es-tranged', made unfriendly; alienated.

Es'tu-a-ry, a river or arm of the sea in which the tide rises.

Eu-lo'gi-um, formal praise.

Eu'pho-ny, agreeable sound.

E-van'ish-ing, fleeting; evanescent.

E-vap-o-ra'tion, passing away in vapor; changing to vapor.

Ev-o-lu'tion, act of unfolding.

Ex'ca-vate, to hollow out.

Ex-cheq'ner, treasury.

Ex-ha-la'tion, effluvium; vapor; steam.

Ex-hil'a-rāt-ing, enlivening; cheering.

Ex'i-gen-cy, demand; pressing need.

Ex-pa'tri-ate, to banish; to expel from one's country.

Ex'pe-dite, to hasten.

Ex'pi-ate, to atone for; to make satisfaction.

Ex-punge', to blot out.

Ex'tant, existing.

Ex-u'ber-ance, great abundance; overflowing plenty.

Ex-u-da'tion, sweating; oozing out.

Fa (*Scotch*), fall; lot.

Fa-cil'i-tate, to make easy; to remove difficulties.

Fan-tas'tic, fanciful; whimsical.

Far'del, a bundle; a pack or load for the back.

Fas-ci-na'tion, charming; enchantment.

Fas-tid'i-ous, over-nice; hard to please.

Faun (*Myth.*), a god of fields and shepherds.

Fe-cun'di-ty, fruitfulness; fertility.

Fes-toon', a garland or wreath hanging in a curve.

Feu'dal, pertaining to a feud, that is, a right to lands on condition of service to a superior.

Film'y, composed of a thin skin or web; like a cobweb.

Fin'i-cal, over-nice; affectedly exact.

Fir'ma-ment, the sky; the canopy of the heavens.

Flu'ent-ly, in a flowing, easy manner.

Fo-ren'sic, relating to courts of justice, or legal proceedings.

Fos'sil, a substance dug from the earth.

Fran'kin-cense, an odorous resin.

Fri'ar, a brother or member of any religious order.

Gal'ax-y, the milky-way.

Gal'li-ard, a brisk, gay man.

Gal'van-ism, electricity produced by chemical action.

Gar'ni-ture, furniture; adornment.

Gar-rote', an iron collar used in executions; a collar of the same form.

Gen-e-al'o-gy, list of ancestors; pedigree.

Ges-tic-u-la'tion, act of making gestures; action accompanying speech.

Gey'sers, boiling springs in Iceland.

Ghoul, an imaginary being supposed to prey upon human bodies.

Glade, an open space in a forest.

Glint'ed, glanced; peeped forth.

Glu'ti-nous, sticky; adhesive.

Gos'sa-mer, a fine, filmy substance floating in the air.

Gowd (*Scotch*), gold.

Gra-da'tion, regular progress, step by step.

Graph'ic, vivid; lively; well drawn.

Grat-u-la'tion, expressing joy at another's happiness or good fortune.

Gree (*obs.*), good-will; rank; *to bear the gree*, to be victor.

Gro-tesque', odd; fanciful.

Guid (*Scotch*), good.

Gut'tu-ral, relating to the throat; made by the throat.

Gym-nas'tic, relating to bodily exercise; athletic.

Hack'neyed, worn out by frequent use.

Ha'lo, a circle of light.

Hame'ly (*Scotch*), homely.

Har'bin-ger, a forerunner.

Harp'si-chord, a musical instrument.

He-red'i-ta-ry, descending by inheritance.

Her-met'i-cal-ly, perfectly close; by chemical process.

Hes-per'i-des (*Myth.*), daughters of Atlas, who owned the orchards in Africa, in which golden fruit grew.

Het'er-o-dox, contrary to an acknowledged standard of religious doctrine.

Hi-e-rar'chy, sacred government; the priest-hood.

Hi-e-ro-glyph'ics, sacred picture-writing of the ancient Egyptians.

Hind, a peasant; a servant.

Hod'den (Scotch), humble.

Hu'mid, moist; wet.

Hus'band-ry, economy; farming.

Hy-po-thet'i-cal, based on a supposition, or hypothesis.

I'dlesse, idleness; sloth.

I-de'al, imaginary; unreal.

Ig'ne-ous, pertaining to fire; fiery.

Il-lim'it-a-ble, unbounded; boundless.

Il-lit'er-ate, unlearned; uneducated.

Im'age-ry, figures of speech; figurative language.

Im-mu-ta-bil'i-ty, unchangeableness; stability.

Im-pal'pa-ble, not perceptible to the touch.

Im-pe-rā'tor (Latin), commander-in-chief.

Im-plic'it, implied; undoubting; firm.

In-car'na-dine, to dye red, like blood or flesh.

In-ces'sant-ly, unceasingly; without stopping.

In-com'pa-ra-ble, matchless; unequaled.

In-con'gru-ous, inconsistent; absurd.

In-cor'po-rate, to unite into one body; to form into a body politic.

In-cre-du'li-ty, readiness to believe without sufficient proof.

In-crus-ta'tion, formation of a crust on the surface.

In-cum'ben-cy, state of lying or resting on something; the holding of an office.

In-dec'o-rous, unbecoming; indecent.

In-def'i-nite, indistinct; vague.

In-del'i-bly, so as not to be erased; ineffaceably.

In-dict'ment, formal charge, or accusation.

In-dis'so-lu-ble, not to be dissolved; enduring.

In-dom'it-a-ble, not to be subdued; unconquerable.

In-du'bi-ta-bly, without doubt; unquestionably.

In-duc'tive-ly, by inference; by the inductive method of reasoning.

In-ef-fect'u-al, without producing the proper effect; fruitless.

In-es'ti-ma-ble, priceless; invaluable.

In-ev'i-ta-ble, unavoidable.

In-ex'or-a-bly, firmly; so as not to be moved by entreaty.

In-fi-del'i-ty, unfaithfulness; unbelief; scepticism.

In-flam'ma-ble, easily set on fire.

In-gen'u-ous, open; frank; candid.

In-i'ti-ate, to introduce; to begin.

In-no-va'tion, change; introduction of a novelty.

In-sig'ni-a, badges of office; marks of distinction.

In-sip'id, tasteless.

In'su-læ (Latin), islands; separate houses, i. e. houses standing alone.

In-ten'tive-ly (obs.), closely; attentively.

In-ter-mit'tent, ceasing for a time, or at intervals.

In-tim'i-date, to make afraid; to affright.

In-tract'a-ble, unmanageable; obstinate.

In-trin'sic, internal; real; genuine.

In-tu-i'tion, immediate perception by the intellect; intuitive knowledge.

In-tu'i-tive, perceived without reasoning.

In'un-date, to overflow.

In-ured', accustomed.

In-vec'tive, censure; reproach; abuse.

In-vet'er-a-cy, state of being old; chronic state.

In-vul'ner-a-ble, not to be wounded; secure from injury.

I'ro-ny, saying one thing and meaning another, in mockery.

Ir-ra'di-ate, to enlighten; to illume.

Ir-re-me'di-a-ble, incurable; without remedy.

Ir-rep'a-ra-ble, not to be repaired; irretrievable.

Ir-i-des'cent, having the color of the rainbow.

I'ris, the rainbow.

Is-o-la'tion, detachment; separation from all others.

I-tin'er-ant, wandering; traveling; going from place to place.

Jas'mine, a climbing plant which bears very fragrant flowers.

Joc'u-lar, sportive; witty; facetious.

Joc'und, joyous; blithesome; gay.

Ju-ris-pru'dence, science of law.

Ju'rist, one versed in law; a lawyer.

Lab'y-rinth, an edifice full of winding passages; a maze.

La-con'ic, brief; in the manner of the ancient Spartans.

La-goon', a large shallow lake, having an opening into the sea.

Lam'bent, playing on the surface; touching lightly.

Land'gra-vine, the wife of a Landgrave, or German nobleman.

La'tent, concealed.

Leash, a thong of leather, by which a dog or other animal is held.

Leg'en-da-ry, fabulous; not authentic.

Le-vi'a-than, an immense animal; the whale.

Li-cen'tious, loose; dissolute; unrestrained.

Lim'pid, clear; transparent.

Lin'e-a-ments, outlines; features.

Lit'er-al-ly, according to the letter.

Lord'ling, a petty lord.

Lore, learning.

Lu'di-crous, laughable.

Lu'rid, ghastly pale; gloomy.

Mal-le-a-bil'i-ty, the quality by which a substance may be hammered out.

Ma-nip-u-la'tion, handling; working with the hand.

Manse, a house; a parsonage; a farm.

Man-u-mis'sion, setting free.

Mar'i-time, pertaining to the sea; marine.

Mart, a place of sale or traffic; a market.

Mar'tyr, one who, by his death, bears witness to the truth.

Mar'tyr-dom, the state or death of a martyr.

Masts, the fruit of a forest-tree; nuts; acorns.

Ma-ter'nal, relating to a mother; motherly.

Maun'na (*Scotch*), must not.

Mau-so-le'um, a large and splendid tomb or monument.

Med'i-ca-ment, anything used to heal or cure disease.

Me-di-oc'ri-ty, middle state or degree.

Me'ni-al, a servant; a domestic.

Mere, a pool or lake.

Met-a-mor'phose, to transform.

Met'a-phor, a figure of speech by which a thing is said to be what it resembles.

Me'ter, rhythmical arrangement; measure.

Mewl'ing, crying like a young child.

Mid'rib, the middle rib, as of a leaf.

Mil-len'ni-al, relating to the millennium, or period of a thousand years mentioned in the Scriptures.

Mi-nu'ti-æ, details; minute particulars.

Mi-rage', a deceptive vision seen in the air.

Mis'cre-ant, a vile wretch; an infidel.

Mit'i-gate, to soften.

Moc'ca-sin, an Indian's shoe.

Mod'i-cum, a small quantity.

Mod'u-late, to vary; to change, as the voice, from one key to another.

Mon'as-ter-y, a place of religious retirement; an abbey or convent.

Mo-men'tum, moving force.

Mon'o-dy, a mournful song, sung by one person.

Mon-op'o-lize, to have the exclusive right of sale; to take the whole.

Mon-op'o-ly, an exclusive right of sale.

Mo-not'o-nous, unvarying in sound; tedious.

Mon'y (*Scotch*), many.

Mo-sa'ic, inlaid work, formed by combining pieces of differently colored stones.

Mos'lem (*Arabic*), Mohammedan; a true believer.

Mosque, a Turkish or Mohammedan temple.

Mul'ti-form, having many forms.

Mun'dane, worldly; terrestrial.

Mu-nic'i-pal, pertaining to a corporation or city.

Mu-ta'tion, change.

Mu'ti-late, to maim; to deprive of a limb or other material part.

Mys'tic, obscure; unintelligible.

Myth, a fable.

Myth'i-cal, fabulous.

My-thol'o-gy, a history of the ancient fables and fabulous deities.

Nave, the middle or body of a church.

Ne'o-phyte, a new convert; a beginner; a novice.

Ne-pen'thes, a drug used by the ancients to relieve pain.

No-mad'ic, wandering; pastoral.

No-men-cla'ture, a list of names belonging to a particular service or art.

Nonce, present call or occasion.

Nymph, a goddess of the mountains, forests, meadows, or waters.

O-bei'sance, expression of respect; a bow; a courtesy.

Ob'e-lisk, a tall and slender stone pyramid.

Ob-liq'ui-ty, deviation from a right line.

Ob-lit'er-ate, to blot out.

Ob-liv'i-on, forgetfulness.

Ob'lo-quy, censure.

Ob-scen'i-ty, indecency; impurity.

Ob-se'qui-ous-ness, ready obedience; servility.

Ob'so-lete, disused; neglected.

Ob-tru'sive-ly, without invitation.

Of-fi'cious-ness, excessive zeal; undue forwardness.

Om'i-nous, threatening evil.

Om-nip'o-tent, all-powerful.

On'er-ous, burdensome.

Op'u-lent, rich; wealthy.

O-rac'u-lar, like an oracle; positive.

Os-ten-ta'tious, making a vain display.

Ox-y-hy'dro-gen, produced by the union of oxygen and hydrogen gas.

Pæ'an, a song of victory.

Pag'eant, a pompous show or spectacle.

Pal'e-tot (*pal'e-to*), a peasant's frock; a loose overcoat.

Pal'frey, a saddle-horse.

Pal-la'di-um, a safeguard.

Pal'pi-tate, to beat or throb like the heart.

Pan-o-ram'ic, presenting a complete view; like a panorama.

Pan-ta-loon', a character in a comedy; a buffoon.

Par-a-bol'ic, expressed by a parable; figurative.

Par'a-chute (-shoot), a machine for descending from a balloon.

Par'a-mount, superior to all others.

Pard, the leopard.

Par'ox-ysm, fit; sudden and acute attack; convulsion.

Par've-nu, an upstart; one who has become suddenly rich.

Pas'tor-al, relating to shepherds; rural.

Pa-thol'o-gy, the science which treats of diseases.

Pa'thos, feeling; passion; tender emotion.

Pa-tri'cian, a person of high birth; a nobleman.

Pat'ri-mo-ny, an estate inherited.

Peas'ant-ry, farmers; country people.

Pe-cu'ni-a-ry, relating to money.

Ped'a-gogue, a teacher of children.

Ped'ant, one who makes a vain display of his learning.

Ped'ant-ry, a vain display of learning.

Ped'i-gree, line of ancestors; descent or lineage.

Pelf, money; riches; lucre; gain.

Pe-na'tes (*Latin*), the household gods of the ancient Romans.

Per-ad-ven'ture, perhaps; perchance; possibly.

Per-am-bu-la'tion, walking about or around; tour.

Per'co-late, to ooze; to pass in drops; to filter.

Per-di'tion, ruin; destruction.

Per-en'ni-al, lasting; perpetual.

Per'fi-dy, faithlessness; treachery.

Per'fo-rate, to pierce; to bore.

Per-sim'mon, a small tree bearing a plum-like fruit.

Per-son-i-fi-ca'tion, a figure by which inanimate objects are represented as having life and intelligence.

Per-spic'u-ous, clear; easily understood.

Pet'ri-fy, to change into stone.

Phan-tas-ma-go'ri-a, optical illusions; magic lantern.

Phe-nom'e-na (plural of *phenomenon*), appearances.

Phil-an'thro-pist, a lover of mankind.

Phren-ol'o-gy, the science of determining character by observation of the head or skull.

Phys-i-og'no-my, discernment of character by the face; the face.

Pied (*pide*), variegated.

Pin'na-cle, the highest point; the summit.

Plen'i-tude, fullness; abundance.

Plu-ton'ic, pertaining to Pluto; igneous.

Pol-lu'tion, corruption; defilement.

Pol-y-syl'la-ble, a word of four or more syllables.

Pon'der-ous, heavy; weighty.

Pon'tiff, a high priest.

Por'phy-ry, a kind of rock or stone.

Port'ance, air; mien; demeanor.

Por'ti-co, a porch; a covered space at the entrance of a building.

Po-sa'da (*Spanish*), an inn or tavern.

Po'ten-cy, power; strength.

Po-ten-ti-al'i-ty, state of having power; possibility not reality.

Prac-ti'tion-er, one who practices an art or profession.

Pre-ca'ri-ous, doubtful; depending upon another's will.

Prec'e-dent, something used as an authoritative example.

Pre-con-cert', to consider and agree upon beforehand.

Pred-e-cess'or, one who precedes another in an office.

Pre-dom'i-nate, to prevail; to rule.

Pre-emp'tion, the right of purchasing before others.

Prej-u-di'cial, injurious; detrimental.

Pre-lim'i-na-ry, introductory.

Pre'ma-ture, ripe before the time; unseasonable.

Pre-mon'i-to-ry, warning beforehand; giving previous notice.

Pre-or-dain', to ordain or decree beforehand.

Pre-pos'ter-ous, inverted in order; absurd.

Pre-sen'ti-ment, a notion of what is about to occur.

Pre-ter-nat'u-ral, beyond what is natural; strange.

Pri-mo-gen'i-ture, state of being born first.

Pris'tine, original; primitive.

Prod'i-gal, wasteful.

Pro-gen'i-tor, a father; an ancestor.

Pro'ge-ny, offspring; children.

Pro-sa'ic, pertaining to prose; dull; uninteresting.

Pro'te-an, assuming different forms; like Proteus.

Pro-tu'ber-ant, projecting.

Pru-nel'la, a woolen stuff used for making shoes.

Psal'mo-dy, the singing of psalms or hymns.

Psy-cho-log'i-cal, relating to psychology, or the science of the soul.

Pur'blind, near-sighted; dim-sighted.

Pyg'my, one of a race of dwarfs; a dwarf.

Quaff, to drink in large draughts.

Quag'mire, soft, wet land.

Qua-ter'ni-on, a set of four things.

Qui-e'tus, rest; death; that which silences claims.

Ra'pi-er, a light sword.

Re-ca-pit-u-la'tion, a summary of the chief heads of a discourse.

Re-cip'i-ent, one who receives.

Re-frac'to-ry, obstinate; disobedient.

Re-it'er-ate, to repeat again and again.

Rel'e-van-cy, state of being applicable or pertinent.

Rem-i-nis'cence, remembrance; that which recalls to the mind.

Re-pug'nant, hostile; opposed.

Re-qui'tal, payment; recompense.

Res-ur-rec'tion, act of rising from the dead.

Ret'i-cence, keeping silence; abstinence from speech.

Re-trib'u-to-ry, affording reward; making repayment, or a just return.

Rev'e-nue, annual rents; income.

Re-ver'ber-ate, to resound; to echo.

Rhap'so-dize, to utter wild, rambling thoughts or sentences.

Rhet'or-ic, the art of composition, or oratory.

Rho-do-den'dron, a shrub bearing showy flowers.

Rhythm, measure; harmonious flow of language.

Ro'se-ate, full of roses; of a rose color.

Ro'ta-ry, turning like a wheel.

Roun'de-lay, a kind of song or dance.

Rub'ble, fragments of stone or rock.

Ru'nic, pertaining to the Runes, or inscriptions of the ancient Norsemen.

Rus-tic'i-ty, state of being rustic; coarseness.

Sa-line', containing salt.

Sa-li'va, spittle.

Sanc'tu-a-ry, a sacred place; a church or altar; a place of refuge.

San'guin-a-ry, bloody; blood-thirsty; eager to shed blood.

Sans *French*), without.

Sap'phire, a precious stone of a blue color.

Sarce'net, a kind of thin silk, used for linings, ribbons, etc.

Sar-don'ic, forced (said of a laugh that is assumed to conceal pain).

Sat'ire, a poem ridiculing vice or folly.

Sa'tyr, a deity of the woods, represented as half man and half goat.

Saul *Scotch*), soul.

Sa-vau'na, an extensive grassy plain.

School'men, men taught in the schools of the middle ages, who disputed on nice points of logic and theology.

Scym'e-tar or **Cim'e-ter,** a Turkish sword of a bent form.

Se-crete', to separate; to conceal.

Sec'u-lar, worldly; temporal; occurring once in an age.

Sed'i-ment, dregs; grounds; settlings.

Se-di'tion, opposition to the government; rebellion.

Seeth'ing, boiling.

Sen-ten'tious, full of meaning; expressive.

Sep'ul-cher, a tomb.

Serf, a slave attached to the soil; a bond-servant.

Ser'vile, slavish.

Sham'bles, the place where butcher's meat is sold.

Sheik, an Arabian chief.

Shin'gle, a collecton of stones worn smooth by the action of water, as found on coasts.

Si'en-ite or **Sy'en-ite,** stone composed of quartz, hornblende, and feldspar.

Si-er'ra (*Spanish*), a saw; a mountain chain.

Sign'ior (*seen'yur*), a title of respect among the Italians; Sir; Mr.

Sil'hou-ette (*sil'oo-et*), the outlines of an object, filled in with black.

Si-lo'ah or **Sil'o-a,** name of a pool or fountain in Jerusalem.

Si-lu'ri-an, relating to the Silures, a people of Wales; hence applied to the geological stratum found in that country.

Sim'i-le, a comparison.

Sim'mer, to boil gently.

Sim'per, to smile in an affected manner.

Sin'u-ous, bending in and out; winding.

So'journ, stay; temporary abode.

So-lil'o-quy, a talking to one's self.

Som'er-set, a leap heels over head.

So-no'rous, loud sounding; giving a clear sound.

Soph'is-try, false and deceitful reasoning.

Sor'tie, a sudden sally of troops from a fortress or entrenchment.

Spe'cious, apparently right; plausible.

Sta-tis'ti-cal, exactly stated and classified, especially in numbers.

Stat'u-a-ry, a sculptor.

Sten-to'ri-an, extremely loud.

Ste-ril'i-ty, barrenness; unfruitfulness.

Ster'to-rous, hoarsely breathing; snoring.

Sti'pend, salary; wages.

Stip'u-late, to bargain; to agree.

Stra'ta (plural of *stratum*), layers.

Strat'e-gy, science of military command; generalship.

Strat'i-fied, laid in strata, or layers.

Strin'gent, binding; strict; rigorous.

Stu-pen'dous, astonishing; wonderful.

Sub-ju-ga'tion, conquest; subjection.

Sub-mer'gence, putting under water; inundation.

Sub-or-di-na'tion, inferiority of rank or dignity; subjection.

Sub-ser'vi-ent, promoting a particular end; subordinate.

Sub-ter-ra'ne-an, under the surface of the earth.

Sub'til-ty, thinness; craft; artifice.

Su-per-flu'i-ty, a greater quantity than is needed; superabundance.

Su-per-in-cum'bent, lying or resting upon something else.

Sur-charge', to overload.

Syl'van, pertaining to woods or forests.

Sym'me-try, a due proportion of parts; beauty.

Sym'pho-ny, harmony of sounds; a musical composition for a full orchestra.

Syn'a-gogue, a congregation of Jews; a Jewish church.

Syn'o-nym, one of two or more words of a language which have the same meaning.

Syn'the-sis, composition; putting together.

Sy-rin'ga, a genus or family of plants.

Sys'tem-a-tize, to reduce to a system; to methodize.

Tal'is-man, something used or worn to avert or repel evil; a charm.

Tan'gi-ble, perceptible by the touch; substantial.

Tan'ta-lize, to tease or torment, by disappointing hope or expectation.

Tap'root, the main root of a plant.

Tat-too', a beating of the drum, as a military signal; marks made on the flesh by pricking in fluids of different colors.

Tech'ni-cal, pertaining to a particular art or profession.

Teens, the year of one's age having the termination *teen.*

Te-mer'i-ty, rashness; recklessness.

Ten'dril, shoot of a creeping plant, used for its support.

Te-o-cal'li, name of a Mexican temple; *literally,* house of God.

Ter-res'tri-al, pertaining to the earth; earthly.

Terse, concise; compact and elegant.

The-ol'o-gy, true doctrine relating to God; divinity.

The'o-rem, a truth or proposition to be demonstrated.

The'o-ry, a doctrine or scheme; a speculation.

Ther-mom'e-ter, an instrument for measuring the temperature of the air.

Throt'tle-valve, the valve used to regulate the supply of steam in a steam-engine.

Tin-tin-nab-u-la'tion, tinkling, as of bells.

Tis'sue, fabric; structure; composite substance.

Tit'u-lar, giving a name or title; relating to a title.

Tra-di'tion, oral report from one generation to another.

Tran-scend'ent, surpassing; unequaled.

Tran'sept, the part of a church that projects at right angles from the body.

Trans-i-to'ry, passing; fleeting; short-lived.

Trem'u-lous, trembling; quivering.

Trep-i-da'tion, a trembling from fear; alarm.

Tri-as'sic, pertaining to a geological stratum, called the *trias.*

Trib-u-ni'cian, pertaining to tribunes.

Tri'col-or, the French flag of three colors; any three-colored flag.

Tri'ton, a fabled sea deity of the ancient mythology.

Trit'u-rate, to reduce to powder by grinding or rubbing.

Trou'ba-dour, a minstrel of the South of France, during the Middle Ages.

Typ'i-cal, emblematic; figurative.

Ul'ti-mate, last; final.

Ul-tra-ma-rine', blue; a blue pigment.

U-lys-se'an, pertaining to Ulysses, a famous Greek hero and king.

Un-al-loyed', pure; genuine; unmixed.

Un-bi'ased, impartial; not influenced by either party.

Unc'tion, ointment; act of anointing; fervor.

U-nique' (-*neek*), single; unmatched.

Un-mit'i-ga-ted, not softened; unmodified.

Un-pre-med'i-tat-ed, unstudied; off-hand; extemporaneous.

U-ten'sil, anything used; an implement; a vessel.

U'til-ize, to apply to a useful purpose.

Vac-il-la'tion, act of wavering.

Val-e-tu-di-na'ri-an, an invalid; a person seeking to recover health.

Vas'sal, a dependant; a bondman; a tenant.

Vat'i-can, the palace of the Pope, at Rome.

Ve'he-ment, forcible; violent.

Ver'i-ta-ble, true; real; positive.

Ves'i-cle, a small bladder.

Vest'ure, a garment; clothing.

Vi'a-duct, a structure for carrying a railway across a valley or river.

Vi'a La'ta (*Latin*), a broad street.

Vi'ce Ver'sa (*Latin*), the terms being exchanged.

Vi-cis'si-tudes, regular changes or alternations.

Vir'u-lence, activity in doing injury; extreme malignity.

Vis'ta, a view through an avenue.

Vi-va'cious, lively; sprightly.

Vi-vac'i-ty, liveliness; animation.

Viv'i-fy, to animate; to make alive.

Vo-cab'u-la-ry, a list of words; a dictionary.

Vo-lu'mi-nous, of many volumes; bulky.

Was'sail-er, a reveler; a debauchee.

Wa'ter-Kel'pie, a water-spirit.

Weïrd, supernatural; caused by magical influence.

Wight, a person; a name applied to any one in irony or burlesque.

Wise-a'cre, one who pretends to wisdom; a witling.

Wist'ful, musing; longing.

Yeo'man, a farmer; a freeholder.

Yore, long since; in former time.

Ze'nith, the point directly overhead.

Zin'ga-rï (*Italian*), gypsies.

Zo'di-ac, the space extending eight degrees on each side of the ecliptic, which contains the orbits of the large primary planets.

A DICTIONARY

OF SOME OF

THE MOST FAMILIAR OF BRITISH AND AMERICAN AUTHORS.

In noting the nationalities in this Dictionary it has been found that some authors have lived and labored in more countries than one; that the birthplaces of some have not been the scenes of their literary successes; and that in a number of cases the places of birth are nowhere stated. In like manner, in the matter of dates, in some cases, especially in the earlier periods, uncertainty has been found among the best authorities; and in not a few, conflicts of opinion appear. In all such cases — both matters of nationalities and dates — the weight of authority has been carefully weighed and the best attainable results given.

The following abbreviations have been used, together with a few others apparently too obvious to need pointing out, — the adjectives indicating departments of literary work : —

A. ....American.	Ess. ....Essay.	Philos. ......Philosophical.
Antiq. ....Antiquarian.	E th. ....Esthetical.	Poet. ....Poetical.
Biog. ....Biographical.	E h. ....Ethical.	Pol. ....Political.
Crit. ....Critical.	Fic. ....Fictitious.	Rel. ....Religious.
Dip. ....Diplomatic.	I. ....Irish.	S. ....Scotch.
Domes. ......Domestic.	Lit. ....Literature, Literary.	Sat. ....Satirical.
Dram. ....Dramatic.	Med. ....Medical.	Sci. ....Scientific.
E. ....English.	Meta. ......Metaphysical.	Theol. ....Theological.
Econ. ....Economy.	Mis. ....Miscellaneous.	Trav. ....Travels.
Ed. ....Educational.	Philol. .....Philological.	W. ....Welsh.
Edit. ....Editorial.		

Abbott, Jacob. *A.* 1803 –   . Rel. and Fic.

Abbott, John S. C. *A.* 1805 –   . Biog., Hist., and Fic.

Abercrombie, John. *S.* 1726 - 1806. Horticult.

Abercrombie, John. *S.* 1781 – 1844. Med. and Meta.

Adams, Chas. F. *A.* 1807 –   . Pol.

Adams, Hannah. *A.* 1755 – 1832. Rel.

Adams, John. *A.* 1735 – 1836. Pol.

Adams, John Q. *A.* 1767 – 1848. Pol., Rel., and Poet.

Adams, Nehemiah. *A.* 1806 –   . Rel., Biog., and Fic.

Adams, Wm. T. (*Oliver Optic*). *A.* 1822 –   . Fic. and Trav.

Addison, Jos. *E.* 1672 – 1719. Ess., Poet., and Dram.

Agassiz, Louis J. R. *A.* 1807 – 1874. Sci. and Trav.

Aguilar, Grace. *E.* 1816 – 1847. Fic.

Ainsworth, Wm. H. *E.* 1805 –   . Fic.

Akenside, Mark. *E.* 1721 – 1770. Poet.

Alcott, Louisa M. *A.* 1832 –   . Fic.

Alden, Jos. *A.* 1807 –   . Eth.

Aldrich, Thos. B. *A.* 1836 –   . Poet. and Fic.

Alexander, A. *A.* 1772 - 1851. Rel. and Hist.

Alexander, Jos. A. *A.* 1809 - 1860. Rel.

Alford, Henry. 1810 – 1871. Theol. and Poet.

Alger, Wm. R. *A.* 1823 –   . Theol. and Mis.

Alison, A. *S.* 1757 – 1839. Esth., Rel., and Biog.

Alison, Sir A. *S.* 1792 - 1867. Hist., Law, and Pol.

Allibone, S. A. *A.* 1816 –   . Biog.

Allston, W. *A.* 1779 - 1843. Art.

Alsop, R. *A.* 1761 - 1815. Poet.

Ames, Fisher. *A.* 1758 - 1808. Pol.

Andrews, Prof. E. A. *A.* 1787 – 1858. Ed.

Angell, Jos. K. *A.* 1794 - 1857. Law.

Anthon, Chas. *A.* 1797 – 1867. Ed.

Arbuthnot, John. *E.* 1675 – 1734. Phys. and Sat.

Arnold, Matthew. *E.* 1822 –   . Poet. and Ess.

Arnold, Thos. *E.* 1795 – 1842. Hist. and Rel.

Arnold, Thos. K. *E.* 1800 - 1853. Ed.

Arthur, T. S. *A.* 1809 –   . Fic.

Ascham, Roger. *E.* 1515 - 1569. Ed.

Audubon, John J. *A.* 1782 – 1851. Sci.

Austen, Jane. *E.* 1775 – 1817. Fic.

Aytoun, Wm. E. *S.* 1813 – 1865. Poet., Dram., and Biog.

Babbage, Chas. *E.* 1790 – . Sci.

Bachman, John. *A.* 1790 – 1874. Sci. and Rel.

Bacon, Francis (*Viscount of St. Albans*). *E.* 1561 – 1626. Philos., Sci., Law, and Ess.

Bacon, Leonard. *A.* 1802 – . Theol., Hist., and Ess.

Bailey, Philip J. *E.* 1816 – . Poet.,

Baillie, Joanna. *S.* 1764 – 1851. Dram.

Baird, Robert. *A.* 1798 – 1863. Rel. and Hist.

Baker, Daniel. *A.* 1791 – 1857. Rel.

Baker, Sir Sam. W. *E.* 1821 – . Trav.

Baker, Wm. M. *A.* 1825 – . Biog. and Rel.

Baldwin, J. D. *A.* 1815 – . Antiq. and Poet.

Bancroft, Geo. *A.* 1800 – . Hist., Ess., and Poet.

Banim, John. *I.* 1800 – 1842. Fic. and Dram.

Barbauld, Anna L. *E.* 1743 – 1825. Ess., Biog., and Poet.

Barham, R. H. *E.* 1788 – 1845. Poet.

Barlow, Joel. *A.* 1755 – 1812. Poet.

Barnes, A. *A.* 1798 – 1870. Rel.

Barrow, Isaac. *E.* 1630 – 1677. Sci. and Rel.

Barrow, Sir John. *E.* 1764 – 1848. Trav.

Baxter, R. *E.* 1615 – 1691. Theol.

Bayly, Thos. H. *E.* 1797 – 1839. Fic., Poet., and Dram.

Bayne, Peter. *S.* Ess. and Rel.

Beattie, James. *S.* 1735 – 1803. Poet. and Ess.

Beaumont, F. *E.* 1586 – 1616. Dram. and Poet.

Beckett, Gilbert A. à. *E.* 1810 – 1856. Dram. and Mis.

Beckford, Wm. *E.* 1760 – 1844. Fic., Biog., and Trav.

Beecher, Catherine E. *A.* 1800 – . Domes. and Econ.

Beecher, Chas. *A.* 1810 – . Rel.

Beecher, Henry W. *A.* 1813 – . Rel., Theol., and Fic.

Beecher, Lyman. *A.* 1775 – 1863. Rel.

Behn, Aphra. *E.* 1642 – 1689. Dram., Poet., and Fic.

Bell, Sir Chas. *S.* 1778 – 1842. Sci.

Bellows, Henry W. *A.* 1814 – . Theol.

Benjamin, Park. *A.* 1809 – 1864. Poet.

Bennett, J. G. *A.* 1800 – 1872. Journalist.

Bentham, Jeremy. *E.* 1748 – 1832. Pol. and Law.

Bentley, Richard (*the British Aristarchus*). *E.* 1662 – 1742. Crit. and Ess.

Benton, Thos. H. *A.* 1782 – 1858. Pol. and Law.

Berkeley, Geo. (*Bishop of Cloyne*). *I.* 1684 – 1753. Philos., Theol., and Poet.

Bethune, Geo. W. *A.* 1805 – 1862. Rel. and Poet.

Bickersteth, E. *E.* 1786 – 1850. Rel.

Bigelow, John. *A.* 1817 – . Pol. and Biog.

Bird, Robert M. *A.* 1805 – 1854. Fic. and Dram.

Blackburn, Wm. M. *A.* 1828 – . Rel. and Fic.

Blackie, John S. *S.* 1809 – . Ess., Crit., and Poet.

Blacklock, Thos. *S.* 1721 – 1791. Poet.

Blackstone, Sir Wm. *E.* 1723 – 1780. Law.

Blair, Hugh. *S.* 1718 – 1800. Theol. and Crit.

Blair, Robert. *S.* 1699 – 1747. Poet.

Blessington, Countess of. *I.* 1789 – 1849. Fic., Trav., and Mis.

Bloomfield, Robert. *E.* 1766 – 1823. Poet.

Boker, Geo. H. *A.* 1824 – . Dram. and Poet.

Bolingbroke, Henry St. John (*Viscount*). *E.* 1678 – 1751. Pol. and Hist.

Borrow, Geo. *E.* 1803 – . Fic. and Trav.

Boswell, Jas. *S.* 1740 – 1795. Biog.

Bouvier, John. *A.* 1787 – 1851. Law.

Bowditch, Nath'l. *A.* 1773 – 1838. Sci.

Bowles, Wm. L. *E.* 1762 – 1850. Poet., Esth., Rel., and Biog.

Bowring, Sir John. *E.* 1792 – 1872. Philol., Theol., Polit. Econ., and Mel.

Boyd, Andrew K. H. *S.* 1825 – . Rel. and Mis.

Boyle, Robert. *I.* 1627 – 1691. Sci. and Rel.

Bradstreet, Anne. *A.* 1612 – 1672. Poet.

Breckinridge, R. J. *A.* 1800 – 1871. Theol. and Trav.

Brewster, Sir David. *S.* 1781 – 1868. Sci. and Biog.

Bristed, Chas. A. *A.* 1820 – 1874. Ess. and Mis.

Brontë, Charlotte. *E.* 1816 – 1855. Fic. and Poet.

Brooks, Chas. T. *A.* 1813 – . Poet. and Trans.

Brooks, Maria. *A.* 1795 – 1845. Poet.

Brooks, N. C. *A.* 1809 – . Ed. and Hist.

Brooks, C. Shirley. *E.* 1815 – 1874. Dram. and Fic.

Brougham, Henry (*Lord*). *S.* 1778 – 1868. Biog., Theol., Hist., and Pol.

Brougham, John. *I.* 1814 – . Dram. and Fic.

Brown, Chas. Brockden. *A.* 1774–1810. Fic. and Pol.

Brown, David Paul. *A.* 1795–1872. Dram. and Mis.

Brown, Thos. *S.* 1778–1820. Meta., Eth., and Poet.

Browne, Sir Thos. *E.* 1605–1682. Theol. and Ess.

Browning, Elizabeth B. *E.* 1807–1861. Poet. and Ess.

Browning, Robert. *E.* 1812– . Poet. and Dram.

Browuson, Orestes A. *A.* 1803– . Fic. and Theol.

Bruce, Jas. *S.* 1730–1794. Trav.

Bryan, Mary E. *A.* Poet.

Bryant, Wm. C. *A.* 1794– . Poet., Trav., and Hist.

Brydges, Sir Sam. E. *E.* 1762–1837. Fic., Trav., and Poet.

Buchanan, Geo. *S.* 1506–1582. Hist. and Poet.

Buchanan, Robert. *S.* 1841– . Poet.

Buckingham, Jos. T. *A.* 1799–1861. Crit. and Mis.

Buckland, Wm. *E.* 1784–1856. Sci. and Theol.

Buckle, Henry T. *E.* 1822–1862. Philos. and Pol.

Bulfinch, S. G. *A.* 1809–1870. Rel. and Poet.

Bunyan, John. *E.* 1628–1688. Rel. Fic.

Burgess, Geo. *A.* 1809–1866. Rel.

Burke, Edmund. *I.* 1729–1797. Esth., Law, Pol., and Hist.

Burnet, Gilbert. *E.* 1643–1715. Theol., Hist., and Biog.

Burney, Chas. *E.* 1726–1814. Music.

Burney, Frances (*Mme. D'Arblay*). *E.* 1752–1840. Fic., Dram., and Biog.

Burney, James E. *E.* 1739–1821. Hist. and Biog.

Burns, Robert. *S.* 1759–1796. Poet.

Burritt, Elihu (*the Learned Blacksmith*). *A.* 1811– . Mis.

Burton, J. H. *S.* 1809– . Hist., Biog., Pol. Econ., and Law.

Burton, Robert. *E.* 1576–1640. Philos. and Ess.

Bush, Geo. *A.* 1796–1860. Theol. and Biog.

Bushnell, Horace. *A.* 1802– . Rel., Theol., and Eth.

Butler, Jos. *E.* 1692–1752. Theol.

Butler, Sam. *E.* 1612–1680. Poet.

Butler, Wm. A. *A.* 1825– . Poet.

Byles, Mather. *A.* 1706–1788. Poet.

Byron, Lord. *E.* 1788–1824. Poet.

Calhoun, J. C. *A.* 1782–1850. Pol.

Calvert, Geo. H. *A.* 1803– . Trav., Poet., and Biog.

Camden, Wm. *E.* 1551–1623. E. Antiq.

Campbell, Geo. *S.* 1719–1796. Crit. and Theol.

Campbell, John L. *S.* 1779–1861. Biog. and Law.

Campbell, Thos. *S.* 1777–1844. Poet. and Biog.

Canning, Geo. *E.* 1770–1827. Pol. and Poet.

Carew, Thos. *E.* 1589–1639. Poet.

Carey, Henry C. *A.* 1793– . Pol. Econ.

Carey, Matt. *A.* 1760–1839. Pol. Econ.

Carleton, Wm. *I.* 1798– . Fic. and Mis.

Carlyle, Thos. *S.* 1795– . Biog., Hist., and Ess.

Carpenter, Wm. B. *S.* 1813– . Sci.

Cary, Alice. *A.* 1820–1871. Poet.

Cary, Phœbe. *A.* 1824–1871. Poet.

Catlin, Geo. *A.* 1796–1872. A. Indians and Trav.

Caxton, Wm. *E.* 1412–1491. Hist. and Trav.

Centlivre, Susannah. *E.* 1667–1722. Dram.

Chalmers, David. *S.* 1530–1592. Hist.

Chalmers, Geo. *S.* 1742–1825. Hist., Pol., Biog., and Crit.

Chalmers, Thos. *S.* 1780–1847. Theol., Eth., Pol. Econ., and Sci.

Chambers, Ephraim. *E.* 1740– . Cyclo.

Chambers, Robert. *S.* 1802–1871. Hist., Biog., and Mis.

Chambers, Wm. *S.* 1800– . Hist., Trav., and Mis.

Channing, Wm. E. *A.* 1780–1842. Theol.

Charles, Elizabeth. *E.* 1826– . Fic.

Chatterton, Thos. *E.* 1752–1770. Poet.

Chaucer, Geoffrey. *E.* 1328–1400. Poet.

Cheever, Geo. B. *A.* 1807– . Rel., Trav., and Mis.

Chesterfield, Lord. *E.* 1694–1773. Letters.

Child, L. Maria. *A.* 1802– . Fic., Biog., and Mis.

Choate, Rufus. *A.* 1799–1859. Pol. and Ess.

Churchill, Chas. *E.* 1731–1764. Poet.

Cibber, Colley. *E.* 1671–1757. Dram. and Poet.

Claiborne, John F. H. *A.* Biog. and Hist.

Clapperton, Hugh. *S.* 1788–1827. Trav.

Clare, John. *E.* 1793–1864. Poet.

Clarendon, Earl of. See HYDE, EDWARD.

Clark, L. G. *A.* 1810–1873. Edit. and Mis.

Clark, W. G. *A.* 1810–1841. Poet. and Mis.

Clarke, Adam. *I.* 1760–1832. Theol. and Biog.

Clarke, McDonald. *A.* 1798–1842. Poet.

Clarke, Mary Cowden. E. 1809- . Fic. and Concord. to Shakespeare.

Clarke, Sam. E. 1599-1682. Rel. and Biog.

Clarke, Sam. E. 1626-1700. Theol.

Clarke, Sam. E. 1675-1729. Theol.

Clay, Henry. 1777-1852. A. Pol.

Clemens, Sam. L. (Mark Twain). A. 1835- . Fic. and Trav.

Cobbett, Wm. E. 1762-1835. A. Pol., Hist., and Ess.

Cobden, Richard. E. 1804-1865. Pol.

Coffin, R. B. (Barry Gray). A. 1826- . Fic. and Mis.

Colenso, John W. E. 1814- . Theol.

Coleridge, Hartley. E. 1796-1849. Poet., Biog., and Ess.

Coleridge, Sam. T. E. 1772-1834. Poet., Dram., Philos., Pol., and Ess.

Collier, J. P. E. 1789- . Crit. and Biog.

Collins, Wilkie. E. 1824- . Fic.

Collins, Wm. E. 1720-1756. Poet.

Colman, Geo. E. 1733-1794. Dram.

Colman, Geo. E. 1752-1836. Dram.

Combe, Andrew. S. 1797-1847. Sci.

Combe, Geo. S. 1788-1358. Sci., Rel., and Law.

Comstock, John L. D. A. 1789-1858. Sci. and Hist.

Congreve, Wm. I. 1670-1729. Dram.

Conrad, R. T. A. 1805-1858. Dram.

Cook, Eliza. E. 1817- . Poet.

Cooke, John E. A. 1830- . Fic. and Biog.

Cooke, P. P. A. 1816-1850. Poet.

Cooper, A. Ashley. E. 1621-1683. Pol.

Cooper, A. Ashley. E. 1671-1713. Mis.

Cooper, Sir Astley P. E. 1768-1841. Sci.

Cooper, J. Fenimore. A. 1789-1851. Fic., Biog., Hist., and Trav.

Cooper, Thos. A. 1759-1840. Law and Pol.

Coverdale, Miles. E. 1485-1565. Rel.

Cowley, Abraham. E. 1618-1667. Poet.

Cowper, Wm. E. 1731-1800. Poet.

Cox, S. S. A. 1824- . Pol. and Trav.

Coxe, A. C. A. 1818- . Poet. and Trav.

Coxe, Wm. E. 1747-1828. Hist., Biog., Rel., and Trav.

Cozzens, Fred. S. A. 1818-1869. Fic. and Mis.

Crabbe, Geo. E. 1754-1832. Poet.

Cranch, C. P. A. 1813- . Poet.

Cranmer, Thos. E. 1489-1556. Rel.

Crashaw, Richard. E. Died 1650. Poet.

Croker, John W. I. 1780-1857. Hist., Biog., Fic., and Ess.

Croly, Geo. I. 1780-1860. Fic., Poet., Hist., Biog., Dram., Pol., and Rel.

Crowe, Catharine. E. 1802- . Fic., Dram., and Mis.

Cruden, Alex. E. 1701-1770. Concordance.

Cudworth, Ralph. E. 1617-1688. Meta.

Cumberland, Richard. E. 1732-1811. Dram.

Cumming, John. S. 1810- . Rel.

Cunningham, Allan. S. 1785-1842. Biog., Fic., and Poet.

Curtis, Geo. Wm. A. 1824- . Ess., Trav., and Fic.

Dabney, R. L. A. 1820- . Pol., Biog., and Theol.

Dana, Chas. A. A. 1819- . A. Cyclo. and Mis.

Dana, Jas. D. A. 1813- . Sci.

Dana, R. H. A. 1787- . Poet., and Fic.

Daniel, Sam. E. 1562-1619. Poet. and Hist.

Darwin, Chas. E. 1809- . Sci.

Darwin, Erasmus. E. 1731-1802. Poet. and Sci.

Davenant, Wm. E. 1605-1668. Poet.

Davidson, James Wood. A. 1829- . Biog. and Crit.

Davis, A. J. A. 1826- . Spiritism.

Davy, Sir Humphry. E. 1778-1829. Sci.

Dawes, Rufus. A. 1803-1859. Poet.

DeBow, Jas. D. B. A. 1820-1867. Pol. Econ.

Deems, Chas. F. A. 1820- . Rel. and Poet.

DeFoe, Dan. E. 1663-1731. Fic. and Poet.

Dekker (Decker), Thos. E. 1638- . Dram.

Denham, Dixon. E. 1786-1828. Trav.

Denham, Sir John. E. 1615-1668. Poet.

DeQuincey, Thos. E. 1785-1859. Fic. and Ess.

Derby, Geo. H. (John Phœnix). A. 1824-1861. Mis.

DeVere, M. Schele. A. 1820- . Philol. and Mis.

Dick, Thos. S. 1774-1857. Sci. and Rel.

Dickens, Chas. E. 1812-1870. Fic.

Disraeli, Ben. E. 1805- . Fic., Pol., Biog., and Poet.

Disraeli, Isaac. E. 1767-1848. Biog. and Fic.

Dodd, Wm. E. 1727-1777. Theol.

Doddridge, Philip. E. 1702-1751. Theol.

Doddridge, Philip. A. 1772-1832. Pol. and Law.

Donne, John. E. 1573-1631. Poet.

Douglas, Gawin. S. 1475-1522. Poet.

Drake, Jos. R. A. 1795-1820. Poet.

Draper, John W. A. 1811- . Sci., Pol., and Hist.

Drayton, Michael. E. 1563-1631. Poet., Fic., and Hist.

Drummond. Wm. *S.* 1585–1649. Poet.

Dryden, John. *L.* 1631–1701. Poet. and Dram.

Dunbar, Wm. *S.* 1465–1530. Poet.

Dunlap, Wm. *A.* 1766–1839. Biog. and Hist. Art.

Duyckinck, E. A. *A.* 1816– . Biog. and Hist.

Duyckinck, Geo. L. *A.* 1823–1863. Biog.

Dwight, Tim. *A.* 1752–1817. Theol. and Poet.

Eastlake, Chas. L. *E.* 1793–1865. Art.

Echard, Lawrence. *E.* 1671–1730. Hist.

Edgeworth, Maria. *E.* 1767–1849. Ess. and Fic.

Edwards, Jonathan. *E.* 1629–1712. Theol.

Edwards, Jonathan. *A.* 1703–1758. Meta. and Theol.

Edwards, Richard. *E.* 1523–1566. Poet.

Eggleston, Edward. *A.* 1837– . Rel. and Fic.

Eliot, George. See LEWES, MARIAN C.

Eliot, John. *A.* 1604–1689. Rel.

Elizabeth, Charlotte. See TONNA, C. E.

Elliott, Ebenezer. *E.* 1781–1849. Poet and Pol.

Elliott, Wm. *A.* 1788–1863. Pol. and Dram.

Ellis, Sarah S. *A.* 1812– . Fic. and Mis.

Elyot, Sir Thos. *E.* 1495–1546. Ess. and Mis.

Emerson, R. W. *A.* 1803– . Ess., Biog., and Poet.

English, Thos. Dunn. *A.* 1819– . Poet. and Fic.

Erskine, Thos. *E.* 1750–1823. Law, Pol., and Fic.

Espy, Jas. P. *A.* 1785–1860. Sci.

Evelyn, John. *E.* 1620–1706. Sci., Philol., and Mis.

Evelyn, John. *E.* 1654–1698. Poet. and Crit.

Everett, Alex. H. *A.* 1792–1847. Pol., Biog., Ess., and Poet.

Everett, Edward. *A.* 1794–1865. Rel. and Ess.

Faber, Geo. S. *E.* 1773–1854. Theol.

Fabyan, Robert. *E.* 1450–1512. Hist.

Fairbairn, Pat. *S.* 1805– . Theol.

Falconer, Wm. *S.* 1730–1769. Poet.

Faraday, Michael. *E.* 1791–1867. Sci.

Farquhar, Geo. *I.* 1678–1707. Dram., Poet., and Ess.

Fay, Theo. S. *A.* 1806– . Fic.

Felton, C. C. *A.* 1807–1862. Ed.

Ferguson, Adam. *S.* 1724–1816. Hist. and Philos.

Ferguson, Robert. *S.* 1750–1774. Poet.

Ferrier, Mary. *S.* 1782–1855. Fic.

Fielding, Henry. *E.* 1707–1754. Fic.

Fields, Jas. T. *A.* 1820– . Poet. and Mis.

Finch, Francis M. *A.* 1827– . Poet.

Finlay, Geo. *S.* 1800– . Hist.

Fitzhugh, Geo. *A.* 1810– . Pol.

Flash, H. L. *A.* 1837– . Poet.

Fletcher, Andrew (*of Saltoun*). *S.* 1653–1716. Pol.

Fletcher, John. *E.* 1576–1625. Dram.

Flint, Tim. *A.* 1780–1840. Biog. and Fic.

Folger, Peter. *A.* 1618–1690. Poet.

Foote, Sam. *E.* 1721–1777. Dram.

Foote, Wm. H. *A.* 1794–1869. Hist. and Rel.

Ford, John. *E.* 1586–1639. Dram.

Forney, J. W. *A.* 1817– . Pol. and Mis.

Forster, John. *E.* 1770–1843. Ess. and Rel.

Forster, John. *E.* 1812– . Biog.

Fowler, Wm. C. *A.* 1793– . Ed., Pol., and Hist.

Fox, Chas. J. *E.* 1749–1806. Pol. and Hist.

Fox, Geo. *E.* 1624–1680. Rel.

Fox, John. *E.* 1517–1587. Biog.

Francis, Sir Philip (*Junius*). *E.* 1740–1818. Pol.

Franklin, Ben. *A.* 1706–1790. Pol., Eth., and Sci.

Freneau, Philip. *A.* 1752–1832. Poet. and Mis.

Frost, John. *A.* 1800–1859. Hist. and Biog.

Froude, Jas. A. *E.* 1818– . Hist., Fic., and Rel.

Fuller, Margaret. See OSSOLI.

Fuller, Thos. *E.* 1608–1661. Hist. and Rel.

Gallagher, Wm. D. *A.* 1808– . Poet.

Gallatin, Albert. *A.* 1761–1847. Pol. Econ.

Galt, John. *S.* 1779–1839. Fic., Biog., and Dram.

Garrick, David. *E.* 1716–1779. Dram. and Poet.

Gaskell, Mary E. *E.* 1822–1866. Fic. and Biog.

Gay, John. *E.* 1688–1732. Poet.

Gayarre, Chas. E. A. *A.* 1805– . Hist. and Fic.

Gayler, Chas. *A.* 1820– . Dram.

Gibbon, Edward. *E.* 1737–1794. Hist.

Gifford, Wm. *E.* 1757–1826. Ess. and Poet.

Giles, Chauncy. *A.* 1819– . Theol.

Giles, Henry. *A.* 1809– . Ess., Theol., and Crit.

Gilfillan, Geo. *S.* 1813– . Biog. and Crit.

A A

Gillies, John. *E.* 1747 – 1836. Hist.

Gilman, Caroline. *A.* 1794 – . Fic. and Poet.

Gilman, Sam. *A.* 1791 – 1858. Rel., Poet., and Mis.

Gladstone, Wm. E. *E.* 1809 – . Pol. and Antiq.

Gleig, Geo. R. *E.* 1795 – . Fic., Rel., Hist., and Biog.

Glidden, Geo. R. *A.* 1808 – 1857. Sci.

Godwin, Parke. *A.* 1816 – . Hist. and Edit.

Godwin, Wm. *E.* 1756 – 1836. Fic., Biog., and Pol.

Goldsmith, Oliver. *E.* 1728 – 1774. Poet., Fic., Dram., Hist., and Sci.

Good, John M. *E.* 1764 – 1827. Sci. and Poet.

Goodrich, Sam. G. *A.* 1793 – 1863. Hist., Trav., Fic., and Poet.

Gore, Catherine G. F. *E.* 1799 – 1861. Fic.

Gower, John. *E.* 1320 – 1402. Poet.

Grahame, Jas. *S.* 1765 – 1811. Poet.

Gray, Asa. *A.* 1810 – . Sci.

Gray, Thos. *E.* 1716 – 1771. Poet.

Greeley, Horace. *A.* 1811 – 1873. Edit. and Mis.

Green, Wm. H. *A.* 1825 – . Philol.

Greene, Robert. *E.* 1560 – 1595. Dram. and Fic.

Griffin, Gerald. *I.* 1803 – 1840. Fic.

Grimshaw, Wm. *A.* 1782 – 1852. Hist.

Griswold, R. W. *A.* 1815 – 1857. Biog. and Crit.

Grote, Geo. *E.* 1794 – 1871. Hist. and Biog.

Hale, Sarah J. *A.* 1790 – . Fic., Poet., and Mis.

Hall, Edward. *S.* 1788 – 1844. Trav. and Poet.

Hall, Jos. *E.* 1574 – 1656. Rel. and Sat.

Hall, Robert. *E.* 1764 – 1831. Theol. and Pol.

Hall, S. C. *E.* 1804 – . Fic.

Hallam, Henry. *E.* 1778 – 1859. Hist., Pol., and Crit.

Halleck, Fitz-Greene. *A.* 1795 – 1867. Poet.

Hamilton, Alex. *A.* 1757 – 1804. Pol.

Hamilton, Sir Wm. *E.* 1788 – 1856. Meta. and Ess.

Hannay, Jas. *S.* 1827 – 1873. Fic., Crit., and Ess.

Hart, John S. *A.* 1810 – . Biog., Ed., and Rel.

Harte, Francis Bret. *A.* 1838 – . Poet. and Fic.

Hawks, Francis L. *A.* 1798 – 1866. Hist. and Rel.

Hawthorne, N. *A.* 1804 – 1864. Fic.

Hay, John. *A.* 1839 – . Poet. and Mis.

Hayne, P. H. *A.* 1831 – . Poet.

Hazlitt, Wm. *E.* 1778 – 1830. Crit. and Poi.

Head, Sir F. B. *E.* 1793 – . Trav. and Pol.

Headley, J. T. *A.* 1814 – . Biog. and Fic.

Heber, Reginald. *E.* 1783 – 1826. Poet.

Helps, Sir Arthur. *E.* 1818 – 1875. Ess., Hist., and Biog.

Hemans, Felicia D. *E.* 1794 – 1835. Poet.

Henry, Matt. *E.* 1662 – 1714. Rel.

Hentz, Caroline L. *A.* 1804 – 1856. Fic.

Herbert, Geo. *E.* 1593 – 1633. Poet.

Herbert, Henry W. (*Frank Forester*). *A.* 1807 – 1858. Fic. and Mis.

Herrick, Robert. *E.* 1591 – 1674. Poet.

Herschel, Caroline L. *E.* 1750 – 1848. Sci.

Herschel, Sir F. W. *E.* 1738 – 1822. Sci.

Herschel, Sir John. *E.* 1790 – . Sci.

Herschel, Sir John F. W. *E.* 1792 – 1871. Sci.

Hervey, Jas. *E.* 1713 – 1758. Rel.

Hervey, Thos. K. *E.* 1804 – 1859. Poet.

Hildreth, Richard. *A.* 1807 – 1865. Hist.

Hillard, Geo. S. *A.* 1808 – . Hist., Trav., and Crit.

Hirst, Henry B. *A.* 1813 – . Poet.

Hitchcock, Edward. *A.* 1793 – 1864. Sci. and Rel.

Hobbes, Thos. *E.* 1588 – 1679. Pol. and Philos.

Hodge, Chas. *A.* 1797 – . Theol.

Hoffman, Chas. F. *A.* 1806 – . Fic. and Poet.

Hoffman, David. *A.* 1784 – 1854. Law and Fic.

Hogg, Jas. *S.* 1772 – 1835. Poet.

Holcombe, Wm. H. *A.* 1825 – . Sci. and Theol.

Holland, J. G. *A.* 1819 – . Fic., Poet., Biog., and Hist.

Holmes, Mary J. *A.* – . Fic.

Holmes, O. W. *A.* 1809 – . Poet. and Fic.

Holt, John S. *A.* 1826 – . Fic.

Home, Henry (*Lord Kames*). *S.* 1696 – 1782. Law and Crit.

Home, John. *S.* 1724 – 1808. Dram. and Hist.

Hood, Thos. *E.* 1798 – 1845. Poet. and Mis.

Hook, Theo. *E.* 1788 – 1841. Fic. and Mis.

Hooker, Richard. *E.* 1553 – 1600. Rel.

Hope, Thos. *E.* 1770 – 1831. Trav. and Art.

Hopkins, Mark. *A.* 1802 – . Theol.

Hopkinson, Francis. *A.* 1737 – 1791. Poet.

Hopkinson, Jos. *A.* 1770 – 1842. Poet.

Horne, John. *E.* 1722 – 1808. Dram.

Horne, R. H. *E.* 1803 – . Dram. and Mis.

Horne, Thos. H. *E.* 1780 – 1862. Theol. and Hist.

Hosmer, Wm. H. C. *A.* 1814 – . Poet.

Howard, Henry (*Earl of Surrey*.) *E.* 1516 – 1547 Poet.

Howells, Wm. D. *A.* 1837 – . Poet., Fic., and Mis.

Howison, Robert R. *A.* 1820 – . Hist. and Biog.

Howitt, Mary. *E.* 1800 – . Fic., Poet., and Mis.

Howitt, Wm. *E.* 1792 – . Fic., Rel., and Mis.

Hudson, Henry N. *A.* 1814 – . Crit.

Hughes, Thos. (*Tom Brown*). *E.* 1823 – . Fic. and Mis.

Hume, David. *S.* 1711 – 1776. Hist. and Philos.

Hunt, J. H. Leigh. *E.* 1784 – 1859. Poet. and Ess.

Huntington, J. V. *A.* 1815 – 1862. Poet.

Hurlbut, Wm. H. *A.* 1827 – . Edit. and Trav.

Huxley, Thos. H. *E.* 1825 – . Sci.

Hyde, Edward (*Earl of Clarendon*). *E.* 1608 – 1673. Hist., Biog., and Pol.

Inchbald, Elizabeth. *E.* 1756 – 1821. Dram. and Fic.

Ingelow, Jean. *E.* 1830 – . Poet. and Fic.

Ingersoll, Chas. J. *A.* 1782 – 1862. Hist., Poet., and Dram.

Ingraham, Jos. H. *A.* 1809 – 1866. Fic. and Rel.

Innes, Cosmo. *S.* 1662 – 1744. Hist.

Irving, Edward. *S.* 1792 – 1834. Rel.

Irving, Washington. *A.* 1783 – 1859. Hist., Biog., and Fic.

Ives, Levi S. *A.* 1797 – 1867. Theol.

James, G. P. R. *E.* 1801 – 1860. Fic., Hist., and Poet.

James, Henry. *A.* 1811 – . Theol.

Jameson, Anna. *E.* 1797 – 1860. Art. and Mis.

Janney, Sam. M. *A.* 1801 – . Biog., Poet., and Rel.

Jarves, Jas. J. *A.* 1818 – . Trav. and Art.

Jarvis, Sam. F. *A.* 1787 – 1851. Theol.

Jay, John. *A.* 1745 – 1829. Pol.

Jay, Wm. *A.* 1789 – 1858. Biog. and Pol.

Jefferson, Thos. *A.* 1743 – 1826. Hist. and Pol.

Jeffrey, Francis. *S.* 1773 – 1850. Crit.

Jerrold, Douglas W. *S.* 1803 – 1857. Poet. and Fic.

Jewsbury, Maria J. *E.* 1800 – 1833. Poet. and Mis.

Johnson, Sam. *E.* 1709 – 1784. Philol., Fic., Poet., and Biog.

Johnston, Jas. F. W. *S.* 1796 – 1855. Sci.

Jones, Chas. C. *A.* 1831 – . A. Antiq.

Jones, Joel. *A.* 1795 – 1860. Theol.

Jones, John B. *A.* 1810 – 1866. Fic.

Jones, Sir Wm. *E.* 1746 – 1794. Philol., Dram., and Law.

Jonson, Ben. *E.* 1573 – 1637. Dram.

Judd, Sylvester. *A.* 1813 – 1853. Fic. and Rel.

Judson, Emily (*Fanny Forrester*). *A.* 1817 – 1854. Fic. and Poet.

Junius. See FRANCIS, SIR PHILIP.

Kane, E. K. *A.* 1820 – 1857. Trav.

Keats, John. *E.* 1796 – 1821. Poet.

Keble, John. *E.* 1792 – 1866. Rel. and Poet.

Keith, Alex. *S.* 1791 – . Theol.

Kendall, Geo. W. *A.* 1807 – 1867. Trav. and Hist.

Kennedy, John P. *A.* 1795 – 1870. Fic.

Kent, Jas. *A.* 1763 – 1847. Law and Pol.

Key, Francis S. *A.* 1779 – 1843. Poet.

Kimball, Richard B. *A.* 1816 – . Fic. and Trav.

Kinglake, Alex. W. *E.* 1811 – . Fic. and Hist.

Kingsley, Chas. *E.* 1819 – . Fic., Rel., Trav., and Poet.

Kinney, E. C. *A.* – . Poet. and Fic.

Kip, Wm. I. *A.* 1811 – . Rel. and Hist.

Kirkland, Caroline M. *A.* 1801 – 1864. Mis.

Kitto, John. *E.* 1804 – 1854. Rel.

Knight, Chas. *E.* 1791 – 1873. Hist. and Mis.

Knowles, Jas. Sheridan. *I.* 1784 – 1862. Dram.

Knox, John. *S.* 1505 – 1572. Theol.

Krauth, Chas. P. *A.* 1823 – . Theol. and Hist.

Kurtz, Benj. *A.* 1795 – 1865. Theol.

La Borde, Max. *A.* 1804 – 1873. Sci. and Hist.

Laing, Malcolm. *S.* 1762 – 1818. Hist.

Laing, Sam. *S.* 1810 – . Trav. and Rel.

Lamb, Chas. *E.* 1775 – 1834. Ess., Fic., Dram., and Poet.

Lander, Richard. *E.* 1804 – 1834. Trav.

Landor, W. S. *E.* 1775 – 1864. Dram., Poet., and Mis.

Lanman, Chas. *A.* 1819 – . Trav. and Biog.

Lardner, Dionysius. *I.* 1793-1859. Sci.

Latham, R. G. *E.* 1812- . Philol.

Latimer, Hugh. *E.* 1472-1555. Rel.

Lawrence, Wm. B. *A.* 1800- . Law.

Layard, A. H. *E.* 1817- . Antiq.

Lecky, W. E. H. *E.* - . Eth. and Philos.

Lee, Eliza B. *A.* 1794- . Fic. and Biog.

Lee, Hannah F. *A.* 1780-1865. Fic. and Biog.

Lee, Nat. *E.* 1658-1691. Dram.

Legaré, H. S. *A.* 1797-1843. Hist. and Law.

Leland, Chas. G. *A.* 1824- . Trav. and Poet.

Leland, John. *E.* 1506-1552. Antiq.

Lemon, Mark. *E.* 1809-1870. Dram. and Mis.

Leslie, Eliza. *A.* 1787-1857. Fic. and Mis.

Lester, Chas. E. *A.* 1815- . Biog., Fic., and Pol.

Lever, Chas. J. *I.* 1806-1872. Fic.

LeVert, Octavia W. *A.* 1820- . Trav. and Ess.

Lewes, Geo. H. *E.* 1817- . Biog. and Hist.

Lewes, Marian C. (*George Eliot*). *E.* 1820- . Fic.

Lewis, Geo. C. *E.* 1806-1863. Pol. and Hist.

Lewis, Matthew G. (*Monk Lewis*). *E.* 1775-1818. Fic. and Dram.

Lewis, Tayler. *A.* 1802- . Theol., Eth., and Crit.

Leyden, John. *S.* 1775-1811. Hist. and Poet.

Lieber, Francis. *A.* 1800-1872. Pol. and Pol. Econ.

Lillo, Geo. *E.* 1693-1737. Dram.

Lindsay, Sir David. *E.* 1490-1568. Dram. and Poet.

Lingard, John. *E.* 1771-1851. Hist.

Lippincott, Sara J. (*Grace Greenwood*). *A.* 1823- . Fic., Ess., and Mis.

Livingstone, David. *S.* 1815-1873. Trav.

Locke, John. *E.* 1632-1704. Meta., Pol., and Ess.

Lockhart, J. G. *S.* 1794-1854. Fic., Biog., and Crit.

Longfellow, H. W. *A.* 1807- . Poet. and Fic.

Longstreet, A. B. *A.* 1790-1870. Fic.

Lossing, B. J. *A.* 1813- . Hist. and Biog.

Lovelace, Richard. *E.* 1618-1658. Poet.

Lover, Sam. *I.* 1797-1868. Fic.

Lowell, Jas. R. *A.* 1819- . Poet., Fic., and Crit.

Ludlow, Fitzhugh. *A.* 1837-1870. Trav. and Fic.

Lunt, Geo. 1807- . Poet. and Fic.

Lyell, Sir Chas. *E.* 1797-1875. Sci. and Trav.

Lyly, John. *E.* 1553-1600. Dram.

Lynch, Wm. F. *A.* 1805-1865. Trav.

Lytton (*Lord*), Sir E. Bulwer. *E.* 1805-1873. Fic., Dram., and Poet.

McCabe, Jas. D. *A.* - . Biog., Hist., and Fic.

Macaulay, Catharine. *E.* 1733-1791. Hist. and Eth.

Macaulay, T. B. *E.* 1800-1859. Hist., Ess., and Poet.

McCosh, Jas. *A.* 1811- . Theol.

McCulloch, J. R. *S.* 1789-1864. Pol., Hist., and Pol. Econ.

Macdonald, Geo. *S.* 1826- . Fic.

McIntosh, Maria J. *A.* 1803- . Fic.

Mackay, Chas. *S.* 1814- . Poet. and Mis.

Mackenzie, Henry. *S.* 1745-1831. Fic.

Mackenzie, R. S. *A.* 1809- . Fic., Poet., and Biog.

Mackintosh, Sir Jas. *S.* 1765-1832. Pol., Hist., and Crit.

Macpherson, Jas. *S.* 1738-1796. Poet. and Hist.

Madden, Sir Fred. *E.* 1801- . Antiq.

Madison, Jas. *A.* 1751-1836. Pol.

Maginn, Wm. *I.* 1794-1842. Ess. and Mis.

Mahan, Asa. *A.* 1799- . Theol. and Eth.

Mahon, P. H. Lord. *E.* 1805- . Hist.

Mahony, Francis (*Father Prout*). *I.* 1800-1866. Ess. and Mis.

Malthus, Th. R. *E.* 1766-1834. Pol. Econ.

Mandeville, B. *E.* 1670-1733. Eth.

Mann, Horace. *A.* 1796-1859. Eth. and Trav.

Manning, Anne. *E.* 1812- . Fic.

Mantell, G. A. *E.* 1790-1852. Sci.

Marlowe, C. *E.* 1564-1593. Dram.

Marryat, Capt. F. *E.* 1792-1848. Fic.

Marsh, Geo. P. *A.* 1801- . Philol. and Mis.

Marshall, John. *A.* 1755-1835. Biog. and Law.

Martineau, Harriet. *E.* 1802- . Fic., Rel., Trav., and Hist.

Marvell, Andrew. *E.* 1620-1678. Poet. and Crit.

Massey, Gerald. *E.* 1828- . Poet.

Massinger, Philip. *E.* 1584-1640. Dram.

Masson, David. *S.* 1823- . Ess., Crit., and Biog.

Mather, Cotton. *A.* 1663–1728. Rel.
Maturin, Chas. R. *I.* 1782–1824. Dram. and Fic.
Maturin, Edward. *A.* – . Fic. and Poet.
Maury, M. F. *A.* 1806–1873. Sci.
Maverick, Aug. *A.* – . Biog. and Mis.
Mayer, Brantz. *A.* 1809– . Hist.
Mayhew, Henry. *E.* 1812– . Fic.
Mayo, Wm. S. *A.* 1812– . Fic.
Meade, Wm. *A.* 1789–1862. Rel.
Mellen, G. *A.* 1799–1841. Fic. and Poet.
Melville, H. *A.* 1819– . Fic. and Trav.
Merivale, Chas. *E.* 1808–1875. Hist.
Middleton, H. *A.* 1797– . Pol.
Mill, Jas. *S.* 1773–1836. Pol. Econ.
Mill, J. S. *E.* 1806–1873. Pol. and Pol. Econ.
Miller, C. H. (*Joachin Miller*). *A.* 1841– . Poet.
Miller, Hugh. *S.* 1802–1856. Sci. and Trav.
Milman, Henry H. *E.* 1791–1868. Poet., Dram., and Hist.
Milnes, R. M. *E.* 1809– . Poet. and Trav.
Milton, John. *E.* 1608–1674. Poet., Pol., and Rel.
Minot, Geo. R. *A.* 1758–1802. Hist.
Mitchell, Donald G. *A.* 1822– . Fic.
Mitchell, John R. *A.* 1793–1858. Sci. and Poet.
Mitchell, Maria. *A.* 1818– . Sci.
Mitford, Mary R. *E.* 1786–1855. Fic., Dram., and Poet.
Mitford, Wm. *E.* 1744–1827. Hist.
Moir, D. M. *S.* 1798–1870. Ess., Poet., and Fic.
Monboddo, J. Burnet (*Lord*). *S.* 1714–1799. Philos.
Montagu, Mary W. *E.* 1690–1762. Mis.
Montgomery, Jas. *S.* 1771–1854. Poet.
Moore, C. C. *A.* 1779–1863. Poet. and Philol.
Moore, Frank. *A.* 1828– . Hist. Coll.
Moore, Thomas. *I.* 1779–1852. Poet. and Fic.
More, Hannah. *E.* 1745–1833. Dram. and Fic.
More, Sir Thos. *E.* 1480–1535. Pol. and Fic.
Morgan, Lady Sydney. *E.* 1789–1859. Fic. and Trav.
Morris, Geo. P. *A.* 1802–1864 Poet. and Dram.
Morris, Wm. *E.* 1830– . Poet.
Morton, Sam. G. *A.* 1799–1851. Sci.

Motherwell, Wm. *S.* 1798–1835. Poet.
Motley, John L. *A.* 1814– . Hist.
Moultrie, Wm. *A.* 1731–1805. Hist.
Mudie, Robert. *S.* 1777–1842. Sci.
Müller, F. Max. *E.* 1823– . Philol. and Mis.
Mulock, Dinah M. *E.* 1826– . Fic.
Murchison, Sir R. *E.* 1792– . Sci.
Mure, Wm. *S.* 1799–1860. Lit. Hist.
Murray, Lindley. *A.* 1745–1826. Philol. and Rel.
Napier, Sir Chas. Jas. *E.* 1782–1853. Law.
Napier, Sir Chas. John. *E.* 1786–1860. Hist.
Napier, John. *S.* 1550–1617. Sci. and Rel.
Napier, Sir Wm. F. P. *E.* 1785–1866. Hist.
Neal, John. *A.* 1793– . Fic., Poet., and Dram.
Neal, Jos. C. *A.* 1807–1847. Fic. and Mis.
Newman, John H. *E.* 1801– . Theol.
Newman, Fred. Wm. *E.* 1805– . Theol.
Newton, Sir Isaac. *E.* 1642–1727. Sci. and Theol.
Newton, John. *E.* 1725–1807. Rel.
Nicoll, Robert. *S.* 1814–1837. Poet. and Rel.
Nordhoff, Chas. *A.* 1830– . Trav., Fic., and Mis.
Norton, Mrs. C. E. S. *E.* 1808– . Poet., Fic., and Mis.
Nott, Josiah C. *A.* 1804– . Sci.
Oliver, Peter. *A.* 1821–1855. Hist.
Opie, Amelia. *E.* 1769–1853. Fic.
Osgood, Frances S. *A.* 1812–1850. Poet.
Osgood, Sam. *A.* 1812– . Rel. and Trav.
Ossoli, Margaret Fuller d'. *A.* 1810–1850. Crit. and Mis.
Otis, Jas. *A.* 1725–1783. Pol.
Otway, Thos. *E.* 1651–1685 Dram.
Owen, David D. *A.* 1807–1860. Sci.
Owen, John. *E.* 1616–1683. Theol.
Owen, John J. *A.* 1803–1869. Ed. and Rel.
Owen, Richard. *E.* 1804– . Sci.
Owen, Richard. *A.* 1810– . Sci.
Owen, Robert. *A.* 1771–1858. Mis.
Owen, Robert D. *A.* 1801– . Mis.
Paine, Thos. *A.* 1736–1809. Pol. and Theol.
Paley, Wm. *E.* 1743–1805. Theol. and Eth.
Palfrey, John G. *A.* 1796– . Hist.
Palgrave, Sir F. *E.* 1788–1861. Hist.
Pardoe, Julia. *E.* 1808–1862. Fic. and Trav.
Park, Mungo. *E.* 1771–1805. Trav.

Parker, Theodore. *A.* 1810–1860. Theol.

Parkman, Francis. *A.* 1823– . Trav. and Hist.

Parnell, Thos. *E.* 1679–1718. Poet.

Parsons, Theoph. *A.* 1797– . Theol. and Ess.

Parton, James. *A.* 1822– . Biog. and Ess.

Parton, Sarah Payson (*Fanny Fern*). *A.* 1811–1872. Fic. and Mis.

Patmore, Coventry. *E.* 1823– . Poet.

Paulding, Jas. K. *A.* 1778–1860. Fic.

Payne, John H. *A.* 1792–1852. Dram.

Peabody, A. P. *A.* 1811– . Rel.

Peck, Wm. H. *A.* 1830– . Fic.

Penn, Wm. *A.* 1644–1718. Theol.

Pepys, Sam. *E.* 1632–1703. Mis.

Percival, Jas. G. *A.* 1795–1857. Poet.

Percy, Thos. *E.* 1728–1811. *Reliques.*

Phelps, Almira L. *A.* 1793– . Sci., Fic., and Mis.

Phillips, Ambrose. *E.* 1675–1749. Dram.

Phillips, John. *E.* 1676–1708. Poet.

Phillips, Edward. *E.* 1630–1680. Philol.

Phillips, Wendell. *A.* 1811– . Pol.

Pierpont, John. *A.* 1775–1866. Poet.

Pike, Albert. *A.* 1809– . Poet.

Pinkerton, John. *S.* 1758–1821. Hist.

Pise, Chas. C. *A.* 1802–1866. Rel. and Poet.

Plumer, Wm. S. *A.* 1802– . Rel.

Poe, Edgar A. *A.* 1811–1849. Poet., Crit., and Fic.

Pollard, E. A. *A.* 1838–1873. Hist., Biog., and Pol.

Pollok, Robert. *S.* 1799–1827. Poet.

Pope, Alex. *E.* 1688–1744. Poet.

Porson, Richard. *E.* 1759–1808. Crit.

Porter, Anna M. *E.* 1780–1832. Fic.

Porter, Jane. *E.* 1776–1850. Fic.

Potter, Alonzo. *A.* 1800–1865. Pol. Econ. and Rel.

Powell, Thos. *A.* 1809– . Dram. and Biog.

Praed, W. M. *E.* 1802–1839. Poet.

Prescott, Wm. H. *A.* 1796–1859. Hist. and Ess.

Preston, Margaret J. *A.* 1838– . Poet.

Priestley, Jos. *E.* 1733–1804. Philos. and Sci.

Prime, Sam. I. *A.* 1812– . Trav. and Rel.

Prior, Matt. *E.* 1664–1721. Poet.

Procter, Adelaide A. *E.* 1825–1864. Poet.

Procter, Bryan W. (*Barry Cornwall*). *E.* 1790–1868. Poet. and Dram.

Purchas, Sam. *E.* 1577–1628. Trav.

Pusey, Edward B. *E.* 1800– . Theol.

Quarles, Francis. *E.* 1592–1644. Poet.

Quincey, Josiah. *A.* 1744–1775. Pol.

Radcliffe, Anne. *E.* 1764–1823. Fic.

Raguet, Condy. *A.* 1784–1842. Pol.

Raleigh, Sir W. *E.* 1552–1618. Hist. and Poet.

Ramsay, Allan. *S.* 1685–1758. Poet.

Ramsay, David. *A.* 1749–1815. Hist. and Biog.

Ramsey, J. G. M. *A.* 1797– . Hist.

Rawlinson, Geo. *E.* 1815– . Hist and Rel.

Raymond, H. J. *A.* 1820–1869. Journalist.

Read, Thos. B. *A.* 1822–1872. Poet.

Reade, Chas. *E.* 1814– . Fic.

Reed, Henry. *A.* 1808–1854. Crit. and Hist.

Reed, Wm. B. *A.* 1806– . Biog. and Ess.

Reid, Mayne. *I.* 1818– . Fic.

Reid, Thos. *S.* 1710–1796. Meta.

Reid, Whitelaw. *A.* 1839– . Hist. and Edit.

Requier, A. J. A. *A.* 1825– . Poet.

Ricardo, David. *E.* 1772–1823. Pol. Econ.

Richardson, Chas. *E.* 1775–1865. Philol.

Richardson, Sam. *E.* 1689–1767. Fic.

Ripley, Geo. *A.* 1802– . Rel. and Crit.

Ritchie, Anna C. Mowatt. *A.* 1820–1870. Fic. and Dram.

Rives, Wm. C. *A.* 1793–1868. Biog., Hist., and Eth.

Robbins, Eliza. *A.* – . Hist. and Mis.

Robbins, Royal. *A.* 1787–1861. Hist.

Robertson, Fred. W. *E.* 1816–1853. Rel.

Robertson, Wm. *S.* 1721–1793. Hist. and Biog.

Robinson, Edward. *A.* 1794–1864. Philol. and Theol.

Roche, Regina M. *E.* 1765–1845. Fic.

Rogers, Henry. *E.* 1814– . Theol.

Rogers, Sam. *E.* 1763–1855. Poet.

Roscoe, Wm. *E.* 1753–1831. Biog. and Mis.

Rossetti, Christina G. *E.* 1830– . Poet.

Rowe, Nich. *E.* 1673–1718. Poet. and Crit.

Rowson, Susanna. *A.* 1761–1824. Fic. and Dram.

Ruschenberger, Wm. S. W. *A.* 1807– . Trav. and Sci.

Rush, Benj. *A.* 1745–1813. Sci., Pol., and Ess.

Ruskin, John. *E.* 1819– . Art.

Russell, Wm. *S.* 1741–1793. Hist., Fic., and Poet.

Russell, Wm. H. *E.* 1816– . Trav. and Mis.

Sabine, L. *A.* 1803– . Biog. and Mis.

Sackville, Thos. *E.* 1536–1608. Poet.

Sala, Geo. A. *E.* 1827– . Fic. and Trav.

Samson, Geo. W. *A.* 1819– . Trav. and Ess.

Sands, Robert C. *A.* 1799–1832. Biog. and Fic.

Sargent, Epes. *A.* 1812– . Dram. and Poet.

Sargent, Winthrop. *A.* 1825–1870. Hist.

Savage, Richard. *E.* 1698–1743. Poet.

Saxe, John G. *A.* 1816– . Poet.

Schaff, Philip. *A.* 1819– . Theol., Hist., and Eth.

Schmucker, Sam. M. *A.* 1823–1863. Hist., Biog., Theol., and Dram.

Schmucker, Sam. S. *A.* 1790–1863. Theol., Biog., and Trav.

Schoolcraft, H. R. *A.* 1793–1864. A. Indians, Hist., and Trav.

Scott, Sir Walter. *S.* 1771–1832. Fic. and Poet.

Scott, Wm. A. *A.* 1813– . Rel.

Sedgwick, Caroline M. *A.* 1789–1867. Fic. and Trav.

Selden, John. *E.* 1584–1654. Pol. and Law.

Sewell, Thos. *A.* 1787–1845. Sci.

Shakespeare, Wm. *E.* 1564–1616. Dram. and Poet.

Sharpe, Sam. *E.* – . Antiq. and Hist.

Shaw, Henry W. (*Josh Billings*). *A.* 1818– . Mis.

Shea, John G. *A.* 1824– . Hist. and Rel.

Shedd, Wm. G. T. *A.* 1820– . Hist., Ess., and Rel.

Shell, R. L. *I.* 1794–1851. Dram. and Pol.

Shelley, P. B. *E.* 1792–1822. Poet.

Shelton, F. W. *A.* 1814– . Fic. and Poet.

Shenstone, Wm. *E.* 1714–1763. Poet.

Sheridan, R. B. *E.* 1751–1816. Dram.

Sherlock, Thos. *E.* 1678–1761. Theol.

Sherlock, Wm. *E.* 1641–1707. Theol.

Shillaber, Benj. P. (*Mrs. Partington*). *A.* 1814– . Mis. and Poet.

Shirley, Jas. *E.* 1596–1666. Dram.

Sidney, Algernon. *E.* 1621–1683. Pol.

Sidney, Sir Philip. *E.* 1554–1586. Fic. and Poet.

Sigourney, Lydia H. *A.* 1791–1865. Poet.

Silliman, Benj. *A.* 1779–1864. Sci. and Trav.

Simms, Wm. G. *A.* 1806–1870. Fic., Poet., Hist., Biog., and Ess.

Skelton, John. *E.* 1460–1529. Poet.

Smedley, F. S. *E.* 1815–1864. Fic.

Smiles, Sam. *S.* 1816– . Biog. and Ess.

Smith, Adam. *S.* 1723–1790. Pol. Econ.

Smith, Albert. *E.* 1816–1860. Fic.

Smith, Alex. *S.* 1830–1867. Poet.

Smith, Charlotte. *E.* 1749–1806. Fic. and Poet.

Smith, Goldwin. *E.* 1823– . Hist. and Mis.

Smith, Horace. *E.* 1779–1849. Poet. and Fic.

Smith, Jas. *E.* 1775–1839. Fic. and Poet.

Smith, John Pye. *E.* 1774–1851. Rel. and Sci.

Smith, Seba (*Major Jack Downing*). *A.* 1792–1868. Fic. and Mis.

Smith, Sydney. *E.* 1771–1845. Pol. and Ess.

Smith, Thos. B. *A.* 1810–1871. Hist. and Antiq.

Smith, Thos. S. *E.* 1788–1861. Sci. and Philos.

Smith, Wm. *E.* 1814– . Dictionaries.

Smollett, Tobias G. *E.* 1721–1771. Fic. and Hist.

Smyth, Thos. *A.* 1808– . Rel. and Sci.

Somerville, Mary. *E.* 1780– . Sci.

South, Robert. *E.* 1633–1716. Theol.

Southey, Robert. *E.* 1774–1843. Poet., Hist., and Mis.

Southwell, Robert. *E.* 1560–1595. Poet.

Southworth, Emma D. E. N. *A.* 1818– . Fic.

Sparks, Jared. *A.* 1794–1866. Biog. and Ess.

Spencer, Herbert. *E.* 1820– . Philos.

Spencer, J. A. *A.* 1816– . Hist. and Rel.

Spenser, Edmund. *E.* 1553–1599. Poet.

Sprague, Wm. B. *A.* 1795– . Rel. and Biog.

Squier, E. Geo. *A.* 1821– . A. Antiq.

Stanhope, P. H. (*Earl*). *E.* 1805– . Hist. and Biog.

Stedman, E. C. *A.* 1833– . Poet.

Steele, Richard. *E.* 1671–1729. Ess.

Stephens, Alex. H. *A.* 1812– . Pol.

Sterne, Lawrence. *E.* 1713–1768. Fic. and Rel.

Stewart, Dugald. *S.* 1753–1828. Meta., and Pol. Econ.

Stillingfleet, Edward. *E.* 1635 – 1699. Theol.

Stirling, Wm. *S.* 1818 – . Hist. and Biog.

Stith, Wm. *A.* 1689 – 1755. Hist.

Stoddard, Richard H. *A.* 1825 – . Poet.

Stowe, Harriet B. *A.* 1812 – . Fic.

Street, A. B. *A.* 1811 – . Poet.

Strickland, Agnes. *E.* 1806 – . Biog., Fic., and Poet.

Strother, D. H. (*Porte Crayon*). *A.* 1816 – . Trav. and Mis.

Stuart, Moses. *A.* 1780 – 1852. Theol. and Philol.

Suckling, Sir John. *E.* 1609 - 1642. Poet.

Sullivan, Wm. *A.* 1774 – 1839. Pol., Hist., and Biog.

Sumner, Chas. *A.* 1811 – 1874. Pol.

Swain, Chas. *E.* 1803 – . Poet.

Swinburne, A. C. *E.* 1843 – . Poet.

Swinton, Wm. *A.* 1834 – . Philol. and Hist.

Swift, Jonathan. *E.* 1667 – 1745. Fic., Pol., and Poet.

Talfourd, Thos. N. *E.* 1795 – 1854. Dram. and Ess.

Tappan, Henry P. *A.* 1806 – . Eth. and Theol.

Tautphœus (*The Baroness*). *E.* – . Fic.

Taylor, Henry. *E.* 1800 – . Dram. and Poet.

Taylor, Isaac (*of Ongar*). *E.* 1759 – 1829. Fic.

Taylor, Isaac. *E.* 1787 – 1865. Rel.

Taylor, Bayard. *A.* 1825 – . Trav., Fic., and Poet.

Taylor, Jeremy. *E.* 1613 – 1667. Rel.

Taylor, Thos. (*the Platonist*). *E.* 1758 – 1835. Trans. of Plato and Aristotle.

Taylor, Tom. *E.* 1817 – . Dram. and Fic.

Temple, Sir Wm. *E.* 1628 – 1699. Pol. and Ess.

Tennent, Jas. E. *E.* 1804 – 1869. Hist. and Mis.

Tennyson, A. *E.* 1810 – . Poet.

Terhune, Mary V. *A.* – . Fic.

Thackeray, W. M. *E.* 1811 – 1863. Fic. and Mis.

Thatcher, Benj. B. *A.* 1809 – 1840. Am. Indians.

Thirlwall, Connop. *E.* 1797 – . Hist.

Thomas, F. W. *A.* 1811 – 1864. Poet. and Fic.

Thoms, Wm. J. *E.* 1803 – . *Notes and Queries.*

Thomson, Jas. *E.* 1700 – 1748. Poet.

Thoreau, H. D. *A.* 1817 – 1862. Trav. and Mis.

Thornwell, Jas. H. *A.* 1811 – 1862. Theol.

Thorpe, T. B. *A.* 1815 – . Fic. and Mis.

Tickell, Thos. *E.* 1686 – 1740. Poet.

Ticknor, Geo. *A.* 1791 – 1871. Hist. and Biog.

Tighe, Mary B. *E.* 1774 – 1810. Poet.

Tillotson, John. *E.* 1630 – 1694. Rel.

Tilton, Theo. *A.* 1835 – . Edit., Fic., and Poet.

Timrod, Henry. *A.* 1829 – 1867. Poet.

Todd, John. *A.* 1800 – . Rel. and Trav.

Tonna, Charlotte Elizabeth. *E.* 1792 – 1846. Fic.

Tooke, John Horne. *E.* 1736 – 1812. Philol.

Townsend, J. K. *A.* 1809 – 1851. Sci. and Trav.

Trench, Richard C. *I.* 1807 – . Theol. and Philol.

Trescott, Wm. H. *A.* 1823 – . Pol. and Hist.

Trollope, Anthony. *E.* 1815 – . Fic.

Trollope, Frances. *E.* 1778 – 1863. Trav.

Trollope, Thos. A. *E.* 1810 – . Fic.

Trowbridge, J. T. *A.* 1827 – . Fic., Poet., and Trav.

Tucker, Beverly. *A.* 1784 – 1851. Fic. and Law.

Tucker, Geo. *A.* 1775 – 1861. Hist., Biog., Fic., and Ess.

Tucker, St. Geo. *A.* 1752 – 1827. Poet. and Law.

Tuckerman, H. T. *A.* 1813 – 1871. Crit. and Fic.

Tudor, Wm. *A.* 1779 – 1830. Edit., Biog., Trav., and Mis.

Tupper, M. F. *E.* 1810 – . Poet.

Turnbull, Robert. *A.* 1809 – . Rel.

Turner, Sharon. *E.* 1768 – 1847. Hist.

Tusser, Thos. *E.* 1523 – 1580. Poet.

Tuthill, Louisa C. *A.* 1799 – . Fic. and Mis.

Tyler, Sam. *A.* 1809 – . Philos. and Biog.

Tyndale, Wm. *E.* 1484 – 1536. Trans. of Bible.

Tyndall, John. *E.* 1820 – . Sci.

Tyng, S. H. *A.* 1800 – . Rel.

Tytler, Alex. F. *S.* 1747 – 1813. Hist., Biog., and Law.

Tytler, Patrick F. *S.* 1791 – 1849. Hist. and Biog.

Udall, Nicholas. *E.* 1506 – 1564. Dram.

Upham, Thos. C. *A* 1799– . Theol. and Meta.

Usher, Jas. *E.* 1580–1656. Hist., Rel., and Antiq.

Vanbrugh, Sir John. *E.* 1666–1726. Dram.

Vaughan, Henry. *W.* 1621–1695. Poet.

Vaughan, Robert. *E.* 1795–1868. Biog., Pol., and Theol.

Verplanck, G. C. *A.* 1787–1870. Crit. and Mis.

Victor, Metta V. *A.* 1831– . Fic. and Poet.

Walker, Jas. B. *A.* 1805– . Rel.

Wallace, H. B. *A.* 1817–1852. Art. and Crit.

Waller, Edmund. *E.* 1605–1687. Poet.

Wallis, Severn T. *A.* 1816– . Hist. and Ess.

Walpole, Horace. *E.* 1717–1797. Dram. and Mis.

Walton, Izaak. *E.* 1593–1683. Biog. and Mis.

Warburton, Wm. *E.* 1698–1779. Theol.

Warburton, Eliot B. G. *I.* 1810–1852. Fic. and Trav.

Ware, Henry. *A.* 1764–1845. Rel.

Ware, William. *A.* 1797–1852. Fic. and Crit.

Warfield, Catharine A. *A.* 1817– . Fic. and Poet.

Warner, C. Dudley. *A.* 1829– . Ess.

Warner, Susan. *A.* 1818– . Fic.

Warren, Sam. *E.* 1807– . Fic.

Warton, Jos. *E.* 1722–1800. Hist. and Crit.

Warton, Thos. *E.* 1728–1790. Crit. and Hist.

Waterton, Chas. *E.* 1782–1865. Sci.

Watson, Henry C. *A.* 1831–1869. Hist. and Fic.

Watts, A. A. *E.* 1799–1864. Poet.

Watts, Isaac. 1674–1748. Hymns.

Wayland, Francis. *A.* 1796–1865. Eth., Pol., and Theol.

Webb, Chas. H. *A.* 1835– . Mis.

Webb, Jas. W. *A.* 1802– . Ess. and Trav.

Webber, Chas. W. *A.* 1819–1856. Fic.

Webster, Daniel. *A.* 1782–1852. Pol.

Webster, John. *E.* 17th Century. Dram.

Webster, Noah. *A.* 1758–1843. Philol.

Weems, Mason L. *A.* 1759–1825. Biog. and Mis.

Welby, Amelia B. *A.* 1821–1852. Poet.

Wells, David A. *A.* 1827– . Sci. and Pol. Econ.

Wesley, John. *E.* 1703–1791. Theol. and Rel.

Wesley, Sam. *E.* 1664–1735. Rel. and Poet.

Wesley, Sam. *E.* 1690–1739. Poet.

Whately, Richard. *I.* 1787–1863. Theol. and Logic.

Wheaton, Henry. *A.* 1785–1848. Law.

Whelpley, Sam. *A.* 1766–1817. Hist. and Theol.

Whewell, Wm. *E.* 1795–1866. Philos. and Sci.

Whipple, E. P. *A.* 1819– . Crit. and Ess.

Whiston, Wm. *E.* 1667–1752. Sci. and Rel.

White, Gilbert. *E.* 1720–1793. Sci.

White, H. Kirke. *E.* 1785–1806. Poet.

White, Jos. Blanco. *E.* 1775–1841. Rel.

White, R. Grant. *A.* 1822– . Philol. and Crit.

Whitefield, Geo. *E.* 1714–1770. Rel.

Whitman, Sarah H. *A.* 1813– . Poet.

Whitman, Walt. *A.* 1819– . Poet.

Whitney, W. D. *A.* 1827– . Philol. and Crit.

Whittier, John G. *A.* 1808– . Poet.

Wilberforce, Wm. *E.* 1759–1833. Rel. and Pol.

Wilde, R. H. *A.* 1789–1847. Poet. and Biog.

Wilkes, John. *E.* 1727–1797. Pol.

Wilkinson, John G. *E.* 1798– . Hist.

Willard, Emma C. *A.* 1787–1870. Hist. and Mis.

Williams, Wm. R. *A.* 1804– . Rel.

Willis, N. P. *A.* 1806–1867. Poet., Fic., and Mis.

Wilson, Alex. *A.* 1766–1813. Sci.

Wilson, Henry. *A.* 1812– . Pol.

Wilson, John (*Christopher North*). 1785–1854. *S.* Poet., Fic., and Mis.

Winslow, H. *A.* 1800–1864. Rel. and Eth.

Winslow, M. *A.* 1789–1864. Rel. and Philol.

Winthrop, John. *A.* 1587–1649. Hist. and Mis.

Winthrop, Theo. *A.* 1828–1861. Fic.

Wirt, Wm. *A.* 1772–1834. Biog. and Ess.

Wiseman, N. *E.* 1802–1865. Theol., Fic., and Ess.

Wolcot, John. *E.* 1738–1819. Poet.

Wolfe, Chas. *I.* 1791–1823. Poet.

Wood, Geo. *A.* 1799– . Fic.

Wood, Ellen P. *E.* 1820– . Fic.

Woodworth, Sam. *A.* 1785–1842. Poet.

Woolsey, Theo. D. *A.* 1801– . Law and Theol.

Worcester, Jos. E. *A.* 1784–1865. Philol.

Wordsworth, Wm. *E.* 1770–1850. Poet.

Wotton, Sir Henry. *E.* 1568–1639. Poet. and Ess.

Wyatt, Sir Thos. *E.* 1503–1542. Poet.

Wycherley, Wm. *E.* 1640–1715. Dram.

Wyckliffe, John. *E.* 1324–1384. Trans. of Bible.

Yonge, Charlotte M. *E.* 1823– . Fic. and Hist.

Youatt, Wm. *E.* 1777–1847. Domestic Animals.

Young, Edward. *E.* 1684–1765. Poet.

Young, Thos. *E.* 1773–1829. Antiq.

THE END.

www.ingramcontent.com/pod-product-compliance
Lightning Source LLC
Chambersburg PA
CBHW030945110726
47900CB00004B/1141